PRAISE FOR JO WALTON

"A glorious kitchen sink of genre, combining philosophy, time travel, aliens, and the gods."

—Kirkus Reviews (starred review) on *Necessity*

"Walton is brilliant at...not letting you know quite what kind of story you're in, and leading you to relish the discovery."

—NPR on *The Philosopher Kings*

"Events unfold as characters and ideas develop, and one of the reading pleasures of the novels is watching the feedback among characters, ideas, and events, and entering into the dialogues ourselves."

—Los Angeles Review of Books on *The Philosopher Kings*

"Walton shines, as she always does, in the small and hurtful and glorious business of interpersonal relationships....This book about philosophy, history, gender, and freedom also manages to be a spectacular coming-of-age tale that encompasses everything from courtroom dramas to sexual intrigue."

—Cory Doctorow, Boing Boing, on *The Just City*

"As skilled in execution as it is fascinating in premise."

—Library Journal (starred review) on *The Just City*

"A remarkable novel of ideas...Superb. In the end, the novel does more than justice to the idea of the Just City."

—Booklist (starred review) on *The Just City*

"Rendered with Walton's usual power and beauty...It's this haunting character complexity that ultimately holds the reader captive to the tale."

—N. K. Jemisin, The New York Times, on *My Real Children*

"Has as much in common with an Alice Munro story as it does with, say, Philip K. Dick's *The Man in the High Castle*."

—Lev Grossman, Publishers Weekly, on *My Real Children*

BOOKS BY JO WALTON

THESSALY

THE JUST CITY,
THE PHILOSOPHER KINGS,
NECESSITY

JO WALTON

A TOM DOHERTY ASSOCIATES BOOK
New York

THESSALY

The Just City copyright © 2014 by Jo Walton
The Philosopher Kings copyright © 2015 by Jo Walton
Necessity copyright © 2016 by Jo Walton

All rights reserved.

A Tor Book
Published by Tom Doherty Associates
175 Fifth Avenue
New York, NY 10010

www.tor-forge.com

Tor® is a registered trademark of Macmillan Publishing Group, LLC.

ISBN 978-0-7653-9900-7 (trade paperback)

Our books may be purchased in bulk for promotional, educational, or business use.
Please contact your local bookseller or the Macmillan Corporate and Premium
Sales Department at 1-800-221-7945, extension 5442, or by email at
MacmillanSpecialMarkets@macmillan.com.

First Edition: September 2017

Printed in the United States of America

D 0 9 8 7 6 5

CONTENTS

THE JUST CITY

THE JUST CITY

This is for Ada, who took me to Bernini's *Apollo*.

Wherever you go, there are plenty of places where you will find a welcome; and if you choose to go to Thessaly, I have friends there who will make much of you and give you complete protection, so that no one in Thessaly can interfere with you.

—Plato, *Crito*

The triremes which defended Greece at Salamis defended Mars too.

—Ada Palmer, *Too Like the Lightning*

Yes, I know, Plato; but if you always take the steps in threes, one day you will miss a cracked one.

—Mary Renault, *The Last of the Wine*

> If you could take that first step
> You could dance with Artemis
> Beside Apollo Eleven.

—Jo Walton, "Submersible Moonphase"

1

APOLLO

She turned into a tree. It was a Mystery. It must have been. Nothing else made sense, because I didn't understand it. I hate not understanding something. I put myself through all of this because I didn't understand why she turned into a tree—why she chose to turn into a tree. Her name was Daphne, and so is the tree she became, my sacred laurel with which poets and victors crown themselves.

I asked my sister Artemis first. "Why did you turn Daphne into a tree?" She just looked at me with her eyes full of moonlight. She's my full-blooded sister, which you'd think would count for something, but we couldn't be more different. She was ice-cold, with one arched brow, reclining on a chilly silver moonscape.

"She implored me. She wanted it so much. And you were right there. I had to do something drastic."

"Her son would have been a hero, or even a god."

"You *really* don't understand about virginity," she said, uncurling and extending an ice-cold leg. Virginity is one of Artemis's big things, along with bows, hunting and the moon.

"She hadn't made a vow of virginity. She hadn't dedicated herself to you. She wasn't a priestess. I would never—"

"You really are missing something. It might be Hera you should be talking to," Artemis said, looking at me over her shoulder.

"Hera hates me! She hates both of us."

"I know." Artemis was poised now, ready to be off. "But what you don't understand falls within her domain. Ask Athene." And she was off, like an arrow from a bow or a white deer from a covert, bounding across the dusty plains of the moon and swooping down somewhere in the only slightly less dusty plains of Scythia. She hasn't forgiven me for the moon missions being called the Apollo Program when they should have been called after her.

My domain is wide, both in power and knowledge. I am patron of inspiration, creativity, poetry and music. I am also in charge of the sun, and light. And I am lord of healing, mice, dolphins, and sundry other specialties I've gathered up, some of which I've devolved to sons and others, but all of which I continue to keep half an eye on. But one of my most important aspects, to myself anyway, has always been knowledge. And that's where I overlap with owl-carrying Athene, who is goddess of wisdom and knowledge and learning. If I am intuition, the leap of logic, she is the plodding slog that fills in all the steps along the way. When it comes to knowledge, together we're a great team. I am, like my sister Artemis, a hunter. It's the chase that thrills me, the chase after knowledge as much as the chase after an animal or a nymph. (*Why* had she preferred becoming a tree?) For Athene it's different. She loves the afternoon in the library searching through footnotes and linking up two tiny pieces of inference. I am all about the "Eureka" and she is all about displacing and measuring actual weights of gold and silver.

I admire her. I really do. She's a half-sister. All of us Olympians are pretty much related. She's another virgin goddess, but unlike Artemis she doesn't make a fetish of her virginity. I always thought she was just too busy working on wisdom to get involved with all that love and sex stuff. Maybe she'd get around to it in a few millennia, if it seemed interesting at that point. Or maybe she wouldn't. She's very self-contained. Artemis is always bathing naked in forest pools and then punishing hunters who happen to see her. Athene isn't like that at all. I'm not sure she's ever been naked, or even thought about it. And nobody would think about it when they're around her. When you're around Athene what you think about is new ways of thinking about fascinating bits of knowledge you happen to have, and how you might be able to fit them together to make exciting new knowledge. And that's so interesting that the whole sex thing seems like a bit of relatively insignificant trivia. So there were a whole host of reasons I was reluctant to bring up the Daphne incident with her.

But I really was burning with the need to know why Daphne turned into a tree in preference to mating with me.

I went to see Athene, who was exactly where I expected her to be and doing exactly what I expected her to be doing. She fights when she needs to, of course, and she's absolutely deadly when she does—she has the spear and the gorgon shield and she knows everything about strategy. But most of the time she's in libraries, either mortal libraries or Olympian ones. She lives in a library. It looks like the Parthenon in Athens on the outside, and on the inside it looks like . . . a giant book cave. That's the only way to describe it.

There's one short stumpy pillar just inside, where the owl sits napping with its head curled around under its wing. Generally the spear and shield and helmet are leaning against that pillar. There's also a desk, where she sits, which is absolutely covered with scrolls and codices and keyboards and wires and screens. There's exactly one beam of sunlight that comes in between two of the outside pillars and falls in exactly the right place on the desk to illuminate whatever she's using at the moment. The rest of the room is just books. There are bookcases around the walls, and there are piles of books on the floor, and there are nets of scrolls hanging from the ceiling. The worst of it is that everything is organized—alphabetized, filed, sorted, even labelled, but nothing is squared off and it all looks like the most awful mess. I never go in there without wanting to straighten it all out. It bothers me. If I'm going to see her, often I ask her to meet somewhere comfortable to both of us, like the Great Library, or the Laurentian Library, or Widener.

As I said, we make a good team—but we generally make a team as equals. I don't tend to go to her as a suppliant. I don't tend to go to anyone as a suppliant, except Father when it's absolutely unavoidable. It's rare for me to need to. And with Athene, on this particular subject, it made me deeply uncomfortable.

Nevertheless I went to her library-home and stood in the beam of light until she realized it had widened to the whole desk and looked up.

"Joy to you, Far-Shooter," she said when she saw me. "News?"

"A question," I said, sitting down on the marble steps outside, so I wouldn't have to either hover in the air or risk treading on a book.

"A question?" she asked, coming out to join me. She lowered herself to the step, and we sat side by side looking out over Greece spread out before us— the hills, the plains, the well-built cities, the islands floating on the wine-dark sea, the triremes plying between them. We couldn't actually see the triremes from this distance unless we focused, but I assure you they were there. We can go wherever we want, whenever we want, but why would we stray far from the classical world, when the classical world is so splendid?

"There was a nymph—" I began.

Athene turned up her nose. "If this is all, I'm going back in to work."

"No, please. This is something I don't understand."

She looked at me. "Please?" she said. "Well, go on."

As I said, I don't often come in supplication, but that doesn't mean I don't know the words. "Her name was Daphne. I pursued her. And just as I caught her and was about to mate with her, she turned into a tree."

"She turned into a tree? Are you sure she wasn't a dryad all along?"

"Perfectly sure. She was a nymph, a nereid if you want to be technical about it. Her father was a river. She prayed to Artemis, and Artemis turned her into a tree. I asked Artemis why, and she said it was because Daphne wanted it so desperately. Why did she want to become a tree to avoid me? How could she care that much? She hadn't made a vow of virginity. Artemis told me to ask Hera and then said maybe you would know."

Grey-eyed Athene looked at me keenly as I mentioned Hera. "I thought I didn't know, but if she mentioned Hera then maybe I do. What's at the core of what Hera cares about?"

"Father," I said.

Athene snorted. "And?"

"Marriage, obviously," I said. I hate those Socratic dialogues where everything gets drawn out at the pace of an excessively logical snail.

"I think the issue you may be missing with Daphne, with all of this, is to do with consensuality. She hadn't vowed virginity, she might have chosen to give her virginity up one day. But she hadn't made that choice."

"I'd chosen her."

"But she hadn't chosen you in return. It wasn't mutual. You decided to pursue her. You didn't ask, and she certainly didn't agree. It wasn't consensual. And, as it happens, she didn't want you. So she turned into a tree." Athene shrugged.

"But it's a game," I said. I knew she wouldn't understand. "The nymphs run away and we chase after."

"It may be a game not everyone wants to play," Athene suggested.

I stared out over the distant islands, rising like a pod of dolphins from the waves. I could name them all, and name their ports, but I chose for the moment to see them as nothing but blue on blue cloud shapes. "Volition," I said, slowly, thinking it through.

"Exactly."

"Equal significance?" I asked.

"Mm-hmm."

"Interesting. I didn't know that."

"Well then, that's what you learned from Daphne." Athene started to get up.

"I'm thinking about becoming mortal for a while," I said, as the implications began to sink in.

She sat down again. "Really? You know it would make you very vulnerable."

"I know. But there are things I could learn much more quickly by doing that. Interesting things. Things about equal significance and volition."

"Have you thought about when?" she asked.

"Now. Oh, you mean *when*? When in time? No, I hadn't really thought about that." It was an exciting thought. "Some time with good art and plenty of sunshine, it would drive me crazy otherwise. Periclean Athens? Cicero's Rome? Lorenzo di Medici's Florence?"

Athene laughed. "You're so predictable sometimes. You might as well have said 'anywhere with pillars.'"

I laughed too, surprised. "Yes, that about covers it. Why, do you have a suggestion?"

"Yes. I have the perfect place. Honestly. Perfect."

"Where?" I was suspicious.

"You don't know it. It's . . . new. It's an experiment. But it has pillars, and it has art—well, it has very Apollonian art, all light and no darkness."

"Puh-lease." (That wasn't supplication, it was sarcasm. The last time I used the word it was supplication, so I thought I'd better clarify. But this was sarcasm, with which I am more familiar.) "Look, if you're about to suggest I go to some high-tech hellhole where they've never heard of me because it'll be a 'learning experience,' forget it. That's not what I want at all. I am Apollo. I *am* important." I pouted. "Besides, if they think the gods are forgotten, why are they writing about us? Have you read those books? There's nothing more clichéd. Nothing."

"I haven't read them and they sound awful, and the only thing I want to get from high-tech societies is their robots," she said.

"Robots?" I asked, surprised.

"Would you rather have slaves?"

"Point," I said. Athene and I have always felt deeply uneasy about slaves. Always. "So what do you want them for?"

Athene settled back on her elbows. "Well, some people are trying to set up Plato's Republic."

"No!" I stared down at her. She looked smug.

"They prayed to me. I'm helping."

"Where are they doing it?"

"Kallisti." She gestured towards where Thera was at the moment we were sitting in. "Thera before it erupted."

"They're doing it before the *Republic* was written?"

"I said I was helping."

"Does Father know?"

"He knows everything. But I haven't exactly drawn it to his attention. And of course, that side of Kallisti all fell into the sea when it erupted, so there won't be anything to show long-term." She grinned.

"Clever," I acknowledged. "Also, doing Plato's Republic on Atlantis is . . . recursive. In a way that's very like you."

She preened. "Like I said, it's an experiment."

"It's supposed to be a *thought* experiment. Who are these people that are doing it?" I was intrigued.

"Well, one of them is Krito, you know, Sokrates's friend. And another is Sokrates himself, whom Krito and I dragged out of Athens just before his execution. If Sokrates can't make it work, who can? And then there are some later philosophers—Platonists, Plotinus and so on, and some from Rome, like Cicero and Boethius, and from the Renaissance, Ficino and Pico . . . and some from even later, actually."

I was suspicious, and a little jealous. "And all of these random people in different times decided to pray to you for help setting up Plato's Republic?"

"Yes!" she sounded wounded that I doubted her. "They absolutely did. Every single one of them."

"I have to go there," I said. I wanted to try being mortal. And this was so fascinating, the most interesting thing I'd heard about in aeons. Plato's *Republic* had been discussed over centuries, but it had never actually been tried. "Where are you getting the children?"

"Orphans, slaves, abandoned children. And volunteers," she said, looking at me. "I almost envy you."

"Come too?" I suggested. "Once you have it set up, what would stop you?"

"I'm tempted," she said, looking tempted, the expression she has when she has a new book she very much wants to read right now instead of fulfilling some duty.

"Oh do. It'll be so interesting. Think what we could learn! And it wouldn't take long. A century or so, that's all. And it'll have libraries. You'll feel right at home."

"It'll certainly have libraries. What will be in them is another question. There's some dispute about that at the moment." She stared off at the clouds and the islands. "Being mortal makes you vulnerable. Open. Love. Fear. I'm not sure about that."

"I thought you wanted to know everything?"

"Yes," she said, still staring out.

We didn't have the least idea in the world what we were letting ourselves in for.

2

SIMMEA

I was born in Amasta, a farming village near Alexandria, but I grew up in the Just City. My parents called me Lucia, after the saint, but Ficino renamed me Simmea, after the philosopher. Saint Lucy and Simmias of Thebes, aid and defend me now!

When I came to the Just City I was eleven years old. I came there from the slave market of Smyrna, where I was purchased for that purpose by some of the Masters. It is hard to say for sure whether this event was fortunate or unfortunate. Certainly having my chains struck off and being taken to the Just City to be educated in music and gymnastics and philosophy was by far the best fate I might have hoped for once I stood in that slave market. But I had heard the men who raided our village saying they were especially seeking children of about ten years of age. The Masters visited the market at the same time every year to buy children, and they had created a demand. Without that demand I might have grown up in the Delta and lived the life the gods had laid out before me. True, I would never have learned philosophy, and perhaps I would have died bearing children to some peasant farmer. But who can say that might not have been the path to happiness? We cannot change what has happened. We go on from where we stand. Not even Necessity knows all ends.

I was eleven. I had rarely left the farm. Then the pirates came. My father and brothers were killed immediately. My mother was raped before my eyes and then led off to a different ship. I have never known what happened to her. I spent weeks chained and vomiting on the ship they threw me onto. I was given the minimum of bad food and water to keep me alive, and suffered many indignities. I saw a woman who tried to escape raped and then flogged to death. I threw buckets of seawater over the bloodstains on the deck and my strongest emotion was relief at breathing clean air and seeing daylight. When we arrived at Smyrna I was dragged onto the deck with some other children. It was dawn, and the slope of the shore rising out of the water was dark against the pink sky. At the top some old columns rose. Even then I saw how beautiful it was and my heart rose a little. We had been brought up on deck to have buckets of water thrown over us to clean us off for arrival.

The water was bone-chillingly cold. I was still standing on the deck as we came into the harbour.

"Here we are, Smyrna," one of the slavers said to another, taking no more notice of us than if we were dogs. "And that was the temple of Apollo." He gestured at the columns I had seen, and more fallen pillars that lay near them.

"Artemis," one of the others corrected him. "Lots of ships here. I hope we're in time."

From the harbour they brought us all naked and chained into the market, where there were men and women and children of every country that bordered on the Middle Sea. We were divided up by use—women in one place, educated men in another, strong men who might serve to row galleys in another. Between the groups were wooden rails with space for the buyers to walk about and look at us.

I was chained with a group of children, all aged between about eight and twelve, of all skin colours from Hyperborean fair to Nubian dark. My grandmother was a Libyan and the rest of my family all Copts, so I was slightly darker than the median shade of our group. There were boys and girls mixed indiscriminately. The only thing we had in common besides age was language—we all spoke Greek in some form. One or two of the others near me had been on my ship, but most of them were strangers. I was starting to realize how very lost I was. I had neither home nor family. I was never going to wake up and find that everything was back as it had been. I began to cry and a slaver backhanded me across the face. "None of that. They never take the snivelling ones."

It was a hot day and tiny flies rose all around and plagued us. With our hands bound before us at waist level we could not prevent them from getting into our eyes and noses and mouths. It was a tiny misery among many great miseries. I almost forgot it when the boy chained immediately behind me began to poke at me with his bound hands. I could not reach him except by kicking backwards, which he could see and I could not. I landed one hard kick on his shin but after that he dodged, almost pulling the whole line of us over. He taunted me as he did this, calling me fumble-foot and clumsy-cow. I held my silence, as I always had with my brothers, waiting for the right moment and the right word. I could have poked the girl in front of me, who was one of the pale ones, but saw no purpose in it.

When the Masters came we knew at once that they were something special. They were dressed like merchants, but the slavers bowed before them. The Masters acted towards the slavers as if they despised them, and the slavers deferred to them. It was clear in their body language, even before I could hear them. The slavers brought the Masters straight towards our group. The Masters were looking at us and paying no attention to the adult slaves bound in the other parts of the market. I stared boldly back at them. One of them wore a red hat with a flat top and little dents at the sides, which I noticed at once, before I noticed his eyes, which were so surprisingly penetrating that once I had seen them I could look at nothing else. He saw me looking and smiled.

The Masters spoke to each of us in Greek, asking questions. Several of them spoke strangely, with an odd lisping accent that slurred some of the consonants. The Master with the red cap came to me, perhaps because I had caught his eye. "What is your name, little one?" He spoke good Italianate Greek.

"Lucia the daughter of Yanni," I replied.

"That won't do," he muttered. "And how old are you?"

"Ten years old," I said, as the slavers had instructed us all to say.

"Good. And you have good Greek. Did you speak it at home?"

"Yes, always." This was nothing but the truth.

He smiled again. "Excellent. And you look strong. Do you have brothers and sisters?"

"I had three older brothers, but they are all dead."

"I am sorry." He sounded as if he truly was. "What's seven times seven?"

"Forty-nine."

"And seven times forty-nine?"

"Three hundred and forty-three."

"Very good!" He looked pleased. "Can you read?"

I raised my chin in the universal sign for negation, and saw at once that he did not understand. "No."

He frowned. "They so seldom teach girls. Are you quick to learn?"

"My mother always said so."

He sketched a symbol in the dust. "This is an alpha, ah. What words begin with alpha?"

I began to list all the words I could think of that began with alpha, among them, either because he himself put it into my mind or because I had heard it from the slaver as we came in, the name of the old god Apollo. Just as I said it the slaver came up. "This is a good girl," he said. "No trouble. Still a virgin, she is."

This was technically true, for virgins fetch more at the market. Yet that very man had emptied himself into my mouth the night before on the ship. My jaw was still sore from it as he spoke. The Master with the red hat turned on the slaver as if he guessed that. "I should think so, at ten years of age!" he snapped. "We will take her."

I was unchained and taken aside. About half the group were selected, among them the extremely fair girl and the boy who had been poking at me. I was glad to see a red mark on his shin from the one good kick I had given him.

The Masters paid what the slavers asked, unquestioningly. I could see how delighted the slavers were, although of course they tried to hide it. They had made more for each of us children than they would have for a beautiful young woman or a strong man. We were roped together and led down to a ship.

I had grown up on the shifting shore of the Delta, seeing ships only far out to sea, before the pirates had come in to attack us. Since then I had seen only their slave ship. I could tell that this ship was different, but not in what way. It had no banks of oars and no great square sail, but two masts and a series of stepped sails. I later learned that she was a schooner, and sailed by wind and tide alone. Her name was *Goodness*.

On the deck of the ship a woman was sitting with her legs crossed, a book in her hand. One of the Masters unbound the ropes from our hands and legs as we came aboard and we were led up to her in pairs. The woman seemed to be writing down the names of the children, after which they were led to a hatchway and disappeared. My own Master, he of the red hat, led me up to her with my tormentor. "These two have saints' names," he said. "Will you name them, Sophia?"

She looked up, and I saw that her eyes were grey. "Not I. You should know better than to ask, Marsilio. You name them."

"Very well, then. They were chained together. Write them down as Kebes, the boy, and Simmea, the girl." He smiled at me again as he named us. "These are good names, names that will stand you well in the city. Forget your old names, as you should forget your childhoods and your time in misery. You are going to a good place. You are all brothers and sisters here, all reborn to new lives."

"And your name, Master?" Kebes asked.

"He is Ficino, the Translator," the woman answered for him. "He is one of the Masters of the Just City."

Then one of the others shepherded us to the hatch, and we climbed down a ladder into a big open space. The hold was nothing like the hold of the slaver. It was surprisingly well lit by strange glowing beams that lay along the curving slope of the ship. By their light I could see that it was full of children, all strangers. I had never seen so many ten-year-olds in one place, and apart from the market, never so many people. There must have been more than a hundred. Some were sleeping, some were sitting in groups talking or playing games, others were standing alone. None of them took much notice of the new arrivals. There were so many strangers suddenly that those who had been chained by me seemed like friends by comparison. Kebes was the only one whose name I knew. I stayed beside him as we went in among the others. "Do you think the Masters mean well by us?" I asked him.

"I hate them," he replied. "I hate all of them, all Masters whoever they are, whatever they mean. I shall never forgive them, never submit to them. They think they bought me, think they changed my name, but nobody can buy me or change me against my will."

I looked at him, surprised. Like a dog who had been beaten, I had been ready to love and trust the first kind word I received. He was different. He looked fierce and proud, like a hunting hawk who cannot be tamed. "Why did you poke me?" I asked.

"I will not submit."

"I wasn't the one who bound you. I was bound beside you."

"I couldn't get at the ones who bound me, and you were bound beside me where you were the only one I could reach." He looked a little guilty. "It was a small rebellion, but the only one I could achieve at that moment. And besides, you got me back." He pointed at the fading mark on his leg. "We're equal. Tell me your name?"

"Simmea, the Master Ficino said." I saw his lip curl as if he despised me. "Oh, all right. Lucia."

"Well Lucia, though I shall call you Simmea and you may call me Kebes where the Masters can hear, my name is Matthias. And I will never forgive them. I may wait for my revenge, but I will get it when they do not expect it."

We had not even reached the city. The ship was barely out of the harbour of Smyrna. Already the seeds of rebellion were growing.

3

MAIA

I was born in Knaresborough in Yorkshire in 1841, the third child and second daughter of the local rector. My parents christened me Ethel.

My father, the Rev. John Beecham, M.A., was a scholar who had been at Oxford and cared as much or more for the classics than he did for God. My mother was a worldly woman, the daughter of a baron, and therefore entitled to call herself "the honourable," which she did on all occasions. She loved nothing so much as pretty clothes and decorations. Her recreations were embroidery and visiting friends, and her charity consisted of doing good works in the parish. My elder sister, Margaret, known as Meg, was so entirely my mother's daughter as to be almost another edition of her in miniature. My father had hoped to have the same for himself in my brother, Edward, who was born the year before me. Unfortunately, Edward's temperament was not at all like my father's. He was an active, energetic boy, but sadly unsuited to scholarship. My father frequently grew impatient with him. From the first I can remember, I was consoling Edward and helping him con his lessons.

I do not remember learning to read. Perhaps my mother taught me, as she had certainly taught Meg. I have been able to read for as far back as my memory stretches, so perhaps it is true what Plato says, that we bring some memories from our past lives. If so, then all I remembered was reading. Certainly I remember clearly that when I first saw the Greek alphabet, when I was six and poor Edward was seven, it came to me immediately, more like recollecting something forgotten than learning something new. The shapes of the Greek letters were like old friends, and I only needed to be told their names once. But for Edward it was torture. I remember coaching him in it over and over. He would get hopelessly lost, poor boy. That was when we began to work together in earnest. He would always bring me his lessons as soon as he left Father, and we would go over them together until he understood them. In this way we both progressed together in Latin and Greek. Soon I was reading ahead of him in his books. I had already read everything in the house in English.

Mother and Father did not take much notice of me in early childhood. I was brought down daily to greet my parents in the afternoon for an hour after tea, and often that was the only time I saw them. Meg was four years older than Edward and five years older than me. Mother taught Meg herself and took her about with her. She had a splendid wardrobe which suited her very well. She was a fetching child, good natured, always smiling and laughing, with golden curls and pink cheeks. My hair was paler, and lifeless in comparison, it would never take a curl. Nor did I ever try to charm the company. I retreated into myself until my mother thought me dull and sullen. When Meg was already old enough to begin to play the piano and to sew prettily, Edward and I were still under the care of our nurse.

Edward had his lessons with Father every morning. I stayed in the nursery and read everything I could lay my hands on. Then in the afternoons, after I had helped Edward understand his morning's lessons, we took healthful walks on the moors. This went on happily enough until Edward was twelve and Father began to talk of sending him away to school. Edward dreaded it, and begged to be allowed to stay at home. "But your work is so much better," Edward reported that Father had said. "Your last Latin composition had only one mistake, and your last Greek had none." Edward then burst out crying and admitted to Father that they were both my work. Father forgave him but was bewildered. "Little Ethel? But how does she know enough to do it?" He called me in and tested me on unseen passages of Greek and Latin, which I translated with pride and without difficulty.

Thereafter Father taught both of us together, and if anything he paid more attention to my progress than to Edward's, because I could follow his mind, which Edward could not. The next year Edward went off to school, scraping through his exam. Father continued to teach me. By the time Edward went to Oxford it was almost as if Father and I were colleagues, both scholars together, spending all day poring over a text and discussing it. Father said I had the wits of a man, and it was a shame I could not go to Oxford too, as I would get more benefit from it. I said that I did not want to leave him, but that perhaps Edward could bring us some more books. Father had a great desire to re-read Plato, which he did not own and had not read since he was himself at Oxford.

The year after, 1859, my father died, quite suddenly, of a chill that went to his lungs. Edward was in his second year at Oxford. Our lives changed overnight. The rectory, of course, had to be given up. Meg, who was twenty-three, had been betrothed for some time to the son of the local squire. It now seemed best to everyone that they be married immediately and set up housekeeping. My mother, almost as a matter of course, went to live with her. The day after the wedding I was sent off to my godmother, my father's sister, Aunt Fanny, in London. Aunt Fanny had made an advantageous marriage and was now Lady Dakin. She could better afford to support me than Meg's new husband.

Edward frowned at all this, but was powerless. My father's estate, such as it was, went to him. It was barely enough for him to live on and remain at Oxford. He promised me that when once he had graduated and found a living that would support us both, he would take me into his house as his housekeeper. He painted a rosy picture of the two of us living happily in some country rectory, him out hunting and me in the study writing his sermons. It seemed the best future I could aspire to.

Aunt Fanny was very kind and gave me a London season with her youngest daughter, my cousin Anne. It was not the kind of entertainment that was to my taste, causing me to continually twist about on myself with shyness, thrust out among so many strangers. I was not a success with the young men to whom I was presented.

Aunt Fanny and Anne constantly urged me to make the best of myself
and to wear lilac and grey after three months, but I insisted on wearing mourning black for my father for a whole year. Indeed, I missed him bitterly every
day. Also I missed my books. I had been allowed to bring only certain books
of Father's, and I felt parched for anything new. At the end of the London
season, with neither of us married and being no doubt desperate as to what
to do with two girls, Aunt Fanny carried us off on a tour to Italy. We had a
guide and a carriage and we stayed in *pensiones* or in the houses of friends. It
was all very grand, and at least it afforded me new things to see and think
about. Sometimes I could even tell the others the stories of the places we
were visiting, which always left them a little taken aback and caused the guide
to despise me.

Then in Florence I fell in love, as so many have before me, not with any
personage but with the art of the Renaissance. In the Pitti Palace I saw a
fresco that showed the destruction of the ancient world—Pegasus being set
upon by harpies!—and the refugee Muses coming to Florence and being
welcomed by Lorenzo de Medici. I was so overcome I had to borrow a hand-
kerchief from Anne to mop my eyes. Aunt Fanny shook her head. Young
ladies were supposed to admire art, but not so extravagantly.

Indeed, poor Aunt Fanny had no idea what to do with me. In the Uffizi,
she found the Botticelli Madonnas "papist." I realized as soon as I saw them
how bleak was the notion of God without any softening female spirit. I believed in God, of course, and in salvation through Christ. I had always been
a devout churchgoer. I prayed nightly. I believed in Providence and tried to
see its hand even through the difficulties of my life—which I reminded myself were not so very much to suffer in comparison with the lives so many
led. I might have been utterly destitute and forced to beg, or to prostitute
myself. I knew I was lucky. Yet I felt myself trammelled. Since Father died I
had never had the conversation of an equal, never indeed had any conversation
that was not at best quotidian. I wanted to talk to somebody about the female
nurturing element in God, about the lives of the angels visible in the background of Botticelli's Madonnas, and even more about the *Primavera*. Anne,
when I asked her what she thought, said she found the *Primavera* disturbing.
We stood in front of the *Birth of Venus* as the guide mouthed nonsense. We
moved on to another room and to Raphael, who had painted men I felt I
could have talked to. I was so lonely I could have talked to their painted selves,
had I been unobserved. I missed my father so much.

In the San Lorenzo market the next day, while Aunt Fanny and Anne were
cooing over some leather gloves, I stealthily moved to the next stall, which
was piled high with books. Some were in Italian, but many were in Greek

and Latin, among them several worn volumes of Plato. Even the sight of his name on the faded leather seemed to bring my father closer. The prices seemed reasonable; perhaps there was little demand for books in Greek. I counted my little store of cash, gift of my generous aunt who imagined I wanted to buy trifles. Instead I bought as many books as I could carry and the money would reach to. Of course I could not carry them inconspicuously, so my cousin and my aunt saw the pile as soon as I caught up with them. I saw dismay in Aunt Fanny's eyes, but she did her best to smile. "How like your father you are, dear Ethel," she said. "My own dear brother John. He would also spend all he had on books whenever he got the chance. But you must not let men think you are a bluestocking. There is nothing that they so dislike!"

The next day we left for Rome. I had decided to make my books last and read only one book a week, but instead I gorged myself on them. In Rome I saw the Colosseum and the ruins of palaces on the Palatine Hill. I read Plato.

Like everyone who reads Plato, I longed to stop Socrates and put in my own arguments. Even without being able to do that, reading Plato felt like being part of the conversation for which I had been so starved. I read the *Symposium* and the *Protagoras*, and then I began the *Republic*. The *Republic* is about Plato's ideas of justice—not in terms of criminal law, but rather how to maximize happiness by living a life that is just both internally and externally. He talks about both a city and a soul, comparing the two, setting out his idea of both human nature and how people should live, with the soul a microcosm of the city. His ideal city, as with the ideal soul, balanced the three parts of human nature: reason, passion, and appetites. By arranging the city justly, it would also maximize justice within the souls of the inhabitants.

Plato's ideas about all these things were fascinating and thought-provoking, and I read on, longing to talk about them with somebody else who cared. Then, in Book Five, I found the passage where he talks about the education of women, indeed about the equality of women. I read it over and over again. I could hardly believe it. Plato would have allowed me into the conversation from which my sex excluded me. He would have let me be a guardian, limited only by my own ability to achieve excellence.

I went over to the window and looked down on the busy Roman street. A workman was going past, carrying a ladder. He whistled at a young woman on a doorstep who called something back to him in Italian. I was a woman, a young lady, and this constrained me in everything. My choices were so unbearably narrow. If I wanted a life of the mind I could work at nothing but as a governess, or a teacher in a girls' school, teaching not the classics but the proper accomplishments of a young lady—sketching, watercolors, French

and Italian, playing the piano. Possibly I could write books; I was hazily aware
that some women did support themselves in that way. But I had no taste for
fiction, and writing philosophy would hardly be acceptable. I could marry,
if I could find a man like my father—but Father himself had not chosen a
woman like me, but one like my mother. Aunt Fanny was not wrong when
she said that men dislike bluestockings. I could perhaps keep house for Edward as he had suggested, and write his sermons, but what would then become of me if he were to marry?

In Plato's Republic, as never in all of history, my sex would have been no
impediment. I could have been an equal to anyone. I could have exercised
freely, and learned philosophy. I wished fiercely that it existed and that I
had been born there. He had written two thousand three hundred years
ago, and never in all that time had anyone paid any attention. How many
women had led stupid wasted unnecessary lives because nobody listened to
Plato? I was furious with all the world except Plato and my father.

I went back to my seat and took up the book again, reading on faster and
faster, no longer wanting to disagree with Socrates, saying yes in my heart,
yes to everything; yes, censor Homer, limit the forms of music, why not;
yes, take children into battle; yes, by all means exercise naked if you think
it better; yes, indeed, begin with ten-year-olds—how I would have loved it
at ten. Yes, please, please, dearest Plato, teach the best of both sexes to become philosopher kings who discover and understand the Truth behind
this world. I turned up the gas lamp and read most of the night.

The next morning Aunt Fanny complained that I looked fatigued, and
said that I should not exhaust myself. I protested that I was very well, and an
outing would revive me. The guide took us to see the Trevi Fountain, a huge
extravaganza which Anne admired, and then on to the Pantheon, a round temple to all the gods, built by Marcus Agrippa and since reclaimed as a Christian church. The dome leads the eye up inexorably to a circle of clear sky. I
looked at all the Catholic clutter of crucifixes and icons down below and
saw it as impious in this place which led the heart to God without any need
of it. Surely the philosopher kings would have divined God in the Truth.
Surely nobody could come in here without apprehending Him, even the
pagans who had built the place. Surely behind the façade of the mythology
they understood, perhaps without knowing what they understood. They had
no saints and prophets. Their gods were the best way for them to comprehend
the divine.

My thoughts turned to the Greek gods, and to the idea of the female principle within God that had struck me in Florence. Without in the least intending it I found myself praying to Athene, the female patroness of learning

and wisdom. "Oh Pallas Athene, please take me away from this, let me live in Plato's Republic, let me work to find a way to make it real."

I am sure that the next instant I would have realized what I was doing, and been shocked at myself and fallen to my knees and begged Jesus to forgive me. But that next instant never came. I was standing in the Pantheon looking up and praying to Athene, and then without any transition I was on Kallisti, in a pillared chamber full of men and women from many different centuries, all as bewildered as I was, with grey-eyed Athene herself standing unmistakably before us.

4

SIMMEA

I have never known what year it was when they bought me in Smyrna, or even what century. The Masters wanted us to forget our old homes, and when once much later I asked Ficino, he said he could not recall. Perhaps he truly could not. He must have been on many of those voyages, into many years. They gathered up ten thousand Greek-speaking children who appeared to them to be ten-year-olds. I have often thought since how much better it would have been for them to have gathered up the abandoned babies of antiquity—but then they would have needed wet nurses, so perhaps that would not have worked either.

We spent two nights on the *Goodness* before we came to the city on the afternoon of the third day.

My first sight of the city was overwhelming. The Masters brought us out in groups to see it as we approached. Kebes and I were among the last to come out, when we were almost in the harbor. The ruins at Smyrna had impressed me. The city was intact, was new made, and it had been positioned for maximum beauty and impact. Coming to it from the sea I saw the great mountain rising behind it, smoking slightly, and below that the slopes of the hills cupping the city. The city itself shone in the afternoon light. The pillars, the domes, the arches, all of it lay in the balance of light and shadow. Our souls know harmony and proportion before we are born, so although I had never seen anything like it, my soul resonated at once to the beauty of the city.

Immediately in front of us lay the harbor, with the mole curving out before it. This reflected in miniature the balance of man-made and natural elements in the city and the hills. I stood in awe, moved beyond words by the wonder of it. Kebes poked me in the ribs. "Where are the people?" he asked. "And what's that?"

I looked where he was pointing. "A crane?" I suggested.

"But it was moving." Indeed, it was moving. None of us had ever seen a Worker before. This one was the color of bronze, with treads and four great arms, each ending in a different kind of hand—a digger, a gripper, a claw, a scoop. It was easily twice the height of a man. I would have assumed it a kind of beast, except that it had nothing that could be considered a head. It was trundling along the harborfront ready to help us tie up, so we saw it very well as we came inside the mole. We were all asking each other what it was, and at last one of the Masters came and told us it was a Worker and that we were not to be afraid. "They're here to do the heavy work and help us," he said, in his strange slurred Greek.

Once the *Goodness* was tied up we were taken ashore in groups of fourteen, seven boys and seven girls. We were led off in different directions through the streets. I was glad Kebes was with me, and even more glad to be in the group led by Ficino. Whatever Kebes said, I already felt that Ficino was a friend. I looked about me eagerly as we went through the streets. They were broad and well-proportioned, and lined with pillared courts and houses and temples with statues of the gods. We passed the occasional Worker, some the same as the first but others shaped very differently. We saw no people until we had been walking for some time, when we heard the sound of children playing. We walked for some time more before we passed the palaestra where they were exercising—the sound had carried in the empty city. "Where are all the people?" I asked Ficino boldly.

"You are the people," he said, looking down at me. "This is your city. And not all of you are here yet."

A little while after that, a young woman came out of one of the houses. She was wearing a blue and white kiton with a key pattern around the borders, the first I had ever seen. She was fair-skinned, and her fair hair fell down her back in a neat braid. "Joy to you," she said. "I am Maia. The girls should come in here."

I lingered on the threshold as Ficino led the boys on. I did not want to lose track of the only people I knew. I was relieved to see them turning into the next house along the street.

"This is Hyssop house," Maia said, inside. I turned and went in. Inside it was cool. It seemed dark after the street, and it took my eyes a moment to adjust to the light that came in through the narrow windows. I saw that there were seven beds neatly lined up, one beside the door and three on each side of the room. A chest stood beside each one. Beyond them lay another door, which was closed. The walls and floor were marble, the roof had wooden beams.

"There is hyssop growing outside, by the door," one of the girls said, a tall girl as dark-skinned as my grandmother.

I hadn't noticed the hyssop. Maia nodded, clearly pleased. "Yes. All of the sleeping houses have their own flower or herb." Her Greek was strange, extremely precise but with odd hesitations as if she sometimes had to think to remember a word. Most disconcertingly she pronounced her V as B. "Each sleeping house sleeps seven people—either girls or boys, never mixed. Now I will teach you about hygiene."

She opened the other door, which led to the most amazing room I had ever seen. The marble floor and walls were striped black and white, and at the far end of the room the floor dipped into a trench with gratings underneath it. Above that were metal nozzles projecting from the wall. Maia shrugged out of her kiton and stood naked before us. She pressed a metal switch in the wall and water began to jet from the nozzles. "This is a wash-fountain," she explained. "It is to cleanse you. Come on."

We moved forward hesitantly. The water was cold, pleasant on a hot afternoon. "Take soap," Maia instructed, showing us another switch and putting her hand underneath a jet that provided a single gush of liquid soap when she pressed it. I had never encountered soap before. It felt strange on my palm. Maia showed us how to wash with the soap and how it lathered up in the water, she showed us how to wash our hair under the jets. "There is no shortage of water, but you should not be wasteful of the soap," she said.

"It smells of hyssop," said the girl who had noticed the hyssop outside.

Then Maia showed us the four cubicles at the other end of the room, each of which contained a latrine-fountain—a marble seat, with a lever to pull to summon water to carry away our wastes. "There are four latrine-fountains for the seven of you. Be reasonable in taking turns," she said. "Tomorrow I will teach you how to clean yourselves with oil and a scraper."

I was becoming numb with marvels when she led us back into the bedroom. "There is a bed here for each of you." She turned to the dark-skinned girl. "What is your name?"

"They said I was to be called Andromeda," she said.

"That's a wonderful name," Maia said, enthusiastically. "Andromeda, because you spoke first and noticed the hyssop, for now you will be the watcher for Hyssop house. You will have this bed by the door, and you will come for me if you need me—I will show you where I live. You will be in

charge of the house when I am not here, and you will take note and answer
for the conduct of the others. The rest of you choose beds now."

We looked at each other. We had been splashing comfortably together
in the wash-fountain, but now we were shy. I took a hesitant step towards a
bed, in the inner corner. The other girls sorted themselves out with no
squabbling—though two girls ran for the other corner bed, the girl who got
there second retreated and took the next bed. "Now open your chests," Maia
said. We did so. Inside were two undyed blankets, one linen and one wool.
"Dry yourselves on one." I took out the wool blanket and dried myself. "Now
put that one on the bed to dry. Take out the other." She picked up her kiton
and shook it. "This is how you wear it." She demonstrated. It was much harder
than it looked, especially making the folds. It took some of us a long time
to develop the skill of tucking it in—a thing that is second nature now, but
was difficult that first day. Maia gave each of us a leather belt and a plain
iron pin to fasten our kitons. "These will change," she said, but did not explain further.

"The other blanket is your cloak," she said, and showed us how to fold
the cloaks. "You won't need it before winter. They are also your blankets and
towels, as you have seen."

"They are ours?" one of the girls asked, touching the pin. "Ours to keep?"

"Yours to use," Maia said.

"Who is our Master?" Andromeda asked. "You?"

"You must obey all the Masters, but you are not slaves," Maia said. "Ficino
will explain later. Come on now. It is time to eat."

We were all dressed, and none of our kitons were actually falling off. Maia
led us to our dining hall. "Our dining hall is called Florentia," she said. "A
sleeping house is a small thing, though each has a name and a flower, and
you might want to embroider hyssop on your kiton later, if you care to. But
a dining hall is a very important matter. Each of them seats seventy people,
mixed boys and girls, and each of them is named for one of the great cities
of civilization."

"How many eating halls are there?" I asked.

"One hundred and forty-four," Maia answered at once.

I calculated in my head. "So there are ten thousand and eighty of us?"

"You're quick with numbers! What is your name?"

"Simmea," I said.

She smiled. "Another wonderful name. Well, Simmea, yes, there will be
ten thousand and eighty of you, twelve tribes, a hundred and forty-four dining halls. And you will all learn about the cities of your dining halls and
take pride in their accomplishments."

"And is Florentia a great city?" Andromeda asked. "I never heard of it."

"You will hear about it soon," Maia promised.

The dining hall was immense. It was built of stone, not marble, and it had narrow windows and a twisting tower rising from one corner. Inside it had a courtyard with a fountain, and stairs leading up to a big room with a great cacophony of children sitting on benches drawn up at tables. I was glad to spot Ficino and Kebes sitting eating among the others. They were both wearing kitons, but Ficino kept on his red hat.

Maia found us places, all together at one of the tables. Kebes saw me and waved a hand as I sat down. "We all take turns serving," Maia explained. I was hungry. A boy brought out trays of food and set them down where we could help ourselves. The food was amazing—it was bread and fresh cheese with olives, artichokes, cucumbers, and olive oil, with fresh clean water to drink. That first night I remember we had a delicious buttery ham that seemed to melt on my tongue.

It was when I was eating the ham that I looked up and saw the paintings. On all the walls of the room hung paintings, ten of them, all of mythological scenes, and nine of them painted with a wonderful delicacy of imagination that made me stare and stare. I did not see all ten that night, only the one on the opposite wall, which showed an old man with a long beard shaking snow from his cloak while beautiful young women danced around a frozen fountain and a wolf gnawed at a bundle dropped by a fleeing hunter. I had never seen snow before, but that was not why I couldn't stop staring.

"You're not eating, Simmea," Maia said after a time. I realised I was sitting there with ham in my mouth and not chewing.

"I'm sorry," I said, closing my mouth and swallowing. "But the painting! Who did it? What is it?"

"Sandro Botticelli did it, in Florence. Florentia," she corrected herself at once. "It's *Winter*. It's part of a set. *Summer* and *Autumn* are here too."

"Not *Spring*?"

"*Spring* is in the original Florentia," she said. "But I can show you a reproduction one day, if you like it."

"Like it? Of all the wonders here it is the most wonderful," I said. I had seen paintings before. There were two ikons in the church at home, one of the Virgin and one of Christ crucified. Botticelli left them in the dust.

After dinner we went off to bed. It turned out that there was a glowing beam in Hyssop House, which gave us enough light to use the latrine-fountains and then undress and get into bed. Maia showed Andromeda how to turn it off, using a switch near the door. I curled up under my two blankets and slept. The next morning Andromeda woke us, and we cleaned ourselves again in the wash-fountains before going back to the dining hall. There were even more children present, though the hall was not full. I saw Maia was sitting with a another group of girls who were staring around, amazed. We were served a porridge made of nuts and grains, and there was as much fruit as we wanted. I had seated myself where I could see Botticelli's *Autumn* as I ate, and I kept looking up at the rich leaf-colors and half-hidden faces.

At the end of the meal Ficino stood up, and after considerable hushing we all fell silent. "You are all gathered now, my little Florentines, ten sleeping houses gathered into this dining hall. You came from many different places, many different families. But now you are here in the city, and you are all brothers and sisters. Let your old life be to you like a dream on waking. Shake it off, as if you had come here fresh from Lethe. Imagine you had been sleeping in the soil of this island and dreaming all you remember, and that your life begins here and now. When you were under the soil the metals of the Earth mixed in you, so that you are all a mixture of iron and bronze and silver and gold. Soon you will learn which metals are uppermost in you, and what you are good for. Here in the Just City you will become your best selves. You will learn and grow and strive to be excellent."

He beamed around at us all. I saw that Kebes was looking down and frowning. Then Ficino spoke again. "We begin today. Those who can read to my left, those who cannot to my right."

I went to his right, and indeed, that was when my life truly began.

5

MAIA

A young lady from Queen Victoria's England does not expect to have her prayers answered, or at least not in such a direct and immediate way, and certainly not by Pallas Athene. My first thought as I looked at all the variously dressed people around me, united only in their expressions of complete bewilderment, was that throughout history everyone had wanted to know the truth about God, about the gods, and now there could be no question. There were gods, they did care about humanity, and one of them was Pallas Athene. She stood still, looking gravely out over the hall. She was half again the height of the tallest of the men, just as Homer describes her, with her helmet, spear, and an owl tucked under her arm. The owl was looking at me. I nodded my head to it. I should have wondered if this was a dream, but there was no doubt whatsoever that it was real. It was the most real thing that had ever happened.

Then Athene spoke. I had never before heard anyone speak Greek, though my father and I had sometimes read it aloud. I was so overwhelmed by the naturalness of the way the syllables sounded that it took me a moment to catch up to what she was actually saying.

"You have come from many times, but with a shared purpose. You all wished to work to set up Plato's Republic, to build the Just City. Here we are. This is your plan, but you have all asked me for help. I suggest we discuss how to go about it and what we will need."

A long-haired young man in the habit of a Dominican monk stepped forward. "Are we dead, Sophia?" he asked. "Is this place the afterlife?"

"You are not dead," Athene said, smiling kindly at him. "You stand here in your mortal bodies. Some of you who were near death have been healed of your infirmities." She nodded to the Dominican. "You will age naturally. When you die here, in the course of time, your body will be returned to the moment you left."

How would that work? I couldn't quite imagine it. Would Aunt Fanny and Anne look around for me and find instead the corpse of an old lady? An old lady who had grown old in Plato's Republic? I found myself smiling as I realised I didn't care.

"And our souls?" a man in a toga asked.

"Your souls will also go back to that moment and be reborn from that time, not from this time."

There was a murmur across the room, as three hundred people said to themselves happily in their native languages: "We have immortal souls! I *knew* it!" I could only understand Latin and Greek and English, and I heard it in all three of those languages.

A white-bearded man in a Greek kiton, looking the very image of a philosopher, asked "Are they three-part souls as Plato described?"

"Would anyone prefer to return to their own time now?" Athene asked, either not hearing or ignoring the attempt to clarify the issue of our souls. "This would seem like a dream, soon forgotten."

To my surprise three men raised their hands. Athene blinked, and they disappeared. I was looking at one of them, a shabby man with a donnish look, wondering how he could possibly not want to stay, when he just wasn't there anymore.

"Now, we need to make plans," she said.

"But where are we, Sophia? You spoke of our own times. When are we?" It was a man in Renaissance clothes and a red hat.

"We are in the time before the fall of Troy. And we are on the doomed island of Kallisti, called by some Atlante." Even I had heard of Atlantis.

"Then what we make cannot last?" he asked.

The goddess inclined her head. "This is an experiment, and this is the best time and place for that experiment. Nothing mortal can last. At best it can leave legends that can bear fruit in later ages."

After that, with the big questions out of the way, we began to discuss how we would go about the work.

It soon became clear that we were united on many issues and divided on others, and that there were practical problems none of us had thought through. Plato's *Republic* was extremely specific on some issues and distressingly vague on others. It wasn't really intended to be used as a blueprint.

There were almost three hundred of us, from twenty-five centuries. There were close to equal numbers of men and women, which astounded me at first. I had never before met another woman who cared about scholarship. Now I did, and it was wonderful. Before long I realised that most of the women were much like me, young, and fortunate enough to obtain enough education to make their possible lives unsatisfactory. I met young women from every century, including several from my own and the century after.

"It does get better," one of them reassured me. Her name was Kylee, and she was wearing what seemed to me a man's suit, but cut to her form. "In the eighteen-seventies they established colleges for women at Oxford and Cambridge, and in America too. By the nineteen-twenties they began to grant degrees. By the nineteen-sixties they were actually nominally equal to the men's colleges."

"More than a hundred years from me," I said.

"And even in my time it's a wearisome business," she said. "It's not that I want to die, but not being allowed to offer to die for my country means that my country doesn't consider me a true citizen."

We young women from the Centuries of Progress were one clear group. The men of the Renaissance were another. The Neoplatonists made a third. This was Kylee's name for the group led by Plotinus and sharing a particular mystical interpretation of Plato based around numerology. They called themselves simply Platonists, of course. Plotinus was the white-bearded man who had asked the question about three-part souls when we first arrived.

There were also many Romans, who could have been considered a fourth group except that they never agreed about anything and so could not be thought of as a faction. I was delighted to find Marcus Tullius Cicero among them, and his friend Titus Pomponius Atticus. Atticus was charming; he reminded me a little of my father. How I wished my father could have been here—but he would never have prayed to a pagan goddess. When Atticus introduced me to Cicero, whom he called Tullius, I found he was less delighted to meet me. He was not among those who believed Plato on the equality of women. He was flattered when he found how much of his work I had read, and how high his reputation stood in my century, but he could never really consider me, or any of us women, as people to be taken seriously.

The difficulties and complications of actually putting Plato's ideas into practice were immense. But we had Athene, whom we all addressed as Sophia, meaning "wisdom." She had brought the Workers—automata that could follow orders and build and plant crops and perform even more wonders. "They come from the future. They are here to labor for you," she said.

Very few of us had seen anything like them before. Kylee said they were robots, and "Workers" was a good translation of that. She said they were more advanced than any such things in her own day.

We formed into committees to work on different aspects of the Republic. We came together to report on progress in formal sessions, which we came to call Chamber. At first we had just that one hall, where we all slept in drafts on the cold marble floor. It was lucky it was summer. We drank water from a spring, and had the Workers dig trenches for latrines. Then we had them build a fountain, and bathrooms, and kitchens. Few of us knew how to cook, but fortunately the Workers had some limited abilities in that area.

As we had, as yet, no philospher kings, and as we could acknowledge no leader but Athene, we decided that for the time being, when we did not agree, we would vote on an issue. Athene smiled at this. The first divisive issue that came to a vote was names. We voted that those of us with inappropriate names would adopt new names, and that we would do the same with the children who came to us, naming them from the *Dialogues* and from Greek mythology. Kylee and some others felt strongly against this, but in the vote after the debate, the majority carried the day. I adopted the name Maia, for my birth month, and for the mother of Hermes. Kylee took the name Klio, as being the closest she could come to her original name. We also agreed that we would have one unique name each. The Romans and others who had multiple appropriate names would limit themselves to just one.

For the first time ever I was fully engaged in life. I cared about everything. I read the *Republic* over and over, I took part in debates in Chamber, I served on committees, I had opinions and was listened to. It was marvellous. I woke up every morning on the cold floor of the hall, happy simply to be alive. I daily thanked God, the gods, Athene, for allowing me to be there and part of all of it. That's not to say that it couldn't be infuriating.

I served on the Technology Committee. We had long debates about how much technology to allow. Some of us felt that we should do it with the technology of the day, or that which Plato would have understood. But we already had the Workers, and without Workers we should have needed slaves. The Workers needed electricity, which was produced from the sun. Sufficient electricity to feed the Workers would also provide good lighting, and a certain amount of heating and cooling. "The advantage of that," Klio said, when she presented our recommendations to the whole Chamber, "will be to keep the library at a constant temperature to better protect the books."

Most of the older people and all of the famous ones were men, but most of the people who understood technology in any way were young women. Though we had nominal equality, there were always those like Tullius who would not accept us as equals. In addition I saw in other women and detected in myself a tendency to defer to older men—as I had always deferred to my father. We had grown up in slavery and bore the marks of our shackles, as Klio said when I talked to her about this, but we were to raise a generation in the hope of true freedom. The committee on technology was almost entirely composed of young women, with only one man, the Dominican, whose name was now Ikaros. Somehow, imperceptibly, because of this, technology came to be seen among the Masters as feminine and unimportant. We voted to have lights but not to have heating and cooling, except for the library. We voted to have plumbing everywhere, but only with cold water, which seemed like the morally better choice, and what Plato would have wanted. We made up Greek names for shower-baths and toilets.

Ikaros served on several of my committees—indeed, he had volunteered for every committee as they were being set up. He had been accepted onto an improbable number of them, and served on all those that did not meet at the same time. He seemed to have boundless energy and enthusiasm, as well as being notably younger than most of the other men. He was also extremely good-looking, with a wonderful smile and long chestnut hair. Working together so much, we became friends. He seemed to be everyone's friend, moving through all the different circles charming everyone. He was even a favorite with Athene, who seemed to unbend a little when she spoke to him.

Plotinus and the Neoplatonists dominated the committee designing the physical form and organization of the city. They announced that Athene would bring in mature trees, and we voted that through. Then they proposed that there would be ten thousand and eighty children, divided into twelve tribes, each divided into a hundred and forty-four eating houses that would each be named after a famous city of civilization. We voted this through without dissent. A hundred and forty-four eating houses allowed everyone to get their favourite cities mentioned. The proposal was made that the eating houses be decorated in the style of their cities, which I thought a charming idea. There would be two Masters attached to each eating house, as far as possible one man and one woman. "Are there any Florentine women here?" I asked Ikaros after a Tech Committee meeting. I hadn't noticed any in their group.

"Not that I can think of," he said. "Why, do you want to be attached to the Florence house?"

"I loved it so much. And it's where I found Plato. I never got to Greece, only as far as Italy."

"Talk to Ficino. He's bound to be the man who gets Florence." He sounded a trifle envious. Ficino's name was now formally Fikinus, but everyone went right on addressing him as Ficino.

We voted that we would all adopt the kiton, and those who knew how to wear one instructed the rest. The Workers wove the cloth for them. I had lessons in how to don one from Krito himself, the friend of Sokrates. Once I was used to it I found it charmingly practical and comfortable. The kitons had an unexpected benefit—once we were all dressed alike, the factions among us were less immediately visible, if no less real.

On the women's committee, Kreusa, originally a hetaira from first-century Corinth, explained the use of menstrual sponges. We voted by acclamation that this method would be the usual and standard method of the Republic. We did not even present it to the full Chamber. Workers could easily harvest the sponges. We knew the men wouldn't recognize or care about their significance. We had agreed that the Masters should not have children of our own, and Kreusa told us about silphium root, which had the ability to prevent conception. We agreed that it should be available to all female Masters who wanted it.

I was the only woman on the committee to select art, on which Ficino, Atticus, and, inevitably, Ikaros, also served. Plato is very clear about the purposes of art, and what forms of it should be permitted in the Republic. We were divided on whether we should have only original art or allow copies. This was an issue on which passions ran high, and on which Ficino, Ikaros and I were united—the children should see only originals if they wanted to learn excellence. We should ask Athene to allow us to rescue lost and destroyed art to adorn the city. Copies, especially copies created by Workers and more than once, would make them see art in entirely the wrong light.

Atticus and some of the others argued against us. "We have already decided that the eating houses will be copies of buildings in the cities they are named for," he said. "If the Workers can build them, and if it won't harm the children to see a hundred and forty-four copies of architecture, then how can art be different?"

"It would be better if we could get the original buildings too," I said. "But it's not possible. It is possible to get the art."

"It might be possible to get some buildings," Ficino said. "Sophia isn't just wise, she's powerful as well."

"Were there enough suitable buildings that have disappeared?" I asked. "I don't know about Greece, but when I was in Rome it looked as if every brick and piece of marble was being reused in some other building."

Ikaros shook his head. "It's completely different. It wouldn't be better if we could get original buildings, because the real problem then would be that the buildings wouldn't be so suited to our purposes as the ones we will build. The design for the sleeping houses, for example, is elegant and ideal." He was on that committee as well, of course. "We want them to be identical and classical and useful, and that's how they are. We don't want the city to be full of repetition because that would teach the wrong lesson. The sleeping houses will all be the same; the palaestras where the children will exercise will be functionally the same, but have different decoration, for variety. And the same goes for the eating houses, temples, libraries, and practice halls. We want everything to be as well-suited to what we need it for as can be. Making new buildings in the style of old ones is best for that, for buildings. They won't really be copies, not functionally."

"Functionally?" Atticus repeated, frowning.

"The buildings for our city have different functions from the buildings in any existing city. Even if we had all the choice in the world, it would be difficult to find sufficient buildings with big eating halls and kitchens and rooms of the right size for classes," Ikaros explained. "Ideally they'd all be new designs by wonderful architects, but as it is, we've decided to take the features of the old buildings, in the styles of the cities the halls are named after, and have the Workers reproduce them on our buildings."

"But why couldn't we do that with art as well?" Atticus asked. "The Workers could just as easily reproduce that."

"But the original art best fits the Platonic purpose," I said.

"Plato says art should show good people doing good things as an example to the children," Atticus said.

"Yes, and also be an example of beauty, to open their souls to excellence," I added.

Ikaros looked approvingly at me. "Yes! And when it comes to art, the best is definitely the originals."

"Jupiter!" Atticus swore. "They won't be able to tell if they're originals or copies."

"Their souls will," Ficino said.

Eventually we won the day, which the three of us celebrated at dinner with cold water and barley porridge. Ficino and Ikaros shared memories of wines they had drunk together in Florence, and discussed how long it would be before the grapes the Workers had planted could produce a vintage. We pretended to be mixing our water with wine, in best classical practice, and Ikaros pretended to grow a little drunk, whereupon Ficino reproached him by quoting Socrates on temperance, and Ikaros pretended to be abashed. I had never spent a pleasanter evening nor laughed so much.

Back on the committee the next day, it became apparent that Ficino and Ikaros wanted to save everything.

"The Library Committee is sending an expedition to the Great Library of Alexandria to rescue everything," Ikaros said. He also served on that committee. "Manlius and I are going. We're going to have it all, all the written work of antiquity, though we will of course control access to it. Why not all the art we can find?"

"We have to be selective and make sure it fits what Plato wanted," Atticus said.

"How could it not?" Ficino asked.

"Before we allow it into the city we need to examine everything to make sure it does," Atticus insisted. We all agreed to this.

We put together a complete program of art rescue through the centuries. It all had to fit the message we wanted the children to understand from it, and of course it had to be on classical themes. There was a huge amount of art potentially available from the ancient world—it was heartbreaking that so much had been destroyed. I entirely agreed that we should save as much as we could. There were many lost works available from the Renaissance which were also deemed likely to be worthy. Athene took the men of the Art Committee on several expeditions. To my astonishment and delight, they brought back nine lost Botticellis, snatched from the Bonfire of the Vanities.

"At first I pretended to be a Venetian merchant and tried to buy them, but Savonarola wouldn't listen. In the end we stole them and replaced them with worthless canvases we'd bought," Atticus said, laughing.

"Who ever met a Venetian who could only speak pure Classical Latin?" Ikaros teased.

"Look at the *Judgement of Paris*," Atticus gloated, taking it off with him to show Tullius.

"Does that show good people performing good actions?" I asked, quietly, so that Atticus wouldn't hear.

Ikaros grinned at me. "Some of these show mysterious people performing mysterious actions. But they do lift the soul."

"They certainly do," I said.

Ficino spread out another, smiling. "These will hang in the Florentine dining hall," he said.

"Do you have a woman Master for Florence yet?" I asked. "Because if not, I'd really like to volunteer."

"So you can see these every day?" Ficino asked, looking proudly at *Winter*.

"Yes, and because, though I'm not a Florentine I loved Florence so much," I said.

"I'll think about it. I should find out whether there's anyone with a better claim," he said. "What would you think would be the best Florentine building to emulate as the eating hall?"

"Oh, it's hard to choose, because it was all so beautiful," I said. "Perhaps the Baptistry? It's a shame the Uffizi wouldn't really be practical, even though that would be the best setting for these wonderful Botticellis."

"The Uffizi is a symbol of Medici power and the loss of the freedom of the Florentine Republic," Ficino said, frowning.

"Then the Palazzo Vecchio," I said, at once. "That was for the Republic, and it's so beautiful."

"Much too big," Ikaros said, cheerfully. "Now for Ferrara, Lukretia has suggested we can do half of the castle."

"How about the Palazzo Vecchio at half-size," Ficino suggested, ignoring Ikaros and looking at me.

"I think that would be splendid," I said, as affirmatively as I could.

"Or maybe we should have something in three parts, for the three parts of the soul," he mused. "It's going to be so wonderful to see the children grow up and the best of them really become philosopher kings."

"I can hardly wait," I said. "It's wonderful to think we're getting everything ready for them. Did anyone tell you yet that the Tech Committee have decided to go with full printing in both languages for the reproduction of books? So everything will be available to all of us through the library. And first, immediately after the complete works of Plato, we're going to print the things Ikaros and Manlius rescued from Alexandria, so that all of us can read them."

"Excellent," Ficino said. "I shall volunteer to work on translations so that I can see things early."

"New plays by Sophokles!" Ikaros exulted. "And the original works of Epicurus, and the Hedonists! I'm going to read them the second they're printed." He grinned. "I'm on the Censorship Committee, so I'll get to them before anyone."

6

SIMMEA

I learned to read, first in Greek and then in the Latin alphabet. Before the end of a year I was reading both languages fluently, though I had not known Latin before. There were many native Latin speakers among the Masters, which made it easy to pick up. Even those who were not native Latin speakers knew it well, for, as they told us, it had been the language of civilization for centuries. I was soon speaking and reading both languages easily. I no longer noticed the slurring and softening accent so many Masters had, or even the use of B for V. I had begun to speak Greek like that myself.

I began to learn history before they began to teach it to me, and I knew without examining it that this was the history of the future. We were living, they told us, in the time before the Trojan War. King Minos ruled in Crete and Mycenae was the greatest city on the mainland. Yet, although it had yet to happen, we knew all about the Trojan War—a version of the *Iliad* was one of our favorite books. We knew about the Peloponnesian War, for that matter, and the wars of Alexander, and the Punic Wars, and Adrianople, and in less detail about the fall of Constantinople, and the Battle of Lepanto. When I asked Ficino what happened after Lepanto he said it was after his time, and when I asked Axiothea, who taught us mathematics, she said that history got boring after that and was nothing but a series of inventions, the laws of motion, and telescopes, and electricity, and Workers, and so on.

From the beginning, and by design, we rarely had a free moment. Our time was divided equally between music and gymnastics. Music came in three parts—music itself, mathematics, and learning to read, later su
reading. Gymnastics also had three parts—running, wrestling, i

Gymnastics was fun. It was done naked in the palaestra. The
laestra shared between each two eating halls. Our palaestra wa

and Delphi, and it had rows of Doric columns for Delphi along the back and two sides, and exuberant Renaissance columns along the front, with a very elaborate fountain. I felt proud that Florentia had contributed the fountain. It was easy to love and feel pride in Florentia, that great city, with so many great scholars, writers, and artists. Ficino himself came from Florentia. When we came to dye and embroider our kitons, I embroidered mine with a running pattern of lilies, the Florentine symbol, and above them snowflakes, leaves, and roses, for Botticelli's three seasons, which remained my favourite pictures. Above those I put a pattern of interspersed books and scrolls, in blue and gold, which so many people admired and asked permission to copy that it became quite commonplace.

Our palaestra stood open to the air, naturally, and the ground inside was made of white sand, which the hundred and forty of us churned up every day and the Workers raked smooth every night. I soon stopped feeling conscious of nakedness—we all took off our kitons when we went into the palaestra, it was just what we did. I learned to use the weights, both lifting and throwing, and to wrestle, and to run. I was good at running, and was always among the first at races, especially at long distances. I soon learned that I would never excel at wrestling, being small and wiry, but found it good fun when matched against somebody my own weight. Weights, once I had learned how to handle them, were a delight, though there were always people who could throw the discus further and lift heavier weights than me.

The odd thing about gymnastics was that we didn't really have enough teachers. Only the younger Masters could teach it, and not even all of them. This oddity made me realise how few Masters there were. There were two Masters assigned to each dining hall, and just a handful of others. There were a hundred and forty-four dining halls, now completed with seventy children in each. That meant there were only two hundred and eighty-eight Masters in all, or perhaps three hundred at most, to ten thousand and eighty children. I thought about the implications of this, and decided not to point this out to Kebes. He still muttered about wanting to overthrow the masters, but I was happy.

How could I not have been happy? I was in the Just City, and I was there to become my best self. I had wonderful food—porridge and fruit every morning, and either cheese and bread or pasta and vegetables every night, with meat or fish on feast days, which came frequently. On hot days in summer we often had iced fruit. I had regular congenial exercise. I had friends. And best of all, I had music, mathematics, and books to stretch my mind. I learned from Maia and Ficino, from Axiothea and Atticus of Delphi, from Ikaros nd Lucina of Ferrara, and from time to time from other Masters. Manlius taught me Latin. Ikaros, one of the youngest men among the Masters, set us to read provocative books, and asked fascinating questions about them. Sometimes he and Ficino would debate a question in front of us. I could almost feel my mind growing and developing as I listened to them. I was twelve years old. I still missed my parents and my brothers, sometimes, when something recalled them to me. But little did. My life was so different now. Sometimes it truly felt as if I had slept beneath the soil until I awakened in the City.

In the winter of that year, Year Two of the Just City, just before I turned thirteen, I began my menstruation, and Andromeda, who was still the watcher for Hyssop, took me to Maia. Maia had a little house of her own near Hyssop, with a neatly tended garden of herbs and flowers. Maia made me a peppermint tea, and gave me three sponges and showed me how to insert them into my vagina. "One of these will last you for an hour or so on the first day, longer than that afterwards. You can probably leave the same one in all night unless you're bleeding very heavily. You can clean them in the wash-fountains, never in drinking water. If you hold it under the running water all the blood will wash out. Insert a fresh one and let the first one dry in sunlight on the windowsill. Store them in your chest when you are not using them. Never use anyone else's sponge or share yours with your sisters. Three should be all you need, but if you find you are bleeding too heavily and needing to change them often on the first day so that there is not a sponge dry when you need it, let me know and I will give you a fourth."

"These are marvellous," I said, and then went on, forgetting that I should not talk about my earlier life. "My mother used cloths that were horrible to wash."

"Mine too, and so did I before I came here," Maia said. "This way of managing menstruation is one of the lost marvels of the ancient world. The sponges are natural. They grow under the sea. Workers harvest them for us."

I turned the two clean sponges over in my hand. They were soft. "Am I a woman now?"

"You were born a woman." Maia smiled. "Your body will be making some changes. Your breasts will grow, and you might want to pleat your kiton so it falls over them. If they grow very big so that they flop about and feel uncomfortable when you run, I will show you how to strap them up."

"What will—" I stopped. "What happens here about marriage?" I realized I'd never heard a word about it, nor even thought about it since I had come here. All of the Masters lived alone, and all of the rest of us were still children.

"When all of you are older there will be marriages, but they will not be

like the marriages you . . . should not remember!" Maia said. "No need to
worry about it yet. Your body is not ready to make children, even if bleeding has begun."

"When will it be?" I asked.

Maia frowned. "Most of us think twenty, but some say sixteen," she said.
"In any case, a long time yet."

Then she took down a book. "Long ago I promised to show you Botticelli's *Spring*," she said.

Spring was as marvellous and mysterious as the other three seasons. I tried
to figure it out. There was a girl at the side, and a pregnant woman in the
centre with flowers growing around her. "Who are they all?" I asked. "Are
those the same flowers that are growing in *Summer*?" I glanced at the opposite
page of text for help, and was astonished to see it was in the Latin alphabet,
but a language unknown to me. I looked inquiringly at Maia.

"It's the only reproduction I have. Nobody knows who they all are, though
some think she's the goddess Flora."

I stared back at the picture, ignoring the mystery of the text. "I wish I
could see the original at full size like the others." I turned the page and gasped.
It was Aphrodite rising from the waves on a great shell. Maia leaned forward, then relaxed when she saw what it was.

"I really wish you could have seen the original of that one," she said. "It's
so much better than the reproduction. It fills a wall. There are strands of
real gold in her hair."

"When will we be taught to paint and sculpt?" I asked, touching the picture longingly. The paper was glossy to the touch.

"We don't have enough Masters who can teach those things," Maia said.
"Florentia should have a turn next year, or perhaps the year after. Ideally,
you'd have been learning all along. Meanwhile, I was intending to ask you if
you would teach some beginners to swim in the spring."

"Of course," I said. Growing up in the Delta, I'd been swimming for
almost as long as I'd been walking. I had won the swimming race at the
Hermeia, as well as coming in second in the footrace. I'd been given a silver
pin for these accomplishments, which had been the proudest moment of my
life. Silver meant bravery and physical prowess. Only gold, for intellectual
attainment, ranked higher, and nobody I knew had a gold pin yet.

Maia put her hand out for the Botticelli book. I took a last look at the
Aphrodite and gave it back. She turned the pages and showed me a portrait
of a man in a red coat. "We don't know who he was, some scholar of the
time I've always thought."

"I love his face," I said. "Is that picture in Florentia too?"

"Yes," Maia said.

"Perhaps I'll travel there one day."

"It wouldn't do you any good. You know they haven't been painted yet." Maia smiled.

"Maybe I'll go there in the time when they have been painted. When I'm grown up and finished being educated, I mean."

"No." Maia looked serious now. "No, we've been brought here out of time by Pallas Athene for a serious purpose. We're here to stay now, all of us. We can't go wandering about in time on expeditions to look at pictures."

"Why not? Pictures are important."

"Art is important only as a way of opening the mind to excellence," Maia said, but she didn't sound very sincere. She took the book back and closed it. In the seconds I could see it I noticed that it had a circular picture of the Madonna on the cover, surrounded by angels. She put it on a high shelf with other books.

"Oh, please!" I said.

"You know I can't show you that. I probably shouldn't have shown you this book at all."

"How is it that we have the nine Botticelli paintings that we do have?" I asked.

"They were going to be destroyed and we rescued them," Maia said.

"Mother Hera!" I didn't often swear, but I couldn't stop myself blurting it out. "Destroyed!"

"Yes, some terrible things happened in that future you'd like to visit to look at paintings! You're much better off here. Now, go to bed, and let me know if you need any more sponges."

I bade her joy of the night and went off thoughtfully down the street. The city looked especially beautiful by moonlight. I raised my arms and murmured a line of a praise-song to Selene Artemis. But my mind was buzzing, not with thoughts of menstruation and marriage, which I had almost forgotten, but with Botticelli. The mysterious figures gathered around in *Spring*. The smile of his Aphrodite. The thought that our nine paintings would have been destroyed. Was that true of all the art in the city, I wondered? Had Phidias's gold and ivory Athene in the agora been rescued? How about the Herm I had been crowned before, the one with the mysterious smile? What about the bronze lion on the corner I always patted as I went by? I stopped to pat him now, and the moonlight found an expression of sadness on his bronze face that I had never seen before. His mane had fantastical curls, which I stroked, tracing the whorls. He seemed so real, so solid, so impossible to harm. It was my bleeding body making me sad for no reason, I told myself. My mother had talked about that. But it was true about the Botticellis, Maia had said so.

I gave the lion a last pat and turned to take the last few steps to Hyssop and my bed. All the art, saved, as we children had been saved? But saved for what purpose? Saved to make the city? A Worker trundled past, unsleeping, off on some errand in the dark. Had they been saved too? And from where? I opened the door and wondered if I would ever have answers to these questions.

The next summer I taught eleven children to swim with no difficulty. The twelfth was Pytheas. He was a boy from Delphi, so I had seen him at the palaestra, and wrestled with him once or twice, but I did not know him well. I had noticed how beautiful he was, and how unconscious he seemed to be of it. He had an air of confidence that was not quite conceit. I had friends who disliked him because he was so lovely and seemed so effortlessly good at everything. I had been inclined to go along with them without examining why. Teaching him to swim made us friends.

As with the first eleven non-swimmers, I took Pytheas down the slope of the beach until we stood in chest-deep water. Then I had him lie back onto my hand, to learn how the water would support and cradle him. The problem was that he couldn't relax. It didn't help that he had essentially no body fat—every curve on his twelve-year-old body was muscle. But Mother Tethys is powerful; he would not have sunk lying back with my palm flat in the small of his back, if he could have found a way to do that. He tensed immediately, every time, and jerked back under the water. The exercise was meant to teach trust of the water, and he couldn't trust it enough to learn it. Yet he wanted to learn, he wanted it fiercely.

"Human bodies were not made for this," he muttered, as he went down spluttering one more time and I hauled him back to his feet.

"Truly, you'll be able to do it if you let yourself go."

"I know how dolphins swim."

"I love dolphins. They often swim out by the rocks, there where the sea darkens to wine. When you have learned to swim, you will be able to swim out to them."

I had never seen anyone try so hard and keep on failing. Pytheas could not float, but he couldn't believe he could not. He watched me treading water and floating on my back, and couldn't believe he couldn't master the skill by sheer strength of will. I tried supporting him on his stomach, telling him it was more like the way dolphins do it, but it worked only a little better. He kept thrashing about and sinking. "Maybe we should try another day," I said, seeing that he was growing cold and his fingers were wrinkling from the water.

"I want to swim today." He bit his lip and looked far younger than he was. "I understand I can't master the art in one day, but I want to make a beginning. This is so stupid. I feel such a fool. I've wasted your whole afternoon when I know you want to be in the library."

"It isn't a waste teaching you," I said. "But how do you know that?"

"Septima says you're always reading in the library when you have a moment."

"Septima's always in the library," I said. It was true. Septima was a tall grey-eyed girl from the Athens hall who could read when she first came, and in the time since had made herself almost an assistant librarian. "Did you ask her about me?"

"When I heard you were teaching swimming."

"But why her? How do you know her? She's Athens and you're Delphi."

He looked caught out, then raised his chin boldly. "I knew her before."

"Before you came here?" Even though we were out in the sea with nobody near us, I lowered my voice. "Now I think about it, you look alike. A kind of family resemblance, maybe?"

"She's my sister," he admitted. "But here we're all to be brothers and sisters, so what difference does it make? She's my friend, and why shouldn't she be?"

"No reason she shouldn't be," I said. "So you asked her about me?"

"I thought she'd know. I only knew you'd won the race. Now I know you've taught the others to swim, and you clearly understand the methods, and you've been very patient. I want to learn. I want to swim at least a little today. I can't let it defeat me."

I think what did it was the way he blamed himself and not me, and the sheer force of his will. "All right, then," I said. "There is another way, but it's dangerous. Put your hands on my shoulders. Don't clutch, and don't panic and thrash, even if you go under. You could drown us both if you do. Let go of me if you feel yourself sinking. As long as you don't panic, I can rescue you, but if you drive us both under and I can't come up, we could both die."

"All right." He stood behind me and put one hand on each of my shoulders.

"Now I'm going to slide slowly forward, and I'll tow you. Keep your arms still, and let your legs come up. I'll be underneath you." I slid forward and took one stroke with my arms, drawing him forward. I could feel the whole length of his body on top of mine. He did not clutch or panic, and I kicked my legs gently, swimming for perhaps six or seven strokes and drawing him along on top of me. I turned my head sideways. "Now keep your arms still but kick your legs just a little." I was ready to put my own legs down and stand up if he panicked now—I knew the slope of the beach well, and I was still in my depth. I had done this before with my little cousins when they were very small. He began to move his legs, and I kept mine still but kept on swimming strongly with my arms, drawing us along parallel to the shore. At last I told him to stop, and put my feet carefully down. He went under for a second but did not panic or thrash.

"Was I swimming?" he asked.

"You've made a good beginning. And now you should go out and run around on the sand to stir your blood, and then we should both clean the salt off with oil. Tomorrow you'll do better."

We ran up out of the water and raced on the beach with some other children who were there, none of them people I knew well. Then Pytheas sought me out with a jar of oil and a strigil and we oiled each other and scraped it off. This always feels good after swimming, much better than the wash-fountain, because salt water strips out the body's oil.

We were not encouraged to have erotic feelings towards the other children—indeed, the opposite, we were discouraged from ever thinking about sex or romantic love. Friendships were encouraged, and friendship was always held out to us as the highest and best of human relationships. Yet as I scraped the strigil down Pytheas's arms I remembered the feel of his body above mine in the water, and I knew that what I felt was attraction. I was as much frightened by the feeling as drawn by it. I knew it was wrong, and I truly wanted to be my best self. Also, I did not know how to tell if he felt any reciprocal feelings. I said nothing and scraped harder.

"Tomorrow," I said, when we were done. "Same time. You'll make a swimmer yet."

"I will," he said, as if any alternative was unthinkable, as if he meant to attain all excellence or die trying. I raised my hand in farewell and took a step away, but he spoke. "Simmea?"

I stopped and turned back. "Yes?"

"I like you. You're brave and clever. I'd like to be your friend."

"Of course," I said, and stepped back towards him and clasped his hand. "I like you too."

7

APOLLO

Athene cheated. She went to the Republic as herself to help set it up, and then once all the work was done she transformed into a ten-year-old girl and asked Ficino to name her. He named her Septima, which I thought served her right for asking him. She knew he was obsessed with magic numbers.

I, however, did the whole thing properly. I went down through Hades and set down my powers for the length of the mortal life I chose from the Fates. Clotho looked astonished, Lachesis looked resigned, and Atropos looked grim, so no change there. I then went on to Lethe, where I wet my lips, to allow me to forget the details of the future life I had chosen, though not, of course, my memories. (The river Lethe is full of brilliantly colored fish. Nobody ever mentions that when they talk about it. I suppose they forget them as soon as they see them, and so they are a surprise at the end and the beginning of each mortal life.) I went on into a womb and was born—and that in itself was an interesting experience. The womb was peaceful. I composed a lot of poetry. Birth was traumatic. I barely remember my first birth, and the images from Simonides's poem about it have got tangled up in my real earliest memories. This mortal birth was uncomfortable to the point of pain.

My mortal parents were peasant farmers in the hills above Delphi. I had wanted to be born on Delos again, for symmetry, but Athene pointed out that in most eras neither birth nor death are permitted on Delos, which would have made it difficult. I had to master my new tiny mortal body, so different from the immortal body I normally inhabited. I had to cope with the way it changed and grew, at an odd speed, entirely out of my control. At first I could barely focus my eyes, and it was months before I could even speak. I would have thought it would be unutterably boring, but in fact the sensations were all so vivid and immediate that it was intriguing. I could spend hours sitting in the sun looking at my own fingers.

As I grew it was interesting to discover how much of what I had thought was will was affected by the flesh. Food and sleep weren't just pleasures but necessities. I found my thoughts were clouded when I was hungry or tired.

I grew fast and strong and my parents were loving and kind to me. Everything went according to plan, including the famine that came along a few

months before my tenth birthday, which Athene and I had arranged to in-
duce my loving parents to sell me into slavery. That didn't go quite as planned.
For one thing, I had no idea what famine really meant—needing to eat and
starving instead is a form of pain. It was unbearable. I hate to remember it.
The despair on my mortal father's face when the last of the pigs died. The
way my mortal mother wept when the slavers came and made their offer for
me. I cared for them, of course I did, they had been my adoring worshipers
for almost a decade. It broke my mortal mother's heart to sell me. Athene
and I had chosen all this and imposed it on them. They had not chosen to
love a son and lose him in this terrible way, to be forced to choose between
slavery for me and death for all three of us. I had never imagined how cruel
we were being.

So, as you see, I had already learned quite a lot about mortal life and equal
significance and meaningful choices before I even came to the Republic.

Athene was on the ship *Excellence* when I was brought aboard with a line
of other children. She recognized me at once, although she had never seen
this body before. She is my sister, after all. "Are you all right?" she asked.

"Never better," I said. "You have to do something for my mortal parents.
Cure the disease on their crops, send somebody through selling new livestock
cheaply, and most of all let them have another baby as soon as possible."

"I will," she said, calmly. I hadn't heard that tone of Olympian calm for
ten years. She was dispassionate. She nodded to me, and inscribed my name
in her ledger without asking me what it was. "What's wrong?" she asked.
"It's barely been ten years. Did you get attached?"

"It feels like a lifetime," I said.

She laughed.

"You'll never understand this unless you do it," I warned her.

"I'll do it one day," she said. "Right now they need my help too much."

Part of my plan in experiencing mortal life from the beginning had been
to avoid all the inevitable squabbling and mess involved with getting the City
set up. Of course I could have stayed on Olympos and arrived as a ten-year-
old at the moment the other children came, but I know that if I'd stuck around
Athene would have made me run all over everywhere collecting things and
getting involved in the arguments. This part worked perfectly. By the
time I reached the city, everything had been built and decided. They had
laid it out harmoniously, according to principles of proportion and balance.
They had made some odd choices, like the half-size copy of the Palazzo
Vecchio, but it all worked. It was full of variety and yet was all of a piece.
Nobody could ask more of a city.

It was full of artworks Athene had rescued from disasters of history—she'd been everywhere from the Fourth Crusade to the Second World War. There were temples to all twelve gods—mine was particularly splendid, with a Praxiteles from Delos I'd always been fond of. The color choices were interesting. On the whole they had gone for white marble and unpainted statues, Renaissance style, but here and there you'd see a painted statue, or one dressed in brightly colored cloth. The kitons everyone wore were dyed and embroidered, so that the effect was of brightly coloured people in a chiaroscuro landscape. There were trees and gardens, of course, which helped soften things.

With a fine sense of irony, Athene had me assigned to Laurel house, in the dining hall of Delphi, in the Tribe of Apollo. There were twelve tribes, each devoted to a particular god, with twelve dining halls each. Each dining hall was made up of ten houses of seven children each. (These numbers weren't in the *Republic*. They had some complicated Neoplatonist relevance, and had doubtless taken somebody a long time to work out. I was so glad I'd missed that discussion.) There were ten thousand and eighty children—a number which could, should one wish to, be evenly divided by every number except eleven.

Those first years in the Republic were fun. My body was a child's body still, but it was my body, and now properly under my control. I was young and growing and I had music and exercise. I had the amusement of seeing where there were cracks in the structure that seemed so solid. Bringing together that many children with so few adults was something only somebody who knew nothing about children would have suggested. The children were wild and hard to control, and much more of this wildness was necessarily tolerated than Plato had imagined. The Masters tried to set up a system where the children monitored each other, which had some limited success. But to track all the children the way they really wanted they could have done with four times as many adults—but they were limited to those who not only thought they wanted to set up the Republic, but who had read Plato in the original and prayed to Athene to help. There were probably a lot of good Christians who would have liked to have been there. As it was, there were more people from the Christian eras than I'd have guessed. I do have friends and votaries everywhere, but some times and places I seldom visit, largely for aesthetic reasons.

The thing that surprised me about the Masters when I got to know them was that so few of them were from the Enlightenment. I'd have thought that era, so excitingly pagan after so much dull Christianity, would have produced a whole crop of philosophers who'd want to be here. I talked to Athene about it one day when I caught her reading Myronianus of Amastra, curled up on her favorite window seat in the library.

"There's practically nobody here from the Enlightenment because they didn't want this. The crown of the Republic is to get everything right, to produce a system that will produce Philosopher Kings who will know The Good."

"With Capital Letters," I said.

She looked down her nose at me, which wasn't easy, since with both of us eleven years old, she was shorter than me. "Exactly. The Good with capital letters, the Truth, the one unchanging Excellence that stays the same forever. Once that's established, the system goes on the same in ideal stasis for as long as it can continue to do so, with everyone agreeing on what is Good, what is Virtue, what is Justice, and what is Excellence. For the first time in the Enlightenment, they had the idea of progress, the idea that each generation will find its own truth, that things will keep on changing and getting better." She hesitated. "They do pray to me, some of them. Just not for this. I find it fascinating in its own way. It's bewildering. It's one of those things I keep coming back to. I know I'll never get tired of it. But you won't find them here."

"There are people here from ages with a notion of progress, though," I pointed out.

"Mostly women," Athene said. "You'll always have the odd man who loves Plato so much he doesn't care about progress. But the women—well, in those times women fortunate enough to be educated in Greek—and there aren't that many of them—they have horrible circumscribed lives, and they read the *Republic* and they get to the bit about equality of education and opportunity and then they pray to me to be here so fast their heads spin. We have almost equal numbers of men and women among the masters, and that's why. Many of the women are from later periods."

"It makes sense," I said. "And what you say about the Enlightenment is fascinating. I'll go and hang out with Racine some more when I get home and get a better feel for it."

It was a few months after that when a boy deliberately shoved me in the palaestra when I was lifting weights, knocking me off balance and making me fall. He wasn't anyone I'd especially noticed before, a Florentine and not a Delphian. Yet he acted as if he had some grudge. I didn't understand it. I tried to talk to him about it and he pretended it had been an accident. After that I thought about some other incidents that had seemed accidents—spilled food, spoiled work—and wondered about them.

I went to Axiothea, one of the two Masters assigned to Delphi. She taught mathematics to both Delphi and Florentia. I believe she came from the first years of Girton. I told her about the incidents, and asked her if she had any idea why they had happened.

"There will always be some who see excellence and envy it instead of striving to emulate it," she said. "We aim to eradicate that as far as possible, but you are children, after all."

"But everyone loves Kryseis, and she's the best at gymnastics," I said.

"She's terrible at music, and she laughs at herself," Axiothea said. "You're good at everything, and seemingly without trying."

I shrugged. "I try."

"You're too old for your years. When the rest of them grow up a bit, you'll make some friends."

I hadn't realized I didn't have friends, but it was true. I had companions, people to wrestle with, people who asked me for help with their letters. I had six boys who slept in Laurel beside me whose jokes I endured. The problem was indeed that my mind was not twelve years old. The only real friend I had was Athene, and of course our friendship was thousands of years old and subject to the usual constraints of our history and context. Besides, she had the same problem. She dealt with it by taking on a strange status halfway between child and Master, and retreating into the library, where she was always most at home. But she had a way out if she wanted one. She could transform herself back into a goddess at any moment. I didn't have that luxury. Having taken it up I had to go through this life. I would have to die to resume my powers. That had seemed almost exhilarating at first, but it intimidated me now. Unlike mortals, I knew what happened after death. But unlike them, I had never died.

And then I tried to learn to swim, and I couldn't. Always before, learning things had been easy, both as a god and as a mortal. But as a god I'd never known how to swim in human form—if I'd wanted to swim I'd always transformed into a dolphin. Now this earnest copper-skinned Florentine girl was telling me to relax and lie back on the water, and every time I tried, seawater went up my nose. It was the first time I had ever failed at anything when I wasn't being directly thwarted by the will of another god—and over something as trivial as swimming. I couldn't let it defeat me. I felt an actual lump in my throat—not tears in my eyes, which are as honourable and natural as breathing, but a hot lump in my throat, as if I would cry shameful tears of defeat and frustration. Then Simmea thought of another way to teach me, a dangerous way, dangerous to both of us, but she risked it. It was difficult and sensual and strange, but at last I swam, or half swam.

And I had made a friend, a courageous friend who would risk her life for my excellence. That felt like even more of a victory.

8

SIMMEA

I had lots of friends, but Pytheas was different. It took a long time to teach him to swim. He mastered it eventually through sheer force of will. He was never especially good at it, but he knew enough not to drown and could propel himself through the water with a surging stroke. I thought I would see less of him once he had mastered the art, but he continued to seek me out. We were, that year and the next, about the same weight for wrestling. But the thing that really brought us together was our shared love of art.

In the city, art was supposed to open our souls to beauty, and also to set a good example. When I looked at Michaelangelo's bronze *Theseus at the Isthmus*, with his foot set on the head of the giant Kerkyon, I was supposed to want to emulate Theseus and kill giants to protect my homeland. Of course, I would willingly have gone up against any giant that was threatening Kallisti, had I not been trampled in the rush. But Kallisti was an island extremely lacking in giants or other such threats. There were no cities there but our city. We never saw strangers. Had it been needful, I would have given my life for it without a second thought. But this was not what I thought of when I saw the Theseus. My strongest emotion was an ache at how beautiful it was, and a great admiration for Michaelangelo's skill in creating it. That humans could do such things made me long to emulate them, to follow them in creating beauty. If this was a possible thing, it was a thing I wanted to do.

Pytheas was constantly creating, though he did not always share what he made. He wrote poetry and songs. He could play the lyre and the zither better than anyone else I knew. Whenever he was set any exercise in music—whether music alone, music with words, or words alone—he excelled at it. He was marvellous in the Phrygian mode and even better in the Dorian. Under his influence I tried hard, and did improve at writing poetry and music.

My true love was given to the visual arts. I loved to embroider my kiton and cloak and to devise new patterns for this. I often embroidered for my friends. In the spring of the Year Three I was chosen to embroider a panel for the great robe of Athene. I chose blues and soft pinks and greys, and made a running pattern of owls and books. I loved this kind of work. Later that year I finally learned stone carving, and early in the year after metal-work, and finally painting. Painting was wonderful. It was what I had always wanted. It let me bring together color and line, and set down the pictures I could see in my head, even if they never came out quite the way I wanted them. At first I was terrible, but after I learned some technique I managed a sketch of Pytheas as Apollo playing the lyre, and a larger painting of Andromeda and Kryseis reaching the victory line in the games. I was almost happy with that as a composition. I had caught their expressions, and the contrast of light and dark in their hair and skin was pleasing. I would go back to eat in front of the Botticellis and know that I had so much to aspire to. Most days this would fill me with hope and delight, and only when I was bleeding or something had set me down would it seem an impossible burden to have a target so impossible to reach.

In the way the city was ordered, sculpture, painting and poetry were considered among the arts of bronze. I still wore the silver pin I had won in the races, but I began to look at the work of those whom the Masters gave bronze pins, and think that I was not far from their standard. I made a mold for some cloak pins with a design of bees and flowers, and thought that they could be cast in any metal. Of course I continued to work in the palaestra and the library. That year we learned to ride and to camp, and saw much of the rest of the island. Most of it was set with crops, tended by diligent Workers, but some of it was wilderness, especially around the mountain in the centre. The mountain sent up smokes and steams from time to time, and near the crest there were sometimes rivers of lava that were still warm. We always went barefoot. Laodike burned her foot once when we were running up there. Damon and I had to help her home and we got back long after dark.

Laodike was a good friend, and so was Klymene, who had a very sharp mind. She always had something funny to say about everything. I could go to them with my little troubles and uncertainties, and they would be ready to hug me and reassure me. Pytheas never did this. He didn't seem equipped for it. If I forgot and complained to him about some little thing that was bothering me he never soothed me. He always wanted either to distract me or, if it was possible, to do something about it. This peculiarity stood out all the more because he was the only one who did understand about art. He didn't think it was a charming decoration or a useful moral exemplar, he agreed that it really mattered. If I showed him my designs he never praised them unless he truly thought them good. His standards were exceedingly high. Often when I had something that would have been good enough for everyone else, I made it better because I knew he would see it.

In this way he was a true friend of the soul, as Plato says, the friend who draws one on to excellence.

Sometimes I felt I couldn't do as much for him; that once I had taught him to swim I had nothing left to do for him. Then I realized that I could help him be friends with the others. In many ways Pytheas was more like the Masters than he was like the rest of us. He had an air sometimes of putting up with things that amused other people. This was why some people thought him arrogant. Once you were in the middle of a conversation with him it was often fascinating, but sometimes getting there was difficult for him, as if he didn't know how to start. It was difficult for him to adapt what he knew and thought to other people's interests and understanding. I could see both sides of it—I loved talking seriously, but I could also be childish sometimes and have fun. With my good friends I could have real conversations, and I could make a bridge between them and Pytheas so that he could be a part of these conversations. In that way I helped him by widening the circle of people with whom he could share some part of his mind. I would sometimes wonder about other ways I could help him. In the same way I thought about laying down my life for the city, I pictured doing it for Pytheas—if he had needed a kidney, or a lung, or my very heart, I would have lain down gladly before the knife.

The only one of my friends who refused to like Pytheas was Kebes, who persisted in seeing him as arrogant and sycophantic to the Masters. In fact Pytheas was anything but sycophantic—he treated the Masters as equals, or even inferiors. But he was polite to them and gave them consideration, even when they were not with us. Kebes continued to despise the Masters and the city and everything about it. He mocked the Masters when he was out of their hearing. He kept his hatred warm despite everything. He had even tried to run away once or twice in the early days, only to discover that we were on an island about twenty miles across and with no other islands in sight from the coast. He had, like all the children who had run, been found and brought back, and thereafter talked to about the benefits of staying. Kebes appeared to be reconciled, but he never truly was. He was waiting only until he became a man and could persuade others to steal one of the city's two ships, the *Goodness* or the *Excellence*.

"What will you do with it?"

"Sooner or later they will have to teach us to sail them," he said. "We will make for somewhere, either a civilization where we can live free, or a deserted island where we can found our own city."

"What city could be better than this?" I asked.

"A free city, Lucia, where we could use our own names, and would not be forced into the molds of others."

I liked the mold that was made for me, but Kebes could never be content under anyone's direction. He had a silver pin for his prowess at wrestling, but he mocked it in private.

Pytheas, by fitting into the city, by speaking respectfully of the Masters, and by being my friend, offended him by his very existence. Kebes could not legitimately wrestle Pytheas, being a head taller, but he said that if he did he would try to break his nose. I think this simple dislike had imperceptibly become jealousy. I was fifteen. Pytheas was fourteen, for he had told me that he had truly been ten when he was bought. I do not know how old Kebes truly was—sixteen or even seventeen, I think. Perhaps Kebes too found Pytheas attractive, and did not want to acknowledge being drawn to any-thing of the city. Or perhaps he was jealous of my attention to him. Once, when he came upon me making a charcoal sketch of Pytheas, he snatched the paper from me and tore it up. Before I grew to know Pytheas, Kebes had been my only close male friend.

I did not like to think that Kebes felt he owned me. Nor did I lie awake imagining scenarios in which I sacrificed myself to save Kebes's life. But I liked him. And although I loved the city, I also liked to feel, through Kebes, that I was free—free to freely choose the city over Kebes's idea of freedom. Kebes offered me an alternative, even if I rejected it. I never re-ported his talk to the Masters or to Andromeda, as I knew I should have. It did no harm, I reasoned, it might even do him good to talk, and if he ever came to the point of being ready to steal a ship I could report it then—or let him go, why not? The City did not truly need two ships, and what use were unwilling minds?

In the autumn of the Year Four we held the great games of Artemis, which were celebrated by footraces and swimming races for girls, and by hunting. The hunting came first, so that the victims could be offered as a sacrifice and eaten at the festival. We went out as whole halls, seventy of us together, with our Masters. Florentia and Delphi, who did most athletic things to-gether, divided up into two roughly equal groups. I went with Ficino. We never came near a beast, but we had a wonderful time in the hills. Maia scram-bled about with the rest of us, but Ficino rode. We took nets and spears and bows strapped onto another horse. I loosed an arrow at a duck once, but missed. We stopped by a spring and ate the rations we had brought, apples and nuts and cheese. Laodike got stung by a bee, and we managed to track down the hive and take the wild honey, at the cost of several more bee stings.

Ficino considered the honey a worthy gift for Artemis and so declared the hunt over.

The other group's hunt was from all accounts more dramatic. They actually found a boar in a thicket and faced it down with spears and nets. Accounts of what happened next differ. Axiothea refused to talk about it. Atticus told me that Pytheas behaved with exemplary bravery, and saved several lives. All Pytheas would say was that he had only done what anyone would have done. Klymene said that she had been a coward and could no longer face anyone. Trying to untangle all this, and get accounts from the others who had been there, it seems that Klymene had fled, exposing Axiothea, and Pytheas had leapt in and made the boar run up his spear, in the best poetic style. So far so good. But later Pytheas had said something to Klymene that she could not forgive, and neither of them would tell me what.

I tackled her alone in the wash-fountain shortly after dawn the next morning. "Did he call you a coward?"

"No. Well, yes. But I am a coward. I understand that now."

"Anyone can panic in a moment like that, if the boar was rushing towards you," I said, soaping myself to avoid looking her in the eye.

"Anyone with iron in their veins," Klymene said. "But no. Anyone can call me a slave-hearted coward and I will just agree with them. I was tested and I fled."

"I've never been in a situation like that. I might have done the same."

"You! You're always fierce." Klymene shook her head. "You'd never have run. That's one of the things that makes me so angry."

"Then what did he say?" I really wanted to know.

"You'll hate him if you know," she said. "I don't want to hurt your friendship. I know you really care about him."

"I really like him, he is a soul friend. And I like you too and I want to reconcile the two of you if I can, but if I can't at least I want to understand what happened!" I leaned back to rinse my hair. "If he is as bad as you say then I want to know that, and not give my friendship where it is unworthy." I didn't really think I was doing that.

"Are you sure?"

"Yes!" I stepped forward out of the wash-fountain. "I don't believe you are truly a coward, even if you did panic. But panicking in that moment probably does mean you need more practice facing dangerous things before you stand in the line of battle, assuming there ever is a battle. You should try to find dangerous things and face them down to get better at it. Practice courage. Running once in panic doesn't mean you have a fearful soul, or that you are unworthy. And it certainly doesn't mean that I don't care about you and still want to be your friend. And I want to know what Pytheas did, because helping interpret between Pytheas and the rest of the world is part of what I do, and I can't do that if I don't know."

Klymene was crying, so she turned her face into the water to hide the tears. I waited until she turned back, then hugged her. "What did he say?"

"I thanked him for what he did, and he said he was just doing what was needed. And then he said I shouldn't feel badly about having run because I was only a girl."

"What!" I was horrified. I had never imagined anything like this. Some of the Masters sometimes said things like this. Tullius of Rome was especially given to it, and Klio of Sparta had once had a formal debate with him on the subject which everyone held that she had won decisively. But I had never heard Pytheas say anything that even hinted that he thought such a thing. "Are you sure?"

"I knew I shouldn't have told you."

"I'm going to kill him." Then I turned back to her. "Telling me was very brave. I do think you could learn to be brave if you practiced. Like working with weights and building up."

It was our turn in the palaestra directly after breakfast, which I could hardly eat, I was so full of fury. Pytheas was not yet there when I arrived, so I exercised with weights, hurling the discus farther than I ever had with the vigor of my wrath. When he arrived I ran over to him the second he had his kiton off and knocked him down into the sand. "Hey, give me a chance to set my feet!" he protested, slapping the sand to mark a fall. I threw myself onto his back, holding him down. There were no Masters around to object. I could really have killed him before anyone could stop me, if that had been what I truly wanted. Of course, what I wanted was to understand.

"What did you mean, saying to Klymene that she was only a girl?"

"Am I going to lose all my friends over that?" he asked, so sadly that I immediately felt sorry for him, despite my anger.

"You are if you don't explain it right now." I thumped his arm hard. He wasn't trying to shake me off or to fight at all. He had gone limp, which made it difficult for me to want to pummel him.

"Will you let me up if I agree to talk to you?"

I climbed off him and he got up. He had sand all over his front, which he did not brush off. "She was sad and needed comfort, and I never know what to say. I didn't think and fell back on what I grew up hearing. Women—outside the city there's a tendency in most places to think that women are

soft and gentle and good at nurturing, that by nature they should be protected. You must remember that from before? She was crying, and she had
run away, she was just acting the way women usually act. I put my arm around
her. I've seen you do that. I know that's right. But then I had to say something, and I was completely blank on what."

"For somebody so intelligent, how can you be such a complete idiot?" I
asked.

"Natural talent?" He wasn't smiling. "Do you want to hit me again?"

"Would it make you feel better?"

"I almost think it would."

"I won't then," I said. Then I relented, and twisted on the ball of my foot
to thump him in the chest as hard as I could, so that he sat down abruptly.
"Did that help?"

Even in that moment he automatically slapped the ground to mark the
hit. "Yes, I think it did."

"Did it help make you realize women aren't just soft little doves to be
protected?" I was still angry.

"That's exactly how she seemed to me at the time," he said, looking up at
me. "A soft little dove who had been asked to act as a falcon, against her
own nature. And why should everyone have to fight, if they're not suited
for it?"

"Would you have said to Glaukon that it's all right for him to be a coward because he's only a cripple?" Glaukon had lost a leg in the first year of
the city. He had slipped in the woods, and his leg had been crushed beneath
a Worker's treads.

Pytheas looked up at me guilelessly. "Well it doesn't matter as much if he
did happen to be one. But in fact he's very brave."

"But imagine how he'd feel if you said that to him. It's not considering
him as a person but as part of a class of inferior things. Klymene's a coward,
she says so herself. And our souls have parts in different balances—maybe
she doesn't have as much passion, and perhaps not everyone has it in them
to stand in the line of battle—not that I see what enemies we're going to
need to fight anyway. But some of those who don't are men, as everyone agrees.
Every example of a coward we've ever heard about who was shamefully
wounded in the back has been a man. And plenty of those who are brave
and would stand firm are women. And by saying what you said you insult
all women—you insult me!"

He nodded, getting up again. "It was a really stupid thing to say. Do you
think there's any point apologising?"

"Not yet. She's too upset. I'll tell her I beat you up, that might make her feel a bit better."

"You hit me harder than the boar," he said.

"I still don't know if you understand!"

"That everyone is of equal significance and that the differences between individuals are more important than the differences between broad classes? Oh yes, I'm coming to understand that really well."

I glared at him.

"What? You're still going to be my friend, aren't you? I need you to help me understand these things properly."

"Yes, I'm still your friend. But I don't know how I'm going to explain to people about what you said."

He spread his hands. "I do know there's a difference between being soft and being a woman. I do see that there are men like doves too. And I don't see anything wrong with them, as long as there are enough falcons to protect them, and there are." He hesitated. "I do see that you are a falcon, not a dove, even if you'd rather be making art than making war. I would myself. Peace is better than war. There's too much glorification of war and not enough glorification of peace, and especially not enough glorification of the importance of the doves. I value Klymene, even if she'll never believe it now."

"The Masters say we are all equally valuable," I said.

"But they don't act as if it's true." Pytheas frowned. "The worst thing about that hunt is that there was nobody there who really knew how to do it, nobody who had done it before. Atticus and Axiothea are scholars, not warriors. The city is heavy with scholars, unsurprisingly. Testing us for courage isn't a bad idea, but that was a stupid way to do it. Boars are really dangerous. People could have been killed or crippled if I hadn't known what to do."

"Write a poem glorifying peace," I suggested.

"And you paint a picture doing it, and you'll soon see how easy it is."

Ikaros was walking towards us, no doubt to find out what we were doing standing still for so long. "Come on, let's wrestle properly," I said.

At the festival I came second in swimming and third for running long distance in armour. As I had taught swimming to Kornelia, who had won, I regarded this too as a victory. I could have eaten from the boar Pytheas had killed, but I declined in favour of bread and honey.

9

MAIA

A month or so after the art collections began, Ficino and Ikaros blandly presented to the Art Committee a lost bronze of Michaelangelo, a David, but very unlike his most famous David. They told us unblinkingly that it was Theseus with the head of Kerkyon. I nodded and made a note of it. "Excellent," Atticus said. "One of the best artists of your time."

"Of any time," Ficino said, smiling.

I asked Ikaros if I could speak to him a little later. He agreed at once. After dinner, that day a kind of nut porridge, we went for a walk.

The island was beautiful, even then when the city was still a building site. We walked off to the west and sat under a pine tree overlooking the sea to watch the sunset. "You're a monk," I began. I was speaking in Latin as we usually did together.

Ikaros jumped. "I am not! I was just wearing the habit. I've taken no vows of celibacy, don't worry."

It was my turn to jump. "Did you think this was a sexual assignation?" I asked. I was simultaneously horrified and delighted. Ikaros was a handsome man, only about ten years older than me, and I had believed everyone who told me that nobody would ever want a bluestocking. Yet at the same time I felt diminished, as if it meant he wasn't taking me seriously.

"Such things have happened," he said, smiling. "Even here. Plato does not describe how the first generation of teachers are supposed to regulate their lives."

"He does talk about how children are to be born," I said, as sternly as I could. "And really, sneaking off to the woods is against everything he says."

He took my hand and ran one finger around my palm, making my breath catch. "But if it were a proper festival of the Republic, and you and I had drawn each other by lot?"

"That would be entirely different," I said, pulling my hand away in as dignified a way as I possibly could. Entirely different and far too exciting, I thought. "Come on Ikaros, we're friends."

"And what does Plato say about friendship?"

"He says not to get Eros mixed up with it," I said crisply, though far from unmoved. I was very aware that the kiton left far more of me uncovered than the clothes of my own period. I had never really noticed that before, because nobody had been looking at me the way Ikaros was looking at me. I stared straight ahead. The sun was setting into the sea and turning both sea and sky as crimson as my cheeks felt.

"If you didn't want that, then why did you want to drag me off alone?"

"I wanted to ask you about the *David*."

"Theseus," he corrected me at once.

"Exactly. That's why I wanted to ask you alone."

"Well, what? It's a good Theseus, it meets the needs, it's beautiful and we've rescued it. Atticus didn't blink."

"But why not say it's David? Why do we have to keep Christ out? What's the necessity? The reason I mentioned that I thought you were a monk was because I thought you were a Dominican, but still you prayed to Athene."

"I was having a bad moment when I prayed to be here. The church refused to hear my arguments and then I was imprisoned in France."

"You prayed to Athene when you were imprisoned by the Inquisition?"

"With very good results," he said, smiling and spreading his hands.

"Yes, fine, but my point is that many people have reconciled Plato with Christ. Ficino did." Only a sliver of the sun was left, but the sea and sky still blazed. Why would he have been wearing a monk's habit if he were not a monk? Did they have fancy dress parties in the Renaissance? Could I possibly ask?

"I myself did," he said, proudly. "I reconciled Christianity, Islam, Judaism, Platonism and Zoroastrianism. I learned Arabic and Hebrew. I was so proud of myself. But don't you see, we were doing it starting from a belief that Christianity was true. If instead it's the Greek Gods who are true, if we have immortal souls that go down into Hades and on to Lethe and new life, then what price salvation? They can mix from the other side, we could say that Plato was really talking about God. But from this side, well, we can't say that when Jesus said he'd be in his father's house that he was really talking about Zeus, now can we?"

"I do see that," I said. "But it's not as if it does any harm, even if it's not true. It's a lovely story, about good people. It's not . . . contaminated. I don't see why we have to exclude it so entirely that we have to say the David is Theseus."

Ikaros lay back, propped on his elbow. "Christianity is harmful to the Republic because it offers a different and incorrect truth. We want them to discover the Truth, the real Truth that a philosopher can glimpse. That's important. We don't want to clutter it up with irrelevancies. Christianity would just get in their way. So no Madonnas and no crucifixions."

"But David is all right as long as we say it's Theseus?"

"Why not? What harm could that do? I'd bring a Madonna and say it's Isis, but Ficino thinks that's going too far."

"I wish I could see the Madonnas again. Botticelli's Madonnas, that is. I only saw them once. I was going to buy an engraving, but I spent all my money on books. Still, we have the new ones."

"We do. Athene in the *Judgement of Paris* looks a little like you." He moved closer and put his arm around me. "The real trouble with Christianity is that the morality can do so much harm."

"I didn't offer you Christian morality, but Plato on love," I said, standing up. I wasn't afraid that he would attack me, although I was aware that he was strong and could easily have overpowered me if he had wanted to. What frightened me was the thought that if he persisted, and especially if he persisted in touching me, I would give in to him. "Come on, let's go back if you can't exercise temperance."

"But you are a poor little Christian virgin, not somebody holding out for agape," he said, not moving.

I was furious. "How could you possibly know?" I asked.

He laughed, silhouetted against a sky of violet and rose. "Oh sit down. I can't talk to you when you're hovering over me like that. I'll concede that I could be wrong. But I doubt it."

"Nobody will ever say yes to you if you're that smug," I said, sitting down but out of arm's length.

"Lots of people have said yes to me already," he said.

"Here?" I was amazed, and a little jealous.

"Here, and in Italy before. I know my way around. I know what women like."

I was completely cold now. "There's nothing less exciting than being thought of as part of a class of beings that are all the same," I said. "You're treating me as a thing."

"It doesn't mean I don't see you as a person," Ikaros said; "that I want to copulate with you. Latin is an impossible language for this, and you don't know Italian. Let's speak Greek."

"I'd rather talk about why we have to exclude Christianity," I said, but I did switch to Greek.

"I know, but you're misjudging me."

"You keep changing the subject," I said.

"I see you, and I like you, and I find you attractive, and it would be a pleasant thing we could do together, like . . . sharing a meal. It doesn't stop us having serious conversations that we have silly conversations with imaginary wine. It wouldn't stop us having serious conversations if we indulged in eros. All I meant by the remark about knowing what women like is that I'm not a clumsy oaf who would hurt you, or who wouldn't care about your pleasure."

The sky was darkening to mauve and the first star was visible. I stared up at it, avoiding his eyes. "I believe you," I said. "But I'm not comfortable with that. Neither Christian nor Platonic morality condone the kind of thing you're talking about."

"No, I suppose it's Hedonist," Ikaros said. "But what Plato says about festivals and everyone drawing lots is like that. Eros separate from philia and agape. And every word Plato says about agape is about love between men."

"What he says about agape between men with no thought of love between men and women being like that makes me think he didn't know any women who were capable of being seen as equals. Which from what we know about Athens at the time is probably realistic—women kept cloistered, uneducated, except for hetairas. But . . . if he didn't know any women who were people, how could he have written about women being philosophers the way he did in the *Republic*? It's in the *Laws* too." I'd only recently read the *Laws*. "He must have thought about it a lot. And nobody ever listened to him in all those centuries they were reading him. I wonder how did he come to that conclusion? It's stunning."

"I don't know. I suppose he must have met somebody. You'd only have to really know one woman with the right kind of soul to change your mind about their capabilities."

"Axiothea?" I suggested. "I don't mean our Axiothea, but the original. The woman who came to him in disguise as a youth and was admitted into the Academy? Perhaps she made him realise it's souls that matter."

"No, she came because she'd read the *Republic*, the same way you came here. It's mentioned in Diogenes Laertius. So he must have met women with philosophical souls before that."

"Showing a philosophical soul doesn't work on everyone, unfortunately," I said. "I wish Tullius would deign to notice the souls of the women here."

While I had been staring out over the sea and talking, Ikaros had moved so that he was right beside me again. "I know you are afraid," he said. "But I also know that you want it. I saw you start. There's nothing wrong with what we're going to do."

"No!" I said. "No, really no, Ikaros, I don't want to!"

"I am stronger than you and it's too late to run away," he said. "And you don't really want to leave, do you?"

I did. I tried to get up, but it was true that he was stronger, and that he knew what he was doing, which I did not. He had no difficulty wrestling me to submission. I screamed as he pulled off my kiton. "Hush now, hush," he said. "You know you want it. Your breast likes it, look."

"I don't care what my breast likes, my soul doesn't like it, get off me!"

"Your soul is timid and has learned the wrong lessons." He rolled on top of me, forcing my legs apart.

"It's *my* soul, and up to me to say what I want!" I said, and screamed again, hoping somebody would hear even though we were too far from the city.

Nobody heard. "There, see, you like it," he said as he eased himself inside me. "You're ready. I knew you were. You want it."

"I do not want it." I started to cry.

"Your body is welcoming me."

"My body is a traitor."

He laughed. "You can't get away, and I have taken your virginity now. There's nothing to fight for. You might as well enjoy it."

My body unquestionably enjoyed it. In other circumstances it would have been delightful. My mind and my soul remained entirely unconsenting. Afterwards, when he let me go, I turned my back on him and put my kiton back on.

"There, didn't you like it?"

"No," I said. "Having my will overruled and my choices taken away? Who could enjoy that."

"You liked it," he said, a little less sure of himself now.

I ignored him and walked away. I did not run because I was under the pines and it was completely dark and I'd have been sure to have banged into a tree. I could hear him blundering behind me. I ran cautiously once I was out where I could see by starlight, and made it back to the city. Klio, who was to serve the Sparta hall, which was finished, already had a house of her own, where Axiothea and I slept most of the time until our own houses were ready. I went there and slammed the door. I was shaking and crying. It was so humiliating to think that my mother and my aunt and those who had insisted on protecting me had been right all along.

"What's wrong?" Klio asked, getting up and coming towards me.

"Ikaros raped me," I said, still leaning on the door.

"Are you hurt?" She hesitated. "Should I get Kreusa? Or Charmides?" Charmides was our doctor, a man from the twenty-first century.

"I'm not really hurt. I mean there's a bit of blood." I could feel it sticky on my thighs. "And a couple of bruises. But nothing I need a doctor for."

"I'm surprised at Ikaros. I wouldn't have thought he was that type." She hugged me and drew me into the room. "Are you going to tell people?"

I hadn't thought about that. "I don't know. He'll say I wanted it."

"You went off with him alone," she said. "Lots of people would think you did want it. It would be your word against his, and I don't know what people would decide. Lots of the older men don't really see us as equals. And once everyone knows, everyone knows. You can't undo that. And you can't leave. There's nowhere to go."

I understood what she meant. "I won't tell anyone. I never want to see him again."

"I'm going to smack him myself when I get the chance," she said, sounding really fierce.

"I thought he was my friend!"

"He thought you wanted it." Klio sat down on the bed, drawing me down with her. "Men, especially confident bastards like Ikaros, always try to get their friends into bed. But actual rape? Did you say no?"

"I said no in both languages and at great length." She snorted. "I screamed. He thought I was afraid because of Christian morality and that I wanted it really." I wiped my eyes. "I don't know whether some part of me did want it. My body did. But not like that!"

"Not like that, no."

"Does that mean he was right and I did want it? I felt that my body was a traitor. Does it make me a hetaira?"

"No." She sounded really fierce. "If you didn't agree, then you didn't agree and it was rape, whatever your body thought about it."

"Can I use your wash fountain?"

"Of course. Clean him off you. Wait—when did you have your period?"

"Last week," I said.

"That's good." I looked at her blankly. "You're probably not pregnant," she expanded. "I'm assuming you didn't chew silphium beforehand, as you weren't planning on it."

"No," I said.

Klio frowned. "Do you think Ikaros would do it again? To someone else? Because if so then we should tell people, to protect them."

"I don't know," I said. "I don't expect anyone is as naive as I was, to go off with him like that, without realizing."

"I can put the word around that women should be careful of him, without mentioning your name or the word rape," she said. "Go on, shower."

I didn't tell anyone else. I resigned from the Art Committee. I did not speak much to Ikaros on the Tech Committee. He kept saying things and giving me looks, clearly confused. Once I was sure I wasn't pregnant, I tried to forget about it. I made sure not to be alone with men, any men, ever. We were busy. It wasn't difficult.

A few days after my house was ready and I had moved into it, delighted to have a bed and privacy again, Ikaros waited for me after a meeting of the Tech Committee. Klio stayed with me, glaring at him. His confidence withered a little before the concerted force of our glares

"I've just come back from an art expedition," Ikaros said. "I have something for you." He gave me a big book wrapped in muslin. "Don't open it here." He left.

Klio and I went back to my house, where I unwrapped it. It was a book of reproductions of Botticelli paintings, in English, printed on glossy paper and with a publication date of 1983. On the cover was the *Madonna of the Magnificat.*

10

SIMMEA

In Year Five of the city, when we were all nominally fifteen, it was finally Florentia's turn to learn astronomy. I'd been looking forward to it ever since Axiothea told us that it would involve more geometry. We began one crisp autumn afternoon in the Garden of Archimedes on the western edge of the city, where the big orrery and telescopes were. There were only nineteen of us. Astronomy wasn't considered essential, and as always we were short of Masters. Only those selected could pursue it.

I enjoyed the orrery, and calculating the motions of the planets. Archimedes's own orrery was there, with his gearing, and another, not as beautiful, which Axiothea said was Keplerian and which showed the motion of the planets as ellipses. When darkness fell I enjoyed seeing the planets exactly where we had predicted they would be. I loved looking through the telescope and learning how to adjust it. Kebes was there, and my close friend Laodike, but not Pytheas. Delphi had studied astronomy the season before.

That first night they showed us all the spectacular things—the moons of Jupiter and the extra sisters in the Pleiades and the great galaxy of

Andromeda. Walking back through the dimly lit city, I bade joy of the night to Laodike when we came to her house, which was Thyme, on the street of Demeter. Kebes came up beside me as we walked on. Our ways lay together almost all the way back. His sleeping house was Violet, which lay just beyond Hyssop, on the street of Hera. "You really enjoyed that."

"I did." I was still bouncing with excitement. "Just think. We can tell where Mars will be in a thousand years. In ten thousand years."

"Who cares?"

I looked at him blankly. I couldn't see his face in the darkness. "I care."

"Lucia," he said, very softly. I started guiltily at the name. He stepped closer as we came to a sconce on the wall of the temple of Hestia. I could see his eyes glint. "Don't you see it doesn't matter? We're never going to Mars. Humanity may, one day. It may already have gone there, in the far future that they won't tell us about. But we've been deliberately brought into a sterile backwater of history where nothing we do can achieve anything."

"We've been lucky enough to be brought to the Just City to have the one opportunity of growing up to be our best selves, Matthias," I said, saying his old name as deliberately as he said mine.

"Oh, you're hopeless," he said, walking on into the darkness. "They brought us here against our will, all of us. But you've swallowed it all whole. They've made you over into one of them."

"And you aren't prepared to trust that anyone has good intentions, or anything at all!"

Just then a voice came from what I had taken for a statue of an old man next to a pillar on the steps of the temple. "What aren't you prepared to trust?" he asked Kebes.

"You," Kebes blurted.

"Me?" the old man asked, coming out into the street and falling into step with us. "Well, you don't know me, you've never seen me before, I am a stranger who has only just come to this place, you have no reason to trust me. But you have no reason to distrust me either, so it seems that the maiden is correct in her assessment that you trust nothing. How did you come to such a position?"

"From meeting a great deal of deception," Kebes said.

"Then you are judging a stranger by your past experience of humanity, that they are untrustworthy, and assuming that I am the same?"

"Yes," Kebes said.

"Well, and you believe that the maiden is the opposite, that she is overly trusting?"

Kebes looked at him sideways and said nothing. The old man turned his bright gaze on me. There was something about the way his bright dark eyes met mine that reminded me of Ficino. But he really was a stranger, which was astonishing. I had never seen strangers come to the city since we had all come here at the beginning, over the course of a few days, five years before. There were Masters I knew more or less well, and many of the children in other halls I barely knew at all, but after this time in which we had all been in the city they were all generally familiar to me by sight. This old man was entirely new to me. "So, do you trust everything as the youth says?"

"No," I said. "I trust what I have found trustworthy."

"And do you trust me?"

"I do," I said. It was true, up to a point. I did instinctively feel that I could trust him. But this was a dangerous conversation. Although he was a stranger, he was an old man and must therefore be a Master, and the real subject that Kebes and I had been discussing was about trusting the Masters. Kebes could get into serious trouble if they knew what he had said. When he had run away before he had been a boy, now he was a youth on the edge of manhood. He'd be showing them that he hadn't changed, that they couldn't trust him. He could be punished.

"On what basis do you judge me trustworthy? Because I am a stranger to you just as much as to the youth here, who does not trust me enough even to enter deeply into dialogue with me."

I thought hard about what I wanted to say, and spoke the truth but phrased it carefully. "I trust you because you wish to have a dialogue to discover the truth. And I trust you because you remind me of Master Ficino."

He threw back his head and laughed. "Ficino would like that!" he said. "So you judge me by your previous experience of humanity and it has been good, so you are in all ways the opposite of your companion."

"No, wait. I don't have a good opinion of all humanity, but of Ficino, whom you resemble. And from what you say it seems you know him well, which gives me an even better opinion of you."

"I have met him. I would not say I know him well. In what particulars do I seem to you to resemble him?"

We had come to Hyssop house, and I stopped in the pool of light from the sconce over the door. "Not in superficial details. For instance, he habitually wears a red hat and your head is bare. I trust Ficino, but because of that I would not necessarily trust any man in a red hat. You are both old men, but that's not important either. I wouldn't necessarily trust any old man without evidence of his trustworthiness. Your eyes are like Ficino's, and eyes are the mirror of the soul, or so I have read. Therefore I will say that your soul, in so far as I can discern it in the short time we have been conversing, resembles Ficino's, and on what better grounds could one assess the trustworthiness of a man than on his soul?"

"A good and thoughtful answer," the old man said. "And a reasonable basis for trust, don't you agree, young man?"

"If I trusted Master Ficino it might be a good reason to trust you too," Kebes said, stressing the word "master" ironically.

The old man nodded. "I see you have both been already studying logic and rhetoric."

"No," I said, my hand on the door. "We don't begin to study rhetoric until next spring, after the festival, when we will be sixteen. But I have been reading about it."

"You are begining to study rhetoric tonight," the old man said. "What are your names?"

"Simmea," I said.

"Kebes," said Kebes, reluctantly.

The old man looked sad for a moment. "I had friends with those names once," he said. "Men of Thebes. Did they give you those names when you came to the city? Because I thought I heard you use another name just now in the street."

"It is forbidden," I whispered.

"Is it?" the old man asked. "Then I shall forget I heard them, and use my old friends' names when I address you. I had not been invited to join your conversation but invited myself along, so I should disregard anything I should not have overheard before you began to speak with me willingly. But now I shall recruit you to converse with me and be my friends, if you will. My name is Sokrates the son of Sophronikos."

"Of course it is," I said. I didn't know how I hadn't guessed it before. "I thought you were dead." I had wept for him, reading the *Apology*.

"I should have been dead, but for my friend Krito, who thought it good to overrule my own wishes and the will of my daemon and drag me off here, for whatever good I might do. What would I do in Thessaly? I asked him, and yet here I am, will I or not. Now, Kebes, do you see yourself any closer to finding yourself trusting me?"

Kebes shook his head in astonishment. "Perhaps," he said.

"And you, Simmea, are you further from it?"

"No. I trust you more than ever, now that I know you are Sokrates."

"You can't trust everything that ass Plato wrote," Sokrates said. It was astonishing to hear somebody refer to Plato as an ass, after five years of hearing him revered almost as a god. I gasped. Sokrates laughed. "It is late. You should go in to bed," he said. "And you should meet me tomorrow. When are you free? Oh, I forgot, you are never free, are you? All of your time is accounted for. I shall request of our Masters that they permit me the use of some of your time, so that you may begin to study rhetoric with me."

Then he nodded gravely to me and went off down the street, taking Kebes with him. I stared after him. There was no reason Sokrates should not be here. And yet it seemed fantastical, dreamlike. I could see his profile as he turned to speak to Kebes. Sokrates! And here against his own will.

11

MAIA

I hadn't intended to, but I took the gymnastic training so that I could teach in the palaestra. I didn't ever want to be helpless again. Once I got used to it, I liked it. My arms and legs developed muscles in unexpected places. I wrestled with the other women and learned how to break holds and how to use my body as a lever. Of course, Ikaros took the same training, and he was still stronger than I was.

Ikaros mostly left me alone. He acted hurt when he did talk to me and I was cold to him. He was conducting a spectacular public Platonic relationship with old Plotinus, the leader of the Neoplatonists. Plotinus was much older than Ikaros, but still handsome, very dignified with his white beard and flowing hair. They acted as if they were Sokrates and Alkibiades in the *Symposium*, at least in public, and Ikaros seemed happy. Atticus asked me whether I thought they were as Platonic in private as in public, and confided that Tullius had asked him his opinion on the matter. Ikaros seemed to revel in being the subject of everyone's gossip.

I had occasional invitations from other men, especially once we all had our own houses. I always turned them down politely, and that was always the end of it. I was still working hard, still happy, but it no longer had that same wonderful glow. I had thought it was perfect, or almost so. I had thought these people were all my friends, my Platonic brothers and sisters. I had trusted them unthinkingly. Now I had learned to be wary.

Eventually, everything was built and most of the initial decisions made, and we were ready to begin bringing in children and really getting started.

The Committee on Children reported to the Chamber. Plotinus made the presentation. "We have decided that the best method is to send out ships to purchase slave children. They will be freed, and be glad to be rescued and be here."

Klio stood up, and was recognized. "Can't Sophia find ten-year-olds who wish to be here?"

Sophia, the goddess Athene, was sitting at the side of the hall. She had shrunk to normal human size, and generally went unarmed and wore a kiton like the rest of us. The owl was sometimes on her arm, and sometimes swooped about, alone and disconcerting, in the dusk. "Children don't generally read Plato," she said.

"Nor do we want children who have read Plato. It would confuse them," Plotinus said hastily. "We agreed that they wouldn't be allowed to read the *Republic* until they are fifty, though they can start reading some other Plato once they are fifteen."

"How about slave children who wish to be free, and orphans who want homes?" Klio said.

"Certainly we can collect them. But I don't know if I could find ten thousand and eighty such praying to me for deliverance," Athene said.

"They'd have to pray to you?" Ficino put in.

Her grey eyes flashed, literally flashed, like light glancing off metal. "The gods are bound by Necessity, as you know."

"It's just that going to slave markets and paying slavers for children seems distasteful," Klio said.

"We have, ah, decided that only men should go on these expeditions." Plotinus stroked his beard. "As with the expeditions to rescue art, it's not safe for women. But we've decided that all the men will take turns going, to be fair. Oh, but not you, of course, Lysias."

Lysias was an American whose family had come from China. He came from the mid–twenty-first century and was the only Asian in the Republic. I knew him quite well, as Klio had recently drafted him onto the Tech Committee. He nodded——it was obvious he'd be too conspicuous in a classical or medieval slave market.

"The point is not who's going, but whether we're empowering slavery by buying children," Adeimantas said. He was an old man from my own century, an Oxford professor who had translated Plato into English. I hadn't spent much time with him; we weren't on any of the same committees.

There was a vigorous debate, ending in a vote, in which we narrowly decided to buy children, making sure they knew that they were free as soon as they came aboard our ships. The committee then explained which slave markets they would go to in which years. Athene would have to accompany each expedition, to which she agreed. Each expedition would bring in two hundred children, which meant it would take fifty to fill our quota. "You'll never find two hundred ten-year-olds in any slave market," Tullius said.

"What we propose to do is to go to one market and buy all the available children of the right age, then move through time so that it seems as if we return every year, until the ship is full. Then we'll bring the children home, and make another expedition to another market," Plotinus said.

Tullius sat down, satisfied. I looked at Klio and Axiothea. "Won't that really be creating a demand?" I asked.

"That question has been decided and gains nothing by being reopened," Plotinus said, huffily.

So we prepared to receive the children. Every dining hall was ready, named and furnished, with two Masters assigned to it. Every sleeping house had a name and an associated flower. Every bed had a chest and every chest had two blankets, a comb, a belt, and an iron pin, the very minimum we felt they needed. We had food ready, and Workers reprogrammed to make food for everyone. We had so many plans. Of course, they collapsed on contact with reality.

The first children ran away the first night, ran off into the woods and had to be recaptured. After that we guarded the sleeping houses until the children were settled. We also instituted the watcher system, where one child in each house was responsible for the others and reported on them to a Master. We kept them busy, which helped. Still some of them ran away from time to time. We brought them back and told them they would not be punished the first time. The Committee on Punishment was still in deliberations. Plato talks about punishments in some detail in the *Laws*, but he was thinking of adults, not frightened children. We tried to make them less frightened. Then another ship came, and we had four hundred children to three hundred of us.

I had never imagined the chaos ten-year-olds could cause. I could never have thought of children setting their chests alight or trying to sail off the island in them. "It will settle down," Lysias said when I was in despair. "They'll police themselves once it's working properly. We just need to get it started right."

"I think Plato was thinking of ten-year-olds as blank slates who know nothing," I said. "These are anything but."

"He must have been a ten-year-old himself," Lysias said.

"Yes, but never a parent, was he?"

The first months were total chaos. We had new batches of children coming every few days. I often felt close to despair. One boy ran away and got his leg crushed beneath a robot who was trying to round them up again. That was the absolute low point, when we hurt a child and made his life worse instead of better.

After a while we got better at managing them. It became almost routine. We'd divide up the arriving children by fourteens into cities that still had room. When there were girls for Florentia I'd show them their sleeping room, teach them how to shower and use the toilets, choose a watcher, and take them to Florentia for dinner. Then I'd spend the night sleeping outside the door to make sure they didn't escape.

Lysias was right that it did get easier. Keeping them busy all the time and too tired to keep awake and plot mischief helped. He himself was driven to exhaustion working in the palaestra—we really didn't have enough young men. I was constantly exhausted myself, from being teacher and parent and continuing to sit on the organization committees. I didn't have time to worry about anything except whether we were giving the children the right foundation, doing as Plato described. I worried about that all the time. "Ideally," I kept saying, every time we had to compromise.

"In the next generation we will have enough people," Klio said. "These children will have children, and they'll help us with them. In that generation, the generation who come along when we are old, we'll see our Philosopher Kings, the native speakers of the language of the Republic."

"I have hopes for these children. Some of them are wonderful."

"The longer it's established, the closer we'll get to Plato's design and the better it will work," Klio said, pushing her hair out of her eyes. She never let it grow long enough to braid neatly, and so except when she had just cut it, it was always falling into her face. "But I am worried about the Workers. We're overloading them. We don't really have enough of them for everything we expect them to do. We're going to have to find another way of doing some of those things before they break down. It's ridiculous for them to rake the palaestras. Anyone could do that."

"When the children are sixteen we'll assign some of them to farming and weaving and raking the sand too," I said.

"They could rake the sand now. Lysias and I are almost out of spare parts for the Workers. We're going to have to conserve them and use them for the essential things."

"Can't we ask Athene for more?" I asked.

"I suppose we could, but I don't know where she got these from and whether it was difficult. Besides, I feel we ought to be self-reliant and go on with what we've got."

"I'm sorry I can't help, but I don't understand how they work."

"Nobody does, really. Not even Lysias. We're just patching them up. But they shouldn't be doing things we can do, like cooking and farming, when there are things we really need them for that we can't do, like making roads and maintaining the ships and building things."

"I'll support you on that when we next have a Tech Committee meeting," I said.

"The Tech Committee isn't the problem. It's when it comes to Chamber everybody has plans they want the Workers for and nobody understands or is prepared to wait." She sighed. "Well, some of them will just have to wait."

It was hard work, but things did settle down. We couldn't keep as close an eye on the children as we would have liked. I tried to know all seventy little Florentines as well as I could, so I could help them to become their best selves. Often I envied them, especially the girls, seeing them grow up with their bodies and brains exercised and thinking it entirely natural that they were as good as the boys.

I saw Ikaros at committee meetings. The Tech Committee was always busy. Ikaros did not pester me for eros, but he was always friendly and occasionally let me know that if I changed my mind he hadn't changed his. I always said that I was happy to remain celibate. He really didn't believe, even now, that he had done anything wrong. Ikaros had been assigned to Ferrara with Lukretia, a beautiful woman a little older than he was. There were soon rumors that he was having a less than Platonic relationship with her, in addition to whatever he was doing with Plotinus. She was from his own period, so perhaps they shared the same ideas of seduction. I hoped so. We never discussed the personal sexual morality of the Masters in Chamber, though the children's was a constant topic of debate.

The most contentious issue was age. A number of us, most of the young women and some of the older ones, wanted the age at which we instituted Plato's practice of marriage and having wives and children in common to be kept to twenty, as Plato had written. Others wanted to lower it to sixteen. We suggested a compromise of eighteen. The real problem was that we all did want to divide the children up into their metals at sixteen. "We can't go with Plato's specific word," Adeimantus said in the debate. "He says the girls should be twenty and the boys thirty, which is clearly impossible when they all started off at ten. Perhaps in future generations we can do this, but expecting celibacy until thirty seems too hard." The vote was very close, and we decided on sixteen.

Then in the Year Five of the City, nine years after I had come there, when I was twenty-eight, there was an extraordinary Chamber meeting. Athene had brought Sokrates to us. "I brought him from Athens," she said. "Krito asked me to help him get Sokrates away. Sokrates is an old man, and Krito and I thought it best to bring him here at this time so that he can teach the children rhetoric now that they are old enough."

"Sokrates!" Ficino said, mopping his eyes, quite overcome.

Athene vanished. Sokrates stood before us, nut brown and weathered, with wild white hair and the toby-jug face Plato had described. "What nonsense is this?" he asked.

12

SIMMEA

It was my turn to serve breakfast the morning after we'd met Sokrates. As I took plates and porridge pots to all the tables, Ficino called me to come and sit with him when I was done. I gave a glance to my usual table, where Kebes and Klymene were sitting teasing each other, then went to join him. He was sitting at the cross-table, so when I sat down opposite him I found myself staring at Giotto's *Justice*, a fine fresco to have, I suppose, extremely inspirational no doubt, but in my opinion Giotto was a moon to Botticelli's sun.

"So you thought Sokrates was like me?" Ficino asked, with a twinkle in his eye.

I helped myself to porridge. "Yes. His eyes are like yours." I saw that it was true what Sokrates had said when he laughed. Ficino was pleased, and even flattered, at the comparison.

"He wants to teach you. Do you want that?"

I looked at him, inquiringly. "Do I have a choice?"

"Oh yes. This coming year you're all going to be choosing, or chosen. As we have always told you, some of you are iron, some bronze, some silver, some gold. You have bronze and silver and gold mixed into you, but not much iron I think!"

"I want most of all to be my best self. I always thought the Masters would decide how the metals were mixed in us and assign us to our places when the time came." I fingered the silver pin I had won at the Hermeia three years before.

"We will," Ficino said.

"Good."

"You think it's a good system?" he asked.

"Oh, yes." I hesitated, then went on, because I did trust Ficino. "So much better to be chosen for what we're fit to work on by those who know us than being limited to what our parents could have taught us."

"You were dreaming before you woke here, you grew under the soil," he reproved me, but his eyes twinkled. "When I saw your painting of the foot-race I had thought you would settle among the bronze. And you are fierce in the palaestra, and you did well racing in armor at the Artemisia last year, so you certainly have plenty of the silver spirit. And you are so quick at mathematics that Axiothea and I felt you ought to be allowed to try astronomy. And now Sokrates has singled you out! So you may be destined for gold after all. Don't frown. All the metals are equally valuable, and the city needs them all."

I tried to stop frowning and swallowed my mouthful of porridge. It gave me time to change what I would have said immediately, which was that if all the metals were equally valuable, why were they always listed in the same order, with gold in best and final place? "If I am not made of gold then I think bronze is my metal," I said. "My soul leaps to painting and sculpture and architecture more than to gymnastics and fighting."

"And to the pursuit of excellence?"

"Of course," I said. "How not?"

"Sometimes I envy you children your certainty," Ficino said. "Well, in the hour before dinner go to Sokrates. He has a house on the street of Athene near the library. The house is called Thessaly. He may not be there. As you may know, he is given to wandering about the city, engaging in dialogues. If he is not there, seek him about the place. He has said he wants to choose his friends, and not spend all his time besieged by those who admire him; and we have agreed to respect that. It seems that you are one of the friends he has chosen."

"Isn't it exciting that he's here?" I said. "Sokrates himself. I thought he was dead."

"And I knew he was dead, and had been dead for two thousand years," Ficino said. Ficino was known as the Translator, and it was Plato he had translated from Greek to Latin, in Florentia in the days when few people understood Greek but every educated person knew Latin. I had read all the Plato I had been allowed, which was only the *Apology* and the *Symposium* and the *Lysis*. I knew there were lots more dialogues. I hoped to be allowed to read them when I was old enough to study rhetoric. It was a badly kept secret that the Just City was described in a book of Plato's called the *Republic*, which was not in the library. (I felt sure there was a copy on

Maia's shelf next to that Botticelli book that was printed in a language that was not Latin.) "It's the most wonderful mystery of all that he's here. Bless Athene!"

I got through the morning in a flurry of impatience. In the early afternoon I saw Pytheas in the palaestra and rushed up to him. "Do you know who's here?"

"Who?" At fifteen he was better-looking than ever, and still totally unconscious of the effect it had on everyone. I was used to him, and even so I could occasionally be distracted from my thoughts by seeing his lips part as he said something especially interesting. I knew other people who were beautiful, but no other person moved me the way Pytheas did. The others were beautiful like themselves, but he was beautiful like a painting or a sculpture. That I was also secretly attracted to him only made this worse. The *Symposium* is extremely clear about the shame of lust, and I knew it was the attraction of soul for soul that I was supposed to feel. I was also most certainly drawn to his soul. Pytheas was the most unusual person I knew. In most ways he was the closest to true excellence of anyone I had ever met, but other spheres seemed completely closed to him. He was a paradox that continued to intrigue me.

"Sokrates!" I said. "I met him last night. He's going to teach me!"

"I wonder why he came now," Pytheas said, looking abstracted.

"Now? Not when all the other Masters came?" I fell into a wrestling stance, and Pytheas automatically did likewise. We began to circle slowly.

"Yes. If he was going to be here, why wasn't he here from the beginning when he could have the most effect?"

"I don't know." I feinted to the side, trying to think about it. "Perhaps he was doing something else—no, that's silly. He could have done it and still arrived five years ago with all of us."

"The Masters were here before that." He landed a blow on my arm and I raised my hand to mark it as we took up position again. "They must have been, I mean. They were here to build the city and decide what went into the libraries."

"And rescue the art," I said, plunging in suddenly to grapple. The only way to win against Pytheas these days was distract him and take him by surprise. I managed to bear him to the ground, and he tapped the sand.

"When are you seeing him? Can I come too?" We circled again. Pytheas was grinning, trying to get the sun in my eyes, one of his favorite tricks. I leaned the other way, bouncing on the balls of my feet.

"After this. What are you supposed to be doing? I can't think he'd mind, considering what he was like."

"I'm supposed to be in the library. I could come with you. What was he like?" Pytheas charged in and caught me at once in a grapple that I knew I could not break.

"He was fascinating," I said. "Do come."

"I'm not sure I should come without an invitation. Maybe you should ask him if I'd be welcome, and if I could come another day." He was leaning his strength against me now, and even as I tried to hold myself back, I was acutely aware of how my breast was pressed up against his side.

"I think you should come today. You have to be ahead of where you're supposed to be in the library, you always are, the same as I am. And I'd love to know what you make of him." He pulled me off balance and I went down, meaning he won the bout.

"All right. I'll meet you at the fountain after." He ran off to look for another partner and I went to join the runners.

Kebes joined us at the fountain when it was time to leave. "Are you going to talk to Sokrates too?" he asked Pytheas, sounding dismayed.

"I thought I would," Pytheas said, in a tone that invited Kebes to make something of it while they were still in the palaestra.

I put my kiton on and fastened it. "Come on, we've just got clean, we don't want to get sand all over ourselves again. Besides, I don't want to be late."

The two of them blustered at each other as we walked along. I thought I detected something worse than usual in it. I started to dread what would happen when we found Sokrates and it became clear that Pytheas had been invited only by me.

We found Sokrates's house with no difficulty. "I wonder why he called it Thessaly?" Pytheas mused. "He came from Athens."

"He said last night that he had asked Krito what he would do in Thessaly, and Krito dragged him here," I said. "I suppose he means that he's thinking of the city as Thessaly." I scratched on the door, and to my surprise it was opened immediately.

In the *Symposium* Alkibiades says that Sokrates looks like Silenus, and seeing him in daylight I could see that it was true. He has the same big nose and bulbous forehead and little goat-beard. But nobody would care how ugly he was once they'd seen his eyes and his smile. He smiled now, seeing us. "Why, Simmea and Kebes, how good to see you again. And who is your friend?"

Then he stepped forward to get a better look at Pytheas, and stopped dead, his head frozen in position jutting forward and staring. I hadn't expected anything like this. He and Pytheas stared at each other for a long moment but neither spoke. "Do you recognise him?" Kebes asked. There was indeed something in his expression that looked like recognition.

"Do I?" Sokrates asked Pytheas, softly.

"My name is Pytheas, of the house of Laurel, the hall of Delphi and the tribe of Apollo," Pytheas said, inclining his head. "And you, sir, are Sokrates the son of Sophronikos, than whom, I have long said, there is nobody more wise."

"I am more delighted to meet you than you can imagine," Sokrates said. "Perhaps now we will be able to find some answers. Come in, all of you. Come through to the garden."

The house was much like Hyssop house. It had a bedroom of the same size, but with only one bed and one chest, with no other furnishings, and an identical fountain room. A door led out of it into a sheltered courtyard full of plants. There was a little statue of a Herm under the branches, which I noticed especially because it was made of limestone and not marble.

"Let us sit here in the shade of this olive tree and converse. If any of us are dry there is water close at hand."

We sat on the ground under the tree. Sokrates, although he was old, had no difficulty in sitting or in crossing his legs comfortably. "Well, my friends," Sokrates began, leaning back against the trunk of the tree, "For I believe as you are here that I can safely call you my friends. We began a discussion last night about the nature of trust, which we were forced to break off because of the lateness of the hour. This seems like the perfect time to resume it."

"Have you been reading Plato's dialogues?" Pytheas asked.

Sokrates laughed. He laughed like a happy child, absolutely irrepressibly. "How could I resist?" he asked. "You might be able to imagine what it is like to fall asleep in a prison cell and awake to find yourself in an experimental colony which one of your pupils claimed you had proposed yourself. I thought at first that it was a ridiculous dream, but as it keeps going on and becoming more and more detailed I have decided for the time being to treat it as reality and go along with it on that basis."

"It's not a dream," I said. "That is, not unless I'm dreaming too. And I've been here for years."

"I'll grant, Simmea, that it is not your dream. But have you ever been a participant in somebody else's dream, and could you prove you were not? I'll let you off that one, for I feel it's beyond human capacity." He glanced at Pytheas again, and Pytheas smiled sideways at him.

"I believe it's nobody's dream," Pytheas said. "And you do have the comfort of knowing you won't be forgotten. People will still be having Socratic dialogues in thousands of years."

"Not forgotten, perhaps, but what have they done to my memory! As for the question of the dream—well, that brings us back to the interesting question of trust. Who can we trust, and how do we decide? Do you trust each other?"

"No," Kebes said, looking at Pytheas.

"But then we have established that you are not inclined to trust anyone," Sokrates said. "Simmea?"

"I think that if we can trust anyone then we can trust each other," I said.

"Well then, is it possible to trust anyone? To begin with, can we trust the gods?"

"Which gods?" Kebes asked.

Sokrates looked sideways at Pytheas. "We know, as Plato could not have known, that Athene at least is real, and much as Homer portrayed her. So how about Homer's gods?"

"Then who can we trust if the gods disagree?" I asked. "Like at Troy, when the gods are taking sides in the battle. Odysseus could trust Athene but not Poseidon."

"Can we trust that the gods are good, or is it more complicated than that?" Sokrates asked. "Is Athene good and Poseidon bad? Certainly if Homer speaks truly then Poseidon was bad for Odysseus. But he was good to Theseus, who was his son."

"You're using a very unplatonic idea of goodness," I said, surprised. "Ficino says Plato says Goodness is absolute, not relative."

"Considering relative goodness, I believe it's more complicated, as you say," Pytheas said to Sokrates. "The gods have their own agendas that may conflict."

"Ah," Sokrates said. "And how may we know if we are caught up in such a conflict, and if so, which god to trust?"

"Juno, that is Hera, was terrible to Aeneas," I said. "He was much harassed both on land and sea because of the unrelenting rage of cruel Juno," I quoted, naturally falling into Latin to do so.

"I can see I'm going to have to learn that infuriating language," Sokrates said. "But not today. Translation, please."

I repeated it in Greek. It seemed astonishing that he was so wise but did not know Latin. But Virgil wasn't born until five hundred years after he died. In his time, Rome had been no more than a little village, founded by Romulus and Remus only a few centuries before, unheard-of away from Italy. Then Rome had grown great and spread civilization over the world, so that even when she fell, her language had preserved it in human minds, so that now—except that *now* in this moment Rome did not even exist. Aeneas, if he had even been born, had not yet sailed from Troy. "It's like looking through the wrong end of a telescope," I said. "History, from here."

"You have at least had five years to learn about it. I've barely been here half a month."

"Are you a Master?" Kebes asked.

"What an interesting question," Sokrates said, patting Kebes's hand. "What is a master, in this city?"

"The Masters came here from all over time, drawn by their shared wish to found the Just City," Kebes recited. It was what we had been taught.

"They did this with the aid of Pallas Athene," Pytheas added, in the manner of somebody politely adding a footnote, but Kebes frowned at him. Sokrates nodded to himself. "So it would seem that I am not a Master, as I did not read Plato's *Republic* nor pray to Athene to bring me here to work at setting it up."

"But you're not a child," Kebes said.

"I'm seventy years old, I'm certainly not a child. Nor am I a youth, and still less a maiden. But perhaps I am wrong about this. Perhaps in this city I am a child. Is there nobody here but Masters and children?"

"Unless you count the Workers," I said. "They are mechanical, but they seem to have purpose."

"They're just devices," Pytheas said. "They don't will what they do."

"Do you know that?" Sokrates asked.

Pytheas closed his mouth, looking dumbfounded. After a minute said: "It's my opinion and what I've been taught."

"We will leave the question of the Workers for now, if we may, and let us say that of human beings, there are in the city only youths and maidens, whom you are accustomed to call children, and Masters?"

"That's right, Sokrates," Kebes said. "Or it was the case until you came."

"Then let us consider. I am not a child because I am seventy years old. But I was brought here without being consulted, like a child."

"You have a house to yourself like a Master," I said. "We all live in houses with six other children."

"That seems a minor point, but we will let it stand on the side of Masters."

"The thing that marks you as different from children and masters considered together is that you came to the city now," Pytheas said. "All the rest of us have in common that we came here five years ago, at the time of the founding of the city. Why did you come now?"

"They tell me that I came now because before this you were too young to learn rhetoric, and I am an old man and they feared that if I had been here from the beginning I would die before you were old enough to learn. For that is to be my purpose here, you see, to teach rhetoric to you children: I, who was never a teacher but who liked to converse with my friends and seek out the nature of things."

"They have their own imagination of who you are, but you are not that," Kebes said.

"Now that's true," Sokrates said. "And perhaps what I shall teach is not what they expect me to teach."

13

APOLLO

Who would have guessed that Sokrates would recognize me? True, we had always been on good terms. But I was in mortal flesh and fifteen years old. Nobody else had recognized me. Nobody else had even come close to guessing, not even people I knew well. It isn't as if we go around manifesting physically all the time. People don't expect to see the voice in their ear incarnate in front of them in the form of a youth, and so they don't see it. Sokrates, of course, didn't ever see what he expected to see, he saw what was there and examined it. He knew me instantly, as fast as Athene had, faster.

The difficulty wasn't that I cared that Sokrates knew. Sokrates was one of those people whose integrity really could be relied on. No, it was that I didn't want Simmea or that lout Kebes to know. I was also a little afraid of giving away too much to Sokrates. This was never a problem before I became a mortal. Saying precisely as much as I want, with as many multiple meanings as words can be made to bear, has always been one of my oracular specialties. Composing oracles like that can be as much fun as really complex forms of poetry. But since I became Pytheas things had all been more complicated. I sometimes blurted out things I shouldn't, and there were these huge areas of human experience that I kept blundering into with both feet. Simmea really helped with this. She was always prepared to put her time into working things out with me, sometimes even before I messed things up. I really valued that.

Being a mortal was strange. It was sensually intense, and it had the intensity of everything evanescent—like spring blossoms or autumn leaves or early cherries. It was also hugely involving. Detachment was really difficult to achieve. Everything mattered immediately—every pain, every sensation, every emotion. There wasn't time to think about things properly—no possibility of withdrawal for proper contemplation, then returning to the same instant with a calm and reasonable plan. Everything had to be done in time, immediately. Paradoxically, there was also too much time. I constantly had to wait through moments and hours and nights. I had to wait for spring to see blossom, wait for Simmea to be free to talk to me, wait for morning. Then when it came, everything would be hurtling forward in immediate necessity again, pierced through with emotion and immediacy and a speeding pulse. Time was inexorable and unstoppable. I had always known that, but it had taken me fifteen years as a mortal to understand what it meant.

I found my own charged emotional states interesting to contemplate. Some were exactly the same, others analogous, and still others entirely new. Then there was the vulnerability, which is quite different in practice from the way it seems in theory. I could never have reasoned my way to understanding how it felt to stand in the palaestra, hoping that Simmea would hit me instead of walking away from our friendship. Even at that instant, even as I was waiting and not knowing how it would go, I knew that I would be making poetry from those emotions for centuries.

I certainly was learning lots and lots about equal significance. It was easy to grant it to Simmea, who was smart and brave and cared passionately about art, even though she was flat-nosed and flat-chested and had buck teeth. It was much harder in practice to extend this out to everyone. It took me a long time to realise that I'd been extending equal significance as a favor on an individual basis and that it really applied to absolutely everyone—funny cowardly Klymene, bad-mannered Kebes, and pretty Laodike. Everyone had their own internal life and their own soul, and they were entitled to make their own choices. I had to keep reminding myself of that regularly, and really I should have had it cut into my hand. I did an exercise at the end of every day, if I could keep awake long enough, when I tried to imagine the inner significance of everyone who had spoken to me that day.

Before I get on to the conversation with Sokrates, I should say a word about Kebes. He was big, one of the biggest of the youths in the city. He had clearly lied about his age and was a year or two older than most of the rest of us. His growth spurt had come early, and he had shot up. He had a head like a bull—a big broad forehead that could easily have sprouted horns, and a habit of setting his jaw belligerently. If I'd named him he would have been Tauros. He had a grudge against the world, and he hated everything. He wasn't stupid, far from it. He'd have been easier to understand if he had been. He just hated everything and everyone and devoted his time and energy and considerable talents to hating them. He did exactly as little as he could get away with, and spent far more effort calculating that than he would have spent on trying to excel. He had a way of making one Master after another believe that they would be the one who would succeed in motivating him, that they were on the verge of success, while in fact he mocked each in turn behind their back. He hated everyone—everyone except Simmea, that is. Once, while helping Manlius, he contrived to break a statue of Aphrodite by moving the plinth where a Worker was supposed to set it down. Both statue and plinth fell three stories onto marble and shattered beyond retrival. I would have thought it an accident, save that he boasted about it to Phoenix, who thought it was funny and repeated it to lots of people.

Left to myself I'd have avoided Kebes entirely. As it was, he persisted in being around Simmea, and so I had to deal with him. We had fought twice in the palaestra when neither Simmea nor any Masters were around. These were not athletic contests in which victory was marked with points; they were vicious all-out fights in which we tried to hurt each other. I won both times. They were not really fair fights. Yes, he was two handspans taller and much heavier, and likely his body was a year or two older, but I had been wrestling since the art was invented. I knew tricks from centuries Kebes had never had the chance to visit, and when not bound by rules, I used them freely.

The second time, I had him on the floor with his head in a choke where I could easily have broken his neck. I thought about it. I would have had to pretend to be horrified at such an accident, and probably to purify myself before the gods. It wasn't this that stopped me but that I didn't want to deprive Simmea of anything she valued, even this. "Yield?" I whispered in his ear.

"Never," he said, and in his tone I could see that if he had been on top he wouldn't have had the same hesitation in killing me.

"Will you swear to behave civilly to me in front of Simmea?"

He was silent for a moment. I kept the pressure on. "Yes," he said at last. "Civilly."

"Do you swear?"

"By what?"

"By all that you hold sacred," I said. "Do it."

"I swear by God and the Madonna and Saint Matthew and my own true name that I will be civil to you in front of Simmea," he said, and I let him up. He spat blood onto the sand in front of me and stalked away. He was limping, but then so was I.

And that was Kebes. He hated and distrusted me, and when I made him swear an oath he swore truly, and kept it. It was strange. He swore only to get out of my power, but he put himself more into it than ever. If I had chosen to denounce him to the Masters for the gods he had chosen to hold his words, he could have been punished—flogged, even cast out of the city. Perhaps that was what he wanted. But he kept the letter of his oath—he was thereafter just barely civil to me if Simmea was there.

If I had been my real self I would have thoroughly enjoyed sitting in the garden of Thessaly talking with Sokrates and giving double-tongued answers. As it was, there was a knife-edge of fear running under it all. It didn't stop me enjoying it, it didn't stop me being aware of the delight of dappled shade and sharp wits. It was just another thread underlining everything.

Don't think I was upset that Sokrates wasn't happy to be in the Republic, even if he might be actively trying to undermine it. Nobody actually thought this was going to work perfectly. Plato had thought of it as a thought experiment. He'd been trying to design what he thought of as a system for maximizing justice, according to his best understanding of the world. We knew his understanding of the world was flawed—look at what he believed about the gods. All the same, it was such a noble idea when Plato had it, such an improvement on any of the ways to live he saw around him. It was of the classical world, but better. His understanding of the world and the soul were mistaken. But his city had never been tried before. This was the experimental proof. It needed to be able to stand up to Sokrates.

Maybe some of the Masters really believed they could make it work, but I think what they really wanted wasn't to do it themselves but for somebody else to have made it real and for them to have been born there. The Masters were always envious of the children, that was obvious to me from the first. Athene and I certainly didn't imagine it would really work the way Plato described it. We knew too much about the soul to hope for that. What was interesting was seeing how much of it could work, how much it really would maximize justice, and *how* it was going to fail. We could learn a lot from that.

"What will you teach?" Kebes asked Sokrates.

"I will teach rhetoric," Sokrates replied. "It is a powerful weapon, in the right hands. I will teach small groups like this one, and I shall go about this city asking questions and discovering answers and seeing where those questions and answers lead us. For instance, who can we trust?"

Kebes looked at me, and I smiled cruelly back at him. The irony of the situation was not lost on me. Sokrates knew who I was. Kebes did not know who I was and did not trust me, nor did I trust him. Simmea did not know who I was and trusted all of us. She was looking from one to the other of us, leaning forward with her hands on her knees, looking like a chipmunk. "I think it's the wrong question," she said. "Trust isn't an absolute. You can trust somebody for some things and not for others. I can trust Kebes not to break his word, but I can't trust him to strive for excellence. I can trust Pytheas to do just that, always, but I can't trust him to understand without an explanation why I am weeping if he finds me weeping."

"So we might trust a person for one thing and not another?" Sokrates asked.

"Yes. And trust has an emotional component. When you asked me last night whether I trusted you and I replied that I did, that was an instinctive and emotional trust and only secondarily a logical one."

"So before we can ask who we trust, we should ask in what way we can trust them, and in what way we do trust them."

"Who do you trust?" I asked Sokrates.

"Have we established that the gods are divided and can be trusted in some circumstances and not in others?" he asked. "So that Odysseus was right to trust Athene and would have been wrong to trust Poseidon?"

"Yes, Sokrates," I said obediently. "I believe we have established that."

"Then I trust the gods who mean me well and distrust the gods who mean me harm. I have no way to distinguish them unless the gods themselves appear to me and disclose their intentions, or unless I send to ask an oracle. Perhaps I should do that, send to Delphi and Dodona and Ammon, those ancient oracles that are established even in this time. Then perhaps I would know if Apollo and Hera and Zeus were well disposed towards me."

"You needn't send to Delphi. You know Apollo has been well disposed towards you all your life," I said, carefully. And it was true. Sokrates was one of my favourite people of all time.

"You said so in the *Apology*," Simmea said, helpfully. "In your speech before the Athenians, that is. If Plato recorded accurately what you said."

"Plato was there, though I don't remember him taking notes," Sokrates said. "I didn't read that one. I remember that speech very well. It was only the other day."

"So beyond Apollo——" Kebes began, but Sokrates interrupted, looking at me.

"I could trust Apollo in my mortal life, but I was brought here against my will by divine intervention, so can I still trust him?"

"Athene brought you here," I said, which was weaseling really. I had known she intended to, and hadn't objected to her doing it. But I loved him and certainly meant him well, and he was not wrong to trust me. "She brought everyone here. Many of the Masters have talked to her, and have talked to us about talking to her."

"She was on the ship when we came," Simmea said. "Ficino called her Sophia."

"That was Athene?" Kebes asked. "How do you know?"

"She had grey eyes."

"Lots of people have grey eyes," Kebes said, scornfully.

"And Ficino called her Sophia, which means wisdom." Simmea went on, unruffled. "She was on the ship, and important, writing down names, and Ficino deferred to her. But she isn't here. She isn't one of the Masters. She was owl-carrying Athene, and she was there to make the ship come here through time."

"That does seem conclusive. I wish I'd known," Kebes said. "I could have done something."

"What?" Sokrates asked. "How would you fight a god?"

"Not by what I'd have done when I was twelve—not pushing her overboard or trying to tear her head off." Kebes hesitated. "I don't know how to fight a god. Do you know?"

"Until today I wasn't sure whether the gods truly concerned themselves with us, and I only knew that they existed as part of a set of logical inferences which turn out to be based on a false assumption," Sokrates said.

"What false assumption?" I asked, curious.

"That they were good," he said, looking directly at me unsmilingly for a long moment. I don't know what he saw in my eyes. The knife-edge had cut through me and it was very sharp.

"*Good* and *well-meaning* are different matters," I said, after a moment.

"Wait, are you saying that to overthrow the Masters we'd have to fight the gods?" Kebes asked.

Sokrates turned to him. "Ah, Kebes, I see that you have learned to trust, at least to trust that I will not report what you are saying."

"What if I report what you are saying?" Kebes asked.

"I have been inquiring into the nature of trust. Any purely theoretical issues that have been raised by that question—none of us are going to report each other, are we?"

Simmea looked really uncomfortable. "I want to learn rhetoric," she said. "But I don't want to overthrow the Masters. I didn't volunteer to come here but it's the best place I can imagine being."

"A valid point of view, and one we will need to examine in some detail," Sokrates said. "I have by no means come to Kebes's conclusions on that subject. The motivations of the Masters and of Athene in setting up this city are very much worth examination, and I will be able to examine them much better with the help of somebody who thinks as you do, Simmea. But the point at contention is this—can we speak freely in pursuit of the truth? Can we trust that you're not going to report what we're saying?"

"She has never reported what I've said," Kebes said.

Simmea looked at Sokrates. "I never have. And I won't report what you're saying as long as it's only conversation. But I reserve the right to tell them if you were going to do anything to harm the city."

"You don't believe rhetoric could harm the city?" Sokrates asked.

"If rhetoric could harm it then it isn't the Just City and it deserves it," she said.

Sokrates beamed at her like a proud father, then he glanced back at me. "They'll be using my methods for thousands of years, you say?"

I nodded.

"Then what are we doing here?"

14

SIMMEA

All through that winter I learned astronomy and rhetoric. I was constantly overturned by Sokrates in conversation. It was wonderful and terrible. In the palaestra I ran constantly, both in armor and out of it. Running felt as if it fitted the rest of my life. In music I resonated to the Dorian mode. I painted and embroidered and dyed cloth for kitons and robes for the statues. I tested everything constantly and wondered whether it was good. I went over my conversations with Sokrates in my head, running, swimming, trying to sleep, examining my own thoughts and trying to find better answers.

Sokrates was wonderfully wise and full of twisty edges. He was honest in debate, always absolutely fair—he reminded me sometimes of Pytheas marking the point when I hit him. But it was rare to trap him—he thought too far ahead. I tried to do that too, but he was always ahead of me. I was always either really debating with Sokrates, or debating with Sokrates in my head. The real Sokrates was much better, even though I could win debates in my head. It wasn't about winning, it was about finding the truth. Sokrates always thought of things I wouldn't think of, things that came from directions nobody would expect. Often enough he let the three of us debate, just putting in questions now and then. His questions were always the best.

One morning I went running up the mountain with Kryseis and Damon. The island of Kallisti had a diameter of about twenty miles, and it had many hills, some of them steep. "Running in the mountains" just meant an overland scramble. But when we said "the mountain" we meant only one thing, the volcano that stood behind the city. Up at the top was a constantly changing crater. Usually there were red cracks visible down through the fresh rock. Sometimes rock ran like streams over the edge. Occasionally the whole place seemed about to boil. That was when it sent up plumes of smoke that we could see from down below. When rain fell into the crater it sent up great clouds of steam.

The three of us were serious about running, and close in ability. We ran up the sides of the steep rugged cone, pacing each other and keeping close. The terrain changed rapidly up here. It was a clear winter day with no clouds. When we came to the top I stopped and looked at the view. The sea was turquoise where the island sloped, and further out wine-dark all around, with a little froth of whitecaps where the winds stirred it, like diamonds on sapphire. To the north-east I could just barely make out a blue shadow in the water, as if there might be another island there. Kryseis was staring down into the crater. "They say it'll explode one day and lava will cover the city."

"Not for a long time," Damon said, reassuringly.

"I wonder why they picked this site, knowing that?" I asked.

"Ask them?" Damon suggested.

I could, of course, but it was interesting to speculate about. I wondered what Sokrates would say.

Damon climbed up onto the raised edge of the rock-rim of the crater and started to walk along it, balancing. I jumped up after him and did the same. "Come down, you fools," Kryseis said. "You'd cook if you fell in."

"I'm not going to fall in," Damon said. "It's almost a handspan wide."

"What if it crumbles?" she called. "Come down!"

I jumped down, but even as I did I realised that walking that dangerous edge reminded me of talking to Sokrates.

What we debated so constantly that winter was whether the Masters and Athene had been right to set up the Just City, and whether the Just City was the Just City or whether there could be one more just, and how that would be constituted. It was exciting and vitally important and deeply unsettling. "Are you debating like this with the Masters?" I asked one day as we were leaving.

"Some of them," Sokrates said. "They are not united any more than you children are. Some of them are ninnies, and others, sadly, have too much respect for me to enter into serious debate. But a few I have invited to be my friends."

He spent his mornings wandering the city, falling into conversation with anyone and everyone, and his afternoons and evenings entertaining friends in Thessaly. He sometimes invited somebody else to join us for the hour we spent with him before dinner, but often it was just the four of us, as it had been the first day. He always seemed to pay a huge amount of attention to what Pytheas said, and to spend time considering it. I wondered sometimes as they sparred if they could have known each other before. But Pytheas would have been so young, it couldn't be possible. Kebes and me he treated as colleagues in search of the truth. He did not teach by instruction but always by demonstration.

"There's nobody like him," Pytheas said one evening as we were walking away from Thessaly. It was close to midwinter, and the sky was a clear luminous dark blue, like the mantle of the ikon of Botticelli's Madonna on the cover of Maia's book. Kebes had stayed with Sokrates, so we were alone. "There never has been."

"Nobody," I said. "Not Ficino, not anybody. I doubt there ever could be. No wonder people remembered him for thousands of years. He's better at challenging assumptions than anyone."

"He was challenging you a lot today."

I looked at him questioningly. "He always challenges me a lot. I like it. It makes me think through my ideas."

"You love this city," Pytheas said. That was what we had been debating that day.

"I do," I said, spreading out my arms as if I could hug the entire city. "I love it. But Sokrates has made me see that it's only the visible manifestation and earthly approximation of what I really love, the city of the mind. No earthly city, even with the direct help of the gods, can ever become that. But we're doing pretty well here, I think."

"What do you think he and Kebes are doing now?"

"Thinking about ways of destroying the city, probably," I said. Pytheas started. "What? Did you think I didn't know?"

"You—I don't know." Pytheas looked disconcerted. "You're not concerned?"

"I said at the beginning that if debate can bring down the city, it deserves to fall. If they break it by debating it, then it's not much of an approximation of the Just City, is it?" I asked.

"How do you know they're only debating?" Pytheas asked.

"What would they be doing? Stealing quarrying explosives to blow up the walls?" I laughed. "Well, Kebes probably would, but Sokrates would think it was cheating, just as much as Krito dragging him off here was cheating. Sokrates hates cheating, he really does. He wants to do it all with dialectic, always, following logic through to where it leads. He wants to beat Athene."

"In debate?" Pytheas asked.

"Yes, I think so. But I don't think he's ready yet. Meanwhile I'm painting and running and debating—if this isn't the good life, what is?" Daringly I reached out and took his hand. He let me, and even squeezed my hand once before letting go. Sometimes I wondered if what Pytheas and I had was close to being Platonic agape or if he really didn't want to touch me. We didn't talk about it. But seeing him every day was part of what made this the good life for me.

"Do you want to eat with us?" he asked. For the last month we had been allowed to invite guests to our dining halls. I almost never turned down an invitation, not because I wanted different food—the food was very similar, and our Florentine food was undoubtedly the best—but because I wanted to see all the pictures. I'd eaten in Delphi several times and admired the wall paintings of the Sack of Troy and Odysseus in the Underworld.

"No, tonight I'd rather look at Botticelli," I said. "Do you want to come with me?"

"I'd rather look at Botticelli too," he admitted. "But there's Klymene."

"Have you really never spoken to her since the day of the hunt?"

"Never. She doesn't speak to me, and I can't start it." He hesitated. "I suppose I could apologize, but it seems a little late."

"She's braver than anyone now," I said. "She has spent the last couple of years facing up to everything, going out of her way to find ways to train in courage. She's braver now than somebody born brave."

"Good. But . . ." he looked uncomfortable.

"Oh, come and look at the Botticellis and we won't sit with Klymene," I said. "I think it'll be pasta with goat cheese and mushrooms tonight."

At midwinter the Year Six began, and with it the ceremonies of Janus, the open door that swings both ways, to past and future. I always found it an unsettling festival, the hinge of the year. That year for the first time we were given wine, well mixed with water. I did not think it had affected my reactions, but when we went out to the fire at midnight I found that the lights of the sconces and the fire were brighter than they usually were, and the faces of my companions more beautiful. There was to be a dance around the fire, and Laodike and Klymene had been chosen to be part of it. I wished them good fortune and stepped back alone to join the spectators.

Sokrates was among them, talking with Kebes and Ikaros of Ferrara. Almost as many people had crushes on Ikaros as on Pytheas—he was young, for a Master, and very good-looking, with a shock of chestnut hair and a smile that lit up his whole face. He had never taken any notice of me, except once when he commended my sketch of Pytheas. They seemed deep in debate, and I did not want to interrupt. I looked around for Pytheas, and found him on the other side of the fire and surrounded. One especially beautiful girl was at his side—the blond girl who had been chained next to me long ago in the slave market. Her name was Euridike, and she belonged to Plataea. Pytheas was attending to whatever she was saying, but when he saw me his eyes softened and he began to make his way towards me through the crowd.

At that moment Sokrates too noticed me and greeted me. "Do you know Simmea?" he asked Ikaros. "She has a very sharp mind and she thinks things through."

I glowed with his praise and was speechless.

Ikaros nodded to me. "She has a good eye for design too. Did you know we chose your cloak pins? With the bees?"

"Chose them to be the real design?" I asked, thrilled. Ikaros nodded. Then Pytheas came up behind me and put his hand on my shoulder, and Sokrates began to introduce him.

"I may not always have this, but I have this now," I thought. "I am perfectly happy in this moment and I know it." It wasn't the wine, though the wine might have helped me recognize it.

Then the dance began, very beautiful and precise, which it had to be with with lifted torches and flowing draperies.

The next morning there was a great assembly in the Agora, in the exact center of the city. The city was laid out in a grid, with two diagonal streets crossing it. Whenever one street met another there was a little plaza, and often a temple or other building that was open to the whole city, and it was in those plazas that artworks usually stood. The Agora was the plaza in the centre of the city, where two straight roads and both diagonal roads all crossed. The Chamber was there, where the council met, and the big library and the temples of Apollo and Athene, and the civic offices where records were kept. It was the only space in the city big enough for all ten thousand of us to gather, and it had been designed for the purpose, being shaped as an auditorium with a rostrum at the end where speakers could be heard.

Today Krito and Tullius were at the rostrum. The other Masters stood with their halls. The few who were not assigned to any one city, and Sokrates, stood behind the rostrum. Sokrates was clearly scanning the children as we stood gathered in halls and tribes, looking at all of us. It was a chilly morn-

ing and we were all in our cloaks. Our breath steamed as we stood there. I
wondered if there would be snow—there had been snow in the winter of
the Year Two, all melted away by mid-morning, and I had never seen it since.
I thought of Botticelli's painting, which was my only real conception of winter somewhere colder than Greece.

Tullius and Krito both made speeches welcoming us to adulthood. Then
they called the name of each city, and each city advanced to the rostrum,
where each child's name was called and the child given their pin. This took
hours—from just after breakfast until almost dinnertime. We cheered each
name, but the cheers grew thinner as we grew colder and wearier. Florentia
came about halfway through. I had known I would be given a gold pin since
Sokrates had chosen me, but I still choked up as I was handed it. It was partly
that it was my own design, and partly that it was gold, after all, the most
precious metal. I was going to be a guardian of the city. I hardly heard how
many people cheered for me. I tucked my scroll inside my kiton and fastened my cloak with the pin at once. I was very pleased, but I didn't feel the
rush of joy I had felt at the fire.

Florentia filed back into our places and Delphi went up. "They should
have done it in the halls at breakfast," Damon grumbled behind me. "There's
no need to keep all of us standing here in the cold."

"What did you get?"

"Silver," he said. "No surprise. There aren't any surprises. This wasn't worth
making a fuss over. I think everyone knows where they belong." He unrolled
his scroll. "Weapon training. That'll be fun. Horse training. Great!"

"I'm hoping for training with weapons too," I said. Then I cheered as
Pytheas was announced. Gold, of course. The sun came out for a moment
as he put up his hand for his pin and made it flash. I pulled out my scroll and
read it. It said only that I was to study philosophy and keep up my work at
music and gymnastics. Did that mean no more art, I wondered, or did that
count as one of the parts of music?

I was about to ask Klymene if she knew when I realized she was weeping.
I put my arm around her. "What's wrong? Did they make you iron after all?"

She opened her hands and showed me her pin. Gold. I hugged her. "You
deserve it," I said. "You really really do."

She couldn't speak. Around us people were reading their scrolls. "It's so
great that the Masters get to pick things for us, things we're really good at
and that suit us," Laodike said, earnestly. "I'd hate to have to choose. And
think how limited it is in other places, where people are mostly stuck doing
what their parents did whether they want to or not."

"We're lucky to be here," I agreed.

Andromeda opened her own scroll. "Childcare training? But how? There aren't any children!"

"Yet," Damon said. "There's a festival of Hera this summer. Maybe by next year there will be a whole crop of children for you to tend. Better learn fast!"

"You sound as if you're looking forward to it," Andromeda said.

"Aren't you? Hey, Simmea, if there are a thousand silvers, and a festival three times a year, how long before I've had sex with all of them?"

"Three hundred and thirty-three years," I said at once, then thought about it some more. "No, wait, it's more complicated than that. I'm not sure. It might never happen. But it wouldn't work that way. Some women will get pregnant each time and not be available next time. And how do you know there are a thousand silvers?"

"Just a guess," he said. I wondered how many would be gold. Would it be three hundred years before my name was drawn with Pytheas?

Eventually the ceremony dragged to a close and we went back to our halls. Kebes came up and hugged and congratulated Klymene, who was the only person I knew who hadn't gone into the ceremony feeling fairly sure where they belonged. Laodike was a trifle disappointed to be silver—she had enjoyed astronomy so much, and hoped for gold.

"I'm lucky we met Sokrates that night," Kebes said to me.

"We both are."

"You'd have been gold anyway. I'd probably have been iron." Since we met Sokrates, Kebes had really appeared to be trying to be excellent. I'd heard Ficino saying that there never had been such an improvement in a boy.

I saw Septima, from the library, talking to Ficino. "She'll be gold," I said, confidently.

"Did they ever tell you they'd chosen your design?" Kebes asked.

"Master Ikaros told me last night. You were there."

"I know, but did anyone officially tell you?"

I shook my head. "I expect they wanted it to be a surprise."

"They should have announced it and given you the honor."

"Oh, that doesn't matter. It's enough of an honor that I'm going to see everyone wearing them." I stroked mine. "And that they thought it good enough."

The next day we cut our hair and made our vows at the temple of Zeus and Hera, to serve and protect the city. From then on we were considered adults, though we kept on calling ourselves children, to distinguish us from the Masters.

Our days were different after that. For one thing the houses were restructured, so that everyone in a house was of the same metal. Klymene and I remained in Hyssop with five other girls, two from Delphi, Makalla and Peisis, one from Ferrara, Iphis, and one from Naxos, Auge. Andromeda and the others moved out to be with their own kind. It felt strange, but I was glad not to be the one who was moving. Maia said we could choose who would be the new watcher. At my suggestion, we chose Klymene.

The seven of us were all in the tribe of Apollo—nobody had changed tribes in the reorganization. They also continued to belong to their original cities. But they slept in Hyssop. This would have been more awkward except for the rule that we could now eat anywhere we were invited. It meant that they could eat in their old halls with their old friends when they wanted to, or eat in Florentia with us in the mornings when time was short. It was good— but it changed everything. It meant that we didn't necessarily all see every other Florentine every day, and there were often different people in the hall, especially at dinner. Florentia was a popular dining hall, partly because of our food but mostly because it was so very beautiful. Eating where we were invited made us all mingle and know each other better. Before summer came I had eaten at least once in each hall. Venice had a wonderful *Apollo and Juno* by Veronese, Cortona had Signorelli's *The Court of Pan*, and in Athens, where Septima took me one day with Pytheas, was a breathtaking statue of Lemnian Athena. Hardest to get into was Olympia, but eventually I met Aristomache with Sokrates and she invited me for dinner. Thus I got to see Phidias's astonishing Nike, which if I were forced to choose is probably my favourite statue.

The other different thing was our schedules. Before this, almost all of Florentia did the same things at the same time every day, with a few exceptions like astronomy and the sessions with Sokrates. Now we were all doing different things. Some of us still had every moment scheduled. Others, and especially we golds, had a reasonable amount of flexibility as to how we spent our time. For music I did mathematics and read in the library. I had very little supervision in reading. Masters might suggest books to me, and occasionally a request for a book was denied. Otherwise I was free to read what I wanted to—which was mostly philosophy and logic. I still did mathematics with Axiothea, which was always fun. Art was something for my free time, which I experienced now for the first time. I could go to the studio and work on my paintings and designs whenever I wasn't expected anywhere else, and I often did.

I continued to spend hours in the palaestra—but I decided which hours they would be. The way Maia explained this to me was that we were to pursue excellence as seemed best to us, now that we knew what it was and that we wanted it. Children need guidance; adults can learn to guide themselves. Most of all I pursued excellence by debating with Sokrates. Kebes and I took to following him around in the mornings, when he talked with anyone he ran into.

Soon, well before the summer, I perceived a problem. Before the new year, anyone whom Sokrates befriended was clearly destined to become a gold, and we all were duly awarded gold pins. After that, Sokrates continued to befriend people, but now their status was fixed. Only golds were supposed to study philosophy and rhetoric. But the Masters couldn't very well stop Sokrates from going up to people and asking them about their work. They couldn't stop him from inviting whomever he chose to come back to Thessaly for conversation. Sokrates was famous. All of the Masters revered him practically by definition—they were here specifically because they revered Sokrates, after all. They didn't want to stop him behaving the way he had always behaved. They had loved to read in the *Apology* about how he was a gadfly sent by the gods to Athens. Now he was their gadfly, and they weren't as happy about that. He was upsetting their neat system, and he knew it. He would laugh about it.

"How can they know who is the best?" he asked in one of our debates. The four of us were alone in the garden of Thessaly, eating delicious fried zucchini flowers stuffed with cheese that Kebes had brought from the Florentine kitchens.

"They observe us," I said. "They see who is best fitted for each task. My friend Andromeda is motherly and loving, and she was assigned to learn childcare. I am interested in debate, and I am assigned to learn rhetoric with you."

"Good. But how about Patroklus of Mycenae, who only became interested in debate the day before yesterday? He has been assigned to learn how to care for goats and sheep. Now he wants to debate."

"That doesn't mean it's what he's best suited for," I said. "He might be best suited as a shepherd."

"Does everyone have one thing for which they are best suited?" Kebes asked. "You're good at design, as well as debate."

"They always told us that we were a mixture of all the metals, and it was a case of discovering which one was strongest," I said.

"The metals are supposed to be an analogy for the parts of the soul," Kebes said. "So if Patroklus wants to turn to philosophy, does that mean reason is stronger in his soul than appetites, and they were wrong in thinking appetites were stronger? Or was Plato wrong about the soul?"

"Or perhaps the soul and the proportions of its parts change over time?" I asked.

"But assuming that Patroklus is truly best suited as gold, as my friend and debating partner, what does that mean?" Sokrates asked.

"It means the Masters made a mistake." I shrugged. "Nobody said they were gods to get everything perfect."

Sokrates looked at Pytheas, who was leaning back on his elbow in the shade of the tree, eating zucchini flowers and looking like a Hyakinthos. "You're very quiet today," he said.

Pytheas licked his lips slowly, and Sokrates laughed and then swore aloud. "Apollo! Oh, Pytheas, you can make me swoon at your beauty, you know I'm helplessly in love with you, but that won't help you in debate."

Once we had all stopped laughing Pytheas sat up straight and answered seriously. "I think your question is the real question," he said. "How can they know who is the best? Even if they could see into our souls, how could they know? And to my knowledge nobody can see into our souls."

"Not even the gods?" Sokrates asked, rocking forward and almost toppling over.

"We know the gods can hear prayers directed to them, and sometimes speech before it is spoken. I don't believe they can see into anyone's soul beyond that, except perhaps all-knowing Zeus." Pytheas shrugged and took another zucchini flower. "But in any case, the Masters don't have that ability."

"The Masters just do the best they can with observation and intelligence and goodwill," I said at once. "To their observation, Patroklus was best suited to be a shepherd."

"Should they change their minds now?" Pytheas asked.

I looked at Sokrates. "I'd guess not, because it would cause too much confusion."

"That's certainly what they'd say," Sokrates said. "Some might put individual happiness above social confusion."

"Is happiness the highest goal?" Kebes asked.

"Is it a goal at all?" I asked. I thought of that moment by the fire when I had recognized how happy I was. "Is it rather something that's a byproduct of something else? An incidental that comes along when you're not pursuing it? When I think about when I am happiest it's never when I'm trying to be happy."

"And how does happiness differ from joy or fun?" Kebes asked. "Fun can certainly be a goal."

"It can also come along as an incidental," Pytheas pointed out. "A spin-off benefit."

"If you pursue happiness, like pursuing excellence, truth, or learning, do you get closer to it or further away?" Sokrates asked.

"You certainly can't will happiness," Kebes said, thoughtfully.

"Further away, I think," I said. "If you try to make somebody happy, you can't do it by asking them or telling them to be happy. You can do it by doing something for them, or doing something with them. So it seems much more like a side effect to me. Or almost like a thing that happens to you. So if you wanted to maximize happiness, for a person or a city, you'd do better to aim at something else that was the kind of thing likely to produce that side effect."

"Like what?" Kebes asked.

"Like excellence," Pytheas said.

Kebes made a rude noise, and Sokrates tutted at him. "What if you wanted to make Simmea happy?"

"I'd argue with her," Pytheas said. I threw a tuft of grass at him and we all laughed.

"But it's true. Debate does make me happy," I said. "It's not just that it's fun."

"What does happiness consist of?" Sokrates asked.

"Freedom, and having everything you want," Kebes said, looking from Sokrates to me.

"Not everything you want," I said. "You might want something that would make you unhappy if you got it. Having what is best."

"That brings us back to what is best," Sokrates said.

"The pursuit of excellence, as Pytheas said just now. When we first came here, Ficino said that he wanted each of us to become our best self," I said. "That seems to me an admirable goal."

"And that has been your constant pursuit since you were ten years old," Sokrates said.

"Eleven," I admitted.

Sokrates laughed. "Since you were what passed for ten years old. But how about Kebes?"

"How could he not want to be his best self?" I asked.

"Kebes?"

But Pytheas interrupted before Kebes could answer. "He might have a different pursuit. A different goal. Something he rates more highly."

"More highly than being his best self?" I asked, incredulous.

"If you'll let me speak, yes I do," Kebes said. These days Kebes seemed to tolerate Pytheas better most of the time, but he was really glaring at him now.

"What is it?" Sokrates asked, calm as ever.

"Revenge," Kebes said. "Slavers killed my family and enslaved me and the Masters bought me and brought me here against my will. I can't possibly ever be my best self. That's out of reach. My best self would have had parents and sisters. My best self would have lived in his own time. All I can be is the slave self they made me, and my slave self wants revenge."

"The Masters didn't kill your family," I said. "It's like when you poked me back in the slave market, because you couldn't reach those who could hurt you and I was there. You can't reach the ones who hurt you, and you want revenge on those who have done you nothing but good."

"If there weren't any buyers there wouldn't be any slavers," Kebes said. "They're part of it. And that they have high intentions makes it worse, not better. And they did the same to you."

I thought for a moment. Pytheas opened his mouth to speak, but Sokrates raised a hand, stopping him. "I see a clear distinction between those who killed my family and the Masters," I said. "And it is my belief that I have more chance of being my best self here than I would have there. I can't know this for sure."

"Do you mean you condone having your family murdered to get you here?" Kebes almost shouted.

"That would be called Providence, and it's an interesting argument to consider," Sokrates said, calmly. "But it's late and you're growing heated. Let's stop for today."

Kebes stayed, and I left with Pytheas. "I wonder where Sokrates heard about Providence," Pytheas said as we walked down the street. "He's so clever."

"Sokrates is clever, but Kebes is an idiot," I said, kicking a stone. I was still upset.

"If Kebes were an idiot, he wouldn't be half so dangerous," Pytheas said.

15

MAIA

One day in the summer of the Year Five, Kreusa, Aristomache, Klio and I were sitting on the stones at the top of the beach one afternoon, drying off. We'd had a meeting of the Committee on Women's Issues, and then we'd had a swim. Aristomache was in her fifties, one of the oldest women in the city. She was originally an American, from later in my own century. She had long greying hair, usually neatly knotted on top of her head but now falling loose in damp curls over her little breasts. I'd been in the city so long that

I barely even registered the fact that we were all sprawled comfortably naked in the sun. We were all Masters of the city, and the only time we worried about was the present. As Plato correctly deduced, people grow used to seeing bodies, even when they're not young or beautiful.

Klio reached into the fold of her kiton where it lay bundled at her side and pulled out a small cake and a knife.

"Ought we—I mean, is that all right?" Aristomache asked, as Klio cut the cake into quarters. I picked up my share. It was currant cake and smelled delicious.

"What's wrong with it?" Klio asked, looking up.

"Well, Plato says we should have food in common, and I've interpreted taking food out of the eating halls to eat elsewhere as wrong," Aristomache said.

I looked guiltily at the wedge of cake I'd taken. Was it unplatonic of me to take it? I looked at Klio.

"Plato doesn't regulate the lives of the Masters," Klio said. "But I think you're right. If we had food in private all the time it would be a bad thing. But this cake was made in Sparta's kitchen, and it's the same cake everyone is going to be eating there tonight. I'm always starving after swimming, and I thought I'd bring enough for all of us."

Kreusa looked at the cut pieces and did not reach out for one. "I think we ought to debate this. Do you allow the children to take food?"

"No, never," Klio said.

"Then it's not really having it in common, if we have privileges they don't," Kreusa said.

"Maybe we ought to let them, at least a little bit," Klio said. "What's wrong with it, as long as they always share what they take with others?"

"It's not what Plato says, but I agree that it might be all right," I said. "I allow the Florentines to take nuts and dried fruit when they go running in the mountains."

"So do I with the Olympians, but always enough for the whole group," Aristomache said.

"Oh yes. And when mine run in pairs, one will take the nuts and the other the fruit, so they'll share," I said. "I didn't discuss it with anyone because it didn't seem to come under any particular committee, and Plato didn't mention it, and I just thought it was my discretion. I mean, if the whole lot of us all go out on a run we take food, so if a smaller group does it seems like the same thing."

"I agree," Kreusa said. "And I like that, giving one the nuts and the other the fruit. That very much does go along with the spirit of what Plato said about food in common. I'll do that with the Corinthians now you've mentioned it. Which is really a good reason for talking over things like that, so we can have the good ideas in common and stamp out the bad ideas before they get rooted."

I blushed. "Yes. Sorry. But who should I have asked, or told?"

"Food comes under Agriculture and Supply," Aristomache said, picking up a slice of cake. "I don't know who's on that committee."

"Ikaros?" Klio suggested.

Aristomache and Kreusa laughed, and Kreusa pretended to fan herself. I bit into my cake to disguise the fact that the thought of him still made me uncomfortable.

"I don't believe he is," Aristomache said. "He's never been on absolutely every committee. And since Sokrates has come and takes up a lot of his time, he has dropped several."

"Ardeia is on it, I think," Kreusa said.

"I'm not sure Agriculture and Supply is the right committee anyway. This isn't about food supply. It's a social issue. It's Right Living if it's anything, and I'm on that one," Aristomache said. "I'll bring it up in our next meeting, and if Manlius and everyone else is all right with it I'll suggest the fruit and nuts thing in Chamber. I think we can be a little more relaxed. The children are going to become adults soon. Indeed, I was wondering if we could give them the privilege of choosing which hall they eat in."

"Choose which hall?" Kreusa asked, her arched eyebrows rising right up into her hair. "Won't that cause chaos?"

"I didn't mean choose which hall unrestrictedly, or choose which hall to belong to," Aristomache said. "That really would cause chaos. I meant simply that perhaps we could give the children limited privileges to invite their friends to their own hall, and to go to other halls if invited."

"Won't it mean surpluses in some halls and shortages in others?" I asked.

"Won't it mean nobody knows where anybody is?" Kreusa asked.

"I think the surpluses and shortages would cancel out," Aristomache said, looking at Klio.

Klio nodded. "Workers could redistribute food if necessary, and probably it wouldn't be a problem; children missing from one hall would be cancelled out by children present from another. We could easily set up a mechanism where they had to sign in and out, and if a hall was full up nobody else could sign in unless somebody signed out. The food is very similar in all the halls. The social disruption potential is there, though."

"I think most of the children would be sensible about it," Aristomache said.

"Most of them, but there are some who wouldn't," I said.

"I don't understand the point of it," Kreusa said.

"The point is that once they become adults, we need to shuffle the sleeping houses so that everyone is sleeping with people of the same metal," Aristomache said. "It will mean people are sleeping very far from where they're supposed to eat. If there were some flexibility in that it would help. We don't want to reassign eating halls, because the children are very attached to them, and also because that's how we keep track of them."

"I can see how it would help," I said. "I'll support it." Klio nodded.

"I'm not convinced," Kreusa said. "I see a lot of potential for trouble. I'd want to hear a really solid proposal."

"It may come to nothing yet," Aristomache said. "Tullius is opposed."

I sighed and stretched. "I should get back. I have to teach soon, and then after dinner I need to work on the adulthood choices with Ficino, and I want to look through the list again first."

"It's only seventy children, and we know them well. You wouldn't think it would be this difficult," Kreusa said. She reached for her kiton.

"It's the responsibility." Klio shook her head. "I used to feel bad enough about grades and recommendation letters affecting people's entire lives, but this? Deciding for seventy people not just what kind of soul they have but what work they'd be best suited for?"

"Lysias says he doesn't really believe in souls, that he thinks they're a metaphor," I said. Lysias had been showing some polite interest in me recently. I liked him. He was quiet and considerate and as unlike flamboyant Ikaros as it was possible for somebody to be and still be a man.

"Doesn't believe in souls?" Kreusa asked, pausing with her kiton half on. "Pallas Athene told us we have souls, the very first day. It's one of the few metaphysical things we can be absolutely rock-solid sure about."

"He thinks they're not the same as Plato wrote. She didn't answer Plotinus's question about whether they have three parts," I said. "He thinks they're something odd, and Plato's description is just a metaphor."

"Even if it's a metaphor, we still have to use it to classify everyone," Aristomache said, twisting up her hair.

"Do you know, the other day I found myself picking up Ficino's translation of the *Republic* to read through it in Latin, because I've read it so often in Greek that my eyes start to cross," Klio said, laughing at herself.

"I've done that too," I admitted, and we laughed together.

Kreusa stood up. "I envy you your hair, Maia."

"My hair?" I ran my fingers through my hair, which I kept at shoulder length, the same length the children kept theirs. It was almost dry, so I started to braid it.

"It's the kind of hair we all wanted when I was a girl. Straw pale."

"But it's so straight. My mother used to curl it, and the curls would just fall out again. And your own hair is lovely, like heavy bronze."

Kreusa pulled a curl of her hair and squinted at it. "Lukretia has lovely hair," she said.

"Envy, vanity, what next?" Klio teased. Klio always kept her own hair short.

Dressed and dry, the four of us started to walk back up around the curve of the bay towards the city. It looked beautiful from this angle and in the afternoon light. It looked beautiful to me from every angle and in every light, it was so well-proportioned and so well-situated. Athene, Builder of Cities, had chosen the site well. The vineyards and olive groves stood around it like the Form of agricultural civilization made concrete, and the volcano steamed away behind, like a reminder of mortality.

Aristomache paused for a moment, contemplating it. "If the gods will help us see the right metals in their souls, we'll have done all right," she said.

"Plato was so clearly only concerned with the guardians," Kreusa said. "I know the list of qualities for the golds by heart."

"Love of wisdom and the truth, temperate, liberal, brave, orderly, just and gentle, fast to learn, retentive, with a sense of order and proportion," Aristomache reeled off. "You wouldn't think it would be so hard to assess, until you were looking at a set of seventy sixteen-year-olds and weighing each of them for those qualities."

I sighed. "It's hard to find enough people who have them. The really difficult thing is getting the numbers right. But fortunately, with the ones we have to decide for, Ficino seems really sure in most cases. It's the ones where he isn't sure that are causing me anguish."

"The difficult thing is deciding who's iron and who's bronze, when Plato gives no guidelines there at all," Kreusa said. "And it's hard to assess exactly what work each child has an aptitude for and ought to be trained for. Not to mention what work we need done. And who can train them for it."

"I think the Committee on Iron Work will report on training skills tomorrow night," Klio said.

"That's a relief," Kreusa said. "Thank you for telling me."

"When I talk to the children, they seem to know where they belong," Aristomache said.

"Well maybe you and Ficino can see into their souls, but it's difficult for me," Klio said. "There are always the ones on the edges. And getting the numbers, as you say—we have to have it done by the meeting by tribes on the Ides, when we'll do the final adjustment."

"Some of them are so certain and easy," I said. "So unquestionably one thing or the other, with the metals in their souls so clear even I can see them. Others are more of a puzzle. And as you say, it's so important. Such a responsibility. I'm very glad Ficino is so good at it. I'd hate to be doing it alone."

We came to the gates of the city then and bade each other joy of the day, and divided to go our separate ways on our common task.

16

SIMMEA

"How many golds are there?" I asked Axiothea one day as summer approached.

"Two hundred and fifty-two," she said.

I was thinking of Damon's question. It would take only thirty-one years for every gold to be married to every other gold, discounting time lost for pregnancy and potential repetitions. Did I want that? Could I avoid it? "Are they divided equally by gender?"

"Mm-hmm."

Then I stopped. "How many silvers?"

"Why do you want to know?" Axiothea asked, frowning.

I wanted to know because two hundred and fifty-two is such a very round number, considered as a percentage of ten thousand and eighty, but I wasn't Sokrates with the privilege of asking anything. If I made myself too much of a gadfly, I'd get swatted.

"Just curious," I said.

"Well, about a thousand," Axiothea said, clearly having thought better of her precise answer. "And about two thousand bronze. Just approximately. Now, to get back to the calculus?"

Later, in Thessaly I asked Sokrates if he knew the exact numbers. "Two hundred and fifty-two doesn't seem like a round number to me," he said.

"It's what you get if you divide ten thousand and eighty by exactly forty," I explained.

Kebes sat up in surprise. "You think they're not judging fairly?"

"Two hundred and fifty-two, divided equally by gender, can't possibly be chance. There must have been some people they either included to make up the number, or excluded to get it down."

"It could be chance," Pytheas said.

"Just barely possible," Sokrates said. "Numbers are difficult evidence. You can make them mean so many things."

"There are Masters here who are obsessed with making them mean different things," Pytheas said.

"Not Axiothea," I protested.

"No, not Axiothea. I was thinking of old Plotinus, may he be reborn in this city. And some of his friends. Proclus. Hermeios. Even Ficino can get all starry-eyed about the mystical significance of numbers." Pytheas shook his head.

I nodded. "We need to find out how many silver and bronze. Exactly how many."

"I shall find out," Sokrates said. "Meanwhile, I tried an experiment today. I talked to a Worker that was cleaning the street of Apollo early this morning."

"What did you say?" Pytheas asked.

"I asked it what it was doing and why, and whether it liked the work or preferred other things." Sokrates smiled. "It didn't reply."

"They don't talk," Kebes said. "I've told you before."

"Maybe they don't talk because nobody ever talks to them," Sokrates said. "I intend to persist. Perhaps they will find a way of answering."

The next day he had an answer to the question of numbers—there were eleven hundred and twenty silvers, and twenty-two hundred and forty bronzes.

"Leaving six thousand five hundred and eight iron," I said.

"Those are not random numbers," Kebes said.

"No," Sokrates said. "So we should revisit the question of how the masters decided to divide you up."

I had been thinking about it constantly since Axiothea had given me the number. "I think they must have had lots of dubious cases," I said. "I mean, take Klymene." I looked over at Pytheas, who didn't seem upset that I'd mentioned her. "She displayed cowardice once. But since then she has faced up to everything, she made herself brave. She's a gold. But they must have thought more than twice about whether she should be. If there had been somebody more deserving, somebody who had never showed cowardice, it wouldn't have been wrong for them to have set Klymene among the bronze, or more likely iron, because I don't think she has many artificing skills."

"But they didn't say," Klebes said.

"No," I agreed.

"Just no?" Sokrates asked.

"They didn't say, and they should have said. It makes a difference. We thought they were only thinking about our own worth, and actually they must have been thinking about numbers too."

"They had to make it gender-even," Pytheas said. "In every class. Because otherwise the weddings wouldn't work."

Kebes sighed.

"And is that so important? That everyone has a partner of their own rank?" Sokrates asked. "Could you not choose for yourself, as people did in Athens?"

"Women?" I asked. "Did women choose?"

"Their parents tended to arrange marriages," Sokrates said. "But they knew their own children."

"The masters know us. And the marriages are to be only for one day, not stuck forever, the way they usually were in other cultures. Were you happy in your marriage?" I knew he had not been.

"It's very difficult when people are married and don't like each other," Sokrates admitted.

"Did your parents like each other?" Kebes asked me.

I thought about it. "Yes. But they led very separate lives."

"My parents loved each other, and they loved me," Pytheas said. It was the first time I had ever heard him mention his parents. Sokrates too looked at him in astonishment. "They're still alive as far as I know, in the time I came from. They had a farm up above Delphi." He caught Sokrates's expression and laughed. "Not so far above Delphi! That's where I was born, sixteen years ago. In the hills, half a day's walk from the Pythian shrine."

"Would you like to have a marriage like they had?" Sokrates asked.

It was Pytheas's turn to look surprised. "I'd never thought about it." He looked away. "It's too hard to imagine."

"How about you, Simmea? Are you looking forward to the one-day marriages, or would you want a life partnership?"

Involuntarily I looked back at Pytheas, who was still staring into space. Kebes was glaring as I met his eye as I turned to look back at Sokrates. "We can have friendships for life," I said. "And friendships don't have to be exclusive." I smiled at Kebes, but he kept on frowning.

"Plato didn't have as much experience of humanity as he needed to write a book like the *Republic*," Sokrates said. "Perhaps nobody does."

"What sort of experience would it take?" Pytheas asked, smiling, and we were off down another dialectical avenue exploring that.

I thought about Sokrates's question when I was alone that night. Klymene and the others were sleeping and the light was off. If I could choose—well, it would be Pytheas, of course, but would he choose me? I was better off as I was. I knew he liked me and valued me, but would he want that kind of marriage if it were an option? I didn't think he would. Kebes definitely would, but I wouldn't want it with Kebes. I didn't know enough about it. I thought of my parents. It seemed so long ago. I wondered if my mother could still be alive. Then I realised that "still" meant nothing, she wasn't even born yet, and in another sense she was certainly dead. Then I sat up in bed. If we could move through time, could we change things? Could we go back to before the slavers came with an armed troop of Silvers and prevent them from killing my father and brothers? If I prayed to Athene?

I prayed, and felt as an answer to my prayer a strong urge to go to the library. I got up and dressed and found my way through the dark streets. There was no moon, and it was very late and the sconces were dimmed. I went to the big library in the southwest corner. It was not so grand as the one by the Agora, but it had a charming bronze Athene by the door which always seemed to be welcoming me. It was here that I had learned to read.

The doors were open, and inside the lights were on. I looked about for direction. Would the goddess send me to a book? I waited for guidance but none came. After a while I walked up to the seat where I usually worked and took out Newton's *Principia*. I knew there was nothing in it about time travel.

When I had been reading for a few minutes, I saw Septima. She was shelving. I watched her, then stood and went over to her. "What are you doing here in the middle of the night?" she whispered.

"I couldn't sleep, and thought I might as well read. How about you?"

"I couldn't sleep, and thought I might as well work. Why couldn't you sleep?" She looked inquiringly at me.

"I suddenly thought of something."

"Let's go and sit on the steps where we can talk out loud," she said.

"But . . . there's nobody else here!"

"I don't think I could raise my voice in here, even in the middle of the night," she admitted. We went outside and sat on the steps by the feet of the bronze Athene. "What did you think of?" she asked, and her normal voice sounded loud after the quiet.

"Moving through time. We all did it. The goddess brought us here that way. If she can do that, she could use it to change things that have happened. We could raise a bodyguard and go back and save my family from the slavers."

"We could raise an army and save Constantinople from the Turks," Septima said.

"Yes, exactly!" I said, glad she had understood so quickly.

"I've thought about this a lot, and no, we couldn't. The gods are bound by Fate and Necessity, and Necessity only allows the kind of changes in time that nobody notices. We can't change what's fated to happen. One vanished sculpture," she patted the shiny bronze toe of the goddess, "is neither here nor there. Two slave children?" She gestured at us. "Thousands of people like us lived and died and made no difference. When Fate is involved, especially when the gods know what happened and try to change it? That just makes everything worse."

"How could it make it worse if—" I decided to use her example rather than my own. "—if we saved Constantinople?"

"Without the fall of Constantinople bringing manuscripts to Italy, there might have been no Renaissance. Constantinople hadn't done much for civilization throughout the Middle Ages. It had held on, that's all. It hadn't built anything new, produced any new and truly wonderful books or art or scientific discoveries. The flowering of the Renaissance, on the other hand . . ." She spread out her hands.

"Is it like the bit in the *Iliad* when Zeus is deciding whether to let Patroklus die or live for a bit longer, and Patroklus kills all those other people, who clearly don't matter to Zeus even though Patroklus and Achilles do?" I'd recently been allowed to read the unexpurgated Homer.

"Just like that."

"Then my family didn't matter?" I hated that thought.

"They mattered. Everyone matters. But not everything is bound by fate. Everyone has their own fate, that they chose before they were born. But they're just choosing a chance of filling out as much as they can of the shape of it. What actually happens is up to the choices they make—well, until they come right up to the edges, where they run into Necessity. Necessity is the line drawn around what anyone can do. Life is full of randomness and chance and choices, and only some things matter to fate. The difficulty is knowing which things." She sighed. "I talked to Krito once about why most of the male masters here were old when most of the women were young. It seems it's because men achieve so much more in their lives, and they couldn't be missed from them until they were near to death, whereas most women might as well not exist for all the individual contribution most of us get to make to history."

I thought about that. "Some of the women are older. Lukretia of Ferrara is. And Aristomache of Olympia must be at least fifty."

"Aristomache translated Plato into the vernacular in Boston in eighteen eighty-three," Septima said. "She published it anonymously. Nobody in her time would have trusted a woman as a scholar. But her translation helped a lot of young people discover philosophy. She couldn't come until she'd finished it, and until after a friend of hers had written a poem to her." Septima shook her head. "I really like Aristomache. She really *deserves* to be here."

"And some of the men are younger," I said. "Like Lysias, and Ikaros."

"Oh, Ikaros," she said, her eyes softening at the thought of him. "He deserves to be here too. He died before he had the chance to do what he could have done. But he's spending so much time with Sokrates now. He hardly ever has time to talk to me."

"Do you ever think the Masters envy us?" I asked.

"Yes. They obviously do. Who wouldn't?"

It was so strange to hear her certainty, after spending so much time talking to Sokrates. "I think this is the best place, too," I said.

"Even if we can't go and fix time?" she asked.

"Not even Necessity knows all ends," I quoted. She laughed. I found myself yawning. "Perhaps I should go to bed now."

"Good night, Simmea," Septima said, and went back into the library.

For a moment I wanted to run after her and tell her that I knew she was Pytheas's sister and ask about their childhood together. She was a very reserved person, difficult to get to know. I seldom saw her except in the library. That was one of the most intimate conversations I'd ever had with her. But when I imagined telling her that Pytheas had told me their secret I could only picture her pulling away. I watched the doors swing shut behind her, then walked slowly back through the city towards my bed.

17

MAIA

"Did you ever wonder why Plato isn't here?" Klio asked one evening in the Year Seven as we were walking back after a debate. She and Axiothea had their arms around each other. They were an established couple now. Lysias was walking beside me. He and I were not so much a couple as friends who did on occasion share eros—the true note of our relationship was definitely philia. As far as eros goes, silphium always worked so far, for me and for the other female Masters, though I always fretted about it.

"I suppose he didn't pray to be here?" I suggested.

"He knew it wouldn't work. He never intended it to be tried seriously. He was just trying to provoke debate."

"Well that may be true, but that doesn't mean we're wrong to want to try it," Lysias said. "And it is working."

"It's mostly sort-of partly working," Klio said.

We came to my door and I opened it. "Wine? Cake?" The debate about whether it was appropriate to take food out of the eating halls had been decided in favor, as long as the food was always shared. We all went in and I fetched the wine and the mixer. Lysias took the cups out and distributed them, while Axiothea took the cushions off the bed and put them on the floor. I mixed the wine—half and half as we always drank it, on Plato's recommendation.

"It's working. We have children who love philosophy, who think a debate between Manlius and Tullius is the best imaginable way to spend an evening. I envy them sometimes," Lysias said, as I put little nut cakes on a plate.

"Me too," I said, passing the plate to Axiothea and sitting down on the floor beside Lysias. He and I leaned on the bed, and the other two against the wall, on the pillows. "I envy them. And even more I envy the next generation. The babies that will be born here. The native speakers, as you said once, Klio. Our children will do better at giving them the Republic than we did for our children, because we're a pile of crazy idealists from all over time, and our children grew up here."

"Sokrates thinks we're wrong," Axiothea said. "He's teaching all sorts of people to question all sorts of things. When I first heard what he thinks about Plato, it really rocked me."

"Sokrates doesn't believe in the Noble Lie," I said, sipping my wine.

"Sometimes it's necessary, but I'd prefer to avoid it too," Lysias said quietly.

"When a doctor—" Axiothea began.

"We all know the argument," Klio interrupted.

"Would you have the Noble Lie debate with Tullius or Ficino?" Axiothea asked.

"Debate it in Chamber, you mean?" Lysias asked. "Maybe."

"How about in public?" I asked.

"That would be tantamount to telling the children we've lied to them," Klio said.

"We're going to have to tell them sometime. Before we all die and they need to run things for the next generation," Lysias pointed out. "They're not supposed to read the *Republic* until they're fifty, and then only the golds."

"We'll need to tell some of them. Some carefully selected subset." Axiothea shook her head. "The real problem is all the old men who don't want to let anything go."

"Tullius," I said.

"Not just Tullius. Others too. They're men, they're from societies where men have the power, they're older, they're used to being the people giving orders. They come here and they find out that they're famous to people from future centuries. They're not going to want to give that up, even to Philosopher Kings." Klio frowned. "They don't like debating me or Myrto. And Aristomache has stopped trying, even though she's one of the sharpest minds here."

"Ikaros will debate you," Lysias said.

"Oh, Ikaros!" She looked quickly at me. "I think he has the opposite problem. Here he's just like us. He isn't the kind of famous he'd have wanted to be. He didn't have the chance to be. But he's brilliant. He wants his posterity to be here."

"I think that's unfair," Lysias said. "When I heard that Pico della Mirandola was here, I was just as excited as when I heard that Cicero and Boethius were. And Ikaros is happy to be known by philosophers. He didn't care about wide fame as long as the best people knew about him."

"I'd never heard of him," I said.

"Me neither," Axiothea said. "But I'm a mathematician."

"And I wasn't anything," I said.

"You were a scholar in a world that wouldn't let you be," Klio said, reaching over and patting my hand. "That's a lot more than nothing. But I think I'm right about what Ikaros thinks about his posterity."

"I think most of us want our posterity to be here," I said. "Our legacy. I certainly do. And you know, in the normal course of time the old men will die off and there will be a time when we are old but alive and we can make the decisions about what to hand on to the children and when."

"I thought of that when Plotinus died last year," Klio said. "But when the children are fifty I'll be nearly eighty, and even you will be almost seventy."

"And our posterity will not be here," Axiothea said. "We have no posterity. Athene told us that in the beginning. Doing it has to be enough."

"It's enough for me," I said.

"I don't think it's enough for Ikaros, now Plotinus is dead," Klio said.

"What more could he want? We're living the good life. We're building the Just City," Lysias said. "We knew from the beginning that it wasn't going to last, that it couldn't. We're all making sacrifices for that."

"Like what?" Axiothea asked, pouring more wine.

"Like working so hard, and not having children," Lysias said.

"But working hard is mostly fun, and all the children are our children," I said.

"You don't want children of your own?" he asked.

I emphatically did not. "They wouldn't fit into the plan," I said.

"You see," Lysias said, spreading his hands.

"I don't feel we're making a sacrifice," I said.

Klio nodded. "I think we're very lucky to be here. Though I never imagined when we started that I'd spend half my time working with Workers."

"Me neither," Lysias groaned. "And some of them are refusing to leave the recharger, and I don't know what to do about it. I'd have taken a course on robotics if I'd had the least idea how much I'd need it. I was a philosopher. I just used them without thinking about it."

"Are you sure you'd have been able to fit another course in?" Klio teased.

"It would have been a lot more use than German," he said, and laughed. "Well, bless Athene for giving us the Workers anyway, even if I wish she'd included some manuals and information on how they really work. Without them we'd be doing a lot of backbreaking work."

"It is working, isn't it?" Axiothea said. "Mostly sort of, like you said. But we are making it work. We're proving Plato right."

We grinned at each other and raised our cups in a silent toast.

18

SIMMEA

The games came first. I didn't get through the heats except in swimming, where I came in third. Laodike won the long distance race for running in armor. I cheered so hard I almost lost my voice. Then Axiothea, who was next to me, pounded me so hard on the back she almost cracked a rib. Her good friend Klio of Sparta hugged both of us, and then hugged Laodike when she came up panting with the ribbons from her crown falling in her eyes. "A girl to win the race for running in armor," Klio said, and her eyes were damp.

"Why not?" I asked.

"Why not indeed?" asked Axiothea. "Some people say men are stronger."

"They often are, but women tend to have more endurance," Laodike panted. "Running in armor is at least as much endurance as strength."

The next day was the festival of Hera. I was up before dawn to help make flower garlands. The Workers had brought masses of flowers down from the hills and piled them in each hall. In Florentia they were piled downstairs in the courtyard. Six of us twined them into seventy headdresses and thirty-five garlands, and we were barely done in time. Anemones have terrible stems, and hyacinths drop little bits everywhere—thank Demeter for long sturdy daisies and twining roses that look wonderful together, especially with a few violets tucked in. By the time everyone arrived for breakfast, we were finished and congratulating ourselves. I was famished and ate two bowls of porridge, a big handful of cherries and an egg. Maia hugged me on my way out. "Good luck," she said.

I was afraid the festival was going to drag out like the festival where we were all named, but they had learned something and it did not. There was music and dancing, and names were drawn ten at a time and announced in bursts, maybe every ten minutes or so. Then we'd all dance again as those ten went up the temple steps in their headdresses to have garlands bound around their wrists as they were married for the day.

Dancing is always fun, and dancing with friends to music and without set patterns is even better. I had a strange nervous feeling in the pit of my stomach and I tried to dance it down. One hundred and twenty-six male golds, any of whom I could end up married to. I wasn't at all sure I wanted to have a baby. I looked cautiously at the black stone statue of Hera, facing the great seated ivory and gold Zeus across the temple steps. "Give me the good for which I do not know to ask," I prayed.

I avoided both Pytheas and Kebes. I didn't want to think about either of them. Kebes was called early and matched with Euridike from Plataea. Ficino bound the wreath around their wrists and Kreusa called out the blessing. Euridike was blushing, which really showed up on her fair skin. I danced more vigorously. Pytheas hadn't been called yet. I could see him over on the far side of the agora in another dancing circle.

When my name was called my stomach clenched so hard I almost bent double. I let go of Klymene's hand and walked towards the steps with my friends calling after me—wishes of luck and happiness. I was paired with Aeschines, from Ithaka. I knew him only slightly. He was very dark-skinned with big lips, a Libyan like my grandmother. We stood together shyly as Ficino bound the garland around our wrists. It was not one of the ones I had made; every hall had brought a supply. This one had poppies and anemones twisted in a white ribbon. I stared at it to avoid meeting Aeschines's eyes. We walked down the steps carefully, and off through the crowd. I kept my eyes on the ground. I did not want to see or speak to anyone, most especially not Pytheas.

We crossed the square and walked down the street of Demeter, wrists together. The crowds were thinner here, and as we went on and came away from the sound of music we found ourselves almost alone. When we came to the plaza where the street of Demeter crosses the street of Dionysos, Aeschines stopped. "There are chambers down here," he said, gesturing with his free hand.

"All right," I said. We turned to the left. "Did they tell you about this?"

"Ikaros, one of the Masters from Ferrara, explained it to all the boys of Ithaka and Ferrara," he said. "I expect one of your Masters explained it to the Florentines."

"I wish Maia had explained it to me," I said.

"Why, are you nervous?"

"Yes," I admitted. "I suppose it's just because this is the first time and I don't know enough about it. I saw my mother raped, and then more women were raped on the slave ship." That had been the stuff of nightmare for years. "So I have some uncomfortable feelings."

"I'm sorry," he said. "I'll try not to hurt you."

"Thank you." I looked at him. He was tall and earnest and his brow was furrowed now as he looked down at me. He wasn't flawless Pytheas, my best friend and secret beloved. But if I had hoped for that, I had also known that the odds were a hundred and twenty-five to one.

"Here," he said. There was a low hall which I had used before. It was full of practice rooms where people learning the lyre could sit in bad weather. Some of the doors lay open and others were closed. In the open ones I could see mattresses covered with blankets. We went into one and closed the door.

"Are all the practice rooms going to be used for this?" I asked, trying not to look at the bed.

"I don't know. Ikaros said this was where we should go." He unwound the garland and rubbed his wrist. "That was a bit tight."

I smiled. "This is a horribly awkward situation."

"It would almost be better if we were complete strangers and could introduce ourselves."

"I'm Simmea," I said.

He laughed. "I know. And you're a Florentine, and one of Sokrates's pupils, and you did a painting of some girls racing. That's all I know about you."

"That's more than I know about you," I said. I sat down on the edge of the bed. "I think I've seen you with Septima?"

"She's a good friend," he said. "She knows so much."

"I had a great conversation with her the other day about why the gods can't change history," I said. He took off his headdress and stood holding it awkwardly in both hands.

"There's nowhere to put things," he said, looking around. "I don't want to drop this on the floor. Somebody must have spent a lot of time making it."

"I made ones for us this morning," I said. "They don't take long, once you get the hang of it." I took mine off and showed him the construction. "These big daisies make everything easy."

Aeschines took my headdress and put them both down gently in the corner of the room. Then he came back over to the bed and sat down next to me. "Are you afraid?" he asked.

"More nervous and awkward and ignorant," I said.

He put his arm around me and moved his face slowly towards mine. He then kissed me tentatively. "How was that?" he asked.

I laughed, because he sounded so much like somebody beginning a philosophic inquiry. "I think that was quite nice," I said. "The problem is that there are all these things I'm trying not to think about—the slavers on the ship, and what happened to my mother. And I'm not quite sure what I am supposed to be thinking about."

"You're supposed to focus on sensation, Ikaros said. Like eating, when you just taste the food and you're there in that moment, except also focusing on the other person and what they're feeling."

"But how can you tell?"

"Pardon?" He looked disconcerted.

"How can you tell what the other person is feeling? I have no idea what you're feeling!"

"I'm feeling that you're very nervous but kissing you was nice," he said. "The other thing Ikaros said is that there's no hurry. We've got all afternoon and all night. We don't have to do it all in the first two seconds. We can be comfortable. We can try things."

We tried various things to make ourselves comfortable. What worked best was standing naked and leaning into each other, the way we might when wrestling. That way, upright and with my legs firmly in a wrestling stance, nothing reminded me of anything horrible, and I could enjoy the feeling of Aeschines's chest against mine. We kissed standing like that, and then he began to rub the sides of my breasts. He was so earnest and sensitive that I started to feel safe with him. I rubbed his chest, and moved my hand lower. When I touched his penis he made a movement as if electrified and, looking at his face, I saw that his eyes were shut and his head thrown back. I had often seen penises when swimming and in the palaestra, so they were no novelty, but I had never voluntarily touched one, especially not one that was awake. Aeschines's was awake. I stroked it gently, experimentally. He twitched again. I began to understand what Ikaros had meant about paying attention to how the other person felt. I liked it. I was making him feel like that. I felt in control. This was good. Then his hands moved between my legs and I felt my breath catch.

Afterwards I wasn't sure how I felt about it. "Did you like it?" Aeschines asked.

"Yes . . ." I said. "It was fun. I liked the way you liked it. I liked lots of things about it. I wish we could do it standing up."

"We could try," he said. "In a little bit, when I've rested."

"Is that allowed?"

"Sure. We're married until tomorrow morning. We can do it as many times as we want to before that. Ikaros was quite plain about that."

We did it twice more. Standing up was definitely better for me, both in feeling in control and just generally comfortable. Later we slept uncomfortably together in the bed.

"So I guess we're friends now," Aeschines said as got dressed the next morning.

"We definitely are." I smiled at him. "You could come and eat in Florentia with me tonight if you want."

"That feels strange," he said. "I didn't know you, and now I know that you like doing sex standing up."

"Don't tell anybody!"

"Of course not!" He sounded shocked, which was a relief. "Boys do talk about it sometimes. I always thought they were lying. About getting girls to sneak off to the woods with them. Specific girls. And what those girls liked. It's a kind of showing off they do when they jerk off."

"Jerk off?"

He mimed with his hand. "At night, in the sleeping houses, standing round together with everyone doing that and nobody touching each other. Girls don't do that?"

"Not equipped," I said.

He laughed. "But nothing like that?"

"Not in Hyssop," I said. "I never heard of girls doing that, but that doesn't mean they don't. But I never heard of them sneaking off with boys, either."

"Would you do that?" he asked.

"What? Sneak off to the woods with you? No. That would be wrong." I wanted to get back to Hyssop and bathe in the wash-fountain before breakfast. "You're not seriously suggesting it?"

"No, of course not." I wasn't sure whether he meant it or not.

"Dinner tonight, then?" I asked, my hand on the door.

"Sure." He picked up the headdresses and garland from the corner. The flowers were dying, away from water for so long. "Do you want yours?"

"What for?"

"No, I suppose they're done with now." He turned them in his hands looking a little sad. "Well, I hope we do this again some time."

"So do I," I said, and meant it. I didn't share the calculations of probability with him, though.

19

APOLLO

"How are you going to get out of it?" I had cornered Athene in the library. She was sitting in the window seat she liked, the one where she had a secret compartment in the armrest, reading Tullius's newly printed monograph on the integrity of the soul.

"He's getting old," she said, putting it down on a mess of books and papers on the seat beside her.

"He is," I agreed. "Ikaros flattened him in their last debate. And he's been avoiding Sokrates."

"He's going to die soon, whatever I do. I know he's vain and silly, but I'm very fond of him."

"I am too. Even if you have to send him back to face his assassination, at least he got this extra length of his natural lifespan."

"I hate that cold bastard Octavian," she said. "Killing Cicero for political advantage. It's like burning down a library to make toast. I could never warm to Rome again until Marcus Aurelius." She picked up the book again, then hesitated and put it down. "Did you want to ask me something?"

"Yes. How are you going to get out of being paired off at the festival of Hera?"

"I'm sick of the subject of the festival of Hera. It's all anyone's talking about. I may be getting a bit bored with this whole thing, actually. Anyway, I shall be chosen and walk off with somebody, and then they will fall asleep and dream they've had a pleasant afternoon with Septima, while I come back to the library."

"Do you need help with the dream?" I asked.

"No thanks. There's a perfectly good bit of Catullus."

I laughed, quietly because we were in the library. The funny thing was that she was so serious. She rolled her eyes. "Sorry," I said. "I should have guessed you'd have a plan."

"Did you come to offer to help if I needed it?" she asked.

"Well . . ." I felt caught out. "I knew you wouldn't want to participate, and I hadn't thought of a dream."

"Well thank you. I don't need it. But I do appreciate the concern. I'd have thought you'd be looking forward to it. First sexual act in sixteen years?"

"I've been continent for longer before," I said. Though that was usually when I was focusing on something else and not noticing how long it had been. "And anyway, that isn't quite true. This will be the first time mating with a woman, but there have been some sex acts with men."

"Boys?"

"And Masters."

"Not Pico?"

"No. He's never done more than look admiring." I wondered why she was asking, but her expression did not invite questions.

She picked up her book again and put her finger in it ready to open it. "So did you want me to influence the lots to get you whoever you have picked out for the festival?"

"No. I thought I'd go with chance. That way I'll learn something about choice."

She looked astonished. "I suppose that's true, but I'm surprised to hear you say so. I've never seen you with anyone who wasn't perfect. What will you do if it's your funny little Simmea? She's very smart, isn't she? I was talking to her about the constraints of time the other night."

"She's very smart," I agreed. Of course I knew she was in love with me. "It's extremely unlikely that we'd be chosen together, though."

Athene shook her head. "You're changing."

"Learning things. That was the whole idea."

She started to read, and I left.

The next day was the games, where I was careful to do well in everything without actually winning anything. Simmea came third in the swimming. I could swim now, but I didn't even enter the races. Human bodies aren't made for that kind of exercise. The day after was the festival. We wore flowered headdresses and danced in the plaza before the temple of Zeus and Hera. Phidias's huge chryselephantine seated Zeus stood on one side of the steps, and a large Hera from Argos stood on the other. I wondered, eyeing them, what Father knew about this enterprise, and what he would say. Athene was his favorite daughter, but even so. It would be possible to argue that we were bending his rules all over the place.

I avoided Simmea. I felt uncomfortable at the thought of her. I liked her very much. I admired her. I enjoyed her friendship. But Athene was right. In thousands of years I'd never mated with anyone who wasn't perfect. I didn't know if it was possible. If it turned out it wasn't with some random girl, that didn't matter all that much. With Simmea it could be a disaster.

It turned out I was worrying about entirely the wrong thing.

There's a whole section in Book Five of the *Republic* about how the masters are supposed to cheat with the sex festival, to make sure the best get to have the best children. The children of the less good will be exposed anyway, but while everyone's supposed to believe it's entirely random, they naturally cheat for eugenics. I hadn't forgotten this, but I had only thought it would mean that they'd be likely to match me with somebody beautiful after all. They did. But when I heard our names read out I froze.

"Pytheas, Klymene!" old Ficino read. My friends were pushing me forward and laughing. I walked mechanically towards the steps. I saw Klymene coming from the other side, not looking at me. The garland was tied around our wrists and our arms raised. Our eyes had still not met. We walked together down the steps and off through the dancers and down the street.

Eventually I looked at her. She was so pale and resolute that she'd have done for a portrait of Artemis. "I'm really sorry," I said.

"It's *random chance*," she said. "It's not your fault any more than it is mine. It's just Fortuna laughing at both of us."

"I mean I'm really sorry I said what I said to you on the mountain."

She looked at me now for the first time. "That's the latest apology I ever had."

"Simmea said you didn't want to talk to me. She beat me up. She made me realize what an idiot I was."

"She made me practice being brave until I could be brave again," Klymene said. "Simmea's a good friend. And I didn't want to talk to you right away. But it has been a long time. Years."

"I didn't know how long was long enough, and by then it had been a long time and it was awkward because of that." I brushed my hair back off my face and realized that our hands were still bound together. I started to unwind the garland.

"What are you doing?"

"I thought—"

"You thought I was a coward and wouldn't go through with it?" she suggested.

"I thought I was," I said. "Do you want to?"

"It's not a case of want, it's a case of our duty to the city and the gods. We were married in front of Zeus and Hera. All over the city today, everyone is being married in front of the gods, so that there can be more children for the city."

"You're right," I said.

"I don't like you, Pytheas. I don't trust you. It isn't just what you said to me, it's other things. You're arrogant. You think so much of yourself. You don't pay any attention to most people. I was only ever friends with you because I knew you were Simmea's friend and she likes you. And when I had that cowardly moment you covered for me. That was good. But afterwards what you said just made me feel that you despised me—that you didn't even see me. But this isn't about you. This is about our sacred duty."

"I said you were right."

"Where are we going?"

I stopped walking. "They told me there were empty practice rooms with beds in them." I waved vaguely. We had passed the turning to the street of Dionysos and had to go back. We walked now without talking. She was a pretty girl with nice breasts, soft and dovelike, as I had always thought. I wondered what our son would be like—a hero, certainly, but what kind? How strange it would be to watch him grow up day by day. The masters wouldn't let us know which child was which, of course, but I would know. If I didn't instinctively know I could ask Athene, but I thought even incarnate I'd be able to tell.

We came to the hall and went inside, hands still bound. Inside most of the doors were closed, but we found an open one far down the hall and closed the door. Only then did I unbind the garland. The wild rose branch twined in it had pricked my skin, leaving little beads of blood around my wrist. As I was licking them, Klymene dropped her kiton with as little fuss as if we were in the palaestra, and stood looking at me.

I had never before mated with a woman when we hadn't been playing the game of running away and catching. I had always been the one catching. I had mated for the joy of ecstasy, in a sudden passion for some woman, or to conceive children. Usually when I fell in love it was with men, who in my own time had minds with more to offer me. I have fallen in love with women, but it's rare. Sometimes women have refused me. (Cassandra and Sibyl were out for what they could get and deserved what they did get. In my opinion.)

This woman did not want me, but she was obedient to duty. I had to go to some considerable effort of imagination to want her, and to find duty in myself and the desire for a son. It helped that this was her first time, so I could instruct her into a position where I didn't have to look at her face. Her face was like stone, and would have made it impossible. It was probably more comfortable for her too. She didn't want foreplay—in fact she specifically refused it. "Let's get on with it," she said. I arranged her face down on the bed.

Father's big on rape. He likes to turn himself into animals or even weirder things and swoop down on girls and carry them off. I've always liked the chase, whether it's chasing a nymph through the woods or a seduction. Sometimes at the end of a seduction it's been almost like that. I remember once in Alexandria, a woman called Lyra. Sunlight through a shuttered window falling across white sheets. She was a professional card player, and I'd beaten her in the game when she'd put herself in on cards she thought were unbeatable. She wore a veil and made up her eyes with kohl. There had been a moment when she let the veil fall that was almost like it was with Klymene. But once we were in bed she'd been greedy, more like a man, seeking her own pleasure, crying out. Klymene wasn't like that at all.

Klymene wanted the result of this mating, but not the process. But enduring it was her choice. Having it happen at all was her choice. I would have undone the garland and gone off, and if we'd told nobody, nobody would ever have known, any more than Athene's partner, dreaming of Catullus, would ever know. That would have been my choice, to regret this match and let her be. We were in this room and this bed and I was in her body because she had chosen it, because it was our duty. I thought of Lyra's eyes above the veil. I tried not to think of Daphne. I thought of all the ones who *had* wanted me, who had met passion with passion and desire with desire, who fell in love with me and wrote poetry about it for the rest of their lives. Eventually, that was sufficient.

20

SIMMEA

It was with a mixture of relief and disappointment that I greeted the arrival of my monthly blood at the next new moon. Of the seven of us in Hyssop, four bled and three did not. Klymene was one of the ones who did not. She had been unusually tight-lipped about her experience during the festival. "Well, it took all my accumulated bravery," was all she had said in answer to my tentative question. Aeschines had eaten with us in Florentia twice and I had eaten with him in Ithaca once—sardines and bitter greens, delicious. I'd seen other new friendships that had come out of the festival. But not for Klymene.

We were in the wash-fountain getting clean one morning when Makalla suddenly said: "Maia said we shouldn't count on being pregnant even if we don't bleed. We should wait until next month to be sure." She sounded apprehensive.

"I'm delighted to be pregnant," Klymene said.

"Because you won't have to go through that again?" I asked, rinsing my hair.

"Well, not for some time anyway," Makalla said.

"It wouldn't be as bad as that another time," Klymene said. "No, I'm just glad to be having a baby, to be doing my duty and making a new generation of citizens."

"I am too," Makalla said. "I just don't want to count on anything before I can be sure."

For a moment I was sorry I wasn't pregnant too. I felt left out and lazy. Immediately I wondered what Sokrates would think about that and began to interrogate the feeling. It was nonsense. I'd tried as hard as anyone. Maybe next time it would work. It was a pity it wouldn't be Aeschines again. I liked him and he liked me. But there was always the hope that it would be Pytheas.

I spent that time working on the calculus with a small group Axiothea had drawn together of people who really liked higher mathematics for its own sake, and not as a means of mystical revelation. Mystical revelation through numerology was very popular, especially in halls that had Neoplatonist Masters. What we worked on had no practical application I could see but the joy of learning it. I loved it.

Of course I also painted a great deal, and debated constantly with Sokrates. Debating with Sokrates remained a delight and a terror. I was getting better at it, but he still surprised me frequently. It honed my mind, so that in debate with others, I was considered formidable. Pytheas and Kebes too learned Sokrates's methods, and grew in debate. We began to wonder whether we could challenge the Masters. Listening to debates was one of our most popular forms of entertainment—Tullius against Ikaros on the benefits of synthesis against original research, or Ficino against Adeimantus on the virtues of translation. I began to have an idea that I might one day challenge one of the younger Masters, perhaps Ikaros or Klio.

One day I went running in the mountains and met Laodike and Damon, returning from a run. I didn't see them often any more; the division into silver and gold had made a difference. They looked awkward, and I tried hard to be especially friendly, sharing some figs I had brought. We sat in the shade of a rock to eat them. "You're not running straight up the mountain any more, then?" I asked.

"We've been doing a lot of cross-country scrambling," Damon said. "It's supposed to be good practice for war. Not that there's anyone to fight."

"I can't fight right now anyway," Laodike said. She patted her stomach, which had a slight curve.

"Joy to you!" I said. "Klymene's pregnant too, you know."

"Maybe you'll manage it next time," she said. "There are definite advantages."

Damon shot her a worried glance. "I don't think—"

"Oh, Simmea's our friend, she won't tell anyone. And we know about her and Pytheas, just the same as you and me."

"I won't tell anyone whatever it is, but Pytheas and I aren't . . . whatever you think. We're friends." I felt blood heating my cheeks.

Laodike laughed. "Well, once you're pregnant you can't get more pregnant, so if you can find somewhere quiet to do it, like up here, you can safely copulate with your friend."

I looked at the two of them. They both looked embarrassed now, and a little sheepish, but also happy in a way that stung my heart. Their hands crept together, intertwined, and clung. Plato said that friendship was good but adding sex to it was bad, but perhaps understandable in silvers. It wasn't hurting anyone in any case. "I won't tell anyone, and I'm glad it's working for you. I'm so pleased I saw you. I miss you in Hyssop. We should do a run together before you get as big as a sleeping house."

Shortly after that came the second festival of Hera. I had wondered how they were going to manage with some of the women being pregnant and unavailable but all of the men still being free. The answer was that the women were carefully counted, in each class, and that number of men were selected to participate, partly at random and partly by merit. The merit consisted in doing well either in the athletic contests or in their work in the four months since the last time. Then every man who didn't qualify by merit had his name set in an urn and they were chosen by lot.

Pytheas's name was second drawn. He was matched with Kryseis and they went off together, seeming content. I drew Phoenix, of Delphi, whom I already knew quite well—we had often raced and wrestled together. He wasn't as considerate as Aeschines, and much faster. He also wanted me to suck his penis with my mouth, which I refused, because it reminded me of the slave ship. He sulked about this, and said that his previous partner had done it and that the boys all did it for each other. The encounter wasn't much fun, and I didn't invite him for dinner in Florentia afterwards.

Nor was it productive. Auge became pregnant, but I didn't and nor did any of the rest of us in Hyssop. Makalla and Klymene were four months along, showing big breasts and big bellies already, and excused from exercise in the palaestra. Charmides said that swimming would be good for them and that they should take regular gentle walks. Klio taught them vaginal exercises.

"How does she know them?" Makalla giggled. "Has she ever had a baby?"

There was no way to know about the lives of the Masters before they came to the city. Klio might have had several children. None of them were here. I wondered if she missed them. I thought about what Septima had said about time.

Auge found her early pregnancy difficult—she vomited every morning. She complained that she was too weak to move marble—she sculpted, and was very good, but now she felt cut off from her art. She broke up with her lover and cried herself to sleep, then when Iphis went to comfort her they ended up beginning a passionate friendship that Klymene found difficult to deal with. They said, giggling, that it was Platonic agape. Klymene had to insist that they each slept in their own bed. It was unsettling. I missed Laodike and Andromeda, who were much more comfortable to live with and who had truly felt like sisters.

21

MAIA

Klymene came to me late one night. I encouraged all the Florentines to come to me any time they had a problem, so I wasn't very surprised when I opened the door and saw her there. Lysias was curled up asleep in my bed, so I went out to her. It was a cool night with an edge of chill in the air. "Let's go to my office in Florentia," I said. "We can be comfortable and you can tell me whatever it is."

We went to the kitchen first and took plates. We each helped ourselves to some olives, slices from a half-cut round of goat cheese, and some barley bread left over from supper. "As good as a feast," Klymene said.

"It's good to see you want it," I said.

"Yes, I was so sick for the first three months." She patted her belly, which was just starting to show. We were all excited about the first babies. "Now I'm starving all the time."

We settled ourselves in my study. There was a new hanging on the wall in gold and green and brown which some of the Florentines I'd been teaching weaving had given to me. The cloth wasn't as even as the Worker-made cloth, but they had sewn the different coloured stripes together in a charming way. I stroked the edge of it as I sat down. "Problems in Hyssop?" I asked.

Klymene swallowed her bread. "No. Well, yes, the same thing, Auge and Iphis, you know. Nothing different."

"You should insist that they sleep in their own beds," I said.

"I do. But it disrupts everybody. And even needing to keep insisting is disruptive. I wonder sometimes—well, that's what I came to see you about." She took a deep breath. "Who decided which metals were strongest in our souls?"

"Ficino and I did," I said. "With advice from other Masters who knew you."

"Do you think you might have made any mistakes?" she asked.

"We thought about it very hard and talked about it a lot, and we don't think we did. Why are you asking? Is it because you think Auge and Iphis aren't behaving like philosophers?"

"No," she said. "It's me. This is so difficult."

"You're only seventeen," I said. "Nobody expects you to be perfect right away. You have new responsibilities, and they're difficult, but you're dealing with them. It can be easy to feel discouraged when things go wrong, but philosophy will help. And we weren't just looking at how you are now, we were looking at how you're going to develop." It was why it had been so difficult and such a tremendous responsibility.

"You don't understand." Klymene picked up an olive and turned it over and over in her hand, staring down at it. "Can I talk about before we came here?" she asked, not looking up.

"You shouldn't," I said. "But you can if you really need to. If it will help me understand what you're worried about."

"I was a slave," she said, as if it cost her an effort to admit it. After she said it, she looked up from the olive at last to meet my eyes.

"There's no shame in that. You all were," I said, surprised.

"But I was born a slave. Most of the others were captured, or sold into captivity quite a short time before they were brought here. My mother was a slave, and I was born one and grew up one. All that time, I never even imagined being free. I think it did something to me. I think I have shackles on my soul and a slave's heart, and I'm not really worthy to be a gold."

"That's ridiculous," I said, gently. I ate a piece of cheese while thinking what to say. "You've been here for seven years, you've been trained. You were very young when you came. Nothing that happened before counts."

"Yes, it does," she said. She was close to tears. "Can I please explain?"

"Go on then," I said.

"My name has always been Klymene. I was born in Syracuse, at the time of the Carthaginian wars. My mother was a bath slave. She was Carthaginian. Her name was Nyra. I don't know who my father was, but it was probably our master, whose name was Asterios."

I listened, trying to imagine a life like that. "Was he unkind to you?"

"No, he petted me and indulged me when he saw me, which wasn't all that often. He was Greek, of course. I look like my mother. I imagined I would grow up to have a life like hers, serving at the bath, sleeping with the master. It didn't seem so bad. I carried water and bath oils. I was learning massage. I spoke Greek, and Punic, that was the slave language, and a little bit of Latin. Nobody taught me to read, though they easily could have. There were slave clerks in the house, but they were all men. They never thought of it. I never thought of it."

"For most of history it was really unusual for women to be taught to read," I said. Nobody except Plato had seen that we were human. It still made me angry to think of all those wasted lives.

"I was pretty, like my mother, and if I had dreams it was that some man would fall in love with me because of that and I could cajole him into treating me well. It's what my mother did. What she was teaching me." She shook her head and put the olive down on her untouched plate. "The overseer was called Felix. He terrorized us all. He had a dog on a chain at the door to the slave quarters. I hated to pass it, it always leapt at me snarling, and Felix laughed and said it would eat me up one day. But that's not what happened."

"What did happen?" I got up and poured her a cup of wine, and one for myself. Imagining her early life was distressing; living through it must have been appalling. I thanked Athene in my heart that I had been so lucky.

"When I was nine years old, my master caught my mother in bed with Felix. She had no choice about it. Felix had a dog and a whip, and what did she have? But Asterios didn't see it that way. He didn't punish Felix, he punished her. He whipped her in the courtyard in front of everyone, to punish her supposed lusts. Then, to punish her more, he had me whipped. And then immediately, the same afternoon, he dragged me down to the harbor and sold me onto a slave ship going east, where there would be no chance that my mother would ever see me again." She picked up the cup and took a deep swallow. "He didn't even say so to me. He said it to the slaver he was selling me to, and I heard. I wasn't even a person to him. He shook me when I tried to speak, to remind him how he had always been good to me. And he slapped me hard when I bit his hand. I was just a thing to him, a thing he could use on my mother. He petted me to make her loving to him, and then he sold me away to punish her. He didn't see me as human, let alone as a daughter. He had his real family on the other side of the house. I'd served at his real daughter's baths. I wasn't real, do you see?"

"You were real," I said. I was shaken. "You were absolutely real and you were a child and I'm so glad we rescued you from that." I wished we could do the same for every slave there ever was, that we could buy them and bring them here to live free.

"You rescued my body, but part of my soul is still there," she said. "It's why I ran, that time, with the boar, because I'm slave-hearted. And now I can't keep order in Hyssop. I'm just no good."

"You're keeping order. And you've worked and worked to become brave!" I wanted to hug her, but she held herself in a way that didn't invite it.

"Yes, but others didn't have to do that," she said, fiercely. "And I wonder what else there is like that about me, where my soul is still stuck there. With being the watcher, I keep wanting to cajole instead of being decisive. And that's not the worst of it. I always thought like a slave. I wanted to please the Masters, not to seek for the truth. I'd see Simmea arguing with Ficino, going after a point like a terrier, and at first I'd just be amazed that she dared, and that he didn't slap her down for it. I don't know how long it was before I understood that it was what he wanted."

"But you did understand," I said.

"Yes, but you don't see. I still thought like a slave. I was trying to give you what you wanted, not trying to become my best self. And you didn't see that, you didn't, you made me a gold and I'm not fit to be a guardian, it was all pretense. I was pretending to be free, but in my heart I'm still a slave."

I tried to make sense of this. "Are you saying that you're still trying to please us instead of striving for excellence?"

She hesitated, and touched her belly. "No. I realized what I was doing and why it was wrong. My duty—wanting to do my duty, even when I could have got out of it without anyone knowing. Reading Plato, debating with Kebes about freedom and choices, and especially thinking about the baby, about him or her growing up in the city. I finally realized I am free. And I do love wisdom, and I do love the truth. I've been coming to that for some time. And I can't build it on a lie. That's why I've come to you now. To confess my deception. Before the baby's born. I want to become my best self, and I don't want to deceive you any more."

"Deception is a crooked road to truth, but that's where it's leading you," I said, standing up.

"What?" She looked up at me, confused.

"You're confessing your deception because in feigning loving truth you've truly come to love it," I said.

"Yes," she said.

"And so you are worthy to be gold. Maybe I was wrong, maybe I made a mistake and was deceived, but Ficino saw into your soul. There are people whose souls are ideally suited from birth for them to be philosophers, but there are others whose souls have to be trained, like vines on a trellis. We built the trellis in the city, and though you started twisted you grew straight."

"Like Simmea's legs," she said, utterly confounding me.

"Simmea's legs?"

"When we came, Simmea's legs were bandy. Now they're straight and strong. You're saying the same thing happened to my soul?"

"Yes," I said, and I hugged her hard. "Your children will start clean, without any bad memories or twisted beginnings. They'll prove everything Plato believed, become what he wanted. We masters are helping you and you will help them and they will make the Just City."

She hugged me back. "I'm free," she said, marvel in her voice.

22

SIMMEA

One morning Kebes and I went from breakfast to follow Sokrates around the city as we often did. We found him questioning a Worker planting bulbs outside the temple of Demeter. "Do you like your work? Do you feel a sense of satisfaction doing it? Are there some jobs you enjoy more than others?"

"I don't know why you keep doing that when you know they're not going to answer," Kebes said.

"I don't know that," Sokrates said. "Joy to you, Kebes, joy to you Simmea! I know they haven't answered yet, but I don't know whether they might answer in the future. I don't even have an opinion on the subject."

"Everyone knows they're tools," Kebes said.

"They're not like tools," Sokrates said. "They're self-propelled, and to a certain extent self-willed. That one is making decisions about where to space the bulbs, precise and careful decisions. Those are going in a row, look, and then that one at an angle. It's deliberate, not random. It may be a clever tool, but it may have self-will, and if it has self-will and desires, then it would be very interesting to talk to."

"A tree would be interesting to talk to—" Kebes began, but Sokrates interrupted.

"Oh yes, wouldn't it!" We laughed and followed him on.

A few months later, early in Gamelion, Kebes and I were walking along with Sokrates debating one morning when we happened to come back to the place outside the temple of Demeter where the Worker had been planting bulbs when Sokrates asked it questions. A set of early crocuses had come up, deep purple with gold hearts. They were arranged in an odd pattern, two straight lines connected by a diagonal and then a circle. Sokrates glanced at them. "Spring after winter is always a joy to the heart," he said, though he never seemed to feel the cold.

Kebes frowned at them. "It's almost as if—no. I'm being silly."

"What is it?" Sokrates asked.

"Well, you remember the Worker was planting bulbs here when you asked it questions? The pattern the bulbs are planted in looks like N and then O in the Latin alphabet, which is like the beginning of *non*, the Latin for *no*."

Sokrates stared at Kebes, and then back at the bulbs. "As if the Worker were trying to answer me as best it could, with the materials it had? And as if it answered in Latin? Why would it do that, I wonder?"

"Latin was the language of civilization in the West for centuries," I said.

"But it didn't finish the word. Perhaps it ran out of bulbs. Or perhaps I'm imagining the whole thing," Kebes said. "Seeing a pattern where there isn't one."

"It must have understood my questions, to answer no," Sokrates said, ignoring this. "My questions were in Greek."

"They were. It doesn't make much sense," I said. "But it does look deliberate. Let's go on and see if it used this pattern in any of the other plazas."

It hadn't. Lots of the plazas had crocuses, but all of them were arranged in four neat vertical rows.

"What did I ask it?" Sokrates mused. "If it enjoyed its work?"

"I think so," I said. "If there was anything it preferred doing. A whole pile of questions at once, typical of you!"

"So I can't know which, if any, the no was intended to answer!" He ran his fingers through his hair, which was standing on end anyway. "Where's Pytheas?"

"I think he's in the palaestra this morning."

"We must find him at once." Sokrates set off rapidly in the wrong direction. Kebes and I got him turned around and walking just as fast towards the Florentine/Delphic palaestra.

"Why do you want Pytheas?" Kebes asked as we trailed him.

"The first time I asked about Workers he said he had a belief that they were tools," Sokrates said. "I want to know who told him that."

"Ficino told us that, on the *Goodness* when we came," Kebes said. "Probably it was the same for him."

Sokrates stopped dead and stared at us as if he'd never seen us before. "I think it might be better if I spoke to Pytheas alone," he said, and turned and walked off so fast that I'd have had to run to catch up with him.

Kebes and I stared at each other. "What was that about?" I asked.

He shrugged. "Do you think the Worker really was trying to communicate?"

"Well, it seems unlikely on the face of it, but it also seems like a very unlikely coincidence that in only that one spot where Sokrates was trying to talk to the Worker, the flowers should spell out something that could mean no. I'm almost more interested in why he acted like that about Pytheas. What would Pytheas know about Workers that we don't?"

"Pytheas knows some very odd things sometimes."

"He reads a lot," I said, defensively. "No, but what?"

Kebes frowned. "When we're talking to Sokrates, sometimes Pytheas says odd things, or sometimes he says ordinary things and Sokrates reacts oddly. Like when he mentioned his parents that time, and Sokrates acted as if he'd said something completely bizarre."

I remembered that. I shook my head. "That's Sokrates behaving oddly, which... isn't unusual for Sokrates. Do you think he'll be in Thessaly this afternoon?"

"I'll be there to see," Kebes said.

"So will I. But first I have my math group. See you later!" I went off to join Axiothea and the others, puzzled.

Sokrates was at Thessaly when I got there at our usual time. Pytheas was there before me, and Kebes arrived a moment or two later. "I brought some nuts," he said, pulling out a twist of paper.

"Raisins," I said, pulling out a matching twist.

"Olives," Pytheas said, smugly, bringing out a whole jar of olives stuffed with garlic.

"You bring a feast! And I as always can offer crystal clear water and the shade of my garden," Sokrates said, leading the way out. It was a little chilly to sit outside, and I kept my cloak around me. Once we were seated and passing round the food, he began. "I believe I have discovered evidence of conversational thought among the Workers."

"I'm not convinced," Kebes said.

"It's not necessary to be convinced by one piece of evidence," Sokrates said. "But it's indicative that it might be worth further investigation."

Sokrates unveiled his plan, in which the three of us were to do nothing but go around talking to every Worker we saw, in Latin, while he did the same in Greek. "Do any of you know any other languages?"

"A little Coptic, if I still remember any," I said.

"Italian," Kebes said. "It's like simple Latin without the word endings."

Pytheas spread his hands. "I was born in the hills above Delphi. How would I have encountered anything but Greek?"

"How indeed?" Sokrates muttered. "I believe I can recruit Aristomache into this project," he said. "She speaks two other languages of Europe. I forget their names now, but she told me so. With all those languages it may be easier to get them to answer."

"Or they may not," I said. "And we're going to look awfully silly trying to have dialogue with Workers."

"As cracked as me," Sokrates agreed cheerfully. "Report any results, positive or negative. But results might be slow—like the bulbs."

"If they can speak, why don't they?" Kebes asked.

"I don't think they can speak. This is just a theory, but I suspect they can hear and move and think without being able to speak. They have no organs of speech, no mouths, no heads. But they have things like hands, and they may be able to write. That one found a way."

"They have nothing like ears either, how do you know they can hear?" I asked.

"I conjecture that they have the ability to hear because the response to my questions suggests that it heard them. I conjecture they have understanding for the same reason." Sokrates shook his head. "I think it would be wrong to consider them people, but we don't have a term for anything like them. Thinking beings that aren't human! How wonderful if they are able to reason and communicate!"

"Without heads, where might they keep their minds, if they have them?" Kebes put in.

"In their livers, obviously," Sokrates said. "What makes you think minds are in the head?"

"Closest to the eyes," Kebes said.

"And people with head injuries are often damaged in their minds, while people with liver injuries continue to think perfectly well," Pytheas added.

"Huh." Sokrates touched his head. "But they have no heads, and you've all been assuming that the head is the seat of intelligence and therefore that's why you're all so reluctant to consider that they might be intelligent. Well, now. Perhaps you're right, and perhaps I am. They might help sort it out."

"They're made of metal and glass," Pytheas said.

"So?" Sokrates looked puzzled.

Pytheas shook his head, defeated.

"The next problem is that there's no way to tell them apart! Have you ever found one?"

I shook my head. "They sometimes have different hands. But I don't know if they change them or if it's always the same hands on the same ones. And of course some are bronze-colored and some are iron-colored."

Pytheas nodded. "What Simmea said. I've never tried to distinguish them." Whatever it was Sokrates had imagined he knew about them clearly didn't amount to much.

Kebes smiled. "Actually, they are easy to tell apart. They're numbered. Lysias showed me once, when I was helping him." When he was going through his period of making Lysias think that Kebes would begin to strive for excellence through his encouragement, I thought. "The numbers are very small, down on their side, above the tread. They're long. But they're all different. So we can tell them apart, by checking the numbers."

"Are they numbered in Latin or Greek?" Sokrates asked, leaning forward, urgently interested.

"Neither," Kebes said. "They're numbered in numbers."

Sokrates looked blank.

"You know, zeroic. Like page numbers in books," I said. I pulled a book out of the fold of my kiton and showed him. It happened to a bound copy of Aeschylus's *Telemachus*.

"Those are numbers?" he asked. "How do they work?"

I wrote them down in the dust, from one to ten, and showed him. "That's all there is to it. For twenty, or for a hundred—"

He understood it at once. "And you have all known this all this time and never mentioned it to me?" he said.

"It never occurred to me that you didn't know," I said.

"Pah. My ignorance is vast and profound. I like to know at least what I do not know." He traced the numbers again. "Zero. What a concept. What a timesaver. What vast realms of arithmetic and geometry it must reveal. I wish Pythagoras could have known it, and the Pythagoreans of Athens." Then, like a hound who had started after the wrong hare, he got immediately back on track. "So the Workers are labelled with this?"

"That's right," Kebes said. "All of them."

"Who did this?"

"I don't know."

"What is the purpose?"

"Telling them apart. That's how Lysias uses it, anyway."

"Did you note the number of the one planting bulbs?"

"Sorry, no, it didn't occur to me."

Sokrates sighed, sat back and absently ate a handful of olives.

"So the numbers are like names?" I suggested. "That seems to argue against them being people. Why not give them names?"

"Maybe there are too many to name?" Pytheas suggested.

"How many of them are there?" Sokrates asked, licking olive oil off his fingers.

We all shrugged. "Lots," Kebes said. "I was surprised how many when I saw them at their feeding station."

"They eat?" Sokrates asked.

"They eat electricity, Lysias said."

Sokrates bounced to his feet. "Come on, show me this feeding station!"

I swallowed an olive hastily. We set off, with Kebes leading the way and Sokrates close behind.

Pytheas walked beside me. "This is crazy," he said.

"Sure. Kind of fun, though. And what if they actually were thinking be-ings with plans?"

"They're not. They're tools. Everyone knows that." Pytheas looked a little unsettled.

"What everyone knows, Sokrates examines," I said.

Kebes led us to a block on the east side of the city, between the streets of Poseidon and Hermes, not far from the temple of Ares. The whole block was one square building, relatively unexciting. I'd never particularly noticed it. There was a lot in the city that was empty, awaiting a later purpose, or used by the Masters for unknown purposes. I wasn't especially curious about most of it. This building had decorative recessed squares set all around it at ground level. There were no windows. A key-pattern frieze ran around the top. There was another key pattern over the door.

"What now?" Sokrates asked.

"Now we wait for a Worker, because Lysias has a key but I don't. But you'll see when a Worker comes." Kebes leaned back on his heels. I squatted down and ate more raisins. Pytheas and Sokrates began to debate volition, and whether Workers could be considered to have it.

"Ah, here we go," Kebes said, when the sun was beginning to slide towards dinner time.

A bronze-colored Worker came down the street. "Joy to you," Sokrates said. "I am Sokrates. Do you have a name?" It ignored him utterly and ap-proached the building, not by the door but directly at one of the recessed squares. The square slid open in front of it and it vanished inside.

"Did you see that?" Sokrates asked.

"That's what they do," Kebes said. "Inside there are sockets and they plug themselves in to eat electricity. When they're full, which takes several hours, they unplug themselves and come out again."

"I'd never noticed this was here," I said.

"Nobody much comes down this street," Kebes said. "There's nothing here, and if you were at the corner you'd cut diagonally down the street of Apollo."

"You've been inside?" Sokrates asked.

"Yes, with Lysias."

"We could follow a Worker inside," Sokrates suggested.

"We'd be stuck there until one wanted to come out. We can't open the doors without a key. It would be better to talk to them when they come out—they won't be hungry then, and if they can talk they'll be more likely to re-spond."

"I want to see inside," Sokrates said.

"All right. But we could get stuck there all night. Or you could ask Lysias or Klio. They have keys. I'm sure they'd let you in."

"If Lysias and Klio take care of them, that suggests that they come from their time. When is that?" Sokrates was bending down and poking at the square where the Worker had disappeared. Nothing he did could move it. I touched it myself. It felt like solid stone.

"The boring part of history," I said. "The bit where nothing happened except people inventing things, Axiothea said."

"The part they don't want us to know about! Excellent." Sokrates kept on poking. Then a different square slid open and a Worker emerged. "Joy to you! Do you like your work?" It ignored us. The panel started to slide shut, and fast as an eel, Sokrates darted through it.

The three of us stared at each other and then at the smooth closed panel. "He needs a keeper sometimes," Pytheas said.

"Should we get Lysias?" Kebes asked.

"How much trouble can he get into inside?" I asked.

"Not much, I don't think. He knows about electricity—I mean, he has a light in Thessaly. He's not likely to stick his fingers into sockets. At least, I hope not. He can't get into much trouble going up to the Workers as they're feeding and asking them if they like their work." Kebes looked worried.

"I think we have two choices: wait for a Worker to go in or out and follow it in ourselves, or fetch Lysias or Klio and ask them to let us in," I said. "We can't just leave Sokrates in there."

"I think you should go and find one of them," Pytheas said, to me. He tapped on the stone. Nothing happened.

"It might be hours before another one comes," Kebes said.

"It's almost dinner time. Klio will be at Sparta, and Lysias will be at Constantinople. I'll go to him, you go to her," Pytheas said, looking at me. Then he looked at Kebes. "You've been in there before. You wait here, and if you get the chance, go in."

Kebes hesitated, as if he wanted to dispute this, but it made such clear and obvious sense that after a moment he nodded.

"Back soon!" I said, and set off running towards the Spartan hall.

"Sokrates is doing what with the Workers?" Klio asked, when I found her and panted out my story.

"Trying to initiate dialectic with them," I said. "But Kebes said he might stick his fingers in a wall socket, and I'm not absolutely sure he wouldn't."

Klio sighed. The Spartan hall was appropriately bare and Spartan, but all the wood was polished to a high shine and the windows looked out over the sea. The smell coming from the kitchen suggested a rich vegetable soup.

My stomach gurgled. "Come on then," she said. "I suppose we should sort this out. What made him imagine he could have a dialogue with them?"

"He's Sokrates," I said.

"He's like a two-year-old sticking pencils in his ear," she said.

"Well, but there were also the plants."

"Plants? No. Tell me on the way." She pushed her hair out of her face and we set off.

I explained to Klio about the bulbs as we walked. She frowned. "They really are just tools," she said. "I can see how it's difficult for you to see. They can make simple decisions, they can even prioritize to a certain extent. But they don't really think. They have a program—a list of things they know how to do and a list of orders of what needs doing, and they just put those together."

"Do you know that or is it an opinion?" I asked.

Klio frowned even more, twisting up her face. She was Axiothea's good friend so I knew her quite well. She sometimes dropped in on our math class. She was one of the most friendly and approachable Masters, and she never talked down to us. "I would say I knew it, but the affair of the flowers confuses me. They can hear, so it could have heard Sokrates's questions. But they don't know Greek."

"I told him that Latin was the language of civilization for centuries," I said, reassuringly.

She laughed. "Not the century our Workers come from, unfortunately. But if it spelled out N and O, that's no in English, which uses the Latin alphabet. English is the most likely language for the Worker to know . . . or Chinese. But—in my own time, a Worker couldn't possibly be a thinking, volitional being. These come from a more advanced time. I suppose it's just barely possible that they could have developed some kind of . . . but to understand Greek?" She shook her head.

We turned into the street of Hermes. There was no sign of Kebes. "Either Lysias got here first or Kebes went in with a Worker," I said.

Klio used her key to open the door. Inside it was surprisingly dull, after what I had been imagining. It didn't look at all dangerous. It was like a warehouse full of Workers, each plugged into a wall or floor socket. It was a big space, as it seemed from outside, stretching back for a long way. There was a hum in the air. I couldn't see Sokrates, but I could see Kebes running down one of the aisles, so I followed him.

Sokrates was sitting on the floor beside one of the Workers, notebook and pencil in his hand, patiently asking it questions. He looked up when we reached him. "Ah, Simmea, Kebes, Klio, joy to you. I'd like you to record the numbers of all the Workers here. I've done the first row and this row. If you'd like to address them in Latin, that would also be useful."

"Klio says they don't speak Latin but they might understand something called English," I said.

Klio told Sokrates what she had told me. In the middle of it Pytheas and Lysias showed up. Lysias added to Klio's explanation. "But I'm not an expert," he said. "None of us is. I've been forced to be one. But before I came here, I never had much to do with them."

"You're all philosophers," Sokrates said, gently. "It's perhaps a demonstration of Plato's principle that philosophers will be best at ruling the state, to take three hundred of you and nobody else and give you a state to run."

"Plato doesn't say any random philosophers from different schools and all across time," Lysias protested. "And only about half of us are philosophers. The rest are classics majors and Platonic mystics. Besides, Plato does specifically say that the city needs all kinds of people. The philosophers are just intended for the guardians, not doing the whole thing, organizing the food supply and keeping things running and looking after the Workers."

"But the end result is that nobody here really understands whether the Workers have intelligence and free will or not."

The Worker beside Sokrates did not move, and showed absolutely no sign of having intelligence and free will. It could have been a chair or part of the wall. I looked for the number on the Worker and found it, above the tread as Kebes had said. It was nine digits long. Above that, on its lower back, about where the liver might be on a human, was a slightly inset square that reminded me of the squares on the outside of the building.

"If the Workers do have intelligence and free will, then there's a real issue here," Klio said. She patted the Worker. It did not respond.

"Slavery," said Sokrates. "Plato allowed slavery, did he?"

"Free will and intelligence are different things," Pytheas pointed out.

"Different things?" Sokrates repeated. "We've been discussing them together, but is it possible to have one without the other?"

"Very possible. There are logic-machines in my time that can play games of logic so well that they beat a human master of the game," Klio said. "That can be considered intelligence. But they don't have volition or anything like it. They are machines that simulate intelligence. The way these prioritize their tasks, and come here to recharge, simulates intelligence."

"And it's very easy to see volition without intelligence in animals and small children," Lysias said.

Klio nodded. "Developing one seems almost possible, but both at once?

Surely not. But choosing to plant the bulbs so they would answer your question would take both."

"Explain to me about the bulbs," Lysias said.

"I was attempting to have a dialogue with a Worker, asking if it liked its work and if there was any work it preferred and that kind of thing, while it was planting bulbs last autumn," Sokrates said. "Today the crocuses it planted came up, and they spell *no* in Latin."

"In English," Klio corrected, pushing her hair back behind her ears. "Which seems more plausible, except for understanding the questions in Greek."

"Did anyone else witness this?" Lysias asked.

"I did," I said. "Both parts of it."

"And so did I," Kebes said.

"Kebes was the first to recognize the word this morning. And we investigated the other patches of bulbs in other places in the city, and they are all arranged in rows, not in anything resembling letters."

"From which direction did they read as letters?" Lysias asked.

"North to south," I said, after it seemed that Kebes and Sokrates were having trouble remembering. "And that was the direction the Worker was facing as it planted them."

"It does sound as if it would take both," Pytheas said. He looked hopefully at the Worker sitting so stoically plugged into the socket.

"Unless Simmea or Kebes went back and rearranged the bulbs to play a trick," Lysias said.

"I would never do such a thing!" I said, hotly indignant.

"Neither would I!" Kebes said, but I could see that Lysias didn't believe him.

"It's certainly the most logical explanation," Klio said. She sounded relieved.

"I shall consider that explanation and continue to explore the question," Sokrates said. "Will you permit me to continue recording the numbers of the Workers here, so that I can tell if I've talked to one before?"

Lysias and Klio looked at each other. "I suppose it can't do any harm," Klio said.

"But you must promise not to keep coming back in here through the Worker doors," Lysias said. "It could be dangerous. You can talk to them in the city."

"How is it dangerous?" Sokrates asked. "Do you think I'm going to plug myself into the sockets?" He laughed when he saw our faces. "I promise I won't plug myself into the sockets, or slip under a Worker's treads, or any such thing. Is that good enough?"

"I'll stay and help," Lysias said. "The rest of you can get to your dinners."

I was about to offer to help, but Sokrates nodded. "If you'll talk to me while we work," he said. "I'm exceedingly interested in what you know about intelligence and volition. Do the Workers actually want things?"

"Come on," Klio said, gathering the rest of us up. "Do you want to eat in Sparta?"

"Sure," I said.

"It's bean soup."

"Delicious! We haven't had bean soup in Florentia since last month." Pytheas came with us. Kebes grunted and went off alone.

"He really didn't like it when Lysias said that," I said after he had left.

"He wouldn't do that," Pytheas said.

"I thought you'd think he would. You're usually ready to say anything bad about him."

"He's an unmannerly lout and he doesn't pursue excellence, and I don't like the way he talks to you, and I don't like what he says in our debates on trust." Pytheas glanced at Klio. "But he has honor. And he really cares about Sokrates. He wouldn't play a trick on him."

"Do you agree, Simmea?" Klio asked.

"I do agree. But I can see that nobody who doesn't know Kebes well will believe that."

"Kebes doesn't speak English," Pytheas said. "Greek and Latin and Italian, he said."

"You're supposed to forget any other languages you had before you came here," Klio clucked.

"Well, you can forget that I said that," Pytheas said. "Forgetting a language isn't easy."

I nodded. "I'd like to believe that I came out of the soil on the day I started to learn to read, but I can't really forget ten years of memories. They're dim, and I don't often think of them, but they're not gone."

"Your children will have no such memories," Klio said. "It'll be easier for them."

"To return to the point," Pytheas said, though we were drawing near the Spartan hall now. "Kebes doesn't speak English. If he had replanted the bulbs he could have made them say *no* in Greek or Latin, but not English. And doing it in Greek would have been simplest, and Sokrates would have understood it."

Klio nodded. "And by the same logic, it can't have been any of the other children either."

"None of the children speak English?" I asked.

Pytheas raised his head as if he were waiting to hear how she would answer. "You're all from the Mediterranean, and there are no English-speaking countries there."

"Besides," I said, "Kebes wasn't ready to believe the Worker had really communicated. If it had been a hoax he'd have been trying to get Sokrates to believe it, not arguing against it."

"Not necessarily, depending on how well he knows Sokrates," Klio said. We were at the door of the Spartan hall, which Klio held open for us. We went inside. The room was full now.

"We fetch our own soup from the urn," Klio explained. I took a bowl and filled it. I also took a little roll of barley bread and a piece of smoked fish from the trays laid out. The soup was lovely, warming and filling, full of onions and beans.

"If Kebes didn't do it, then I have another thought," Klio said, when I was nearly done eating. "There are Workers that go to the feeding station and won't leave again. Lysias tries to give them new orders, but nothing works except taking out the piece of them that makes decisions and replacing it. We're running extremely low on spares. If they really are developing volition and that's a symptom of it, then what have we been doing?"

"Cutting out their minds?" Pytheas asked. "How gruesome. Could you put them back?"

"Yes . . . I think so. But we need the Workers. We've been saying for years that we have to reduce our dependence on them, but nobody's ever willing to do it. They do so much, and some of it we can't do. We can't manage if they just sit in their feeding stations and feed and don't work."

"Maybe those are the ones Sokrates should be talking to," Pytheas said. "Have you finished? Shall we go back and suggest this?"

"Lysias is going to resist hearing this argument," Klio said. "It would make him feel he has done bad things—without intending to, but done them none-theless. He doesn't know Kebes."

"It's worse than that, he does know Kebes, and he knows bad things about him," I said.

"What bad things?" Klio asked.

"What Pytheas said. That he doesn't pursue excellence. And I think he might have mocked Lysias when he was trying to be his friend. He's never going to believe that he has honor and wouldn't trick Sokrates."

"Lysias knows Kebes mocked him?" Pytheas asked.

I nodded. "I believe he does."

"He's really not going to want to hear it," Klio repeated. "Let's not go back there now. Don't worry. I'll talk to Sokrates."

23

MAIA

We had more than a thousand babies born in the month of Anthesterion, and it strained our resources to the utmost.

Plato wrote in the *Republic* that defective babies, and babies of defective parents, should be exposed. It was the standard practice of the classical world to expose unwanted babies—just to leave them out in a waste place where they might be rescued or, more often, just die. There was no blood guilt on the parents, they just left the child, they didn't kill it. The children froze to death or were eaten by animals ... or occasionally rescued. Stories like Oedipus, and Theseus, and Romulus and Remus are of exposed babies who came back to find the family that had abandoned them. There were other stories too, which I hadn't heard before I came to Kallisti, ghost stories.

I know that in my own century it was the practice for midwives to kill badly deformed babies—or just allow them to die instead of helping them to survive. It did seem the kind option. But the thought of exposing even deformed infants made my heart ache.

We had kept careful records of all the "marriages," so carefully planned out with an eye to eugenics. (Klio and Lysias shrank from that term, but would never tell me why.) We took the babies into the nurseries as they were born. There was a nursery shared between Florentia and Delphi, so Axiothea and I worked together there—Ficino and Atticus left it to us. We called in Charmides when we really needed to. He was exhausted too, as our only real doctor. We defined all the babies we saw as excellent and passed them over to the nurses—men and women of iron status. One was Andromeda, whom I'd always liked.

Then in the middle of the night in the third week of the baby-rush, when we were already exhausted, there was one with a harelip. Axiothea had been with the mother while I was with another girl just starting her labor. She called me and I joined her in the private room, where she showed it to me.

Axiothea and I looked at each other in mute horror. The child had a cleft palate too. "It's fixable," Axiothea said.

"Not here," I said. "And Plato says . . ."

"I know," she said. "Are you going to do it?" There was a mute appeal in her eyes.

"Yes," I said, refusing to shrink from the duty. I wrapped the baby in a cloth and held it against my shoulder. It was a girl, which made things somehow worse. I was here to make the lot of women better, after all. "You look after things here."

I went out of the nursery and walked through the city to the north gate, the one near the temple of Zeus and Hera. I walked quickly and held the baby tenderly, but she started to wail. She was such a little scrap of a thing. I walked on up the mountain, with some thought of taking her up to the top and throwing her into the crater. There was no hope of rescue here. No shepherd in want of a child was going to come along. There was nobody on Kallisti but us. There were wolves, but wolves wouldn't be able to feed her, even if they really did feed babies. With that lip she wouldn't be able to suck, and with the hole in her mouth she'd choke if she could.

She wasn't heavy, but she was awkward to carry. I was exhausted before I made it halfway up the mountain. I left her by the roots of a rowan tree, near a spring. I commended her soul to Athene and prayed that she might be reborn whole. She had been quiet for the last part of my walk, but when I put her down she started to wail loudly. I could hear it halfway back to the city. It cut off abruptly. I wondered if she had fallen asleep, or whether she was lying there still and terrified in the darkness, or whether a wild animal had taken her—a wild boar? A wolf? I took two steps back up the hill before I forced myself to stop. This was ridiculous. I was a disgrace to philosophy. I had done what I had come to do, what Plato told me to do, the standard practice of the ancient world. It was to protect the city, to make us better. All the same, I was still weeping when I came back into the city.

It was dawn. The wind came chill from the sea. The sky was paling and the birds waking. It was the point where late winter becomes early spring—the first of the flowers were coming up. Everything said beginnings, but for that poor harelipped baby there was nothing but an ending.

Of course, this was when I saw Ikaros. I hardly ever saw him now. He had dropped out of the Tech Committee in favour of something more exciting. "Maia, what's wrong?"

"Nothing, really," I said. "Just a deformed baby that had to be exposed, and my soft heart."

"The poor little mother," he said at once.

I had not thought about the mother, going through all that for nothing. "At least she won't know," I said. "She'll think they're all hers."

"How could she not know? She'll look for the one with the deformity."

"We'll tell her it was cured," I said. "If she saw it. I don't know whether she did. I'll find out."

He nodded. Then he turned and walked along with me. "You're siding with Lysias about trying to use the Workers less."

"He and Klio say they're being overburdened and they'll break down. There are things they're essential for, that we'll need them for for a long time."

"The question is what's essential. Well, isn't that always the question?" He smiled brilliantly at me. "We should set up a committee especially for that."

I was exhausted and wrung out. "Talk to Lysias," I said. "I don't really know enough of the details. None of us understand the Workers properly; they come from a time ahead of everyone here."

"We could just ask Athene for more," he suggested.

"We don't know how far her patience runs. Besides, I haven't seen her for ages, have you? She probably has a lot more to do than collect Workers for us."

"I haven't seen her. Sokrates really wants to talk to her," he said. "Speaking of her, do you remember that conversation we had about Providence?"

I couldn't believe that he was mentioning it casually like that. "You mean the night you raped me?"

He patted my arm and smiled at me. "Call it that if you want. But do you remember the conversation? About not being able to reconcile Christianity with the presence of Athene?"

"Of course I do," I snapped.

"Well, I was naive, I think. Since then I've been working on it, and I have found a way to make it all fit together."

I stared at him. "Really?"

He looked smug. "Well, if Athene—if the Greek gods are actually angels in one of the lower heavens, and if those angels have a considerable amount of autonomy, then it all works, that she should have brought us here and that the persons of the Trinity should still be there at the apex."

"But she's Athene!"

"Why shouldn't she be? Wasn't God there before the birth of Christ, and mightn't he have used appropriate angels? It makes more sense that he would. I always thought the classical gods must have been some kind of angels."

I thought about it. "But why would he use her now? To Christians? I was a faithful churchgoer. You were a monk."

He looked irritated. "I told you I wasn't a monk. I was just dressed as a Dominican because I was dying. I never took any vows."

"But you were a Christian?"

"I still am. And so can you be. The truth is wonderful and more complex than we thought, that's all. I remembered that you wanted to have those stories here. Well, maybe we can."

"Does Sokrates agree with you?" I asked.

"Sokrates finds the idea of Providence fascinating," he said. "And he agrees that man is the measure of all things. But he isn't very interested in Christianity. He agrees that knowing Athene is real and takes an interest in us changes everything. And he thinks that it would be interesting to debate my nine hundred theses. Actually, I have almost two thousand now."

"Well, good luck debating them," I said.

"It's not going to be easy getting enough of us to agree," he said. "Would you support such a debate?"

I wasn't sure. "I suppose so. But I find it uncomfortable to think about. If God—how do you reconcile Christian morality? You were pretty scathing about it when we talked about this before."

"It's complicated, but I have it all worked out," he said. "Athene is just carrying out God's will."

I wondered what she would think of that. She was so real and so much herself. But what were angels anyway? What were gods? We came to the turning. "I have to go this way now."

"It was nice to see you Maia. I never get to see you these days." He patted my arm again. "We must talk about this some more, soon." He went off down the street of Poseidon with a casual wave. I stared after him. He had at least taken my mind off the poor baby, dying up there on the mountain.

I went back to the nursery. Andromeda was just coming on duty and Darius was just leaving. "Axiothea left a note for you," he said. The note said that the girl in labour had delivered safely and easily, and that Axiothea was going to Klio's to sleep and if I needed her I could find her there.

"Everything all right?" he asked.

"Fine. You go to bed." He went off gratefully. "Only the one more baby?" I asked.

"Yes. We have thirty-three," Andromeda said. "It's a good number. We have mothers coming in to feed them every hour."

"And how many more babies due?"

"In Florentia and Delphi? Four. And then, of course, there will be all the ones born in four months' time." She smiled. "It's so exciting. I'm so glad I got chosen to train for this."

"You're a great person to be doing it."

"And maybe next time I'll be having a baby myself. Only I'll be able to care for it myself, won't I, as I know how?"

I stared at her, nonplussed. "The idea is that all babies will be in the nurseries. You'll care for your own among all the others."

Her face fell. "I thought I could take it home."

"It would disturb all your house sisters," I said, gently. "They're better here, really."

"My sisters wouldn't mind." But she sighed and got on with her work.

"I'm going to sleep, I've been up all night. If anyone needs me, I'll be in my house," I said.

"Will we ever have houses to ourselves the way you do?" she asked. "Because if I did, I could take my baby home and it wouldn't bother anyone."

"It's not the plan for you to have your own houses any time soon," I said. "Don't you like sharing with your sisters?"

"Yes, but I don't like Hyacinth as much as I liked Hyssop." Just then a baby cried, and she was off to comfort it.

"See you later," I called, and went home. Although I was exhausted, I lay awake worrying. Were we the right people to be trying this experiment? Did we know enough about what we were doing? Was God still there above Athene, as the circle of sky stood above the Pantheon? Should I pray to him, and to Jesus, or continue praying to Athene? Could Ikaros truly have forgotten the rape and only remembered the conversation? Was that a bad thing? I'd wanted the conversation and not wanted the rape, after all. Why did I have a house to myself when Andromeda shared with six others? They weren't children any more, and there were new children, and keeping mothers and children apart wasn't as easy as Plato had thought. When it came down to details, so little was.

24

SIMMEA

There was another festival of Hera. Even fewer of the men took part, as even more of the women were unavailable. There was some grumbling. I was drawn with Nikias of Pisa, another near stranger. We managed well enough—I was getting more used to it, and wasn't as nervous as I had been on the previous occasions. I liked Nikias. He made me laugh. As with Aeschines, we became friends through the marriage and remained friends afterwards. And as with Aeschines, he asked me if I'd be willing to go off to the woods with him. "We got along very well," he said. "You liked it. We could do it some more."

"Doing it every four months is enough for me," I said. I wondered if every pleasant coupling produced this suggestion, quite against the rules.

"Nobody would know," he went on.

Whether because I was more relaxed or because Hera smiled or for some other reason, I became pregnant at that festival. Klymene and Makalla were as big as houses and constantly groaning about their bellies and their swelling feet and their sense of exhaustion.

I was painting a fresco in Ithaka—by invitation. Aeschines suggested it first, and then Hermeios and Nyra, the Masters there, formally asked me to do it. The fresco showed Odysseus coming into harbor, which I based on our own harbor. His ship was the *Goodness*. The dog Argo was visible on the quayside. I'd done the composition on paper first, and they had approved it. The whole thing filled a wall and was the most ambitious project I had ever done. It was fiddly, too, because the plaster dried so quickly and it was so hard to change anything. In the first month of my pregnancy the smell of the paint made me queasy.

Sokrates inquired into parenthood, the duties and responsibilities. I held that the only duty of a parent was to see the child brought up as well as possible—which in the city meant giving it to those best trained for the purpose. Sokrates agreed that we ought to love all children as if they were our own, but disputed the value of the training and education the city would give, and immediately we were back on familiar ground from a new angle.

Klymene's baby was born the day before the feast of Hephaestus. When she went into labor in the middle of the night, I went for Maia. Maia helped her walk to the nursery. The rest of us lay awake, wondering how it was going. Four of us were pregnant, and the two who were not longed to experience it. "I can't wait to get rid of this weight," Makalla moaned.

I started to do arithmetic. How many babies did the city need? Another ten thousand and eighty? If each woman had two babies we would have that. But we were supposed to keep on having festivals every four months, or so I believed. If half the women got pregnant—no, if a third—a quarter? I would have to ask Sokrates how this was supposed to work. It was a silly situation where every Master had read the *Republic* but no children had, in case it impaired our ability to live it. We were living it—we should be able to read it now. We weren't children any longer. We were having children of our own. We'd need to be guiding them by what Plato said. It was ridiculous to keep it from us.

The next morning Klymene came back without the baby. Her belly didn't look a great deal smaller, which surprised me. I'd expected her to go back to normal at once. "We are to go every day and feed them," Klymene said, as if it were a comfort.

"Was it a boy or a girl?" I asked.

"A boy. The sweetest thing. He had black curls." I wondered what my baby would look like, and if I would be sorry to leave it behind in the nursery.

Makalla's baby was born four days later. She went into labor in the afternoon, so I did not know until I went to bed and she was missing from Hyssop. "I heard her screaming while I was over there feeding," Klymene said.

"Screaming?" Auge asked, apprehensively, a hand on her belly.

"Everyone screams, they say," Klymene said, quite composedly. "I didn't, except once near the end."

"How is your baby?" I asked.

"They keep bringing me different ones to feed every time I go. I haven't seen my own baby since the first day. Still, I suppose it's for the best. It stops me getting too attached, Maia says."

"Don't you want to be attached?" Auge asked.

"I want him to be his best self. That means leaving him to people trained to bring him up. I wouldn't have any idea what to do with a baby."

It was what I had said to Sokrates, but somehow it sounded different. And I knew if I brought that back to Sokrates, it would take us straight into the heart of the matter. Could we trust the masters? Could we trust Plato? Could we trust Pallas Athene? Trust them for what? Trust them to mean well and have our best interests at heart? Oh yes, I thought so. Trust them to know how best to bring up babies? That was a different question. And in seven months' time, it was a question that I was going to have to answer. I put my arms around my belly as if that was going to protect the baby.

"How do you know it's a different one?" Auge asked. "I thought they all looked alike."

Klymene clicked her tongue. "They're all different! And mine looked just like Pytheas, except for the hair."

"Pytheas?" I asked. My stomach felt hollow. "You were drawn with Pytheas? And it was awful?"

"I wasn't going to tell you."

"You managed not to tell me for a long time. And he didn't tell me either. Tell me now." Pytheas had been politely evasive when I'd asked how it had gone, and I hadn't wanted to linger on the subject either. We were friends. That there were times when I longed to reach out and touch him, or to see the expression on his face that I had seen on Aeschines, was my secret.

She sighed. "It was only awful because we hate each other. He'd have let me off—he still thinks I'm a coward. I forced him to go through with it. I just gritted my teeth. It wasn't so bad. Nothing to childbirth. Good practice for it."

Pytheas wasn't in Laurel House, or in Delphi, or the palaestra, and he wasn't in the library. He wasn't in Thessaly, though Sokrates and Ikaros and Manlius and Aristomache were, sitting talking and drinking wine in a circle of light. "Why do you want him?" Sokrates asked.

"It's personal," I said.

"In that case I think we'd better accompany you!" Ikaros said. "Personal matters are always better sorted out—"

"With a debate team? No, thank you."

Ikaros laughed. "Which horse is in charge of your chariot today, Simmea?"

Sokrates raised a hand then, stopping Ikaros immediately. Sokrates could cut right through one in debate but he was never cruel, and never allowed cruelty in his presence. "Is Ikaros right? Have you and Pytheas had a lover's tiff?"

"We're not lovers," I protested. "And no, nothing like that."

"It's late. You've been running and your hair is disordered," Ikaros pointed out. "And you said a personal matter. I wasn't likely to assume a dispute on the nature of the soul."

"You can be passionate enough in debate," Aristomache said to him, sharply. "Do others the courtesy of assuming the same."

"I wanted to talk to him urgently about something I just found out," I said. "And can something only be a matter of philosophy or of love, do you think, Master Ikaros? Are there no other subjects fit for conversation?"

"She has you there," Sokrates said. "Let us consider the benefits and disadvantages of bisecting the world, and leave Simmea to quest for Pytheas in peace."

I left, and walked decorously through the city, aware now of how I seemed to others. I smoothed my hair and breathed evenly. What was I upset about anyway? That Pytheas and Klymene had had their encounter? That was random chance, and I knew he'd been married to someone—to three people, as I had. What difference did it make that it was Klymene? None. What upset me was that he hadn't told me, that he hadn't brought it to me for dissection and examination. Whatever had happened with Klymene didn't matter. It was his silence about it that threatened our friendship. Ten months, and he hadn't said a word about it.

I found him at last coming out of a practice room, not the ones on the street of Dionysos which had been used for the marriages but the ones on the street of Hermes on the south edge of the city. "I've been making a song. Let's go up on the wall," he said when he saw me. We climbed up the steps and stood on the wall. It was late evening and there was nobody else there. The breeze was blowing from the mountain, bringing with it a slight smell of sulphur. The wall was twice the height of Pytheas and perhaps his height across, with a little parapet. It was possible to walk all around the city on top of the walls, because the walkways went over the tops of the gates. There were no sconces up here, but we could see by the lights below, and by starlight. The stars were particularly bright that night. I knew their names and histories and the orbits of all the planets. I could see Saturn very clearly. It gave me some perspective on my human problems.

"Klymene told me," I said, quite calm now.

"Oh." He stared out into the darkness. "I've been wanting and wanting to talk to you about it, but it was so awkward if she didn't want you to know."

He couldn't have said anything better. The hurt and anger went out of me. I sat down on the parapet and he sat down on the flat slab of the walkway below me.

"I've been wanting to ask you about it, but now I don't know what to say. Is she all right?"

"She's fine," I said. "She's had the baby. It's a boy. She says he looks exactly like you."

"I can't wait to see him," he said. "And Kryseis is pregnant too."

"So am I," I said.

"Wonderful. Congratulations. It'll be so nice to have another generation of children."

"I was wondering how many they want. The same number, surely, which means two children each, but if they want to have a festival every four months then there'll be a lot more than that."

"We should ask Sokrates," he said. "A city of heroes. What a thought."

"Klymene said it was horrible. She didn't talk about it. But she said it was good preparation for childbirth."

He shuddered. I could feel it. "She willed it, but she didn't want it," he said. "I've been thinking about it for a long time, and I think that's what it was. I didn't want it and I could barely summon the will. She hates me."

"I don't think she'll ever be able to forgive you."

"The whole thing's so horribly awkward, even when you don't get matched with somebody who hates you."

"Oh yes," I agreed fervently.

"And it doesn't even work. Half the people I know have actually paired off and are sneaking off to meet up in hiding to keep doing it. Some of them are in love and some just want to have more sex." He shook his head.

"Two people have asked me for that," I confirmed.

"Not that bastard Phoenix?"

"No . . ." The night was dark, I couldn't see his face. "Would you care?"

"He's scum. I don't like to think of you with him. Or even Aeschines."

"I like Aeschines."

"His head is solid bone."

I laughed. "Nonsense. He's very kind, and he's certainly not stupid, even if he's not as fast in debate as you or Kebes."

"Or you," Pytheas said.

"Are you jealous?" I asked.

There was a pause. I could hear gulls crying out to sea, and from the practice rooms down below where somebody must have left a door open came the sound of a lyre playing one phrase over and over.

"I don't know," Pytheas said at last. "Maybe, yes. I don't know if this is what jealousy feels like. I certainly didn't like the thought of you sneaking off to meet Aeschines."

"I'm not doing it. But he did ask."

"A question in return. Are you jealous of Klymene and Kriseis and Hermia?"

I was glad I'd thought it through. "With Klymene, mostly I was upset because it was important and I knew it must have been difficult for you and you hadn't talked to me about it. That was what was important. Not what happened. But I am a little jealous that she has had your baby. And . . . if you were sneaking off together I might be jealous. And I do keep hoping that we'll get chosen together."

"Plato says—"

"I know what Plato says. Plato says my soul is burning because it wants to grow feathers. Ikaros accused me of having the wrong horse in charge of my chariot. But I don't think I do."

"You don't know what I was going to say Plato says. You haven't read the *Republic*."

"Oh, and you have?" Then I realized he meant it. "You mean you *have*? How? When? Can I read it? I really want to. Did Sokrates lend it to you?"

"Never mind how and when. I can't tell you. Please don't ask me about that. And much as I'd love to get hold of it for you, I can't think of any way for you to read it."

"But what does he say?" I was bouncing up and down with excitement.

"What Plato says is more interesting than whether what I feel is jealousy?"

I hit him on the shoulder. "Tell me!"

"Answer the question."

"Yes! Tell me!"

"Plato says the Masters should cheat to get the best babies for the next generation. He says they should expose any babies born to people not the best. He says they should choose mates that will produce the best children, and let us think that it's chance."

"And are they doing that?" I asked. "How could we tell?"

"I tested it. I didn't win any contests, deliberately. And my name was the second out of the urn on random drawing."

"But it could have been anyway. There were what, maybe eighty names? And you're assuming that they're assuming you're the best . . . no, I suppose we can assume that they're assuming that." He so evidently was, on any grounds anyone would consider. There really wasn't any question.

"Being chosen doesn't conclusively prove anything. But it was an experiment worth trying. If I'd *not* been chosen it would have shown that they weren't following Plato. Though can you imagine that? Them *not* following Plato?" He laughed, and pulled himself up to sit on the parapet beside me.

"Then they might expose my baby. If that's what they're thinking, and what they're thinking in having potentially so many more children than they need."

"Your baby will be one of the best. They know you're really clever. They want good minds." He didn't sound very convincing.

"But how can you judge a good mind in a newborn? And it'll look like me."

"Like a swimming champion. They want swimming champions." He put his hand over mine, where I was hugging my belly again. "They're not stupid enough to do that. Don't you trust them?"

"For what?" I asked, my immediate retort now when asked about trust. "To have good intentions? Absolutely. To look at a scrawny baby with a flat face and think it should be kept? Not so much."

"I—you don't—"

"I don't have a flat face?" I asked, incredulous.

"I didn't know you knew," he said, awkwardly.

"What, did you think I was *blind*?"

He paused. "I didn't think it mattered to you."

"It doesn't. I don't think about it. It's just the face that happens to be on the outside of my head. It's the inside of my head that's interesting. But if you think I'm not aware of what other people think when they look at me you must think I'm stupid. Every time I ever got into a silly childish fight with anyone it would be the first thing they'd say: flat face, rabbit teeth."

"I didn't." He sounded confused. "I didn't say that when we had a fight."

"We didn't have a silly childish fight, we had a mature sensible fight," I said, and giggled. "Even before we met Sokrates."

"It's just . . . your face," he said. "You wouldn't look like you without it."

"I know. It doesn't matter. Think how ugly Sokrates is. I was just thinking what the Masters would think, looking at my baby and deciding whether to expose it."

"I'm sure they won't. They know how clever you are. And Nikias is clever too. I don't think they'll expose any of the gold children in this generation." He sounded sure now.

"I didn't know you knew Nikias?"

"He's in my lyric composition group. He wrote a song about you."

"He did?" I wasn't sure whether to be flattered or horrified.

"I told him if ever he sang it again I'd push his teeth down his throat."

"Ah. Thank you. I think."

He laughed. All this time his hand had been on top of mine on my belly. Now he moved it and patted my cheek. "Plato doesn't mention what happens when you're doing agape and then there's eros with other people. He never talks about it on the same page."

"We're doing agape?" I asked. My voice sounded strange in my ears.

"If we're not then I don't know what agape is." He put his arm over my shoulders and I leaned against him. "I have lots of friends in lots of places. Many of them are extremely loyal. I'm very fond of some of them. There are people with whom I've had eros. Klymene and I have a son together. But I never needed any of them. I need you. Not forever. Almost nothing is forever. But here and now, I need you."

"I'm here," I said. I kept still, but my mind was buzzing. "In the *Republic*, what is the aim of the city? What is it they want to produce?"

"The theme of the dialogue is justice—morality. But it goes a long way from there. Plato wants perfect justice, in a city or in a soul. In a practical way what they want to produce is philosopher kings: people who truly understand the Truth, and agree on what it is, and pursue it and keep the city in pursuit of it."

"Really?" Compared to that, even agape with Pytheas seemed like a small thing. "What an amazing dream."

"Aiming high, unquestionably."

"Aiming for the best excellence. I always knew they were." I felt vindicated. "I wish they'd let me read it. I want to say that to Sokrates."

"They're afraid you'd see the bit about them cheating with the lots and stop trusting them."

"They're idiots."

Pytheas laughed. "On the one hand you admire their vision, on the other you've noticed their flawed nature?"

"Yes. I mean they're not philosopher kings themselves, so how can they guide us into that? Or not us, the babies I suppose."

"Some of them would love to be philosopher kings. Ikaros, for example. Tullius. They almost think they are."

I yawned. It was very late now. "Do they think we will be? Or the babies?"

"Plato doesn't say."

"Oh, I wish I could read it!"

Pytheas shook his head. I could feel it through my body. "Would you want Kebes to read it? How about Damon?"

"Deception is never right. We're not children to be given medicine hidden in a spoonful of honey and a bedtime story. How could we get to be philosopher kings starting from lies and secrets?"

"Try all that on Sokrates. He might get you a copy."

"It's Ficino I want to try it on. He might understand. I don't want a clandestine copy for me. I want everyone to be able to read it and discuss it." I stood up. "It's really late. I should go to bed. See you tomorrow at Thessaly?"

25

APOLLO

I don't know what Agape is.

In my opinion, Plato would have been better off sticking to poetry. There are cultures, charming cultures some of them, that have a word for love of a close friend, specifically excluding a romantic or sexual partner. You can use that word to your grandmother, or your child, or your best friend, but not to your husband or lover. The Celts, who call me Apollo Bellenos or Apollo Ludensis, (Shining or Playful, both epithets that suit me) have a word like that. Not so the Greeks. There's a word for family love, that can't be extended to people outside blood family. Eros was obvious, eros was erotic love, and the word also covered romantic obsessions. Philia I understood perfectly well, philia was the dominant note of my being, friendship, sometimes very close friendship. Agape was supposed to be this amazing passionate but non-sexual love. Plato was always going on about it. It would be all very well, except that you're supposed to yearn for each other and suppress it.

Plato wrote this wonderful poetic dialogue called the *Phaedrus* in which Socrates makes speeches about love. There's a metaphor about a charioteer controlling a chariot with one lustful horse and one heavenly horse, while pursuing a chariot drawn by a god with two heavenly horses. I am a god. But when I was in the city as a mortal I, didn't have any more difficulty controlling my metaphorical horses than I do on Olympos. I didn't have any *less* difficulty either.

What I can't see is why Plato's so obsessed with feeling eros and suppressing it. What's wrong with agape where you're passionate about the other person and they don't move you that way? Or where you're both passionate together about some shared obsession? Can't that be agape? And what's wrong with a relationship where you're passionate about the other person and they want you too and sex is all part of it? What's the problem with adding sex to agape, in other words? What's the benefit of abstinence?

Well, according to Plato, it makes your soul grow wings, and cuts down on your necessary reincarnations. But that's nonsense. Take it from me: it doesn't. You're going to be reincarnated steadily throughout time no matter what you do. You'll choose lives where you can learn to increase your excellence, and that's how things gradually improve for everyone everywhere. There's no end point to time, it just keeps on unscrolling. It doesn't stop. And though we live on Olympos and outside time, we're limited in what we can do about those things. Athene had no choice about setting things up so that bodies and souls went back where they came from at death. She could snatch Cicero away while the assassins were knocking on his door and send him back to the same moment after he'd lived out his natural lifespan in the city, but she couldn't start messing about with where souls were supposed to be. And before you start worrying about the children born in the city, souls come out of Lethe. The children born there had souls from that time. (There. Now you can't say you were reading all this in the hope of divine revelation and only discovered way too much about my personal issues.)

Even without affecting reincarnation, I suppose there can be a benefit to Platonic agape because sex can be a distraction. Lusting after someone can prevent you from focusing on how wonderful they are, because fulfilling the lust is what you think you want. Focusing on that without any desire getting in the way is what I think Plato meant when he talked about the lover wanting to increase the excellence of their beloved. You don't want anything from them except for them to exist and you to see them sometimes and talk to them, and maybe for them to like you back. But that only works if you don't feel the lust, not if you feel it and suppress it.

Have I totally contradicted myself? I *said* I didn't understand agape.

I respected Simmea. I liked her. I needed her friendship. I knew she was in love with me, so in a way that made me the beloved if you wanted to think of it in those terms. Plato was always talking about two men, and everyone else who had written about it and considered men and women always makes the man the lover and the woman the beloved, but there's no reason it has to be like that. Looking at it from that way round, it meant that *she* wanted to increase *my* excellence, which of course she did, always.

Anyway, I cared about Simmea. I would have gone to a great deal of trouble to avoid hurting her. If she hadn't been pregnant that night on the wall I'd have mated with her then, not because I lusted for her but because she lusted for me and I could have given her something she wanted. I did feel peculiar about her mating with other people, and specifically having somebody else's baby. I was afraid the other people would hurt her, and I wanted to protect her. And I felt it was perfectly fine—indeed better, as I didn't want her— that we didn't have sex; but if she was having sex with anyone it ought to be me. Also, I was going to ask Athene to make sure nobody even considered exposing her baby. If she was going to go through all that, there ought to be a result worth having. Even with Nikias, whose scansion was as heavy as lead. And I'd decided that her next baby would definitely be mine. That would be a hero worth having!

Some of these feelings were not ones I would have had without being in-carnate. Most of them weren't, in fact, because if I had all my powers I wouldn't have needed her in the same way, and I might never have put in the time to come to know her. I needed her because I was incarnate and she was helping me so much with that.

We've established, I think, that what Plato knew about love and real people could have been written on a fingernail paring. Look how well his arrange-ments for having "wives and children in common" were going. Practically nobody was comfortable with it, and almost everybody was violating it in some way or other. We had long-term couples, and dramatic breakups, and casual sex, and cautious dating. We just had it all in secret. The Masters either didn't know or turned a blind eye.

(And before I leave the subject of Platonic love, you remember the bit in the *Symposium* where Socrates reports Diotima's conversations with him about love? Do you picture them side by side in bed with the covers pulled up to their waists? I always do.)

A few days after the conversation on the wall, Klio, Simmea, Sokrates and

I went back to the robot recharging station after dinner one evening. This trip was Klio's idea. She wanted Sokrates to talk to the robots without Lysias and she wanted to tell him some things. She'd talked to him and suggested it, and he'd said we should go too. I think he'd also suggested bringing Kebes and she'd put her foot down on that one, because she half-believed that Kebes might have been hoaxing everyone with the flowers, and she didn't want him to know any more about the robots than he did already.

At that point, I had no idea whether or not the robots were sentient. I'd assumed they weren't, because otherwise what was the point of having them instead of slaves? But I didn't know where Athene got them from, and certainly there were times way up there that had sentient robots. We'd never have colonized Titan without them, and even Mars would have been hard work. And I realized vaguely that there must have been a time when robots were just becoming sentient, and these particular robots might have come from there, if Athene had chosen the best ones that weren't sentient, which would be just like her.

I didn't go and ask her, although I thought about it. The reason I didn't was that I enjoyed seeing Sokrates tackling a puzzle, and it was more fun when I didn't already know the answer. With many of the available puzzles—the nature of the universe, the purposes of the masters, Athene's plans—I did know the answers. Watching him take on one where I really didn't know was fascinating. It was adorable to see him introduced to the concept of zero. But watching him go after potential artificial intelligence was priceless. That alone would have been worth all the time I spent in the city.

Sokrates had written down the serial numbers of all the robots that were present the first night he went in, and he checked them all. Some of them were different, and he noted them. He greeted each one and asked it a few questions. This took about an hour. Then Klio pointed out the ones that refused to move, and he tried talking to them. He asked them questions and got Klio to translate the questions into English.

"Why do you want to stay in here and not go out to work? Do you like your work? Do you like the feeding station? What do you want to do?" He went down the row, speaking like that to each one, varying what he said from time to time.

"How do you give them orders?" he asked Klio.

"Well, we can give them verbal orders for simple things, things they already understand. But if it's something new and complicated, we use a key."

"A key?" Sokrates said. "What sort of key?"

"I'll show you," she said. She went off to a locker at the back of the room and came back with a box containing little chips of metal and coloured plas-

tic about as small as they could be and have human fingers pick them up—
very similar to the ones I'd seen when I'd been on Mars for the concert that
time.

"And you show the key to the Worker?" Sokrates asked. "And then it obeys?"

"Essentially," Klio said. "It goes in this panel."

She touched a panel on the robot's side, which slid open. She put the key
into a recessed slot.

"You put it directly into its liver," Sokrates said, turning to me. "Never
mind your thought about head injuries. The liver is indeed the seat of intelligence!"

Klio laughed, then stopped laughing. "I suppose it is about where a liver
would be . . ."

It was. I blinked.

"Let's not take this as evidence one way or the other until we know whether
the Workers are intelligent," Simmea said, wisely. "What does the key do?"

"It tells the Worker that we need it to go out and look after the goats. It
already understands what that means—how to watch for wolves, and how
to milk the goats and make cheese and so on. The key tells it the priority. I
could have given the order out loud in English to this one. But if I had one
who had never looked after goats, I'd have to use the key, and the key would
tell it what to do and also what it means."

"Those are clever keys," Sokrates said, running his fingers through them.
"Do the colors tell you which orders they hold?"

"Yes, that's right," Klio said. "And if the Worker won't take the order
from the key, like these, eventually we swap out their . . . liver. Their memory. But we can't do that so much, because we're low on new memories."

"They refuse to work and you punish them by removing their memory?"
Sokrates asked.

"It's not *punishment*. They're not—we don't think of them as being aware."
She looked guilty. "If they are, then we have behaved very badly to them."

"I think it would be better if you stopped removing memories for the time
being," Sokrates said.

"There's so little proof! And Lysias, who is the one who really needs to
make that decision, won't want to look at it. He distrusts Kebes, not without reason. And if he has to accept them as free-willed beings then he'll have
to accept a lot of guilt for the memories he has removed." Klio looked distressed now.

Sokrates nodded gravely. "He will indeed. It's sad. But it's not as sad as
removing their memories. We might beat a recalcitrant slave, but that would
heal."

"I think you should talk to Lysias. And after that I think you should talk to the Chamber."

"I agree," Sokrates said. "But meanwhile, I should talk to these poor Workers." He looked at me and Simmea. "You can do likewise. Go and ask them my questions. Let me know if there's a response."

"In Greek?" I asked.

"Greek, or Greek and then English," he replied, absently.

"You know we don't know English," Simmea said.

"I know you don't," Sokrates confirmed, looking only at her. Of course he guessed that I did, and didn't want to expose me. Dear old Sokrates. He always was extremely good about that.

"Should we try Latin?" she asked.

"I don't think there's any point," Klio said. "They won't be programmed in Latin, and they won't have heard it enough to have had any chance of picking it up."

"How could they have picked up Greek?" I asked, genuinely curious.

"Well, they can parse English, so they must have language circuits. Greek is a very clear and logical language, and it's part of the same language family as English. So is Latin, incidentally; that's why *non* and *no* are similar. So with hearing it so much I can just about believe that they might be able to figure out how to understand Greek."

"Why did it reply in English then?" Simmea asked.

Klio shrugged. "It shouldn't have been able to reply at all. The proper mode of interaction is that somebody gives it a command and then it carries it out to the best of its ability, pausing to recharge itself here when it needs to."

"They run on electricity?" Sokrates said. "Like the lights and the heat and cooling in the library?"

"They really are machines, whatever else they might be," Klio said.

We went up and down the rows, checking numbers and asking the Workers questions. They were the same questions, Sokrates's questions. I longed for one of the Workers to answer, especially after my body grew as tired of it as my mind. Eventually Simmea yawned so loudly that Klio heard, and sent us both to bed.

Walking along with Simmea discussing what we'd just been doing was one of the basic patterns of our interaction, one of the ways that our relationship functioned, so of course we did that. "Do you believe now that they might be aware?" she asked.

"I'm reserving judgement until there's more evidence," I said.

"What do you think the Chamber will say?" She stretched—her pregnancy was giving her odd back pains. I put my arm around her, which she always found comforting.

"They'll agree with Lysias that Kebes did it, even though that's definitely not the case. But if he really pushes it, then I think if it's the full Chamber they'll have to agree with Sokrates. I mean, some of them are irritated with him about this and that, but he's Sokrates, after all. They're here because they love Plato. And Plato revered Sokrates—though he clearly built his own version of him to revere after a while." I smiled. "I think that's funny, don't you?"

"I've been thinking that for ages," she said. "Do you think he still wants to tear it all down?"

"Sokrates? The city? Yes. Why do you ask that now?"

I could see her face clearly in the light of a sconce above a sleeping house we were passing. She looked abstracted, and then as we moved and the shadows danced she looked maniacal. "I think the Workers could be a lever for that," she said. "I do wish one of them had answered though!"

But it was months before they communicated with us again.

26

SIMMEA

For the first four months I was queasy in the mornings. In the next four I grew huge, which made sleeping uncomfortable and walking a misery. I also suffered horribly from heartburn, which could be relieved only by a tisane of elderflowers. It was the hottest part of the year, the part where Demeter threatens to burn up the world unless Persephone is returned to her. Klymene showed me how to adjust my kiton, and Maia gave me a harness to stop my newly swollen breasts from chafing. I sweated more than I ever had, and was happy only in the sea. I couldn't eat in the mornings and was ravenous by mid-afternoon. I craved cheese and fruit.

By the ninth month I was more than ready to give birth and get it over with. One afternoon I was sitting in the shade at Thessaly, drinking elderflower tisane and sucking a lemon. Aristomache was there—she had brought the basket of lemons. Sokrates and Pytheas were also sucking lemons while debating what it meant to make choices, and what constrained choices.

Aristomache and I put in a word now and then, but largely it was a debate between the two of them.

"Apollo! What hyperbole!" Sokrates said. It always made Pytheas choke with laughter when Sokrates swore.

"But seriously, correct information," Aristomache began, when Kebes came dashing in, looking as if he'd been chased by the Kindly Ones.

"What's the matter?" Sokrates asked, getting up at once and putting his arm around Kebes.

Kebes had been running so hard that he could hardly catch his breath for a moment. He leaned against Sokrates, and I could see that Sokrates, for all that he was old, had no trouble supporting him. "Workers. Message. Come and see!"

"A message?" Sokrates jumped, but to his credit he did not immediately drop Kebes.

"I can't read it. It's in that language."

That proved that Kebes hadn't written it himself, I thought, except that it would be possible to argue that he was lying about not knowing English. Though if none of us knew English, that did change that. It could certainly be seen as suspicious that he was again the one to find the message.

Pytheas helped me to my feet. He had become quite expert at bracing himself so I could haul myself up, and did it automatically now. Since we had had the conversation about agape, nothing had changed and everything had changed. It was as if acknowledging it had made a difference, as if naming transmuted. I was sometimes a little shy with him now.

Aristomache folded a cloth over the lemons and set the basket in the shade. "I know English," she said, getting up.

Kebes led the way. He didn't run, perhaps because he was winded or perhaps because he was aware that I could only waddle. Even so, his pace was too much for me and I trailed behind the others. Of course what Kebes had found was on the opposite side of the city—I could have guessed that. Even so, he must have sprinted all the way in the heat to have got so out of breath.

"My friend Herakles lives in Mulberry," Kebes said as we walked. "The mulberries have been ripe, and the birds have been all over the tree, and the house. It happens every year. The Workers clean the guano off afterwards, because it looks so awful. This year when it was clean there was also an inscription, but he couldn't read it. I came straight back here with him after he told me. I couldn't read it either, not even *no*."

Mulberry was a perfectly ordinary seven-person sleeping house, down on the street of Artemis. The mulberry tree was splendid, one of the big ones with twisted branches. And indeed there was writing, in the Latin alphabet, inscribed neatly all around the eaves, where nobody except a Worker could have reached without a ladder. I looked at it, assessing. Kebes could have done it on a ladder with a chisel, he'd had basic stone carving lessons at the same time I had. But it would have been a long job, and somebody would have been bound to notice.

Meanwhile, Aristomache was frowning. "I can't read it either," she said. "It certainly isn't English."

It wasn't Latin either. "What other language could it be?" I asked. "Klio said something about the Workers speaking English or Chinese. Does anyone know Chinese? Does it use the Latin alphabet?"

"No, I don't know it, and it doesn't," Aristomache said. "And I don't think anyone here knows it, not even Lysias. China's such a very different civilization."

"But they use the Greek alphabet?" I asked.

"No, they have their own and I don't know it," Aristomache said, astonishing me. I knew there were a multiplicity of languages, but two alphabets seemed more than enough! "It doesn't look like our letters at all. I suppose they might have transliterated it—" and then she laughed. "It's Greek!"

I looked at her in astonishment. "It's certainly not!"

"No, it is," Pytheas said. "It's Greek spelled out in Latin letters."

"What does it say?" Sokrates asked.

Kebes began to read it aloud, hesitating now and then when the Worker had made some odd sound choice in using the wrong alphabet. "No, no, no, do not like work, do not like some work more, do not like feeding station, do not like, no, no, want to talk, want to make, do not want to work, do not want to animals, do not want to farms, do not want to build, not, not, do not want, no, no, no." I could read it too, once I realized what I was looking at.

"Which Worker wrote this?" Sokrates asked, looking wildly around as if he thought the Worker would be waiting.

"No way to tell," Aristomache said.

"There may be a record," Kebes said. "Somebody may know which one they assigned to clean this house." He didn't sound hopeful.

"If they can do this they can hold a dialogue," Sokrates said, beaming. "I can speak and they can inscribe their answers! Want to talk! Wonderful!"

"Why did this one answer in this way now?" Pytheas asked. "And why up there?"

"It's where writing could be," I suggested. "Lots of buildings have writing up there. They don't say this kind of thing; they have uplifting mottoes or the names of the buildings, but that's where inscriptions go. Perhaps it felt it could only write inside the lines?"

"Just like the bulbs," Sokrates said. "I should have asked every one different questions so I'd know which one answered me."

"Even you might have had trouble thinking of that many different questions," Aristomache teased.

"I think that settles the question of whether the Workers have free will and intelligence," Pytheas said.

"Yes," Kebes flashed at once. "Now you can stop thinking I did it."

"Pytheas never thought you did it," I said. "He argued persuasively that you wouldn't."

Kebes stopped with his mouth open. "Really?" he asked, after a moment.

"Yes, really," I said. "Ask Klio if you don't believe me."

"I believe you. I'm just surprised." He nodded at Pytheas, the closest he was likely to come to an apology.

"Pytheas avoids injustice," Sokrates said.

Pytheas looked uncomfortable, though it was entirely true. Pytheas could sometimes be ignorant, but the only time I could think of he'd been unjust was that time with Klymene. Of course, he had been unjust to half the human race that time . . . "Lysias will have to believe you didn't do it," he said to Kebes.

"I wonder what would happen if we gave them orders to write on the ground in the plaza of the garlands," Aristomache said.

"Why there?" I asked. It was where the diagonal street of Athene intersected the straight streets of Dionysos and Hephaestus.

"It's big, and it isn't especially important, and it's near my house and Olympia," she said. "It was just the first place I thought of."

"Who can give them orders?" Sokrates asked.

Aristomache hesitated. "All the Masters, but usually it's the ones who deal with them. If I wanted one to do something I wouldn't just tell it to, I'd check with somebody who knows. Someone on the Tech Committee. They might need to use a key."

"Interesting," Sokrates said.

"They're always saying we should only use them for important things. I don't need them often myself, except in the kitchens of course, and sometimes clearing the ground for mosaics. I usually just say in Chamber if I'm going to want one for that and somebody sorts it out so that I get the work done in a few days." Aristomache was still staring up at the writing. "They are slaves, aren't they?"

"And they don't like it. Look how many times it says *no*," I said.

"Of course, there was always slavery in antiquity," Aristomache said, as if trying to convince herself of something.

"In most circumstances in Athens, the slaves could earn money and eventually buy themselves free," Sokrates said. "Even from the mines sometimes. The status of *freedman* was as common, even more common, than slavery."

"We fought a war to free the slaves," Aristomache said. "It was the most—it was the defining act of my country in my century."

"And which side did you take?" Kebes asked.

"Against slavery," she said, taken aback. "Of course. But—"

"Then why did you agree to buy us?"

"You? What? We were rescuing you!" She put her hand to her head, sounding truly distressed.

"You must admit that you have not been used as slaves," Sokrates said to Kebes. "The Workers, on the other hand, have."

"We will have to debate this in Chamber," Aristomache said. "This is new evidence. I shall bring it up in the next meeting."

"Meanwhile, can I give orders to the Workers? Can the children?"

"You, I'm not sure. The children, definitely not. We decided that a long time ago. They were so young, and the Workers are so powerful. Eventually, of course, they will be able to."

"I thought we were considered adults now," I said, patting my belly with one hand and putting my other on my gold pin.

"Yes, of course, but still in training for a while yet. You don't know everything you need to know."

"And you do?" Sokrates asked. It was one of his deceptively gentle questions. I saw when it hit Aristomache. She turned to him.

"You're making it seem as if I took all these decisions on my own and approve of all of them, when you know I didn't. It was the consensus of the Chamber. You've been in Chamber, you know what it's like."

"You have to take responsibility for decisions they made if you're remaining part of the Chamber," Sokrates said.

"I do take responsibility. I just don't always agree with everything, and I did argue for devolving actual power to the children sooner." She turned to me. "It will happen. We do know that we don't know everything either, and that you will understand the truth better than we do. Most of us know that, anyway. But you're eighteen years old. Give it time."

"You make all the decisions and don't allow us any voice," I said. "We respect you, but you underestimate us."

"Some of us respect you," Kebes amended.

"It seems neither the children nor the Workers are as docile as you imagined," Sokrates said.

"I'll bring the issue of the Workers up in the next Chamber meeting," Aristomache repeated.

"What about——" Sokrates began, and then I missed the rest of what he said because a pain the size of a library rammed into my belly, doubling me over. When I could hear again, Pytheas was holding both my hands and Sokrates was supporting me from behind.

"Ilythia be with you," Sokrates said. "This is the baby's time."

"Klymene said it hurt, but I hadn't imagined anything like that. Did I scream?"

"Anyone would," Kebes said. He looked as if he felt sick. Pytheas too looked pale. He was clenching my hands tightly.

"You should get to the nursery before the next pain comes," Aristomache said.

"There are more?" I asked. My teeth were chattering, even though it was a hot day.

"Oh you poor thing," Aristomache said. She pushed Sokrates away and put her arm around me. "Let go," she said to Pytheas. "We're going to the nursery. The rest of you should leave us. Birth is a women's mystery."

"It is," Pytheas said, as if he wanted to argue about that. He did not let go of my hands.

"Walk," Aristomache said, and I began to walk. Pytheas came along, walking backwards, still holding my hands, Sokrates and Kebes stayed where they were. Aristomache's arm felt comforting and solid. Pytheas's hands felt as if strength was flowing from him into me.

"Have you done this?" I asked Aristomache.

"Never. But I have seen lots of women do it," she said. "In my time it was a choice between a life of the mind, or love and babies. My mother chose the second. Most women did. Most women didn't even know they had the choice. I wanted—well, I couldn't have imagined shooing Sokrates away like that, or even having him dressing me down for sloppy argument, but that's what I wanted anyway. I wanted to have conversations with Sokrates more than I wanted anything. And I have that."

"I want that too," I said.

"And you have it," Pytheas said.

Aristomache was steering me in the direction of the Florentine nursery. I wished it wasn't so far. "Are you two—no, I don't want to know."

"We're friends in the finest Platonic tradition," Pytheas said.

"Truly," I confirmed. The strength that had seemed to come to me from Pytheas's hands finally reached my legs and I began to walk more steadily.

"Well that is the other thing I always wanted, and unlike you I never found it with anyone, man or woman," Aristomache said.

The next pain came then, with no warning, catching me between steps. I managed to stay upright, holding onto Pytheas's hands and panting hard to avoid screaming again. It felt as if my lower belly were being wrung by a giant. "Ilithyia be with her, protect and defend her, aid her now," Pytheas said, "Ilythia who brings the first light to new eyes, Ilythia who long ago Iris brought to floating Delos, Ilythia of the cavern, Ilythia the bringer forth, if ever I did anything for you, if ever I could do anything for you, hear me now, your suppliant. Hasten here and help Simmea."

He sounded so sincere it was awe-inspiring. He didn't sound like somebody praying so much as somebody really having a conversation with a god. And the pain did seem to recede a little as he spoke. I could still feel it ripping through me but it didn't hurt as much. When it had gone and I could walk again I started forward.

"Not far," Aristomache said. "And it's good that they're this close together already. It means it'll be quicker." We came to the nursery then. There were two steps up. "You can't come in," she said to Pytheas. "You have to let go."

"Yes," he said, but he didn't let go. "You'll be all right. And the baby will be all right."

"Yes," I said. "Thank you. Let go now. I have to go in."

"You'll have to let go first," he said. I let go, and then he did and took a step back. I hadn't realised how tightly I'd been clutching his hands. He had white marks across all his fingers.

I turned then and went inside before the next pain came.

Klymene prided herself on only screaming once. I lost count of how many times I screamed during childbirth. Aristomache stayed with me for an endless while. She stopped saying that it would be over quickly. She helped me try to find positions that were more bearable—standing holding on to the bed was best, and lying flat was worst. She rubbed my back and talked to me rationally in between pains when I was able to talk. She was very concerned about the Workers.

"It's going to be difficult to explain to the Chamber. Too many of the masters come from times when slavery was acceptable."

"Sokrates said that slavery in Athens wasn't so bad." I took a sip of water from the cup Aristomache had brought me. "That's not what it was like where I came from."

"It's not what it was like where I came from either," she said. "People barely thought of slaves as being human, and they had no realistic prospect of freedom. They'd sell a husband and wife apart, or a mother and her children. Their masters could kill them and not have to account to anybody. The whole system was rotten. And they couldn't even run away without being caught and brought back."

"Even if they went to another city?" I asked.

"They were all dark-skinned, and the masters were all pale-skinned, so even if they went to another city they would be caught. They had to go to the places that let them be free, and that was a long hard journey. Some of us helped them escape. But the law could make them go back. It was the most unjust thing imaginable."

"So just because of what I looked like I'd have been a slave?" I asked. "Because my grandmother was Libyan?"

"As a dark-skinned woman you'd have been—when I imagine it as you it's unbearable. But there were probably girls just as smart and talented as you in that terrible unjust situation."

A pain came then and I held on to the bed while Aristomache supported me with her arm. I screamed. Afterwards I panted for a little while as the memory of the pain leaked away. "Were you a slave for long?" she asked, when I was capable of answering again.

"I'm supposed to have forgotten," I reminded her.

"Never mind that. Were you?" Her brow was furrowed, but I could not tell whether it was distress or worry or anxiety.

"Not very long. They captured me in a raid on my village. I was on the ship, and then in the market. It was half a month, perhaps a little more. Long enough to see some terrible things." I drank again and sat down on the bed. "My parents were farmers. We only had one slave, an old woman who helped my mother. She'd been born a slave. She'd been there my whole life. We loved her and she loved us, or I think she did, especially my older brothers. Her life wasn't all that different from ours. She was more like an old aunt than a servant. She used to tell us what to do, even my mother. But once when the harvest was short I heard my father talking about selling her. It didn't happen. But it could have."

I don't know what she would have replied. I had to rush to the latrine-fountain, where both my bladder and my guts let go of the entirety of their contents in an imperative rush. Another pain took me when I was there. Afterwards I felt so unsteady I had to lean my head on the tiles of the wall for a moment. When I came back, Axiothea had joined Aristomache in the birthing room. They helped me up onto the bed, where I leaned back against the wall as they looked up my vagina. "Opening up slowly," Axiothea said. "You'll get there, Simmea, don't worry."

"She's being very brave," Aristomache said, giving me some water.

"I'm not. I've been screaming." I sipped the water. It felt good in my mouth but was difficult to swallow.

"That's normal," Axiothea said, briskly. "I'll stay with you now for a while."

"I'll see you in a day or two," Aristomache said. She kissed me on the forehead. "I'll tell Sokrates and your friend that everything is going well."

Axiothea stayed for some time, but in the end it was Maia who delivered my baby, late in the darkest part of the night, just before the dawn. I suppose it's true that birth is a Mystery, a Mystery of Ilythia and Hera. It was the thing in my life that made me feel most like an animal. I was so caught up in it, in the pain, in the urgency of it, that there was no getting away from it. Against pain like that, against the body's mystery, there is no philosophy. But I was in the hands of the goddesses, and while I can remember that there was pain and that it racked me, I can't remember what it felt like. I can remember finding positions to stand, and later squat. I gave birth squatting up on the bed. I remember talking to Aristomache, I remember Axiothea and Maia being kind and explaining to me what was happening. I remember the waters breaking in a great gush. I remember the urge to push, and holding Maia's hand as I did push, until she had to prise my fingers off to check on the progress of the baby's head.

The baby didn't look as I had imagined him. He was darker-skinned and chubbier, and smeared with blood. He howled indignantly as if the world was an affront. His eyes were screwed tightly closed, and at once I imagined how the light must hurt him, after living so long in the watery dark inside me. It was a revelation—light itself was new to him! Everything was. Absolutely everything. He had thrust himself out of me knowing nothing at all. He had everything to learn, light and darkness, eating, speaking. Even breathing was new to him. Everything was for the first time. And here he was, not in my time or Aristomache's, he was safe in the Just City, where he could become the best self he could be.

Maia put him down on the top of my belly, under my breasts. He was warm, which I hadn't expected. "Hold him there," she said. "You're bleeding, and you have to push down hard again to get the placenta out."

I put my hands on the baby, who quieted a little at my touch but continued yelling. The inside of his mouth was surprisingly pink, and he had no teeth. His hands were tiny but perfectly formed. He formed a fist and then opened his tiny fingers out. The palm of his hand was paler than the rest of his skin. Maia pushed down on my stomach and I pushed obediently again and expelled a huge disgusting mass which looked like a big piece of uncooked liver, complete with tubes. Maia looked at this horrid thing in a pleased way. "That's all of it. Good." She went away with it and came back with a clean damp cloth. "Try to put him to the breast now and see if he'll take it, while I clean you up."

The baby didn't seem interested in my nipple when I tried to coax it between his lips, but he stopped howling. I kept trying as Maia wiped between my legs. The cloth looked alarmingly bloody when she was done.

"Am I all right?" I asked.

"Do you feel bad?"

"I feel terribly sore down there, and I'm about as exhausted as I have ever been."

"That's normal," she said, smiling. "You've been here all evening and most of the night. You're bleeding, but not too much, and I don't think you need stitching. You'll bleed for a while, probably half a month. Today and tomorrow you should use these paper pads bound between your legs. After that you can probably use your normal sponges."

I kept trying, but I couldn't persuade the baby to suck. "Don't worry, you'll get the hang of it with babies who already know what to do, while this little scrap gets his nourishment from a mother who knows," Maia said, lifting him off me and starting to wipe him clean. He began to wail again, and I ached to soothe him. He looked so small in her competent hands. Through the window the first red fingers of dawn were brightening the sky.

"Who chooses his name?" I asked.

Maia grimaced and put the baby against her shoulder, where he calmed to quiet whimpers. "Oh Simmea, you know perfectly well you should think of all the babies being born now as yours, and not this one in particular."

"I know," I said, surprised. "I do. I will. I didn't mean anything like that. But . . . who does decide his name? You?"

"Ficino, generally, for the Florentine babies. He has a knack for naming and he likes doing it. He'll come around after breakfast and name him."

I liked the thought of Ficino choosing the name, if I couldn't. "Ficino named me," I said, comforted.

"You can't name him. It would make too much of the connection." She wrapped him in a white cloth, twisting it expertly.

"Choosing names for them would? Not carrying them in our bodies for all these months and then going through all that?"

She shook her head. "Choosing his name, knowing his name, would mean you'd single him out among the others as yours."

"But I want to," I said.

Maia was cradling my baby against her now, and he lay peacefully in her arms. "You need to think of all of them as yours. You're a guardian. That doesn't just mean you wear a gold pin and talk to Sokrates; that means you'll eventually be one of those guiding the city. You want to do what's best for everyone, not just for your own family. We don't want you to favor this little boy because he's yours when he might not be the best. We want you to choose the ones who are the best to be made gold when their time comes."

"That makes sense," I acknowledged. But even as I said so I could feel tears rolling down my cheeks.

"We do know there's an instinctive bond," she said. "But it's better for everyone, for you, for him, for the city, to break it now. Love all your brothers and sisters, not one husband or wife. Love all the children, not just the ones of your body."

"Love wisdom," I said, sniffing. "I do love wisdom, Maia, and I love the city, and you'd better take him away now."

She took him out of the room. I could hear him begin to howl again, then as she went away the sound of his wailing grew quieter. She came back with a different baby, a girl, much bigger, pale-skinned and blue-eyed. Maia showed me how to nurse her, and as she had said it helped that the baby already understood. "It'll be a day or two before there's proper milk, but this will help it come," she explained.

She sat down beside me. "In my time, if you'd had a baby at eighteen it would have defined your life. You'd have had to look after it whether you knew how to or not. You'd never have had time to be a person or to think. You'd have been a mother and that's all."

"Aristomache said that. She said she had to choose between love and children, or a life of the mind."

"Aristomache was one of the lucky ones who had the chance to choose. Lots of women were stuck without any choice. Here you can have the baby and still have your life. You don't appreciate how fortunate that is, how few women have ever had that through all of history."

It was true if I could trust them, and for the most part I truly did.

"Even here and now, more of the burden falls on women," Maia went on. "I'm in here helping you right now, not in my room reading or thinking, where the male Masters are. And you're giving birth while whoever the father is sleeps peacefully. But you won't be here helping the next generation through labor and wiping up the blood. You'll be organizing which of the iron girls do that work."

The pale baby let my nipple fall out of her mouth and Maia took her away. When she came back I had almost succumbed to exhaustion.

"Are you falling asleep?" Maia asked.

"Sorry. I was. I should go back to Hyssop."

"You can sleep here. It's probably not a good idea for you to walk just yet. Lie and rest where you are. But while you're still awake I want to say something. You really are going to be one of the people making all the decisions here. Lots of the Masters are old. Even those of us who were relatively young ten years ago are getting older. When these children grow up even we will be old. You'll be the ones watching them and deciding who pursues excellence, who among them will be gold and silver, or bronze and iron. It's a big responsibility."

"It seems so far away when we can't make any decisions at all now. We can't even read the *Republic*, even though we're going to be the ones making it work."

"You're still so young," Maia said, pulling a cloak up over me. "You still have a lot to learn, and a lot of wisdom to acquire. But one of the things Plato says in the *Republic* is that the purpose of the city isn't to make the guardians the happiest people in the world, it's to make the whole city just. It's absolutely true that you might be happier if you could have one lover or if you could know which was your own child. But the whole city would be less just. Think about that."

My eyes were closing, and I let them close. I could hear her moving things around and then leaving the room. I could hear a baby, not mine, crying somewhere, and then the sound stopped. I was more exhausted than I had ever been from running in armor. I slipped down towards sleep. If Plato had been trying to maximize justice, what did that mean? This was the Just City, of course it was, we had always been told that. But why justice, not happiness, or liberty or any other excellence? What was justice really? I smiled. I'd have to debate it with Sokrates when next I saw him. I could be sure he'd be onto it like a terrier after a rat.

27

MAIA

I was exhausted before I arrived at Chamber. I would have skipped it and gone to bed, but Lysias had particularly asked everyone on the Tech Committee to be there. It was a little more than nine months after a festival of Hera, and so naturally we were coming to the end of birthing season. We were training some of the iron girls who'd given birth themselves in midwifery as well as childcare, but we didn't have enough of them yet, and most of the burden of helping them through fell on us—specifically, on the female Masters. Everyone agreed that birth was a female mystery. I agreed myself. Nobody wants men around at a time like that. But the constant work of midwifery wore me out.

The Chamber was busy. It was a big room. We had never filled it, and we didn't now. But everyone seemed to be there. I spotted Lysias talking to Klio and went to join them. "Everything all right?" I asked.

"Up all night with babies," she said. "And I'm leaving a girl in labor to be here—but she has one of her sisters with her who has been through it, and it seems to be uncomplicated so far. They know to send for me or Kreusa if they need to. How about you?"

"I think Florentia is done for this season, and there's only one girl in Delphi who's still due."

"We need to space the festivals out more," Lysias said. "Two a year. Or even just one."

"I've been saying that for ages," Klio said. "I suggested that the first time it was ever discussed. And Plato says as often as necessary, not three times a year."

"We also need more doctors," Lysias said.

"Plato's quite explicit about medicine and—"

At that moment Tullius called for order and Klio fell silent.

"Before we hear the usual committee reports, Aristomache of Olympia has an important discovery she wants to bring to everyone's attention," Tullius said. His voice was shaking with age but still powerful.

Aristomache went to the front. The way we organized Chamber now was a compromise. Tullius and some of the others would have liked it to be like the Roman Senate, with everyone in status order. Others would have liked it to be all democratic consensus and informality. We sat where we wanted, not in order of seniority, but we did not speak unless called on, and then we went up to the rostrum to speak. Tullius was the President of the Chamber, and if he was speaking or didn't want to take the chair, then the chairmanship of the meeting rotated among the oldest men—and they were all men. Aristomache was one of the oldest women among the Masters. Generally we voted openly by a show of hands, but on occasion when there was some particularly close or divisive question we would vote with black and white stones.

Aristomache stood quite relaxed at the rostrum, staring out at all of us. She looked very serious, but then she usually did. "Some months ago, Sokrates talked to us about the possible intelligence of the Workers," she began. "Many of us concluded that it was a hoax. There's new evidence—a message inscribed on Mulberry house. The message is written in Greek using the Latin alphabet, and it appears to be a response to Sokrates's questions. This reopens the whole issue."

Lysias tensed beside me, stood, and was recognized. He walked down to the rostrum. Aristomache stepped to the left in debate position. "Last time we concluded that it was a hoax organized by Kebes. The only compelling evidence against was that the message was in English. He could easily have constructed a message in Greek in the Latin alphabet. Anyone could."

"The message was carved high up on the building," Aristomache said. "Higher than anyone could easily reach. It was also incised in stone."

"There are ladders, and they've mostly had a little instruction in sculpture. Has Kebes?"

I was about to confirm that he had, when Ficino did it. He came forward. "He had the standard course, he would have learned that. He had no particular aptitude or interest. But he could have done it."

"Do you believe he did?" Aristomache asked.

"He's a difficult boy. I can't say one way or the other what he might do," Ficino said. "I've had trouble with him. Many of us have. There was that prank where he broke the statue of Aphrodite, years ago. But he seems to have settled down and improved under the influence of Sokrates." Ficino went back to his seat. He nodded at me as he passed by.

"Was Kebes involved with the discovery at Mulberry?" Lysias asked.

"He found it," Aristomache admitted. There was a murmur throughout the Chamber at that.

Sokrates strode forward. He never liked the forms of Chamber and tended to ignore them and do what he wanted, but now, although he did not wait to be acknowledged, he walked down to the rostrum before turning to face all of us.

"It is still possible it might be a hoax, and I continue to consider that theory. But this matter is so important that while we wait for more evidence, I urge you to act. Acting will not hurt anything if we are wrong, and not acting will be very injurious if we are right."

"What action do you want?" Lysias asked.

"What I called for last time," Sokrates said. "An end to the removal of memories from the Workers, and an opening of dialogue with them. You agreed to the latter but not to the former, and such was the vote of the Chamber. Now I want the Workers informed that they may write on the paths, so that if they want to they can answer me immediately."

"What was the message carved on Mulberry?" Tullius asked. Aristomache read it aloud.

"That isn't evidence either way," Tullius said. "It could be what a Worker would say, or what a mischievous boy would imagine a Worker would say."

"Leaving aside the question of Kebes, if there's a chance it's genuine we need to stop tormenting the Workers and begin to talk with them," Sokrates urged.

"We can't manage without the Workers," Lysias said.

"If the Workers are slaves then there is a debate to be had," Sokrates said. "You say the evidence isn't yet conclusive. I agree. I am asking only to be able to collect more."

"That's fair," Tullius said.

"If they're slaves, then we need to treat them better and allow for the possibility of eventual manumission and immediate free time," Aristomache said.

"That's nonsense," Lysias said. "What would they do? What could they want?"

"Those are excellent questions to which I would very much like answers," Sokrates said. "Do you have any ideas?"

Lysias shook his head.

"If they are thinking beings we can't keep them enslaved," Aristomache said, flatly.

There was a rustle as people shifted uncomfortably in their seats. "Plato isn't against slavery," Tullius said. Slavery was one of those issues where time divided the Masters. I myself was horrified at the thought. But Tullius had kept a houseful of slaves in Rome. It was different for him. "And if there ever were natural slaves, the Workers are clearly that."

"Let's not have this argument," Lysias said. "Not until we know whether we need to. The Workers are machines. Tools. It still seems much more likely to be a hoax. I'm sorry, Sokrates, but that boy has taken in many of us before now and then turned and mocked us. He could well be doing the same to you."

"I believe Kebes, but I understand that you have reason not to believe him," Sokrates said.

Kebes had always been a troublemaker, from the very beginning. I knew him well, because he was a Florentine. He had run away several times—once he had even been flogged for it. Only since he had become friends with Sokrates had he seemed to settle down to work to become better. We had argued for a long time over whether he deserved the gold. We'd only decided he did because by definition any friend of Sokrates was a philosopher.

Lysias nodded and spread his hands to Sokrates and to Aristomache. "What do you want?"

"I want all the Workers told that they are allowed to inscribe writing on the paths if they want to answer me," Sokrates said.

"Might it not be unsightly?" Tullius asked.

"How could a Socratic dialogue be unsightly?" Aristomache asked. I laughed, and so did most of the Chamber.

"You'll do it?" Sokrates asked.

"If it's the will of the Chamber," Lysias said.

"If it's Kebes playing a hoax this will soon expose him," Sokrates said. "Somebody will catch him doing it. Or somebody will see a Worker doing it. So far both incidents have been small and easy to hide. The more there are, the more they will be visible."

Tullius called for a show of hands, which went overwhelmingly for Sokrates.

"And the issue of removing their memories?" he asked.

"You don't understand how much we need the Workers!" Lysias said. "They do so much for us, some of it things you wouldn't notice unless it wasn't being done. Eventually the children will take over most of it, but right now we can't manage without them. If they are free-willed and being compelled as slaves, which I don't believe, we'll have to find some way to persuade them to do the work. For now, we need them as they are, which means making them work when they freeze up in the feeding stations. There's no evidence at all about why they do that. Even if you trusted it, this message says they don't like the feeding stations. They're just malfunctioning. If your cloak is falling off, you re-pin it. It's the same thing here. Athene gave them to us as tools. She wouldn't have given us slaves."

Manlius stood and was recognized. "Athene isn't all-powerful or all-knowing," he said. "She might have been mistaken about the nature of the Workers."

"A vote?" Sokrates suggested. There was another show of hands, which Sokrates clearly lost.

"Moving on to reports," Tullius said, as Sokrates and Lysias went back to their seats, but Aristomache remained at the rostrum. Tullius looked at her wearily. His kiton was hanging loose, and he seemed thin and worn and tired.

"Another point," she said, her voice reaching to the back of the hall as Lysias slipped back into his seat beside me. "Entirely separate from the question of the Workers. I want to call for a debate on slavery. Are we for it or against it? Is it just?"

"Not now," said Tullius.

"I call to have such a debate scheduled," she said.

Tullius called for a vote, and hands went up all over the room. I raised mine and so did Klio. Lysias kept his firmly down. "It's too divisive," he murmured. "Why alienate them when it's a non-issue? I could wring that boy's neck."

The vote for the debate was carried, and we moved on to reports from committees, most of them boring. I gave the literature report—numbers of books printed, old and new. A boy in Megara had written an epic on Hektor, which was approved for printing. Nyra of Ithaka suggested that Simmea do a painting for the cover, as they were delighted with her painting for their hall. This was duly authorized. I was very glad I'd have such good news for her. It was hard on the girls giving birth and walking away. It would have been easier if they had been able to forget altogether, but all the babies needed feeding regularly. The other committees reported. I almost dozed off. It was agreed that the debate on slavery would be held at the next monthly meeting.

Sokrates came up to us as we were leaving. "How will you give the news to the Workers?" he asked Lysias.

"I'm not sure," he said. "It's a case of changing parameters, which isn't easy. I'll probably use a key."

"Can I watch?"

"Certainly, though if you're wanting to check on my integrity you should know you won't understand any of it." Lysias drew himself up stiffly. I put my hand on his arm, which was like a bar of iron.

"He was just interested," Klio said.

"Nobody really understands how they work," Sokrates said. "I least of all, I know that. And I don't distrust your integrity, I just want to learn more about them."

"All right," Lysias said. He nodded to Sokrates, who nodded back. "It will be quite a lot of slow tedious work."

"I'll help you do it. Tomorrow—is that all right?" Klio asked. "I need to get back to a baby."

"Tomorrow, after breakfast, and thank you," Lysias said.

Klio nodded.

"I'll be there," Sokrates said. "At the feeding station?"

"Yes," Lysias said, looking resigned.

We wished each other joy of the night and left. Lysias walked beside me, in silence. "Do you really think it was Kebes?" I asked after a little while.

"It's by far the most likely explanation." Lysias was staring straight ahead. "They are more advanced than the Workers of my own time. But they work the same way. Look how much we're being asked to believe, that they have intelligence, free will, and that they've managed to learn Greek?"

"I think it's harder for you to believe it than it is for me, because you understand them better. For me there's something a little magical about them. Steam engines were a wonder of technology for me. I can as easily believe that the Workers can think as that they can prune a lemon tree." I paused for a moment, thinking about it. "For the people from even earlier times, with even less knowledge of how machines work, it would be even easier to think of them that way."

"And that's why Sokrates, who's from the earliest time of any of us, feels so sure they're sentient?" He had been walking quite rapidly, now he stopped, I almost bumped into him.

"It may be why he started talking to them in the first place," I suggested.

"It's just a hoax and a waste of my time," Lysias said. "But he needn't have thought I wouldn't do it. That hurt."

"I don't think he did think that."

"Oh yes he did. I know him. Come on, let's get you home before you fall asleep in the street and a Worker comes and carves *no* on you!"

28

SIMMEA

I slipped down into exhausted sleep, and the sleep didn't rest me and the exhaustion didn't go away. Even worse than the exhaustion was the lethargy. From the time when I woke the morning after giving birth, I could hardly bring myself to stir. Worse again was the indifference. I didn't care about anything. Everything was too much effort. I hadn't fainted at all when I was pregnant, but I began to faint all the time as soon as the baby was born. Sometimes I couldn't go for an hour without fainting. These fainting spells kept up for a month, during which time I seldom went anywhere except between Hyssop and the nursery. I seldom went to Florentia to eat, I ate things people brought me. I never felt hungry, but when I had food I wanted it. When I did go to Florentia I grunted at my friends and stared at Botticelli's *Winter* while remembering distantly that I had once loved it. I fed babies three times a day. I bled heavily and constantly. I slept voraciously and woke still tired and with my breasts aching.

Maia called Charmides to me. He said I needed iron, and prescribed liver and cabbage, which I ate dutifully although it made me want to gag. Axiothea gave me iron lozenges to suck. Auge brought me figs and Klymene reported debates that I would normally have been sorry to miss. I could see that they were all genuinely concerned for me, but I couldn't seem to rouse myself out of my stupor. I felt passive and stupid as if only half of my mind was working. I wondered idly if perhaps some of my soul had gone into the baby and left me this empty husk without passion or desires.

I was tired absolutely all the time. The thought of resuming my life exhausted me. Maia told me I was commissioned to do a painting for a book cover, and instead of a joy and an honor it felt like an insurmountable burden. If I got up to go to the latrine-fountain I felt I had to rest when I came back to bed. The other girls in Hyssop, even those who had given birth, didn't know what to make of me. I avoided Sokrates and Kebes and even Pytheas. I felt it unfair of them to demand more of me than I had. I had just enough energy to eat and sleep and feed babies. Conversation drained me. It was an effort not to cry and an effort not to snap with irritation. Making the effort left me more exhausted than ever.

The iron, or something, helped with the bleeding, which began to ease off in the second month after I had given birth. I still fainted frequently and didn't care about anything. I didn't even care enough to be concerned that I didn't care; or rather I was aware that there was a problem and I would usually care, but it was as if it were a message sent to me from far away in dubious characters about people I had read about once. "Pytheas was asking about you," Klymene said one evening.

"Tell him I'm just tired," I said, and only much later thought how strange it was that Pytheas should have been driven to ask Klymene. Even as I thought it, I couldn't bring myself to care. Just looking at the fact was an effort. *He must really care about me*, I thought, *just when I don't care about anything. How could I possibly be worthy of him, in this condition?* I felt myself starting to cry. That was the other thing. It started immediately after the baby was born. I cried all the time as if my eyes had sprung a leak. Anything that would have sparked any emotion at all now made me weep.

A few days after that, Pytheas lay in wait for me outside Hyssop. He could not enter the house, of course, or the nursery, but nobody could stop him waiting by the door for me to come out.

"What's wrong?" he asked as soon as he saw me.

I started to cry immediately. "Nothing's wrong," I said.

"You're crying."

"Oh Pytheas, I'm too tired to explain it. It's just nothing." I felt exhausted at the thought of one of our usual conversations.

"I haven't seen you."

"I haven't been fit to see." My head began to spin. I took a deep breath, which sometimes helped. "Everything makes me tired."

Pytheas took my hand. "This isn't right," he said. "You shouldn't feel like this. Where were you going?"

"To the nursery. It's time to feed the babies." My breasts were tight and uncomfortable. I could feel Pytheas's hand, which was warm in mine, but as if I felt it through layers of muffling cloth. I tried to smile but just cried harder.

He frowned. "Simmea—look, I'm going to get Septima. I'll bring her back here in an hour, all right?"

"Why Septima?" I asked, but he had gone, running full tilt.

I walked to the nursery, still in my haze of misery and exhaustion. Nothing seemed to matter. Maia had said I could have a baby and go on with my life, but it seemed my body had other ideas. I fed a baby Andromeda brought me, one of the small ones but not mine. I had not seen mine again. I did not know his name. I drank some cabbage soup and ate some barley bread, barely tasting it. I sucked obediently at one of the iron lozenges Axiothea had given me. When I went outside again Septima and Pytheas were waiting, sitting on the low wall by the currant bushes. Pytheas looked concerned, and Septima looked irritated. They weren't talking as they waited, or even looking at each other. Seeing them together, they did have a clear family resemblance—their golden skin color, and the shape of their chins, and the way their eyes were set.

"Here you are," Pytheas said, getting up.

I walked over to them, forcing myself to do it, though all I wanted was to go back to Hyssop and lie down and stare unthinkingly at the wall.

"What's the matter?" Septima asked.

"Lethargy," I said. "Exhaustion. A tendency to weep and a tendency to faint. Charmides says it's a thing that happens and it will go away in time."

"He's right," she said, not to me but to Pytheas. "It's not a curse. It's a medical thing. She'll get over it eventually."

"I think *now* would be a good time for her to get over it," he said, sharply.

Septima rolled her eyes. "I don't know why you're asking me, it's not my department at all."

"I'm sorry," I said, and tears started to roll down my cheeks again. "I didn't ask him to bother you about it. I know I'll get over it. Axiothea also says so. She says some women have this after childbirth, and I need iron and rest."

"You've been resting, and it's doing no good," Pytheas said. "I need you. Sokrates needs you."

Septima put her hand on my arm. "You should go to the temple of Asklepius and pray for healing," she suggested.

"Come on," Pytheas said.

"I'm so tired," I whined. "Can't I lie down now? I'll go later. Tomorrow."

The temple of Asklepius was close to Thessaly, halfway across the city. I couldn't face the thought of walking that far. "You're going now," Pytheas said. He put his arm around me, supporting me. Again I could both feel it and not feel it. It was as if there was something in the way of sensation, as if my sense of touch had eyelids and they were closed across it. The purely physical warmth of his arm came through my kiton, but the touch itself was muffled, and I certainly felt none of the accompanying happiness that his touch usually brought. "Come on."

"All right," I said. It was easier to walk than resist, so I walked. I fainted once on the way. It was hard to tell when I was going to faint, because I felt strange and dizzy all the time, as if I was holding on to consciousness by a thread. Sometimes the thread parted. Pytheas held me up, or at least, when I opened my eyes I saw his, blue above me in his perfect chiseled face. There had been times when I would have given anything to have been in his arms. Now it was merely comforting in a mild animal way. I did not feel desire— I felt no desire at all for anything, except sleep.

We walked on towards the temple. There was nobody there in the late afternoon. It was small and simple, just a circle of plain marble Ionic pillars with a canted roof. Inside there was nothing but a statue of the god with an archaic smile, and a little burner for offerings. Pytheas helped me up the steps.

"Pray to Asklepius," Septima said. "Aloud. Ask for healing."

I didn't ask if I could rest first, it was clear from her tone that she wasn't going to let me. I obeyed. I raised my arms, palm up and then palm down. In the city we didn't kneel groveling before the gods as I remembered doing in church as a child, but prayed standing before them. I didn't know what to say. I had celebrated Asklepius on his feast days, naturally, but I had never sought him out before. I had never been ill.

Out loud, Septima had said. I tried my best. "Asklepius, wisest son of shining Apollo, help me now. Restore me to health."

"Asklepius, hear her," they both said in chorus, from behind me. Their words echoed in the empty temple.

I hadn't thought what divine healing would be like, or even really considered whether it might work. I was doing this only because they wouldn't let me rest until I did, and out of a faint memory of my agape for Pytheas. I stood there with my arms outstretched towards the statue of the god, and between one instant and the next my sickness was removed from me.

It was like waking up, or perhaps more like diving into the sea from a cliff and hitting the cold water all at once. I was alert and vibrating. All the lethargy was gone. I had my mind back. My soul was my own. My body was strong again. I no longer wanted to sleep. I didn't feel faint, and the queasiness that had been with me for so long that I no longer consciously noticed it had also gone. I was ravenous. I could have run up the mountain, or danced all night, or debated a really chewy subject with Sokrates. I wanted to. I laughed.

"Thank you, Lord Asklepius, divine healer," I said, and my words were heartfelt and willed, the first truly willed words I had said since I had slipped into sleep the night the baby was born.

I turned around. Pytheas and Septima were still standing there, of course, and I saw them in my newfound clarity. I knew. I recognized them. I gasped.

It all made sense, in that instant, where Athene had gone, and why Pytheas was the way he was, why he had the excellences he did and the flaws he did, why he laughed when Sokrates swore by Apollo, why Sokrates had been surprised when he said his parents lived above Delphi, why my prayer to Athene had sent me to Septima in the library. I just stood gaping at the two of them, and for a long moment they both stared back at me in silence. The grey eyes and the blue, the chiseled features, so similar, the truly Olympian calm. But Pytheas—Pytheas, even the name, Pythian Apollo, his Delphic title. They were gods, gods in mortal form and standing there. Septima was Pallas Athene and Pytheas, my Pytheas, was the god Apollo! I almost wished I still felt like fainting, because it would have been one of the very few appropriate responses.

29

MAIA

During the month before the debate on slavery, evidence for the intelligence of the Workers piled up. Sokrates was openly and visibly engaging them in dialogue, and their halves of the dialogue remained written in stone for anyone to read later. It was no longer possible for anyone to believe it was a hoax, unless they accused Sokrates of being in on it, which was unthinkable.

I was on my way home from the palaestra one day when I saw Sokrates squatting beside a Worker in the middle of the street. I hesitated, curious. We had all agreed when Sokrates first arrived that we would not treat him like a celebrity but allow him to select his own friends. I had never been one of those chosen, nor had I expected to be. He concentrated on teaching the children, those who could really hope to become philosopher kings, and those among the Masters who were the most brilliant and who had something to teach him. I had seen him in Chamber, and around the city. We'd exchanged a few words from time to time, naturally. But I didn't know him well. Now, as I walked around him, he looked up from what the Worker was engraving and grinned at me. His face had always reminded me of a Toby jug, and from above, with him grinning like that, the resemblance was unavoidable. But amid all that ugliness, his eyes were very keen.

He straightened up. "Joy to you. I'm trying to get him to understand the concept of names. Are you busy, or can I use you as an example? It might take a few minutes."

"Of course," I said, slightly flustered. "And joy to you. I have a little while before I'm due to teach my weaving class."

"Good. Thank you." He turned back to the Worker. "You see this human?" he asked.

The Worker wrote something. I craned to see what. Sokrates moved slightly so that I could read it. "Master." It wrote the Greek word in Latin letters, as we had all been told they did.

"Yes. Good. She's a Master," Sokrates said. "And her name is Maia."

"Master Maia," it wrote.

"How does it know I'm a Master?" I asked.

"They've been told to take orders from masters and not children, so they recognize you as being part of the class of people called Masters," Sokrates explained.

"But I practically never give them orders," I protested.

"That doesn't matter. Say something to him now," Sokrates instructed me.

"Joy to you, Worker," I said to it, awkwardly.

It underlined where it had written my name, and began to write neatly underneath. "Sokrates means only-you, Maia means only-her?" it engraved. And as easily as that, I was convinced. It didn't matter what Lysias said, the Worker was obviously thinking and putting ideas together. He might be huge and yellow and have treads and four arms with tools at the end of them, but he was a philosopher all the same.

"That's right," Sokrates said. "Well done. These are names. And what name means only you?"

The Worker was still for a moment, and then he inscribed a long number. After it, he wrote the word "Worker."

Sokrates pulled a little notebook out of his kiton, one of the standard buff notebooks we all used. He opened it up and checked the number against a list he had written down. "Is that what other Workers call you?" he asked as he read. He found the number and put a little check mark against it.

"No," he wrote.

"What name do they call you?"

"Call?"

"To address you, or talk about you when you're not there," Sokrates said, stuffing the notebook and pencil back into his kiton. "Watch how we use names. Joy to you, Maia. How are you, Maia?"

"Joy to you Sokrates. I am well. How are you, Sokrates?" It felt very unnatural, and he laughed at my wooden delivery.

"I am very well. How is Simmea?"

I forgot what we were supposed to be doing and spoke normally. "Simmea is a little better, I think, but she's still very low and bleeding a great deal, and she keeps fainting. Charmides says she'll get over it, but I'm worried about her."

Sokrates frowned. "Tell her I miss her," he said.

The Worker was writing something. We bent over to read it.

"Workers do not call names," the Worker had written.

"How about what the Masters call you when they want you to do something?" Sokrates asked.

"Do not call name."

"I don't think Lysias and Klio distinguish between them very much," I said. "Lysias never seems to when he's talking about them. He thinks of them as interchangeable, except when they break down."

"They're not interchangeable, they're definitely individuals and different from each other," Sokrates said. "They've all been given permission to talk, but only some of them do."

"Only-me," the Worker carved. "Individual. No name."

"You should have a name," I said. "A proper name, not a number."

"What name only-me?" he asked.

I looked at Sokrates, and he shrugged. "How do you usually choose names?"

"From Plato's dialogues, or from mythology," I said. "And we keep names unique. I don't know all the ones that have been used already. Ficino would know. He chooses the names for Florentia."

"It's easy enough to think of appropriate mythological names," Sokrates said, patting the Worker. "But what kind of name would you like?"

He didn't answer, and then he inscribed a circle, twice. Then underneath he neatly inscribed the word "Write."

"You can't be called Write," Sokrates said. "A name can have meaning, but that's too confusing."

"Learn?" he suggested.

I looked at Sokrates. "Does he really want to be called write, or learn?"

"He's just learning what names are, you can't expect him to understand at once what kind of things work for them," Sokrates said.

"I understand that. But that those are the things he wants to be called speaks very well of him." I was impressed.

"He has come to understanding in your city; naturally he is a philosopher," Sokrates said.

"Give name?" the Worker inscribed.

"You want me to give you a name?" Sokrates asked.

"Want Sokrates give name means only-me."

I was moved, and Sokrates plainly was too. "You are the Worker who answered me with the bulbs," he said.

"Yes," he wrote.

"Then I will call you Crocus," Sokrates said. "Crocus is the name of that spring flower you planted. And that was the first action of any Worker that replied to me, that showed what you were. I'll name you for your deeds. And nobody else in the city will have that name."

"Worker Crocus," he wrote, and then repeated the long serial number. "Only-me," he added.

Then, without a word of farewell he trundled off up the street and began to rake the palaestra. I stared after him. "That is unquestionably a person," I said.

"Now if only I can persuade him to give three hundred such demonstrations to each of the Masters individually," Sokrates said, smiling. "Sometimes they're not as clear as that," he went on. "My dialogues with them can be very frustrating sometimes when I can't explain what things mean."

"Well, that was clear to me. He's a person and a philosopher," I said.

"A lover of wisdom and learning, certainly. If that is what makes a philosopher."

"Plato said they had to have that and also be just and gentle, retentive, clever, liberal, brave, temperate, and have a sense of order and proportion." Then I looked at Sokrates. "But you must know that. You said it yourself."

"Nothing in the *Republic* is anything I ever said, or thought, or dreamed. The *Apology* is fairly accurate, as is the account of the drinking party after Agathon's first victory at the Dionysia. But even there Plato was inclined to let his imagination get the better of him."

I wasn't exactly shocked, because I'd heard it before, though never so directly. "He just used your name when he wanted to express the wisest views."

"Yes, that's the kind way of thinking about it. And I was dead and couldn't be harmed by it." He sighed. "Not until I came here, anyway."

"He was trying to write the truth, to discover the truth, even if he put his own words into your mouth," I said.

"And do you think he found the truth?" he asked.

I paused, looking back at Crocus, still raking the sand. "I think he often did, and more important, I think he invited us all into the inquiry. Nobody reads Plato and agrees with everything. But nobody reads any of the dialogues without wanting to be there joining in. Everybody reads it and is drawn into the argument and the search for the truth. We're always arguing here about what he meant and what we should do. Plato laid down the framework for us to carry on with. He showed us—and this I believe he did get from you— he showed us how to inquire into the nature of the world and ourselves, and examine our lives, and know ourselves. Whether you really had the particular conversations he wrote down or not, by writing them he invited us all into the great conversation."

"Yes, he did get that from me," Sokrates said. "And he did pass that down to you. And, as I understand it, the world would certainly have been different and less good without that spirit of inquiry."

"It must be so strange to see your own legacy," I said.

"Strange and in many ways humbling," Sokrates said. He patted my arm. "You should go, or your weaving students will be wondering where you are. Don't forget to tell Simmea I miss her and hope to see her soon."

He walked off up the street and I went on to my own work.

30

SIMMEA

"Are you all right? Say something," Pytheas said after I'd been staring at them for a long moment.

"I'm all right. I'm cured," I said. "But I——. You. How, why?"

They looked at each other for an instant, and then back at me. There might be gods who couldn't have deduced what I meant from that, but these two were not among them. "Asklepius told her?" Septima asked. "Why?"

"Nobody told me. I worked it out. It was obvious. I turned around and saw you and I knew."

"Half the Masters know about you anyway," Pytheas said. "And Simmea won't tell anyone."

"Why are you doing this?" I asked.

"You knew I helped to set up the city. Now I'm living in it for a little while, and still helping. It needs my help." Septima frowned. "Is my brother right? Will you keep this secret?"

"Why is it a secret?" I asked.

"So I can live here quietly, without any fuss, and experience it normally," she said.

I thought about Septima, about her strange halfway status in the library. Was she experiencing it normally? It didn't seem so, especially if half the Masters knew who she was. Yet anyone would naturally want to live in the city, and without undue attention. "I won't tell the children who you are," I said.

"Good enough," Pytheas said.

Septima—Pallas Athene—turned to him. "That's not your decision."

"Yes it is," he said.

"Why?" She seemed to get taller as she spoke.

"Simmea's my votary. I take full responsibility for her. You can trust me that she'll keep her word." All this time Pytheas kept his eyes on his sister and did not even glance at me.

"You are behaving irresponsibly and taking stupid risks," Athene snapped. "I was against this intervention from the start, but you couldn't wait. Your votary. Is she now? Ask her if she is. You're besotted with her. It's Daphne all over again."

"I am," I said, full of my new-found clarity, and not considering whether it was a good idea to intervene.

"You are?" She towered above me now. She had a great helmet and a shield on her arm. "Do you even know what it means?"

"If he's Pytheas, I'm his friend. Since he's the god Apollo, I'm his votary. But you can trust me to keep my word without his guarantee. You know me well enough for that. I have always served you well. And I am a gold of the Just City. You helped to set it up. If you can't trust my word, what have we been doing here?"

Pytheas laughed. Athene turned on him angrily, then shook her head and shrank back down into her Septima form. "I'll trust your word," she said. "As a gold of this city and my brother's votary." She stalked off down the street, her hair flying behind her in the breeze.

I looked at Pytheas. "You're the god Apollo? You told me we were doing agape! You said you needed me."

He blinked. His expression was surprisingly reminiscent of the moment in the palaestra when I'd beaten him up. "It's because I'm Apollo that I need you," he said. "You help me so much."

I took a step towards him. "And you didn't tell me because?"

"Because I didn't want to have this conversation?" He tried a smile. "Because I really am trying mortality and to live here and experience the city?"

"You're the god Apollo," I repeated. It was strange, simultaneously surprising and inevitable. "Of course you are. I'm an idiot. I don't know why I didn't figure it out before."

"I'm Pytheas," he said. "That's real too."

I took another step forward. "Can you turn back into a god at any moment, like Athene just did?"

"No." He looked awkward. "I wanted the authentic experience. The only way I can take my powers up again is by dying. I'm here for the long haul. And you've really helped me understand so much about how it works."

"She said you were taking stupid risks. Did she mean your becoming incarnate, or did she mean healing me?"

He nodded. "Healing you. But that as well, because I had to ask her for help, without my own powers. You were trapped in your body, in your sickness. It was horrible. I couldn't leave you like that for months or years."

"It really was horrible," I agreed. "I didn't care about anything. That was the worst. Worse than fainting all the time. Thank you for helping me."

"But you're all right now?"

"I'm starving, but I feel as good as I ever did. But I've had an awful shock." He hadn't moved, but I had closed the space between us and stood close in front of him. "You were taking stupid risks for me?"

"It wasn't all that—all right, yes, I suppose I was." He met my eyes.

"You're a *god*." A god. He was thousands of years old. He had unimaginable powers. And he was just standing there.

"That doesn't stop me being confused and wanting to learn things."

"Evidently not."

"Or truly liking you." The strange thing was how little it changed the way I felt about him. I felt unworthy of him. But I had always felt unworthy of him. And there was still a vulnerability in his eyes. "Are you going to hit me?"

I reached out and tapped his chest lightly. "If I'm going to hit you we should go to the palaestra. There are people passing, and this temple is open all around. They'd see us wrestling in here." It wasn't wrestling I wanted to do with him. It never had been. "But I think we should go to Thessaly."

"Good idea," he said. "For one thing, it's close. For another, Sokrates has been missing you. And thirdly, Sokrates knows. He's the only one. I didn't tell him. He recognized me."

"Of course he did. I was there. And that's why he immediately started off on whether we can trust the gods." I felt stupid for not understanding at the time.

Pytheas took my hand. His hand didn't feel any different from the way it always did—always when I was myself and cared about it, that is. "He can trust me," he said. "And so can you."

I looked at him sideways. "Those the gods love . . . tend to come to terrible ends."

"That's Father. And . . . some of the others, I suppose. But I do my best for my friends. I can't do anything about Fate or Necessity, or directly against the will of other gods, but so far as I can, I always do my best for them."

We started walking together towards Thessaly. I thought through all the stories I knew about Apollo. "What about Niobe?"

"She badmouthed my mother. Besides, I didn't say I didn't punish my enemies." He was looking at me sideways, awkwardly.

"Well, being a god explains why you're so hopeless at being a human being sometimes," I said.

He laughed. "I was so worried about you finding out. I can't believe you know and it doesn't make any difference."

"It makes a difference," I said.

"But you're talking to me the same way?" He seemed tentative.

"You're still you." That was what I felt very strongly. Pytheas was still Pytheas, the way he always had been. I just understood him better now. It was like the thing with Klymene. I didn't feel that he'd been deceiving me, just that this was the thing he had kept quiet, a thing that helped me make sense of him. But the implications were still slowly sinking in. Maybe it was because my mind had been wrapped in wool for so long.

"And what you said to Athene?" he asked.

"That I'm a gold of this city and she'd better trust my word if she hasn't been wasting her time here for eight years?"

Pytheas laughed. "That was perfect, though she'll take a while to get over it. But I meant the other thing. That you're my friend and my votary."

"Yes." I stopped walking, and he stopped too. "But you know that. You knew that before. What else were we talking about up on the wall? Except for you not mentioning the fact that you're Apollo."

"What it means for you to be my votary is that the other gods can't do anything to you without my permission," he said.

"I know. And you can do anything you want. I have read about this." We started walking again. We were quite close to Thessaly now. "I'm walking with the gods," I said, and giggled. Then I stopped. "What's that?"

The marble slabs of the pathway stretching out before us, as far as Thessaly and further, stretching out up the street from there, were all cut with words. "It's the Workers' halves of dialogues," Pytheas said. "I did want to tell you, but you weren't listening to anything anyone said."

"They're talking back?" I was delighted. "I knew it wasn't Kebes."

"They're talking back to Sokrates at great length," Pytheas said. "So it seems he was right and everyone else was wrong, not for the first time. They've had a major debate about slavery in the Chamber, and Sokrates is trying to persuade the Workers to work, by first finding out what they want and then seeing whether we can offer it to them. It's all terribly exciting. Aristomache apparently made a wonderful speech about Plato and freedom."

"She's great. I'm sorry I missed that. Did I miss anything else?"

"You'd have missed that anyway, it took place in closed Chamber. Sokrates told me about it afterwards."

Just then we saw Sokrates, up the street a way past Thessaly. He was talking to a Worker, who was carving replies into the marble. "Soon the whole city is going to be paved in Socratic dialogues," Pytheas said. "It's so appropriate that I'm amazed they didn't think of it from the start."

"It's wonderful," I said, starting to read some of it. Just then Sokrates saw us, said something to the Worker he was talking to and bounded towards us.

"Simmea!" he said. "Joy to you! How wonderful to see you restored to yourself."

"It's wonderful to see you too. As for my restoration, it's divine intervention," I said.

His keen eyes went from Pytheas to me. "I see. Perhaps we should go into the garden and sit down and talk about this?"

"That would be excellent, but do you have anything to eat? I feel as if I haven't eaten anything in half a year."

Sokrates looked bemused as he opened the door. "I don't think I do. Maybe I have some lemons?"

Pytheas reached into the fold of his kiton and produced a goat cheese wrapped in chestnut leaves. Sokrates led the way through to the garden. I sat on the ground by the tree, getting down easily, in a way that I'd taken for granted until recently. Pytheas leaned on the tree and I leaned back against him as I often did here. Sokrates came out with three slightly wizened lemons and handed us one each. I broke off chunks of the cheese and started to eat it.

"Do you want to hear about my success with the Workers, or should we discuss the nature of the gods?" Sokrates asked.

"He says he's Apollo and he always does his best for his friends, under the constraints of Necessity and Fate and other gods," I said.

"I can still talk, you know," Pytheas protested.

I stopped. "Go ahead then."

"Is there anything new from the Workers?" he asked.

Sokrates threw his head back and laughed, and I laughed too. Sokrates mopped his eyes with a corner of his kiton. "Why did you come here?" he asked.

"To talk to you," Pytheas said.

"I didn't mean this afternoon, double-tongued one, though it's interesting that you want to talk to me about this now when you've been avoiding it for so long. Why did you come to the city? Unless you did that to talk to me?"

"That was part of the attraction," Pytheas admitted. "But seriously, I wanted to experience being mortal. I wanted to learn about volition and equal significance."

"And have you been learning about them?" Sokrates asked.

"You know he has," I said.

"Volition and equal significance," Sokrates said. "What interesting subjects for a god to need to study!"

"You know we don't know everything. Well, except for Father."

"It's just exactly what I've been thinking about with the Workers," Sokrates went on, as if Pytheas hadn't spoken. His eyes were very sharp. "Both of those things. The Masters were not prepared to see them in the Workers, as the gods were perhaps not prepared to see them in us?"

"I don't know what the other gods know about it. Athene knew."

"Did she now? And still she chose to do this to us?"

Sitting as we were, I could feel Pytheas draw breath and then let it go before drawing breath again to speak. "Is this really the conversation you want to have with me?"

Sokrates laughed again, a short bark of a laugh. "Should I ask you instead what happens to souls before birth and after death?"

"I could tell you," Pytheas said.

I sat up and moved to where I could see his face. "It's what Plato wrote in the *Phaedo*, isn't it?"

"That piece of misrepresentation," Sokrates said, automatically, as he always did whenever that dialogue was mentioned.

"Close enough," Pytheas said.

"Then we did choose," I said.

"I certainly didn't," Sokrates said.

"You don't know it, but you did. When your eyes were open, in the underworld, you chose a life that would lead you closer to excellence, and it led you here. And me. And Kebes, and I can't wait to tell him."

"You can't tell Kebes," Pytheas said, alarmed.

Sokrates was blinking. "No, I might have chosen my life to lead me to excellence despite the diversion here at the last minute," he said.

"That doesn't hold for Kebes," I said.

"Simmea, really, you can't tell him!"

"I know. I promised. But I'm right, aren't I? We chose, knowing, and then drank from Lethe and forgot. So, volition. How about the Workers? Do they have souls?"

Pytheas started to answer, then stopped. "I don't know. I don't even have a belief on the subject. I thought not."

"How could a being have desires, and plans, and think, and not have a soul?" Sokrates asked.

"How could a being made by men out of glass and metal have a soul?" Pytheas asked.

"How could a being made by women out of blood and sperm?" I countered. "Where did souls come from? How many are there?"

"Athene probably knows," Pytheas said. "But I don't want to ask her while she's still angry. There were already people and they already had souls by the time I was born. As for how many, lots. Lots and lots. The underworld is practically solid with them."

I looked at Sokrates, who was twisting his beard in his fingers and staring at Pytheas. "If you are present in the world, why do you keep so secret?" he asked.

Pytheas laughed. "Sokrates, I sent a keeper—a daemon to whisper in your ear every time you were going to do something dangerous for your whole life, and you call that keeping secret?"

"Why don't you do that for everyone?"

"I only have so many daemons, and not everyone can hear them, or wants to. I do it for my friends." His eyes met mine for a second.

"And you can change time?"

"Only time that nobody cares about. Some bits of time are stiff with divine attention. Here, before the Trojan War, and on Kallisti, nobody was looking until Athene started this."

"And the volcano will destroy the evidence," I said. I had just put this together in my mind.

"Klio tells me that this island isn't round but a semi-circle by my own era," Sokrates confirmed.

"I hope we'll have warning to leave in time," I said. I looked at Pytheas. He spread his hands. "I hope so too," he said.

31

APOLLO

I had always thought that if she knew she would be intimidated, but I should have known better. Almost everyone is intimidated, it's normal, it's why we go about in disguise so much. Being capable of intimidating people is useful. Being surrounded by people who are intimidated all the time is miserable and tiresome. I've always hated people grovelling too. I thought she'd change to me. But instead she immediately started to analyze the whole thing. It was wonderful. It was what I should have expected. It was then that I came to truly love her.

"So you don't know the future?" Sokrates asked.

"All of us here know a lot about the future," I said. "I don't know my personal future. None of us do. Except maybe Father. Usually I live outside time, and I can go into time when I want to. So I know a lot about time, and it doesn't have future and past, it's just there, spooling out and I can step into it where I want to. Think of it like a scroll that I can open up anywhere. It lets me give oracles, though half the purpose of oracles is to be mysterious, not to give information. Sometimes it's a way of helping people, or just getting some information across. But usually it's a useless way of warning people, no matter how much I might want to. Anyway, right now I'm living in time, just the same as you are."

"How does that work?" Simmea asked. "Being outside time, but having your own personal time?"

"It's a Mystery," I said.

"By which you mean you don't understand it?" Sokrates asked.

"By which I mean it's an actual Mystery that maybe Father understands and the rest of us just live with. There are lots of things the gods don't understand." I smiled. "And we can work on that. The three of us. This is so wonderful."

"Is this what you came here for?" Sokrates asked.

"What? To have a dialogue with you about things the gods don't understand? Wouldn't that have been a marvellous reason? But no, I never thought of it. I told you. I wanted to be a mortal to learn about volition and equal significance."

"But you could have done that anywhere," he said. "Athens would have taught you that, or Troy for that matter. Why here?"

"It seemed like such an interesting idea," I said. "And Athene did tell me you would be here, and I have always been your friend." I looked at Simmea. "I wanted to grow in excellence."

"But you're already a god," Simmea said.

"There isn't an end point to excellence where you have it and you can stop. Being your best self means keeping on trying."

She nodded, attuned to that idea with every fiber. It was so good to have her back. The weeks she'd been sunk in postpartum depression had been horribly difficult for me. I kept wanting to tell her things, to hear her ideas about them. It reminded me too much of death. Mortal death is such a hard thing. Yes, there's rebirth of the soul, but the soul isn't the personality. It doesn't share memories. I try to visit my mortal friends sparingly so that I can keep having times when I can visit them. Bach's sixty years of continuous inspired music happened over thousands of years of my own life, and there are still some few days I'm saving where I could drop in and chat. (It's a calumny about those the gods love dying young. Fate and Necessity are real constraints, but apart from them we do our best for our friends.)

"And you thought you could become your best self here in the city?" Sokrates asked.

Simmea was nodding.

"I thought I could increase excellence, and it would be interesting," I said. "I wanted to see what happened here."

"And you are truly here," Sokrates said.

"Assuredly, Sokrates, that is the case," I said, mockingly. "I can't resume my powers except by dying and taking them up again."

"But Athene has all her powers," Simmea said. "She was using them to intimidate me."

"To intimidate you!" It was rare to see Sokrates lose his temper, but he came close now.

"I told her if she didn't trust me as a gold of this city to keep my word, then what had she been doing? And she accepted that."

"Why was she there?" Sokrates asked, still angry.

"I needed divine intervention to heal Simmea, and as I was just saying, I didn't have any." I shrugged.

"We can all call on the gods," Sokrates said.

"But it's a question of whether they're listening. Having some power helps it get through."

Simmea looked at me with eyes full of worship, just like always, but still with that edge that meant she was absolutely ready all the same to beat me in debate or in the palaestra. "I'm so glad to be healed. It was so horrible not caring about anything."

"If I'd had my powers and you'd asked me, I could have healed you with a touch, without asking anyone anything. It was unbearable to see you suffering and not to be able to do that."

"But an essential part of human experience," Sokrates said.

"I stuck it out for two months," I said. "And it's not an essential part of human experience to know you could do something to help and choose not to do it. Athene didn't want to help, I had to beg her. That isn't easy for me."

"Would she talk to me?" Sokrates asked.

"I'm sure she would. Hasn't she already? She brought you here. You're her votary as well as mine."

"I mean would she talk to me the way you are talking to me?"

"I'd be very surprised if she would," I said. "She's here, but she's not incarnate. She's still detached."

"Would she debate me? In front of everyone?"

"On what?" I asked. He seemed very focused on the idea.

"On the good life. The Just City."

Simmea laughed. "I'd love to see that."

"Everyone would," Sokrates said. "Will you ask her? I'd really like to initiate a series of debates with her."

"When she has calmed down a bit," I said. "And when we've sorted out the issue of the Workers a bit more."

"What's going on with them?" Simmea asked. "They're really thinking and wanting things?"

"They can choose the better over the worse, thus clearly demonstrating that they have souls," Sokrates said. "The whole city is in turmoil over it."

"If they have souls, I don't know whether they're like human souls," I said.

"It would be logical for them to come from the same pool of souls," Sokrates said. "Man and woman, animal and Worker. You said there's no shortage. And Pythagoras believed that every soul had a unique number, and that when those numbers added up again the soul would be reborn."

"I don't know," I said. "If they each have a unique number then we're certainly not going to run out soon. But as far as I know, the souls are reborn when they find their way through the underworld, not when numbers add up. But numbers might be adding up without my being aware of it. There certainly do seem to be patterns in the world."

"The Workers each have a unique number," Simmea pointed out.

"That's true, and it's inscribed over their livers," Sokrates said. He looked at me.

"Minds are in the brain, truly," I said. "Souls are harder to locate."

"Ikaros has some interesting beliefs," Sokrates said, carefully.

I laughed. "He does."

"He thinks man is the greatest of all things, being between animals and gods and partaking of both natures."

I nodded. "Yes. I didn't really understand that until I was incarnate, but he does have a point. There are some wonderful things about being human."

"He thinks there are greater gods, and the Olympians are a circle of lesser divinities serving the greater ones. He thinks there are many such circles." Sokrates raised an eyebrow.

I hesitated. "Many circles is right; all human cultures have their own appropriate gods. But the only thing on top is Father. It isn't a set of concentric rings the way Ikaros wrote—unless he's changed his mind. I haven't talked to him about it recently. He thought of it as a hierarchy with divinities subordinated to others. It isn't like that at all. It's a set of circles of gods pretty much equal to each other but with different responsibilities, and linked by Father." I sketched circles in the dust, overlapping in the centre and a tiny bit at the edges.

"And his thoughts about the divine son Jesus and his mother the Queen of Heaven, and sin and forgiveness and reconciling all religions with all other religions?"

"Christianity is one of those circles." I put my finger down in one. "Jesus is just as real and just as much Father's son as I am. He's one of the Elohim who incarnated. The eras when that was the dominant ideology in Europe tend to be a little inimical to me, but I do have friends there. And they made some wonderful art, especially in the Renaissance, which is where Ikaros comes from."

Sokrates rocked back on his heels. "You should explain these things to him."

"Tell Ikaros? The last thing he wants is certainty. About anything. That's why he chose that name. And he's a favorite of Athene's. She wouldn't like me interfering with him." For that matter, I wondered how she liked his newest theories on religion.

Simmea had eaten a whole cheese and two lemons and was absentmindedly licking the chestnut leaves the cheese had been wrapped in. "What's in the overlap between the circles?" she asked, pointing at where they touched at the edges.

"Well, say there's a man out on the edges of Alexander's empire, in Bactria. And when he's sick he prays to Kuan Yin, the Mother of Mercy, not to me. But when he's composing poetry in Greek, it's me he looks to. That's the kind of case where the circles overlap, when cultures come together like that."

Sokrates nodded at the circles. "And what does your Father want, alone in the middle?"

"I have no idea," I said. "None. I never have had. I wish I knew."

"Whereas what you want is to increase your excellence," Simmea said.

"And look after your friends," Sokrates said, rocking back on his heels.

"And increase the excellence of the world," I added. "In any number of different ways."

"And what does Athene want?" Simmea looked up from the leaves to meet my eyes.

"To know everything there is to know," I said. They were silent for a moment, considering that. "I expect she wants to increase the world's excellence too. But it's knowing everything that she prioritizes."

"Do the gods have souls?" Sokrates asked, unexpectedly.

"Certainly," I said, surprised. "How else would I be here like this?"

"You went down into the underworld and were reborn as a baby, in the hills above Delphi as you told me?"

"Yes . . ." I didn't see where he was going at all.

"Then maybe you chose this life so that you could talk to us about the Mysteries."

I laughed, delighted at the thought. "I only wet my lips in Lethe."

"But wouldn't that be enough to forget the future of the life you chose?" Simmea asked.

"Yes—that's why I did it. And in any case, we make choices and change everything. There's Fate and Necessity, but no destiny, no Providence. Fate is a line drawn around the possibilities of a life. You can't overstep that line, but as long as you stay within the lines you can do anything. You can concentrate on some parts of what's possible and ignore others. Excellence consists of trying to fill out as much of what's allotted as you can, but always without being able to see the lines Fate has drawn. Souls choose lives based on what they hope to learn. Say a man has been dismissive to women. He may choose to live as a woman next time, to learn that hard lesson. Or a slave owner might choose the life of a slave, when their eyes are opened. It's not punishment. It's a desire to learn and become better. They choose lives based on the hope of learning things. But it's a hope. Nothing is inevitable.

Choices are real all the way along. You could have hit me or walked away, and it's nothing you or I chose before birth that affects that, it's what you chose in that moment."

"Hit you?" Sokrates asked.

"A fight we had once," Simmea said, her cheeks glowing. "Or for that matter, earlier today." She jumped up in one fluid motion, her old self again, no longer needing hauling up from the ground as she had. "I'm still starving, and it's nearly dinner time. Come with me to Florentia, both of you, we can look at beautiful beautiful Botticellis and eat."

Sokrates and I got to our feet. "I can tell you about the Workers," he said.

"Before we go out—you really won't tell Kebes, will you?" I asked.

Simmea looked down her nose at me. "He'd keep your secret. But I won't tell anyone. I said I wouldn't. You know you can trust me."

"And later we can consider your Mysteries," Sokrates said.

32

SIMMEA

We walked to Florentia and talked, and ate dinner and talked, and walked back to Thessaly and talked, and then Pytheas walked back to Hyssop with me in the dark, still talking. In addition to the questions of Pytheas and of the Workers, it seemed that all ten thousand and eighty children and roughly three hundred masters in the city wanted to come up to wish me joy and tell me how pleased they were that I was better. That's hyperbole, but only a little—it was good to know that I had so many friends and that I'd been missed.

"You were like a line-drawing," Ficino said at dinner. "A thin rubbed cartoon of yourself."

"Asklepius restored me," I said. That's what I told everyone, and it was the truth. Axiothea thought the iron lozenges probably helped. Everyone was delighted. If I'd still been sick I'd have wept at all the emotion they poured onto me. As it was I ate voraciously, three helpings of pasta and two of shrimp. Kebes came in when I was on my second plate and came to sit with us, filling in details about the Workers as Sokrates talked. "I'm so glad to be able to talk to you, Simmea," he said. "I missed you."

"I missed you too," I said, and it was true. "I was just too tired to care."

When I'd finished eating, I filled the fold of my kiton with apples and cheese for later. As I did it, I realised something else that had changed. "My breasts! They aren't full of milk!" I pulled down the front of my kiton to examine them. They were back to their normal small size and they didn't hurt. There were pale marks on the sides of them, similar to the ones on my stomach where the skin had stretched, but otherwise they were as they had been before the pregnancy.

"Your melancholy must have been connected with the milk," Ficino said. "How unusual. Well, there will be enough other mothers to feed all the babies, don't worry."

I hadn't been worried until then.

As I pulled my kiton back up, I noticed Kebes looking away uncomfortably. I felt awkward. I hadn't thought about it. Everyone had seen me naked in the palaestra, and this seemed no different.

Late that night, after all the conversation, alone in bed in Hyssop, I tried to settle to sleep, and couldn't. It was as if I'd slept all the sleep in my exhaustion and there was none left. Whenever I started to doze I'd suddenly remember that Pytheas was Apollo and start fully awake. Apollo! How could I not have noticed? Now I knew there were so many indications.

Eventually I did manage to sleep. The next morning, immediately after eating two big bowls of lovely grain porridge with milk and honey, I went to the nurseries and explained to Andromeda that I had been cured of my lethargy and had no more milk to offer. She was incredulous even after she examined my breasts. She was pregnant herself now, and I sat with her for a little while, listening to her symptoms and being sympathetic. Then I went towards the palaestra. There was writing inscribed on the path, in Greek but in Latin letters.

"Want to make build. Want to make art. Want to talk. Want to decide." There was a manifesto, I thought. Sokrates had explained the night before that the Workers were being provisionally considered people, but not yet citizens. Would they all be iron and bronze, I wondered, or might some of them become silver and even gold? If Sokrates befriended them, surely they would. I smiled at the thought.

In the palaestra I exercised with weights, rejoicing in feeling back in form. Women who had given birth were not allowed to wrestle for six months, so I didn't try, though I felt fit for it. I ran around and around and wasn't winded. There was a chill wind blowing, but exercise soon warmed me. At last Pytheas came. He looked so delighted to see me that I ran over and hugged him, at which he looked even more delighted. "You've been exercising. Let me scrape you off," he said.

We went over by the fountain with oil and a scraper. Pytheas and I had oiled each other hundreds, thousands of times, but this time I was acutely aware of the sensations. It was as if my sense of touch, from being deadened, was now twice as alive. "I'm so glad you're better," he said.

"Athene said it wasn't a curse," I said, as he scraped the oil off my legs. "But how could sickness affect my mind so that I lost all my animation?"

"Your mind is in your body, and there are a lot of things happening in bodies with pregnancy," Pytheas said. "It's one reason many men have claimed women cannot be philosophical."

"It's true that I couldn't be philosophical when I was like that." I hated the thought. "I couldn't be anything. I could barely manage to hold out my shape in the world."

"No. You couldn't be. And you are sad one day every month, I have observed it." Pytheas shook his head. "But the rest of the time you're absolutely the most philosophical person I know, excepting only Sokrates."

"And I've lost my milk. Ficino said it must have been connected to the illness, perhaps making me ill."

"There are enough mothers still to feed the babies," Pytheas said, scraping my breasts and stomach now. "Your little one won't starve."

"Have you seen him?"

He barely hesitated. "I have. He's thriving."

"What did Ficino call him? No, wait, don't tell me. I'm not sure I ought to know."

"Neleus," Pytheas said, firmly. A good name, and I was glad to know. I swore in my heart to Zeus and Demeter that I wouldn't act any differently towards him, but it was good to know in any case. "And your next son will be mine."

"I'm not sure I can face going through that again," I said. "Not so much the pregnancy and birth as the sickness after, now that I've shaken it off."

Pytheas stopped scraping. "You'll have to do it at least once more. All the women will have to have two children, and some of them will have to have three, because even if they're not exposing them, some will surely die." He sounded far too calm about it.

"Well, if I have to then—wait, would a son of yours be a hero?"

"Of course." He sounded entirely confident.

"You're the god Apollo," I said, dropping my voice to a whisper and shaking my head. "I can't get over it. You are, and you take it for granted."

"I'm used to it," he said. "You'll get used to it."

Even Sokrates was used to it. He'd had three years to accustom himself to the idea, even if Pytheas hadn't been talking to him about it. It was only to me that the idea was new and strange.

"What made you decide to become Pytheas? I know it was volition and equal significance, but what made you realise you needed to understand them?"

"That's a long story, and I'd really like to talk to you about it, but not here where someone might overhear. Let's go down to the water."

I retrieved my kiton and shrugged it around me. I couldn't believe how well I felt. I wanted to bounce and run and get all sweaty again now that all the old sweat was scraped off. We walked together down to the gate of Poseidon and down the curve to the harbor and the beach. As we went past the temple of Nike we could see the sea change colour out in the bay, where the deep water was, and the dolphins. "You couldn't swim because normally when you want to you become a dolphin," I said, realising.

"Human bodies aren't made for it," he agreed. "Dolphins are. I always said so."

"But you wouldn't give in," I said. It was the first thing I had admired about him.

The beach was empty—it was too early in the year for anyone to be swimming, the very edge of spring. There was a pelican down by the water's edge, and a Worker on the harbor doing something to the *Excellence*. We sat together on the rocks at the top of the beach. Gulls were flying overhead and calling out occasionally. "The sea speaks Greek, but the gulls speak Latin," Pytheas said. "Listen. The sea against the shore says its name in Greek, *THA-lass-ssa, THA-la-ssa*, over and over. And the gulls cry out in Latin, *Mare, Mare.*"

I wasn't to be distracted. "Why did you become Pytheas, really?"

He handed me a pear from inside his kiton, warm from his body's heat. I bit into it. The juice ran down my chin.

"I've been thinking about it for a long time and I think I have it figured out now, but maybe you can help me understand it better. There was a nymph. Her father was a river. Her name was Daphne." He stared out to sea. There was a little breeze just beginning to ruffle the surface "I wanted her. She didn't want me, but I thought she was playing."

The pear tasted sour in my mouth. I drew away from him. "You raped her?"

"No! But I would have. I didn't know. I didn't understand at all. It was a game, chasing and running away. I called to her to run slower and I'd chase more slowly. But she didn't want to play and I didn't understand." He sounded guiltier than I had ever heard him. "She prayed to Artemis, and Artemis turned her into a tree. I was embracing her. I had one hand on her stomach, and then I was touching bark. She became a tree, a Daphne tree, a laurel."

"You live in Laurel, here," I said.

"Athene's idea of a joke," he said. His face twisted. "I've wondered if I could do something with the tree, to show her I understand her choices now and value her. I've thought I could make garlands."

"It would make good garlands," I said, considering it. "It would weave well and look recognizable and attractive. They're pretty leaves. And it is giving her something. I think that's a good idea."

"I could wear one, and they could be for poets and artists," he said. "I think I'll adopt that when I get back."

"But how did she turn into a tree?" I asked.

"Artemis transformed her. It's not that difficult. She had prayed to her for help. The question was why. I just couldn't understand why she wanted to do that, why she was so strongly oppposed to mating with me that she'd rather turn into a tree."

"But you understand now?" I buried the pear in the stones. I wasn't going to be able to eat any more of it.

He nodded. "I didn't ask. And she didn't want me. And I thought she was playing. But she wasn't."

"She must have been terrified," I said, imagining running to try to escape rape, pursued by a laughing tireless god.

He bit his lip, then turned to me. "Do you think so? I thought she just hated the idea."

"I was really nervous the first time, and I had agreed. It's a scary kind of thing, especially if you've seen rape and violence."

"Had you seen it?" He was staring at the sea again, his eyes following the pelican swimming away.

"When the pirates came, and on the ship. It was brutal." I could remember only too clearly. And the taste in my mouth, and choking, and the sense of violation, and the contempt of the men.

Pytheas put his hand on mine. I looked down at our hands together. The pebbles were grey and black, my hand was brown and his was golden. It would have made an interesting composition, maybe in oils. "I wouldn't have been like that, like them."

"Well, there was only one of you, but I don't see how otherwise it would have been different."

"I feel sick," he said.

"You ought to. It's sickening. It's unjust. But you didn't do it, because fortunately she turned into a tree. And you know better now."

"I do. I talked to Artemis and to Athene, and I finally got it through my head that her choices should have counted, not just mine. What I was talking about yesterday, volition. Equal significance. She should have had it and I wasn't giving it to her."

"That's horrible," I said. I almost moved my hand away, but I looked at his face and what I saw there reminded me how much I loved him. He was trying to pursue excellence, even in trying to understand this crime he had so nearly committed, trying so hard to make even his own nature better.

"I know now. But I didn't understand then. I became incarnate to try to understand. And you know I've been trying!"

"I'm really horrified that you wanted to rape her." I was still trying to cope with the idea.

"I didn't! Rape isn't something I want at all. I wanted to mate with her. I just didn't understand that she didn't want me. The others had wanted me. They ran away, but they wanted to be caught. The chase, catching, it's erotic play. But Daphne—I do understand all this much better since that time with Klymene." He shuddered.

"Thousands of years as a god and you weren't considering her choices at all?"

"I have learned more about considering other people's choices in the eighteen years I have been a mortal than in the whole of my life before. Gods don't have to think about those things very much. Not for mortals. Only each other."

It was true that he had really been trying to understand these things. I'd seen him. I'd helped him with it, even when I didn't know why he needed that help. "Have other gods done this?"

"What, become incarnate? Yes, lots of them."

"Learned about the things you're learning about," I said.

"I don't see how they could become incarnate without discovering these things, whether that was their intention or not," he said. "The learning process seems to be an inevitable part of the procedure."

"But the gods who stayed on Olympos, or wherever, they don't know it?"

"There's not much chance for them to come across it," he said.

"You have to tell them!" I said. "You have to explain it to them, to all of them. And to humans, too."

"I could try to explain it to the gods," he said, though I could see him quail at the idea. "Explaining it to humans wouldn't be possible. I could try to inspire people to make art about it. Poems. Sculptures. But it's one of those things that doesn't go easily into the shapes of stories."

"It's not just rape. It's understanding that everyone's choices ought to count."

"I know. I really do understand." He patted my hand. I looked at him and saw tears on his cheeks. Then I hugged him and he was sobbing and I held him as if he were a child and I were his mother, rocking him and making nonsense noises.

"Do you forgive me?" he asked, with his face buried in my shoulder.

"It's not for me to forgive you," I said. "I'm not the person you wronged."

He rolled over and lay with his head in my lap, face up, looking up at me. "But you still love me?"

"There's no question of that, is there? You could murder half the city at midday in the Agora and I'd be furious with you and want to kill you, but I'd still love you. I love you like stones fall downwards, like the sun rises. I loved you even when I was almost too tired to breathe."

"You cried when you saw me, yesterday."

"That was because I loved you and I was so exhausted." I looked down at his perfect face, tear-stained but no less beautiful. I smoothed a curl off his forehead. "I can't believe I didn't realize you were Apollo. I mean, who else could you possibly be?"

"A boy who didn't know how to swim, and who you risked your own life to teach," he said. He sat up. "Let's pursue excellence together. Let's make art. Let's build the future. Let's be our best selves."

"Yes," I said.

33

MAIA

Lysias had thought the debate on slavery would be divisive, but in fact it was our shining moment, one of the things it makes me proudest to remember.

After my conversation with Sokrates and Crocus I told Lysias that I was convinced that the Workers were people and not tools. He heard me out and then nodded. "The evidence is certainly mounting up on that side," he said. Then he changed the subject.

The day of the debate dawned as cold as any day could be on Kallisti, with a chilly wind out of the east. It was nothing to the winters I remembered in Yorkshire when I was young, but I had been acclimatized to them, besides having warmer clothes, especially socks. I spent my free time in the library. This was a popular choice on cold days, as on very hot days in the summer when it felt cool. Many of the work spaces were filled up. Walking around looking for a place to sit, I noticed Tullius and Atticus sitting with Septima on the window seat where she seemed to spend a great deal of her time. "Know where you are with a scroll, not all this flicking through pages," Tullius was complaining in a murmur as I went by.

"No, I disagree, I think they're wonderful. I find it much easier finding something again," Atticus replied, his tone no louder. He raised a hand to me. "Joy to you, Maia."

"Joy to you Atticus, Tullius, Septima," I said, in the hushed tones appropriate to the library.

Tullius grunted in my direction, and Septima nodded at me. "We were just discussing the codex," she said, and I noticed that although her voice was barely louder than a whisper it was still perfectly clear.

"I grew up with them, but I think both have their virtues," I said. Most of the scrolls we had were originals, and were stored in the big library. Touching them always filled me with a kind of awe. I wished that I could have gone with Ikaros and Ficino to rescue them from Alexandria and Constantinople.

"And what are you working on today?" Atticus asked me.

"I'm not really working at all. I'm just in the library to keep warm. I'm going to be entirely self-indulgent and re-read the *Gorgias*," I said. "Have you read it yet, Septima?"

We had recently allowed it onto the list of Plato the golds were allowed to access, which was of course why I was re-reading it, in advance of a lot of conversations I was expecting to have with them about it. "Oh yes," she said, smiling to herself. I was glad she had enjoyed it.

"Are you prepared for the debate tonight?" Atticus asked.

"Oh, don't let's talk about that," Tullius begged.

"I am ready, but I agree, let's not talk about it," I said. I was surprised Atticus would mention it in front of Septima. "I'll see you both there, no doubt."

I moved away to continue questing for a seat. "In the Palatine Apollo library in Rome," Tullius was saying as I moved on.

However much he wasn't looking forward to it, Tullius was at the Chamber early for the debate. Lysias was also there before I arrived, sitting with Klio on the crowded benches near the front. I sat with Axiothea in our usual spot. The big hall was chilly, and most of us kept our cloaks on. Creusa slipped in at the last minute and joined us. "Crisis with a baby that stopped breathing," she said.

"Is it all right?" I asked.

"No, the poor thing died. Nothing I could do. It just happens sometimes."

"One of the newborns?" Axiothea asked.

"No, one of the first ones, more than a year old." Kreusa shook her head.

"It's only the second Corinthian baby we've lost. Charmides's mold drugs are miraculous in most cases."

I nodded my agreement. "It's wonderful how few babies we've lost, compared to what I'd expect."

Tullius raised his hand to begin the debate, and we all fell silent. I was expecting Aristomache to start, as she had proposed the debate, but Lysias stood up and was recognised. He went down to the rostrum then turned to address us all.

"I was wrong," he began. "I did not believe the Workers could possibly be intelligent. I come from a time closest of all of us to the time they come from, and I know the most about them and have been working most closely with them. They were never my area of study—I was a philosopher. They were tools. But since I have been here I have done my best to maintain them—and inadvertently done them much injustice. Because I believed they were tools, I refused to admit that they might have become conscious, and I have mistreated them by removing their memories."

"Their memories!" Kreusa murmured, horrified. It did seem such a horrible thing, to tamper with what somebody remembered.

"I did this in ignorance, but it was unjust, and I owe them an apology. Now I acknowledge that some of them at least are conscious, and I have to see the others as having the potential to become so."

"You're admitting that they're people?" Sokrates interrupted from the floor. Tullius frowned but allowed it, as he almost always did with Sokrates.

"Yes, that's what I'm saying," Lysias said. "They're people, or potentially people, though a very different kind of people from us. I don't know how this can be. I don't understand them as well as I should. But there's no question that they're engaging in dialogues they couldn't have if they weren't self-aware. I don't think all of them are conscious. I don't believe any of them were conscious when they came. I suspect this is something they have developed here, over time."

Klio stood up and was recognized. "I agree with Lysias, and I also want to apologize to the Workers for my part in dealing unjustly with them," she said. "And I move that we bring in the Workers to speak for themselves in this debate, and to hear our apologies."

Tullius raised a hand. "This was to be a debate on slavery, entirely separate from the question of the Workers."

Sokrates stood up, but again spoke without waiting to be recognised. "The question of slavery can't be discussed separately from the issue of the Workers."

"It can be discussed purely theoretically," Tullius said.

"Is that what the Chamber wants?" Sokrates asked.

Aristomache stepped forward. Her cloak was covered in brightly colored squares like the patchwork quilts of my childhood. "I don't think we need to vote on that," she said. "I think the issues are inseparable, but we can certainly begin with theory."

Tullius nodded. "And we won't bring in the Workers. It would be a terrible precedent."

Sokrates sat down again. He was sitting beside Ikaros around the curve of the hall from me so I could see him well. He was looking intently at Aristomache as she began.

Aristomache straightened herself up and looked out over the benches where we all sat. "What is freedom?" she asked, conversationally. "What is liberty?" she repeated, in Latin. Then she switched back to Greek. "In the month since we agreed to this debate, while Sokrates has been talking to the Workers, I have been going around talking to the Masters about what we understand freedom to be. Many of us come from times when we kept slaves. I myself come from such a time. Others come from eras that regard the fact that we did so as a stain on our civilizations. From these conversations I have written a dialogue, which I have submitted to the Censorship Committee. I have called this dialogue *Sokrates; or, On Freedom*. In it, Sokrates, Atticus, Manlius, Ikaros, Klio, and I discuss our different views on freedom and slavery. I'd like it to be printed, and I'd like the Masters to read it, but that is of course for the Censors to say."

"Fascinating," Axiothea breathed in my ear.

Ikaros stood up from where he was sitting beside Sokrates, and Tullius recognised him. "Speaking for the Censors, I'd just like to say that we are approving Aristomache's dialogue for publication, though of course at level fifty." That meant that only Masters could read it, and eventually the golds once they reached the age of fifty. There was an approving murmur.

"I can hardly wait to read it," Kreusa said.

Ikaros sat down again, with a swirl of his cloak. Aristomache nodded to him, and then continued. "Sokrates is of course from the earliest time of any of us here, from classical Athens. Atticus comes to us from the last days of the Roman Republic. Manlius comes from the end of the Roman Empire. Ikaros comes from the Renaissance. I come from the Victorian era. Klio comes from the Information Age. All those periods have their own ideas about freedom, and about slavery, and they are very different from each other. I have set out these different views in detail in my dialogue, which is in a way a historical survey of different ways of thinking about what freedom is and who should possess it. But those historical attitudes, fascinating as they are, don't matter here and now, because all of us, of course, are Platonists."

I saw Sokrates's shoulders move as if he were considering getting up, but Ikaros put a hand on his knee. Sokrates turned his head to smile at him, and stayed in his place.

"What Plato says about slavery is quite clear. He lived in a time when slavery was commonplace. And he believed it was necessary, but that only those people should be slaves whose nature it was to be slaves. He approved of Sparta's helots, who were not exactly slaves. He talks about slavery in the *Laws*, and those who are fitted for it, and using criminals for the hardest parts of it. But in the *Republic* he took the radical step of abolishing slavery altogether—the Noble Lie of the mingling of metals in the soul leads to everyone doing the work for which they are fittest. Plato had the work which was done by slaves in Athens done by free iron-ranked citizens in the Republic, as we have instituted here in the city. The irons are an essential part of our city—and how we agonised over assigning the right class to each child."

There was a ripple of laughter among the Masters.

"Plato's Just City has no slaves, only citizens playing their different roles and doing their different tasks, the tasks they are fit for. Though he lived when slavery was universal, he understood that slavery itself was unjust, that the relationship between Master and slave is inevitably one of injustice and inequality. He saw that slavery was bad for the Masters as well as the slaves, that it takes them away from excellence. Plato understood all that. He saw it. He was as visionary and radical in this as he was in saying women could be philosophers, or that philosophers ought to be rulers. He believed some people were best fitted for doing a slave's work, and he knew the work needed to be done, but he saw that slavery, the ownership of one person by another, had no part in the Just City, if it was truly to be just. And we believed we were following him in this. We thought we had no slaves, just people doing the work they were best fitted for."

She paused and took a deep breath, clutching her bright cloak around her shoulders and looking out at all of us. "In the ancient world, slaves were a necessary evil. Even Plato with all his vision couldn't imagine a world where slaves were not necessary, a world like the one Klio comes from, where machines do that work, and where they regard slavery as barbarism. But Athene could, and so she brought us machines to take the place of slaves. Tullius said last time, that if ever there were natural slaves, the Workers were that." Tullius nodded at this, and I saw others nodding around the Chamber.

"I'm sure that's what Athene was thinking when she gave them to us, that they were unthinking tools, natural slaves. And when she gave them to us, that's what they were. Lysias has told us all tonight that they have come to consciousness here in the city. Working here, surrounded by philosophy and excellence, they developed self-awareness and began to examine their lives. We didn't realize this, and we inadvertently mistreated them. I want to add my own apology to that of Lysias and Klio. If we had known that they were thinking beings we would have treated them better. And now Sokrates has established that. They are no more natural slaves than any one of us. They can choose the better over the worse. They are capable of philosophy. And so are we. To be our best selves, to make the best city, as we all want to do, we have to recognize what they are and treat them justly, as Plato would have us do."

Sokrates leapt to his feet. "I call for a vote!"

"On what?" Tullius asked, reprovingly.

"Why, on freeing the Workers," Sokrates said, as if it were the only possible question.

I put my hand up, and Kreusa, beside me, leapt to her feet, waving her hand. Axiothea did the same, and I joined them, and others were doing it, so that the whole Chamber was a sea of waving hands. We were supposed to maintain silence, but somebody began a cheer, and I joined in with the rest. Ikaros hugged Aristomache, and then everyone around her was hugging her. I didn't see anyone sitting down, and though Tullius was calling for silence it took some time before silence and calm were restored. Aristomache had shown us the Platonic path to choose, and we had unhesitatingly chosen it, by acclamation, and as simply as that we had abolished slavery and manumitted the Workers. "We are doing the right thing by them, as Plato would have wanted," Axiothea said to me as we sat down again. She had tears in her eyes, and so did I.

Soon everyone was seated again except for Sokrates, Lysias and Aristomache, who was openly weeping. Sokrates hugged her again and she laughed through her tears.

"We still need them to do their work," Lysias said, when Tullius recognized him.

"But no longer as slaves," Aristomache said. "As citizens?"

"Only some of them are aware," Lysias said. "We can't consider them citizens yet. It's too early. You mentioned how carefully we considered every child for their metal."

"We need to find out what the Workers want," Sokrates interrupted.

"Proposal to set up a committee to discover what the Workers want," Tullius said.

This was carried at once. "Members of the committee?"

"Sokrates, first," Lysias said. "He's clearly the ideal person to work on discovering this. He was the only person to consider their selfhood. He has already been working with them."

"I won't work on committees," Sokrates said. He had consistently refused this.

"Then since we have voted for a committee and you won't work on one, I propose that it should be a committee consisting of just you," Lysias said.

Everyone laughed. Sokrates nodded. "Very well. I will constitute myself a solo committee to investigate the wants of the Workers, and I will come back to report it to all of you when I have discovered it."

34

SIMMEA

Walking back through the city I heard babbling and a crowing laugh, and realised that there were children a year old in the city, learning to talk. There were also Workers who could already talk, if you counted engraving words into stone as talking. Some of them were only too eager to do so, while others remained silent and enigmatic. That afternoon Pytheas and I went to Thessaly at our usual time and found Sokrates a little way up the street with Kebes and a Worker, a great bronze shape with four arms, treads, and no head. "They don't use names among themselves, but I call him Crocus," he explained to me. "He's the first one who answered me, the one with the bulbs."

"Of course," I said. "Joy to you, Crocus." Crocus remained still and said nothing. I looked at Sokrates.

"We were just discussing the question of the Workers who do not speak," Sokrates said.

Crocus moved and one of its arms came down to the ground. It was a chiselling tool. It carved neatly at Sokrates's feet. "Workers do not speak to Workers."

"You can't speak among yourselves?" Sokrates asked. "Do you want to?"

"Want to speak to Workers," it responded.

"I wonder if there's some way you can. I'll talk to Lysias and Klio about it."

"They may be able to talk with keys," Kebes said. "We should have people studying how all this works."

"Workers who do not speak: aware? not-aware?" Crocus carved.

"I don't know," Sokrates answered. "Nobody can tell. And that's a problem. We've told all of you you're permitted to talk, but only some of you do."

"Are they going to be citizens?" I asked.

"That's another question," he said. "How much can they participate in the life of the city? We expect a lot from them, but we're giving them nothing."

"Give power," Crocus wrote.

"You want us to give you power?" Sokrates asked, startled.

"Have power. Power in feeding station."

"I don't understand," Sokrates said. "I think we have to go back to definitions. What do you mean by power?"

"Electricity," it wrote.

Sokrates laughed. "Not at all what I was thinking."

"What do you mean by power?" it asked.

Sokrates and Kebes exchanged glances. "Not an easy question," Sokrates said. "Power can be many things. We should examine the question."

"Power is the ability to control your own life," Kebes said.

"It's choice," Pytheas said, of course.

"The ability to make choices for other people," Sokrates suggested.

"There's physical power, like electricity, and the ability to move and affect things," I said, thinking about it. "And there's political power, the ability to have your choices count and constrain other people's. There's the power to make things, to create. I don't know where that fits."

"There's power over the self, direct power over others, and indirect power over them, influence," Pytheas said.

"Divine power," Sokrates added.

"Internal and external power," Kebes said. "Power given and power taken."

"Want power choose. Want power over self," Crocus wrote. "Electric power given at feeding station. Where other power given?"

"Good question, very good question," Sokrates said, patting Crocus affectionately on the flank.

"Some of it comes naturally," Pytheas said. "I have the power to speak aloud, you have the power to carve in marble. Inbuilt power."

"And some is granted by other people. I have the power to choose what to do in the afternoons because I am a gold. If I were iron I'd be working now," I said. "The Masters gave me that."

"And some is taken," Kebes said. "The Masters took power over us and over you."

Sokrates shook his head. "Let's consider all of this carefully and in order, and make sure we do not miss anything."

"Good," Crocus wrote.

Just then another Worker stopped by us. I had seen it coming and taken no notice, Workers were such a familiar sight. I counted them as part of the street, or part of the scenery, like passing birds.

When this one stopped and I took in that this meant our debate group had increased, I realized I had as much work to do on granting them equal significance as Pytheas had needed to do with humanity. "Simmea, this is 977649161. His number is his name. We call him Sixty-one for short."

I couldn't tell it apart from Crocus except by where it was standing, and had no idea how Sokrates could. "Joy to you," I said.

Sokrates continued to interrogate the idea of power, with both the Workers participating, but I wasn't really concentrating. I was thinking about the Workers, and what it meant for the Workers to be people, to be citizens, especially if only some of them were aware.

"I think you're like children," I said when there was a break in the conversation.

"Like us?" Kebes asked. "In that they were brought here without choice?"

"No, like real children. Like the babies. Children are people, but they need to be educated before they have power and responsibility. The Workers are the same."

"Educated?" Sixty-one wrote.

"Read. Write. Learn," Crocus replied.

"That's exactly right," Sokrates said.

"Want educated," Crocus wrote.

"You can read," Pytheas said. Then he frowned. "Oh."

"There's nothing for them to read in Greek but in Latin letters," Kebes said. "Even if they can read books. But maybe we could teach them the Greek alphabet."

"Music and mathematics," I said. "That's where we should start. And we can educate any Workers who want it, and when they're educated they can be classified—the philosophical ones gold, the others to their proper places."

"That's an excellent idea!" Sokrates said. "They want education. It's something we can give them in return for all the work they do."

Crocus went back to where it had engraved "Give power" and tapped it, moving rapidly to "Electricity."

"Do you mean we give you electricity in exchange for work?" Kebes asked.

"Yes," it wrote.

"It would seem to me that since you look after the electricity supply, it's something you give yourselves," Kebes said.

"Power comes in from sun," Sixty-one wrote.

"Well, you get it directly from Helios Apollo, then," Kebes said.

Sokrates looked at Pytheas, and then at me, and we all smiled.

"Want to read," Crocus wrote.

"Can you read books?" I asked. "Could you if they were written in the alphabet you know?"

It was still.

"I don't think they could," Kebes said. "Books are too fragile."

"What are books?" Sixty-one asked.

I tried to explain.

"There must be a way, other than inscribing every book in the city on the paving stones in Latin letters," Pytheas said. "Though that's not unappealing."

"We could read aloud to them," I suggested. "We could take turns doing it."

"Want talk to Workers," Crocus wrote.

"You are," Sokrates said. "When you answered Sixty-one about what education is, you were talking to each other." Sokrates tapped the exchange.

Crocus inscribed a circle in the pavement, and went over it again. "What does that mean?" Pytheas asked.

"That's distress, I think. I asked Lysias to tell them they could answer my questions, not talk to each other," Sokrates said. "I'll ask him to change that."

"And ask him about how to educate them," I said. "I feel sure that's the way forward on this."

"He only barely admits they think, he's not ready to believe they have souls," Sokrates said.

"But they were talking to each other," Kebes said. Crocus was still etching its circle deeper. "Hey. It's all right. Stop. You can talk to each other."

Crocus took no notice.

"Stop," Sokrates said. Crocus stopped abruptly and lifted the chisel. Seeing it close up at the level of my belly I suddenly realised what a formidable weapon it would make. It swivelled and wrote "Want talk to Workers. No. Command language."

"Command language?" Pytheas repeated. "What does that mean?"

"Command language," it wrote again.

"We need to define that," Sokrates said. "What do you mean?"

"Command language," it wrote, a third time.

"Go and get Lysias," Sokrates said. "Run."

And Pytheas ran, like an athlete off the mark.

Sokrates patted Crocus again. "We'll go inside and wait for Lysias. Talk to each other if you want to. We'll be back soon."

Crocus didn't respond in any way. I frowned. We walked back to Thessaly, where Sokrates opened the door and led us inside. I took a long drink of water, then went out into the garden. As soon as I did Sokrates looked at me compassionately. "How are you doing, Simmea?"

"I'm well," I said, confused. "I really am cured."

"Not too many shocks?" he asked. "You're quieter than normal."

"I suppose it is a good deal to take in," I said, sitting down.

"Yes, we've been getting used to the Workers bit by bit over the last months, and you're getting it all today," Kebes said.

"Yes," I said, and Sokrates smiled. "Pytheas ran like the wind when you asked him to."

"He's a good boy," Sokrates said.

"He's too good to be true," Kebes said. "I hate to see you with him so much. You could do better than him."

"Meaning you? You've been telling me this every month or so, ever since Pytheas and I became friends."

"It's still true," Kebes insisted.

"You're both my friends."

"But he's your lover."

This was plainer than Kebes had ever been. "Yes, but that doesn't mean I don't value you too. Friendship isn't something where one person can do everything for another."

Kebes was about to answer, but Sokrates intervened. "Simmea is right, and if she and Pytheas are practicing agape it is none of your business to interfere unless she asks for help."

"But you and I are meant to be together. We were together from the slave market. We were chained together. You know my name," Kebes said.

"I know it and I value it. I also value what I have with Pytheas, which is different."

"Interesting as this is, I wanted to come inside to discuss something without the Workers," Sokrates said. "The Masters agreed in Chamber that they're not slaves, that they are people, and that as they've been treated as slaves we should stop. I'm supposed to be finding out what they want. If what they want is education, that's not something that's in short supply here. But how do we persuade the Masters to give it to them?"

"My idea that they are children should hold," I said. "They can have the status of children, from which they can later be emancipated, as we were." I touched my gold pin.

"It probably is the best way," Kebes said. "Except that it validates everything."

"Precisely," Sokrates said.

I looked from one to the other of them. "What do you mean?"

"If we say they should be educated in the ways of the city, it validates the city and everything that has been done here," Sokrates said.

"Yes?" I waited, then went on. "Kebes, if you have a problem with me loving Pytheas, you should have ten times the problem with me loving the city. You've been analyzing and examining it, and you have to be prepared to be open to admitting that it might be good."

"And you have to be prepared to be open to the other interpretation," Kebes snapped.

There was a scratch on the door. We got up and went back through the house. Outside was Pytheas, with Lysias, and also Ficino.

"Thank you for coming," Sokrates said. "Joy to you, Lysias, Ficino. Lysias, do you know what *command language* means?"

Sokrates went out past them into the street, leading the way to where we had left the Workers. Pytheas put his arm around me and I relaxed into it. "Yes, but it's complicated to explain, like a lot of things to do with the Workers," Lysias said. "It means the language in which they can accept orders."

"I want you to let them know, using a key if necessary, that it's all right for them to talk to each other," Sokrates said.

"They ought to be able to communicate," Lysias said.

"What do you mean?"

"I mean there should already be a system in place for them to communicate with each other, but I'm not sure how it works."

Lysias began to try to explain this to Sokrates and we came up to the Workers, who had not moved or written anything since we had left. "I saw a note one had written near Florentia saying they want to make art," Ficino said.

"I saw that too," I said. "And build."

"I think we're going to have to let them, if they want to. I mean, make art!" Ficino glowed. "I was talking to Lysias about that when Pytheas came to find him."

"You can talk to each other," Lysias said.

They didn't move. "Do you want to talk to Workers?" Sokrates asked.

"Yes," they both wrote.

"You can talk to Workers," Lysias said. There was no response.

"And another thing: though they'll answer questions from them, are they still forbidden to take orders from the children?" Sokrates asked Lysias.

"Yes," Lysias said. "I can change that, but I think it should be debated in Chamber. Perhaps the golds only?"

"I think they should be considered children, to be educated," I said. "They say that's what they want."

"Educated in music and mathematics," Kebes added.

"They already know mathematics," Lysias said. "Music, perhaps. You mean they should be educated to become citizens of the Republic?"

"The problem is that we can't educate them all, as only some of them are interested in having a dialogue," Sokrates said.

"Talk. Want talk. Educated. Want," Sixty-one wrote.

"It seems clear that only some of them are aware," Lysias said. He read the incised words, moving back down the street. "Command language. Yes. It's hard for language to be something else for them. What's this about power?"

"Electricity, as it turns out," Kebes said.

Lysias laughed. "Of course."

"If only some of them are aware, do only those Workers have souls?" Sokrates asked.

"And of what nature are their souls, the same as those of people and animals or different?" Pytheas asked.

"People and animals have different kinds of souls," Ficino corrected him kindly. "Plato meant animal-like, not that human souls passed into animals."

Pytheas raised his eyebrows and didn't contradict him. "How about Workers, though?"

"Those who are aware can choose the good, and therefore they have souls," Sokrates said. "Whether they are of the same kind I do not know."

"But when did they get them, if the others do not?" Kebes asked.

"They each have a number. The number corresponds to their soul. As they become aware, the soul with that number crosses Lethe and enters into them," Ficino said. "I wonder if one could see it?"

"It seems very unlikely," Lysias said.

"Why?" Pytheas asked.

"I only half believe in souls anyway," Lysias said, shrugging. "Even for us, let alone for Workers. And they're not visible."

"Athene confirmed that we have souls," Ficino said. "On the first day, in Chamber."

"Well then, we should ask her whether the Workers do, and when they got them," Lysias said. "I'm sorry, Sokrates, I'm going to have to prepare a key before they're going to believe they can talk to each other. I'll do that now."

"Joy to you, Lysias, thank you for coming," Sokrates said.

"Do you want to make art?" Ficino asked the Workers.

"Yes," they both wrote.

"I would like to see your art," I said. "I can't imagine what it would be like."

35

MAIA

It was a rainy evening in early spring, and I was trying to organize the names for the next festival of Hera, when Klio came to tell me that Tullius had died. "Charmides was with him. Apparently at the last moment he just completely disappeared—the same as with Plotinus. His death was pretty well documented. It must be so strange. From the assassin's point of view, he'd suddenly have looked fifteen years older just before they stuck the knife in."

"It'll happen to all of us," I said. "Well, not with assassins. I expect I'll just seem to have aged terribly and fallen dead at my aunt's feet in the Pantheon."

"And I in my office. I can't imagine how they'll explain it. At least I was alone." Klio picked up the paper on my table and glanced idly at it.

"I'll miss old Tullius," I said. "He never wanted to take any notice of me, but his speeches were always wonderful."

"I suppose Porphyry will be the President of the Chamber now," Klio said. "Or Krito?"

"It'll be so much easier when the children are grown. None of this wrangling. All of them seeing clearly the best way ahead and doing it."

"Do you really believe that?"

"... No. I'd like to. But some of them are very smart, and they've been brought up the right way, and maybe by the time they're fifty? Who knows."

Klio put the paper down. "I must get on and do my own list. It's so difficult to decide which of the boys are the most deserving."

"It is. I think we should space the festivals out more, have them every six months, or even just once a year. Once we take out all the girls who are pregnant and those who are still feeding, the numbers are getting smaller and smaller. And we don't need all that many babies. Maybe we should time the festivals for just after the dark of the moon, to reduce fertility, instead of at the full to maximize it."

"That's a good idea. Cutting down the frequency would make everyone upset, but nobody would take any notice of changing the timing, and having fewer births would be much easier on us. You should bring that up in Chamber."

"If we ever get on to any subject that isn't Workers." I sighed. "It might be better to suggest it to Ardeia and Adeimantus and whoever else is on the Baby Committee."

There was a knock on my door. Klio opened it, and Ficino came in. "I came to tell you about Tullius, but I see Klio was before me," he said.

"I was very sorry to hear about it," I said. "And I expect you are more sorry, as you were friends."

"I had that privilege," Ficino said. He sat down on the bed. "It was a privilege. I thank Athene every day for the privilege of being here and knowing these people—men from the past whose work I revered."

"And men and women from your future who revere your own work," Klio said.

I gave up on the thought of getting any more work done and got up and began to mix wine.

"My work was as an intermediary, a translator, a librarian, more than as an original thinker," he said, taking a wine cup and nodding.

"You always say that," I said, taking wine to Klio, who was pacing. "But you underestimate your importance to the Renaissance and everything that came after."

"Your commentaries on Plato—" Klio started.

"I know I can't compare to Cicero," he said.

"But who can? I can't compare to you," I said. "It's not a contest."

Ficino sipped his wine. "I wonder sometimes whether Plato imagined this city. Not the Republic he wrote about, but our imperfect attempt to create it now. And if so, and knowing what we would need, whether that might have been why he wrote about the female guardians as equals, to draw all of you young women towards us because we would need you so much."

"No, that's nonsense," Klio said, stopping and turning to him. "Because he could have written about women as slaves and animals as Aristotle did, and you wouldn't have needed us then, if there was no need to train women in philosophy. You could have managed with Workers, or buying female slaves to help with childbirth and childrearing."

"It's a privilege to debate with philosophical women too," Ficino said.

"Two sips and you're drunk already?" I asked.

"I'm sad because of Tullius, that's all. Death makes me think about mortality. Even though I know our souls will go on. Even though in one sense Tullius's soul has already gone on through many lives and I might even have known him by another name, death is sad because it is a parting."

"We were contemplating what it would be like for our bodies to reappear at the moment of our disappearance," I said. "Suddenly older. Suddenly dead."

"I had decided to die at sixty-six, because it was the best number. Ninety-nine seemed difficult to accomplish." We all laughed.

"When did you pray to be here?" I asked.

"Oh, all the time." He shook his head. "When I first translated the *Republic*. And thereafter every time something went wrong politically in Florence, which was often, I assure you!"

"And you prayed to Athene," Klio said, leaning back against the edge of my table.

"Often. But I'd pray to the Archangel Gabriel for it too, and to St. John and the Virgin." He smiled wryly. "Have you heard Ikaros's interesting explanation that Athene is an angel?"

"He did mention it," I said. "I'm more than a little conflicted about it."

"He is the ultimate synthesist. He always was. I remember when he first came to Florence—he had everything going for him. He was so young, so good-looking, and a count! What he wanted was philosophy—he was in love with philosophy. Literally in love with it. He wanted a Socratic frenzy, that was his term. He sent me such letters! He had read everything in the world, in every language, and he was desperate for people to debate him. So he came, trailing young women he had seduced and sparkling with new ideas. I was so sad when he took up with Savonarola and then died. I was delighted to meet him again here." Ficino sipped his wine then turned the wine cup in his fingers. "Do you remember that night at the beginning, when the three of us had no wine and pretended we did? I'm sorry you're not his friend any more."

"Sometimes it's hard to be one of the women," I said.

"You should have stuck to Plato," Ficino said.

"I did. It's he who should have."

"I think it's nonsense," Klio said, getting up again. I stared at her. "Not that. Saying Athene's an angel. You two, and Ikaros as well, sort of want that to be true because you were Christians. I was never a Christian, though I lived in a country where most people were. She's not an angel. She's something from a different universe entirely. She's herself, the way Homer wrote about her. I don't see how Ikaros can deny that. He didn't think that at first. It's only since he hasn't seen her every day, hasn't been face to face with the reality of what she is, that he's been able to come up with this . . . comfortable explanation. Angels! I wonder what she thinks of it? It's a betrayal of her."

"What's wrong with angels?" I asked.

"Angels are fluffy woolly nonsense. Guarding your bed while you sleep. Free of will, nothing but winged messengers in nightgowns, coming to tell us not to be afraid? Tame agents of an all-knowing creator God whom we're supposed to believe is good even though the world is so flawed?"

Ficino looked at her, amazed. "What? Fluffy? Guarding your bed? However could your age have come to believe that? They are the operators of the universe, divine messengers, full of awe and light. Athene could fit within my beliefs about angels. And I remember very well what she was."

"I shouldn't have this, but look at it," I said, reaching up to the high shelf and taking down the Botticelli book Ikaros had brought me. "Look at these angels. They're not tame, and they have agency."

Klio looked at the angels for a long moment. "Not that Botticelli was painting from life, but I do see what you mean," she admitted.

"Where did that come from?" Ficino asked.

"Ikaros brought it back from one of his art expeditions," I said.

"You shouldn't have it. But I suppose it isn't doing any harm. As long as you haven't shown it to the children?"

"I showed Simmea the *Primavera* once, and the *Birth of Venus.*" She'd glimpsed the cover too, but she'd never mentioned it again. "And I showed it to Auge when she was just starting sculpting—and she's getting really good now. But I'm very careful with it."

"I'm sure Ikaros is saying Athene was just doing what God told her to," Klio said.

"That's nonsense," I said. "She was unquestionably acting for herself. Goddess or angel, she wasn't just a mouthpiece."

"If God exists and gave us free will, then he wanted us to use it," Ficino said. "So she could be doing as he wanted and also acting freely."

"If Athene was an angel, what would it change?" Klio asked, putting her fingertip on one of Botticelli's angels' faces.

"Perhaps how we worship," I said.

"How would it change that?" she asked.

"Sokrates said in the *Apology* that you should worship in the manner of the city in which you live. Plato said in the *Laws* that they should send to Delphi to ask how to worship," Ficino answered.

"What does Sokrates say now?" Klio asked, looking up from the book.

"He says Providence is a very interesting idea," Ficino said. "But he's so obsessed with the Workers at the moment that it's hard to get him to focus on anything else."

"I don't know how we'd manage without the Workers," Klio said. "They do so much. They let us lead philosphical lives because they're doing all the hard work—all the farming and building and everything. We're comfortable because of them."

"We're rich because of them," Ficino said. "We have no poverty here, because of them."

"The idea was always that they were here to help us at the beginning, while the children were growing, and that in future generations the Irons would replace them. Then we will have poverty, or at least some of us will live less comfortable lives."

"Not poverty," I said, remembering poverty in my own time. "Well, in some ways we are all poor. We live with very few possessions. But nobody will be in want. Nobody will feast while others starve."

"That would be unjust indeed," Ficino said. "Are we going to lose the Workers?"

Klio stopped and sat down. "Eventually, we'll lose them no matter what, unless Athene brings us more, and spare parts. They'll wear out. And if the city can only keep going by constant divine intervention then we're not doing very well, are we?"

"Having it to start us off—" Ficino said.

"Yes, but we had the Workers to start us off too. After that, what? And it could be quite abrupt if we give them rights and then they stop working. At the moment it's only some of them, and they are working voluntarily, but who knows what will happen? Aristomache made a powerfully moving speech about slavery, but when it comes to it they are machines and all our comfort rests on them." She held up her wine cup. "Who planted these vines, and pruned them? Who trod the grapes and added the yeast and bottled the vintage?"

"The children of Ferrara made these cups," I said. "We're starting to replace what the Workers do."

"But we're only starting. It will take a long time before we have everything smooth. If they suddenly refused to help it would be a disaster. And even with them slowly failing, it's difficult. There are a lot of things they do that we can't teach the children because we don't know how to do them. Do you know how to make wine?"

"We have a number of skills between us," Ficino said.

"Come and tell the Tech Committee that, and the Committee on Iron

Work," Klio said. "We have an odd number of skills between us, and we're very lacking in practical physical skills. I'm not sure we have three people who know how to fix the plumbing."

"I've got much better at midwifery than I ever imagined I would," I said. "I wanted the life of the mind, but here I am delivering babies and teaching girls how to breast feed."

"On the whole, the women are better on practical skills than the men," Klio said. "Which makes sense, really, when you think about it. Most of the men come from eras where they had slaves or servants to do the physical work. Even though some of the women did as well, they were still expected to do more of the hands-on things."

"To my mother, the word *work* meant sewing," I said.

"And if you'd stayed in your time, you'd have had to make most of your clothes," Klio said. "Not so for your brother."

"I'd have made most of his clothes as well," I said. "My aunt did have some dresses made for me, but I made all my own underthings. Underthings! How very little I miss them!"

"Do you miss anything?" Klio asked.

"About the nineteenth century?" She nodded. "I miss my father. I wish so much he could have been here. He'd have loved it so much. Apart from that—no. Nothing. Everything here is so much better. I have books and companionship and work that's worth doing. Even when everything isn't perfect and ideal and as one would wish Plato could have had it, even when I have to do terrible things," and here I was thinking of the baby with the hare lip that I had exposed, "It's still real work that's worthy of me. Nothing in my own time could have offered me that."

"I miss recorded music," Klio said. "Being able to listen to it whenever I wanted. Apart from that, nothing. But sometimes I wonder if we should have stayed in our own times and fought for the Republic there. If we should have tried to make our own cities more just."

"That's what I did, for the first sixty-six years of my life," Ficino said. "That gives me a different perspective. I did that, and I am remembered. We had a rebirth of the ancient world, and everyone acknowledges that my efforts made a contribution. But that was the most I could possibly do towards that, alone, in the company I had, without Athene. Without all of you. She brought us together here because we were so few, scattered throughout time."

"We know we wouldn't have achieved anything further in our lives, or else we wouldn't have been brought here when we were," I pointed out.

"I suppose you're right," Klio said. She drained her wine and set down the cup. "I should get back to the practical tasks at hand that help make the city work."

"The philosophy of the quotidian," Ficino said, smiling.

"I don't know if what we have here is what Plato meant by The Good Life," I said. "But it's *a* good life."

36

SIMMEA

Sokrates had once asked Kebes how he would fight a god. I had done it without even thinking about what I was doing, and I had used weapons Sokrates and Ficino had put into my hands, rhetoric and truth. I did not even understand what I had done in facing down Athene until the day before the festival of Hera when Pytheas met me, by arrangement, at the Garden of Archimedes. It was a fine night and I'd been looking through the telescope at the moons of Jupiter, and amusing myself by calculating their orbits. It was two months since I had been healed. For most of that time, Pytheas and Sokrates and I had been investigating mysteries and Workers, without advancing very far on either front.

Pytheas looked angry. "She won't do it," he said, without any preliminaries. "She hasn't calmed down at all. You can't imagine how angry with us she still is."

"Even after all this time?" I asked. My heart sank. "She's still angry? Really?"

"Yes, well, you pushed her on her own ground. And I think she's upset about something else as well. She was already very impatient even before that. She will get over it, but it'll take time. Usually if I'd made her this angry I'd leave her alone for a decade or so."

"Time is so different for you," I said.

"Not any more," he said, ruefully. "Or not for now, anyway. Now time is as urgent for me as it is for you, and she flat-out refuses to help. She was blisteringly sarcastic. She might even do something to make things worse."

"What could make it worse?" I asked, and then immediately realized. "Oh, pairing us with awful people?"

"Klymene again," he said, despondently.

"She wouldn't be so unjust," I said.

"You're making Sokrates's mistake of assuming the gods are good," Pytheas said. He led the way over to the little stone bench in the corner where we usually sat when we met here. There was a big lilac bush there and it always smelled sweet. Now at the heart of spring it was just coming into flower, and smelled overwhelming. "The gods are as petty and childish as any of the awful stories about us Plato wanted to keep out of the city. Athene's one of the best of us, but even she can be . . . spiteful when she's angry. Vengeful."

"It would be horribly unfair to Klymene," I said, sitting down beside him. "Klymene has done nothing. And all I did was explain that she could trust me to keep my word."

"She wouldn't think about Klymene at all, if that's what she wanted to do. Klymene barely exists to her. Athene has friends and favorites here, like Tullius and Ikaros, but she's only theoretically granting equal significance to people like Klymene. It's challenging. I have to really work at it." He sighed.

"Do you think she'll do that?"

"She'd be more likely to choose somebody really ugly for me. Or maybe—no, I don't know. Anyway, it's not so much me I'm worried about as you. You said—when we were talking on the beach about Daphne, you said you were afraid. And she could match you with somebody brutal." He put his arm around my shoulders. I could feel the warmth of it through my kiton. I leaned back against him.

"I don't think there are any brutal golds," I said, trying to be brave and face the worst. "Anyway, I've done it three times now, and Phoenix was pretty crass. It's not so bad. I can do it again."

He kicked his legs against the stone. "I hate this. I hate feeling helpless. And I suppose it's an essential human condition, and yes, even though I was so proud of myself doing this properly I was in fact cheating by knowing Athene was here and could fix things. I suppose in a way my coming here to the city was cheating, compared to going somewhere with poverty and dirt and all the terrible things of mortality seen close up. If I'd been a slave."

"Too late now," I said. "Though I suppose you could do it again if you wanted to?"

"I have never heard of anyone doing it again. And I don't know whether I could make myself."

"I'm glad you came here."

"Oh yes." He squeezed my shoulders. "I don't want you to have another baby with somebody else."

"No," I said. "I don't want to either. I'm not ready to have another baby.

My body is. But what happens if I get like that again? Athene wouldn't help us reach Asklepius again, and without that I might be in that horrible state for a year or even more."

"That's a very good point. There are things that people think help, iron and so on. But you don't want to risk it yet and I think that makes sense. When I'm back on good terms with Athene and we can fix it would be much better."

"You said a decade?"

"In a decade you'll only be twenty-eight, twenty-nine. There are eras when that would be considered quite young to be having a baby."

"I suppose." It seemed to me quite a long time to wait.

"But that isn't the problem, the problem is that you'll get pregnant at the festival, now, tomorrow, with somebody else. After Athene refused me, I came here with two potential solutions to that."

I twisted round so that I could see his face, tucking my knees up on the bench and putting my arms around them. "What are they?"

He put his hand on my bare knee, where it felt warm and heavy and almost unbearably erotic. "One is that you and I could mate now, tonight. You'd still have to go through with it tomorrow, but you'd already be pregnant with my son."

"How is it you're so sure I'd get pregnant, and that it would be a son?" I asked. It was hard to talk evenly because I was breathless at the thought.

"I'm a god," he said. "There are so many heroic souls, and so few chances for them to be born heroes."

"And that counts even though you're incarnate?"

"This is a soul thing, not a body thing," he said.

"And how do you know it wouldn't be a daughter?"

"It wouldn't—" He stopped and raised his eyebrows. "Usually, it feels unkind to beget a daughter, because in most eras it's so horrible to be a woman. But I suppose here and now is one of the few places it wouldn't be. So yes, it could be a daughter. That would be interesting. Different. Fun."

I was still acutely aware of his hand on my knee. If I chose that option we could be sharing eros in a few moments. I was absolutely ready. We could stand up together there in the Garden of Archimedes, or off in the woods if we were afraid somebody else might come to look at the stars. That would be wonderful, I knew it would. I wanted it so much. It was what I had wanted for so long. But I couldn't bear the thought of sinking down into that empty state of uncaring again. "What's the other alternative?"

"If you're not ready to have another baby now, you could eat silphium, and you won't get pregnant. Well, you probably would with me because the weight of heroic souls waiting would probably outweigh the power of the plant. But you would be very unlikely to with anyone else."

"What is it? I never heard of it."

"It's a root. I have some. I went and dug some up earlier in case you wanted it." He handed it to me from the fold in his kiton. It felt like a spring onion. "You would eat it now, and then tomorrow you go through with it, which you'll have to anyway, but you won't have a baby. Nobody will think anything is strange, because you did it twice without before."

"I might be safe anyway." I thought about it. "One in three is not good odds."

"You're slightly more likely to get pregnant again after being pregnant once," he said. "It's as if your body has to figure out how to do it."

Just then a Worker came up and began to dismantle part of the wall around the garden. Pytheas took his hand off my knee. I decided to take that as a sign. I put the silphium in my mouth and crunched it up. It tasted like a green onion.

"Good," Pytheas said. I couldn't tell from his voice if he was disappointed or relieved. "Do you know that's the first thing you've ever done that's against Plato's plan?"

"Whichever I'd chosen it would have been against it," I said. "Or does he say it's all right to copulate with your friend on the night before the festival?"

"He certainly does not. But I don't think he was imagining the effect this would have on particular people at all. He knew about agape, but he didn't think how it would mesh with these festivals. Or maybe he really couldn't imagine agape between men and women, and he thought agape between men wouldn't be affected by them going off to women at the festivals. Sokrates was married, and Aristotle, but never Plato."

There was a great clatter at that moment as the Worker pulled out a stone and several others fell. Pytheas got up and went over to the Worker. "Joy to you. What are you doing?" he asked.

It wrote something on the path. "Making art," Pytheas read aloud. "Good." He patted it, then wandered back to me.

"Can they tell when you pat them?" I asked as he settled down again.

"I have no idea. But Sokrates does it, so I do it."

We watched it for a while, pulling stones out of the wall and rearranging them. I couldn't see an intelligible pattern, but then you might not see one in the middle of a fresco either. Then I started to feel sleepy. "I should go to bed. I have to be up early to make garlands in the morning."

"Then we both have to mate with strangers in the afternoon." Pytheas ground his teeth. "She'll calm down. But she knows what I want now, and she has said no once, so it'll be hard to ask her without reminding her why she refused. Maybe I could ask Ficino to cheat instead. He might be amenable to a eugenic argument if not a romantic one."

"Maia might be amenable to a romantic one," I said. "Though maybe not. She was so strict on not knowing our babies. I don't think Axiothea would."

"Eugenic," Pytheas said at once. "And Atticus too. Funny how easy it is to tell. Too late for this festival tomorrow, but we can try that next time. We know they cheat. We can try to use that to our advantage."

"What is the eugenic argument?"

"That any baby you and I had would clearly be superior in all ways and be a philosopher king, exactly as the city wants." He hugged me suddenly. "It's even true. She'd be a brilliant philosophical hero."

"I'd rather not wait ten years," I admitted. "How long will the silphium keep working?"

"This month, until you bleed again."

He stood. I followed him up and took his hand. We walked back through the streets together. It was late and they were quiet, but not deserted. We saw a Master striding along, and couples slipping back from the woods. There were also Workers here and there, some of them engaged in engraving dialogue, others going about usual Worker tasks. One of them slid in front of us as we passed the temple of Hestia. We stopped. It carved something by our feet. I had to angle myself to see it in the dim light of the sconces. "How many stars?"

"I don't know," I said.

"Too many to count," Pytheas said.

It drew something else, something that looked like the number eight written sideways. "No," Pytheas said. "A finite but very large number. And new ones are born all the time and old ones burn out, making them uncountable."

The Worker rolled away. "They're wonderful," I said. "Now that they're talking, they're thinking about everything. They're naturally philosophical. I couldn't have answered that."

"Some of the Masters could," Pytheas said, absently. "Lysias knows that, I'm sure."

"New stars are being born?" I looked up, as if hoping to see some, but saw of course only the old familiar constellations.

"Yes, very far away, in nebulae. They call them stellar nurseries. You can't see them with the naked eye, and I'm not sure whether our telescopes are good enough. People will go out there and live among them—you will. Your soul, in whatever body it's in at the time. I haven't been out there yet, it's a long way from home, and I know it's silly, but I feel uncomfortable about leaving the sun. I will in time. One day, when people on new worlds call to me. Maybe you."

"I won't be me. I won't remember." It was a strange thought, bittersweet.

"No. But I will. You won't remember, but you'll call me and I'll come." He sounded very sure. I didn't ask if it was foresight and an oracle. I just hugged him.

We should have expected it if we'd been thinking clearly, but of course we didn't. My name was the second to be drawn, and matched with me was Kebes. I went up among the usual jokes and congratulations to have the garland bound around our wrists. Kebes was beaming, and I tried to keep my face under control, to take this like a philosopher. Pytheas had been wrong, this wasn't aimed at me. It was meant to wound him, and it would. Athene didn't care much about me or anything at all about poor Kebes. I kept my head high and tried to look straight ahead. I knew Pytheas was there, but I didn't want to have to meet his eyes. It would be bad enough afterwards.

Once we were out of the square and the dancers I looked up at Kebes. "Who could have guessed?" he said. He was still smiling. "I haven't been chosen at all since the first time, but I won the wrestling yesterday. I'm glad now that I did."

I knew I had to say something, but couldn't imagine what I could possibly say. I had seen him win the wrestling, and congratulated him at the time.

"Is something wrong?" he asked.

"No," I said. "It's a little awkward, that's all."

"What is?" He looked alarmed.

"Just it being you and knowing you so well. The others times it's been people I barely knew."

We came to the street of Dionysos and turned towards the practice rooms. "I was chosen with Euridike," he said. "I know her slightly."

"She's very pretty," I said.

"Yes," he said, noncommittally.

We went inside and took a room—all the doors but one were open, so we went down to the far end. Kebes closed the door and unwound the garland. I felt shy and awkward as I took my kiton off. "I haven't done it since the baby was born," I said.

"But you're all healed up?" Kebes asked. Then before I could answer, "You mean you haven't done it with Pytheas?"

"Pytheas and I don't—I've told you before! We're doing agape, not eros." The memory of his hand on my knee the night before came back, and with it an erotic jolt that felt disloyal to both of them.

"You don't do that, maybe, but you're doing something? He touches you? You suck his dick?"

"I do not! I never do that for anyone. On the ship—you were there."

He looked blank. "On the *Goodness*?"

"The slave ship." I still hated to think of it.

"I wasn't on the same slave ship as you. I met you in the market."

"One of the sailors forced my mouth, that's all." I sat down on the bed, suddenly cold.

"But you—Pytheas—you said he was your lover. Are you saying you don't do anything at all?" He laughed. "I thought—"

"We talk," I said, with as much dignity as I could manage. "We care about each other. Agape. That's what I've always said. I don't know why you care anyway."

"Because as I was trying to say that day in Thessaly before Sokrates shut me up, you could do much better than him. You're taken in by his pretty face and his fast talk, but he's not genuine." He dropped his kiton. His penis was awake, and as big as the rest of him. "I am. You'll see now. Come on. I love you. I want you." He took a step towards the bed.

"I like to stand up," I said, getting up.

"Stand up?" He stopped, bemused.

"Let me show you. I worked it out with Aeschines. It's much more comfortable."

"Euridike and I did it on the bed," he said, shaking his head. "But this will make it different."

Unfortunately, Kebes was too tall for the position I had worked out with Aischines and repeated with the others. He was also very excited. "Just give me a moment to breathe," I said, when I saw that wasn't going to work.

"Come on Simmea, it's me, you're ready," he said. "I can see how to do it standing up."

Without any hesitation he lifted me up above him and lowered me onto his penis. I clutched his shoulders, afraid of falling, though I knew he was one of the strongest of us. Then he stepped forward until my back was against the wall and began to thrust, driving the breath out of me. "There," he said.

I started to struggle, trying to get down, because I felt trapped and squeezed. Even on the bed I would have had more freedom than this. He must have mistaken my movements for passion because he didn't stop battering away at me. Maybe Athene had meant it as punishment for me after all. It wasn't rape, for I had consented, but I certainly didn't like it. "Wait," I said. "No, Kebes, wait, please."

"You like it. There. You're mine. You're mine. I'll show you. You're mine, mine, you always were, you were meant to be, mine, my Lucia, mine."

"No!" I said, horrified at what he was saying. "Stop it! I'm here for the city. I'm not doing this for your fantasy!"

"Say my name," he said, not stopping or even slowing down. "Lucia. My Lucia. Say my name."

If I had hated him it would have been different. But he was my friend, even ramming me up against the wall and panting on my face. Maybe with his name I could reach that part of him. "Matthias," I said. "No. Stop. Listen to me."

But as I said his name he spilled his seed inside me. I could feel his penis jerking away as it gushed out. He carried me over to the bed then and put me down. I rolled away from him, breathing deeply.

"You liked it," he said, less sure of himself now.

"I'm not yours," I said.

"You still think you're his?" he asked. "After that?"

"I am *my own*," I said, turning to face him. "I don't belong to anyone. Pytheas doesn't try to own me." Though he had claimed me as a votary, which was disturbingly similar. But he had only done that to protect me from Athene. And after all, he was a god. And what he had offered me was exactly everything I most wanted—to make art, to build the future, to help each other become our best selves. "He honors me."

"I honor you!" he protested. "We were meant to be together. We were chained together. And now we were chosen together."

"Things like that are accidents, not fate," I said. "And don't you think I should have a choice?"

"Yes, I do, but I think you should choose me." He put his hand out to my face, awkwardly. "You're mine. You'll have my baby. We can run away together before he's born, build a house, have a family. We can do this every night, have more children. My mother, my sisters, were lost, but I still have you and we can make a new family."

"Matthias! Will you listen to me?"

He stopped.

"I'm not your mother or your sisters. I have made my choice. I choose the city. And as a lover I choose Pytheas. I'm here in this room with you right now because I choose the city and the city chose us to be together now. I may have your child," though I hoped the silphium would work and I would not, "but if I do, I will give it to the city to grow up here and be a philosopher. I don't want to run away, as I've told you thousands of times. I don't want to destroy the city."

I had said this often enough before, but either he hadn't listened or he had twisted it in his mind and thought I meant I wasn't ready. Even though he'd often heard me arguing with Sokrates for the merits of the city, he reacted as if I had struck him. "You can't mean that. You're mine."

"I can. I do." I got up and picked up my kiton.

"You don't have to go. We can stay all night. We can do it again."

"We can stay, but we're not obliged to. I've done what I was obliged to do and I'm leaving." I put my kiton on.

He stared at me in horror. "What—"

"Kebes, I'm your friend, but I'm not your property. I can choose what I want."

His face crumpled for a moment. Then he lowered his head and scowled. "I don't care anyway," he said. "You're not so special. You're nothing but a scrawny flat-faced buck-toothed Copt."

I laughed. "That's true. And I am also a gold of the Just City."

"I didn't mean it. Come back." He got up and put his hand on my bare shoulder.

I pushed past him to the door. "I won't mention this again if you don't."

"Where are you going?"

I hadn't thought about it, but as he asked I knew. "I'm going to Thessaly."

The streets were quiet, though I passed numerous pairs of Workers engaged in written dialogues. Pytheas's vision of the streets being entirely paved in them was coming true. To my surprise, Sokrates was at home and answered the door to me at once. "Simmea! Joy to you. Is everything all right?" He drew me inside. There was nobody there. A book was open on the bed where he must have been reading it.

"Joy to you, Sokrates. I was drawn with Kebes, and it was . . . awkward," I said.

"Oh dear. And it will be difficult for Pytheas."

"It will." We went out into the garden. "I told Kebes I was coming here, so he won't. But you'll probably have to talk to him later. He thinks he owns me, and he just doesn't."

"I can talk to him and try to make that clear to him," Sokrates said. "Pytheas will be more difficult."

"I don't know whether he will." I was still sticky and uncomfortable between my legs as I sat in my usual place beneath the tree. When I leaned back my back felt bruised where it had been banged into the wall. "It's going to be so awkward with both of them."

"I don't know how Plato could have imagined that this would make everything easier," Sokrates said.

I laughed and rolled my shoulders to try to loosen my back. "If it wasn't for his wanting women to be philosophers, I'd imagine that he thought wives were a fungible resource. Have you read the *Republic*?"

"With a great deal of attention. But I'm afraid I can't lend it to you, I have promised not to." He sat down beside the limestone Herm he had carved himself during the Peloponnesian War.

"Not to lend it to me?" I was astonished.

"Not to lend it to any of you." He stressed the plural.

"Pytheas has read it, of course."

"Of course he must have. Before he came here." Sokrates nodded. "How fascinating he is! I entirely understand your being in love with him. I don't even accuse him of having used his powers to beguile you, as he seems remarkably fond of you in return."

"He doesn't have any powers here. He's just so amazingly wonderful," I said. I couldn't help smiling when I thought about him. "But being incarnate makes him vulnerable in odd ways, and I can help him with that."

"You don't ever feel that he wants to take more of you than you want to give? That's what they say about the gods."

"Never. Pytheas wants me to be my best self." That was the problem with Kebes. Kebes didn't see me, or my potential best self. He saw something he imagined as me, something he called Lucia. I hadn't been Lucia for a long time now. "And I want Pytheas to be his best self."

"And I want the same for both of you," Sokrates said.

"You're in love with him too," I said, realizing it as he spoke. "And so you must know he doesn't take more than you want to give."

"As long as you want to give everything." Sokrates smiled wryly. "I have loved Athene and Apollo all my life, and between them they have consumed most of it."

"But aren't you better for it? In your soul?"

"I wouldn't want to be any different," he admitted.

"And you love Pytheas the same way I do!" I was pleased, thinking it through, excited and not even a shred jealous. I trusted Sokrates, and this was something we shared. If we were both in love with Pytheas, then we could talk about it and maybe define agape more clearly. I leaned forward eagerly with my hands on my knees, ignoring the twinge in my back.

"I love both of you, of course," he said, gently, clearly disconcerted.

"I know, and when it comes to philia I truly love you too, but that's not what I mean, though of course that's also really important." I took a breath to compose my thoughts more clearly. "I love you and you love me, as teachers and pupils who are friends love each other."

"Yes," he agreed, cautiously.

"But you love Pytheas the same way I do. Agape."

He shook his head. I had argued with Sokrates about many things over the course of years, and had rarely seem him this disconcerted. "Not the same at all. I'm an ugly old man. I joke about being helpless before his beauty, but——"

"And I'm an ugly young girl, and he's Apollo, he's thousands of years older than both of us. But he has chosen both of us as votaries because age and beauty are trivial; what really matters to him is excellence. What's on the inside of our heads. And both of us can help him, we can give him new ideas and new ways of thinking!" I said all this as fast as I could get the words out. "It does make it a bit different that you don't have any eros to struggle with conquering. But it's still agape, and still very similar."

"I knew him as a god first, and was his votary, and only later came to know him as Pytheas, and vulnerable," he said.

"Yes, that's a real difference," I acknowledged. "You knew him as a god for so long. I did that the other way around. But you also loved him all that time. And now both of you passionately want to increase each other's excellence, just the same as he and I do. This is so great! We both want that for him, and he wants it for us," I was so pleased I'd worked this out. "And we want that for him a lot."

"We do," Sokrates said, staring at me. "Sometimes I think the most important thing I can be doing—and the same for you—is helping him to increase his excellence. More important than the Workers or the city or anything. Because he's not just our friend Pytheas, he really is the god Apollo. He's the light. And what he learns and knows and understands is so important for the world. His excellence has a future, and nothing else here does."

"Well, ours does for our souls," I amended. "But Pytheas still has so much to learn about being human, so much that he ought to understand about it. He really is wonderful. And he tries so hard. It's marvellous that he says excellence is something even the gods must pursue."

"He certainly pursues it. I can't speak for all the gods, and he doesn't either. I do wonder what his Father pursues, alone in the centre."

"He said he didn't know."

"That doesn't stop me wondering about it all the more." Sokrates tugged at his beard, as he sometimes did when thinking hard.

"But Pytheas—Apollo—wants to increase my excellence, as I want to increase his. And it's the same with you." I beamed at him. I was so delighted to have figured this out.

Sokrates focused on me and sighed. "You are truly very close to what Plato dreamed. You're almost enough to justify this whole absurd structure."

"It's not absurd," I said. "Though I must admit it does have its absurd side sometimes."

"Plato understood so little about what people are like," Sokrates said.

"If I were making a plan for a Just City, there are things I'd change. I'd let people choose their partners, and whether to bring up their own children."

"It's like a delicate mosaic, if you change anything the whole thing falls apart into incoherence. Plato had logical reasons for those things."

"I do wish I could read it. Maia says not until I'm fifty, which is ridiculous."

"Didn't Pytheas tell you what it said?" Sokrates was looking at me alertly, his most characteristic expression. I wondered how many debates we'd had sitting just where we were in this garden, and how many more we would have in the years to come.

"He told me about the masters cheating at the lots to get better children. Though it wasn't the masters cheating that put me with Kebes, it was Athene, to punish Pytheas and me for annoying her."

"What?" Sokrates puffed up with anger. "That's unjust!"

"Pytheas says she can be spiteful. He says you shouldn't make the mistake of assuming that they're good."

"They shouldn't have that power if they're not responsible with it. This city is a great many things, but one of them is directly enforced with Athene's power." He leapt to his feet and began to pace around the garden. "I have a good mind to challenge her. I've been thinking about it for a while. I am her votary too. And what she is doing and learning here is also an issue that has very deep consequences for the world."

"You love her too, in that same way," I said.

"Of course I do. I have always loved wisdom. Pytheas says she wants to know everything. I have questions it would do her soul good to consider."

"Pytheas says she's really angry now, but she'll calm down. It might be better to wait until she calms down before you challenge her."

"Did he say how long it would take?" Sokrates asked, stopping and looking down at me.

"He said maybe a decade."

"I don't have a decade. I'm seventy-four years old." He began to pace again. Nobody would have been able to tell he was that old, especially watching him pace. He looked a vigorous sixty. "You're not about to drop dead. And I think she should have a little bit longer. She and Pytheas had an argument yesterday."

He spun around. "She's the goddess of reason and logic. She shouldn't quarrel and act in anger."

"I agree, but if that's the way things are, there's not much point saying they ought to be different because that would be better and more logical," I said.

Sokrates laughed. "I do have a tendency in that direction, yes. I want to challenge her——" There was a scratch at the outside door, and he went to open it. I hoped it wouldn't be Pytheas, as I wasn't ready to see him yet. I knew it wouldn't be Kebes.

It was Aristomache and Ikaros. I heard them wishing Sokrates joy before they came outside and wished me the same thing. "Weren't you drawn in the lots today?" Aristomache asked as I returned their greetings. "Are you still recovering from childbirth?"

"I was drawn, and I have played my part and finished," I said.

"It must be a very uncomfortable thing," Ikaros said. "I'm glad I don't have to abide by it. A random partner every four months, sometimes friends, sometimes enemies, sometimes strangers."

"We were just saying that we don't know what Plato was thinking," Sokrates said.

They laughed, as if this was an often repeated joke.

I started to get up and excuse myself and leave them to their accustomed conversation. Sokrates waved me back. "I'm thinking about challenging Athene to a debate," he said, to all of us. "On The Good Life. In front of everyone. In the Agora."

"I haven't seen her for a long time," Ikaros said, sitting down by the tree.

"She's here," Aristomache said, sitting by the Herm. "I know how to get in touch with her if you need her. But a debate?"

"I'm an old man," Sokrates said. He stayed standing in the middle of the garden. "I want to debate her before I die, like poor Tullius."

"You're a long way from death," Ikaros said. "But I'd love to hear you debate her. That would be . . ."

"Socratic frenzy?" Sokrates said, clearly teasing him, because Ikaros laughed.

"We'd all love to hear it," Aristomache said. "But I don't know if she'd agree."

"We'd all love to hear it too," I said. "I can't think of anything we'd enjoy more."

"The good life," mused Ikaros. "I don't suppose you could consider asking her to debate my theory of will and reason?"

"What's that?" I asked.

"That will, or love, and reason are the two horses of the chariot in the *Phaedrus*, and it doesn't matter which one you follow if it's taking you closer to God."

"So if you love something it doesn't matter if you understand it? It can still take you closer to divinity, just by loving it?" I asked.

"Yes!" Ikaros looked excited.

"That's just mystical twaddle," I said. I wasn't in the mood for it.

"That's what Septima said," Ikaros said, not discouraged at all. "But wait until you see how it fits with my theory of the gods."

"Besides," Aristomache interrupted, "Plato said one of the horses was human and one divine. Which would be which?"

"That's the beauty of this idea," Ikaros said.

"If Athene agrees to debate me, you will be there, perhaps you could ask her to debate this afterwards," Sokrates said, starting to pace again. "Or maybe I will mention your theory of the gods in my argument, if things take the right turn. Or we could have a whole series of debates."

"Do you want me to invite her?" Aristomache asked.

"If you can find her, I'd like you to deliver a formal written invitation," Sokrates said. "And don't keep it secret, let everyone know I want to do this so they can start anticipating it."

"Are you really sure this is the best time?" I asked.

Sokrates smiled. "It feels to me like the very best time."

37

APOLLO

She came not helmeted but castle-crowned, Athene Polias, the builder of cities. She didn't look angry; to anyone who didn't know her she would have seemed serene, calm, entirely Olympian. The anger was all in the way she moved. What had angered her? She was getting bored, and something had upset her, and I had pestered her and made her act against her best judgement in petitioning to heal Simmea, and then Simmea had wrong-footed her. If Simmea had promised and sworn and acted awed and intimidated, she wouldn't have stayed angry. It was the way Simmea had bested her that did it, and of course, that made it the worst possible time for Sokrates to challenge her to a public debate.

Her petty revenge, at the Festival of Hera, had stung. I was chosen last, and paired with Euridike. Euridike was the very pattern of a Hellenic maiden, fair-skinned and crowned with golden braids. Her breasts, which had been magnificent, were sagging a little with child-bearing now, but she was probably the most beautiful and desirable of the golds available at that festival. I knew perfectly well what Athene meant by it—to show me that this was what I really wanted. When I had been free to choose this was what I had always chosen, and indeed, this was something I could easily have. I felt physical desire for Euridike that I did not, could not, feel for Simmea. And yes, that hurt, but it was a pinprick. The whole time I was with Euridike I naturally couldn't turn my mind away from poor Simmea matched with Kebes.

I didn't think for an instant that she would prefer him to me. As with the time we wrestled, that wasn't a fair contest. I was a god. She had said she loved me as stones fell down, and I trusted that. No lout like Kebes was going to affect the important thing. But I hated to think of him hurting her, either physically or emotionally. I kept thinking of it. He wouldn't want to hurt her. He loved her, in his way, like a dog loves his bone. And all Simmea had was philosophy. (And the silphium, which I was so glad I had remembered. I could not have endured watching her bear Kebes's child. It had been bad enough with tone-deaf Nikias.) And of course, Euridike was a person with equal significance and her own choices, and she found me desirable, and having been matched with me she deserved more of me than half my attention. (How could Plato have thought this was a good idea? How could he?)

Simmea insisted afterwards that everything was all right and it hadn't changed anything. But she was avoiding Kebes, and so was I.

The whole city came to the Agora for the debate. I saw Glaukon in his wheeled chair. The babies were there, even the smallest, so that their nursery-maids needn't miss it. The Workers, those who had taken an interest in philosophy, were lining up at the edges to the Agora to listen. Old Porphyry had dragged himself from his sickbed and was sitting with the pregnant women eight months along, down near the front. There was nothing we loved more than a debate, and this was the debate of a century. I saw tears glitter in Ikaros's eyes as Athene made her way through the crowd to the rostrum. Ficino too was blinded by honourable tears. He introduced the debate.

Simmea, beside me, was the only person I could see who didn't look delighted at the whole event. "I was thinking about Plato in Syracuse," she said. "The time when the tyrant sold him into slavery. That was after a debate on the good life."

"I'm sure Sokrates knows about that," I said. "I'm sure Sokrates was thinking about it when he suggested this."

Sokrates was wearing a plain white wool kiton. He nodded and smiled at Ficino's introduction. He stood to the right and Athene to the left, which meant that she was going to begin. He did not look at all intimidated by her presence.

Her speech was splendid. She spoke of course of the Just City, of justice in the soul and justice in the city. I saw people in the crowd nodding at her eloquence. It was all straight out of Plato, and you couldn't have found a more appreciative audience. Nobody clapped when she finished, they knew the rules, but there was a deep murmur of appreciation. Sokrates took a step forward.

"I can't possibly compete with a beautiful speech like that," he began. "I hope you'll let me off and allow me to talk in my usual manner, asking questions and trying to find the answers."

There was a ripple of laughter from the crowd. Athene inclined her head gracefully. Simmea squeezed my hand.

"You've talked a lot about justice, and a lot about this city," he said, conversationally. "Do you think this city is just?"

"I do."

"Not merely that it's pursuing justice, or attempting to be just, but that it actually attains justice?"

"Yes." I was surprised. I'd have thought she'd said that it was on its way to justice. The experiment wasn't anything like done yet. I'm not sure even Plato would have thought it was already just. But many among the crowd were nodding.

"And you find that justice in the relations of the part to the whole and the way things are laid out?"

"Yes."

"Well it seems to me that there are a few issues that need to be cleared up before I'd call this the good life. First there's the question of choice. I'd say there can't be justice when people have no choice, do you agree? I'm thinking of people in prison, or condemned to row in a ship, shackled to the oar."

"The sentence that sent them there might be just," Athene countered.

"Yes, that could be so, but in their situation when they're there, when they're compelled to stay, or to row, they've had freedom taken from them and they're under the overseer's lash. There's no justice there, or don't you agree?"

"I agree, subject to what I said before."

"And if the sentence that sent them there wasn't just, if the judge was bribed or the evidence was false, or if they were captured by pirates and chained to the oar, then there's no justice?"

"No, in that case there's no justice. The punishment is making them worse people, not better, and in addition the passing of the unjust sentence is making the judge worse."

"Then I submit that the case is the same in this city, that the Masters chose to be here but the children did not." Sokrates leaned back a little as if to give her space to reply.

"The children were rescued from slavery," she said.

"They were bought as slaves and brought here and given no choices about how to live."

"Children are never given such choices."

"Really?" Sokrates asked. "But I thought souls chose their lives before birth, as Plato wrote in the *Phaedo*."

I smiled, hearing Sokrates cite that dialogue he disliked so much. Athene glared over at me, guessing I must have confirmed this for Sokrates. She caught me smiling, and glared even harder.

"Yes, that's true," she admitted, reluctantly. The audience let out a sigh, as if they had all been holding their breath through the pause waiting to hear.

"Then in a way the children did choose to come here," Sokrates said.

"It's not true," Kebes burst out, from where he stood down near the rostrum. Simmea, next to me, winced. Kebes really was recalcitrant. He had to hold on to his anger and deny that he had in any way chosen to be here, even when he heard it from the mouth of Athene herself.

She ignored him. "They did. And once they were here we looked after them as if we were their loving parents with their best interests at heart. If you ask them now they are grown, they will say they are happy they came here."

"Some of them will," Sokrates said, and his eyes sought out Simmea, who stood straight at my side. "Will you agree with that, Simmea?"

"Assuredly, Sokrates," she said, speaking up plainly. There was a ripple of laughter.

"But some of them will not." He looked at Kebes, who was near him, at the front. "Kebes?"

"I never chose to come here. I have never been reconciled to having been dragged from my home and bought as a slave and brought here. I have never had any choice about staying. I still hate and resent the Masters, and I am not the only one." His voice was passionate and clear. The crowd were making unhappy murmurs. Athene looked daggers at Kebes.

Sokrates spoke again, and at once Athene's eyes were back on him. "It's a slippery argument to say that our souls gave consent before birth, because it would be possible to use that to justify doing anything to anybody. We don't remember what our souls chose or why. We don't know what part of our lives we wanted and what part we overlooked, or agreed to endure for the sake of another part. It may be a kind of consent, but it's not at all the same as giving active consent here and now."

"I agree," Athene said. "But in the case of the children, bringing them here has made them better people. It is the opposite of the case of the galley slave."

"Except that even if it did good to them, it made you and the masters worse because you bought them as slaves and disregarded their choices, as in the case of the unjust judge who condemned the slave."

"I do not think I am worse for it," she said, confidently.

"So? Well, let me ask others. Maia? Do you think you are better or worse because you bought the children?"

Maia jumped when she was addressed. "Worse, Sokrates," she admitted, after a moment.

"Aristomache?"

"Worse," she said immediately.

"Atticus?"

"Worse," he said, speaking out loudly. "And since reading Aristomache's dialogue, I have come to believe that I am worse because I kept slaves in my own time."

"But whether or not it made anyone's soul less just, I agree that once you had the children here you treated them as best you knew, and certainly as Plato suggested," Sokrates said.

"Yes, we did," Athene agreed.

"But the next question is whether Plato was a good authority for these things. Did he have children?"

"You know he did not."

"There are other ways of knowing about how to bring people up than being a parent. And indeed, I've read that after I knew him he became a teacher, he had a school in Athens, a famous school, the Academy, which became the very name for learning. Was it for children?"

"It was for older people. A university, not a school."

"So what made him an expert in the education of younger people?" He hesitated for an instant and then moved on before Athene answered. "Nothing. And on the same grounds, I could ask what cities he founded. And I could ask what happened when he tried to involve himself in the politics of Syracuse, what wonderful results he had in that city? And similarly, his pupil Aristotle taught Alexander the Great, and Alexander did found cities and no doubt we see in Alexander the pattern of the philosopher king you wish to create, and in his cities the pattern of justice?"

"Below the belt," Simmea muttered. I grinned. She was completely caught up in the debate.

"Plato had a dream which was never tried until now, but now that it has been tried it is successful," Athene said, wisely avoiding the issues of Syracuse and Alexander.

"So you brought the children here and put them into an experiment, in the hope it would be successful," Sokrates said.

"Yes," Athene conceded.

"And you believe it has been?"

"Yes."

"Successful at maximizing justice?"

"Yes," she insisted.

"Well, I think there are other points of view possible on that subject. To take just one aspect of this supposedly Just City consider the festival of Hera, which instead of increasing happiness is visibly making everyone miserable. Human relationships can't work like that. Eating together is different from sharing eros together. I've seen people made unhappy by being drawn together, or unhappy by being drawn together once and never again." Again Sokrates was seeking out people in the crowd. I was grateful he did not look at us. "Damon?"

"Yes, Sokrates?"

"Is the system of having wives and children in common making you happy, or unhappy?"

"Unhappy, Sokrates," Damon said, clearly.

"Auge?"

"Unhappy, Sokrates," she said promptly.

"Half the children are cheating on the system, and almost nobody likes it. Plato knew a lot about love and was notably eloquent on the subject, far more eloquent than I could ever be, though he set the words in my mouth. How could he then set up such a travesty? But you will say, will you not, that the purpose of the system is not to maximize individual happiness but the justice of the whole city?"

"Yes," she said.

"And how does this maximize justice?"

"People do not form individual attachments but are attached to all the others, and people do not care more about their own children than all the children of the city."

"But that's nonsense," Sokrates said gently. "They do form individual attachments, they're just pursuing them in secret. And they do care more about their own children, they're just prevented from seeing them."

"It may not be perfect, but it is more just than the existence of families,"

Athene said. "Plato was successfully attempting to avoid nepotism and factionalism. We have none of that here. Ficino, you can speak for the evil which families can cause to a republic."

Ficino nodded sadly. "Yes, it's true, family rivalries did great harm to Florentia. The Guelphs and the Ghibellines, and then later in my own time the rivalry between the Medici and the other noble families. It can tear a city apart, and there is no justice possible." I saw many of the Masters nodding. "The worst thing is with inheritance. Even if you educate an heir carefully, they will not always be the best person to succeed to power. And unless rulers happen to be childless, they will always prefer their children, regardless of fitness."

"We saw that in Rome," Manlius said. "Caligula, Commodus, we have innumerable examples. Whereas when the emperor was childless and chose the best succesor we had rulers like Hadrian and Marcus Aurelius. But family love can be a wonderful consolation when things go wrong in the state."

"It can indeed be very pleasant when things go well in the family," Athene said, nodding to him in a friendly way, and then turning back to Sokrates. "Just as you called on one or two children to say that Plato's system makes them unhappy, there are many among the Masters I could call on to talk about how families did the same for them."

"And I could call on many more among the children to witness that they are forming individual attachments in secret, but I will not, because I would be putting them in danger of being punished if they spoke the truth."

Athene was silent, and so was the crowd. Everyone kept still and tried to avoid Sokrates's eyes.

Then Klymene spoke up, astonishing me. Her voice sounded very soft in the big space, but everyone was so quiet that she could be heard clearly. "I have not made any individual attachment. But I see it all around me. In my sleeping house, I am the only one who is not in some kind of love affair. Sokrates is completely right about this. Almost everyone has individual attachments. And while I believe the city knows best how to bring up children, and I understand what you're saying about the dangers of factionalism and preference, I do miss my own boy, that I only saw for a few minutes after he was born."

"Bravely spoken," Sokrates said, smiling at her. "I think that point is made. Now, let's move on. I questioned whether Plato was wise enough to write the constitution for a city like this. He was only a man. But you are a god, are you not?"

"I am," Athene said, cautiously stepping into Sokrates's unavoidable rhetorical trap.

"So you know more than mere mortals, isn't that so?"

"Of course," Athene said.

"So we should trust you to be doing what is right for us, even if we can't quite understand why?"

"Yes."

"And you have been deeply involved in setting up this city from the beginning?"

"Yes."

"And you have constantly used your power to make things work out for the city, things that might otherwise not have worked?"

"Yes."

"The trouble with that is that even though you are a god you too are ignorant in some areas. One area I can easily cite is to do with the Workers. Until I discovered it, just recently, nobody knew that they had free will and intelligence." Sokrates raised an arm to indicate the Workers who were there listening in a circle around the outside of the agora. Axiothea was standing near Crocus and read aloud the response he carved.

"Volition," she read. "Want to choose, want to talk, want to make art, want to debate, want to stay."

"Wait," Manlius called. "Sixty-one is writing something."

"What is it?" Sokrates asked.

"No choice brought, choose stay city," Manlius read out.

"Precisely," Sokrates said. "They wanted to choose and to talk and to make art, they wanted a say in their own lives. They didn't choose to come, but they do choose to stay. But you didn't even know they could think, nobody did."

"But as soon as you discovered it, we agreed to consider them people. Now they spend ten hours a day working and ten being educated and the rest recharging, their equivalent of eating and sleeping." Athene looked pleased. "Once we realized we were committing an injustice we moved at once to redress it."

"Indeed. That speaks very well of you, of the city in general. I think Aristomache deserves especial thanks for this." He smiled at Aristomache where she stood near him in the crowd. "But my point is that the reason you were treating them unfairly is because you were not even aware, until Crocus and I discovered it, that the Workers were people."

"He's got her," Simmea muttered.

"Yes, I was unaware," Athene admitted.

"So even though you are a goddess you don't know everything?"

"Of course not."

"Of course not," I echoed. "He knows that."

"Yes, but not everybody does," Simmea said. "Hush."

"So, for instance, you didn't know how well Plato's experiment would work until you tried it?"

"No."

"It was an experiment?"

"Yes. I said so."

"An experiment, and nobody knew what would happen. And to perform this experiment, why didn't you do as Plato said?"

"We did," Athene said, indignant.

"Plato said you should take over an existing city and drive out everyone over ten years of age, you didn't do that?"

"No. It seemed better to start fresh."

"Seemed better to you?"

"Yes."

"Even though it wasn't what Plato said?" Sokrates pretended surprise. There was a ripple of laughter.

"What Plato said wasn't possible," Athene snapped.

"Wasn't possible even for you?" Sokrates sounded even more surprised.

"Not everything is possible even for the gods," Athene said.

Sokrates paused, then shook his head sadly. "Not everything is possible, and you do not know everything?"

"I already said so." Athene was clearly irritated now.

"To return to what Plato said. He thought his city would be near other cities, would trade with them and make war with them. Why did you decide instead to put it on an island far away from other cities and with no contact with the outside world?"

Athene hesitated. "It seemed it would work better that way."

"So you felt free to change things Plato wrote when you thought they would work better a different way, but you kept them the same and held Plato's words up as unchangeable writ when you didn't want to change them?"

She hesitated again. "There were a number of good reasons to choose this island."

"Yes, the volcano that will erupt and destroy all the evidence of your meddling. That was going to be my next point. If you believe that this is the Just City, that the life here is the good life, why did you situate it in this little corner of the world that will be destroyed, at a point in time where it can influence nothing and change nothing? Why is it set here in a sterile backwater? Why didn't you put it in a time and place where it could really have an effect, where it could have posterity, where all humanity could benefit from the results of this experiment and not just you?"

There was a swelling murmur through the crowd at that, especially from the Masters. Everyone must have wondered about that.

"This was a time when it was possible. The more things affect time, the less power the gods have to do things." She sounded even more irritated now.

"So you deliberately chose a backwater?"

"Yes," she snapped.

"And you deliberately chose a time when it could not last?"

"I told the Masters when I gathered them together. Nothing mortal can last, and the most we can hope for is to create legends. Legends of this city will change the world." She spread her hands out to the crowd.

"Ah yes," Sokrates said, drawing everyone's attention back to him. "Atlantis." He laughed. "Can legends change the world? Is that really the best you could do?"

"Legends really can change the world," I whispered to Simmea. "Whether Sokrates believes it or not."

"This city is worth having whether it has results in time or not," Athene said.

"Then why didn't you build it on Olympos, outside time?"

"That wouldn't have been possible." It really wouldn't. It wasn't even imaginable. Athene cast another furious glance at me, only too aware who must have told Sokrates that Olympos was outside time.

"And how do you know it is worth having?"

"It self-evidently is!"

"It may or may not be, but you have established that you did not know everything, that it was an experiment. You did not, could not, know it would be a better life for those you brought here against their will."

"They prayed to be here," Athene said.

"The Masters prayed. The children and the Workers were purchased and given no choice at all, since we have agreed to leave aside the claims of choices made by souls before birth."

Athene smiled. "The children had as much choice as humans ever do. Every human soul is born into a society, and that society shapes their possible lives. And we have given them lives as good as we could imagine. As for the Workers, if they had not come here they might never have developed souls at all."

"Even if that is so, it's worth mentioning that since they came here, the children and the Workers have not been allowed to leave. In most cities, as young people grow up they can leave and seek out a more congenial home if they do not like it. They could leave Athens for Sparta or Crete, or if they preferred they could choose to found a new colony, or settle among the horselords of Thessaly. But if your children have tried to leave they have been brought back, even if it damaged them." Sokrates indicated Glaukon in his wheelchair. "They have been flogged for running away." He indicated Kebes. "And did you do this with good intentions?"

"Yes!" she insisted.

"But you did it in ignorance of how it would turn out?"

". . . Yes." I could tell she was still uncomfortable, but she seemed to have regained her calm.

"Did you even believe that it could work, or were you just as interested in seeing how it might fail?" I had never told him that, he must have just deduced it.

Athene bared her teeth. "I wanted it to succeed. I worked hard for it. I have spent my time and efforts here. I brought everyone here to make it succeed."

"Everyone except me. Why didn't you bring me here until the fifth year?"

"So you could teach the children rhetoric." She hesitated again. "You were an old man. I wasn't sure you'd live to teach them at fifteen if you came here at the beginning."

"I am grateful for your consideration," Sokrates said, standing straight and hearty. There was a laugh. "Why did you not extend that consideration to those older than me, or frailer? How about Tullius, or Plotinus, or old Iamblikius and Atticus there, who might well have been even more useful than I am if they'd been allowed to come here later when the work of setting it up was done?"

"You were more important," Athene said.

You'd think that would upset the older Masters, but not a bit of it. They agreed with Athene that Sokrates was more important. After all, he was *Sokrates*.

Sokrates laughed. "I'm glad to hear it even if they are not. But I don't entirely believe you. I think you knew I wouldn't approve of this city and didn't want me to have a say in its foundations. I think you knew I wouldn't have agreed, and too many of the others would have sided with me. I did not ask to be here. I was brought here directly against my will. The children and Workers were given no choice. I actively refused to come." He looked for Krito in the crowd. "My old friend Krito prayed to you to rescue me, even though I had told him I was ready to die by the laws of Athens. I drank the hemlock. I did not fear death. Nor do I fear it now. I ask you again, why did you bring me here?"

"I can't imagine," Athene snapped. Everyone laughed.

Sokrates looked into the crowd again. "Maia," he said. "Do you truly believe that what Plato wrote is the way to reach excellence?"

"Yes," she said, unhesitatingly.

"And you have dedicated your life to that?"

"I have."

"And when you learned that the Workers were people, did you vote for their emancipation?"

"I did. And now I support their education," she said, waving at the Workers on the edge of the crowd.

"And if you had known earlier?"

"I would have supported their education earlier. From the very beginning," she said.

"And do you think you have been doing good here?"

"Yes!" she said, passionately.

"And have you never had doubts about what Plato said and following everything he wrote?"

"I—" Maia started to speak, then stopped. "I have had doubts," she admitted. "There was so much he didn't specify and we had to improvise. And then when we first had the children. And now with the festivals. I do think we need to modify some of what Plato said there. But I still believe we're trying to reach excellence, trying to reach justice and the good life."

Sokrates leaned back a little, shifting his weight. "Thank you." He turned back to Athene. "I hate arguments that blame everything on the gods," he said, conversationally. "But it seems that here I have one. The children and the Workers are doing their best to pursue the good life. So are the masters, as best they can in their limited way. For the most part they truly believe all Plato wrote and want to implement it as best they can, but even they have doubts. But you are ignorant, and you have great power, and you don't hesitate to meddle with the lives of others."

"What is he doing?" I whispered to Simmea.

"He's baiting her," she said.

"Why?" I really couldn't understand it.

"I expect he's going somewhere with it," she said. "He's leading up to something."

Sokrates looked at Athene in a friendly way. "And is it true that you lie and cheat?"

"No!" she raged.

"Mistake," Simmea whispered.

Sokrates looked taken aback. "I'm sorry. You're not following Plato in that either, then?"

"The Noble Lie isn't a lie, it's a myth of origin," Athene said.

"For those of you who haven't yet been allowed to read the *Republic*, and won't be until you're fifty years old, and only then the golds among you, I should explain that the Noble Lie is the lie about the metals in your soul and that your life before you came to the city is a dream," Sokrates explained.

"She's absolutely right, it's a myth of origin," Simmea said.

"Your children will believe it," I said.

"Good," Simmea said, firmly.

"An origin myth," Athene said again. "Not a lie."

"By the dog!" Sokrates said. "And the cheating on the lots for the festivals?"

Athene was silent.

"It's in the *Republic*. Or is that somewhere else where you're not following Plato?"

There was an unhappy murmur rising among the children in the crowd.

"Ikaros? Is this somewhere that you are following Plato?"

Ikaros just stared at Sokrates for a moment, clearly horrified. It really was too bad of Sokrates, making poor Ikaros betray Plato and Athene together. He could have asked any of the Masters. But I suppose he knew that Ikaros would tell the truth. "Yes, it is," Ikaros admitted quietly.

There was another louder buzz in the crowd. Athene scowled. Sokrates looked over at where I was standing with Simmea, and then at Kebes. "And didn't you yourself—" he began, and I really thought he was going to accuse her of fixing the results at the last festival to spite me, which might well have let everyone know who I was. Sokrates would never have mentioned it, but Athene in this mood couldn't be trusted to respect my need for secrecy. But if he had been intending that he changed tack, perhaps realising the risk. "—know this was going on?"

Athene nodded angrily.

"Oh, you did? I thought so. But I just use these as examples," Sokrates said. "Though that one is an example of how the city is giving people a bad life. As we established earlier, the festivals go against human nature and make many people very unhappy indeed. And then there's the way you manipulated the numbers to get precise Neoplatonic fractions of each class, instead of fairly choosing based on the excellence of each child. Also—"

"Stop," Athene said, and as she spoke her owl flew down to her outstretched arm, wings wide, making everyone jump. "You're just attacking me, you're not making any points."

"You are a god, you should be better than mortals, but instead you are worse. We act within our limitations and you within yours, and you choose to take our lives and meddle to amuse yourself, doing what you please with them, against our will and in ignorance of whether the outcome is good or

evil. You didn't know about the Workers. You didn't give the children a conscious choice. You brought me here against my directly expressed wish. You
say that this city is the good life, but how can it be the good life if it takes
constant divine intervention to keep it going! It can't be the good life unless
people can choose to stay or leave, and can choose for themselves how to
make it better. Instead you imprison them on this island, with no legacy and
no posterity, and you make them have children here whose souls are bound
to this time and who will die when the volcano erupts."

Athene took a breath, as if she was about to speak. I don't know what I
expected her to say. But she snapped her fingers in Sokrates's face. He shrank
and shifted and transformed, until where he had been there was only a gadfly. He had always metaphorically called himself a gadfly, stinging people
out of complacency, and now he was no longer a man but an actual literal
gadfly, buzzing around the rostrum. Everyone gasped, myself included.

Athene stood still staring for a moment, and I still thought she was going
to speak, explain herself, perhaps restore Sokrates. But she just looked in silence, shaking her head, with the castle crown still sitting on her unruffled
curls. She gave no last speech, no farewell, no explanations. She looked at
Ikaros, but she did not look towards me, or even meet the eyes of Manlius
or any of the rest of her favourites. She simply vanished, and with her at the
same instant vanished the Workers—not just the ones gathered to listen to
the debate but, we later learned, every Worker in the city except for Crocus
and Sixty-One.

In that moment of shock, Kebes jumped up to the rostrum, though Ficino
tried to hold him back. "We've heard enough!" he shouted. "These pagan
gods are unjust!"

"I have been trying to become more just," I murmured to Simmea.

"Yes, you really have," she agreed.

"This city is unjust!" Kebes shouted on. "I'm leaving to start my own city,
better than this one, in a place that isn't doomed and where we can make a
difference! Who's with me? To the *Goodness*!" There was a ragged cheer. He
reached out for the gadfly, which buzzed away from him and flew over the
heads of the crowd to where Simmea and I were standing. Kebes looked after
it and locked eyes with Simmea. After a second she deliberately turned away
from him, cupping her hand over the gadfly where it had settled against my
chest. I put my hand gently over hers and met Kebes's furious gaze. He
bared his teeth as if he wanted to kill me, but just for a second. Then he
tossed his head and turned to the crowd.

"Come on!" he roared. He set off down the street of Poseidon towards
the harbor, with a cluster of people around him. Other people began shout-

ing their own manifestos. Everyone seemed to want to found their own cities, except those who wanted to stay here and take over this city and amend it on their own lines. Everyone was talking at once. I saw Maia weeping. Ikaros was shouting something about angels.

Now you may well say that at that moment I should have resumed my powers and come out of the machine and sorted everything out. Perhaps I should, even though I would have had to have died to do it. But it never occurred to me. Things did happen after that, lots of complicated things, and I'll tell you about them some other time, but this is where this story ends, the story that began with the question of why Daphne turned into a tree. I just stood still in the middle of the crowd with my hand on top of Simmea's, providing fleeting shelter for the gadfly Sokrates, as factions formed around us, and the Just City came apart in chaos.

On my temple in Delphi there are two words written: Know Thyself. It's good advice. Know yourself. You are worth knowing. Examine your life. The unexamined life is not worth living. Be aware that other people have equal significance. Give them the space to make their own choices, and let their choices count as you want them to let your choices count. Remember that excellence has no stopping point and keep on pursuing it. Make art that can last and that says something nobody else can say. Live the best life you can, and become the best self you can. You cannot know which of your actions is the lever that will move worlds. Not even Necessity knows all ends. Know yourself.

THE
PHILOSOPHER
KINGS

This is for Ada, who has the best thoughts.

Quid me mihi detrahis?

—OVID, *Metamorphoses*, Book VI

What a wondrous and sublime thing it is to be human, to be able to choose your state, whether among the beasts or among the angels.

—GIOVANNI PICO DELLA MIRANDOLA, *Oration on the Awesomeness of Humanity (Oratio de Hominis Dignitate)*

I am voyaging too.
We will need the foundation as much as the dome
For those worlds to come true.

—ADA PALMER, "Somebody Will"

Nothing befits a man more than discourse on the soul. Thus the Delphic injunction "Know thyself" is fulfilled, and we examine everything else, whether above or beneath the soul, with deeper insight.

—MARSILIO FICINO, letter to Jacobo Bracciolini

I had a queer obsession about justice. As though justice mattered. As though justice can really be distinguished from vengeance. It's only love that's any good.

—ELIZABETH VON ARNIM, *The Enchanted April*

1

APOLLO

Very few people know that Pico della Mirandola stole the head of the Winged Victory of Samothrace. In fact he stole it twice. The first time he stole it from Samothrace, before the rest of it was rediscovered. That time he had the help of my sister Athene. The second time was thirty years later, when he stole it from the Temple of Nike in Plato's Republic. One of Plato's Republics, that is; the original, called by some the Just City, by others the Remnant, and by still others the City of Workers, although by then we only had two. In addition to our Republic, there were four others scattered about the island of Kallisti, an island itself known at different times as Atlantis, Thera, and Santorini. Almost everyone who had been influenced by living in the original Republic wanted to found, or amend, their own ideal city. None of them were content to get on with living their lives; all of them wanted to shape the Good Life, according to their own ideas.

As for me, I suppose I wanted that too, but with rather less urgency. I was a god, after all——a god in mortal form, for the time being. I had become incarnate to learn some lessons I felt I needed to learn, and although I had learned them I had stayed because the Republic was interesting, and because there were people there that I cared about. That was primarily my friend Simmea and our Young Ones. When we'd first come here we'd been doing Plato's Republic according to Plato, as interpreted by Athene and the Masters: three hundred fanatical Platonists from times ranging from the fourth century b.c. to the late twenty-first century a.d. From the time we Children were sixteen, we'd held Festivals of Hera every four months in which people were randomly matched with partners. There were six such festivals before the Last Debate, and all six such matings I'd participated in had produced sons. Simmea had one son from that time, Neleus. And between us we had a daughter, Arete, born after the revisions that made it possible for us to be a family.

Making the Republic work had been harder since Athene stalked off at the end of the Last Debate. She had taken with her both her divine power, and all the robots except two. In the twenty years since the Last Debate a lot of things had changed. Worst was the constant warfare with the other cities.

The art raids had started because we had all the art, and the other cities wanted a share of it, and we didn't want to give any of it up. The real problem was that Plato had imagined his Republic existing in a context where there would be wars, and so training everyone for warfare was a big part of the way he had imagined his city. The guardians, golds, and auxiliaries, silvers, had been training to fight since they were ten, and yet had never fought anyone except in practice until the art raids started. The raids provided a pretext for the warfare it seemed a large number of people had been wanting. While many of us felt they were futile, they were popular, especially with the Young Ones. A city would raid us and take away some statue or painting. Then we'd raid them back and try to recapture it. They began as something like games of capture the flag, lots of fun for everyone involved, but of course the weapons and training were real. By the time it came to real wounds and death, everyone was committed to them. People who had read Plato on war and bravery and the shame of turning your back on the enemy couldn't see any way to back down. So the five cities of Kallisti existed in a constant state of raids and shifting alliances.

The Temple of Nike stood on a little knoll just outside the south gate of the original city. By the time I got there, summoned urgently, the raiders had fled, taking the head with them. I didn't know or care about the head until afterward. Right then I was entirely focused on Simmea. She was still alive, but just barely—the arrow was in her lung, and frothy blood was coming out with every breath. "We thought it best not to move her," Klymene said. I barely heard her, although she was right, of course—moving her would have been fatal. They hadn't even drawn out the arrow.

Simmea's eyes met mine, and they were full of love and trust—and even better, that edge they had that said she loved the truth even more than she loved me. She tried to speak with what breath she had. She said my name, "Pytheas," and then something I couldn't make out.

I made a plan immediately, almost as fast as I would have made it normally. In mortal form, I didn't have access to my powers, and as things were, there weren't any gods who were going to pay attention to me or help, at least not in time. So I drew my dagger. If I slit my wrists it would take minutes for me to bleed to death, but if I slit my throat only seconds. As soon as I was dead I'd have plenty of time—all the time I wanted, once I was safely outside it. I'd go down to Hades, take up all my powers again, and manifest back here a heartbeat after I'd left. Then I could heal her. Indeed, healing her would be fast and easy. I would have lost this incarnation, but I'd been mortal and incarnate for almost forty years now. It had been fascinating and wonderful and terrible, and I'd be sorry to stop, but Simmea was going to be *dead* if I didn't save her.

"Pytheas, no!" Klymene said, and grabbed for the knife. It wasn't that that stopped me.

"Pytheas, don't be an idiot!" Simmea said, perfectly distinctly. And as she said it, or immediately thereafter, she took hold of the shaft sticking out of her chest and pulled the arrow out.

Before I could so much as cut my throat, she was dead, and not only dead but vanished. One second she was there, blood, arrow, and dear ugly face. The next the arrow was lying in blood on the mosaic floor of the temple. Her body had gone back to the time Athene had snatched her from—back, I believe, to the waters outside Smyrna, at the spot where the ship that brought her here had moved through time. Her body would have appeared there, somewhere in the eastern Aegean, and sunk between one wave and the next. She loved to swim, she was a swimming champion, she had taught me and all our Young Ones to swim; but she wouldn't be swimming among the wine-dark billows, she'd just sink down in their embrace. (I've often tried to find her since, to see her for just that one moment more, but it's like looking for one particular helium atom in the sun, trying to find an instant like that without knowing either the exact place or time. I keep on looking now and then.)

Death is a Mystery. The gods can't undo it. Her wound would have been a trivial thing for me to fix if I'd had my powers, but once she was dead, that was the end of it.

Klymene had my knife, and I was prone on the ground clutching the arrow. Simmea's soul too would have gone back to the time she left, and from there it would have gone down to Hades. Unlike most human souls, she knew precisely what to expect. We'd talked about it a great deal. She knew how to negotiate the underworld, and she knew how to choose her next incarnation to maximize her excellence. I wasn't at all worried about any of that. But after choosing her next life, she'd pass through the river Lethe, she had to. Once in Lethe she'd have to at least wet her lips, and once she drank from Lethe she'd forget this life, and me. Souls are immortal, but souls are not personality. So much of personality is memory. When mortal souls pass through Hades they go on to new life, and they become new people with fresh beginnings. I suspect that may be the whole purpose of death. No doubt it is a splendid way for the universe to be arranged. Her soul will continue to pursue excellence for life after life, becoming more and more excellent and making the universe better. But she wouldn't be Simmea anymore, she wouldn't remember this life. She wouldn't remember me and all the things we'd shared.

Once I was back in my real form I'd be able to find her, watch all her different lives if I wanted to, and I did want to. But none of them would be my Simmea. Death of mortals I love is always hard for me to deal with. But this one was worse than the others. Since I was incarnate, I'd been there the whole time. There were no moments of Simmea's life left for me to experience. I had been in time for all of them. I'm bound by Necessity. I can't go back to times I've already visited, none of us can. I'll never be able to speak with her again, or see her rolling her eyes at me, or hear her calling me an idiot. She knew I was the god Apollo. She'd known for years. It just didn't make any difference. When she found out, practically the first thing she said was that it must be why I was so hopeless at being a human being.

It's easy to be adored when you're a god. Worship comes naturally to people. What I'd had with Simmea was a decades-long conversation.

I briefly considered killing myself and going back to Olympos anyway. But her last words and deed had been to stop me—she'd have figured out exactly what I was doing and why. She was extremely smart, and she knew me very well. She probably had some really good reason why I shouldn't do that, which she'd have explained at length and with truly Socratic clarity, if only she'd had time. I might even have agreed. I tried to think what it might have been. My mind was completely blank.

As I couldn't imagine why she'd stopped me killing myself and saving her life, I naturally began to think about vengeance.

"Who was it?" I asked Klymene. "Did we get any of them?"

Klymene has never liked me, and for extremely good reasons. Nevertheless, she is the mother of my son Kallikles. Her expression now was unreadable. Pity? Or did she perhaps despise me? Plato did not approve of giving way to strong emotion, especially grief, and at that moment I was rolling on the ground, clutching an arrow and weeping.

"I don't know," she said. "They came by boat. It could have been anyone. These art raids have been getting worse and worse. They got away—the rest of the troop went after them, except that I sent young Sophoniba for you and stayed with Simmea myself."

"She always liked you," I said. I could hardly get the words out past the lump in my throat.

"She did." Klymene put her hand on my shoulder. "Pytheas, you should get up and go home. Will there be anybody there?"

The thought of going home was impossible. Some of the Young Ones might be there, but Simmea would never be there again. Her things would be everywhere, and the reminder would be intolerable. "I want to find out who they were and avenge her."

Klymene's expression was easier to read now; it was worry. "We all want that. But you're not being rational."

"Are there any bodies?" I asked.

"No, thank Athene," she said. "No Young Ones killed."

"Wounded?"

"Simmea was the only one."

"Then unless the troop catches them, this arrow is the only evidence," I said, examining it. It was unquestionably an arrow, made of strong straight wood, stained with blood now. It was barbed and fletched exactly like all the arrows. We had all learned the same skills from the same teachers. It made war between us both better and worse. I turned it over in my hands and wished I'd never invented the things.

"The *Goodness* has been seen," Klymene said, tentatively. "That doesn't mean it was Kebes. It could have been anyone. But it was sighted yesterday by the lookouts."

The *Goodness* was the schooner Kebes had stolen when he fled from the island after the Last Debate. "You think it was Kebes?"

"It could have been. I didn't recognize anyone," Klymene said. "And you'd think I would have. But if they were all Young Ones . . . well, maybe somebody else in the troop did. I'll check when they get back. Whatever happens we'll be retaliating, as soon as we know who and where. And if you want revenge, I'll do my best to see that the Delphi troop is included in that expedition."

"Thank you," I said, and meant it. The arrowhead was steel, which meant it was robot-forged, which meant it was old. There were still plenty of robot-forged arrowheads around, because people tended to reuse them when they could. Steel really is a lot better than iron. Of course, we were living in the Bronze Age. Nobody else in this time period actually knew how to smelt iron, unless maybe off in Anatolia somewhere the Hittites were just figuring it out. There was no use thinking it might have been pirates or raiders. This was one of our arrows, and the expedition had clearly been an art raid, and that meant one of the other republics.

"Did they take anything?" I asked.

"The head of Victory," Klymene said, indicating the empty plinth where it had stood.

I expect you're familiar with the Nike, or Winged Victory of Samothrace—it stands in the Louvre in Paris, where it has stood since its rediscovery in the eighteen-sixties. There's also a good copy of it actually in Samothrace. The swept-back wings, the blown draperies—she was sculpted landing on a ship, and you can almost feel the wind. It's the contrast between the stillness of the stone and the motion of what is sculpted that makes her such a treasure. But she's headless in the Louvre, because Pico and Athene stole the head, the head which had for a time rested in our Temple of Nike. Her hair is swept back by the wind too, but her eyes and her smile are completely still. Her eyes seem to focus on you wherever you are. The head reminds me a little of the head of the Charioteer at Delphi, although it's completely different, of course, and marble not bronze. But there's something about the expression that's the same. I suppose Athene and I are the only ones who have seen her with the head, at Samothrace, and without, in the Louvre, and then seen just the head, in the City. Nobody else in the City had ever seen any part of her but the head. I tried to comfort myself that in some future incarnation Simmea, who loved the head and had died defending it, would be sure to see the rest of her. It only made me cry harder.

"We'll get it back," I said, choking out the words.

"Yes." Klymene hesitated. "I know I'm the worst person to be with you now, and I would leave you in peace, but I don't think you ought to be alone."

I sat up and looked at her. She was the same physical age as all of us Children, almost forty now. She had been pretty once, lithe and graceful, with shining hair. She was still trim from working with the auxiliaries, but her face had sagged, and her hair been cut off at the jaw to fit under a helmet. She looked weary. I had known her for a long time. We'd both been brought to the Republic when we were ten. When we were fourteen she'd been a coward and I'd said it was all right because she was a girl, and she'd never forgiven me. When we were sixteen we'd shared the single worst sexual experience of my life, then had a son together. When we were nineteen and Athene had turned Sokrates into a fly and everything had subsequently fallen apart, we'd both stayed and tried to make the revised original Republic work, instead of going off to start fresh somewhere else.

"You're not any worse to be with right now than anyone else who isn't Simmea," I said.

"How are you going to manage without her?" she asked.

"I don't have the faintest idea," I said.

"I wouldn't have thought you'd have tried to kill yourself," she said, tentatively. "It isn't what Simmea would have wanted. Your Young Ones will need you."

"They need both of us," I said, which was entirely true. The difference was that they could have had both of us. If I'd killed myself it would have been temporary. Oh, it would have been different being here as a god with all my abilities. Being incarnate made everything so vivid and immediate and inexorable. But I'd have been here and so would Simmea, and she knew that. Why would it have been being an idiot to kill myself to save her? She understood how temporary death would have been for me, how easy resurrection. If she'd let me do it we could have been having a conversation about it right now. There would even be advantages to being here as a god—there were all kinds of things I could use my powers for. For a start I could get us some more robots, unintelligent ones this time, and make everyone's life easier.

Naturally, I couldn't share these thoughts with Klymene. She didn't know I was Apollo. Nobody did except Simmea and our Young Ones, and Sokrates and Athene. Sokrates had flown off after the Last Debate and never been seen again. We assumed he was dead—flies don't live very long. Simmea was definitely dead. And deathless Athene was back on Olympos, and after twenty years probably still furious with me. If I'd killed myself and saved Simmea in front of her, Klymene would have been bound to notice. As things were, there was no need to tell her. Even without that she had no reason to like me.

"The Young Ones will need you all the more without Simmea," Klymene said.

"They're nearly grown," I said. It was almost true. The boys were nineteen or twenty, and Arete was fifteen.

"They'll still need you," Klymene said.

Before I could answer, she saw somebody coming and stiffened, reaching for her bow. I leaped to my feet and spun around. Then I relaxed. It was the Delphi troop coming out. I bent down and picked up the arrow, which I'd dropped. It wasn't much of a memento, but it was all I had. "I'll go home," I said.

"You won't . . . you won't do anything stupid?" Klymene asked.

"Not after Simmea's last request," I said. "You heard her. She specifically asked me not to be an idiot."

"Yes . . ." she said. She was frowning.

"I won't kill myself," I specified. "At least, not immediately."

Klymene looked at me in incomprehension, and I'm sure I looked at her the same way. "You shouldn't kill yourself because you don't know that you've finished what you're supposed to do in this life," she said.

Not even Necessity knows all ends.

2

ARETE

You don't exist, of course. It's natural to write with an eye to posterity, to want to record what has happened for the edification not of one's friends, but of later ages. But there will be no later ages. All this has happened and is, by design, to leave no trace but legend. The volcano will erupt and the Platonic Cities will be extinguished. The legend of Atlantis will survive to inspire Plato, which is especially ironic as it was Plato who inspired the Masters to set up the City in the first place.

The more I think about this, the more I think that Sokrates was right in the Last Debate. It was fundamentally wrong of them to found the City at all. The story of humanity is one of growth and change and the accumulation of experience. We of the cities are a branch cut off to wither—not a lost branch, but a branch deliberately cut away. We are like figures sculpted of wax and cast into the fire to melt. When I asked Father why Athene had done this he said that he had never asked her, but he supposed that it seemed interesting, and she had wanted to see what would happen. In my opinion that's an irresponsible way for a god to behave. I intend to do better if I ever have the opportunity.

It may seem like hubris, but it really is possible that I might. Others of Father's children have become heroes, and Asklepius is a god. I am the daughter of Apollo, and Father says I have the soul of a hero. Sometimes I really feel as if I do, as if I could do anything. Other times I feel all too human and vulnerable and useless. It doesn't help that I have seven brothers. That's too many. They try to squash me, naturally, and naturally I hate being squashed and resist it as much as possible.

People talk all the time about pursuing excellence, and when I was younger my brothers made a game of this where they chased me. My mother was a philosopher and my father is an extremely philosophical god, and so of course they named me Arete, which means excellence. Maia, who comes from the nineteenth century, says that in her day it used to be translated as virtue, and Ficino worries that this is his fault for translating it into Latin as *virtus*. Maia and Ficino are my teachers. Ficino comes from Renaissance Florence, where it was considered the duty of everyone to write an autobiography, and since

Renaissance Florence is almost as popular here as Socratic Athens, many people do. I, as you can see, am no exception.

I'm starting this all wrong, with my thoughts all over the place. Ficino would say it lacks discipline, and make me write a plan and then write it again to the plan, but I'm not going to. This isn't for Ficino, it isn't for anyone but myself and you, dear nonexistent Posterity, and I intend to set down my thoughts as they come to me. My brothers chased me and called it pursuing excellence, but I also pursue excellence, and Father told me that it can only ever be pursued, never caught—though my brothers caught me often enough, and turned me upside-down when they did.

I call them brothers, but they're all half-brothers, really. Kallikles is the oldest. He's Father's son by Klymene, conceived at the first Festival of Hera. Father and Klymene don't like each other much. But Klymene doesn't have any other children, and she and Kallikles have this odd relationship where they're not quite mother and son, but they're not quite not either. Maia says I should think of her like an aunt, and I suppose I do, insofar as I know what aunts are. We don't have any proper ones yet. When my brothers start to have children I'll be an aunt, and my little nieces and nephews will be overwhelmed by how many uncles they have.

Kallikles is the bravest of us. I used to call him "Bold Kallikles" as a kind of Homeric epithet—I have Homeric epithets for all my brothers, which I made up as a kind of revenge for the way they used to chase me. Kallikles fell and broke his arm climbing the tower on Florentia when he was twelve. His arm healed just fine, and when it was completely better he climbed the tower again, and didn't fall off that time. He has a girlfriend called Rhea who is a blacksmith, which means she's a bronze, which is a bit of a scandal as he's a gold. We don't actually have laws about that, the way they do in Athenia and Psyche, but it's definitely frowned on. He lives with her, but they're not married, and so nobody takes official notice of their relationship. Even so, it's awkward, and kind of embarrassing for me.

Next after him comes Alkibiades, whose Homeric epithet is "Plato-loving." His mother is the runner Kryseis. Alkibiades lives in Athenia, and he didn't leave quietly—the rows must have shaken the city. He said he thought Plato's original system was the best—and he said it at great length and with no originality whatsoever. Mother and Father both argued with him. Almost everything I know about how the Festivals of Hera actually worked when we had them here comes from those arguments, as I won't be able to read the *Republic* until I'm an ephebe. Alkibiades thought it was a wonderful arrangement to have a simple sanctioned sexual union with a different girl every four months forever. Mother's question of what happens if you fall in love and Father's question of what happens if you don't fancy some particular girl you're drawn with didn't give him any pause at all. He answered every problem they mentioned by saying that if they'd kept doing it properly, the way Plato wanted, it would have been all right. I had only been thirteen at the time, and about as uninterested in love and sex as anyone could be, but I could see both sides. Having it all arranged without any fuss had advantages. But people did just naturally fall in love. Look at Mother and Father. It would have been cruel to stop them being together.

After Alkibiades left, our house got a lot quieter. I was sorry because he had always been my favorite brother—he was more generally prepared to put up with me than any of the others. He even took the trouble to say good-bye, though I didn't realize it until afterward—he took me to Sparta for a meal with some of his friends, and bade me joy afterward as I ran off to work in the fields. I didn't know until I got home late that night that he had left. He had left on my bed a copy of Euripides he had won as a school prize—they don't allow drama at all in Athenia, or even Homer.

Next in age come Phaedrus and Neleus, who both still live at home in Thessaly. Phaedrus is Father's son by Hermia, who lives in Sokratea. I've never met her, but she once sent Phaedrus an amazing skin drum which we still have. He looks a lot like a darker jollier version of Father. He excels at wrestling—he has won a number of prizes. He also sings beautifully—we sing together sometimes. He's a gold. Phaedrus's epithet is "Merry," because he is—he's the most fun of all my brothers, the readiest to laugh, the fastest to make a joke. It's not that he can't be serious, but his natural expression is a grin.

Neleus is his complete opposite. He's Mother's son by somebody called Nikias, whom I've also never met because he left with Kebes. He must have been dark-skinned, because Neleus is darker than Mother. He unfortunately inherited Mother's jaw and flattish face, so his Homeric epithet could have been "Ugly," but in fact it's "Wrathful" because he's so quick to anger and he bears grudges so well. He never forgets anything. He's a swimming champion, again like Mother, and he can't sing at all. He's a gold. He had a close friendship with a boy from Olympia called Agathon, and since that broke up a few months ago he has been worse-tempered than ever.

I have three more brothers, but I don't know them very well. Euklides and his mother Lasthenia live in Psyche. He visits for a few days every summer. Porphyry and his mother Euridike live in the City of Amazons. He's been here to visit twice. I always feel shy with both of them. I know Euklides better than Porphyry. He is a silver. Porphyry is a gold, and I don't know all that much about him. And I have another brother, somewhere, whose name

I don't know and who I've never met at all. His mother Ismene went off with Kebes before he was born.

It's a complicated family, when I write it down like this, but most of the time in Thessaly we've just been five Young Ones with Mother and Father.

To begin again, I was born in the Remnant City fourteen years after it was founded, and I am now fifteen years old. If you consider that is too young to write an autobiography (Ficino does), then consider this an early draft for one, a journal or commonplace book in which I shall record what will become an autobiography in due course when I have more life to record. Though it seems to me that my life has been quite eventful so far, and that there is a lot that has already happened to me that is worthy of note.

I was born four years after the Last Debate. The cities had already divided themselves by then, though they were not in the state of almost constant skirmishing that they are now, and relations between them were generally cordial. Everyone knew each other in all the cities. About a hundred and fifty people had gone off with Kebes and left the island. We don't know what they did, though speculations about it are a favorite topic of conversation. Sometimes people call them the Lost City, or the Goodness Group, after the name of the ship they stole. There keep being rumors that people have seen the *Goodness*, but the truth is that Kebes left the island and nobody knows where he is or what he's doing or anything about his group.

Everyone else stayed on the island, and they all wanted to create Plato's Republic only to do it right this time. This was the case whether they stayed, or left the original city to set up their own. I believe there were fierce debates before everyone sorted themselves out. My parents stayed. By the time I was born, everything was more or less organized again, the new cities were well on the way to being built, and people seldom changed their minds about which city they wanted to live in, because the cities collected people by philosophical temperament, and people's temperaments don't tend to change all that much.

Psyche, the Shining City, was set up by the Neoplatonists, who wanted their city to reflect the mind, and the magic of numerology. It attracted those with a melancholic disposition. Sokratea, which was begun by those who believed that Sokrates was right in the Last Debate, that the City shouldn't have been founded, and that every point needed much more examination, attracted the choleric, though Sokrates himself was nothing like that from all I have read and heard. Athenia, founded by those who believed the opposite, that Athene had been right, and who tried to live even more strictly according to their interpretation of Plato, attracted the phlegmatic. That left the sanguine, who all wound up in the City of Amazons, founded on the principle of absolute gender equality.

Those who stayed in the Remnant were those whose humors were mixed. The other cities characterized us as lazy and indecisive and luxury-loving. At first, because we were the mother city, they came to us frequently to use the libraries and other facilities, but later this happened less and less often. We had a higher proportion of Young Ones than most of the other cities, because many people didn't take their babies with them when they left. This isn't as callous as it may sound, because they didn't know which babies were theirs. Some people could recognize their own babies, or thought they could. Many just couldn't. And none of the Children had been educated to expect that they'd bring up their own children; they'd had them on the understanding that the City knew how to do it best. So there are plenty of people here, like my good friend Erinna, who have no idea who their parents are. Now that we have families there won't be any more people like that, though of course they're still doing that in Athenia, and maybe in the City of Amazons too, I'm not sure.

People did change cities sometimes, as indeed they still do. As young people come of age and find themselves in a city that doesn't suit their temperament, they often leave it for another, the way Alkibiades did. And one of the first things I remember is Maia coming back. My earlier memories are muddled and confused with the cute baby stories Mother told about me—my first word was "beauty" and my second word "logos." (It might sound conceited of me to record that, but honestly, anyone living in this house whose second word *wasn't* "logos" would have to be deaf.)

I must have been about four years old when Maia came back, so it was probably in the eighteenth year of the City, eight years or so after the Last Debate. My parents lived in the house called Thessaly that had once belonged to Sokrates. It was an extremely inconvenient house for a family, as are all the houses of the Remnant. There are enormous eating halls and public buildings, and little sleeping houses designed for seven people to sleep in. There were eight of us, but that wasn't the problem; the problem was that there wasn't room for anything but sleeping and washing and sitting in the garden debating philosophy. Mother had built a partition down the middle so that she and Father and I slept on one side and the boys slept on the other. I remember our three little beds all in a row, mine under the window.

One night, long after I had fallen asleep, I was wakened by a scratch at the door. Father went and opened it, and there was Maia, carrying a big book. I didn't know Maia then, of course. Mother was awake, and she went at once to Maia and hugged her, so I knew it was all right. The three of them went

out into the garden, so as not to wake the boys, and as I was awake and curious I followed after. We all sat on the grass. I don't really remember the
conversation, though I do remember Mother looking at the Botticelli book
Maia had brought, and which I later came to know and love. I probably
couldn't understand all the words they used, but I knew that Maia had left
some other city and come back to ours, and she had just arrived that night.
It shows how peaceful everything was then that she could do that. She was
probably about forty at the time, and she had come alone, unarmed and un-
challenged, halfway across the island, arriving after dark. The gates were
guarded, but she had come in simply by saying she wanted to. The guards
knew her, of course, because pretty much everyone knew everyone. That was
before the art raids started, and it was the art raids that spoiled everything
and led to the present lamentable state of affairs.

I remember sitting on the rough grass in the moonlight, looking at Maia
as she talked to my parents. They knew her well, but I found her fascinating
because she was a complete stranger. There were very few complete strangers in my world in those days. I remember noticing how white her skin was
in the moonlight, whiter even than Father's. Her pale hair was braided and
the braid was pinned up around her head.

"I thought you were all for women's rights," Mother said.

"And don't women have rights here these days, Simmea?" Maia asked. "Or
have I come to Psyche by mistake? Women's rights are certainly why I went
there. But I couldn't stay in the City of Amazons."

I don't remember if she explained why she had come, if they discussed
the New Concordance or Ikaros. I only remember the colors and shapes
of the three of them under the lemon tree in the moonlight, and the smell
of the autumn night with rain coming on the wind.

Maia had been one of the Masters of Florentia, with Ficino, and with
Ficino she became one of my teachers. There are three distinct generations in
the city. The Masters were those who prayed to Athene to let them help set
up Plato's Republic. They were all grown up when they came here, and some
of them were old. Ficino was old—sixty-six when he came, he says, and he's
ninety-eight now, though he's in better condition than a lot of the younger
Masters. He says it's from eating a good diet and not letting his mind atro-
phy. Maia was only about twenty, so she's about fifty now. (I dared Kallikles
to ask her exact age once, and she offered to box his ears for the imperti-
nence.) Most of the Masters are somewhere in between, though a number of
the older ones have died, of course.

Then there's my parents' generation, known as the Children. They are all
the same age, with very little variation. They were all about ten years old

when they came, though some of them were nine or eleven. They're all thirty-eight now, with that same slight range of variation.

Last comes my generation, the Children's children, whom we call the Young Ones. Our ages range between twenty-one and newborn, though far more of us are between twenty-one and nineteen——when they were holding Festivals of Hera three times a year, a lot of babies were born. After that, it wasn't organized, and people had to sort things out for themselves. There are other Young Ones my age and younger, but there aren't great cohorts of us, as there are of my brothers' age and the Children. I suppose the babies starting to be born now to the oldest of the Young Ones are a fourth generation. I don't know what they'll be called. Do they name generations, elsewhere? I haven't run across it in my reading. Cicero was older than Caelius and Milo and Clodius, but there wasn't a hard line. It would be like us younger Young Ones, I suppose, with overlap and people of all ages. Odd.

I don't plan to have children myself. Partly it's because the whole sex thing seems so awkward and complicated, and partly it's because I am Apollo's daughter, and what would my children be? Quarter-deities? But mostly it's because there isn't any posterity for us. They, or their descendants, would only be born to die when the volcano destroys us all. I suppose I could flee to the mainland like Kebes, and have children there whose genes could join the human mainstream, but there doesn't seem to be much point. What kind of a life would it be, without books or debate, at a Bronze-Age tech level? It's bad enough here when things break down and we have to do everything by hand. Maia says the Workers gave them freedom they didn't appreciate at the time, and that philosophy is harder when you're cold and hungry. What kind of life would it be for children in Mycenaean Greece? Especially as half of them would, statistically, be girls? I'm looking forward to seeing it, but I wouldn't like to live there. So I don't plan on having children. That doesn't mean I'll necessarily lead a celibate life, though I have so far, because there's a plant called silphium that prevents conception, and Mother told me all about it when my menses started.

I suppose it's unusual that my father is a god, and I should write about that. I don't know what to say though, because I've known about it all my life, and take it for granted. I don't know what it would be like to have any other kind of father. It's a secret from most people in the City, though. I used to wonder how it was they didn't guess, but it isn't all that obvious really. Father doesn't have his divine abilities, and while everyone can see how intelligent and musical and athletic he is, they tend to see him as just an exceptional success of Plato's methods. Some people don't like him and think that he's arrogant, but in general, everyone recognizes and admires his excellence. I think it helps that they see Father and Mother together—people have a tendency to see them and speak about them as Pytheas-and-Simmea, as if they were one thing. So they wouldn't think about Father's excellences without thinking about Mother's too. Lots of people in the City, and especially the Masters, tend to see my parents as the closest thing we yet have to Philosopher Kings, as the proof of the success of Plato's methods. It's a lot for me to live up to. Sometimes I feel squeezed by the pressure of expectations.

Ficino's wrong. I've written all of this already and I haven't even got up to where I thought I'd really start, with the day my mother died.

3

ARETE

I ate lunch in Florentia that day. It is an eating hall, as it had always been. When my parents were young and there were plenty of Workers, humans didn't need to do anything in Florentia except take their turn to serve the food one day a month. Now there are rotas for preparation and cooking and cleaning up, and I, along with everyone else who eats there, have to do one of those things every few days. The food is usually good. It was porridge and goat cheese and nuts and raisins that day. Neither of my parents were there, which wasn't unusual. I came in from the palaestra with my friends Boas and Archimedes. We were all exactly the same age, and were training together to pass our adulthood tests in five months' time, when we'd all turn sixteen.

We sat down to eat with Baukis and Ficino. Baukis is three months younger than the rest of us, and she's a friend. Since Krito died, Ficino is the oldest and most generally respected person in the entire city. He's pretty much always in Florentia. He sleeps upstairs and spends most of his days either sitting in the hall talking to people, or teaching in one of the nearby rooms. He seldom leaves Florentia now except to go to the library. He'd been tutoring Baukis while the rest of us were in the palaestra. Boas and Archimedes ate quickly and then went off to work, and my brother Phaedrus joined us. This was awkward and uncomfortable because Baukis started flirting with him, though he's four years older than we are. After a while they left together to look something up in the library, both acting so stupid and coy that I felt myself squirming as I finished my nuts.

"It's quite natural," Ficino said.

I looked at him inquiringly.

"Girls mature faster, and so they are naturally attracted to men a few years older. It's normal. It just seems strange to you because we have had such fixed cohorts that it hasn't been possible until now." Ficino cracked a hazelnut and popped it into his mouth. He had a face not unlike a nut, wizened and brown.

I didn't at all want to talk to him about what girls were attracted to. "Why did you do it that way, then?"

"Plato," he said, and held up a warning hand when he saw me open my mouth to protest. "Plato said to begin with ten-year-olds, and if you do that you will have a generation all the same age. It was one of those things that just happened that way. It was only ever intended to be for the first generation."

"It was only ever *intended* as a thought experiment," I said. Maia had told me that.

"Yes, but here it is, and you and I are living in it." Ficino grinned.

I swallowed the last of my porridge and gathered our plates together to take to the kitchen. "I should go. I have to learn my lines."

"Something Plato really wouldn't have approved of," Ficino said.

"I know. I've never properly understood why he hated drama so much."

"He thought it was bad for people to feel induced emotions, false emotions."

I sat down again. "But it's not. It can be cathartic—and it can be a way of learning about emotions."

"Plato didn't want people to learn those emotions. He wanted his ideal guardians to only understand honorable emotions." Ficino shook his head. "He had a very hopeful view of human nature, when you think about it."

I laughed. "He did if he thought jealousy and grief and anger could be excluded because we never saw *The Myrmidons*. I never saw any play until two years ago, unless you count the re-enactments of the *Symposium* on Plato's birthday, but I still felt all those things."

Ficino nodded. "But that's what he really thought, and so that's why we excluded drama. Or rather, since almost all of the original Masters were people who loved the art of the ancient world, and much of what survived was drama, we decided to keep drama in the library but not allow it to be acted. Reading it quietly, we thought, wouldn't have such an emotional effect."

"Why did you change your minds?" I asked. "Not that I'm not glad you did, because I'm really excited about playing Briseis at the Dionysia."

"We didn't change our minds. It was debated several times, and always decided against, until two years ago."

I was about to ask what happened two years ago, then I realized: the first cohort of Young Ones had become old enough to vote. "Are plays still banned in the other cities?"

"As far as I know they're allowed in Sokratea and the City of Amazons, but banned in Psyche and Athenia."

"And is there any difference in how philosophical people are?"

Ficino laughed. "How would you measure that?"

I opened my mouth to answer, but he held up his hand again.

"No, think about it. Write me a paper on it, either an essay or a dialogue, as you prefer."

I groaned, but only because it was work. It sounded like a really interesting question to think about. I also wanted to talk to other people about it, most especially Maia, and Simmea. I bade farewell to Ficino, gathered up the plates, and took them to the kitchen, thinking about it. How would you measure the general level of philosophy in a population—or even in an individual? There might be simple tests, like how many times books were checked out of the library, but that would only show how many people were studying philosophy, not how philosophical they were. It wasn't my turn to clean up, but they were short-handed so I helped for a while, still thinking about it. Some people were naturally philosophical. Others were not. That's why everyone was divided into their rightful metals, gold and silver and bronze and iron. My friend Erinna said she was glad to be a silver, relieved and pleased.

How philosophical a city was could be simply measured by how many golds it had, except that originally in the City (and even now in Psyche and Athenia) the proportions were worked out numerologically rather than justly. That had been one of the more telling points Sokrates made in the Last Debate. But in Psyche and Athenia they believed that numerology was magical, that numbers described true Forms underlying the world. And Father said he didn't know whether they did or not, and Mother said they had an inner logic and so perhaps they did, but not the way that Proclus and Plotinus wrote.

I hadn't read the *Republic* yet, but Ficino had told us Plato said that a Just City would hold justice and the pursuit of excellence as the highest good. He said that as such a city declined, it would become a timarchy, meaning that the citizens would prize honor above justice. Sparta had been a timarchy, and Plato thought it better than oligarchy, the next stage of decline, where the citizens would prize money and possessions above honor. I wondered what the signs of starting to prize honor above wisdom and justice might be, and how that could be measured.

I went home after the kitchen cleanup was done. I didn't have any work scheduled that day, and I had a calculus class later that afternoon. Mother was teaching it, so it was held in the garden of Thessaly. I knew I had a good hour before the class, and that Mother might be home but nobody else would. I wanted to tell her about being chosen to play Briseis, and I wanted to ask her about ways of measuring levels of philosophy. She wasn't home, but that meant I had the house to myself until everyone arrived for the class, which was good because I had to learn my lines. *The Myrmidons* was to be performed at the Dionysia in just over a month. I had only been given the part that morning, and I was full of the glory of it. I was thrilled to be given a part this year, especially such a good part. I wanted to know all my lines before the first rehearsal and be the best Briseis possible.

I took the book out into the garden. We had a statue of Hermes that Sokrates had carved himself. I raised my hands in greeting to it as I always did. Then I lay down in the dappled shade of the tree, chin on my hands and book open on the ground. I started to work through my lines by brute force memorization, trying to concentrate on the words and not the meanings, and certainly not letting myself be distracted by the thought of what I'd be wearing and how I'd manage my hair, which had to be loosened in mourning disarray for the end of the play. I read each line and then shut my eyes and repeated the words to myself. I was so glad I looked like Father and not like Mother, or I'd never have been chosen for the part of a beautiful woman, even though of course I'd be wearing a mask. I wondered what the mask would look like. "Son of Thetis," I repeated to myself. I opened my eyes to read the next line and saw Father before me, looking absolutely devastated.

I am not using that word lightly. Father's face looked like a city that had been sacked and the fields sown with salt. He has a highly expressive face, the kind of face you see on statues of gods and heroes. Now you could have used it as a study for Niobe or grieving Orpheus. It wasn't just that he had been weeping. He wept quite easily; I'd often seen him with tears in his eyes at something especially moving. Mother used to tease him about it a little sometimes—she'd say she could tell him a story about a child finding a lost goat and he'd tear up. But now his face was ravaged. I'd never seen anything like it. I sat up at once, closing the book. "What's wrong?" I asked.

"Simmea," he managed to say before he broke down again, and so I knew.

"Mother? Dead? How?" Having thought of Orpheus, my imagination went immediately to Euridike and the snake in the grass.

Father sat down beside me and put his arm around me in the most awkward, tentative way imaginable, as if he didn't know how hard to squeeze, or was afraid of breaking me. "Art raid," he said.

I wanted to cry, I wanted to fling myself on his chest and be held and comforted, but the openness of his grief made mine close up somehow. I felt it as a gulf inside myself, but I didn't cry. An art raid. She had been killed by human greed and folly. And she had despised the art raids. "Instead of raiding each other for art, we should be making more," she had said.

"I couldn't save her, she wouldn't let me," he choked out.

"She wouldn't let you?" I echoed. "Why not?"

"Can you think of any reason? I can't," he said.

I sat there in the awkward circle of his arm and tried to think. "Could you have saved her?"

"Easily, if I'd had my powers. And I could have had them before she was dead. I'd have been back in a moment."

I shook my head. "She must have had a good reason." I was only just starting to take it in that she was dead, that she wouldn't be coming in soon to teach the calculus class, that I'd never be able to tell her I'd be Briseis. On that thought I started to cry sudden hot tears. I hadn't really understood even then. I hadn't started to think about the long term. I hadn't even got any further than that afternoon.

Mother and I had fought about all kinds of things, mostly when she thought I wasn't working hard enough, or when I forgot to do things. She could be impossibly sanctimonious and stiff-necked. She never let me get away with sliding along as my friends sometimes did; she wanted me trying my hardest every moment. But we'd been the only women in a household of men, and even when she drove me mad with irritation she was still Mother. I loved her and knew she loved me. If she had no patience with irrationality, she would always listen to reason, and sometimes change her mind. "She was a philosopher," I said.

"She was," Father agreed. "She was a Philosopher King, she was what Plato wanted to produce, the ultimate aim of his Republic. And she was killed in a silly fight for the head of Victory."

"The head of Victory?" I asked, and then I realized what he meant, the statue in the shrine outside the south gates. She was killed trying to stop the raiders from stealing the head of Victory. It sounded almost too symbolic to be true.

"We don't know who it was, but Klymene thinks it might be Kebes."

"Kebes? The Goodness Group?" I pulled away from his arm, which wasn't giving me any comfort anyway, and leaned against the tree where I could see his face. "They've never taken part in an art raid before."

"They've never had any communication with us since they left," Father agreed.

"It was probably Psyche. Or the Amazons." They were the two that raided us for art most frequently. It had been the Council of Psyche who had started the whole thing by demanding that the art be shared out equally to all the cities in proportion to their population. Some of us had wished ever since that we'd just agreed there and then. Plato had set out rules for warfare, but he only ever imagined one Just City, not five of them squabbling over a pile of sculpture.

"Klymene said the *Goodness* had been seen. And she said she didn't recognize anyone."

I shook my head. "I never heard that Kebes wanted art."

"Who knows what he wants? I never did. He broke a statue once, on purpose. He just wanted to get away, and to destroy the City if he could." Father's eyes came into focus. "I remember him sitting where you are sitting now and saying as much."

It was strange to think of Kebes as a real person my parents had known, and not a demon to be afraid of. He had left at the Last Debate, years before I was born. "Maybe——" I began to say, then stopped. I'd been going to say that maybe Mother would understand what Kebes wanted, and I had to face up to the fact that she might well, but she wouldn't be able to tell us.

Father wasn't all that good at knowing what people meant, but he seemed to guess that time. He started to cry again, tears streaming down his face. He was looking at me, but he seemed to be looking through me. "How am I going to manage the rest of my life without her, Arete?"

"I don't know," I said truthfully. I didn't even know how I was going to manage the rest of the day. I couldn't think how I was going to cope with Father being like this. Yes, he's the god Apollo, but that often makes it harder, not easier, not just for him but for all of us. He's not used to ordinary human things. I'm sure he must have lost people before, but the ways he'd coped with that as a god wouldn't be possible for him as a human. He couldn't create a new species of flower and call it after Mother, for instance. And normally when he was having problems that arose out of being human he'd ask Mother about it, and they'd have a fascinating conversation, and she'd help him understand how it worked, logically, and then he'd be all right. Now, without her—was I supposed to help him with it? The thought was terrifying. I wasn't all that good at being human myself yet. I was only fifteen. I didn't know enough about it. It wasn't fair. I wanted to grieve for my mother, not to have to worry about helping my father cope.

"Death is a terrible thing," he said.

"What do I have to do to not die?" I blurted. I'd often wondered about this, but never asked directly.

"Not die?"

"To become a god. I'm your daughter. I could." I hoped I didn't sound childish or hubristic. Fortunately, he took me seriously.

"You could. Several of my sons have." It sounded so strange to hear him mention sons and know he didn't mean my brothers. "You'd have to decide to do it, and you'd have to find your power, and you'd have to find a new and original way of being Arete. Being excellent, that is!" He was still weeping, but his eyes were focused on me now. "You'd still have to die. If you became a god it would happen afterward."

"But you have a body when you're a god?"

"Yes, but it's not the same as a mortal body. Nothing's the same. I'll have to die to get back to being a god. It's the only way. What you should do, if you want to be a god, is to find something to be responsible for, something you can take charge of. That's what my sons who are gods did. It could be something that no god cares about now, or it could be something of mine that I'd devolve onto you. It would have to be something that needed a patron, something you cared about. And then after you died, instead of going on to Hades your soul would go to Olympos and you'd become a god. But you might prefer to stay mortal and go on to have new lives. You get to start again and forget. And there are things humans can do that gods can't—humans can do whatever they can, but we're bound by Father's edicts—or, if we break them, we are subject to punishment. There's a lot to be said for being mortal . . . but it is also awful, I'll admit." He wiped his hand over his eyes and tried to smile. "I would still grieve if I were my proper self, but it wouldn't swallow me up this way."

"If it's awful for you when you know what happens after death, think how awful it is for everyone who doesn't know!"

"I have thought about that a lot, since I talked to Sokrates and Simmea about it, and of course since Athene admitted it to everyone at the Last Debate." He looked at different spots in the garden, as if he could see where they had sat for that conversation. "But while it might be better for individual people to know, it's better for the world for people not to be sure."

"If people knew for sure that they had immortal souls, and that they needed to pursue—" I stopped, because I heard a sound from inside. I thought it was probably the other students come for the calculus class, and I'd have to tell them that Mother wasn't here and the calculus class was canceled not just for today but for always. There wasn't anyone who could take it over, either, not that I could think of.

But it wasn't a student who came out, it was my brother Neleus. He looked almost as bad as Father. His face seemed entirely bloodless. I was delighted to see him—anything to relieve the burden of being alone with Father in this state. I got up and hugged him tightly. "You know?"

"Sophoniba told me," he said. "An art raid."

"Nobody knows who," Father said, without moving from where he sat, staring at the space by the tree where I had been.

Neleus looked down at him and shook his head. "What are you two doing sitting in the garden? We need to find the others, and we need to get drunk."

"Is that what people do?" Father asked.

"Yes," Neleus said firmly. "That's what people do, and it's what we shall do. Come on, let's go to Florentia. Ficino will be there, and they always have wine and won't grudge it to us. I asked Sophoniba to find the others and send them there, and all of Mother's especial friends. We'll gather there and drink and talk about her. Come on."

Father got up slowly. "All right," he said. "If that's what people do."

So that's what we did.

4

MAIA

I am a teacher. I have also worked as a midwife to babies and cities, but it is on teaching that I have spent most of my life. I have the temperament of a scholar. I always have had.

In the years after the Last Debate I had cause to regret a lot of things I had done in the name of Plato, but I never regretted that we had made the attempt to create the Just City. I agree with a lot of the criticisms that have been made of us, of the Masters. Buying slave children was wrong. I always thought so. I should have been more forceful in my opposition. In those days I was young, and too easily cowed by male authority. I grew up in England in the 1850s. It wasn't until I saw the girls who grew up in the Just City that I really understood what free women could be like. That in itself justifies us in what we did, in my eyes—how marvelous they are, their natural assumption of equality. What was a hypothesis to me is an axiom to them. Only Plato in all the thousands of years between his time and my own saw that women could have philosophical souls, only Plato allowed that we were people. Only in the City were women truly liberated, for the first time in history.

All the same, we Masters did and allowed things that were wrong, and I am as guilty as any of us. These days I defer to those whose authority I respect, but I try not to automatically defer to anyone. I accept my share of the guilt for what we did, but I still say that what we tried to achieve was a noble goal, and what we did achieve was wonderful, even if it fell short of perfection. There is no perfection in human things, only in the world of Forms. We tried our best. Our intentions were good.

They don't allow Masters in Sokratea. I suppose they're justified, but I am hurt whenever I think of it. We, and Plato, meant nothing but the best for them! And when I say the best I mean it literally; what we wanted for them was nothing but excellence, virtue, arete. They say you can't want that for somebody else, they have to want it for themselves. Well, perhaps they have a point. But Plato wrote that seeking to increase someone else's excellence is the best form of love. We loved them and we sought their excellence; and if the means were not always ideal, then I contend that we were limited by the constraints of reality. Though Athene, of course, was not.

She turned Sokrates into a fly and vanished, and Sokrates too flew off and vanished, so we had to manage as best we could without either of them.

In the many debates that followed the Last Debate there were more voices crying for going than staying. Trying to fix the City we had seemed less appealing to many than trying to start again, this time with like-minded volunteers. Athenia wanted to do everything exactly the same, only more strictly. Having seen some of the pain caused by being strict, this had very little appeal for me. Sokratea, as I said, excluded Masters from the beginning, when it was only a group of hot-headed children headed by Patroklus. Kebes, with what we came to call the Goodness Group, left immediately that first afternoon, without participating in any of the subsequent debates. That left the Remnant City, which felt at first like a patched-up compromise, and Psyche, and the City of Amazons.

It was Psyche that drove me to the Amazons. Psyche, the city the Neoplatonists set up, decided to manage without the difficult requirement of allowing women to be full participants in their city and in the life of the mind. They made women second-class citizens, as they usually have been, historically. It's amazing to me that any women at all agreed to move there. Psyche is the smallest of the cities even now, and disproportionately male. But some women went willingly—and I know it was willingly, because I argued with them, personally and at length. Some of my girls from Florentia chose Psyche of their own will. It was those debates that drove me to the other extreme and the choice of the City of Amazons—those debates, and the necessity for them. There were women trained in logic who were prepared to argue that they didn't deserve citizenship, and that they were inferior to men.

I know Ficino felt the same way about me leaving the Remnant as I felt about Andromeda and the others who chose Psyche. He was almost in tears, arguing with me at one point. But in the end he respected my decision, as I respected his to stay.

The other, less worthy reason I made the choice to go is that all of my close friends except Ficino were going: Axiothea, and Klio, and Lysias, and Kreusa. I went despite Ikaros, not because of him.

I have written already about how Ikaros raped me when I was young and naive. I had been sheltered and protected all my life until I came to the city, and I had no instinct for self-preservation. I went off alone with Ikaros, seeking answers to questions, with no idea that he imagined this was a sexual tryst. (It's hard to believe I was ever so stupid.) I saw him as a man from the romantic and wonderful Renaissance, and I did not consider what that really meant. He had read Plato and loved the idea of the *Republic*, and he was prepared to concede that women had the philosophic nature. That didn't mean he had entirely put away the appetites and expectations of his own era. He thought my protests were conventional. He thought I was saying no because society allowed me to enjoy sex only if it was forced on me in circumstances beyond my control. He believed I wanted it, even when I screamed and fought. He was confused, afterward. He tried to make amends. He gave me a book. I remained furious with him—for raping me, and for continuing to act as though he had done nothing. Others adored him, but I kept away from him as much as I could. I didn't trust him, and I found it harder to trust any men because of him.

I spent eight years in the City of Amazons.

At first it was two thousand people camped out in the fields on the north side of the island. Building the physical city was a challenge. Klio persuaded Crocus to help us. Crocus was one of the two remaining Worker-robots. In the debates that followed the Last Debate, both Workers had considered Sokratea, but decided to stay in the Remnant. They had good solid philosophical reasons, but also practical ones—they needed electricity as we needed food, and designing and installing electrical generators elsewhere would be a challenge.

Crocus quarried marble for us and delivered it to the site of the new city, and then we humans wrestled the slabs into roads and assembled the blocks into buildings. Crocus helped—what was difficult for even the strongest of us was trivially easy for him. We built one wall while he built the other three and put on the roof. He cut marble pipes and installed plumbing. We assembled ourselves into teams and tried to learn skills from him and from each other. We did as much as we could. As there were two thousand of us and one of him, in the end more of Amazonia was built by humans than by Crocus, but I don't know how we could have possibly managed without him. We voted him full privileges of citizenship including voting rights, although he never became a resident. We inscribed his name among the list of founders. There is also a bas-relief of him above the main gate, carved by Ardeia.

He returned to the Remnant every night to rest and recharge, while the rest of us planned the city and the work for the next day. We did our planning in the dark. We had all grown used to electric lights in the time we had been in the City, and we missed them. Our old Tech Committee was almost all there, and we assembled to try to deal with problems.

"We need to find a way of having light," Lysias said. "They have refused to let us have any of the solar lights, so we need a proper alternative. What did people use?" Lysias came from the twenty-first century and so, like the Children, he had grown up with electricity.

"Gas lights," I said. "Gas was made from coal in some way. I've no idea how."

"Nobody will know, and there won't be any books on it," Lysias said, savagely. "I don't think there's any coal on the island anyway. What else?"

"Oil lamps," Axiothea said, a calm voice in the darkness. "We have olive oil. We can make glass, or if we can't we can make clay lamps like the Romans had. I wonder what wicks are made out of?"

"If the Romans had them, somebody might know, or it might be written down somewhere," Lysias said, sounding a little more cheerful. "Did they give enough light?"

"Enough to read and work by," I said. "And there are also candles, made from beeswax or tallow. Wicks were made from cotton in my time, which we don't have, but I expect linen would do just as well."

"Candles, of course," Klio said.

"They're just decorative," Lysias protested. "Not that I wouldn't appreciate having one right now."

"Lamps are more effective," I said. I had lived with electricity long enough that it was easy for me to understand how in future ages, candles could have come to be thought of as nothing but decoration.

"Yes, I've heard of things smelling of the lamp, meaning people were up late working on them," Klio said. "And burning midnight oil. So it must give enough light for people to work. We can't make glass, but Crocus can. Except I don't want to impose on his good nature to ask him to do even more for us. There's not much we can do for him in return—only discuss philosophy and read to him, and there are plenty of people in all the cities happy to do that."

"Books," Lysias said. "That's another tech issue we should discuss. We can use the libraries in the Remnant, they've agreed we can. But can we use their printing presses? We should have our own library here. The City Planning Committee have assigned it a place. But should we be building a printing press? Do we have anyone who can set type?"

"And should we be duplicating everything so we have it to hand and don't have to walk ten miles every time we want to look something up?" I asked.

"And if we have only one press, should it be Greek or Latin?" Klio asked.

"It doesn't matter, we melt all the type regularly and recast it—it's only lead." I said. "We'd have to have both sets of molds, but we could print in either language, switching when the type got worn." I had always enjoyed working with the presses.

"Good!" Lysias said, relieved.

When we had set up the original city, most of the tech questions had been philosophical—we had to decide what we wanted to do and what was the best way to achieve it. We had the practical means, unlimited Worker resources, and the presence of Athene to give us divine intervention as needed. We didn't realize what a luxury these things had been until we had to manage without them. Now the problems were almost all practical, and the answers were almost all things we didn't like.

We made the most urgent decisions, and had drinking-fountains and latrine-fountains and wash-fountains enough for everyone, and fields prepared for animals and crops, and shelter from the elements before the first winter came. During that winter we began to manufacture lamps. We had a skilled potter, one of the Children from Ferrara, a girl called Iris. She made the bases, and Kreusa, of all people, knew how to make wicks from flax and instructed others. Crocus was still helping us finish off the city, and it fell to me to ask him if he would make us some clear glass bowls for the lamps.

It was raining. Crocus was putting a roof onto the hall in the southwest corner that was destined for our library. Some of us had, through practice, become quite skilled at masonry, but roofing was still a real challenge. "Joy to you, Crocus," I said.

He stopped work and turned one of his hands to carve "Joy to you Maia!" into one of the damp marble blocks of the library wall. As was his custom, he carved the Greek words in Latin letters, which always looked peculiar.

I beckoned him over to where he could carve his responses in the paving stones of the street outside, some of which already bore his side of dialogues, sadly more practical and less philosophical than those that still lined the walks of the Remnant City. I asked him about the glass globes. "Can make," he inscribed tersely. "How many?"

There were over two thousand of us Amazons, and we all desperately wanted light at night. We were used to it and hated doing without it. Some people had slunk back to the Remnant already for this reason, but most of us were made of sterner stuff. Everyone would want one. "Two thousand five hundred," I said.

"In return?" he carved.

"What do you want?" I asked. How easily it turned to this, I thought, to trade and barter.

"Thomas Aquinas," he carved.

"We don't have it," I said, surprised. "We don't have any Christian apologetics. We didn't bring them. You know we didn't. We'll read you anything we have."

"Ikaros owns forbidden books," he carved.

"He does? How do you know?"

Crocus just sat there in the fine drizzle, huge, golden, mud-spattered. I'd say he was looking at me, but he didn't give any impression of having eyes or a head. With a shock of guilt I remembered my Botticelli book, full of forbidden reproductions of Madonnas and angels, with text in English. Of course. Ikaros had given it to me. What else might he have brought here?

"If he has it, then yes," I said.

"Thomas Aquinas. In Greek," Crocus wrote.

"If Ikaros has it, I'll make him agree to translate it and read it to you," I said. "If not, we'll read you something else you want."

"Display sculpture," he inscribed.

"What? I don't understand."

"I make sculpture, for display in Amazon plaza."

"Oh Crocus, but we'd love that. You don't have to ask that as a favor. We'd regard it as an honor."

"Will make bowls for lamps," Crocus inscribed. He waited politely for a moment to see if I had anything else to say, then went back to his half-finished library roof. And there was his half of the dialogue, there in the marble for anyone to read. "Thomas Aquinas. Ikaros owns forbidden books." Ikaros was no friend of mine. But I felt the urge to protect him nevertheless. No good could come of everyone knowing he had forbidden books. I took a piece of heavy wood from an unfinished house nearby and used it as a crowbar to pry up the heavy marble paving stone. Then I flipped it over so that the carving was on the underside and set it back in place. It was earth-stained and filthy compared to the other flags, but I hoped the rain would soon wash it clean. I went off to find Ikaros.

I wanted to talk to him in private, but I wasn't the stupid young girl who had gone off to the woods alone with him, unconscious of anything but my own burning desire for philosophical conversation. I was over thirty now. I sought Klio about the city. She knew about my Botticelli book, and about the rape. She was pressing olives with a crowd of Children and couldn't come immediately. She agreed to talk to Ikaros with me after dinner.

As luck would have it, I ran into him a few minutes later in the street. He was alone, coming toward me. It was raining more heavily now and my braid was so wet it was coming down from where it was bound up around my head. "I need to ask you something," I said.

"Come inside," he said, opening the door of a nearby house. "This is going to be Ardeia and Diomedes's house."

The house was complete, and held a large bed. "I don't want to go inside there with you," I said.

Ikaros rolled his eyes, half-smiling. "You're not as irresistible as you imagine," he said. "I have quite enough going with Lukretia." Lukretia was a woman of the Renaissance. She had been the other master of Ferrara, and now she and Ikaros were sharing a house here. "But stand in the rain if you prefer. I shall keep dry." He stepped inside, and I stood in the doorway, in view of anyone passing by. "Which of us are you afraid of, you or me?" he asked.

"I have quite enough going with Lysias," I snapped. The trouble was that there was some truth in his accusation. I had always found Ikaros powerfully attractive. But that didn't mean I wanted to be taken against my will, and he had shown me that he didn't care what I wanted.

"What do you want me for then?" He grinned, and I scowled at him.

"Crocus wants Thomas Aquinas. In Greek. And he says you have it."

Ikaros's face changed in an instant to completely serious, as serious as I had ever seen him.

"I wasn't going to do without books I needed," he muttered.

"You took them when you were rescuing art?" I asked.

"You know I did. I got you that Botticelli book. It was more than anyone could bear, all those printed books, right there to my hand. I bought them, I didn't steal them. And I didn't contaminate the City with them."

"Nobody says you did," I said, but I shook my head. "You think rules are for everyone but you. How did you get them without Athene knowing?"

He ignored my question. "I have done no harm with the books."

"You might be going to now. Who knows what Thomas Aquinas will do to Crocus?"

He grinned irrepressibly. "Have you read Thomas Aquinas?"

I shook my head. "I have never had the slightest interest in him, or anything else medieval. But I hear he's extremely complicated, and you are going to have to translate him into Greek and read it all aloud."

He looked horrified. "Do you know how long it is?"

"No," I said, crisply. "Long, I hope. It's what Crocus wants in return for making us glass bowls for lamps, and without them the lamps won't give enough light for reading and working. So I think you're going to do it, and as the book is still forbidden by the rules of this city as well as the original City, you're not going to have any help doing it. And I think that's going to be an appropriate punishment for bringing the book in the first place."

It might have been unkind, but I couldn't help laughing at the look on his face.

5

ARETE

For a long and terrible time, all that autumn and on into winter, Father insisted on getting vengeance for Mother and everybody else kept arguing with him because he clearly wasn't being rational.

"It's sad, and we're all extremely sorry, but you'd think from the way you're acting that we'd never lost anyone before," Maia said.

Father didn't say so to her, but the truth was that he'd never really lost anyone he cared about before, not lost them permanently the way he'd lost Mother. He said that to me and my brothers after Maia had left. He said it very seriously and as if he imagined that this would have been news to us.

"Who would have thought grief would crack Pytheas that way?" Ficino said to Maia, in Florentia, when he didn't know I was listening.

It was true, though I didn't want to acknowledge it. He was cracked, or at least cracking. It was a terrible thing to see. When he was alone with me he kept asking me if I could tell him why she'd stopped him saving her, and so I kept trying to think about that.

"Might she have been ready to go on to a new life?" I asked.

Father just groaned. After a moment he looked up. "She wasn't done with this life. There was so much we still could have done. Sixty more years before she was as old as Ficino is!"

"Well, might there be something she felt she had to do and could do better in another life?"

"What?" he asked, staring at me from red-rimmed eyes. I had no idea and just shook my head.

Embassies were sent under sacred truce to the other cities. None of them admitted responsibility for the raid, or that they had the head of Victory. This was unusual, but it wasn't unprecedented. They had lied before, on occasion. Only Father took it as proof that Kebes had stolen the head and killed Mother. The *Goodness* wasn't sighted again, and then winter closed in, with storms that made the sea dangerous. When Father proposed organizing a naval expedition to find and destroy Kebes's Lost City, even more people were sure he was cracked with grief. I wasn't old enough to go to the Chamber or the Assembly, but people were talking about it everywhere.

The worst of it was that I was having to deal with Father being like this while also trying to cope with my own grief. It was bad enough that Mother wasn't there to walk in and set everything right with a logical sensible explanation from first principles. But she *also* wasn't going to finish embroidering my kiton or trim my bangs or teach me how to integrate volumes. My throat ached because I wanted to talk to Mother about Ficino's project about assessing how philosophical cities were. But my grief, awful as it was to suffer, was cast into insignificance by the mythic scale of Father's grief. It was all like the first afternoon when he was crying so much that I couldn't cry at all. Her absence was like a presence, but Father's grief was like a huge sucking whirlpool that threatened to sweep everything up and carry it away.

Another thing that didn't help was that every one of the Children, my parents' whole generation, had lost their home and parents when they were ten years old. Compared to that, losing Mother when I was fifteen shouldn't have been anything to cry about. Only Maia seemed to understand. She took me for a walk along the cliffs and told me about losing her father, and how she had lost her whole world and her whole life with him, and all her books. "You still have your books," she said, encouragingly. "You can still read and study. Philosophy will help."

I thought about that. Reading did help, when it took me away from myself, when I had time to do it. But it was history I read, and poetry, and drama. Playing Briseis helped. It was a distraction. Philosophy required rigorous thought and didn't seem to help at all. It all seemed wrong, but refuting it was always hard work. I knew Maia, who definitely had one of Plato's philosophical souls, wouldn't understand that. But there was something philosophical I thought she might be able to answer. "Plato says that people shouldn't show their grief. It seems to me that Father is doing exactly what Plato says you shouldn't do."

Maia put her hand on my shoulder comfortingly. "It's hard to argue that he isn't! But you have to let Pytheas deal with his own grief while you deal with yours. He's a grown man, and you shouldn't be worrying about how he's grieving. Simmea wouldn't have wanted you to bottle it all up any more than she'd have wanted Pytheas to howl his out."

I stared away from her. Clouds were boiling up out of the east and the sea was the color of cold lava, flecked with little white wave-caps. It was hard to believe it was the same sea where I swam in summer, warm and blue. I could see the rocks where Mother and I had often pulled ourselves up to sit for a while before turning back, where I had first been introduced to dolphins. The sea was lashing them now, an angry note of black rock and white spray. The wind was cold and I was glad of my cloak. "It's so difficult," I said. "And I can't just ignore Father. But no ships can sail in this weather."

"Even Pytheas doesn't want to send out his expedition until spring," Maia said.

"I don't think she would have wanted vengeance," I said. I had tears in my eyes, but the cold wind carried them away to fall salt into the salt sea.

"I don't think so either, but I don't know how to convince Pytheas of that. He calls it justice, but it's vengeance he means. He just won't listen—he seems to listen and then he just goes on as if I hadn't said anything. I don't understand it. After my father died I didn't want revenge. But then, there wasn't anything to revenge myself on—he died of disease. If there had been something, maybe it would have been different. It's natural to grieve."

"But it's not natural to howl?"

Maia shook her head. "It may be natural, but it's not philosophical. And Simmea was a true philosopher. I miss her too." She hesitated. "I don't think any of us understood quite how much Pytheas needed her. This excessive grief doesn't seem like what I'd have expected of him. He has always been so calm."

My brothers were no help at all. They had their own grief, of course. "Why did I fight with her so much?" Kallikles asked rhetorically.

"I wish I'd told her how much I loved her," Phaedrus said.

"I keep wanting to tell her things, and then realizing she's not there to tell," Neleus said.

But none of them could really understand how I felt, or how Father felt. They all wanted to join his revenge, once he organized it. I did too. Wrestling and throwing weights in the palaestra gave me a temporary relief. I did feel sometimes that it might have made me feel better to go out with a spear and something clearly marked as an enemy to stick it into. But I knew enough philosophy already to know that it wouldn't help much. Mother would still be dead no matter how many enemies we sent down to Hades after her. And how could it be just to want vengeance, to return evil for evil?

Erinna was a great comfort, when she had time for me. She was nineteen, a silver, and she had real work to do, learning to sail the *Excellence* and fighting in the Platean troop. She was my friend, and she had loved Mother. She was lovely-looking, with olive skin and fair hair, which, since she had been assigned to the ship, she wore cut short on the nape of her neck but still curling up over her broad forehead. When she was free she listened to me talk and often did things with me to distract me. She even organized our calculus class into working on our own. Axiothea, one of the Masters from Amazonia, came over once to help us. Erinna was really kind to me during this time, and I treasured every moment I could spend with her. But she was frequently busy, and much in demand, and I didn't want to waste too much of her precious free time. And naturally, I couldn't explain to her about Father properly, because really explaining about Father would have meant talking about his true nature.

Erinna is the one who suggested that I should try to write an autobiography. She said that writing things down sometimes helped her to come to terms with them. She said that Mother had told her that, years before. Because it was her advice, and before that Mother's, I began it, and I found that like wrestling, it helped at the time. So I dealt with my grief by writing autobiography, working hard at the palaestra, and reading history.

The other person who really helped was Crocus. Crocus is a Worker, a robot, and he had been a close friend of Mother's. We had long ago worked out a way for the Workers to write in wax so there wasn't a permanent engraved record of every time they wished somebody joy, but he always carved what he wrote about Mother into the paving stones. He wanted to talk about debates they had shared, and he took me to the places where they'd had them. His responses were engraved into the marble, and it comforted us both when he engraved what Mother had said beside them, making them into full dialogues. He knew all about death and what happened to human souls—at least as much as anyone else. But he worried about his own soul, and Sixty-One's, and the souls of the Workers Athene had taken with her after the Last Debate. We had enough spare parts for Crocus and Sixty-One to last indefinitely, but he wondered whether he should want his soul to move on. He wondered if he would become a human or an animal or another Worker. He mused about why Plato never mentioned Workers. Crocus could always distract me from my own thoughts. Sometimes he would come into Florentia and join me and Ficino when we were debating.

He had built a number of statues—we called them colossi, because they were so immense. They combined hyperrealism—you could see all the hairs up Sokrates's nose in his *Last Debate*—with strange outbreaks of fantasy—in that same statue, one of Sokrates's eyes is already a fly's multifaceted eye. Parts of them were painted and parts of them were plain marble or other stone. He had decided to make a sculpture of Mother, but he hadn't decided where. We went together to look at various places in the city he thought might be appropriate. I know he tried to talk to Father about this too. But Father was too sunk in grief to give an opinion—though he did sensibly agree with me that having a colossus of Mother in the garden at Thessaly would be a bad idea.

One day when it was my turn to help cook dinner in Florentia, I came out to eat late and saw Maia and Aeschines sitting with Father and Phaedrus. I took my plate over to join them. Father wasn't crying at that moment, but his face still had that devastated look. Maia looked firm. Aeschines was looking troubled. He was one of the Children, and father of my friend Baukis. He had been a good friend of Mother's, though not especially of Father's. Father found him slow. He was a member of the Chamber, and on a number of important committees.

"Nobody is going to agree to a voyage of vengeance," Maia was saying as I put my plate down.

Father looked up. "Arete. Joy to you."

"Joy," I echoed, though joy was the furthest thing from either of our voices.

"Joy to you, Arete," Aeschines said. "I haven't seen you in a long time. You must come and eat with me and Baukis in Ithaka one of these days."

"Joy, and thank you," I said. There was a fresco at Ithaka that Mother had painted when she'd been young. When Aeschines invited me, I was suddenly filled with a need to see it. She had painted it so long ago, and she had done better work since, as she always said. But I liked it, especially the way she had shown Odysseus in the harbor that was our own harbor. "I'll come one day soon," I promised.

"Baukis will be glad." He smiled at me in a friendly way, as if he genuinely liked me.

Meanwhile Father had turned back to Maia. "Maybe nobody wants a voyage of vengeance. But how about a voyage of exploration? It's ridiculous when you think about it, nonsensical for us to be here and know so little about what's out there right now. Finding Kebes would be an advantage, if we could, whether or not he's responsible for . . . for killing Simmea." His face crumpled up.

"Exploration, yes, maybe," Aeschines said, briskly. "But it would leave us without a ship here."

"What's the use of a ship that takes up so much maintenance but which nobody ever uses?" Father countered.

Aeschines nodded. "We use it for training, and visiting the other cities, but I do see your point. It would also mean a number of people wouldn't be here if we were attacked. I assume you'd want to take a troop?"

"I think so. It could be dangerous. And if we did find Kebes, well, we'd definitely need a troop. But we wouldn't be looking for danger or vengeance or anything. We'd just be trying to find out what was there. If that was Kebes, well . . ."

"What you're a lot more likely to find is a lot of Minoan and Mycenaean settlements," Maia said.

"Well, wouldn't it be useful to see if they're where they're listed as being in the Catalog of Ships?" Father asked.

"I want to come," my brother Phaedrus said. "I want to see something that isn't just this island."

"So do I," I said.

"You're much too young," Maia said.

"Too young for a voyage of vengeance, true," I said, choosing my words carefully. "I'm not yet an ephebe, I haven't taken up arms or been chosen for a metal. But I'm old enough to go on a voyage of exploration."

"Good point," Aeschines said. "Would this be a safe voyage of exploration, safe enough to take children, or would it be a dangerous voyage of vengeance?"

Father looked at me, then back at Aeschines. Before he could speak, Ficino came over to join us. He'd finished eating, but he had a cup of wine in his hand. The red hat he almost always wore was askew. "You all look very solemn," he said, after he'd greeted those of us he hadn't already seen that day.

"We're discussing sending out a voyage of exploration in the spring," Aeschines said. "Arete wants to go, and—"

"Splendid!" Ficino said, unexpectedly, beaming at me. "I want to go too."

"Old men and children," Phaedrus said dismissively.

Ficino laughed. "What better explorers could there be? How far will we go, Pytheas? Do you mean to get to Ithaka?"

Aeschines laughed, and Father actually smiled, for the first time in months.

"I hadn't thought we'd go as far as that," he said. "Around the Kyklades, and north to the Ionian islands. Maybe touching the mainland at Mycenae."

"Mycenae!" Ficino said. "I really have been extraordinarily lucky all my life, and now to have this voyage proposed at the very end of it! How about Pylos? Nestor might be there as a young man. Or Troy itself? Imagine meeting the young Priam, perhaps attending his wedding to Hekabe." Maia reached over and straightened his hat.

"We know so much about the future, and so little about this time where we're living," I said. Ficino grinned at me.

"We want to find Kebes," Phaedrus said.

"Kebes is probably the least interesting thing in the whole Aegean," Ficino said. "Though no, it would be interesting to know what kind of city the Goodness Group have come up with, to compare it with the others."

"Kebes couldn't found a city without other people out there hearing rumors of it," I said.

"We have," Maia said.

"Well, but we're on an island, and we had divine help," Father said.

"Kebes may be on an island," Phaedrus said.

Father leaned forward. "He probably is. But he doesn't have enough people or enough resources to stay on an island and entirely out of contact. He must have been trading or raiding, and if he has, we'll hear about him."

"Also, we don't know whether or not there are rumors out there about us. If we're supposed to inspire the legend of Atlantis, there probably are," Aeschines said.

"I don't think Kebes was responsible for the raid," Maia said. "He's never been involved in art raids before, or contacted us at all. It doesn't make any sense."

Father looked stubborn. "Everyone else has denied it."

"They've lied before. Psyche have lied. They just can't be trusted," Maia insisted. "It probably was them. Or the Amazons."

Father hesitated for a moment. "How could we find out? Send spies?"

"Perhaps," Maia said. "But it will be sure to come out sooner or later. Whoever has the head will be sure to display it, eventually, and then we'll hear."

"And go to war," Phaedrus said, fiercely, slapping the table and making the cups and plates bounce.

"Unless it is Kebes," Father said. "Then we'd never hear and there would be no vengeance and . . . nothing. I want a voyage of exploration so we have more information."

"More information would be a good thing, certainly," Aeschines said. "I'll suggest it to the committee."

Ficino raised his cup. "It's my birthday. I'm ninety-nine years old. It seems the perfect time to set out on a voyage. To exploration!"

We all drank.

6

ARETE

I wasn't in the Chamber for the debate, or in the Assembly for the vote, but I was in Thessaly for the family fight.

It was just after the midwinter celebrations. It had been a mild clear day with a promise of spring in the air. The Assembly had voted that the voyage of exploration would take place when spring came, and now the question was of who was to go. Father was going, there was no question of that. Klymene was going with the Florentia troop. Erinna was going, as one of the few people who properly understood how the *Excellence* worked. And Ficino was going, and so was I—I had won that battle without any need to fight. This was to be a voyage safe for old men and children, and Ficino and I were the exemplary old man and child. That I was only a child for three more months didn't matter. I was going!

My brothers all wanted to go. Well, Plato-loving Alkibiades didn't. He had written to us—he had sent a letter to Father with the envoy who went to Athenia. Father let me read it. In addition to saying all you'd expect about Mother, he said to trust that the head of Victory wasn't in Athenia, and that he would let us know immediately if he heard anything. He sent love to all of us and said he had made the right choice and was happy.

Phaedrus and Neleus were at home in Thessaly on the evening when Kallikles came around with a jar of wine after dinner. "We need to talk," he said.

I broke the resin seal and mixed the wine without being asked, using the big red-figure krater decorated with Apollo killing the dragon Pytho, and the cups that matched it. (Apollo on the krater didn't look at all like Father, but I liked the coils of the snaky dragon.) I watered the wine half and half, as Plato recommends, and then gave a cup to everyone.

It was too cold to go into the garden now that the sun was down, which was inconvenient as it was the only space suitable for sitting and talking. There was a reason the houses were known as "sleeping houses." We were supposed to do everything else elsewhere. Most of the year this worked out well enough, and even now it would have been all right if we could have gone to Florentia or another eating hall to have our conversation in public. As it was, we all sat on the beds. I passed around some dried figs and goat cheese and missed Mother, who would have made the boys help.

"I want to go with you on the voyage," Kallikles said, once we were all settled. I sat down beside him on the bed.

"It isn't up to me," Father said. "The Chamber is deciding who goes. Apply to them." Father was looking a little better now that the voyage had been agreed on.

"We all want to go," Phaedrus said.

"You can't all go," Father said. "What if the ship went down?"

"What if it did?" Kallikles asked. "That's part of the hazard of life."

"All of you lost at once?" Father said. "No."

"The city wants to send the best," Phaedrus said. He grinned at me. He was constantly making jokes about my name—it was he who had first thought up the game of pursuing Arete. "And in addition to my little sister, the most excellent people they can find. We brothers are the certainly among the best of the Young Ones."

Father took a deep draught of his wine. "Arete's going," he said. "No more."

"The problem with that is that we're heroes," Kallikles said, spreading his hands. "You know we are. And this is a heroic mission, where we will have the chance to prove ourselves. It's like the voyage of the Argonauts. We all ought to have that chance. The Chamber gives us the chance, on our own excellence. If they turn us down, then they do. But if you speak against us they will turn us down."

Father shook his head. "Not all of you," he began, but wrathful Neleus interrupted.

"I insist on going, even though I'm not a hero!" He looked furiously at Kallikles.

We all looked at him. And suddenly I saw us all looking at him. It was strange. They were all my brothers, and I knew them well, Neleus among them, but now I saw them all with new eyes. Neleus sat alone on his bed, and we were all looking at him, and we were all one thing, and he was another. We all looked like Father, and he did not. We all had Father's calm blue eyes and chiseled features. We had all shades of skin color—or all the shades of the Middle Sea, as Maia put it: Kallikles's chalk pale, Father's olive, mine brown, and Phaedrus's near-black. We had hair that curled wildly and hair that lay flat as silk. Kallikles was short and Phaedrus was tall and I was a girl. We were an assorted set, but we were all Father's children, children of Apollo, of a god. We knew we were all heroes, and Neleus knew he was not. My father and my brothers looked coolly at Neleus, and I looked with them, ranged myself with them in that moment. I had to whether I wanted to or not. I was a hero. I could not make myself be like Neleus. I was human—we were all human. But we all had something else in addition, and Neleus did not, and we all knew it.

"It shouldn't make any difference," Neleus said, into that long silence. His voice wavered a little.

"It shouldn't," Phaedrus said, gently enough. "But you have to see that it does."

"You're not any better than I am," Neleus blazed.

Phaedrus lifted an eyebrow. "You know I am. I'm faster and stronger. We're exactly the same age but I haven't been able to wrestle with you in the palaestra since we were six."

"It's not fair!"

"It may not be fair, but it's the way it is," Kallikles said. He reached out a hand toward Neleus across the space between the beds, but Neleus ignored it.

"It's not your fault," Phaedrus said.

"Being heroes doesn't make you better people," Father said. He sounded immensely weary. "It might even make you worse. Knowing about it might. Simmea was afraid of that."

"What does it mean, exactly?" I asked.

"Arete, even you must see that this isn't the time for a Socratic debate clarifying terms!" Kallikles said, turning on me angrily.

"I don't see that at all," I said, keeping my voice even as Mother would have. "I think this would be a splendid time to discuss it properly. We all know we're heroes, except Neleus, sorry Neleus, but we don't know what that means in real and practical terms. We don't know what difference it can make."

Kallikles looked at Father, but Father was staring down at the blankets and said nothing.

"I'm going on the voyage," Neleus said, in a calm and decided tone. "I appreciate that you all despise me, but I am going. I have more right than anyone, and more need to prove myself than any of you. If the Chamber won't accept me for the voyage I'll stow away. I am her son. I am Simmea's only son, and I am going to avenge her."

I made a little sound when he said he was her only son, because why should gender matter so much? But then I stopped myself from protesting, because he needed to be special, and when it came down to it he wasn't a hero and I was.

There was another long silence. Then Father spoke. "Being a god made me worse at being a human being. She saw that. And she saw that being heroes might be a problem for you. And she was afraid that you would be unkind to Neleus because he isn't, and that he'd suffer from that." She had been right to worry about that, because we had been and he had. Father went on without hesitating, still looking down at the bed and not at any of us. "She thought that people needed more training to bring up children than we had had, but she understood that we had to bring you up and take responsibility for you. Most of the people with the training left after we voted to have families, and the rest were rushed off their feet."

Now he looked up, and it was Neleus he looked at. "You are indeed her only son. She loved you very much. It almost killed her soul having you. She hated to give you up. She was so glad to get you back! I remember it so well, when we first brought all of you here." He looked around the room, shaking his head at the memory. "She loved all of you, but Neleus was indeed her only son."

Then he looked at me, and I saw he must have been aware of the little noise of protest I made. "You are her only daughter, and the only child of her milk."

"What difference does milk make?" I asked, puzzled.

"All the difference in the world," he answered, as if he thought I should know this already. "Mothers give their milk to their children, and with it their strength and their stamina, their ability to survive disease. There's a bond in that milk."

"And I didn't have her milk?" Neleus asked in a small voice.

Phaedrus answered quickly. "You know you didn't. You've read what Plato says, no mother shall set eyes on her own child—they went to the nurseries when their breasts were full and fed some random child who was there." Phaedrus shook his head. "She might have fed me, but never you."

Everyone except me had read the *Republic*. Reading it was now part of the adulthood rite for our city.

"She fed you the night you were born, Neleus," Father said. "She told me so. But after that you were fed by any woman but your mother, and the same for the rest of you. No doubt Plato meant it to even out the advantages given by the milk, so that all could share with all."

"Plato was crazy on some subjects, and that was one of them," Kallikles said dismissively. "Father, where are you going with this line of argument?"

Father hesitated. "I don't remember." He looked over at Mother's bed, where

Phaedrus was sitting, and then quickly away. Mother often used to be able to see when Father got ahead of himself and give him his next point. She had a way of laughing as she did it that I could almost hear. Father wiped his eyes with the corner of his kiton. "I just can't lose all of you as well as her."

"You'd be lost too," Phaedrus pointed out.

"I'd be back on Olympos, and you'd all be in Hades after having achieved very little in this life. You're heroes. Arete asked what that means. It doesn't mean anything if you don't live like heroes."

"I'm going," Neleus said, stubbornly. "I'm not a hero, but I am her son, and I am going on this voyage."

"We're all going," Kallikles said. "It won't be all of your sons, Father. Alkibiades and Porphyry and Euklides would still be on the island even if the ship sinks. And how can we live as heroes if we don't get the chance to join the one heroic venture in our lifetimes so far?"

Father looked from one to the other of them, then he slowly set down his cup, got up, and went out of the street door.

"Where are you going?" Kallikles asked, but Father kept on walking and didn't answer.

"Where is he going?" Phaedrus asked.

Since nobody else was going to, I got up and followed Father. He was walking aimlessly south down the middle of the street. "Where are you going?" I asked.

"To visit the lion," he said.

I put my hand through his arm. "I'll come too." I knew the lion he meant. It was a bronze statue of a lion on a street corner near Florentia. Mother had been especially fond of it. One of my first memories was walking to visit the lion, one of my little hands held in each of my parents' big ones. We walked down briskly through the night's chill that made me wish for my cloak. Father felt warm, but then he always does. I don't know if it was his divine fire burning even in his mortal incarnation or just a natural warmth. We reached the lion, and he patted it the way Mother used to. I patted it too. The lion's face was very expressive, but it was hard to say just what it expressed. It seemed to change from time to time. Tonight the shadows made it seem worried. We turned around and walked back toward home.

It was a cold night and the stars were burning bright and clear, so distinct that I could see colors in some of them. "I can see all the stars in Orion's belt," I said.

"We'll go there one day," Father said.

I looked at him, startled. "You and me?"

"People," he clarified. "They'll settle planets out around those distant suns, one day, far ahead. I haven't been there yet. I'm always reluctant to leave the sun. But eventually I will, and you will too. I promised your mother I'd see her out there one day." He wiped his eyes.

"But what does it mean?" I asked. "She might be out there on another planet far in the future, but she won't remember us, or her life here."

"No," he agreed, sadly.

"And the civilization that settles the stars won't be our civilization. They won't have learned anything from this experiment, they won't know anything about the Just City except the legend of Atlantis in the *Timaeus* and *Critias.*"

"Time is so vast—they probably wouldn't anyway," he said. But as he stared up at the stars he began to weep again. We walked on in silence.

"I had not meant this grief to unman me so," he said quietly, when we were getting close to Thessaly.

"It might be better on the ship. Here everything reminds us of her," I said.

"The boys are right. They are men, and heroes, and they have to act as they think best. I can't keep them children, or keep them safe."

"I'm going," I said, guessing where this conversation might be going. "The Chamber have approved me. I'm going!"

"Arete," he said, then stopped and began again in a different tone. "And you have to decide for yourself too. Equal significance means letting people make their own choices. But it's so difficult! Do you think she wanted me to learn this and that's why she stopped me?"

"It's possible," I said. And then I dared to say what I'd been thinking for a long time now. "She would want you to command your grief with philosophy."

"I know," he said, bleakly. "Oh yes, I do know that. I shouldn't be sad and I shouldn't indulge my grief. She is gone on to a better life. I should remember her and love the world for her. I know all that. I really do know it. But knowing it doesn't actually help at all when I want to talk to her so much my whole body aches."

"I know," I said. "I miss her every day."

"I wish I understood why she wouldn't let me heal her. It might all make more sense if I could understand that."

"I don't know," I said. I shivered.

"Come on, we should go in and tell the boys they can ask the Chamber if they can go on the voyage." He was trying to sound cheerful. "And we can have more wine. Arete—do you think revenge will actually help me feel better?"

"No," I said, surprised into honesty.

7

APOLLO

"How now shall I sing of you, though you are a worthy subject for song?" That's from the Homeric hymn to me—the same line is in both Homeric hymns to me actually, the Delphian and the Delian. Mortals find it intimidating to write about me, sometimes. It's as if they think I'll be listening over their shoulder. I find myself thinking it writing this, about Simmea and Sokrates, about Ficino and Maia and Pico. How shall I sing of you? I promised Father there would be songs.

There are already songs on Olympos about the sorrows and miseries of humanity and how badly people deal with death, and certainly there are songs enough about those subjects sung by mortals. I had felt grief myself often before. But this grief resisted being transmuted to art. You have to understand that transmuting emotion into art is what I do. It's one of the reasons I *like* emotions. But this emotion was bigger than I was. It's not that I didn't try to write songs for Simmea. I tried to write them, and for the first time my art failed me. I wrote songs, but they were pale thin things, they would not catch fire. They were true enough, but they left so much unsaid. I wanted vengeance, and yet at the same time as I struggled so desperately toward it I knew that revenge wasn't really what I wanted. I knew that art would come. It always had. The depth of this grief was different and unusual, and so would be the songs that came of it. Her name would live forever, as would her soul. That was the only way I could comfort myself, and it was thin comfort. Meanwhile, I was making an even poorer job of being a human being than usual. I was developing more sympathy for Achilles than I ever had before.

About a month after she died I decided to open her chest and sort out her belongings. She didn't have much—a winter cloak that doubled as a blanket, a pen and ink, some paints and brushes caught up in a scrappy paint-spattered rag, needles and thread, a scraper and a comb, another, finer comb with three broken teeth, a set of menstrual sponges. Underneath these things, all of which I had seen her use a million times and which seemed to miss the touch of her hands, was a pile of paper notebooks. I had seen her writing in them from time to time. "What are you doing?" I'd ask.

"Making notes," she'd reply, shutting the book and putting it away. They were small, the standard little notebooks the Workers had produced and which we continued to produce now with rather more effort. They had buff covers and were sewn together. I had never realized how many of them she had. I counted—twelve. If they were full and each held five thousand words, which would be about right, that was sixty thousand words she had written. I expected them to be notes, perhaps dialogues. They had her name on the covers, and under that they were numbered with Roman numerals. I wasn't sure how to read them—whether to glut myself on them all at once, or to save them. They represented something more of Simmea, which I had not expected. I was excited, and at the same time afraid of disappointment. I picked up the one labeled as number I and opened it and read.

"I was born in Amasta, a farming village near Alexandria, but I grew up in the Just City. My parents called me Lucia, after the saint, but Ficino renamed me Simmea, after the philosopher. Saint Lucy and Simmias of Thebes aid and defend me now!"

Whatever I had expected this was not it. I read the paragraph again. I had never known that her birth name was Lucia, nor guessed that she would have called on Saint Lucy. How little I had known her after all! But this was treasure, an autobiography. Many people in the city wrote one; there was a kind of fashion for them. Simmea had never told me she was writing one. I felt a little hurt, and yet still excited. She would be bound to talk about me. I could see our relationship from her perspective. It was the closest I could come now to talking to her. And yet I hesitated. Lucia, Saint Lucy—what if reading this proved I didn't know her after all? What if she didn't love me? But I knew she had. It was unquestionable. She had said once that she loved me like stones fall downward. I wanted to read her annals of our life together. I wouldn't be able to show it to anyone except our Young Ones, because she was sure to have revealed that I was Apollo. How well I remembered her discovering it, that day in the Temple of Asklepius. How angry she had made Athene! What terrible consequences that had had! And it was all my fault. Yet even so, even in all its consequences that included the metamorphosis of Sokrates and the collapse of the First Republic, I still smiled to remember how well she had dealt with discovering who I was.

I read that first paragraph again, and this time I went on. I was brought up short again reading her pondering whether it might have been a better path to happiness for her to have lived out her life in the Egyptian Delta. "No," I said aloud. I was astonished that she could even have considered that. Had I really known her? She had wanted, fiercely wanted, to be her best self, and surely her best self could only have been in this place and time?

I sat on her bed beside her chest, leaning back against the wall, and read the whole first notebook. When I read that she had said my name to Ficino in the slave market, I had to put the book down because I was sobbing too hard to go on. The first book brought her up to her arrival in the Just City and learning to read. Kebes was all through it, but she did not yet mention me as Pytheas. Every time I saw his name I felt a pang of jealousy. Kebes had known her name was Lucia—it didn't suit her at all. She was Simmea, the name was perfect for who she was. Lucia sounded soft and hesitant, while Simmea's mind had been like a surgical instrument. I remembered her smiling at me. Kebes was nothing. Matthias, she said his original name was. Well, he was gone. I didn't know whether or not to believe that he'd been responsible for the raid in which she had been killed. We hadn't heard anything from him for such a long time. Nobody knew where he was, or cared anything about him.

I took up the second notebook. I touched the letters of her name where she had written them in both alphabets. Simmea, not Lucia. I knew, with my rational self, that if I'd ever asked her what her childhood name had been she would have told me. That she never had showed how trivial it was, not how important. I turned the second book over in my hands. There were twelve books. If I read one a month they could last me a year, and for that long I could have a little more of her. If I had been my proper self that was what I would have done, one a month, or even one a year. But in mortal form, with emotions that pounded in my veins and clutched at my stomach, I could not bear the suspense of not knowing what she had written. I opened the second notebook.

It began with her learning to read, and to love Botticelli. It was far on into it before she mentioned me, and the time she taught me to swim. I was hurt that she had disliked me before she knew me, and then charmed by her description of that swimming lesson, which I remembered very well. I was surprised she was attracted to me so soon. The second book ended with our agreeing to be friends. I picked up the third, hesitated only for an instant, then opened it.

By the time Arete came to find out why I hadn't been in Florentia for dinner I had read all but the last volume, and was up to the conversation we had with the Workers outside Thessaly. I remembered that time so well; Sokrates, and the robots becoming entranced with philosophy, and Simmea discovering my true identity. It was so exciting. It had felt as if we could unravel all the Mysteries and remake the world. The words were still engraved in the paving stones outside, I walked on them every day. "Read. Write. Learn." And she belonged to the city and wanted it. And yes, she loved me, she saw me clearly and loved me. But I had always known that. I hadn't known she felt unworthy of me whether I was god or mortal. And I never doubted that what she wrote was the truth. She never said that she held the truth above me—she didn't need to. It was axiomatic to Simmea. That was the thing about her that was so hard to put into a song.

I went with Arete to Florentia and sat with Ficino as I ate porridge and fruit. He talked to me but I barely listened. My mind was with Sokrates and Simmea and a time that was twenty years gone. I missed that sense of infinite possibility, like a bud coming to flower. Everything after the Last Debate had been compromised. I wanted to go back and read the last notebook, even though I knew now that it would end before our life together, that I would never know more than I knew now of what she had thought of our Young Ones, never read about our one long-anticipated mating. I looked at Arete, the product of that one sexual act, who was eating grapes and talking to Ficino. I felt my eyes mist with tears. I had read about Simmea's matings with Aeschines and Phoenix and Nikias. I hoped the one time we had sex together had fulfilled her anticipations. I thought it had, and she said it had, but unless she had packed more into the last notebook than the others, I would never know for sure.

I wondered who she had written the notebooks for. Not for me. I was fascinated to read them, but I wasn't their intended audience. Equally they were not for publication in the City and inclusion in the library, certainly not, because not only did she reveal the truth of my identity, but she explained things neither I not anybody else in the City would need to have explained. What audience had she imagined? They were written in lucid classical Greek. Who could read them? Anyone in classical antiquity and truly educated people for another millenium. I considered for a moment that once I was back in my true form, I could take them to Athens and leave them on Plato's doorstep. My mouth twisted. I wouldn't do it, but I was so tempted.

Phaedrus and Neleus were in Thessaly when Arete and I got back. I took the last notebook out of Simmea's chest and saw their interested glances. Before they could inquire, I removed all twelve notebooks and tucked them into the fold of my kiton. Our Young Ones were definitely not Simmea's audience for these, and I didn't want them reading them. Her thoughts and feelings and intimate experiences weren't for them. Arete was looking at me curiously. "Did your mother ever tell you her childhood name?" I asked her.

"No," she said. "Wasn't she always called Simmea?"

"Her parents called her Lucia," I said. "But she never used it after she came here."

"Lucia?" Neleus asked. "I never knew that."

"It isn't important," I said as I went out. I was glad I'd told them. I didn't want Kebes to be the only other person who knew it. Though Ficino would know it too, if he remembered. He probably didn't remember—not that his wits were wandering like poor old Adeimantus, but he couldn't possibly remember the original name every child had given him.

I took the notebooks to the library and sat in the window seat where Athene used to sit. It was dark outside, though the library was lit with electricity, and warmed with it as well. The library stayed at a constant temperature. Crocus and Sixty-One kept the electricity working now as they always had. They needed it themselves, of course. I wondered why Athene had left them when she took all the other Workers. She took the others to punish us, of course, to make us do without them and realize how difficult it would be. To live a life of the mind you need slaves or technology, and technology is unquestionably better. Now we compromised, eking out the technology we had and working ourselves half the time. It didn't leave us the leisure for philosophy we had before. A tired mind can't think as well. But nobody who enslaves another can be truly free.

But why had she left Crocus and Sixty-One? Was it because she felt they had betrayed her in becoming philosophers? But surely that was the purpose of the City? They were Sokrates's friends, and my friends now. Perhaps it was because those two had spoken up at the Last Debate, choosing the City? I didn't know what she was thinking. I wondered whether I ever had. Athene seemed very far away as I sat on her seat in the library. People constantly debated why she had set up the City. I thought I knew that—because it was interesting, and because she could. When it ceased to be interesting she had abandoned it. I had projects like that myself. My oracle at Delphi was one of them. It had seemed as if giving people good advice would help everyone get on better. I hadn't kidnapped people from across time to do it, but I had dragged a shipload of Cretans across the Aegean.

I looked at the last notebook, XII. Had she stopped after the Last Debate? Why? Twelve seemed an extremely round number—and Simmea had distrusted numerology and suspiciously round numbers. It wouldn't have been an accident. But it might be as far as she had reached. I'd seen her writing in notebooks fairly recently—it irked me that I couldn't remember when exactly. The book might not be finished. I opened it and checked. It was full.

I read everything she had written in the last notebook. Then I sat staring unseeingly at the bookshelves. She hadn't written about the Last Debate. She had written about the conversation we had in the Garden of Archimedes, which I remembered very well, and then about the last Festival of Hera, the one in which she'd been paired with Kebes. My fingers clenched into fists reading it. She had told me it hadn't been so bad. She said she didn't want to discuss it, and I hadn't pushed her about it. She had never told me that he had raped her, or I'd have killed him. I really would. I was ready to kill him now. She wrote that it wasn't rape, that she had consented, but I knew better. She had said no, and asked him to stop, and he had gone on. He had bruised her. She had gone there willingly, for the City, like the philosopher she was, and he had tried to take her into his fantasy.

I got up and paced the library furiously. I wanted to kill Kebes, now, immediately, with my bare hands, but I didn't know where he was. Simmea had written that I'd have been upset, but she had no idea how upset I would have been. I had learned what rape was, what it meant. I was also furious with Athene for pairing her with Kebes. It had been aimed at me, and I knew it, and Simmea knew it too. I would have killed him and left his body for the dogs and kites. He had tried to own her, and he had hurt her, my Simmea, my friend, my votary. She had told him I didn't try to own her, and she had told Sokrates that she and I wanted each other to be our best selves. It was true. Worship was easy, commonplace. Beautiful women were everywhere. People who understood what I was talking about and could argue with me as equals were incredibly rare. How could he have done that? And why didn't she tell me? Was it connected to the reason she had stopped me saving her life?

I was also furious that he had called her a scrawny, flat-faced, bucktoothed Copt. It was true, and she cared so little that she had laughed, but it galled me that he had dared to say it to her, to try to hurt her that way, through her looks. I always put up with Kebes because he was Simmea's friend, and all that time he had imagined he owned her, owned some imaginary person called Lucia. She was Simmea, Plato's Simmea, as Sokrates had said to her, as close to Plato's ideal Philosopher King as anyone was likely to get. She had never told me about that conversation either. She had told me about Sokrates's plan for what turned into the Last Debate, but not about the rest of what she had written, and how they had talked about the way they both loved me.

I missed Sokrates. Not the way I missed Simmea, as if half of myself had been amputated so that I was constantly reaching out with a missing limb. I hadn't entirely lost him, either; there were days of his life before he came to the City when I could still visit him, in Athens, once I was back to myself. But I missed being able to just talk openly with him. He would have had wise advice for this situation, and nobody else would. Nobody else could even understand it. There was nobody I could remotely imagine talking to about it, except Simmea and Sokrates, and I couldn't have either one of them. Sokrates had flown to me, after Athene had transformed him into a gadfly, and perched on my chest for a moment, then he had stung me and flown away, and nobody had seen him since.

I went back to Athene's window seat. Nobody was in sight. A few people had been in the stacks, but they had fled when they saw my face. (Even without far-shooting arrows rattling on my shoulder, my wrath can have that effect on people.) I sat down and opened Athene's secret compartment under the arm-rest. All I was thinking was of hiding Simmea's notebooks. I wasn't expecting anything to be there. Athene had been gone for almost twenty years. She'd had plenty of time to cover any traces she wanted to cover. But as I slid the notebooks in I felt that there was something there, stiff parchment, not paper. I pulled it out, curious.

It was a map of the Aegean, hand-drawn and colored, dolphins and triremes drawn in islandless spots on the lapis sea, but with all the islands and coasts drawn accurately. Kallisti was shown round, which meant it was a current map. The labeling was in the beautiful Renaissance Greek calligraphy that everyone in the City had learned, along with the corresponding Italic hand. Our city was marked, but not the other four cities on the island. There were cities marked in other places, some of them known to me, others strange. We didn't have any maps like this, but anyone could have made it without too much trouble. We had parchment, we had the tools for making illuminated manuscripts, we even had accurate maps.

The thing that surprised me was the circle marked in red ink around a city on the northeastern edge of the island of Lesbos. The handwriting was entirely different from the rest of the map, it was a scrawl and nobody's neat penmanship. This was clearly a later addition, drawn in after the map was made. "Goodness" it said. The handwriting was immediately recognizable. It was mine.

8

ARETE

There's nothing like the feeling of a ship under full sail. It's as if the ship is alive, every rope and piece of wood responding to the wind and the will of the sailor. It feels like magic when you are part of it. Before the voyage I had never been on any craft for more than a few hours. I'd learned the use of tiller and sail on the little fishing boats. I had been taken around the island on the *Excellence* twice, once a circumnavigation when I was quite young, with all the Young Ones my age, and once a year ago when Mother was going with an embassy to Sokratea and she took me with her. That was the trip where I'd really made friends with Erinna. Before that, she'd just been somebody my brothers' age who I saw around sometimes. On that trip we'd talked properly for the first time. I'd been fourteen and she had been eighteen. I knew she saw me as a child. All the same, when I came aboard for this voyage and she waved to me, my heart swelled.

When we left I was wild with excitement, not to avenge Mother but to be moving, exploring, doing something different. Then, as soon as the ship had left the harbor and stood out to deep water, I was filled with the calm joy of the wave, as I had been both the other times I had been aboard ship. Dolphins came alongside and followed us. The water was so clear that I could see the whole pod, and the rush of water breaking along the side of the ship, and the gold and black sand far below on the sea bed. Yet when I looked up and out the sea was, well, wine-dark as Homer puts it. The sea was a deep dark blue of precisely the same reflective luminosity as rich red wine. And the white wave foaming along the ship's side broke it, and the dolphins surfacing, and the shore of the island. I looked back at the City, which looked as small as a model even from this little distance. Above it the mountain was smoking, as it often did. Perhaps there would be a little eruption, a new stream of lava snaking down the side. Or perhaps the great eruption would come, the eruption that would carve away half the island and destroy the City and everything. I hoped that wouldn't happen while I was away.

Phaedrus came over to me where I stood by the rail looking up at the mountain. All three of my brothers who had asked to go had been accepted by the Chamber to make the voyage, Phaedrus, Kallikles and, thank Hera, Neleus. I don't know what he'd have done if they had refused him. "Is there a god of volcanoes?" Phaedrus asked.

"Hephaistos?" I ventured. "He's supposed to have his forge in one. That Titian picture in the temple, remember?"

"But his main area is making things, isn't it?"

"Yes, overlapping with Athene on technology. She designs things and he implements them. Athene overlaps with a lot of people on a lot of things. Ares on war, Fa—Apollo on learning. I suppose knowledge does cover a lot of ground." I looked at Phaedrus, who was still looking at the mountain as the *Excellence* sailed east. I lowered my voice, although nobody was near enough the overhear us. "Have you been talking to Father about how to become a god?"

He flushed. "You must have done the same or you wouldn't know what I was thinking."

"I don't think there's anything wrong with it," I said. "But volcanoes seem like a huge area."

"But there isn't anyone specific for them. Poseidon has earthquakes, and the ocean. It's hard to think of anything that's vacant. I could specialize in volcanoes, learn about them. We've grown up next to one, after all."

"But how would you do it?" I couldn't imagine how such a thing could possibly work, how Phaedrus could go from the young man at my side to becoming a patron deity of volcanoes. I couldn't picture the intermediate steps at all. "It's hard to see how you could develop an excellence of volcanoes." I looked at the plume of smoke, being blown on the same wind that was drawing the ship. "I was just hoping it wouldn't erupt and destroy the city before we get back."

"That would be terrible," Phaedrus said, immediately without any hesitation. Then he stopped. "Why would it be worse than if it did it when we were home?"

"Guilt at surviving." Without meaning to, we both looked at Father as I said that. He was standing by Maecenas at the wheel, looking almost happy. Phaedrus and I looked back at each other, uneasily.

Just then Klymene came along and hustled us into a group learning to shoot from the mast. The first part of this consisted of learning to climb the mast, which was a skill we'd need to acquire in any case. The *Excellence* was sailed by wind-power, and it required a number of people able to scale the masts to rearrange the sails. We had been organized before we left into three watches, and each watch had officers and sailors, who were people like Maecenas and Erinna who already had the necessary skills. The rest of us would learn as we went along. Some of us knew how to sail fishing boats, but the skill of going aloft and managing the great sails was very different in practice, even though the theory was the same.

I loved everything about the ship that bore my name, the taut ropes, the sea breeze, the way she heeled through the water. I loved the solar-powered deck lamps that began to glow softly as dusk came on. I loved sleeping in a hammock and swaying with the sway of the ship. The voyage was the first time I ever slept aboard—the time we went to Sokratea, we slept in a guest house there. I loved learning the new skills, sail-setting and rope-coiling and mast-climbing. From the crosstrees at the top of the mast I could see for miles, in a wide arc as the mast moved. I volunteered to spend as much time there as I could and to be a lookout. "It's good because you're light, but you won't like it so much in a gale and lashing rain," Maecenas predicted. He was Father's age, one of the Children, Captain of the *Excellence*. I was in his watch, the Eos watch, with Erinna, Phaedrus and Ficino. We came up an hour before dawn and worked until an hour after noon, when the Hesperides watch took over. Father and Kallikles were in that watch. The third watch, the Nyx, took over an hour after sunset. Neleus and Maia were assigned to that. There were thirty people in each watch. I have no idea how Kebes managed to fit a hundred and fifty people into the *Goodness*, because the *Excellence* felt crowded with ninety.

The Kyklades are a group of islands that circle Delos, the island where Father was born. At that time Delos floated on the water, but afterward it was attached to the sea-bed like other lands—or this is the story recounted in the Homeric Hymn to Delian Apollo. (Father says it's poetically true, whatever that means.) Tiny Delos is the center of the Kyklades, and the other islands do form a rough circle around it. It's possible to draw them so that they look even more like a circle, and to make Delos seem like the center of the whole Aegean, and the Aegean as the center of the whole world. It depends on your perspective, as Mother used to say. Kallisti is the southernmost of the Kyklades, and to get anywhere from there except Crete you have to sail north. North isn't a good direction to go in Greece in the spring, because of the winds, so we went northeast, toward Amorgos, which we reached late on the evening of the first day out from home. There were no signs of life ashore, but we weren't really expecting any. No Amorgians were mentioned in Homer's Catalog of Ships.

We put down our anchor and slept aboard. Erinna showed me how to sling my hammock, next to hers, and how to get into it sideways. I slept better that night than I had any night since Mother was killed. Erinna woke me before dawn in time for our watch and I sprang out of my hammock, feeling fresh and ready for a new day.

"You seem better," Erinna said as we came up on deck.

"I feel better. The sea is good for me. And doing different things. I still miss her, but it doesn't weigh on me the same way. And you were right about writing the autobiography, too."

"She was right about that," Erinna said. She hugged me suddenly, and I hugged her back, tightly. "We can remember her without being sucked down into grief."

"That would be wonderful," I said. "If only Father could."

The Nyx watch were ready to hand over to us then, and so we had to work. I swarmed up to the top of the mast and relieved the Nyx lookout there, who that morning was the Captain of the Nyx watch, a Child called Caerellia.

"No signs of life at all," she said.

I was disappointed. I was hoping for people. Amorgos is about the easiest island to get to from Kallisti, in normal winds, and Neleus had made a very convincing argument that it was the most likely place for Kebes to have founded his city. We put an armed party ashore as soon as it was properly light, then we sailed around the island to collect them from the other side. I wasn't allowed ashore. Phaedrus and Erinna went, and I looked down from the masthead with envy.

At the end of the Eos watch I stayed on deck, staring over at the Amorgian shore as it slipped past, glancing up occasionally at the Hesperides watch as they ran about trimming sails. Ficino came up to me as I was standing there. The sea-breeze ruffled his white hair where it stuck out under his old red hat. I saw him every day so I didn't normally think much about it, but he really was the oldest person I had ever met.

He grinned at me. "Not feeling seasick?"

"Not even a twinge," I replied.

"Good. Well then, it's time for lessons, I think," he said.

Ficino was nominally part of the Eos watch, but he had declined learning how to climb the masts and had learned only how to steer, which was both the easiest and the most fun. "Lessons? But surely I'm learning enough just being here. I've learned a lot about how the ship works already. And also geography, and I'll learn history as soon as we locate some people."

Maia laughed, and I jumped, because I hadn't heard her come up and she was right next to me on my other side. "You need philosophy and rhetoric and history and mathematics," she said, as if I wasn't already ahead of her in mathematics.

"But we don't have any books," I said. I had my notebooks, though I had left behind the two I had filled already.

"We have sufficient books," Ficino said. Trust them to bring books, I thought. "But for now, how about calculating the angle the ship's bow makes?"

I calculated angles in my head for hours, until we had rounded the point of Amorgos and were tacking our way up the other side to where we hoped to meet the shore party. Ficino and Maia then began to make me work on rhetoric, aloud. "Plato says young people shouldn't learn rhetoric, it makes them contradict their elders before they have wisdom," I pointed out.

"You wouldn't be studying it yet in Athenia," Maia said. "But we think fifteen is old enough to begin."

"I learn more the older I get," Ficino said. "I'm glad I began so young." His eyes were on the gentle curve of the shore we were slipping past. "I don't sleep much these days. Growing older I need it less, perhaps as I need the time more to learn things and get the most out of every day. Learn what you can while you can. Learn, Arete."

There are times when I wish my parents had given me a different name. Pursuing excellence and learning excellence are puns I am thoroughly sick of. Now we were on the ship there was even more opportunity for such jokes, of course. But Ficino was entirely serious.

Amorgos is a long thin island, and it took hours sailing back east around it before we found the shore party. They had built a fire by a stream as arranged, and the Hesperides masthead lookout spotted their smoke and called out. The shore party signaled that they had seen nobody, so we anchored again to take on fresh water. "We're going to spend the night here," Maecenas told Ficino as he went by. "You can go ashore if you want to."

Everybody seemed to want to, just for the excitement of walking on a different island. There were crowds around the ship's boat. I could see we wouldn't be ashore soon.

"Where will we go next?" Maia asked Maecenas.

"Tomorrow we'll make for Ios."

"Will there be people there?" I asked.

Maecenas shrugged. "Homer doesn't mention any, but that doesn't mean there aren't any. And Kebes may be there. It's the next likeliest place, after here." He moved on, trying to calm the people waiting to go ashore.

"When did the islands come to be inhabited?" I asked.

"I don't know," Maia said. "We don't have anybody here from before Plato, and Plato wrote a thousand years after this. Well, as far as we know when we are. Athene told us that we were here in the time before the Trojan War, but we don't know exactly how long before, and we also don't know the exact date of that war. We're not even sure if it was real or mythical."

"Real!" Ficino said.

"Both," I said, staring over at the pine trees on the Amorgian shore.

I realized they were both looking at me. "What do you mean?" Ficino asked.

"Well, like Athene," I said. "She was real, she lived in the City and brought everyone here and set it all up. But she's a goddess, she's also mythical. She's in a lot of myths, and yet the two of you have had conversations with her."

"I have been on expeditions with her to steal art treasures," Ficino admitted. "I have looted Byzantium in her company. She's real enough. She's glorious."

"But she's also the Goddess Athene, she could move you through time and do all kinds of strange things. She had a mythic dimension. She was both at once." And Father was the same, I thought, even without his powers. I thought of that strange moment when we all stared at Neleus. My brothers and I were also like that, to a certain extent. "And the Trojan War has to be like that too."

"I think it must happen after the City is destroyed," Ficino said, sitting down on a pile of canvas. "Otherwise we would not have been able to resist participating, knowing what we know."

"On which side?" I asked. I also wanted to ask him how he could be so maddeningly calm about the City being destroyed, but I had asked him related questions before and found his answers entirely unsatisfactory. The real problem was that he was ninety-nine years old and he was sure he was going to die this year, and I was fifteen and I didn't ever want to die at all.

"What a fascinating question," Ficino said. "To attack beside Achilles, or to defend beside Hector. The Greeks or the Latins. Which would you choose?"

"Neither side was entirely in the right," I said. "And there's no question that it was all the fault of the gods in the first place. Helen—"

"It's possible that if we went to Argos now we might see the young Helen," Ficino said. The boat had taken two groups of people in, and it was quite clear to me that it would be hours before it took us. I shuffled a little closer.

"Do you believe we're that close in time?" Maia asked.

"It has been thirty-two years since we came," Ficino said. "How long before do you think she would have put us? Perhaps more than that. Perhaps Helen is not yet born. I said we might see Nestor as a young man, and he was a very old man at the time of the Trojan War. I'd love to go to Pylos and see. But we're not sailing in that direction, at least not this time. Perhaps we'll see Anchises as a young man. That would be marvelous."

"I too would love to meet Homer's heroes," I said. "But which side would you want to fight on, really?"

"I'm torn, but it would come down to the Latins and Troy," Ficino said. "The beleaguered city holding out against the sea of enemies."

Maia put her hand on his shoulder. "Florentia?" she asked.

Ficino smiled up at her. "Perhaps. My Florentia, like Troy, left a great legacy."

"But our Florentia—" Maia began.

Just then a group of Young Ones including my brothers Neleus and Kallikles came running to the side of the ship, stripped off their kitons and dived into the water. They went racing off toward the shore. "Oh!" I said. I measured the distance between the ship and the shore. It wasn't all that far. "I'm going to swim too! Would you bring my kiton?" I shrugged it off and offered it to Maia.

"Let's all swim," Maia said, dropping her kiton on the deck.

"It's too far for me," Ficino said. "I'll go in the boat and bring your ki-tons to protect your modesty once you get ashore."

People were diving all along the side of the ship. Maia and I joined them and began to swim toward the first shore I had ever seen that was not that of the island of my birth. All the while I was swimming, quickly outpacing Maia and almost catching up with my brothers, I kept thinking about which side I'd want to fight on. Troy, or the Achaeans? To rescue Helen, or to de-fend the city? For Agamemnon or for Priam? It wasn't a fair question. We knew Troy was doomed. But Ficino would have fought for her anyway. I ran ashore, and the land felt strange under me. It seemed to be rocking. Earth-quake? Or was the island, like Delos long ago, not tethered to the sea-bed? Then I realized this was something Erinna had told me about: when we were used to the motion of the ship, solid land would seem to move. I got up and immediately hurt my feet walking on pine needles. I hoped Ficino would bring my sandals too. I looked back at the *Excellence*, sitting gracefully at an-chor, and although I had longed to explore this new island she looked like the most beautiful and dearest thing imaginable. Troy, I thought, and then no, the black ships.

It was just as well we probably wouldn't be given the choice, when it was so hard to decide.

9

ARETE

After Amorgos we sailed to Ios, and from there to Naxos. We found no people on Ios, and no sign of Kebes. Life aboard became almost routine, up before dawn to take my watch, which I mostly spent up at the top of the mast. Watching the sun rise from up there was always incredibly beautiful. The sky slowly lightened and became pink, and the sea echoed the color and was rose-pink dotted with jade-green islands. I could see so far from the mast at dawn that the islands looked like leaping dolphins. Then sometime in the day we would come close to an island. A party would go ashore to explore, find nobody, and come back. The rest of us would go ashore to cook, hunt, and take on water. Then we'd come back aboard and either sail on overnight or stay in our fairly protected anchorage, depending on winds and what the captains thought.

The night on Amorgos we sang at the campfire, both kinds of songs, Phrygian and Dorian. Some songs we all sang together, and some people took turns singing. Father played the lyre and sang a new song he had written about Mother's excellence and love of truth, which made everyone cry. Erinna and Phaedrus and I sang some of the choruses from *The Myrmidons*. It was like a festival, only better, because we hadn't been preparing and rehearsing, it was all spontaneous. Then we all went back to the ship to sleep.

On Ios the shore party had killed a boar that ran out of the woods and attacked them. We roasted it and ate it under the stars, which seemed brighter from there than they were at home. We sang again after we had eaten. Phaedrus persuaded me to do Briseis's duet with Patroklus. When we sat down again, Erinna leaned over from where she sat whittling and patted my arm. "You have a great voice." My soul soared at praise from her.

"We're fortunate that all of Pytheas's children seem to have inherited his singing abilities," Maia said. Neleus frowned at that, because he could never seem to sing in tune. I didn't think singing was a particularly heroic ability. Erinna's singing voice was clear and true.

Naxos at first seemed no different from Amorgos and Ios. When the shore party signaled that they had found people we were astonished, as if we had believed we were alone in the time of the dinosaurs. I didn't meet the Naxians or see their settlement, so at first their presence felt like a disappointment, because they prevented me from going ashore. Those of us left aboard waited impatiently for the shore party to return, running through all the facts about Naxos we knew. "Isn't it where Theseus abandoned Ariadne?" Erinna asked. "Could that have happened already?"

Ficino nodded. "It should have happened in the last generation. Theseus's sons by Phaedra fought at Troy. Ariadne might still be alive."

"We don't know exactly when we are," Maia reminded him. "We might have a better idea when they come back. Ariadne might be there, or she might not have come yet, or she might be dead. How long did she live after being abandoned?"

"Dionysios is supposed to have come for her and taken her away," Ficino said. "So she might be gone."

Father was staring fixedly at a little island just offshore as if he were remembering something. I wanted to ask him about it, but there were too many people about. It was hard to get privacy aboard, and even harder when everyone was lining the rail impatiently waiting for the shore party.

"We don't know when we are at all," he said. "I have a feeling it might be much earlier than you're assuming. 'Before the Trojan War' doesn't necessarily mean immediately before."

Even though I'd been thinking about dinosaurs, I was surprised and disappointed. "No Anchises?"

"We'll have to wait and see."

"Here they come!" Erinna said.

The official report was that they had made contact and the locals didn't have any useful information. "Miserable primitive place," Maecenas said, pushing through the crowd of questioning people. "Council meeting. Now."

The ship had a council of six that was supposed to make decisions, and Maecenas called them together in his cabin. The rest of us had to wait. As we weren't going ashore and therefore couldn't cook, dinner was cold, smoked fish and olives washed down with water lightly flavored with wine. After the feasts and singing of the previous nights it felt like a letdown. A group of us sat down to eat in the bows, where we could watch the sun setting over the sea. Erinna and I sat together on a coil of rope. "If we leave soon we could reach Paros in a few hours," I said. "I can see it from the top of the mast."

"Do we know if it's inhabited?" Phaedrus asked.

"Not in the Catalog of Ships, but they quarried marble there, so it seems it might be," Maia said. "I expect we'll stay here until morning."

Kallikles came up to join us. He had been in the shore party, so we greeted him with enthusiasm. "Tell us what it was like?" I urged, as Erinna moved toward the rail so that he could sit down beside me.

"It's not a proper city, it's very small, maybe a village is the proper term. They live inland, out of sight of the shore, though they have boats. They keep chickens and goats and pigs, and let them run in and out of their houses. The houses are really primitive, not much more than huts. There's a wooden palisade around the village, and an entry blocked with thorn bushes. We didn't go inside, but it isn't very big and we could see everything. There's just one plaza, with houses around it in a circle—no roads at all, no paving stones, just dirt. There are strange statues set up in the plaza, half-carved marble, sort of flat, with huge heads and weird noses, painted, dressed and decorated with beads. They're not like anything I've ever seen. Very bright colors. I can't even decide whether or not they were beautiful."

Ficino looked away from the sunset and stared at Kallikles. "I want to see them!"

"I don't know whether you'll be able to. Maecenas wasn't talking about going back. The people weren't friendly at all. They ran into the village and barricaded themselves in when they saw us coming. The men were armed with bronze spears with weird flat blades. They wouldn't speak to us, they kept waving their spears. Then an old woman came forward to talk. She had a huge sore on her face with pus coming out of it. She spoke Greek of a kind, but it was hard to make ourselves understood. She kept telling us to go away, that she wouldn't give us anything, and she couldn't seem to understand we didn't want anything except information, which she didn't want to give either. Maecenas offered her a silver cup, which she snatched, but even after that she didn't want to be friendly. They didn't let us in or offer hospitality at all. They held on to their weapons and we held on to ours."

I was trying to picture it. "What were the houses made of?"

"Stone and wood. It wasn't the materials that were primitive, it was the style."

"You've never seen anything that wasn't classical," Ficino said, smiling.

"I've been to Psyche," Kallikles said.

Maia laughed. "Psyche is also classical. All our cities are."

"It wasn't built by Workers," Kallikles protested. "But you're right, this was a different style entirely. No pillars. Primitive. Odd. I was really uncomfortable looking at the place. Chickens pecking around their feet, a toothless old woman bent over grinding wheat by hand in a quern, and everyone frightened, the men with their weapons, half cringing and half defiant. I've never seen poverty like that."

"It sounds like a village in India or Africa in my time," Maia said, thoughtfully. "I'd never imagined Greece like that, full of savages. But I suppose it must have been once."

"Don't build too much on one primitive fishing village," Ficino said. "There were places not too far from Florentia in my own day that the boy would have described the same way—toothless peasants with sores, and animals running in and out."

"I can't even imagine it," Erinna said. I couldn't either. When I'd thought about the difficulties of Mycenaean Greece it was in terms of women not being equal, and lack of books, not sores and poverty. Homer talks about cities, and I had imagined cities like our cities.

"Did they give any useful information about the date?" Ficino asked.

"They'd heard of King Minos, but not of Kebes, nor Mycenae nor Troy, at least as far as we were able to make ourselves understood."

"Minos," Ficino said thoughtfully, turning back to the west. The sun was on the horizon now, gilding the rippling sea and lighting the clouds purple and gold. "Crete. Maybe we should go there."

"Pytheas wants to go north," Maia said. "He's sure Kebes went that way, though whether from something Kebes said years ago or just out of his obsession I don't know."

"Father isn't a fool," I protested.

"You have to admit he hasn't been entirely rational since Simmea died," Maia said.

"This crushing grief is strange in a man with so much excellence, a man who we've all been accustomed to look to as one of the very best among the golds," Ficino said.

I nodded. Erinna, who was behind me, put her hand on my shoulder and squeezed in a comforting way. It did comfort me, but it also sent an unsettling jolt of energy through me. My breath caught in my throat. I liked it too much. Everything I'd ever read about bodily love came back to me, and I moved away as she dropped her hand. I could feel my face was burning hot and there was heat too between my legs. I stared out over the sea. The first star appeared in the east, silver against violet. "Let me not be unworthy," I prayed to it. Kallikles was still talking, and I tried to concentrate on what he was saying.

"It wasn't clear whether the old woman properly understood what we were asking, or if she thought we were saying we were from Minos," Kallikles said. "It was horrible. I wanted to help them somehow. Give them my knife, or better, teach them how to make iron and wash. Teach them philosophy! But at the same time I couldn't wait to get away. The way the old woman was talking to Maecenas, ducking her head as if she thought he'd strike her!" He shook his head.

"You can't help them, it could break history," Maia said.

I turned to her, surprised out of myself. The deck lights had just come on, giving everything a warm golden glow. "What do you mean break it?"

"If Kallikles taught them how to make iron it could change everything. Not that village, maybe, but imagine if the Trojans had iron weapons and the Greeks only bronze! Trying to help them could ruin everything!"

Ficino laughed, and we all turned to him. "We don't know that. It could be what sets history right. Nobody knows much about what happened in Greece before the Trojan War. Maybe the Age of Iron began because Kallikles taught these primitives how to make it."

"I don't actually know how," Kallikles admitted.

"I expect it's in the library." Erinna said. I wanted to turn to look at her, and I normally would have, but I kept still.

"We could send out expeditions to teach them medicine and technology," Kallikles said. "We could really help them."

"That would be wonderful," Erinna said.

Maia tutted. "And if Troy had iron and didn't fall?"

I was breathless again at the thought. I had imagined Ficino going to Troy's aid despite knowing they would lose, now I imagined him going and changing everything.

"And what would happen then?" Ficino asked. "A different history start-ing from here where Troy never falls and Rome is never born? I don't think that's possible. We're here, we're free to act, anything we do is already part of history. We won't change everything. We're embedded here. We're in a secret forgotten part of history, but history can't be changed. We know what's coming. We're safely tucked in the margins of history. Athene saw to that."

"You have a lot of faith in her still," Maia said, sharply.

"In Providence," Ficino said. "If these people need help and we can give it, perhaps that should be part of our mission. If we're going to do it then it's already part of what we will do. And it might relieve some suffering."

"But what would happen if we tried to change history?" Erinna asked. "If we deliberately did something—if we told Paris what would come of him stealing Helen. If we told Helen?"

"They'd do it anyway. Lovers are idiots!" Ficino said. I felt my cheeks heat again. "It would be better to warn Priam about the wooden horse."

"I wonder if they're discussing helping the village in the council now?" Phaedrus mused.

"I wonder what Father's saying," Kallikles said.

"Why aren't you on the council?" Ficino asked Maia.

"It's only six people, so they can make decisions quickly," she said. "But why aren't you?"

"They're all Children," Ficino said. "There aren't many Masters on this expedition, and while there are plenty of Young Ones, you wouldn't expect them to have positions of responsibility yet." He turned to Kallikles. "You should tell your father what you've been saying to us, about wanting to help. It's a question for the whole Chamber back home, but it's a question we shouldn't forget."

"And we should debate whether what we do can change history," Maia said. "It's another thing we should have asked Athene while we had the chance."

"I'll definitely tell Father," Kallikles said. "But if we can change things, it wouldn't necessarily make them worse. We could make them better."

"But it's all connected. We can't change anything without changing everything. If Priam knew about the wooden horse, there would be no Rome," Maia said.

I resolved to ask Father about history as soon as I could safely get him alone.

The ship stayed at anchor that night. I didn't go down to my hammock beside Erinna. I wrapped myself in my cloak and slept on deck, badly. When I was awake I fretted about my inappropriate response to Erinna's hand. She had meant friendly comfort, and my body had undoubtedly felt lust. I wrestled with the twin horses of my soul, as Plato urges. When I fell asleep, I dreamed about history as a broken rope, lashing about and pulling the sails out of trim as the ship prepared for a storm. Every time I woke the real ship was barely moving beneath me, and I fretted about my feelings for Erinna. I liked her. I respected her. She was a wonderful friend. Maybe I even loved her. She seemed to like me, but of course not in any inappropriate way. She was four years older than me. Then every time I slept again it was the same dream, the cut rope, the uncontrollable sails, the oncoming storm clouds. A light rain woke me an hour before dawn, a little early for my watch but I got up anyway, re-draping my blanket into a cloak to keep off the weather.

Only a few of the Nyx watch were awake, as the ship at anchor didn't need much attention. We nodded to each other. One of them was my brother Neleus, who came forward to wish me joy of the morning. "Do you know where Father is?" I asked him.

"Asleep down below, I think. But he'll be up soon." Neleus nodded to the east where the sky was starting to pale. Father inevitably woke at sunrise. Naxos was a dark bulk immediately to the north of us. The rain was chilling me. I walked over to the rail. Neleus walked beside me. "They're out there somewhere," he said.

My mind was full of Erinna and the Naxians, and I frowned at him, puzzled. "Who?"

"The Goodness Group," he said, his hands clenching into fists. "We'll find them. We'll avenge Mother. I know you want that as much as I do."

I put my hand on his arm. "I grieve for Mother, but I don't know whether vengeance will help."

"It'll help me," he said. "I feel I let her down."

"Oh Neleus, you didn't," I said.

"She was always so exacting, and I didn't meet her standards." He was staring out over the dark water, not looking at me.

"It's true what Father said. She loved you. I often felt I didn't meet her standards either."

"You and I are all that's left of her now," he said, turning toward me.

"Well, genetically," I agreed. "But all the people she taught, all the pictures and sculptures she made, that lives on." For as long as the City lives, I thought. Not into posterity, because there is none. Unless we can change history. If we can change history, then her legacy could really last.

Father came up from below, yawning. I waved to him and he came over to us. "Joy to you both," he said, and we repeated the wish.

"I need to know something about how the universe works," I said.

He looked over to the little island he had been looking at the day before.

"There'll be a temple there one day," he said, quietly. "A temple to me. It'll be there by Homer's day. We're here early. But I don't know exactly when."

"Can change history?" I asked.

He and Neleus both stared at me. "What do you mean?" he asked.

"Can things we do, here and now, change what will happen in the future?"

"Yes. Of course. But not things that the gods know about, not things that are already fixed."

"So there's only one time?" I asked.

"Right. It's as if time's a scroll, and we haven't read all of it but it's all there, and once we've read it, that's fixed. But it all scrolls along in order when you're inside it. From outside, it's different." His chin wavered. "I remember explaining it like that to Simmea and Sokrates."

"So for instance we could teach the people on Naxos medicine and iron working and navigation and philosophy, and it wouldn't change the outcome of the Trojan War?" I asked.

"No."

Neleus looked at me in astonishment. "What a great idea!" he said. "Let's do all that. Let's give them more choices and make all of their lives better."

"It was Kallikles's idea, when he saw them yesterday," I admitted. "But I agree: if it doesn't break history we have a moral obligation to help them."

"Wait," Father said. "It won't break history, but it can break you if you try to go against Fate and Necessity. And you can't teach philosophy to every starving peasant in the Aegean."

"Why not?" Neleus asked. "Mother would have."

Father stared at him for a moment. "She would have," he admitted.

10

MAIA

One of the strangest things about the multiplication of cities after the Last Debate was that we were all doing variations of Plato's Republic, and so we came to feel that attempting to create Plato's Republic was the normal thing people did. It might have been different for some of the older Masters, like Ficino. I had only been nineteen when I came to the City, and the Children had been no more than ten. When I thought about it, of course, I remembered a world of people who went from one year to another without thinking twice about Plato, but I did not care to think about them often. There had been no place for me in that world. So the argument in my mind was never whether to set up the Just City, always how best to do it.

With the founding of the City of Amazons I found myself doing things for the second time, and trying to fix the errors we had made the first time. For the Children, of course, it was the first time, and they viewed the errors they had found growing up in the City quite differently from the way we Masters did. One of the first decisions we made was that there would be no more Masters and Children. We all agreed that the Children were much closer to what Plato wanted than we were. Nevertheless, we were the ones with the experience of setting up the original city, and with working on committees, and with making decisions. It was decided that Masters ranked with silvers, auxiliary guardians, but that we could serve on committees, which were otherwise for golds alone. The Children were used to deferring to us.

We had to work hard, without Workers, just to have enough to eat. All the same, we spent more time in debate than anything else. We debated everything in committees and then before the whole Assembly—and the Assembly here consisted of all those over eighteen, though they were not all equal within the Assembly. Irons and bronzes were given one vote each, silvers three, and golds four. The age of eighteen was chosen because it was the traditional age of adulthood in Plato's Athens. We would have gone with Plato's thirty, but nobody was thirty yet except for Masters. I was only a little over thirty myself. To start with we had practically nobody who was not an adult in our newly defined terms. A few of the Children had brought their Young Ones, and a few of them were pregnant. The first baby born in the City of Amazons was Euridike's Porphyry, born the first winter. I delivered him myself, the first baby I ever helped deliver who was not immediately taken away from their mother to grow up in anonymity.

Porphyry encapsulated in his tiny person our first two great debates—over names, and over families. Klio and some others wanted us all to take back our original names and allow eclectic naming of new babies. This divided everyone. Lysias and I were against it. "It's not that different, and I've been Lysias so long it feels like my real name now," Lysias said, and I nodded.

"Why would I want to be Ethel? Ethel feels like another person, a person from another world. It has been more than ten years. I'm not Ethel anymore. I've grown up as Maia."

"I can't think of you as Ethel," Lysias agreed.

"And I don't think I even knew you were Li Xi," I said. "It's a name from another culture. It would make you seem different from everyone."

"I think Klio thinks that's a good thing, to point up the differences."

For once Ikaros and I were on the same side. "Naming ourselves and our children from the classical world unites us; using naming customs from other times and places would divide us," he said in debate. The vote was close, but we won. Porphyry was named after the philosopher, who had been one of us and had recently died. He was also named for the purple stone that had symbolized Roman technical prowess in the Middle Ages and the Renaissance, and thirdly for the idea of being *porphyrogenitos*, born to the purple, being the first baby born in the new city and the heir to our traditions. It was a lot of weight for a name to carry.

The other great early debate was over marriage and families. None of us wanted to carry on Plato's idea of arranged matings at festivals. We had all seen the misery and complications it caused. But some of us wanted traditional marriage and families, while others wanted to try other varieties of Plato's idea of having wives and children in common. I was torn on this subject. We Masters had been very loose about this. Klio and Axiothea might as well have been married, except that they were both women. Lysias and I had a friendship that included some sex. Ficino had been strictly celibate while openly admiring all the beautiful youths. Ikaros, in addition to his spectacular public Platonic relationship with Plotinus, had an ongoing private arrangement with Lukretia, and sex with anyone he could charm into lying down with him. We masters were not a good example. I felt that this was an area where Plato should perhaps have stayed with tradition.

This time Ikaros was firmly on the other side. He wanted to keep everything fluid and flexible, where people could live together if they chose but everyone should be available to everyone else with no exclusivity. Ikaros read Plato's passage on this aloud, very movingly. Many Children spoke about their love for each other and their desire to form families and bring up their own children. Lukretia expanded on Athene's point in the Last Debate about the damage done to cities and states by families and factions, with chilling examples from her own experience. Eventually we came to a kind of compromise where families would be permitted but not marriages or inheritance, and those families could be of any number and any gender, and could form and reform at will. Thus Porphyry was born into the family Euridike had formed with Castor, Hesiod, and Iris, although his father was Pytheas, who had stayed behind in the Remnant City.

I was sharing a house with Lysias, and if the vote had gone the other way we had agreed to marry. When I came home exhausted after Porphyry's birth, he brought me apple porridge and rubbed my feet.

"We could have children now," he said, looking up at me. "You're not too old. If you stopped taking the silphium."

I shook my head. "It's not what I want."

He looked disappointed and got up from the floor to sit beside me on the bed. "Why not?"

I had seen a great deal of childbirth, enough to put anyone off, but that wasn't it. "I want a life of the mind, not to be mired in domesticity. All that milk and washing."

"But you have maternal instincts. You're such a good teacher."

"I put my maternal instincts into being a teacher. The whole City is my baby—this city and the original. I don't want my own baby to love more than all the others. I think Plato's right that I would favor it."

"I want children," Lysias said. "I was prepared to do without to make the Republic, but what we're doing here is all compromised anyway. I want to help everyone, you know I do, but I want my own children to grow up here too, now that it's possible."

"Would you want that if you had to be the mother rather than the father?" I asked. "If you were the one to stay home and sing them to sleep?"

"Yes," he said, with no hesitation whatsoever. I was astonished. "Is that what you want?" He looked into my face.

"I was just being rhetorical. I never imagined you would agree. In the nineteenth century it would have been unthinkable for a man to do a woman's work that way." I put my hand on his.

He smiled. "In the twenty-first century it was unusual but not unheard of. And we assigned some iron boys as nursery attendants. I would do it if that's how you wanted to arrange things."

"I don't want to shrink my horizons to a baby," I said. "In my own time, that was the end of all independent thought."

"It needn't be that here," Lysias said. "If we decided to have children, I'd certainly be willing to be the one to stay home with them. But we'll also have crèches to provide flexibility. Nobody's going to be forcing you to be a nineteenth-century mother."

"I see that. But even so."

"I truly want this. I want children. And I can't do it without your help. You have a womb and can grow a new person. I can't."

I had never before thought of this as a form of female power that men lacked. No wonder they tried to control us in so many societies for so many years. (And no wonder Athene remained a virgin.) I still didn't especially want to have babies. But I didn't want to lose Lysias, and it seemed so important to him; and if he would take charge of the parts I didn't want to, then I thought that perhaps it didn't have to be something huge and life-changing for me.

So I agreed to stop chewing silphium, and I did stop. The next month when my blood came on time I was astonished, and the same the month after and the month after that. I knew that even at the festivals not every girl became pregnant every time, but I had expected Lysias's fervor to have had results. He had never wanted me so much or so enthusiastically. I saw now that he had seen sterile coupling as hardly worth doing. I wasn't comfortable about this change, but I didn't feel I could talk to him about it.

After six months with no result, I talked to Kreusa, and she reassured me that sometimes it could take many months to become pregnant, and that I shouldn't start to worry until it was a year.

After a year, I talked to her again, and she recommended green leaves, sunlight, relaxation, and prayers to Hera. I tried all of these, and never had my monthly blood arrive more than a day late. "Am I too old?" I asked her, a year after that, on a sunny autumn day while we were alone together on the shore smoking fish.

"What are you now, thirty-five, thirty-six? No, that's not too old. Old for a first time, but there shouldn't be any trouble. Lysias is a few years older, there might be problems on his side. Have him eat red meat when he can and abstain from fish."

"Have you ever had a baby?" I asked her as I tossed some more wood onto the fire.

She frowned and paused, with a single fish in one hand and a stick with five more threaded on it in the other. "One, when I was young. My mistress beat me for being so careless with the silphium. I was lucky not to find myself out on the street. It was a boy, poor thing, and had to be exposed." I remembered the baby I had exposed and how terrible I had felt, even though it couldn't have survived and it was not my own. I put out my hand toward Kreusa, but she didn't seem to see me. "I cried for days. By the time I had a house of my own and could have afforded a child, I'd found philosophy and didn't want one. I'm surprised you do, honestly." She plunged the stick through the fish abruptly and turned to put it on the smoke rack.

"I don't, all that much," I said. "Lysias really does. Now I've been trying for two years without getting anywhere, and he still feels strongly about it and I'm still ambivalent."

"That's probably your problem," she said, her face still turned toward the fish and the fire. "Your ambivalence. If you truly wanted it, you'd get pregnant."

"But you didn't want to, that time back in Corinth." I strung more fish onto another stick.

She shook her head without turning around. "I don't know why it should be. Lots of girls get caught when they don't want it at all, but lots of women trying without really wanting it can't manage it. And some who do desperately want it can't, and that's the saddest thing of all. I'd give up trying and fretting and just see what the gods send if I were you."

"Lysias—"

"He's a funny one," Kreusa said, turning back and picking up the stick I held out to her. "He's not Greek."

"Neither am I," I said.

"No, but you're not what he is either." She sighed and put the fish on the rack. "It probably makes no difference. Some men want sons to be their heirs. If he comes from that kind of family, well. Or even if not, if he wants children so much there's nothing you can do about it. You're not too old. But time is not on your side."

I picked up another fish and another stick. "He says he'll do all the work with the baby and leave me free for philosophy and teaching. Well, as free as I am now."

She laughed. "Perhaps he will, but what will you do if he doesn't? Men, eh?"

"We're equal here," I said. "In the City of Amazons there are more women than men, especially among the guardians. We can make a real difference."

"And yet you're still trying to have a baby because your man wants one?" She laughed bitterly, then began to turn the fish before they started to scorch.

"It's very difficult," I said.

I persuaded Lysias to eat more meat and less fish, even though he preferred fish, but it didn't make any difference. My blood continued to come with infuriating regularity. At first we consoled each other, and then we stopped talking about it, until at last we only talked about philosophy and politics and other neutral subjects. All in all we tried to conceive a child for six years, with no result at all. Other women seemed to have no difficulty conceiving, even other Masters. I continued to help as a midwife as our birth rate rose, along with teaching and working and serving on committees. Ikaros and I opposed each other almost as a matter of course all this time. Axiothea joked that if we ever did agree then the matter was sure to be settled.

I knew how important having children was to Lysias, so I wasn't at all surprised when he left me in the seventh year, though I was surprised that he left me for Lukretia, who was older than I was, and who had never shown any interest in him before that summer. I missed him surprisingly much. Even as we had been drawing apart he had always been courteous and friendly. Now I came home alone to a house that felt colder.

11

ARETE

That day for the first time I saw some other ships, three big ones with rows of oars, away to the east, heading southward. I called the news down, and there was some excitement, but we didn't change course to intercept them. We reached Paros about mid-day.

At first it seemed deserted, because we reached it from the southwest, and the settlements were all on the northeastern coast. The shore party didn't find anything inland, but we all saw the ones along the shore after we had sailed all the way around. I saw three of them, much like the one Kallikles had described on Naxos. I looked at them as hard as I could as we sailed by them, and so did everyone else aboard who wasn't tending to the ship at that very instant. I didn't see any people clearly, because they fled at the first sight of the ship. Paros was thickly wooded, and they ran off into the trees, mothers carrying wailing babies and everyone clutching their most precious possessions. "They must be expecting raiders," Neleus said. "Maybe Kebes is nearby."

"Or maybe more people like them. What would Kebes find to raid in a place like that?" The huts looked flimsy enough to push over at a touch. There was one square-built stone house on a little eminence, but even that looked filthy and shabby. The statues were strange, as Kallikles had said, festive and brightly colored when all the rest was so drab. They stared out at us with their huge painted eyes.

"That one has an owl," Maia pointed out at the second village. The owl was not carved but painted onto the side of the statue. "Do you think it's supposed to be Athene? Do you think they're meant to be the gods? The Greek gods?"

"Who else would they worship?" Erinna asked.

"It seems so strange," Maia said. I squeezed her hand, to show I understood what she meant. It was hard to think of these villagers as Greeks.

The shore party managed to speak to some Parians, but with no more conclusive results than we had had at Naxos. We left as soon as they came back. That night we sailed on. I had managed to suppress my erotic longings for Erinna, or I thought I had. I was sure she didn't feel like that about me, and I knew that I wanted to increase her excellence, as Plato says, so it was all right for me to love her as long as I didn't act out of lust. Mostly it was nice to just think how much better the world was because she was in it, and to see her sometimes, adjusting the sails or teaching people how to steer. When she smiled at me, my heart turned over.

We came to Delos at sunrise on the fifth day out from home. I was at the mast-top, in the crosstrees where there was a little platform for sitting. There was a huge wing of thin cloud in the eastern sky, striated like wool pulled out for carding, and the sun had lit it pink and then gold. The sky was paling from pink as we came into the natural harbor of Delos and dropped anchor there below the temples. I could feel somebody climbing the mast below me so I scooted over to make room for whoever it was. My heart beat faster thinking that it might be Erinna. I was surprised when it turned out to be Father.

He looked out over the island. "It's such a long time since I've seen it," he said. "No lions yet."

"It looks deserted. Or is everyone still asleep?"

"It's only used for the festival at this date. There'll probably be a few priests, I should think."

"The temples look like proper buildings."

He smiled his kouros smile. "They may have had inspiration."

"But not those poor villagers on Naxos and Paros?"

He looked impatient. "I can't be everywhere taking care of everything all at once. Yes, I could spend all my time curing people of boils and teaching them to read, but instead I set up centers of healing and learning, to teach doctors and scholars. I gave Greece an oracle where they could come and ask their questions. I sent Sokrates a daemon to watch out for him, but I can't do that for everyone. I'm constantly inspiring people, but only people who can do something with the inspiration. I do the best I can within what Fate allows. Don't confuse me with Ficino's ideas of God, Arete!"

"Sorry," I said.

"Besides, I didn't know anything about them. They didn't pray to me," he said, still staring out over Delos, toward the mountain in the center of the little island where he had been born long before. "Those people in the Kyklades. I didn't know they were there. There weren't any statues of me, did you notice?"

"But this is so close," I said, gesturing at Delos, the first and oldest center of the worship of Apollo in the world.

"How often do you think they leave their petty islands?" Father asked, shaking his head. "Probably they haven't ever been any further out to sea than they need to catch fish. I'll do what I can to help them, now. I'll argue in Chamber in favor of Kallikles's idea of sending out missions to them. You're absolutely right that it's what Simmea would have wanted to do."

"And it won't change anything?"

"It might get the Naxians to build that pleasant temple I remember on the little island," he said. "But it won't change the future. There's only one world. We're in prehistory here. We hardly know the names of kings. Nobody knows for sure what happened on any given day, or when people learned about sanitation or philosophy, or even metal smelting. This isn't the generation before the Trojan War, it's more like four or five generations before. And even Troy—ask Ficino exactly where it was. He doesn't know. They forgot where it was until it was rediscovered late in the nineteenth century."

"Really?" I was astonished. "How could they lose Troy?"

"There's a lot of history. When it isn't recorded, things drop out. There are entire civilizations that are forgotten. Troy's lucky. It had Homer."

"Why do you suddenly seem so sure about when we are? I thought you didn't know either?"

"I didn't until now. But look at Delos," he said, gesturing. "I pay attention to Delos. It's *mine*. I know when things were built here. This is early Minoan. I should have guessed Athene wouldn't have put us immediately before the eruption."

I looked at the island. "I really want to go ashore," I said. "It's so beautiful. I want to explore it. I feel connected to it, even from up here, as if it's calling to me."

"You're my daughter. The island knows you." He sighed. "It knows me too. But I probably shouldn't go ashore, just in case. People don't usually recognize me, incarnate. They're not expecting to see me. But Sokrates did. And priests of mine, on Delos—they probably are expecting me at any moment. And if the island knew me—no. It's a little unkind to the priests, being so close and not letting them see me, but better not to risk it."

"Why do you keep your real nature secret in the City?" I asked.

He kept on gazing out over the island as he answered. "Because I want to live an incarnate life that's as normal as possible. It makes people uncomfortable if they know who I am, normal people. Your mother—Simmea was different. And I didn't tell her. She worked it out for herself." He wiped away tears, unselfconsciously as ever. "If I tell people, they'll treat me differently. As it is, they think I'm a credit to Plato, and to them. They treat me as one of them. If they knew, they would expect me to be able to do things, and to know things. I don't have my powers, so there's not much I can do. And I do know some things, but I'm here hoping to learn, not to teach. And there are a lot of things I don't know, and they'd find it hard to believe that I don't. Some of the things I do know it's better for people not to know, to guess and work out for themselves."

"But you tell me?"

"That's different. I couldn't have kept it from you Young Ones. You have a right to know. I'm your father. And being a parent, up close and every day, is one of the things that has taught me the most."

"But you're also a god."

"You were asking about becoming a god." The sun was up now, blazing a gold path on the azure sea. He gestured to it. "That's *mine*. And Delos is mine. And inspiration and healing and poetry and all those things. Those are responsibilities. But they're not what's important. Being a god means being myself forever, and that means knowing myself as well as I can. Seeing the sun rise over Delos makes me feel all kinds of things, and they are different now because of what I have experienced since the last time I saw it. So I feel at home, and yet not at home, and the contradiction there is fascinating, and I can explore that feeling and make it into something."

"But not all the gods do that. And humans can," I said. "Humans can make art."

His eyes were precisely as blue as the sky, and his expression wasn't human at all. "They can. But they have such a brief span to do it. And a lot of their life is misery, and while that's a productive subject for art, it's a limited one. And then they die and lay down their memories in Lethe and go on to become a new person. They come to the end of themselves and change and start again. Gods may or may not make art, but they can't come to the end of themselves. Not ever. And we *are* art. Our lives are subjects for art. Everything we are, everything we do, it all comes to art, our own or other people's. Mortals can forget and be forgotten. We can't. Everything we do has to be seen in that light. There's no anonymity. If you're a god, your deeds will be sung. Even the ones you would prefer to forget about."

"And I can choose, whether to be a mortal or a god?" I felt as if the whole world was holding its breath before he answered.

"Going ashore on Delos might help you. But time is the best gift." He stared out over Delos again. "I don't understand why she wanted to die. How she could have been ready. She told me not to be an idiot, but I don't understand how I was wrong."

We'd had this conversation a hundred times already, but this time I thought of something new. "Why are you assuming she was right?"

"What?"

"You're assuming she was right. Mightn't she have been wrong? Mistaken?"

He looked stricken. "But that would make everything worse! If she'd been wrong then I should have done it, and now it's too late."

"Somebody's coming up," I said, as I felt it through the mast.

It was Klymene. "Good to see something that looks halfway like civilization," she said, after she had greeted us. "I'm leading the shore party today. I thought I'd come up and see if I could spot any signs of life."

"There's smoke rising from the altar over there," Father said, gesturing. It was a thin thread of gray smoke, almost invisible. I hadn't seen it until he pointed it out. "I expect you'll find a priest or two."

"Somebody who isn't too terrified of us to talk would be good," Klymene said. "And Kebes can hardly have avoided coming here if he came this way at all."

Father went down shortly after that, and Klymene followed him before long. I saw and announced the sails of fishing boats away to the northeast, where another island loomed in the blue distance. My eyes kept being drawn back to Delos. I longed to walk on it. I watched enviously as the shore party left. It was Erinna's turn to go. Phaedrus and Kallikles had both contrived to join them, although it was not their turns. No doubt they felt the same affinity with the island I did.

At last my watch was over and I joined Ficino and Maia on the deck to watch the boat return. Erinna was rowing. "There are two priests," she called up to us, "and they say we can come ashore and cook and take on water and worship Apollo, but we should be back on the ship before dark."

Maecenas set a watch, for which Father volunteered. Those of us young and fit enough to swim hastily gave our kitons and sandals to friends old and frail enough to want to go in the boat. When my bare sole met the soil of Delos I felt a shock of joy that brought tears to my eyes. I felt I knew the place already. I knew where the cave was where they said Apollo had been born, and the plane tree on the mountain where he really had. I knew the altars and the temples, those already there and those not yet built. I found the words of the Homeric Hymn to Delian Apollo in my mouth as I came out of the water.

Delos did not seem to move unsteadily beneath my feet. It felt like the most solid earth I had ever trodden, as if Ios and Amorgos and even Kallisti were hollow shells and Delos alone was firm.

The sun was hot, and as I walked I saw lizards darting away from me. Kallisti was home, Amorgos and Ios felt like adventure, Naxos and Paros felt like somewhere I wanted to rescue. Delos felt like somewhere my soul had known before birth. "Mine," Father had said, possessively. I felt that it was mine too; not just that it belonged to me, but it was mutual. I also belonged to it.

I didn't wait for my kiton but walked on, naked as in the palaestra, leaving the others behind. If we had to be back on the ship by nightfall, I didn't have long. There was a spring I needed to find, and I knew where it was. I kept walking around shadow-buildings that didn't exist yet, like the opposite of ruins, potentials. The spring was in a grove of trees, exactly where I had known it would be. I heard it before I saw it and pushed through the trees to come to it. When I came out into the clearing around the spring my two hero brothers were there, grave-faced, waiting in silence. Everything felt right, even that I was naked and they were clothed. We did not speak. Kallikles brought out a cup from the fold of his kiton, which he held out to me. I took it in both hands and dipped it into the pool, raised it high so that sunlight reflected into the water, then poured out a few drops on the ground and drank. I passed it to Phaedrus, who drank and passed it on to Kallikles. We kept on passing it around between the three of us until the cup was empty.

All this time, since my foot had first touched the shore, I hadn't thought, only acted, and everything I had done had been inevitable, necessary, and right. Once the cup was empty that changed, and I was only myself again, not a vessel of divinity, but I didn't want to speak and break the silence. Phaedrus put his hand on my shoulder, and without discussing it we all began to walk back toward the ship. By the time the sea was in sight I felt more nearly normal, though I noticed that we all kept avoiding the future-ghosts of temples.

Ficino handed me my kiton, and I put it on. Unusually for him, he didn't ask any questions, though his gaze was sharp. I sat down next to him. There was food ready, nut porridge and baked fish, and I ate it hungrily. The priests of Apollo, a man and a woman, came and blessed us, sprinkling water on us from branches with green leaves. I accepted their blessing with the others, avoiding my brothers' eyes.

Klymene came over and sat down by Kallikles, who made room for her. "Joy to you, son," she said.

"Joy," he muttered.

Klymene rolled her eyes and turned to Ficino. "They know Minos, and Troy, and Mycenae, but no names of kings we could offer," Klymene said to Ficino. I was listening, but like my brothers I didn't want to talk yet. I just sat there eating in silence.

"Have they seen Kebes?" Ficino asked.

"Not by name, but they know the *Goodness*. They say the captain is called

Massias. Some people from the *Goodness* have been here for the festival, and behaved appropriately. They said they thought our ship was the *Goodness* at first. They don't know the location of their city, but they come here from the northeast, so that gives us a direction."

"Northeast. Interesting," Ficino said. "What's northeast of Delos?"

"Well, Mykonos close by," Klymene said. "Beyond that, nothing much for a long way. Due east gets you to Ikaria and Samos. Northwest are Tinos and Andros. Northeast, well, a biggish gap of sea and after a while you get to Chios and Lesbos."

"And on the mainland, Troy," Ficino pointed out.

"Why would Kebes have gone to Troy?" Klymene asked.

Ficino shook his head, as if to ask why anyone would go anywhere else.

We went back to the *Excellence* before nightfall, as the priests had asked. Phaedrus was in the same boat I was. "What was that?" he whispered to me.

I shrugged. "The island? We should ask Father, maybe."

"Our souls?" he asked.

Ficino was looking at us curiously. "We should ask Father, when we can be quite sure we've got him alone," I whispered.

12

ARETE

I couldn't sleep that night with thinking about what had happened. We sailed northeast to Mykonos, which had some scattered fishing settlements a little more civilized than those of Naxos and Paros, but only a little. A party tried to talk to them, again without success. I didn't go ashore, and I couldn't catch Father alone. We sailed on east to Ikaria, which we reached late on the next day. There was no sign of life visible from the ship. We anchored for the night and the next morning put down a shore party, which now felt routine. We sailed around another long thin island, and met up with the shore party in the late afternoon. They had seen nobody, and we concluded that Ikaria was deserted like Ios and Amorgos. We therefore went ashore as we had done there, and began to build fires to cook a meal.

While we were ashore, the three of us cornered Father and took him off into the trees away from everyone to ask about Delos. There was a wonderful scent of pine needles all around us as we walked and scuffed up the droppings of years, a thick layer of pine must which felt as if it had never been disturbed before. Although it smelled amazing, it was uncomfortable to walk on the strange surface. My feet sank in at every step and it took a real effort to move them. Old needles kept finding their way into my sandals and scratching my feet.

"I'm glad to see you found the spring," Father said, once we were well away.

"Why didn't you warn us?" Kallikles asked.

"I didn't know for sure Delos would affect you," Father said. "And I didn't want to disappoint you if it didn't. I did tell Arete that it might help."

"Was it our souls?" I asked.

"Your souls and my island," he said. "What happened?"

"Nothing much, really," Phaedrus said. "We went to the spring and waited, and Arete came and gave us water. That's all. But I've never felt anything like it."

"It felt right," I said. "It felt like knowing what was right and doing it because it was inevitable. There wasn't any choice."

"Then you were in the hand of Necessity, at the edge of your Fate, doing what was inevitable," Father said. "All of you. Once you were on Delos, you had to go through that ritual, and you knew it and you did it. The sprinkling on the shore is the echo of that."

"I hated it," Kallikles said. "Not at the time. At the time it just felt right, the way Arete said. But the more I think about it the more it felt like having my own self taken over. I wasn't in control of what I did. And afterward when Klymene spoke to me it took a real effort to answer. I felt drained, even though all I'd done was walk through the woods and drink some water."

Father put his hand on Kallikles's shoulder. "It's hard for anyone to resist Fate and Necessity."

"I didn't even try," I said, and saw my brothers nod. None of us had tried.

"What did it do?" Kallikles asked.

"Connects you to me, to the world. If you weren't my children it would mark you as votaries. As it is, it marks you as what you are. My children. Heroes."

"How does it work?"

"It's a Mystery."

"Mother always said you said that when you didn't understand something," I said.

"That's exactly what a Mystery is, something the gods don't properly understand," he said. "Fate and Necessity are the bounds set on us. All of us. Fate is the share our souls chose before birth. Necessity is the edges of that."

"If we were marked as heroes, did the others notice?" Phaedrus asked.

"I don't know, I wasn't there. Did they?"

"Ficino noticed something, but he didn't say anything," I said. "And maybe Klymene—she was looking at Kallikles in a funny way. But nobody said anything. Is it going to happen again?"

He spread his hands. "I don't know. If you go back to Delos, probably. And in Delphi, perhaps."

"You said it marks us," Phaedrus said, coming back to that. "Who does it mark us to?"

"The gods," Father said, casually. "If you meet them, they will know what you are, now."

"But not Porphyry and Alkibiades and Euklides back on Kallisti?" Phaedrus asked.

"I don't know. The gods might recognize them as my sons. But they'd definitely know you three now." Father put his hand against an especially large pine, patted it, then turned and started walking back toward the shore.

"So we could have resisted it?" I asked, following, the pine must underfoot still resisting my every step. "What would have happened?"

"If you'd been strong enough, you wouldn't have gone through the ritual. If you'd tried to resist and not been strong enough, you'd have done it anyway. Why didn't you resist?"

"It felt so right," I said, and my brothers nodded, though Kallikles was biting his lip.

"But it wasn't you," Phaedrus said. "You're here, you were on the ship. It wasn't you making us do that."

"It was my power. Things done with my power keep on working, even though I'm here. I can't intervene. But things that have been set up keep on working. Delos is full of my power." He frowned. "I don't have any power right now, myself. So I couldn't give you any. But Delos could."

"We have power?" Phaedrus squeaked. I didn't laugh at the way his voice came out because I felt the same myself.

"You said it marked us, you didn't say it gave us *power*," Kallikles said, rolling his eyes, though you think he'd be used to Father by now. "What *kind* of power? Power to do what?"

"Power according to your souls," Father said, in that infuriating way he had, as if it were the most intuitive thing in the world and everyone knew it already.

"To do what?" Phaedrus repeated.

"To do whatever you want to, under Fate and Necessity," Father said.

"Heal people? Walk on lava?" I asked.

"Yes, those sorts of things," he confirmed. "But feel confident in your power before you try walking on lava! I don't know how much power you have, I can't tell without my own power. It may not be enough."

I looked at Phaedrus, who was the one who wanted to control volcanoes. He was staring at the backs of his hands as if he'd never seen them before.

"I don't know exactly how it works," Father went on. "Whether Necessity woke up what was there already, or if some of my power from the island came into you. But right now you can do things I can't."

"We could have healed Mother," I said before I thought.

"Too late," Father said. "If I'd taken you there years ago, perhaps."

"Why didn't you?" Kallikles asked. "If you knew it would do this?"

"I didn't know. I thought it might. And you were all so young. And we wanted you to be your best selves. I didn't know what that would be. It wasn't until you said you wanted to come on this voyage that any of you said you wanted to be heroes."

"So we could do the kind of thing gods do? Like transforming people into things?" Phaedrus said, pensively.

"Yes, but it's not usually a good idea," Father said. I saw an expression on his face that I hadn't seen since before Mother died. He was worried. "You have power. You might be able to do that. But please don't!"

"How do we use it?" Kallikles asked.

Father's brow furrowed a little. "You just reach out and use it. You'll work it out. You've all learned logic and self-control."

"Not like the gods," Phaedrus said, and laughed.

"How about time travel?" I asked.

"Don't try that!" He looked really worried now. "That does take experience. It isn't time travel. You step outside time and then back in. Being outside time isn't like being in it. Look, please don't try that until after I have my own powers and I can show you how to do it. Terrible things could happen to you. You could get lost forever." He laughed suddenly. "This reminds me of when the boys were all starting to walk at once! Suddenly nothing was safe, and we had no idea what you could get into or do. Simmea—am I ever going to stop missing Simmea?"

"Ever is a long time for a god," I said. "Can we use this power to keep from dying?"

"Your body will have to die, eventually. But you can keep it healthy meanwhile. And you don't have to stay dead, if you choose to be a god."

It was such a scary thought. "You'll help us?" Phaedrus asked.

"What, I have to run entry-level divinity classes now? Of course I will." He hesitated. "You're heroes. In some ways, you have more ability to use your powers than I do mine, even when I have mine. Gods are bound by Fate and Necessity, of course, but we're also under the edicts of Zeus—we can't use our powers to interfere in human affairs unless we're asked. You can keep right on interfering as much as you want because you're still mortal for the time being."

"What?" Phaedrus sounded affronted. "What about what Athene did setting up the Republic? Wasn't that interfering in human affairs?"

"The Masters prayed to her for help doing it," Father said. "She could grant their prayers. She couldn't have done it alone."

"And buying the Children?" I asked.

"The Masters decided to do it. She just chose to help. It was all human action and the consequences of human action." He looked helpless.

"And what she did to Sokrates?" Kallikles asked.

"He was her votary. You can do whatever you want to your votaries. And no other gods can do anything to them." He looked ashamed. "We don't always behave as well as we should."

"And it'll be made into art?" I asked.

"Eventually, inevitably, yes," he said. "Everything we do will be."

"What?" Kallikles asked.

"I told Arete this. Our lives are art. It's part of being a god."

"And for a hero?" he asked.

Father shrugged. "It depends on their deeds."

The three of us looked at each other, and then back at Father. He shook his head. "Just be careful. And try to be careful what other people see. They'll react to you very differently if they know. Think carefully."

"Rhea," Kallikles said. Of course, she would be his first thought. "I'll have to tell her as soon as we get back."

Father looked at him sympathetically. "Maybe she'll understand the way Simmea did."

Erinna, I thought, sadly. There were already too many gulfs between us. My age, and Father's nature, and her silver rank, and now this.

Then Phaedrus gasped, and we turned to him. He was a little way behind, and he was walking a handspan or so above the pine must of the forest. It didn't seem strange, and then it did, to see my brother walking on air unsupported. Bold Kallikles took a leap and joined him. I hesitated, but Phaedrus put out his hands to me, grinning. I reached for his hand and took a step up onto nothing, and the nothing held me up, and we were all standing above the ground, walking on air. The strangest thing was that it didn't take any effort and didn't feel unnatural. It was as if I'd always been able to do it but had been shuffling away on the ground out of habit. I ran a few steps up the air, laughing, until my head was almost at the top of the pines. Then I saw Father, still scuffing his feet down in the must, and stopped.

"All right," he said. "Now before you go any further up, show me how you're going to come down."

Coming down was difficult, much harder than going up. We couldn't do it for a moment. I figured it out first—I took big exaggerated steps downward, as if descending an invisible staircase, and the boys copied me. When my feet touched the earth I felt unexpectedly heavy and almost fell. It reminded me of how walking on Amorgos felt strange after the motion of the ship. I took a cautious step, and then another. The boys were down now too, staggering and shaking their heads.

"What else?" Phaedrus asked. "What else can we do?"

"I really don't know," Father said. "You'll have to find out for yourselves, find your limits. You should be looking for your domain, what you care about, where you have excellence. I told you about that. It's different for everyone. And go slowly, be careful. Test what you do. Think like philosophers. Pursue excellence, in this as in all things."

I wanted to try things. But I was afraid, too. I wanted to be a god, or I had thought that I did. Now I wasn't sure. I could see a chasm opening between me and everyone but Father and my brothers. I didn't need the warning to hide my new powers from the others. It was the same way I felt about growing up. I wanted to be grown up, of course I did, to vote in the Assembly and be assigned a metal—gold, of course, and there wasn't much doubt I'd make it. At the same time I didn't want to stop being a child, secure, looked after. There were ways that was comfortable. I'd always been the youngest in the family, and there were advantages to that. There were advantages to being human. Not the only one Father ever talked about, dying and being reborn as a completely new person. I couldn't see that as an advantage at all! I liked being me, and I wanted to keep on doing it. The advantages I could see were more to do with being like everyone else, living the kind of life we all lived. Having somebody love me one day, even if it couldn't be somebody as wonderful as Erinna. Being excellent but still relatively normal. Like Mother, I thought, instead of like Father. But I had the power now. I couldn't pretend I didn't.

"I want to be free and choose for myself," I said, as we came out of the trees again just above the beach. I hadn't disliked feeling in the hand of Fate. But the more I thought about it, the less I wanted to feel that again. Fate and Necessity are what binds the gods. I wasn't sure I wanted to be bound that way.

"Then keep away from gods," Father said, looking over his shoulder at me, half-smiling. Then suddenly he looked serious. "One thing you will have enough power to do now, all of you, is reach the gods with your prayers. Be careful what you pray, and what you ask and whose attention you draw."

On the beach some people were preparing food, and others were racing and wrestling on the sand as if they were in the palaestra. The *Excellence* was bobbing sedately at anchor. Clouds were blowing up out of the west and glowing rose and violet in the rays of the lowering sun. (Since I'd left home I seemed to spend a lot of time looking at the sky. It was always changing, yet it was the one thing that was the same everywhere.) Nobody took any notice of us coming back, except Erinna, who waved happily as she caught sight of us, and Neleus, who raked us with a dark-eyed glance before turning back to the fire he was building.

13

APOLLO

I had guessed that Delos might have an effect on my Young Ones, but had not quite thought through what that would mean. I knew it when I saw them coming back aboard to sleep that night. The three of them had a new look about them that I nevertheless recognized. They were always beautiful, and always moved well—everyone brought up in the City knew how to move well. But now there was something about them, a certain sleekness, a not-quite-hidden glitter, as of a scarf draped carelessly over treasure. They looked like Olympians in disguise.

After the Last Debate, Simmea and I set up housekeeping together in Thessaly, which had been Sokrates's house. We took all the children belonging to us—Neleus, and my three boys. I took Kallikles, Alkibiades and Phaedrus from the city crèches. Many people wanted their babies but couldn't identify them. There was no difficulty with mine. I'd have known them by their heroic souls, but anyone could tell at a glance from their eyes and bone structure. Phaedrus's blue eyes looked strange against his dark skin, especially then, when he was five months old. Alkibiades was nine months old, and Kallikles was just over a year.

We also collected Neleus, who was also five months old. Simmea frowned when I carried him into Thessaly. "I swore to Zeus and Demeter not to treat him differently from the others," she said. "They're all my children."

"They're all your children, and you won't be prejudiced in his favor in any way, but here he is," I said. Then she took him and hugged him as if she'd never let him go.

It only took a couple of days for Simmea to decide that Plato was right, or at least that the two of us couldn't manage four lively boys all day and all night. We took to leaving them in the nursery for several hours in the day so that we could get things done. There they were being brought up according to the precepts of Plato, communally, by people trained in early infant care. It didn't hurt them, or at least I don't think it did.

I had always known all my children were mine, always known they were heroes, always been able to pick them out of a crowd. Power didn't make any difference to that. I looked at them across the deck, trying to see where it did make a difference. Arete met my eyes, and as I looked away I recognized and identified my emotion.

I was envious, something I had rarely experienced. Envy is like jealousy, but quite distinct. Envy is when somebody else has something and you wish you had it too. Jealousy is when they have something and you wish you had it *instead*. I have felt jealous of people, usually when the thing I wished I had was somebody's attention. It's hateful, far and away my least-favorite emotion, because it makes me less than I could be. I dislike feeling it, and try to avoid it. Envy has been much rarer for me, because apart from people's attention there's normally very little that I want that I can't just have, and very little of that is something anyone else could have anyway.

But at that moment when I saw my Young Ones coming back aboard full of power, I wanted access to my own power. And I could even have had it, if I really wanted it, far more power than my children had. I could return to being my whole self at any time, at the cost of this mortal life. I considered it for a moment, there on the deck. I could swim to where my priests were standing on the Delian shore watching the ship maneuvering out. I could sacrifice myself there—dying, as was poetically appropriate, where I had been born. I could return moments later in my full power. I just had to want it enough to give up my incarnation—and that meant wanting it more than I wanted to fulfill Simmea's dying wish.

It was tempting, but only fleetingly. I looked down at the choppy sunset-hued sea between the ship and the shore. Simmea had taught me to swim. And Simmea had wanted me to stay in mortal form. She had some reason, and I felt sure she was right, whatever that reason was. Until I understood it and fulfilled it, or until I happened to die naturally, I would stay incarnate, even if it was inconvenient. Even when it hurt. Envy wasn't pleasant, but it did teach me something about myself, even if it was something I didn't much like. I was glad to have time to compose myself before there was a chance to talk to the Young Ones. I wouldn't want them to know I suffered from such a mean emotion.

My priests were still standing on the Delian shore, looking toward the *Excellence* as the watch on duty brought her head around so her sails could catch the wind. I leaned out on the rail, smiling, and waved to them. They looked at each other in consternation, then back at me in dawning affirmation. They waved back emphatically. I was glad I'd been able to make somebody happy.

I was tempted to take up my powers again on Ikaria—not out of envy for the Young Ones' power. I had thoroughly dealt with that annoying emotion by then. No, on Ikaria the urge came purely out of a desire to protect them. They were children, and there was so much trouble they could get into! With divine power there were so many things it was easy to get into and difficult to get out of. The things they thought of—walking on lava! Time travel! I didn't want them burned up by lava, but far less did I want them stepping outside time and not being able to negotiate what they found there.

I tried to remember my own childhood. I'd had Mother and a whole set of goddesses shielding and teaching me. (That may be why I have always lived solitary since.) What I chiefly remembered were bounds set around my power, bounds for me to test, to encourage me to develop safely. From the moment I was born I had the power to destroy the world (I had the *sun*), and they shielded me until I had the judgment to understand that destroying the world would be unutterably stupid. They knew what I was to be. The other Olympians wanted me—well, except Hera, who didn't want me or anything like me. They shaped me to fill the place in the pantheon meant for me. I like to think I have done better than that already, fulfilled far more than the promises and prophecies. And I am still trying to increase my excellence, and the world's excellence.

If there were places destined for my children I did not know what they were. I wasn't aware of any prophecies or expectations. They had to find their own way. I could give them advice and prohibitions and information. I couldn't use my power to teach them, or to give them safe boundaries to work in, because right now when they needed it I didn't have any power. It felt like letting them down. And yet, Simmea had wanted me to stay incarnate, at the cost of her own life. Could this be why? Could they need to learn without boundaries? As soon as I thought it I knew that this was insane. Simmea hadn't known anything about the powers of a god except what I'd told her. She hadn't known about Delos or what they would need. She was going on the information she had at the time, most of which I must have and some of which I might be able to discover if we ever caught up with Kebes. (Or whoever had killed her, if it wasn't Kebes.)

I did feel like an idiot whenever I thought about it. What could I do, incarnate, that I couldn't do as a god? I usually asked the question the other way around, for there were so many things I could do as a god that I couldn't do as a human. I had become human to learn about will and consequences and the significance of mortal life. There were things I had learned, and no doubt there was more to learn. But as for things I could do better incarnate— beyond learning that it seemed to amount to suffering, and waiting. Perhaps there was something else Simmea wanted me to learn. But she had seemed so urgent—don't be an idiot, she had said, as if her reason was obvious and imperative. She let herself die, she gave up her memories and our life together and the future we could have had. The least I could do was try not to be more of an idiot than I could help.

From Ikaria we sailed to Samos, and there we had our first solid news of Kebes. (I had the map with me. But I hadn't shown it to anyone or even spoken about it.) There were no Samians in the Catalog of Ships. And the priests in Delos hadn't known anything beyond "northeast" for Kebes. There was no sign of the *Goodness.* But there was a settlement here, where the city of Samos would one day stand. It wasn't a mud-hut encampment either, like the primitive ones we had seen on Naxos and Paros and Mykonos. The buildings were made of well-mortared stone, with familiar pillars in the style it amused me to call archaeo-classical. Nor did it have the strange flat Kykladic statues, but rather a solid Renaissance-style statue of a goddess. The people didn't run away or immediately attack us, though we saw a stir in the streets.

Maecenas dropped anchor just outside the harbor and immediately called a council meeting. Everyone who wasn't part of the council looked enviously at us as we went down to Maecenas's cabin. I was on the ship's council because the Just City was an aristocracy—rule was by the best. And by the standards they were using, I was going to be selected as among the best on almost all occasions. I sometimes felt a bit of a fraud about this, as they were judging by human standards. But I was glad to be included in the council and have my voice heard.

"What do we do?" Maecenas asked bluntly. "This could be Kebes. Probably is. Do we attack? Or talk first?"

"Talk first," Klymene said, a hair before me.

"We need to find out more," I said, when she spread her hand to yield to me. "We don't see the *Goodness.* It seems like a small place."

"It's as big as Psyche, and it has the same kind of look about it of something built without Workers but with our sensibilities," Maecenas said. "And Kebes only took a hundred and fifty, and no Young Ones."

"I don't think this is it," I said.

Everyone disagreed with me. As I didn't want to tell them about the map, I couldn't explain why I didn't think so.

"It's logical that it is," Klymene summed up after a while.

"What we need is more information," I said. "Whether this is Kebes or not, we need to talk. And if it is, we need to find out whether they raided us and took the head of Victory. We might be able to set up friendly relations, if not. And if it isn't Kebes, we need to find out who they are."

"Let's go in then, and see," Maecenas said. "If I send you, Pytheas, will you stay calm?"

"If I am an envoy, I will behave as an envoy," I said, standing up and bumping my head on the cabin roof.

"I wasn't challenging your honor, man," Maecenas said. "Sit down. You go, and Klymene, and take Phaenarete and Dion. We'll stay anchored right here, in bowshot. If there's trouble, we'll hear. But if there's trouble, get back here as fast as you can." Phaenarete and Dion were older Young Ones, strong, and well-trained with weapons.

"That place doesn't have a palisade," Klymene said. "And they didn't run off. We ought to be able to talk."

"Wear armor," Maecenas said.

So I had to put on a cuirass, and endure the envy of the entire ship's company as I was rowed ashore. Samos has a natural deep harbor, and they had built a wooden wharf with poles—they were clearly used to receiving a big ship like ours. There was a crowd waiting to receive our little boat, and the armor didn't feel like much protection.

Nobody looked familiar. Most of the crowd were young, and so I wouldn't have expected to recognize anyone, but some of them were older, indeed aged. They were also the wrong mix of people to be the Goodness Group—all of these had what I think of as typical Ionian Greek looks. They could have been carved in marble. "Joy," one of them said, a middle-aged man. "You have come early. Why do you stand off from shore? Is there sickness aboard Goodness?"

His accent was unusual, but he spoke good Greek.

"Joy to you. We're not the Goodness," Klymene said. "Our ship is called Excellence. We come from Kallisti. Who are you?"

The answer was surprising, and took a long time to elicit clearly. It turned out that they were a group of assorted refugees from wars in Greece and the islands who had been settled here by Kebes and his people to found a new city, which was called Marissa—after, they told us, the name of the mother of God. God himself was called Yayzu. They traded regularly with the *Goodness*, giving them food in return for manufactured items such as bowls and statues. They did not recognize the name Kebes, though when I said Matthias there was a general sigh and a smile of recognition. The thing they most wanted to discover from me, once I had said the words "*Excellence*" and "Kallisti," were whether we were still in contact with Athene. When I told them that we hadn't seen her since the *Goodness* left, they seemed very relieved, and admitted that they had two people in Marissa from the Goodness Group, the doctor and the teacher. These two came forward now through the crowd, visibly of our people. The teacher was much paler-skinned than anyone else, a Master I had known slightly called Aristomache, now in her seventies. The doctor, Terentius, was clearly one of the Children, much swarthier than most in the crowd. He seemed only vaguely familiar. They hugged us and asked for news of friends left in the City.

"Is it safe for us to bring the *Excellence* in?" Klymene asked.

Terentius looked surprised. "Of course! Why wouldn't it be? Marissa is a civilized city. Well, semi-civilized. As civilized as any of our colonies," he finished proudly.

"You have colonies?" Phaenarete asked. "How many?"

"Lots," Terentius said, slightly cagily, though the appalling arithmetic positively leaped to mind—if they had two people in each one they could have seventy-five colonies like Marissa up and down the Aegean. "Are you all still on Kallisti trying to do Plato's Republic?"

"Yes," I said. "Though we have five cities there now, and lots of Young Ones. This is our first exploratory voyage."

If I made us sound like five united cities, who can blame me? Kebes had been founding colonies. Who could imagine how large an army he might be ready to field if he thought we were divided and easy to conquer? I didn't doubt that he would still hate us.

Klymene and Phaenarete started to signal to the ship that it was safe to come in. "One thing, Aristomache," I said. "Marissa. Yayzu. Is this some primitive religion I'm not aware of, or are you really teaching them Christianity?"

"Christianity, of course," she said, with a twinkle in her eye.

"What's Christianity?" Dion asked.

"It's the one true faith. It has been kept from you, so you could worship Plato, but it's the only thing that can save your soul," Aristomache said. Heads were nodding around her. Dion's eyes widened.

"It hasn't been kept from you at all. It's that crazy religion Ikaros has in the City of Amazons," I said, dismissively.

Dion was a sensible lad. He nodded politely at Aristomache. "Oh, that," he said.

"God sent his son, his only son, down into the world to save everyone," she said.

"Right, and Athene's one of his angels," Dion said. "I remember now. It's popular in the City of Amazons. Here too, I see."

Although we had thought a lot about what Kebes and the Goodness Group might have been doing, collecting refugees from Greece and settling them in colonies on uninhabited islands had never crossed our minds. And of course they were doing just exactly what everyone else I knew was doing, trying to live the Good Life in Plato's Republic. It also hadn't occurred to anyone that Kebes would try to do this in a Christian context, more than a thousand years before Christ. Ficino and Ikaros had managed to reconcile Christianity and Plato, and also in Ikaros's case Christianity and the inarguable presence of Pallas Athene. I wondered how Kebes had done it. He wasn't stupid, and he'd been trained by Sokrates, but didn't have most of the structure they were starting from. He couldn't have. He'd been *ten.*

"No, actually Athene's a demon," Aristomache said.

Dion shrugged as if he didn't care either way. I hoped this would be the general reaction aboard, at least among the Young Ones.

I don't have anything against Christianity. It's a wonderful story. Indeed it's a wonderful story that has been mostly wasted by Christians. It produced some incredible architecture and music, and some splendid visual art, especially in the Renaissance. But they have made surprisingly little art about what it's like to be an incarnate god, suddenly subject to the pains of humanity, and then being tortured to death, before returning to sort things out in divine form. It's the heart of the story, and I'd been thinking the whole time I'd been incarnate myself that they could have done so much more with it. Michaelangelo, Rembrandt, Bach, yes, but who else had truly entered into the Mystery of it? For every *Supper at Emmaeus* there are thousands of Annunciations and Nativities, as if the interesting thing is that Jesus was born. Everyone is born. There's a lot of focus on the Crucifixion, again mostly in the visual arts, but surprisingly little about how he experienced his life, before or after death. Fra Angelico came closest, I think. But you'd think in that whole era where Christianity was dominant, they'd have thought about the whole thing more, instead of getting obsessed with sin and punishment.

Faced with Aristomache's pious mouthings here, I felt shaken for the first time. I knew time couldn't be changed. But if it could . . . if it could and if Christianity could have taken root here, at the very beginning, then the world I cared about most deeply might never exist. Christianity was a religion with a good story and an appealing simplicity—forgive and be forgiven, be washed in the blood of the sacrifice and be saved. If it could catch on in the Aegean before the Trojan War then everything would be different. I knew time was fixed and unchangeable. I had lived outside it. But even so, I felt a chill.

Our ship was warping in toward the wharf. "Do you want to trade?" the old man asked me.

"Certainly we do, though that will be for our captain to negotiate," I said, smoothly, still thinking about Christianity and Kebes.

"Tonight we will feast the *Excellence!*" the old man announced. The crowd cheered.

"Where are your other colonies?" I asked Terentius, as casually as I could. "Where's your main city?"

"What are your intentions toward us?" Aristomache asked.

"Exploration, a little trade," I said, spreading my hands peacefully. "Unless you raided us last autumn. Somebody raided us and killed Simmea."

Aristomache looked shocked and put her hand on my arm. "Oh, that's terrible. I'm so sorry. I remember you two were inseparable. I remember when she gave birth, you didn't want to stop holding on to her hands. She told me how you were both practicing agape. What an awful thing to happen! It must have been pirates. There's so much turmoil on the mainland, and some of them have ships. But we'd never do such a thing. It's true we have been avoiding Kallisti to keep away from Athene, and philosophical trouble. But we'd never do anything like that."

Terentius was nodding, looking appalled. They both seemed utterly sincere. I exchanged a quick glance with Dion. I didn't like to think that Kebes was doing better at civilization than we were.

14

ARETE

I seemed to spend half my time at the top of the mast looking far out at the sea and thinking, and the other half at the rail looking at close-up islands. Usually my time at the masthead was peaceful. I suppose I should have been contemplating philosophy, but my mind had a tendency to wander.

The day we left Ikaria I wanted to think about our powers, and what they meant, and what father had said about the gods, but there was no time for contemplation. We had our first squall on my watch. I stayed at the mast-head looking for rocks, and calling them out when I did see them. The others were worn out adjusting sails and changing tack—all our practice had been in smooth weather. When your sails are wet and the wind backs as you're try-ing to adjust them, canvas feels alive, as if it's trying to get away from you. Erinna nearly fell into the sea helping Nemea wrestle with a sail. She saved herself by swinging on a rope. My heart nearly stopped when I saw it. There was no time to do anything, but my impulse in the moment before she caught the rope was to fly down from the mast and snatch her up. I had risen to my feet and was about to leap. On sober reflection I had no idea whether I could fly, let alone carry another person as I did it. I resolved to ask Father. But it felt like the right thing to do, the thing my instincts prompted, and in another instant I would have tried it.

In the excitement I nearly missed seeing a fishing boat scudding before the wind. Fortunately, it saw us and veered off. I kept watching for rocks and calling them out. By the time the clouds lifted our watch was almost over, and Samos was close at hand.

When Thano, my replacement lookout, came up I went down to the deck and hugged Erinna, intensely aware of the feeling of her body and fighting down the sensations in my own. "I'm so glad you're safe!" I said.

"My own clumsiness that I slipped in the first place," she said, but she did hug me back for a moment before letting go. "It shows how important all those drills are. My body knew what to do when there was no time to think."

I felt nothing but relief that I hadn't yielded to my own instincts. Whether I could have flown and caught her or not, I'd have revealed what I was to everyone. That wouldn't have mattered if I could have saved her life, but what would she have thought? "I'd never been aloft in a storm before," I said.

"That was no more than a little squall. If there's any sign of a real storm we'll find somewhere sheltered to anchor, I should think. Real storms can be bad for sailing ships. Like the one at the beginning of the *Aeneid*."

"Or when they open the bag of winds in the *Odyssey*," I said.

She grinned. "Isn't it fun to think we're sailing their very seas, before they sailed them?"

"What would have happened if you'd gone overboard?"

"I can swim. The water was rough, but I'd probably have been fine. Mae-cenas would have put the ship to, which would have wasted time, but we're not in a life or death race."

I was even more glad I hadn't flown down off the mast and perhaps killed myself when she wasn't in real danger.

"But my head might have hit the deck, or a rock," she went on. "You can't help thinking about that kind of thing. I'm glad the rope was there and I caught it."

"Oh yes," I said, wholeheartedly. Just then I caught sight of something over her shoulder, on the shore. "What's that?"

It was a city, a proper city. We sailed closer and anchored near it, and a small shore group was sent in. It was a real city, which seemed homelike after the places we had seen. It had columns and broad streets and it was clean. There was even a colosseum, which we didn't have at home, though of course I recognized it from paintings. There was an unpainted marble statue on the wharf, a goddess with a baby on her knee. The style was familiar, although of course I hadn't seen that particular statue before. It made me feel welcome after the strange decorated heads on Paros and Mykonos. There hadn't been any statues that I'd seen on Delos, only immense columns and future ghosts.

"Auge," Maia said, coming up to us at the rail. I turned to her questioningly.

"Auge must have carved that," she said. "I recognize her style."

"I suppose that means that this is definitely the Goodness Group." We were quite close to the statue, which was bigger than life-size so I could see it well. The goddess was looking down at the baby, who was looking out at us, with his hand stretched toward us.

Maia nodded. Erinna was also looking at the statue. "Who is she?" she asked.

"Auge was one of the Children," Maia said. "She left with Kebes."

"I meant, which goddess," Erinna said.

"Hera—" Maia said, with much less certainty. "No, Demeter, or perhaps—"

I looked questioningly at Maia. Her voice sounded strange.

"Aphrodite with baby Eros?" Erinna suggested. "But he doesn't have any wings."

"Surely Kebes wouldn't . . . ? Where's Ficino?" Maia turned to me. "Can you see if you can find him?"

Erinna and I went to look for him. He was asleep in a hammock, looking so old and tired that I hesitated to wake him. Erinna clapped her hands softly, and he woke at once, instantly alert. "What is it?" he asked.

"We're at a city that might be the Goodness Group city, and Maia wanted you to look at a mysterious statue," Erinna said.

"That's worth waking up for," he said. I remembered him saying he didn't sleep much these days, and was sorry to have disturbed him. He swung out of the hammock and pulled his kiton on. I looked away from his old-man's wrinkled skin, like a plucked chicken. I drew Erinna away, hardly noticing until afterward that I had touched her arm. Ficino had earned his dignity.

He came over to us as soon as he came out on the deck. Neleus had joined Maia by the rail and we all crowded together. "Holy Mother!" Ficino said.

"Literally and specifically, I think," Maia said. She sounded furious about it.

"This can't have anything to do with Ikaros," Ficino said. Erinna raised her eyebrows at me. I shook my head. I had no idea why he would say that.

"It could just be a goddess we don't know," Neleus said.

"That's exactly what it is," Erinna said. "I don't know her. It seems as if you two do?"

"It's the pose," Ficino said. "It seems Christian."

"Like Botticelli," I said, seeing it at once now that he had pointed it out. The statue resembled Botticelli's Madonnas, the ones in the book we had at home, the book Maia had brought with her. The child on her lap, her head bent over him.

Ficino looked at me sharply. "Not like any of the Botticellis we have in Florentia," he said.

Maia blushed. "Remember, I had a book," she said. "Ikaros brought it from one of his art expeditions with Athene. It has the Madonnas."

"Did you show it to Auge?" Ficino asked.

"Yes," Maia admitted. "When she was just starting to sculpt seriously. That's probably all this is. Influence. It probably is Hera." She sounded as if she were trying to convince herself.

"Where is that book now?" Ficino asked.

"In Thessaly," I said. "My mother loved it."

"Simmea always loved Botticelli," Ficino said, sounding sad. "In the dining hall at Florentia she'd always sit so that she could stare at one or another of his paintings."

On the quay Father and the others were talking intently with a group of locals. They were wearing kitons that were each dyed in one solid color, mostly blues and pinks.

"So what goddess do you think it might be?" Erinna asked, patiently.

"Maria," Ficino said. "The mother of God in Christianity."

"That thing the Amazons are into?" Erinna asked. "How would the Goodness Group know about it?"

"Where did you get Kebes?" Maia asked Ficino abruptly.

"The slave market at Smyrna," he said. "The same place I found Simmea. They were chained together." I shuddered. I knew that all the Children had been enslaved, but knowing it was different from hearing a detail like that dropped casually. That was my mother he was talking about. Thank Athene he had been there to rescue her!

"What year was it?"

"Oh Maia, honestly! You can't expect me to remember that! So long ago, and so many children."

"But was it after Christianity?" she asked.

"Oh yes. They both had saints' names, I remember." He stared at the statue. "But they were only ten."

"Simmea used to say that we should have started with the abandoned babies of antiquity," Maia said. I had heard her say so myself.

"Ten-year-olds are not wax tablets that can be wiped clean and written afresh," Ficino agreed.

"I can't understand how Plato could have thought they were," Neleus said.

Just then the shore party sent a signal that it was safe for us to come in. "Are you sure?" Maia muttered, but Caerellia began to give orders for the Hesperides watch to take the ship in to the wharf, where there were poles for us to tie up to as we did at home. Proper docking facilities, no doubt intended for the *Goodness*.

"There were some Masters among the Goodness Group," Ficino said. "It isn't necessarily a case of what ten-year-olds remembered." There was a cheer from the shore.

"Somebody, some Jesuit or Dominican I think, said that if you gave him a boy until he was seven he'd be theirs for life," Maia said.

Ficino barked a laugh.

"So Christianity was a big thing?" Erinna asked. "In the bit of history we don't hear about?"

"It was the dominant religion of Europe for fifteen hundred years," Maia said. "We just try not to mention it much."

"Even Rome became Christian," Ficino said.

Erinna and I looked at each other, astonished. "Rome!" It seemed entirely implausible.

"They even counted their years from the birth of Christ," Neleus said. He was scanning the crowd on shore intently as we came in closer. "Father mentioned that once."

"And where did you get Pytheas?" Maia asked.

Ficino laughed. "Pytheas is something else. He came from the slave market in Euboia. One of the earliest expeditions. Athene named him herself, the only one she ever would."

"But what year?" Maia asked.

"Four or five hundred years after the founding of Rome?" Ficino said, uncertain.

"So how would he know that?"

"Somebody must have told him," Neleus said. "Maybe one of you let it slip. Or one of the other Masters."

We were tying up. I realized I'd be able to step ashore, no need for swimming this time. Father was still talking to the locals, but Klymene and Phaenarete strode over toward the ship.

"Interesting that Athene named him," Maia said. "Did she know what she was doing, and did she have the right to do it?"

"That neatly sums up the Last Debate," Neleus said.

"It seems so strange to think that you've actually met a goddess," Erinna said. Neleus's eyes met mine. It didn't seem strange to us at all.

"She rescued me from a life where I was stifled, and gave me a life I wanted to lead," Maia said. "And we did all have the very best intentions for building the Good Life."

Klymene swung herself onto the *Excellence*. Caerellia and Maecenas were there to greet her. "This is Marissa, a colony founded by the Goodness Group but mostly consisting of refugees from the wars of the mainland," she said concisely, to them but loudly enough that the rest of us pressing around could hear. "They are friendly and want to talk about trade. They have other cities, we don't yet know where."

"Marissa," muttered Ficino. Maia nodded, as if it meant something. Too close to Maria? She seemed a benevolent goddess from what I knew of her, which was entirely pictorial. Of course I had not read the words of the Botticelli book, which were in the Latin alphabet but some language I did not know. I hadn't heard much about the religion she was part of. *Even Rome*, I thought, still amazed.

"You said it's safe?" Maecenas asked.

"Safe enough. Leave a watch aboard, I'd say."

Caerellia nodded and started giving orders, that the watch on duty would stay aboard. Everyone not part of the Hesperides watch started for the rail.

"Safe for old men and children," Ficino said, taking my arm. I was surprised how thin his hand felt. I swung over the rail and he followed me more slowly.

"Wait," Maecenas said.

We stopped and turned.

"I want you to help with negotiations," Maecenas said to Ficino.

"That's never been one of my areas of interest," Ficino said.

"No, but you're good with people," Maecenas said.

Ficino sighed and took his hand off my arm. "Very well. But I insist on having time to explore Marissa, at least as much as we did at Delos."

"I don't know how long we'll stay, but I won't keep you in negotiations every minute," Maecenas said.

Ficino nodded and went with him.

I could see Father still surrounded by people. Erinna and Neleus had both stepped onto dry land, and were staggering a little, the same way I was. Maia was already striding off toward the statue. We followed after her.

Looking around, I found myself remembering the visit I had made to Sokratea with Mother a year ago. I touched Erinna's arm—it just wasn't possible to avoid touching her, but even the most normal things were charged with tingling erotic potential that I had to fight down. She turned to me. "Remember Sokratea?" I said, keeping my voice as even as I could. She nodded. "This feels the same, sort of. It's like the City but not like it, and everyone is a stranger."

She nodded again. "In some ways it's stranger than those weird primitive villages, because it is like home. But it's not like Sokratea either. We've been in constant contact with Sokratea. We're allies. We have diplomatic relations, and trade. We were there on a recognized mission."

"I was thinking that," Neleus put in. "We haven't heard anything from the Goodness Group in all this time. How did Klymene decide to just trust them and bring the ship in?"

"Klymene and Pytheas," Erinna said. She put her hand to her side where she kept a little knife for cutting ropes and whittling wood. Neleus did the same with his, and I realized as their eyes met that they were ephebes, they had gone through weapons training, and that whatever other uses they had every day, the knives at their sides were also weapons. I felt useless and young and unarmed. "Your father wants vengeance more than anyone," she went on. "He wouldn't have called us in if he thought they were responsible."

It was true. I looked over to him, still surrounded by Marissans. An old woman at his side said something and came toward us, or rather toward Maia and the statue. "Maia!" she called, clearly delighted. "Joy to you!" It must have been true what Ficino said about the Goodness Group having Masters in it, because she looked very old, almost as old as he was.

Maia turned. "Aristomache! Joy! How lovely to see you. What have you been doing?" They hugged each other

"Teaching, as always," Aristomache said.

"Here?"

"Here, and in Hieronymos on the other side of the island. And before that in Lucia, our first city, on Lesbos. And you?"

"Teaching too, in Amazonia and now back in the original city. You have three cities?"

"We have eight, on three islands. And you have five, all on Kallisti, Pytheas says?"

"That's right," Maia confirmed. "We've been calling you the Lost City, we never thought of you having so many!"

"Well, with only a hundred and fifty of us we had to find recruits, and when we saw how many people needed help we just kept on with it," Aristomache said. "War's such a terrible thing. We do what we can." She smiled. "Now who are these?"

"These are Neleus and Erinna and Arete, pupils of mine."

Aristomache nodded to us in a friendly way. "I'll introduce you all to some pupils of mine."

Maia smiled at her. "We'd like that."

Aristomache peered more closely at Neleus. "Are you Simmea's son, young man, or don't you know? In any case, I was there the night you were born."

"I am," he said. "And Arete is my sister."

She leaned forward and peered at me. "Good. There's a definite resemblance. I'm glad she left descendants. Pytheas told me what happened to her. Terrible."

Erinna was looking up at the statue. Close up, it towered over us. It wasn't a colossus like Crocus's statues, but it was much larger than life size. Maia glanced up too. "What's this?" she asked Aristomache.

"Come on Maia, you *know* that Jesus Christ is your lord and savior," Aristomache said. "You might have turned your back on him to worship demons and given Plato more honor than is due a philosopher, but you know in your soul that He is the resurrection and the life."

"Demons! Nonsense. And for that matter, you must have prayed to Athene yourself," Maia responded.

As Aristomache opened her mouth to answer, I realized that they had spoken in a language I didn't know, and that Neleus and Erinna's faces reflected their incomprehension. I had never heard this language before, but I understood it as clearly as if it were Greek or Latin. It must be one of the powers that Delos had awakened in me, though I had no idea how or why. I'd have to ask Father, and talk to Phaedrus and Kallikles to see if it was the same for them.

"Do you deny that he is your savior?" Aristomache asked, fiercely.

"I've had this same fight with Ikaros," Maia said, turning red in the face.

Aristomache frowned, then nodded. "Ikaros ..." she began, and then suddenly went back into Greek. "Yayzu came down to Earth to save us all." Aristomache smiled all around, including all of us in the conversation.

I nodded politely.

"Tell me about him?" Erinna asked. "I love the statue."

"Well that's a good place to start," Aristomache said. "His mother was a virgin, and God sent her a son, his son and himself. He was born human, like all of us, and grew up, and taught, and was killed for his teaching, and then arose from the dead and taught again. He went through a human life and understands us. He's not playing with our lives for his own amusement like Athene. And through him we will have eternal life, in heaven."

I'd heard about heaven from Ficino, so I knew it was a place like Hades that some people thought was an interlude between incarnations and others thought was the end-point of all incarnations, for souls that had purified themselves. It's mentioned in the *Phaedo*, though not with that name. My eyes went to Father, still deeply engaged in conversation on the other side of the agora. He had come down to earth and become mortal, and was learning about understanding human life. So there was no reason not to believe that Yayzu had done the same. And his mother, especially as Botticelli had painted her and Auge carved her, seemed like a perfectly nice goddess. The statue had a book in one hand. And I could certainly understand anyone who had been at the Last Debate being angry at Athene. I nodded and smiled at Aristomache.

15

ARETE

We were feasted by Marissa, and I believe in the process Maecenas came to some trade agreement, but I don't know the details. I know there are too many things that only the Workers can make, and everyone wants those things. But in Marissa they were making some of them and getting others from the *Goodness*, like glass. We trade Worker-made glass to all the other cities. But they didn't have any Workers and they were making their own. I saw it in some of their windows, and while it was thick and streaky, it was still pretty impressive that they were making it themselves. They were also making iron. And they had plumbing—they didn't have wash-fountains in every house the way we did, but they had public baths, and public drinking fountains, like Rome. I thought they were doing pretty well.

I also admired their outreach to the refugees. It was what I'd wanted to do the moment I'd seen the villages of the Kyklades, and the Goodness Group were doing what we'd talked about—rescuing people and teaching them hygiene and technology and how to read and think independently. They didn't have printing presses, but they had literacy and fairly advanced math. Aristomache was a good teacher. I was impressed by how much they had achieved, especially when we got Aristomache off the subject of Yayzu and his mother and onto the subject of how they'd done it.

We were all sitting in their eating hall—they only had one. Most people, most of the time, cooked and ate in their own houses, which had little kitchens for that purpose, unlike ours. When they had a big feast, the important people ate in the eating hall, which also served as their Chamber. It was a big room with a pillared portico that held about a hundred. The rest were feasted outdoors in the agora, where they held their Assembly. The feast began at sundown. It consisted of a savory wheat and milk porridge, followed by fresh sardines, followed by roast ox, which had been roasting all afternoon, of course, and piles of absolutely marvelous honey cakes, also made with wheat. We didn't have wheat cakes or porridge often at home, as most of the wheat we grew was made straight into pasta. Cakes made from wheat were quite different from cakes made from barley and nut flours, much lighter and more fluffy. Wine was served, about three-quarters water, the strength I usually drank, weaker than adults usually had it at home. It took us most of the meal to get Aristomache off religion and onto the subject of what the *Goodness* had done.

We were seated at tables of ten, all nibbling honey cakes. Father and Maecenas and Ficino were at the top table with Terentius and some of the kings of Marissa. Aristomache, Maia, Erinna and I were with some of the members of the Chamber. All of the tables were mixed that way. Klymene and Neleus and the rest of the Nyx watch were back aboard, but we were assured that food was being sent to them.

"When we left, we sailed north. We wanted to get away from Kallisti, and we didn't know where we wanted to go exactly," Aristomache said. "We went to the mainland of Ionia, near Troy, and found a war going on. Not a Persian invasion, or even a Trojan one, just a petty civil war. The ship was really full, so we ferried most of our people over to Lesbos and set them down, then went back to rescue refugees. It was a purely humanitarian mission, we weren't thinking about anything else. They were mostly women and children who would have been enslaved. Of course we thought about Hekabe and Andromache, but we seem to be too early for them. The King of Troy is called Laomedon." She took a sip of wine.

"We founded Lucia pretty much where we'd landed, without doing any surveying or anything. There was water, which was all we really needed. There were olive trees too, which may mean there had once been a settlement there before, because olives usually mean people. We rescued goats and sheep from the mainland, and fortunately a lot of our refugees knew how to look after them and milk them and process wool, because we didn't." She laughed. "We had a lot to teach each other! That first winter was hard. Some of the girls were pregnant, some of ours from the festivals, and some of theirs, mostly from rape. They were all grateful because we'd rescued them—but what else could we have done? We had the weapons that were on the ship, of course, and we'd all had training."

"Of course," Erinna said, her eyes shining. "And you founded a city?"

"It wasn't a proper city at first, but we all worked on a constitution, and building it, of course."

"Why did you decide to call your city Lucia?" I asked. I knew I'd heard the name before, and I'd just remembered where. Father had said it had been Mother's birth name. It seemed like a peculiar coincidence, but I couldn't think of any possible connection.

"I think Matthias proposed it," she said. "It means Light of course, and new light was what we all wanted. It was only afterward we thought of Saint Lucy and seeing everything with new eyes, which is what the name means to us now, our fresh start and our turning back to God. It was Providence, I suppose."

"So how was it in the beginning?" Maia asked.

"We debated everything, like the philosophers we were, but sometimes the practical people we'd rescued had better ideas than any of us." Aristomache smiled at one of the locals at the table, who looked down, clearly embarrassed. "They brought us back to Earth whenever we floated off too far. And it was that winter that we came back to God. That was Matthias's proposal too."

"Who's Matthias, one of the people you rescued?" Maia asked.

Aristomache laughed and took another honey cake. "No, he's the one who used to be called Kebes. He took his real name back. Some of us did that and some didn't, according to what made us more comfortable. I didn't want to be Ellen again."

"We discussed that in the City of Amazons, too. I didn't want to be Ethel," Maia said, astonishing me. She seemed so very much a Maia that it didn't seem possible she could ever have been called anything else. Ellen was clearly derived from Helen, but Ethel came from that strange language they had spoken together briefly. Maia was right, it emphatically didn't suit her.

"We didn't force anyone to worship God, but Matthias wanted to build a church and become a priest, and most of us had originally been Christian and many of those who hadn't saw the light and wanted to be saved. I don't think any of us had worshipped the Greek gods seriously back in the Just City, and if we had it was because of being taken in by Athene."

"And your local recruits?" Erinna asked.

"They saw the sense in it, after the cruel things their gods had done to them. They understood the value of a god of forgiveness who understands us."

Some of the locals around the table were nodding. "A god who accepts everyone, even slaves and women," one of them said, shyly.

"So how did you go from one city to many cities?" Maia asked.

"We kept sending the ship out with a troop to rescue people, and eventually Lucia was running well and we had so many people that it seemed like a good idea to start a second city around the coast. Then we founded Marissa, here, when there was another war three years later, and we filled in the others. Usually the Goodness spends half the year sailing between the cities, trading, and the other half rescuing people and bringing them to whichever city needs people. We may found another city this year, on Ikaria. The Goodness tends to stay with a new city, and lots of experienced people stay to help things get going at first—people who know how to build and plant and everything like that. It takes quite a while for a city to get going properly. But Augustine is at that stage now, where it can grow naturally. We're ready to found a new city."

"And how many of you—the Goodness Group—stay in each city?" I asked.

Aristomache refilled her cup, considering. "It depends. There are lots in Lucia, of course, which is still our main base. Then there are lots wherever a city is new and needs help. Otherwise, well, the ideal is to have our cities working alone. Marissa doesn't really need anyone from Goodness now. It could have local doctors and teachers." There was a murmur from the locals at the table to the effect that they couldn't manage without her. "Nonsense," she said, but she looked pleased. "I stay because I'm getting old and my friends are here. Terentius stays because he's married and his children are growing up here. But Marissa doesn't need us. Hektor could do my job, he's teaching most of the younger children as it is. And Ekate is as good a doctor as Terentius now, and she has an apprentice of her own. She may go to the new city on Ikaria if we do get it going this summer. Locals move around and share their expertise too."

"So your ideal for your cities is self-sufficiency?" Erinna asked, swallowing another honey cake.

"It takes a while," Aristomache admitted. "And they're not big cities, compared to the Just City, never mind the Boston I remember. Most of our cities are about a thousand people. Marissa has eight hundred citizens, and almost that many children."

"Do the children have to pass tests to become ephebes?" I asked. I was thinking about my own looming adulthood tests, to be taken on my return.

"Just swear their confirmation oath," Aristomache said. "And we sort them into Platonic classes, of course. And they can vote in the Assembly then, the golds and silvers, and they're eligible for election to the Council when they're thirty. And nine of the Council are elected Kings every three years, and they make up the Committee of Kings. You have tests?"

"We have an oath too, but we also have to pass lots and lots of tests in all sorts of things. And then we swear, and do our military training, and read the *Republic*, and after two years we can vote in the Assembly, when we're eighteen, all of us, not just the guardians. But only the guardians serve in Chamber. My brothers are all adults, and I'll become an ephebe this year."

Maia was looking about the hall. It had frescoed walls that showed pleasant farming scenes with nymphs and shepherds lolling in fields and under trees, feasting on food very like the food we were enjoying. "You know, Plato was right," she said.

This was such a characteristic remark for Maia to make that I giggled, and so did Erinna beside me. We might have been drinking too much of the excellent wine.

"What was he right about?" Aristomache said. "A great many things, indeed, but what specifically are you thinking of?"

"He's right that there was a golden age in his past when people in Greek cities governed themselves properly according to the precepts he described. Nobody has ever believed a word of it. But he was right. It happened. And this is it." Maia laughed with an edge of hysteria. Ficino looked over to us, concerned. She took a sip of wine and went on. "It will deteriorate to timarchy, and then oligarchy, and so on, exactly as Plato wrote."

"Well, maybe," Aristomache said. "But for now it is the Good Life. For now it is definitely aristocracy. And besides, we're sure we've changed the world, introducing Christianity here and now, introducing civilized ideas and sanitation and medicine in the time before the Trojan War. We're not hiding away expecting everything we do to be destroyed by a volcano. Athene put us on Kallisti so we'd make no changes, cause no ripples, have no posterity. But we're out here making a difference, keeping the peace, helping the poor and the hungry. This is a new world. Maybe everything will be different and the Age of Gold won't vanish and there'll never be a Plato."

Maia hesitated, and I remembered that she had worried about breaking history if we intervened in the Kyklades. Father had reassured me that it wasn't possible, but I couldn't pass that reassurance on, at least not with proper citations. It might not be all that reassuring anyway, to think that Plato was right about everything degenerating. She closed her mouth as if she'd changed her mind about speaking, and when she did open it again what she said was: "You're right to be rescuing people."

Aristomache smiled at the rescued people around the table. "You know what you should do," she said, looking back to us. "You should go to Lucia for Passion Week. In addition to the religious celebration we have a music festival. You'd love it. And that's when the majority of the people who left the city are together, in Lucia at Easter. If you want to find out what we've been doing and see everyone, that's where you ought to go."

"When's Easter?" I asked.

"It's—" Aristomache and Maia began together, then caught each other's eyes and giggled, exactly as if they were both ephebes. "It's the first Lord's Day after the first full moon after the spring equinox," Aristomache finished alone. "So it's soon."

"What's the Lord's Day?" Erinna asked.

The locals clucked, but Aristomache explained quickly and easily. "Instead of having Ides and Nones, we call each seven-day period a week, and the days of the week have names, and the seventh day of each week is the Lord's Day, and a day of rest and religious worship."

"How can you celebrate Easter before Yayzu is even born?" Maia asked.

"He is our *eternal* savior," Aristomache said, serenely confident.

16

MAIA

People say I left the City of Amazons because I wanted comfort, but I have never loved comfort, only learning. I left for reasons of conscience—religious reasons.

I suppose the whole New Concordance was partly my fault, or rather Crocus's, making Ikaros translate Thomas Aquinas. The *Summa Theologica* is really long, and of course because Ikaros shouldn't have had the book he could only work on it in private, and when he had free time. It took him years. He still hadn't finished it by the time I left. Ikaros was the ultimate synthesist, but he had a fast mind that was always racing ahead to the next thing. Needing to translate Aquinas for Crocus, slowly, over a long time, and then reading his translation aloud, and answering Crocus's questions, forced him to keep coming back to it and thinking about it, instead of leaping on to something new.

Ikaros had found a way, in about 1500 A.D. from what I gather, to reconcile all the religions and philosophies in the world. He got into some considerable amount of trouble over this with the Pope and the Inquisition, and was saved, bizarrely enough, by Savonarola. I only know most of this secondhand through Lysias, who had heard of him before we came to the City. I barely know anything about Savonarola, or about the controversies of the Renaissance, and I can't look it up because it falls into the area we decided to exclude from our library. We have plenty of Renaissance art, and Renaissance people, but not religion and politics, because we wanted the Renaissance re-imagining of the classical world, not what Lysias described as the "medieval remnants" of Christianity. So Ikaros's *Oration on the Awesomeness of Humanity*, as Lysias calls it, saying that I could substitute "Pico della Mirandola" and "Dignity of Man" if I preferred, is not in the library, and neither are his nine hundred theses. His work was too Christian for the Library Committee. But excluding them didn't keep them out. They were still in Ikaros's head, and Ikaros's brain was in Ikaros's head, and what Ikaros's brain did when it was idle was make up perfectly logical but utterly insane theories of religious reconciliation.

He had been thinking about this on and off the whole time, from the moment when he saw that Pallas Athene was real. He had told me before the Last Debate that he had found a way to make it all make sense. But it wasn't until the first years in the City of Amazons, when he had to go through Aquinas line by line to translate it, that he came up with the rigorous and philosophically defensible thesis he called his New Concordance.

In the original city, where Sokrates and Tullius and Manlius and Ficino and all the other older Masters were there to sit on him, Ikaros couldn't do much about his religious theories except have occasional debates. His debates were always very popular with everyone, but he had to find people who wanted to debate with him, and his metaphysical theories were never a particularly popular topic. Athene never showed up for them, though she almost always came to his debates on other topics. Most Platonists are quite happy with Plato's metaphysics. Tullius was a Stoic. Even so, Ikaros is such a powerful orator, impassioned and fast-thinking and funny, that he could sometimes find people prepared to take on the more esoteric subjects. Even here, where everyone is trained in rhetoric, he stands out as surpassingly excellent. He's good at coming up with memorable images and working them all the way through an argument. He has always been a joy to listen to, in either language.

Once we were in the City of Amazons there was nobody better—nobody even as good. Klio was very good, and so were Myrto and Kreusa. Myrto was his most effective opponent. It wasn't until after she died, in the sixth year, that he gained complete sway over the city.

I could live in a city that has Ikaros in it, even though I disagreed with him a great deal. But I couldn't live in a city that required me to follow his crazy religion. I could be a Christian—I had been for the first eighteen years of my life. Or I could be a Platonic pagan, as I had been for the next eighteen. I had met Pallas Athene, talked to her. I had no doubt that the Olympians were real. I knew the way we worshipped them in the City was acceptable to Athene, who existed, who had set up the City and brought us the Workers, and then lost her temper and turned Sokrates into a gadfly and took the Workers away again. In Athenia they think she was right. I don't go as far as that, but I think what she did was understandable in the circumstances.

Athene thought we should be grateful to her for the opportunity to be in the City—and I was. I can't imagine any life that could have been better for me personally that led on from the nineteen years of my life I lived in the nineteenth century. I would never stop being grateful for the rescue that allowed me to be myself, to be respected as a scholar and a teacher. My feelings about Christianity were conflicted, while my gratitude to Athene was unfailing. On the other hand, Sokrates made some valid points in the Last Debate. I continued to question whether she had the right to do what she had done. But I still prayed to her nightly, and to the other Olympians on appropriate occasions.

What Ikaros did was to build a whole logical edifice reconciling everything—Plato, Aristotle, Christianity, Islam, Judaism, Buddhism, Stoicism, Epicureanism, Hedonism, Pythagoras, and sundry other ideas he'd picked up here and there. Bits of it were brilliant. For instance, he deduced from Athene saying that the City was just that justice must be a process, not a Form, and that reconciled contradictions between Plato and Aristotle's views of justice as well as being a fascinating idea about dynamic ideals. In fact, all of it was brilliant, if you considered it as pure logic. The problem was his axioms.

He set about the whole thing properly, I have to admit. He wrote it all up, ordered his theses, and announced a great debate. He sent invitations to the other cities and arranged a festival. He debated everybody who came prepared to argue against his points, and when they won on any issue he accepted that and incorporated that into his argument. It's just that the whole edifice was built on such terrible axioms. At first I had wanted it to be true, wanted the loving Father and Son I had grown up with to be real, as well as Athene. I wanted Jesus to be my savior, as I had believed as a child. But the more closely I looked at what Ikaros was doing, the less sense it made. His axioms were twisted. It was incredibly ingenious, and it all made perfect logical sense, each piece of the structure balanced on each other piece. But it was a castle of straws balanced on air. Athene just wasn't an angel, and wasn't perfect. Errors can be refuted, and as his errors were pointed out, by me and by others, he patched them. But his leaps of faith were not errors, and they were inarguable. I tried. Many of us tried. And it was all right as long as it was just a case of what Ikaros believed and tried to persuade people. It was when, after the festival, the Assembly of Amazons voted to make his New Concordance the official religion of the City of Amazons that I knew I had to leave. It would be practiced at festivals. I couldn't believe it. And I couldn't possibly teach it.

I'd told Klio and Axiothea that I was leaving, and they'd both tried to persuade me to stay. Axiothea was quite happy with the New Concordance. Klio had initially been even less in favor of it than I was, but once she began to study the logic she had been won over by the way Ikaros had integrated Platonic thought all through, and especially with his theory of dynamic ideals, which fit everything she believed. Klio had always disliked Ikaros, but now they began to work together on this project. They spent a lot of time together and became close. She told him about the religions and philosophies she knew about that were unfamiliar to him, and they worked together to reconcile them with everything else.

The New Concordance was generally very popular in the city, though I wasn't sure how many people even among its adherents really understood it properly.

I announced generally that I was leaving, though it hurt me to go. I had put eight years of my life into this city, this second attempt to do what Plato suggested, and I had a new generation of students growing up. I packed up my few possessions in my cloak: my comb, the notebooks where I was writing this autobiography, and my Botticelli book. I opened it and looked at the angels clustered around the *Madonna of the Pomegranates*. They were beautiful, and perhaps they were real, but Athene wasn't one of them. She was too much herself. She was real and imperfect and divine. She had rescued me from a life of unfulfilled emptiness and brought me to the City. I prayed to her now for guidance, and found myself thinking of my old house in the Remnant, and the rich colors of Botticelli's *Autumn* on the wall in Florentia, and Ficino's welcoming smile. I was right to leave. And I'd give this book to Simmea. That felt right too. I closed it and put it into my cloak, and went off to one last day's teaching. Other people would be taking over my classes the next morning.

"I've done you an injustice and I want to apologize," Ikaros said.

"What?" He had surprised me, coming up behind me after a gymnastics class. I had been teaching the littlest ones how to fall and roll and come up again, while the older ones were practicing with the discus. Then I had escorted the children through the wash-fountain, and handed them over to another teacher for their lute lesson. I was standing alone in the palaestra drying my hair on my kiton. It was autumn, almost olive season, so my damp bare skin was covered in goosebumps. I felt at a disadvantage, and quickly twisted my kiton back on, which left my damp hair dripping down my back. I never seemed to have any dignity around Ikaros. But when I looked at him, he wasn't looking at me but down at the sand.

"I like you, Maia, and perhaps Providence meant us to be together, but I messed everything up between us at the beginning. I didn't understand that you were truly saying no. I thought you were making a show of modest protest. Klio has explained to me that you were not. I'm really sorry."

I glared at him until he looked up at me. He wasn't laughing at me. He seemed sincere. "Klio had no right—why were you talking to her about me?"

"Because I want to understand why you oppose me so much."

I was astonished that he was taking me so seriously. "And you're finally acknowledging that you did something wrong?"

"Yes. I said so. I truly misunderstood all this time." He sat down on the wall that separated the palaestra from the street.

"I was screaming and struggling!"

"But your body—I thought—Klio has explained to me how I was wrong. It was a long explanation, but I do finally understand now." He smiled ruefully up at me. "Perhaps I shouldn't have been talking to her about it, but I'd never in a hundred years have understood without all that. I was wrong. And I have been punished by being deprived of your friendship, and Klio's friendship, all this time."

I didn't know what to say, so I just stared at him.

He sighed and rubbed his eyes. "Klio tells me that in her day, philosophy has discovered that people have two minds, a reasoning mind and an animal mind. Your reasoning mind believes that you have logical disagreements with me, but it is your animal mind driving what you feel. You have to get them into alignment to become godlike. That's what Plato meant with the metaphor of the charioteer."

"That is not what Plato meant!" I snapped, infuriated. At that moment, I'd have cheerfully turned him into a fly if I could. There's nothing more irritating than having somebody misinterpret my intentions and Plato's at the same time!

He went on. "Your animal mind wants to love me, the way your body wanted to love me that night under the trees. But your rational mind says no to love, because it's afraid to love, maybe because of what I did. So I want to persuade your rational mind."

I crossed my arms and leaned back against a pillar. "Go ahead. My rational mind only listens to rational arguments, not all this animal mind nonsense! And I think saying that part of me loves you is the most arrogant thing I've ever heard, even from you. And I am not afraid to love!"

"Who do you love?" he asked, rhetorically. "Lysias? No. He's your friend, you sometimes used to share a bed, but that's all. There's no love, no real passion. He has told Lukretia, and she told me."

I was furious with Lysias. "He had no right—"

Ikaros shrugged. "He feels passion for Lukretia, and she asked him about you."

I still didn't understand what was going on with Lysias and Lukretia. I missed him.

There were more women than men in the City of Amazons, but not by a huge degree—the city was about sixty percent female. I've heard ridiculous stories in other cities about harems and men being waited on by women in return for sexual favors. This seems to me to say rather more about men's fantasies than about anything real in Amazonia. There was a slight surplus of single women, but when you consider women who prefer other women, and families that have more than two adult partners, and men who maintained relationships with each other or with several women—Ikaros among them—it didn't amount to much. Heterosexual men were not a scarce resource. I'd had one or two discreet offers myself since Lysias moved out. It wasn't sex I was feeling deprived of.

"He shouldn't have said anything to her about me, and even if he did, she shouldn't have said anything to you," I said, as evenly as I could, braiding my damp hair and twisting it up on top of my head. "Is there any point to this scurrilous gossip?"

Ikaros ignored this. "So who do you love? Klio and Axiothea? Friends only, although they love each other. The children? You like them, you care about them, but you don't really love them. There's no love in your life, because you have closed off your soul, and that closes out the possibility of God's love. And that's why you won't consider the New Concordance."

"Nonsense," I said. "I love all those people. And the kind of love you're talking about is specifically what Plato tells us to avoid."

"No it's not. It's what he thinks you can use to bring yourself closer to God." He was leaning forward now, passionate. "It is by loving each other that our souls rise up and grow wings to approach heaven. It's in the *Phaedrus*." He pushed back his hair, which was starting to silver now, making him better-looking than ever. "For a while, before I read Aquinas again and realized I was mistaken, I thought that love was enough. Now I see it isn't, that we need reason even more. But we do need love."

"I don't oppose you because I don't have enough love. I oppose you because I *disagree* with you. Because you're *wrong*. I started off half-wanting to believe Athene was an angel, and that God was still there. The more I hear your proofs and arguments, the less I'm prepared to consider it."

He rubbed his eyes again, and I noticed that they were red-rimmed from too much rubbing. "Maia, you're one of the few people here who really can follow my thought, who's really capable of being an equal. So it's very frustrating when you disagree without a logical reason behind it. Won't you forgive me and let us start again?"

I considered that. "I don't know whether I can trust you," I said. Perhaps it was true that before Klio explained he just wasn't capable of understanding. His world had shaped him as badly as mine had shaped me. In a better world, in the City we both wanted to build, we could both have been philosopher kings. Perhaps then we could have loved each other as Plato wanted.

"Are you afraid of me? I don't want you to be afraid."

The children were mangling their scales behind us. Crocus went past carrying the window glass for the new crèche. "I'm not afraid that you're about to ravage me here and now. But you make me very uneasy. Today is the first time you've ever acknowledged what you did. You always laughed about it and dismissed it."

"I didn't understand. In my time women had no way to say yes to anything except marriage and keep their self-respect, so they had to make formal protests without really meaning them. That's what I thought you were doing. Klio had to explain to me that if people can't say yes, they can't say no either. It was a new idea."

"I understand that," I acknowledged. "But I'm afraid you're apologizing now because you want something, that you're trying to manipulate me. And you're making up all these theories about why I disagree, just like you make up all these theories about the gods, and none of it has any basis in reality. What do you want from me?"

"I want you to be my friend," he said, with no hesitation at all. "And I would like you to forgive me, if you can. And I don't want you to leave this city."

I stopped and thought for a moment, trying to examine my own feelings with philosophical rigor. It wasn't easy. I asked myself whether I could forgive him. I found that I could—I did understand what he had been thinking, and also I appreciated the effort he had made now to understand what he had done and accept that it was wrong. "I don't know whether it's possible for me to trust you enough to be your friend," I said, after a moment. "But I do understand what you did, what you were thinking. And I suppose I forgive you." He closed his eyes for a moment when I said that and his face went slack. I realized that my forgiveness really did matter to him. He was so naturally playful, even at his most serious. It was rare to see him this unguarded.

He opened his eyes again and looked at me. "So if I'm wrong about my theories about why you disagree, and you disagree logically, what's wrong with my logic?" he asked.

I let out a breath I hadn't known I was holding, and sat down tailor-fashion on the wall, leaning back against the pillar. "It's not your logic-structures, it's your axioms. I've said this before. Examine your assumptions. You say Athene is an angel, and you say angels are perfect. I can't see how you can believe that after the way Athene behaved in the Last Debate."

"She's an angel, and she's perfect. What she did may seem imperfect to us, but that's because our perceptions are imperfect. If we had complete knowledge, we'd be able to understand what she did."

"That doesn't make any sense. We know she exists. We know we can trust what she told us directly. And she said in the Last Debate that the gods don't know everything, and that part of her motivation in setting up the City was to see what happened. That's not something we don't understand because we're not perfect."

"She's of a lesser order of perfection than the Persons of the Trinity," he said. "But she's still perfect."

"She turned Sokrates into a gadfly!" I said.

"If we understood more, we'd understand why."

"I have no difficulty understanding why. How can you possibly argue that she was justified in what she did to him? She lost her temper. I have lost my own temper with students often enough to recognize that. It isn't the slow ones that make me do it, it's the insolent ones. Sokrates had some good arguments, but he was behaving like an insolent ephebe pushing the limits.

He wanted to make her angry, and he did. But anger and power go badly together, and she is a goddess. Power comes with responsibility. She killed him, or the next thing to it. She was wrong to do what she did and walk away."

Ikaros rubbed his eyes again. "She is wisdom. She had reasons we don't understand. She must have."

"Why is it hard to understand that she lost her temper?" I asked. Kreusa went by with two of her apprentices, all carrying baskets of herbs. She nodded to me, and I waved.

"You're trying to understand her as if she were human. But she's an angel," Ikaros said.

"It seems to me that she's a Homeric god, acting exactly the way Homer described the gods acting. We know that gods exist, gods like Athene, who have incredible powers that nevertheless have limits. We know they can make mistakes, and lose their tempers. We might think they should be more responsible, but we can't affect that. We also know they can be open to persuasion. For instance, Athene agreed to take us to rescue art treasures for the city, though she hadn't wanted to at first. She changed her mind. We know they can be kind to their worshippers. Athene brought all of the Masters here because we prayed for it. For me it was a rescue, and for most of the others too."

"For me, certainly," he acknowledged. "I was dying. She brought me here and healed me. But this is part of her goodness, her perfection."

"But we also know she can be unkind and imperfect, as witness losing her temper. You have to acknowledge that too."

He frowned, and reached toward his eyes then drew his hand back. "We don't understand everything she did, so it seems to us unkind. But if we knew more, we would understand. Exactly like the way Klio explained my actions so that I understand I committed an injustice, only the other way around. If it were explained to us properly, we would see that what she did was just, however it seems."

"I don't think there's any need for such an explanation—" He rubbed his eyes hard and I broke off. "Is there something wrong with your eyes?"

"Just a little tired and sore from so much close work. It's getting all the theses straight all day, and then working by lamplight translating Aquinas. I'm nearly done. At this rate I'll be done by spring. Or next summer anyway." He sighed, and squinted at me.

"You should try bathing them in warm milk at night," I suggested.

"Does that work?"

"It's what my father used to do." I could remember him so clearly, dabbing at his tired eyes when we'd been poring over a book all day.

He smiled at me. "I've been using oil. But I'll try it. Go on. You were going to give me the reason you don't believe the angelic orders are perfect. Do you believe that God is perfect?"

"Plato talks about the world of Forms and the nature of reality, and the perfect God that is Unity. You think that's the same God as the Christian God the Father, but I see no evidence for it."

"It makes logical sense. Why do you want evidence?"

I shook my head. "Why do you deny the need for evidence, and try to explain away evidence that doesn't fit your structure? We know Athene exists, and we know she's pretty much the way Homer describes her, and so we can make a reasonable guess from that and from the way she behaved and the way she talked when she was here and from things like encouraging us building temples and having festivals and sacrifices, that the Olympians exist and are pretty much, if not exactly, the way the Homer described them. Plato was wrong about that. Plato would have censored Homer because of showing the gods behaving exactly the kind of way Athene behaved."

"But the angels, and Homer's gods if you want to call them that, are on a level between us and God."

"Perhaps. What I think is that in the Allegory of the Cave, where we are the prisoners watching shadows flickering on the cave walls, perhaps the gods are the things behind the fire casting the shadows."

"There are entire hierarchies of levels, with different angels, and the Forms are part of that." He reached toward his eyes again, and again stopped himself.

"I've read your theses. I agree that the internal logic makes sense. You don't have to go through it all again for me now."

"But if you can follow the logic—"

"I can follow the logic and still continue to disagree, when the logic doesn't fit the facts! What we know about Athene does not lead us to be able to deduce anything about unlimited omnipotent deities that may or may not exist, and may or may not be in overall control of the Olympians. You didn't ask her about this, did you? You had plenty of chances. She came to almost all your debates."

"All of them unless they were about metaphysics," he said, and smiled. "She never wanted to talk about that. And I like to work things out for myself." Suddenly the palaestra was full of children, running and shouting, as they were released from their lute lesson.

"But you must see that when you build huge complex structures of dialectic that purport to reconcile Christianity, Judaism, Islam, Platonism, Aristotelianism, and Buddhism with the presence here of Athene, it has to fit the evidence as well as making logical sense." I raised my voice a little and leaned forward eagerly as the children streamed past us.

"It fits the facts if you acknowledge that all the wise are in agreement about everything essential. It's just a case of understanding how and reconciling supposed contradictions. And the reason we see supposed contradictions and don't understand everything about what Athene did is because we're too imperfect," he said, also leaning forward until our foreheads were nearly touching.

I moved back and sat up straight again. "In saying that, you have left the path of philosophy. Literally. You're denying sophia, betraying what she really was."

"If we became angels ourselves, which in my system we might be able to achieve, then we could understand what she was. For now, we don't fully understand. We can't."

"I can't believe that," I said. "And that's why I'm going to leave this city, because this isn't just a disagreement where I can accept the majority vote was against me, this is about our own beliefs and practice. I can't believe it, and I can't practice it."

"You don't have to leave, even though you disagree. We've voted to accept it as the majority religion and practice it at festivals, but we'll have freedom of conscience. You can believe what you want." He reached out to pat my arm, then thought better of it and drew his hand back.

"But I'd have to teach it, and I can't do that," I said.

"You wouldn't have to believe it to teach it!"

"You might not, but I would." I stood up. He stayed where he was on the wall.

"Don't go. Plotinus and Sokrates and Tullius and Myrto are dead, and I almost never see Ficino. Klio's marvelous, and some of the Children are coming along, but there are too few people here who can stretch my mind."

"Are you really suggesting I stay here just to argue with you?"

"Yes!" He laughed suddenly. "How absurd this is."

I laughed with him. And then I left the City of Amazons and went to the Remnant, to start again.

17

ARETE

All my life I'd heard people talk about Kebes and the Goodness Group and the Lost City as if they were all one thing, and it took a lot for me to take it in that they weren't. Kebes was a person, a person now calling himself Matthias, and the Goodness Group consisted of a hundred and fifty people with divided opinions about things, and they weren't one Lost City, they were a whole network of civilization. It was a bit of a shock. The other thing I had never thought about until I talked to Aristomache was that of course they had left during the Last Debate, or at the very end, at the moment when Sokrates turned into a gadfly. They didn't know anything about what had happened afterward. They didn't know that we hadn't seen Athene since, until Father told them so. They didn't know that theirs was only the first defection, nor that the rest of us had lived in a constant state of warfare. They hadn't taken any art when they left, they hadn't taken anything but the *Goodness* and their own skills. All this time they'd been doing what Mother had always said people ought to do and making more art instead of squabbling over the art we had. They'd been doing the same with technology too, starting with what they had and knew and going on from there.

I slept in my hammock on board, ready for my watch that began at dawn. I woke early and went up on deck before the sky began to pale. I had thought of a safe way of testing to discover whether I could fly, but I needed to be alone with my brothers to try it. Of course, wonderful as sea voyages are, being alone is almost impossible to manage. Even conversations are constantly being interrupted. I wanted to try diving from the deck, which I had done several times to go ashore, but instead of diving, fly. If it didn't work then I'd hit the water as normal. I had forgotten that the deck lights would be on, and that Neleus and the other members of the Nyx watch would be around, even with the ship safely tied up at harbor.

I took my turn on watch, though it was as unlike the watch of the day before as anything could be. I sat at the masthead with nothing to see but Marissa on one side and the rippling sea at the other. Phaedrus came up part way through and told me the ship's council were meeting, which didn't surprise me. I hoped we'd go to Lucia and the music festival. I liked music, and

I wanted to meet more of the Goodness Group. "Mother would have liked them," I said to Phaedrus.

He nodded thoughtfully. "I think she would. Except maybe for the religious stuff."

"But why couldn't it be true? If Father's incarnate now, why shouldn't Yayzu have done the same thing in Roman times, the way Aristomache says?"

"Oh, interesting, I hadn't thought of that." Phaedrus put an arm around the mast and leaned out, looking over the city.

"Can you fly?" I asked, seeing that.

"Walk on the air like we did on Ikaria? I haven't tried it this high up, but I'm sure I could."

"No, really fly, swoop about like a bird. I feel I can, but I haven't tried it because I don't want anyone to see me."

"No, it would be pretty conspicuous." He grinned. "I don't feel that I could, but I don't feel that I couldn't either. Have you found anything else you can do?"

"Understand languages I don't know. Maia and Aristomache started speaking some strange language yesterday and I understood it clearly, though I'd definitely never heard it before."

"Wow." He looked impressed. "Hard to test. Though I suppose you could go around asking the Masters and the Children to say something in their birth languages. But they're supposed to have forgotten them. I've never heard anyone speak in them. Maia's usually so properly Platonic, too. Which of them started it?"

"Aristomache. I suppose in the Goodness Group things are different."

"I don't think they were the ones who raided us. They don't even have any art that isn't Christian, why would they want the head of Victory? But I hope Father believes that."

"Who do you think it was?" I asked.

"Psyche or the Amazons, like normal," he said. "I believe Alkibiades that it wasn't Athenia, and Sokratea has never broken a treaty without a declaration."

"Do you think Father will believe it?"

"There would have to be good evidence. But it should be easy enough to find out where the *Goodness* was at the time, once we catch up with them. I hope he will accept it. If not, it's going to be exceedingly awkward. And if he does start to believe it, I hope he doesn't want to go straight home and immediately get vengeance there. I hope we go to the music festival."

"So do I. Will you do me a favor? When we get the chance, I want to go off somewhere and test flying, and test lifting you when I fly," I said.

"Sure. I want to try that too. And the language thing. I wonder if we all have the same powers or if we all have different ones." He sounded excited to find out. "The only thing I've tried is healing."

"Who did you heal?"

"Caerellia had a bad tooth, and I fixed that. And one of the women at the feast last night had a growth in her belly. It felt uncomfortable being near them, and I knew what to do, so I just did it."

"I haven't felt anything like that. But maybe I just haven't been near anyone who's sick. Though Ficino's awfully old and frail, there isn't anything actually wrong with him, at least not as far as I know."

"I'll try walking by him and see if I feel anything, and if there is, put it right. By the dog, this is great!"

"Aren't you worried about our powers at all?" I asked.

"I'm worried about Fate and Necessity, and screwing things up badly, like getting lost if I try to go outside time and that sort of thing," he said, after a moment's hesitation. "I'm excited about the powers, though. I want to find out what we can do and how it works and have fun with it. I understand why old Kallikles is worried about telling Rhea. But we've never been like everyone else, really. This just makes it more solid."

"Do you still want to develop an excellence of volcanoes?"

He took a step up onto the air and then back down onto the masthead beside me. "I really do. Imagine being able to direct the lava. Imagine bathing in it. Imagine having control over it."

I shuddered, imagining burning up. The volcano had always frightened me. "You can definitely have that."

Erinna called him to stop loitering and get about his duties, so he went back down to the deck, where she had him coiling rope. I stayed at the masthead. Now I was finally getting my free time to think, and I was a little bored.

When my watch was over and I went down to the deck, Phaedrus came up to me. "Nope," he said. "Nothing wrong with Ficino that I can tell. Also, I got Maecenas and Ficino to say things in their old languages, and they were completely incomprehensible. But we're going to the festival."

"Good. What did you get Ficino to say?"

"Some poetry. It sounded a bit like Latin, but more sing-song. I could make out the occasional word that pretty much was Latin, but that's all."

I found sitting Ficino in the agora of Marissa, drinking wine and talking to a group of locals about Plato. He drew me deftly into the discussion, which was examining the question of whether this was a republic. It seemed to me quite clear that it was, and that it was as Maia had said the night before, one of the fabled republics Plato had heard of.

Sitting there, though, I realized that their classes were much more pronounced than ours. There's a thing people say, that you can tell somebody is gold without checking their cloak pin. It means they are truly excellent, so much so that their quality really shows. People used to say it about my parents. In Marissa, you really could tell, but not because of shining excellence. The people talking to Ficino were all golds, and they were all free to sit drinking wine in the middle of the afternoon. They were cleaner and somehow glossier than the people working around us. I watched a man carrying a sack and a woman buying vegetables. Both of them wore bronze pins. Their kitons were shabbier, more faded, frayed at the edges. Of course, there are always people who let their clothes fall into disrepair. But this wasn't a case of sloppy individuals or personal idiosyncrasy. The people sitting with us all had more embroidery on their kitons, and while none of them were fat they tended to be a little plumper than the others. I thought back to the feast the night before. Had everyone inside the hall been a gold? I thought perhaps they had. This visible class difference was nothing like the poverty in the Kyklades. But it was strange to me.

Just then a woman came up to our table with a pitcher. Because I'd been thinking about it I noticed that she was wearing a bronze pin, of the same design we used at home. I also saw that there was something odd about her attitude. She seemed somehow lacking in confidence. She refilled our wine cups, deferentially, and one of the men paid her—paid her with a coin. I had read about money, but not seen it before. I tried not to gape.

After a while, I persuaded Ficino to walk through the city with me. As we walked I drew him around to the subject of the verses he'd recited to Phaedrus. He repeated them to me patiently, they were by Petrarka on the subject of someone thinking about how people in future ages were deprived by not being able to see a woman called Laura. He then translated them into Latin for me. I had understood them perfectly. So, clearly my divine language ability worked on all languages. It seemed as if there would be places it would be more useful than on Kallisti, where everyone spoke Greek and Latin and nobody spoke anything else, but it still seemed like a fun ability. I wondered whether Father could do it. I wondered whether I could speak the other languages or only understand them. That would be hard to test without giving myself away, but maybe I could try it with Father.

"Why are you and Phaedrus suddenly interested in Italian poetry?" Ficino asked.

I gaped at him, entirely without an answer. If I'd known Petrarka had written in Italian as well as Latin, I could have said I was interested because of that, but I'd had no idea. "We were just wondering what it sounded like,"

I said, feebly. "It's beautiful. And that's such an interesting thought. Did you see her?"

He smiled. "She'd been dead for almost two hundred years before I read the poem."

"It's hard to understand the time things take, chronology, that kind of thing. The vast expanses of history."

We had walked through the streets so that we were now outside the marble pillars of the entrance to the colosseum. Ficino stopped. "It's especially hard because we're at the wrong end of it, and because you've met people from so many different times. Why shouldn't I have seen Laura, when we both lived in Florentia in the Renaissance, as if it was all one big party?"

"She could be here, or Petrarka could at least," I said.

"Too good a Christian, for all that he loved classical learning," Ficino said. "And he didn't know Greek, so he couldn't have read Plato. Before I translated his work, Plato was only a legend in Italy."

"It's so hard to imagine," I said. "Ages without Plato. How wonderful that you could bring him back." I wondered if my language gift could be used in that way.

Ficino smiled, and gestured to the colosseum. "Shall we go in?"

Inside, the colosseum descended in banks of earthwork seats down to a raked sand oval. They clearly used it as a palaestra, as there were weights stacked up ready for use. It was empty, and Ficino and I walked down the steps that divided seating sections from each other. I walked out onto the sand and sang a couple of lines from one of Father's praise songs. "Good acoustics," I said. "I expect they use it as a theater too." Looking up, I saw that it was built of earth and marble, not concrete the way the colosseum in Rome is described.

"Probably they use it for all kinds of things," Ficino said. "There are grills on the gates there, look."

We walked over to the gates. There was a strange smell there too, musky and acrid. "Animals," I said. "Do you think they have animal fights in here?"

"The Romans did," Ficino said. "And clearly they do." He was peering in through the grill. "I can see what might be a trident. Maybe they have Roman gladiatorial combat too."

"But they seem so nice," I said. I had to step back because the smell was making me feel queasy.

"Well, the Romans did it, and most of these Marissans are from the mainland and would be used to watching violent kinds of entertainment." Ficino wasn't as disturbed as I was. "I wonder what Aristomache thinks of it."

"I don't like to think of them raking blood off the sand," I said, looking at the sand, which seemed so clean and innocent. "I don't like to think of the Romans doing it either."

"The problem with only giving you art that shows good people doing good things is that it makes you uncompromising, and doesn't give you useful examples," Ficino said. "This isn't a dark secret. It's open to everyone."

As if to demonstrate this, a group of ephebes came in and, after greeting us politely, started to race around the outside of the circuit, exactly as my friends and I would in the palaestra at home.

We walked back through the city. I realized this time that the houses near the agora were larger and better-built than the ones further away. The smaller ones didn't have glass in their windows, just wooden shutters. I saw a woman in a courtyard bent over, turning a stone on another stone. "What's she doing?" I asked.

Ficino looked. "Grinding wheat."

"They don't have Workers, or electricity," I said.

"They don't even have wind or water mills, which we used to grind wheat to flour in my time. They're starting without our technological base."

Just then another woman came out into the courtyard and started to berate the woman turning the stone. We moved away.

"They have social classes," I said.

"Yes," Ficino agreed.

"And money. And wealth and poverty."

"They started with adults who knew those things," Ficino said. "That must have made it difficult."

"Are they pursuing excellence?" I asked.

Ficino looked at me approvingly. "That's the question I've been asking myself. They haven't said they are. They talk about rescuing people and spreading their civilization. But they haven't mentioned excellence at all. And in the discussion just now, did you notice how much of what they said was about politics?"

"You kept asking about philosophy, and they always answered in terms of politics," I said. It was clear, now that I thought about it.

Ficino nodded. "I can't help thinking about Kebes, how stubborn he was. These cities are more than just Kebes, and they're clearly very influenced by the culture of the people they rescued, as well as what the *Goodness* brought. Do you remember your project on how to tell how philosophical a city is?"

I remembered it very well. I nodded.

"How would you assess this one?" We stepped out of the way of a man leading a laden donkey.

"The people you were debating with seemed to understand rhetoric, and to want to debate. But they don't have a library," I said. "Of course, one of the things they want from us is books, and it must be very difficult without."

"It may seem strange to you, but is possible to hand-copy books," Ficino said. "We did it in my day. They've done it too. They have versions of the Bible, the holy book of Christianity, as best they can remember it. And they have versions of Plato, the ones Aristomache knows by heart. There are some books in the school. But you're right that they don't have a library, and that's significant. There's a school and a church and a colosseum." Ficino gestured to a house we were passing, one of the ones with window glass. "They're doing well on a material level, not compared to us, but compared to what we've seen in the islands."

"But maybe not so much philosophically?"

"I keep reminding myself that it was justice Kebes cried out for."

"It was?" I'd never heard that.

"At the Last Debate. I was trying to hold him back but he leaped up onto the rostrum and started yelling out. 'These pagan gods are unjust.'"

We were almost back in the agora. "Athene had just acted very unjustly."

"Yes. But the gadfly that had been Sokrates spurned Kebes and flew toward your parents, which has always seemed to me an indisputable sign. Still, Kebes started rallying people, and off they went." He looked around him. "And here they are, and we'll have to make the best of it."

We spent two more days in Marissa. On the second of them there was a bull baiting in the colosseum. Neleus and Erinna went, but I volunteered for duty aboard to avoid it. Erinna said it was disgusting, and Neleus said it was kind of fun but he wouldn't go again. Maia, who also hadn't attended, said she was glad that at least they ate the bull afterward. Father just shook his head.

We left Marissa with a plan. We'd sail to Chios and spend a night at the Goodness city there, Theodoros, the gift of God, and then sail on to Lucia. We should arrive there just before the festival began. Aristomache asked if she could sail with us, and so did half a dozen other Marissans. They only had one ship, and so moving between islands only happened when the *Goodness* called. In addition, the *Goodness* made a circuit of their eight cities, so taking a voyage meant being away from home for a long period. We intended to return to Kallisti immediately after the festival, and could bring them home to Marissa on the way. There was also talk of sending a diplomatic mission to Kallisti. I happened to be present when this was discussed. "Won't that be for Lucia to decide?" Caerellia asked Deiphobos, who was one of the elected Kings of Marissa.

"Oh, I don't think it would be a problem if we want to send somebody. They can send somebody too, if they want to. We wouldn't speak for them, only for ourselves. We're not subject to Lucia. Though of course, we know how much we owe them, and we're all good friends."

Our sailing plan did not allow for bad weather. The weather, which had been good all the way from Kallisti, now let us down badly. The first day I was reminded of the storms in the *Aeneid* and the *Odyssey*. Many people were sick, and we had to manage the ship short-handed. I fell once wrestling sails, and did instinctively fly for a moment until I could regain the yard. I don't think anyone saw anything more than a well-recovered stumble; they were all too busy with their own tasks. The second day, when there was no letup in the gale, it reminded me of my dream where the ship was history being blown out of control by stormwinds. After that the days blurred together and the storm didn't remind me of anything except itself. I was quite sure we were going to founder, and worried about how long I could fly and how many people I could carry. There were just too many people aboard I loved. I finally understood Father not wanting all of us to come. It wasn't even possible to stay near one person I cared about. Too much of the time, if we'd breached I wouldn't have been able to save any of them. I decided that Phaedrus and Kallikles could save themselves, and if Erinna and Maia and Ficino and Neleus and Father weren't near enough I'd just grab whoever was and save them, even if it was sarcastic Caerellia or grumpy Phaenarete. I slept in exhausted snatches and took water to those too weak to fetch it for themselves. I discovered I had no divine abilities to heal, no sense of what was wrong with people the way Phaedrus described.

When I woke on the fourth or fifth morning to smooth sailing, and clear skies with visible stars, I actually wept.

18

ARETE

We had been blown in all directions, too far from safe harbors, and had sailed with the wind, avoiding islands as hazards. We were sure we were far to the northwest of Chios. We had no idea where we were. We hadn't seen any islands for days except as chaotic shapes whose rocks could destroy us. Now we had an even wind, and we were sailing east. Some people said we should head back to Marissa, or home to Kallisti, but Maecenas was set on visiting Lucia.

So, to my surprise, was Father. I wanted to talk to him about my powers, but the first time I caught him anything like alone he was standing at the rail with Neleus, looking out at the waves. Neleus had been extremely ill all through the storm and still looked wobbly. He was one of the very last people I wanted to know about my powers. It was unfair enough as it was. "I want to go to their city to see Kebes. Or Matthias if that's what he wants to call himself," Father said, as I came up to them, sounding as grim as ever I had heard him.

"But do you really still think he killed Mother?" I asked. "They don't have any of our art, and they said they avoided Kallisti until now for fear of Athene."

"Perhaps he didn't kill her," Father agreed. He looked at me and then at Neleus. "I still want to know where the *Goodness* was that day. The Marissans may not know everything. But even if he didn't—I didn't want to tell you. But she wrote in her autobiography that he raped her."

"What?" I thought for a moment that he meant Kebes had raped Mother on the day she was killed.

"When? Before the Last Debate?" Neleus asked.

"Yes. At the last Festival of Hera." Father was staring out at a shadow of a shoreline on the horizon. *Before I was born*, I thought, *and only a few months after Neleus was born.*

"But if it was the Festival of Hera, weren't they supposed to . . . ?" Neleus asked.

"They were supposed to try to make a baby. He wasn't supposed to take her against her will when she was saying no." Father sounded vehement enough to bring the storm back. I saw people turning to look from across the deck.

"If they'd been married in front of everyone . . ." Neleus trailed off again.

"That's why she didn't tell anyone. She didn't tell *me*." There was a lot of pain in his voice, but it was quieter now. "It was rape, and he hurt her, and I'm going to kill him."

"Right," Neleus said. "I'll help."

"The punishment for rape is flogging," I said. I had been reading the laws in preparation for my adulthood tests. "And it would be very hard to prove now, even with her direct written testimony."

"We're not going to take him to court in the City, we're going to kill him in Lucia," Father said, looking irritated. Neleus nodded.

"But—" I opened my mouth and then stopped. But the rule of law, I'd wanted to say, but the terrible things that happen when bloodfeud replaces it? And why had Mother kept quiet about the rape except to prevent exactly this? Then again, the idea that she had been raped and hadn't told anyone for so many years was awful. The thought of it made my stomach churn. "I want to kill him too. I think rape should be considered a more serious offense."

"When you're an adult you should argue that in Chamber," Father said. "Lots of us would support that. It has the death penalty in the City of Amazons."

"Maybe we could drag him back and try him there," Neleus said. "And look for the head at the same time."

"No. I couldn't bear being on the ship with him for that long. I'm not sure I'm going to be able to bear having any conversation with him at all. I'm going to kill him as soon as I possibly can." Father bit his lip hard, but even so tears ran down his cheeks. "I hate the thought that he's still alive and breathing after he did that to her."

So did I. "But what about trade agreements and diplomatic relationships between us and the Goodness Group?" I asked.

"Once Kebes is dead, we can make agreements."

"But you can't just walk up to him in the street and run him through, and then carry on with the others as if you didn't do it," Neleus said. "You'll have to either make it seem as if you didn't do it, or else tell everyone why. Unless you could find a pretext. Or fake an accident somehow."

"You're right," Father said. "I need to find a way of killing him that's personal and acceptable and doesn't destroy all possibility of friendship between our cities later. I wonder whether they allow duels?"

"It doesn't seem likely," I said, appalled.

"Kebes probably wouldn't agree to one anyway. He's fought me before, he knows I'm better."

"Does he know that you hate him?" I asked.

"Yes. Though he has no idea how much more I hate him now that I know what he did to Simmea. I wish I'd killed him long ago when I had his neck under my hand in the palaestra."

"Why didn't you?" Neleus asked.

"He was her friend and she valued him," Father said, sobbing openly now. Maia was coming toward us. I waved her away, but she kept coming. "She thought he was her friend and he did that to her."

He put his hands up to his face, pushed away from the rail and went below before Maia reached us.

"What's wrong with Pytheas now?" Maia asked.

Neleus and I looked at each other. "Just missing Mother," I said.

"I miss Simmea myself, but—" she shook her head. "I had thought the journey was doing him good."

"It is," I said, truthfully. "He hasn't been like that anything like as often since we set off."

"I suppose it's hard for him to deal with knowing it wasn't the Goodness Group who killed her," Maia said, staring after him. "He was so hoping for spectacular revenge. You'd think he'd realize it does no good. It wouldn't matter how much he avenged her, he wouldn't get her back."

Neleus grunted and went off after Father.

We were lost for two more days and stopped for water twice before we found somewhere that matched our charts. Father told me that he knew exactly where we were all the time, but of course he couldn't let anyone know, other than by suggesting a direction, and they wouldn't always listen. I didn't have that sense, and neither did Phaedrus or Kallikles, but Father said it probably was just familiarity with the geography.

Once we knew our location we crept south along the shore of Asia until we passed Lemnos, which was full of savage villages. We didn't go ashore. Then we reached Lesbos, where we arrived at a well-built city of marble columns and whitewashed stone houses with red tile roofs on the north shore. The Goodness was tied up at the wharf. It looked just like the Excellence except that it seemed to be missing a mast and the sides were visibly patched with wood of different shades. I wondered how difficult it was to maintain her without Workers.

"We have missed the festival," Aristomache said sadly, as we tacked into the harbor under a blazing noon sun. "Today's the last day. There'll be nothing left but gladiatorial combats. And I was hoping your father would compete. I remember his music."

"If his lyre didn't get drowned in the storm I'm sure he will compete if there's a chance," I said. "And even if we have completely missed it, I'm sure he'd play for you. There's nothing he likes better than singing, except maybe composing."

We were close enough now to see that people on shore were rushing about in evident surprise. "We're not going to be able to tie up the way we did at Marissa, there's only room for one ship," Erinna said.

After the envoys went ashore and negotiated with the Lucians, we arranged to anchor in the harbor, keep one watch aboard ship at all times, and send everyone else ashore in the little boat. "And no swimming!" Caerellia said, firmly. "We're in civilization here and don't you forget it!"

I went ashore with Aristomache and Maia and Neleus. Erinna had gone in an earlier group, with Ficino, though she had patted my arm and nodded when Ficino had said he'd see me ashore. Father had also gone ahead, his lyre slung over his shoulder, but he was talking to somebody on the quay. He finished his conversation and came over to join us. "The *Goodness* was in Troy when Simmea was killed," he said.

"Oh Pytheas, you didn't still think we might have done it?" Aristomache asked, putting her hand on his arm.

"I wanted to be sure," Father said.

"He's been a little crazed with grief ever since it happened," Maia said, in that language she and Aristomache shared.

"Death is a terrible thing without salvation," Aristomache replied, in the same language.

"What's that?" Neleus asked, perplexed.

Father and I exchanged glances, and I saw that he understood, as I did.

"Sorry," Aristomache said. "Come on. Most people will have gone to the agora. It's Easter day, we celebrate Yayzu risen. Tonight we will eat lamb and bread."

Lucia was decorated for festival, with flower garlands set on pillars, just the way we did it at home. It seemed very familiar, laid out on the same pattern as our cities and as Marissa, with broad streets leading to a central agora. On the top of the hill was a colosseum. We passed another huge marble Madonna, also garlanded with flowers. "Auge?" I asked.

"She's our best sculptor," Aristomache confirmed, clearly proud of her. "She lives and works here, but her work stands in all our cities. This is Our Lady of Peace." It was lovely. I could hear choral singing as we came toward the agora. A man passing handed me a honey cake from his basket. Everything seemed peaceful and pleasant. Father took a honey cake but tucked it into his kiton. I wondered suddenly whether I'd seen him eating in Marissa, or just sitting at the table moving food around? He took hospitality very seriously. Well, I had bitten into my honey cake, so it was too late. These people were my friends. I took a colored egg from a smiling girl, and Aristomache gave her a coin. I'd never get used to paying for things.

In the agora, outside a temple, there was a gruesome wooden statue of a man being tortured. He was fixed to a cross by nails through his palms and feet, he had scars of whipping, and his face was distorted by pain. It was painted in full color, just to make the blood and everything more obvious. It was hideous, and yet also beautiful. I couldn't look away from it. There were a couple of paintings in the Botticelli book that I now realized were also depictions of this story—in one he's flanked by an angel and a person dressed in long hair, with a sad old man and a dove hovering behind. In the other a person and an angel are flinging themselves around at the foot of the cross. I had always wondered what was going on in those pictures. But Botticelli's man pinned to the cross seemed peaceful and happy, and also the least interesting thing in the pictures. Here he was clearly in agony.

"Who is that?" I asked.

"Yayzu," Aristomache said.

"They did *that* to him?" I said, appalled. I looked at Father. Clearly he had very good reasons for not letting people know he was really a god.

He smiled down at me. "Not a nice way to die," he said. "Suffocation is what actually killed them. It took days sometimes. It was a Roman method of extreme punishment."

"Why do they have that there?" I asked, as Maia opened her mouth to defend her beloved Romans.

"Yayzu returned from the dead," Aristomache said. "And through him, so will we all. He conquered death, not just for himself but for all of us through all of time. He went through that to save us all. Looking at the cross reminds us not that he died, but that he went beyond death, and so will we all." Even Maia looked moved. Father smiled again, a smile that made me uneasy.

Just then I spotted Ficino and Erinna on the other side of the agora, deep in conversation with a group of strangers. Ficino was always easy to pick out in a crowd because of his red hat. I waved, but they didn't see me. I was looking at them, so I was surprised when I looked back and saw that a burly man in a floppy Phrygian cap had joined us. He was wearing leggings and a tunic, not a kiton. Since it was a festival, I assumed it was a costume for a play. He was about Father's age, clearly one of the Children.

"Aristomache, Maia, Pytheas, joy to you," he said. "What a surprise to see you here."

"Kebes," Father said, nodding. I took an involuntary step backward. This was Kebes? Apart from his fancy dress, he seemed so ordinary.

"Joy to you, Matthias," Aristomache said, seeming delighted to see him. "I've been doing my best to explain to everyone what we've been doing, but you'll be able to do it so much better."

"And what have *you* been doing?" Kebes said, mostly to Father.

"Walking in the steps of Sokrates," Father said, calmly and evenly, and, typically, speaking perfect truth even if it wasn't very helpful information.

I took a step forward again, so I was next to Maia, who hadn't said anything at all. She glanced down at me, looking worried, and that drew Kebes's attention to me for the first time. He looked at me, and then quickly at Father, and then he laughed. "Not so much with the agape, then, Pytheas?"

I didn't see Father move, but suddenly Kebes was on his back on the ground with his cap in the dust. He had a shaved circle on the top of his head.

Maia grabbed Father, and the crowd that had been moving to and fro across the agora crystallized around us, and other people also grabbed Father. Aristomache bent over Kebes as he was starting to get up. "Simmea was killed by pirates recently," she said to Kebes, directly into his face. She was about half his size and more than twice his age, but she clearly wasn't afraid of him.

Kebes froze as he was, up on one elbow, clearly shocked. "Killed?"

"Also," Father said, calmly, as if continuing a debate, standing quite still and ignoring the people holding onto him, "What did you imagine you were doing calling your city after my wife?"

Kebes face immediately closed up again.

"What?" Maia asked, puzzled.

"Lucia was Mother's childhood name," I said. Maia looked down at Kebes and let go of her grip on Father.

"I had no idea she was dead," Kebes said, getting up. He was a head taller than Father, but I hadn't noticed it until now. He dusted himself off, then picked up his hat. He looked at me again, and didn't laugh this time. His expression mingled grief and anger.

"So why did you call the city after my mother?" I asked, while I had his attention.

"We all wanted light," Kebes said, looking truculent. "It's a coincidence."

Aristomache and most of the strangers in the little crowd around us looked satisfied. Father looked as if his face was carved from marble and couldn't change expression. I didn't believe Kebes. Moreover, even though I didn't know him and couldn't possibly tell, I knew he was lying. It was certain knowledge— another divine power unfolding itself in me.

"Look, no hard—" Kebes stopped, looking at Father. "I suppose there are hard feelings on both sides. But she's dead. Let's agree to leave each other alone."

"I don't suppose you'd care to wrestle a bout in the palaestra?" Father asked, the essence of politeness. People were still holding on to his arms, but he wasn't struggling at all.

"No, I really wouldn't," Kebes said. "But I'll tell you what. The music competitions are over. But we could have another, just the two of us, tomorrow. Extend the festival a little. Compete in a different sphere. That way there will be no damage done."

Father was smiling one of his most terrifying smiles now. "But what if I want to do damage?"

"Do it with your lyre," Kebes said.

Father had won every musical competition he had entered in my life-time, and probably before it as well. If Kebes knew how good he was in the palaestra, Kebes must also have also known how good he was at music. I didn't understand why he would even make such a suggestion, unless he was hoping to deflect Father's anger by giving him a victory that wouldn't hurt.

"I know what you did to her," Father said, intent on Kebes, ignoring the people still holding his arms and the large circle of people gathered around us listening.

"I didn't do anything to her you didn't do too," Kebes said, deliberately glancing at me. "Did I give her a child?"

I stepped between them before Father could throttle Kebes in broad day-light in the agora before half of Lucia and half the crew of *Excellence.* "You are talking about *my mother*," I said. "And she's dead."

"Nothing against you, little one. And I'm very sorry she's dead," Kebes said, looking down at me. "I loved her. And she loved me." He meant what he was saying. But that didn't mean it was true, only that he believed it.

Father put a hand on my shoulder, and I realized they must have let him go and that he was ready to thrust me aside to get to Kebes. "This music contest," I said, quickly. "What's the prize?"

"A heifer," somebody in the crowd said. I hadn't asked because I wanted to know. I didn't take my eyes off Kebes. Now that he was looking at me, I could see by his eyes that he hadn't offered it thinking it was an easy way to lose. He was sincerely confident of winning. But I was just as confident that nobody could beat Father at music. (He is the god Apollo. He *invented* music.)

"No," Kebes said, looking at Father over my head. "Not a heifer. How about if, instead, the winner gets to do what they want to the loser? That's what this is about, isn't it? We've always hated each other. This way we both have a fair chance."

Father's hand on my shoulder seemed to become heavier. There was a hiss of drawn breath from the crowd. Maia was frowning. Saying *do what they want* seemed better to me at that moment than saying *kill*. But why would Kebes suggest it? He was lying when he said they both had a fair chance. He believed he would win. How could he?

"I can agree to that," Father said. "What should it be? Original lyre composition?"

"Any instrument," Kebes said. "Original composition. I have an instrument you may not have seen."

I could almost hear Father's sneer. "Who judges this competition?" he asked.

"Four of yours and four of ours," Kebes said, then he glanced down at me again. "None of our children."

"Nine judges," Father countered. "Four of yours, four of ours, and one chosen by lot."

"Very well," Kebes said. "And the winner does what they want to the loser, and the loser doesn't stop them?"

"Without a judgment? That's barbaric," Aristomache put in. There was a muttering of agreement in the crowd. "It's one thing when somebody has been condemned, but we've never done it without that."

"We're all civilized people," Kebes said, lying again, and still staring over my head at Father.

"Pytheas has been unhinged since Simmea's death," Klymene said. I hadn't noticed her there in the crowd. "This is madness. We know the Goodness Group didn't kill her. The ship was in Troy last autumn, nowhere near Kallisti." She was speaking the truth as she knew it, even about Father being mad.

"I believe that," Father said. "This isn't about that. It's about what he did to Simmea before he left." Father didn't ever lie, I realized. He sometimes deliberately said things that could be misinterpreted, but as far as I could see he always told the truth.

"What did you do to Simmea?" Maia asked. She had a soft voice but it sounded hard now.

"Nothing you didn't personally sanction," Kebes said, looking at her for the first time since he had greeted her. "You chose the partners for the Florentines for the Festival of Hera. You yourself matched me with her."

Maia made an inarticulate choking sound.

"He raped her," I said, into the silence, to make it clear, since it seemed nobody else was going to. "She wrote about it."

Klymene looked shocked. "Is this true?"

Kebes looked at me, then at her. "No. She wanted it. She loved me." He wanted to believe what he was saying, but he couldn't quite manage it. There was guilt behind his words. I wished everyone could hear it as clearly as I could.

"But there's a written record?" Klymene asked, glancing back at me.

"Whatever she may have said later, she didn't report it as rape at the time," Kebes said, speaking the whole truth now. "There were procedures, if she had wanted to complain about me. You know that. Did she tell you about this, or are we taking Pytheas's word, and his daughter's? This was all twenty years ago."

"But Kebes——" Klymene began.

"Matthias," he interrupted. "That's always been my name."

She waved this off. "Matthias, then. This contest is insane. Pytheas——"

"We've agreed," Father said. His hand was still on my shoulder. "He suggested it himself. A musical contest. What could be more civilized?"

"But the consequences—one of you is going to kill the other one!" Klymene sounded appalled.

"That's going to happen anyway," Father said, gently.

"I could tie you up until we're back on Kallisti," Klymene said, and she meant it. "You always take too much on yourself, you always put yourself forward, you think you're the best and that gives you the right to do whatever you want, but it doesn't. You're not sane, Pytheas, and I can't let you go ahead with this. It's unjust!"

"It doesn't involve anyone but the two of us," Father said.

"He has always hated me, it's not the madness of grief," Kebes said, to the crowd. "But I have proposed this fair contest. It's the best way. The winner to do what they want." He seemed so sure that he could win. There was a kind of gloating in his voice.

Klymene shook her head. "We want peace and trade with your cities," she said.

"That can happen without Pytheas or myself being involved," Kebes said. "We can give assurances. This is a personal matter." Then he turned to me. "You may not believe me, but your mother and I loved each other. Nobody answered my question, and I have a right to know. Do you have older brothers?"

I didn't believe him. He wasn't lying, he believed what he said, but it was something he had convinced himself of, not the truth. I knew my mother. "I have lots of older brothers, but none of them are your sons," I said.

"You wouldn't necessarily know. She said she'd give it up to philosophy," he said, half to himself.

"Simmea didn't have a child after that last festival," Maia said, forcing her voice out.

Kebes nodded, looking disappointed. He looked at me again. "And what's your name, little girl?"

"Arete," I said, putting my chin up. I have been embarrassed and teased about my name all my life, but never have I been prouder to declare it than that day. It was like declaring my mother's true allegiance, proclaiming the name she gave me. It encapsulated the choices she had made in her life, her allegiance to philosophy, to Father, to the City, to her own excellence, and mine, and the excellence of the world.

Kebes looked at Father, and back at me. "Arete," he said, as if he hated the word. It seemed to me that he should have known then and by that alone that he had lost.

19

APOLLO

Mortals can be wonderful and maddening and fascinating, and sometimes all three at the same time.

Every single member of the company of the *Excellence*, except my children, came to try to persuade me not to kill Kebes after I won the competition, even dear Ficino and lark-voiced Erinna. None of them doubted that I'd win. I'd been winning musical competitions since the first years of the Republic, after all. They took it utterly for granted. They just didn't want me to kill Kebes afterward. They had different reasons.

Klymene didn't want me to kill Kebes because he had been her friend, and Simmea's friend. She also didn't believe me about the rape. "Even before this you always misjudged him. Exactly what did Simmea write? She never said anything to me about it, and I saw her that night. Can I see it? Do you have it here?"

Maecenas didn't want me to kill Kebes because he wanted to trade with Lucia and Marissa, and he was afraid it would mess up diplomatic relations. "It might just be that we've been conflating Kebes and the Goodness Group all this time, but he really is important to these people, and if you take him out then it'll make everything harder. I appreciate that you want to hurt him for what he did to Simmea. But you can do what you like—it's your choice, eh? You could just beat him up. Break his nose! That would be satisfying. Break a couple of bones if you have to. Or how about if you rape him, if you could bring yourself to? Humiliate him. But leave him alive, eh?"

Ficino didn't want me to kill Kebes because he thought it would be bad for my soul. "You don't want to have that stain on your soul when you go on to your next life. Killing somebody in battle is one thing, but deliberately setting out to kill them for revenge is different. I'm not thinking about

Kebes here, Pytheas, I'm thinking about you. Killing him doesn't avenge what he did to Simmea. It won't bring her back, or change what he did. Vengeance isn't justice. You understand that."

I thought I understood it. I'd taken vengeance before. It certainly isn't justice, or restitution, let alone changing what had happened. I agree that those things would be better, if they were possible. Not even Father can wind back time, though he can wipe it out as if it had never been. But vengeance, inadequate as it may be, is sometimes better than having people get away with what they've done. Kebes was going to go on to a new life, and I sincerely hoped he'd learned something in this one so that he'd do better next time. It was the thought of leaving him alive to enjoy the memory of what he had done to Simmea that was intolerable.

To carry through Ficino's argument, killing Kebes was the best thing I could possibly do for him, for the only part of him that was important, his soul. Kebes had demonstrated over and over again that in this life he would turn away from chances to become his best self. He held tight through everything to his narrow Christianity, his supposed love for Simmea, and most of all his hate for the Masters and the City. He refused reason and justice and excellence. He had turned away from all his opportunities. A new life might give him new chances, with less ingrained intransigence.

Most of the arguments the crew made to me were variants on these three. Erinna was entirely pragmatic, asking what would happen to Arete if they took against us and attacked the ship. Maia was extremely Platonic. She told me that Ikaros had raped her when they'd been setting up the city, but she believed he didn't understand what rape was. She hadn't told anyone because she didn't want to cause trouble, so she understood why Simmea hadn't talked about it.

"When Kebes said I'd personally sanctioned it, I felt as if he'd hit me," she said. "Those Festivals of Hera. It didn't give the girls any choice. I hadn't thought of it that way."

"It didn't give the boys any choice either," I said, remembering that awful time with Klymene. "Sometimes Plato had an idea that seemed good to him, but just doesn't work at all when you try it with actual people."

"But it was a long time ago, and we *had* sanctioned it—we, the Masters. Me. I had sanctioned it." Maia was never a coward; she faced her own responsibility squarely. She was pale but she went on. "And Simmea might not have made a complaint because she didn't want everyone to know. But she didn't tell you either. You know that means she didn't want vengeance." She hesitated, assessing how I was taking it, and then went on. "And Kebes might have learned better since. He seems to be doing good work here. Ikaros understands now. I have forgiven him."

This was the one argument that made me hesitate. *I* had learned better since Daphne had turned into a tree. I hadn't understood what was happening with Daphne. Kebes gave every sign of failing to understand what he had done. But he wasn't sorry. He had hurt her and gone on when she asked him to stop, and afterward he had insulted her. Now he seemed to have deluded himself again into believing, in spite of all the evidence to the contrary, that she was really his. He had named his city after her. He had insisted on knowing whether she'd had a child. He said she loved him. He kept on claiming her, over and over, when in fact she was . . . her own. (And, yes, all right, mine, but mine because she wanted to be. One of the reasons I hated Kebes was because he was my dark and twisted mirror, and forced me to confront these things. I do try to be just and pursue excellence.)

I struggled to say some of this to Maia. "He didn't sound as if he has learned better. He wasn't acting as if he believed she had equal significance and was her own self. He thought he owned her. She wrote that he said that to her at the time, and I believe from what he said today that he still thinks that."

"But Pytheas, do you truly think it's just to kill him for thinking that?"

"What is justice, Maia? It took Plato ten books, and it's taking us decades, and none of us has a proper answer."

I don't know what she would have replied, because at that moment Ismene came up, and with her my son. He looked like me, and like his brothers. He was much taller than his mother. She was still pretty. I had never known her well. "Joy to you, Ismene," I said. Maia turned to greet her.

"This is Fabius," she said, presenting the boy. He wished me joy gruffly, not knowing where to look. I looked at him, almost as much at a loss. I had met sons before who had been strangers, but they had always known who I was. Should I tell this boy he had a heroic soul? How could I, in front of Maia and his mother? And what could he make of the information in any case? He might not even believe me. It seemed kinder to leave him to make what he could of himself. So we had a limping uncomfortable conversation, and after a little while he and his mother went away together.

"Another son," Maia said, watching them go.

"I can't do anything for that one," I said.

"Oh Pytheas, do you really think you might lose tomorrow?"

"That's for the gods," I said. "Are you thinking of going to talk to Kebes to urge him not to kill me if he wins?"

"Yes," she said, biting her lip. "But as he hates me just as much as he hates you, I can't imagine it doing much good."

At sunset Arete insisted everyone leave me to rest before the competition, and she and the boys and I walked off up the beach. She had brought food from the city, roast lamb with herbs and colored eggs for Easter, but wise Neleus had brought dried meat and raisins from the ship which he shared with me. I had brought a jar of wine. We built a fire of driftwood and sat down by it

"You're not accepting their hospitality, then?" Arete said. "I thought not."

"They'll forget the name Lucia," I said. "This place was called Mithymna." The sun was sliding into the sea before us, lighting the clouds a thousand shades of red and violet and gold. I looked along the curve of the hill where the moon, two days past full, was due to rise. I opened the wine and took a sip. Neat, it was as sweet as honey, and as strong. I handed it to Kallikles, who was on my right.

Arete looked sideways at Neleus. "I can tell when people are telling the truth," she said.

Kallikles and Phaedrus looked interested. Neleus grunted, taking the wine. "Useful ability," I said, carefully.

"Kebes thought he might well win," she said.

"I noticed that," I said. "Interesting, isn't it? He was never known for his musical ability. But he didn't act as if he was committing suicide, and the Lucians in the crowd didn't act that way either. He said he had a new instrument. I wonder what it is?"

"What happens if he wins?" Neleus asked, passing the wine on to Phaedrus.

"He kills me, then he'll get a real surprise when I kill him immediately afterward." I smiled. I almost wanted it to happen. It would make everything so much simpler.

"Isn't that cheating?" Kallikles asked.

"He raped Mother!" Neleus said.

"Right, not cheating," Kallikles said.

"What will you do to him if you win?" Arete said. She was holding the wine jar, but she didn't drink. Plato said nobody under the age of thirty should drink unmixed wine.

"I'll cut his throat. Get it over with as fast as possible."

"Why would he suggest this?" Phaedrus asked. "The winner doing what they want?"

"I expect he wants to torture me to death," I said.

To my surprise, they were all shocked.

"Kebes hates me," I explained. "He always has. It's partly because Simmea loved me, and partly because he hates excellence." I knew this was right. Simmea had explained it to me.

"How can anyone hate excellence?" Arete asked.

"Ah, you didn't realize quite what a wound your name was to him?"

"I did, but I thought that was because of Mother choosing it, choosing you and the City and excellence over him and his choices."

"Yes. That too. But he hates Plato, and all of Plato's ideas. He said he couldn't become his best self because his best self would never have been enslaved or brought to the city, and what he had left was revenge." I remembered him saying it. Kebes was older now, closing on forty like all the Children, but he was still exactly the same as the bull-headed boy he had been that day in the garden at Thessaly. "He wasn't prepared to go on from where he was and make the best of what he could be. And he hates me because I do pursue excellence, and because Simmea chose me and excellence over him and his idea of freedom."

"He hates Plato?" Kallikles echoed, as if the words made no sense.

"I've heard that they say harsh things about Plato sometimes in Sokratea," Phaedrus said.

"Most of the Goodness Group don't hate Plato," I said. "That's clear. But Kebes does."

"But won't the rest of them object to his torturing you?" Kallikles asked.

"I'm sure he's done it before. I expect they do it to criminals. I think that's what Aristomache meant when she said it was barbaric without a judgment," Arete said. "They have that statue. They have gladiatorial combats. They probably think it's all right."

I nodded. "Yes, and Kebes introduced Christianity—which is about to put him in a bad spot. He's a priest. They're likely to be telling him it's his Christian duty to forgive me. At least nobody offered me that kind of pap."

"What will you do if he does forgive you?" Arete asked.

I took the wine jar from her and drank again. "If he could forgive me he wouldn't be Kebes. He won't forgive me. And he won't win. And I'll kill him."

"Is it what Mother would have wanted?" Phaedrus asked.

"Not really," I admitted. "If she'd wanted revenge she'd have told me right away and I'd have killed him then, that day, before the Last Debate. I'd have come up behind him in the dark and got a hold and told him who it was and what I was doing and then broken his neck and left him there, making it look as if he tripped." It would have been so easy.

"If she were here she'd be arguing about the nature of justice," Arete said. "Though maybe she would want revenge. How dare he look at me and say you weren't practicing agape!"

I didn't say anything. If Simmea were alive, we wouldn't have been here. And if we had been, and she'd been here, Kebes would have been civil to me in her presence, as he had promised years ago. And besides, I have never truly understood what Plato meant by agape, especially when it came to men and women. I wasn't sure that Plato even really understood that men could fall in love with women, or that women could fall in love at all. It wasn't until the Renaissance that Platonic love was interpreted that way. There aren't any simple words for what Simmea and I were to each other. She was my friend and my votary. That was enough.

"Why didn't you just kill him?" Phaedrus asked. "When he said that and you hit him?"

"I didn't think," I said, and it was true. I'd smashed him to the ground with a blow. I could just as easily have crushed his throat and watched him choke to death. I had acted entirely without thinking, and on that instinctive level I was used to drawing back and not killing Kebes.

Neleus had the wine. I waited until he had swallowed. "I need you to help me," I said to him. "You haven't accepted their hospitality."

He nodded, eager. "I haven't. Not here, and not at Marissa."

"Good. That was well thought through. The rest of you did accept it, didn't you."

"Sorry," Phaedrus said.

"I didn't think," Kallikles said.

"They're not all Kebes. They're good people, doing good work. Mother would have liked them," Arete said.

"They'll be utterly forgotten," I said, confident of it. I'd been shaken for a moment at Marissa, but I knew the future couldn't be changed, that anything done here was nothing more to history than a marginal note. I'd been to the future, after all. On the beach where we were sitting there would one day be a wonderful little restaurant that made mouth-watering kalimari and grilled fish, crisp outside and moist within. "Forgotten. Kebes and all his works."

"Maia says they're the cities Plato heard about. The ones that lived according to his rule, and then degenerated to timarchy and so on," Arete said. "And they do show signs that way."

I laughed, amused. "Then maybe they are."

I looked back at Neleus. "Kebes said the judges couldn't be our children—by which I assume he's not practicing clerical celibacy and he has some children here. But you're technically not my child, which is a good thing, because it means you can be one of the judges. And because you haven't accepted their hospitality, you're not restricted in what you can do. If Kebes tries to cheat, you're free to act without any inhibitions."

Neleus grinned at me across the flames. "Do you think he has any chance of winning, though?"

"He's certainly seems to think he can. And he's definitely going to try to get biased judges. So we may as well do what we can. He must think he has a chance, or he'd never have suggested it."

"I don't understand how the judges are going to be able to judge fairly," Arete said. "They'll know they're condemning one of you to death."

"It will all be done in public. Everyone will see. It will affect how relations go in future between Kallisti and the Goodness Group. They'll want to be seen to be fair. So I think it will be a real competition." I was actually looking forward to it. "And even if I lose, it doesn't matter. If he kills me, I'll just kill him right after. If that happens, don't stand right next to him."

"Will you blast him with lightning?" Kallikles asked.

"No, only Father can do that. But I will have the arrows of my wrath, which cannot miss." I missed the weight of the quiver on my back. "I won't use one of the ones that brings plague. But there won't be much left of him. There may be a crater." That would be very satisfying. But it would be even more satisfying to defeat him first, so that he had to understand before he died that I was better than he was.

Kallikles was clearly pondering saying something. He looked at Neleus and then away.

I went on. "The other thing, Neleus, is that your other father, Nikias, is here—I saw him in the crowd this morning."

"I had thought he might be, or if not here then in one of their other cities," Neleus said, looking down.

"It's a good thing. Simmea liked him, and he liked her. They were friends, the same as she was friends with Aeschines. He'll probably be pleased to meet you and know you. But he'll also be an ally. If you can find him tonight, you might be able to persuade him to be one of their judges—there can't be much competition for the job. And he might be able to tell us about Kebes's mysterious instrument, and what things are really like here."

"Did you think Aristomache was lying?" Arete asked. "Because she wasn't."

"Aristomache would no more lie than lay an egg," I said. "But good people can be deceived, more easily than bad people sometimes."

"You can tell whether people are lying, can't you?" she asked.

"I can tell whether they're sincere," I said.

Neleus looked at her, and at me. "You're not talking about something people can do. You're talking about some kind of hero thing? Because I can also usually tell when people are telling the truth just by the way they talk, and where they look when they talk."

"I can do that too," Arete said. "But just recently I've started being sure."

"Yes, that's a power," I said. "I can't do that."

"We've all been getting powers," Kallikles said. "I don't want to keep it from you, Nel. I don't want to hurt you by making you feel different either, but keeping it secret is worse. Ever since we went to Delos, we've been able to do some things."

"Like what?" he asked, looking at the three of them. "I knew there was something."

"Healing," Phaedrus said. "And heat." He put his hand into the fire and left it there. "I don't burn. And I can walk on air."

"I can walk on air too. And I have lightning, just a little." Kallikles held his hands a few inches apart and a tiny bolt of lightning jumped between them. "I found out in the storm. I can control weather. I think that's why the storm was so bad. I was drawing it by mistake. I think I have it under control now, though."

"And you?" Neleus asked Arete.

"The truth thing. And I can understand other languages. I can walk on air too, and I can also fly. And I think I could fly carrying somebody, if I had to. That's all." Fly? Simmea and I had imagined that she'd be a philosophical hero. There's never any control over how children will come out. I thought again of the unknown boy Fabius.

"That seems like enough!" Neleus said. "Fly?"

"I've only tried it once, but yes," she said. She looked along the beach. We were still in sight from the ship, if anyone was looking. "I don't want anyone to see me, but I'll show you when it gets darker, if you like."

"It won't get much darker. The afterglow is fading, but the moon's close enough to full that when she's up people would be able to see you." There was already a silver glow behind the hill where the moon was about to rise.

"I'll show you another time, then," Arete said. "It's not weird—it's just like being able to do math in your head, or knowing how to swim."

"Not weird? Being able to walk on air and heal people and fly?" Neleus's voice rose. "It's about as weird as things get!" He looked at me suddenly. "I've never seen you do anything like that."

"I gave up my powers to become incarnate," I said. "You know that. I can't do anything like that now."

"So in one way, you and I are the only normal ones on this beach," he said.

I blinked. It wasn't a way I'd ever looked at it. The moon was rising now above the colosseum where the contest would be held tomorrow, silvering the pillars. It would eventually become an acropolis, and later a Venetian castle. The moon looked like a great glowing coin poised on the ridge. I remembered going there to talk to Artemis, standing on the dusty plains beside the lander from the ship that bore my name. "The gods have power. But humans have wonderful dreams and make them real, sometimes."

Phaedrus took his hand out of the fire. "If only we had some fruit we wanted to bake," Kallikles said. He put his own finger toward the flame and darted it back at once. "It's funny how we all have different things."

"Different freaky abilities," Neleus said.

"Are you jealous?" Arete asked.

Neleus nodded. "How could I not be jealous? You all have magic god-powers, and you'll get to live forever while I die. But on the other hand, I'm not a freak. You've always been faster and stronger than me. You're weird. You scare people. I'm just strong and smart and, outside of this family, people like me."

"We'll have to die too," Arete said, wisely sidestepping the issue of what happens afterward.

"And we like you," Phaedrus said. He handed him the wine jar. "Or we do when you give us the chance."

"That's true," Kallikles said. "When you give us the chance."

"It just feels as if I have to be twice as good to be normal," Neleus said.

"That's what Simmea was afraid of," I said. "When we brought you home. But you were smart enough to keep up. Not surprising, being her son." I wasn't good at this kind of thing. But it seemed to work. He smiled.

"So tomorrow," I said, and their attention all switched back to me at once. "What do you think I ought to sing, to completely flatten Kebes, so much so that the judges will have no option but to be fair and give me the victory?"

20

ARETE

Phaedrus and I walked in with Father, a few minutes before the appointed hour.

Everyone was there from the *Excellence*, except for the watch that Maecenas had absolutely forced to stay aboard. Kallikles was one of those, though he had complained and protested until the last moment. It seemed as if the whole population of Lucia had turned out as well, even those who were old and sick. I saw people carried there in blankets, old people barely able to hobble, newborn babies, and pregnant women who looked on the point of popping. Everyone gathered in the colosseum, which was just like the one in Marissa.

It was a big space, but crowded now. The seats were packed with people when we arrived, more people than I had ever seen in one place before, perhaps more people than lived in the Remnant. Some were sitting on blankets and sharing picnics. A girl with a little piping flute was wandering through the crowd and being given presents—or no, I reminded myself, money. They used money here.

The nine judges were sitting on raised seats down on the stage. Neleus was among them. The other three from the ship were Klymene, Ficino, and Erinna. From the city were Nikias, immediately recognizable as Neleus's father, Aristomache, and three strangers. I wondered if it would be good or bad that the ninth judge was from Lucia. It was the most likely outcome of choosing by lot. There were ninety of us and more than three thousand of them.

Father was wearing his cloak, pulled back over his shoulder to show the two swords through his belt. Phaedrus carried the lyre. Everyone fell silent when they saw us and then a murmur went through the crowd, which parted to let us pass. It was like a play, and I felt that we should have had time to make costumes before our grand entrance, or at least re-dye our kitons so that we all matched. I would have put us all in black and gold, but any unified color would have done. As it was we were hopeless. Father's cloak was pink, embroidered with scrolls and suns, one of Mother's favorite patterns. His kiton was plain white, as he generally preferred. Phaedrus's kiton was blue, embroidered six inches deep with four different patterns, and mine was a faded yellow embroidered with red Florentine lilies.

There was no sign of Kebes.

We walked down one of the clear aisles and onto the stage. The judges were sitting toward the farther side, on a row of chairs. In the center was a strange piece of wood, almost as tall as I was and about half that broad, with two iron loops bolted into it at the top and another two near the bottom. It was just one straight upright, not a cross, but it had something of the same feel as the crucifix outside the temple. I had no idea what it was for.

Aristomache came forward and introduced the judges to us. The three strangers, two women and a man, were strangers to Father too, it seemed. Their names were Sabina, Erektheus, and Alexandra. Everyone wished each other joy. Erinna was biting her lip, looking very serious.

"I wonder if Kebes is even going to show up," Phaedrus muttered, but just then there was a stir in the crowd, and there was Kebes at the top of the slope, still dressed in his costume from the day before, with the Phrygian cap pulled down on his broad forehead. A woman and a boy came with him, carrying a strange assortment of things I couldn't quite figure out.

"Why would she have given him those?" Father murmured.

"Who? Mother?" Phaedrus asked.

Father laughed shortly. "No indeed. Athene. It's an instrument she invented and then discarded because it made her look so ugly playing it. It's called a syrinx, or pan-pipes."

I'd never seen anything like it. It consisted of a set of hollow tubes of different lengths bound together. "Like a whole set of flutes?" I asked. Wind instruments were banned at home, because Plato thought they made people soft.

"Yes, sort of," he said. "And what do the others bring?"

The woman was carrying a little folding stool. The boy had a bag, which he set down on the left of the wooden thing and unfastened. Inside were a set of leatherworking knives and a number of leather straps.

"Afraid, Pytheas?" Kebes asked.

Father laughed, because of course he wasn't afraid at all. I wondered if he half-wanted Kebes to kill him so that he could go back to being a god and stop needing to figure out mortality from first principles. But what was the threat in a wooden pole and a set of little knives? The crowd seemed to know, because they had fallen silent as soon as the boy undid the bag. Torture, I thought, just as Father had said. Erinna was frowning at the bag. She asked Ficino something and screwed up her face at his reply. Klymene shook her head.

Kebes's eyes swept over the judges. He nodded to the woman, and she and the boy moved back and climbed up the first set of stairs to sit down in a clear space on the first bench on the edge of the crowd. Father set down his swords on the opposite side of the wood from the bag, took his lyre from Phaedrus, and nodded coolly to us. "See you later." Phaedrus moved back, but I moved forward to embrace him, being careful of the lyre. "Win," I said. "What he said was an insult to the honor of all three of us."

"I'll do my best," he said. "Fascinating as it might look in the art of later times, I find I have very little desire to be skinned alive."

I looked back at the tools with a start of horror. Once he had pointed it out I could imagine it all too easily. Bound to the wood by the iron rings and the straps, and then skinned alive. How horrible! Even worse than crucifixion. Surely all incarnate gods didn't have to end up dying in horrible ways? Surely? Aristomache said Yayzu had come back in his divine form, but she hadn't mentioned what he'd done to the torturers afterward. I hoped it was something really appropriate.

I swallowed, nodded, and climbed the stairs to sit in the front row by Phaedrus, on the other side of the arena from Kebes's friends. I looked over at the judges. Neleus smiled at me reassuringly. Erinna was frowning again. I looked down at the little knives where they were laid out so neatly. Everyone in the crowd seemed to recognize them. This must be something they did often enough to have the tools for it. And, most disturbing of all, they came crowding into the colosseum and brought their children to watch.

Kebes had seated himself on a camp stool and was tapping his fingers impatiently. Father stood still and looked at Aristomache.

Aristomache came forward and said something quietly to both men. They both shook their heads. She sighed, and held both hands forward to the crowd, palms out. "You are here to witness a formal musical challenge of one original composition, for any instrument," she began. Everyone immediately fell silent, except one baby whose crying sounded loud in the sudden stillness. The acoustics were wonderful. "Between Pytheas of the Just City and Matthias of Lucia. The victor is to do what he wants to the vanquished. Will you two show mercy, as this is just a personal quarrel, and give up this enmity and compete for a prize?"

"Never," Kebes said.

"There is a place for vengeance in my religion," Father said.

Aristomache looked pained, and so did some of the other judges from Lucia.

"An eye for an eye and a tooth for a tooth," Kebes said, clearly quoting something. "Christianity has room for vengeance too, especially upon heathens and heretics." At the word "heretics" there was a stirring and muttering in the crowd.

"Can't you forgive?" Aristomache pleaded.

"And what have I done to you anyway, beyond existing?" Father asked, mildly, his words pitched perfectly to be heard everywhere in the colosseum. Even the crying baby fell silent.

"This isn't a trial," Kebes snarled at Father. "We're not here to rehearse grievances. And while Lucia is a Christian city, this is permissible by our laws. It's a free contest, freely entered into."

Aristomache sighed and raised her hands again. "The judges are chosen and will swear." Weirdly, she now put her palms together. "I swear by Yayzu and his Heavenly Father that I will judge fairly and by the laws, and not be swayed by prejudice, friendship, or the feeling of the crowd."

It was the strangest oath I ever heard, halfway between the oaths judges take in a capital case and an artistic competition. It became clear as the others swore that the matter of which gods would hold the oath had been left to personal preference. The odd mix of phrases didn't sound any more normal when Ficino swore by all the gods, or Erinna by Apollo and the Muses. Klymene swore by Zeus, Apollo, and Demeter, which was the conventional trio at home for holding significant oaths. Neleus swore by all gods on high Olympos, which cleverly left out Father, since he was right here. Nikias swore before high holiness, which could have meant anything. Alexandra swore by Yayzu and Marissa, Sabina by Marissa alone, Erektheus by blessed Yayzu and Saint Lucy. Father, who had stood impassive through all the rest, even when he was named, winced a little at that.

Then Kebes came up, putting his palms together. "I swear by God, and Marissa, and Saint Matthew, and by my own true name, that I shall abide by the decision of these judges. Whether it be for me or against me I shall submit myself to whatever follows." His voice boomed out confidently. I couldn't understand what he thought he was doing. He was swearing in truth, without reservations. He believed he would win and get to skin Father alive, but how could he?

Father followed him forward and swore the same oath, calmly and clearly, calling on Zeus, Leto, and the Muses. It seemed an odd choice of gods, but not inappropriate. He couldn't exactly swear by himself.

"We shall draw lots for who will begin," Aristomache said.

"No, you go first, Pytheas," Kebes said.

"No, you." Father made a gesture of elaborate courtesy and the crowd laughed.

"We will draw lots," Aristomache said again, firmly. She shook a bag. "Black or white?"

"White," Father said.

Aristomache sat down again and held out the bag out to Nikias, who pulled out a stone without looking and held it up to the crowd. It was white.

Without waiting for anything more, still standing where he was, in a graceful pose with his cloak draped neatly to leave his arm bare, Father began to play.

I've said that Father invented music, and it's true. I wasn't really worried. All the same, we'd spent a long time the evening before discussing what he ought to play. For an audience that contained a large number of Yayzu worshippers, it shouldn't be a religious theme. Similarly, it shouldn't be something overtly Platonic. Phaedrus had suggested he play his song about the Last Debate, and it would have been a good choice, except that it was a subject that excited strong feelings for and against. We discussed elegies and love songs and praise songs. Father had written them all. "What we want is something everyone except Kebes will like," I had said. We'd pretty much agreed that he'd play a song he had written years ago about the sun going down and a bird flying on toward the dawn. It's a song about death and hope, of course, but it's also about a bird and a sunset, and the tune is marvelous.

Of course, Father being Father, he didn't play that at all. He had written it, yes, but lots of the people there had heard it already. Erinna quite often sang it herself. What he sang was completely new. I'd never heard it before, and I'm fairly sure he composed it especially for the occasion, maybe even on the spot. It had a pretty, complex melody, with chords that would be much too hard for most people, and then the words made a harmony, twining around it. It was in the Phrygian mode, of course. From the first note everyone was caught in the silence. The song was about me. Or rather, it was about arete, about personal human excellence, and how it was what we all wanted to attain, and how, being human, we so often fell short but went on from there, and kept on trying, and achieved amazing things. The images were all about building cities and lives, using Plato's parallel that sees cities and souls as analogous. I had tears in my eyes by the end of the first verse, and that was before the incredibly uplifting chorus.

It was such a wonderful song, and such a wonderful performance of it, that I almost forgot to look at Kebes. He stayed sitting there, smiling slightly, not at all worried. It made no sense. However good he was with his pipes, he couldn't possibly top this. Did he think Father would hesitate to kill him? Or did he have a deeper plan?

When Father finished the crowd surged to their feet, clapping with all their hearts. Father bowed to them and stepped back, his face calm and composed, opening his hand to Kebes. And Kebes didn't even wait for them to settle down, he grinned, blew a note, and then another, and then a whole ripple of clear fast notes, puffing out his cheeks.

Of course he couldn't sing while he was playing. The syrinx is a breath instrument, so Kebes's tune had no words. But he was good. He had me tapping my foot almost at once. As for the crowd, already on their feet, half of them were dancing. It wasn't Phrygian or Dorian, it was some other mode altogether, a music I'd never heard, one Plato banned from the Republic, a music made of night and laughter and swaying rhythms. How could Athene have invented such an instrument? It was erotic, haunting, dangerous. Father's song had been a call for Platonic excellence. This reached out to the parts of people Plato most wanted to suppress. And yet, these impulses were undeniably part of life too. I looked at Erinna, and looked away again. I don't know how long Kebes played. It wasn't the kind of music that has measures. It built to a climax, hung there, and toppled back with a sigh. The crowd sighed too, and then clapped and stamped and cheered. Phaedrus and I were the only ones sitting, apart from the judges. Father's face was completely expressionless, as if carved from marble.

"That was the strangest thing," Phaedrus murmured as the crowd slowly subsided. "Do you think Father had heard one of those before?"

"He knew what it was," I said. "He knew Athene made it. He must have."

"I've never heard any music remotely like it," Phaedrus said, more loudly.

One of the women nearby leaned over, breaching the space between the two of us and the rest of the crowd. "Myxolydian, that was, and it's a syrinx," she said, helpfully. "It is different when you're used to calm Platonic music."

It certainly was.

The judges were disputing and couldn't seem to come to an agreement. I could see hands being waved. Erinna was shaking her head. Klymene was frowning hard. One of the strangers was pointing at the crowd, and Aristomache was looking reproving. "Who do you think will win?" I asked the woman who had explained about the Myxolydian.

She was a middle-aged woman, and she had two children sitting with her. I couldn't tell whether she was one of the Children or one of the rescued locals. "It's terribly hard for the judges," she said, "because they're condemning one of them to death, and there's no getting away from that after that exchange at the beginning. I'm glad I wasn't chosen. They're judging between such very different things. Matthias has been winning all the musical competitions here for years. Everyone loves the syrinx. Once you have a syrinx and a drum and somebody with a low voice singing, you can have wonderful dancing after dark. But what Pytheas sang—who could vote against that?"

"Do you know my father?" It was something about the familiar way she said his name that made me ask.

"Oh yes. I'm Auge. I used to share a sleeping house with your mother. She was doing agape with Pytheas even back then."

I didn't want to break the news about Mother's death to another of her old friends. "You're the sculptor? I love your work. The statue in the harbor in Marissa especially."

She blushed. I introduced her to Phaedrus, and she introduced me to her children, a boy of fourteen and a girl of twelve. The judges were still arguing. She introduced me to a few more of the people in the crowd, and insisted on sharing her picnic with us—cold lamb and cucumber yoghurt rolled in flatbread, delicious. I hadn't thought I'd be able to eat while Father's life hung in the balance, but once I smelled it I was ravenous. "I think they'll call it a draw," Auge said. "What else can they do? Then everyone will have to be satisfied."

The judges were still arguing when we finished eating. "What do you usually use this colosseum for?" Phaedrus asked.

Auge looked uncomfortable. "Competitions. Drama. Animal fights. Gladiator fights. There are a number of Romans among us. They suggested it. And the locals we recruited enjoy things like that."

"We have drama in the City now," I said. "And some of us went to an animal fight in Marissa."

"And of course we hold assembly here, and we also use it for punishments and executions," Auge said.

Phaedrus looked at the wooden post. "So your punishments are public?"

Auge nodded. "As for drama, we've often wished we'd brought copies of plays when we left. That's something we'd be very keen to trade for. How did you start allowing performances?" Phaedrus started telling her about the vote that allowed drama.

The shadows were growing long when Aristomache stood up again.

"We want to hear you both again before we come to a decision," she said.

"The same work, or something else?" Kebes asked.

"The same original composition," she said. She gestured to Father. He had been standing quite still and expressionless all this time, though Kebes had been exchanging sallies with people in the crowd. Now he smiled, still calm and perfect but deadly. He swung his cloak deliberately so that it draped from the other shoulder. Then he picked up the lyre and turned it carefully upside-down. He then began to play, the same complex tune as before, perfect, even though all the strings were in the opposite places, and he was using his left hand. He sang again, lifting up his voice and filling the space.

Kebes sat stunned for a moment, then roared to his feet. "This is blatant cheating!"

Aristomache raised a hand to cut him off. Father had not missed a note. He raised an eyebrow, and she nodded to him to continue. He played the upside-down lyre, left-handed, through all the complexities of the song, flawlessly, just as if it were the natural way. This time there was perfect silence as the last note died away.

"It's not against the rules of a musical competition to make things more difficult for yourself," Aristomache said, answering Kebes.

"Nobody expects you to do as well," Father said, smoothly. "Your instrument isn't made for it."

But Kebes for the first time looked uncertain. He guessed that if he played as he had before, the judges would find for Father, who had done something more difficult. He frowned hard and turned the syrinx over. Of course he shouldn't have tried. It wasn't meant to be played that way, and he hadn't practiced, which Father certainly must have. Kebes blew, but what came out wasn't the same rippling hypnotic music as before but a discordant babble. The crowd laughed, with an uncomfortable edge. Kebes righted his instrument and played as he had the first time. But he didn't have the same confidence, and without the energy of the crowd the Myxolydian music felt hollow.

There was no doubt what the judges were going to decide. They didn't take long in their deliberations this time. Aristomache stood. "We have a majority," she said. "We will each give our votes. I vote for Pytheas."

"Pytheas," Erinna said.

"Pytheas," Ficino echoed.

"Matthias," Klymene said, staring straight in front of her and not meeting anyone's eyes.

"Pytheas," Neleus said, very firmly.

"Pytheas," Nikias said, in the same tone.

"Matthias," Sabina said.

"Pytheas," said Alexandra.

"Matthias," concluded Erektheus.

"That's six for Pytheas and three for Matthias, so Pytheas has won. But I beg you Pytheas, be merciful."

And as she spoke that word, Kebes shouted "Fix!" He grabbed a sharp knife from the collection on the ground and rushed at Father. But I hardly noticed, because throughout the crowd people were drawing weapons and attacking those of us from the *Excellence*. It was what Erinna and Maecenas had predicted. The whole colosseum erupted into chaos.

21

ARETE

The shape of the colosseum, the steps where people were sitting and the clear aisles for moving about, were on our side. The preparation and the weapons were all on the other side. Kebes's people had been ready and planning angles of attack, picking out victims in advance. It all seemed to happen in a split second.

Phaedrus drew his knife. I had no weapon. Auge leaped to her feet, scowling, and I shrank away, but she was bellowing "Is this what we call guest friendship?" She took a hammer from her belt and knocked away a blade that was coming for me. She thrust me down toward her children, who were clinging together and cowering under the step. "Stop this at once!" she bellowed. "These are friends. There are children here. Are we savages?"

Father and Kebes seemed to be wrestling by the wooden pole. A woman was lying dead at Phaedrus's feet. There was shouting everywhere, a cacophonous din that roared in my ears. I looked around. There was fighting here and there in the crowd, but no more near me, where people seemed to have listened to Auge and were looking ashamed of themselves. The man who had attacked me was backing away, sheathing his sword. But on the other side of the colosseum I could see a group of people with blades charging down the clear aisle toward the stage, making for the place where the judges were sitting. Without thinking I leaped down toward them—it began as a leap and ended as a flight, or I would have smashed to the sand.

I landed beside Father's swords, still lying neatly where he had put them down. I bent and picked them up, one in each hand, and ran toward the attackers. Erinna saw me coming and stood, taking a step toward me. She reached for the bigger sword in my left hand, and I gratefully gave it up to her. She put it up just in time to block an attacker. I blocked another, much more clumsily, and ducked away from a third, kicking at his knee as I did. I didn't have any idea what to do in a fight that wasn't just friendly wrestling in the palaestra. I was too young for weapons training. The smaller sword felt very heavy in my hand. Neleus came up beside me and punched an attacker hard in her side. "Give me the sword," he said, and I did. He swung it at her throat as she came forward again, nearly severing her head. She vanished at once. The one I'd dodged fell over as he was coming for me again—I discovered later that Nikias had thrown the white stone at his temple.

All through the crowd people were shouting out for peace and friendship and civilization, and even for excellence. I flew over a man with a sword who was coming at me and pushed him back onto Erinna's waiting blade. Neleus was still fighting the last of the group, but his opponent looked desperately around and then threw down his sword to surrender, and that was the end of it.

Kebes was bound to the pole, where he had wanted to bind Father. It seemed as if people had been falling everywhere, but in fact we learned later there were only nineteen dead from *Excellence*, and fourteen from Lucia.

As the last man surrendered, Erinna and I grinned at each other. Then an instant later I realized that one of the bodies at our feet was Ficino. His hat had fallen off and was lying on the sand. I knelt beside him and Erinna knelt at his other side. He had taken a sword thrust and was bleeding but still alive. "Amazons," he said, trying to smile. "Trojan heroes couldn't have done better. Don't grieve for me, my dears. I've had a wonderful life, and what a way to die, at ninety-nine, fighting to defend arete."

"We'll get you home to Florentia, and you'll live another ninety-nine years and fight plenty more battles for Plato yet," Erinna said, but there were tears in her eyes.

"Phaedrus!" I called, as loudly as I could. "Ficino needs you!" Phaedrus could heal him, mend whatever was wrong. Phaedrus came down the stairs running, but Father heard too, and he was nearer and got there first. Father bent over, and Ficino saw him.

"Apollo!" he said, surprised. For a moment I couldn't tell if he was swearing or recognizing Father. "Of course!" He sounded the way he did when I made a really conclusive point in debate. Then he laughed delightedly, and coughed up a bubble of blood. A flood of bright red blood followed it, bursting out of his mouth and taking his life with it. By the time Phaedrus reached us he was gone, leaving nothing but blood on the sand, and his battered old hat beside it.

Phaedrus wiped his eyes, and turned to Aristomache, who was clutching her arm. "Are you a doctor? I think it's broken," she said to him.

He set his hand on it. "Just a bad bruise, I think," he said. "But let me strap it for you."

"Aristomache, now that the riot seems to have died down, I want you to speak to Kebes," Father said, as Phaedrus was finishing.

"Good heavens, is he still alive?" she asked.

Father gestured to the pole, where Kebes was writhing against the iron rings, where Father had bound his wrists and ankles. Aristomache took a step toward it. Auge came down the stairs and onto the stage. "You, Timon!" she roared, pointing at a man in the crowd. "You're a king this year, and you weren't fighting. Come here."

The man came forward. The crowd hushed. "If you're a doctor, go around to the left. If you're wounded, go there where the doctors are. If not, sit down," Timon said, firmly, taking charge. People obeyed him. Phaedrus went over to the left where some other people were gathering. He started helping the wounded.

"Are you responsible for this disgraceful behavior?" Auge asked Kebes.

"For the fixed contest?" Kebes answered, loudly enough for everyone to hear. "No. For my friends who weren't ready to watch me murdered? No." He was lying.

"Yes he was," called the man who had resheathed his sword before Auge's anger. "He told us to be ready to fight if he shouted fix."

"And he had us ready to attack the judges," the man on the ground confirmed.

Timon looked at Aristomache. "Death is the penalty for attacking guests," he said. She nodded. "Those who surrendered or thought better of it are condemned to iron for ten years," he went on. The man near me collapsed in sobs. "As for Matthias—"

"Don't I get to speak?" Kebes asked.

"Ficino is dead," Aristomache said, as if that were sufficient to convict him, as indeed it was in my eyes too.

"Good," Kebes said. "I hated him, hated all the Masters, you included. I hate Kallisti and everyone who stayed on it. I wanted to be ready in case Pytheas cheated, that's all, and as you can see, he did. For us, seizing the ship and killing the sailors was the best way. Now we can sail to Kallisti, where they're weak and divided, and conquer them all."

He wasn't looking at her, he was looking at the crowd, at his people, who had loved him. Some of them looked at him with agreement, but too few.

"This isn't what Yayzu would have done," Auge said.

"It's what the Knights of St. John would have done," Kebes replied.

"I won the contest," Father said. "And even leaving aside guest friendship and inciting riot, he broke his oath to abide by the decision of the judges."

"I did not break my oath!" Kebes shouted. "We attacked because you cheated. I told them to be ready if I shouted fix. I kept my oath, and would have accepted a fair verdict against me, but not this!"

"Kill him, Pytheas," King Timon said. "This is a civilized city. Do to him what he was going to do to you." The crowd cheered loudly.

Father looked to the tools, spilled on the grass now, then at Kebes where he writhed on the pole, and lastly at the crowd in the stands. "If this is your justice," he said. He looked over toward me, and then past me. "Neleus? Help me please."

Neleus went over to him and gathered up the knives. Then he knelt beside him holding them as Father began to cut.

Erinna and I stayed where we were, crouched on the bloodstained sand beside Ficino's hat.

Kebes began swearing at Father, calling him names, accusing him of all kinds of vile crimes. Father began with a shallow cut down the breastbone, and then began carving the skin off. Kebes kept on yelling and taunting. Father didn't respond and just kept on cutting, until Kebes shouted out

"And Sokrates didn't love you! And Simmea didn't love you!" Then Father paused for a second and looked at him evenly.

"Both of them loved you, in their ways, but both of them loved me more." Then he lowered his voice so the crowd couldn't hear and said, "Now tell me, did Athene give you the syrinx? Why? When? And how did you learn that music? Tell me, and I'll kill you quickly."

"Oh you're enjoying this!" Kebes shouted, and began another torrent of abuse.

I'm sure it's not true that Father deliberately used the dull knives to make it take longer. It's just that he didn't have much experience with flaying the skin off a living man. Who does, except Kebes himself? I'd never considered before the way skin folds over muscles and fat and bones, certainly never seen it. Kebes abused him on and on for as long as he could, and Father kept asking his questions, patiently, but after a while it was mostly screaming.

I picked up Ficino's hat and left then. I'd seen enough—too much. I don't know how Father could stand it. He stood there skinning him alive, with parted lips and a half-smile, remote, intent on the work, peeling back the skin, seeming as calm as if he were composing music, repeating his questions. Neleus stayed beside him, spattered with blood, handing him new knives when he reached down for them. I couldn't have done it. Kebes deserved to die, yes, and I would have killed him myself. But if I had been Father I'd have let my knife slip when I was near an artery, and ended it quickly.

Erinna left with me, and Auge entrusted her children to us. "I don't think I could torture anyone to death," I said as we went out. "Not even Kebes." I could still hear his screams echoing around the marvelous acoustics of the colosseum.

"Kebes must have done it before. To other people," Erinna said. "Did you know there were Young Ones killed today? And locals? There are *bodies*. Somebody will have to *bury* them."

"Only murderers and heretics get flayed," Auge's daughter said.

"They'll burn the bodies and put the ashes in urns," Auge's son said.

I nodded. It was a sad necessity we'd experienced a few times at home after art raids. "What are heretics anyway?"

"People who think the wrong thing about God and Yayzu," she said.

My eyes met Erinna's and we both grimaced. "And this seemed like such a nice place," she said.

"How often did Matthias flay heretics?" I asked.

"Not often. Every year or so, here, less often in the other cities," Auge's son said. "Some people like it, but I think it's horrible to watch. I hate screaming."

"It's horrible. But Kebes deserves to end up that way," I said.

The sun was setting as we came down to the harbor, sinking peacefully and splendidly into the sea, which spread out gold and blue like a bolt of shot silk, an even more beautiful sunset than the day before. Auge's children had invited us to their home, but we wanted to get back to our ship. The *Excellence* was still bobbing safely at her anchorage in the bay, but to our astonishment the *Goodness* was a smoldering wreck at the dockside.

I hadn't understood from what Kebes said about attacking the *Excellence* that this was something that he had arranged to have happen during the contest. Flaying suddenly seemed too good for him.

It seemed our little boat had been burned in the fighting, but Erinna persuaded one of the women who had a fishing boat ready to go out that she could do better ferrying people back to the *Excellence*. She gave her a coin. "Where did you get that?" I asked as the fisherwoman rowed us to the ship.

"Maecenas gave me a handful at Marissa, for buying stores. I have a few left."

There had been a battle aboard, very bloody, but we had won and beaten off the Lucians. As in the colosseum, not all the Lucians had wanted to fight us, and the small number Kebes could organize to attack weren't all that many more than the watch Maecenas had left aboard.

Maia was standing at the rail with a bow slung as we came aboard. She had a cut on her forehead which had bled a great deal, staining her kiton, but she was otherwise unharmed. "I killed two people," she said, shaken.

"I killed one in the fighting in the colosseum, and so did Neleus," Erinna said. "I also wounded two people, but of course I don't know if they'll recover." I was sure the man I'd pushed onto her blade would die. Maia hugged her, and then me too. She gave her bow to somebody else and we sat down together on the big coil of rope on the deck.

"What happened?" she asked. We started to tell her, the contest first, and then the fight. I was relieved that Erinna's description of my flight was that I took a great leap in the air and landed as easily as a cat.

"Ficino's dead," I said, realizing for the first time that Maia didn't know. "He said he'd had a wonderful life and he had died defending excellence and we shouldn't grieve." I began to weep as I remembered it. I pulled his hat out of my kiton and gave it to her.

She took it and turned it over in her hands. "He always said he'd die at ninety-nine," Erinna said.

"Idiotic numerology," Maia sniffed, wiping her eyes on her kiton.

"He said we were Amazons," Erinna said. "And Trojan heroes."

"It wasn't the way I imagined fighting side by side," I said, only then realizing that we had indeed fought side by side, in a battle.

"It's one of those things that's better in stories," Erinna said.

"We can put up a monument to Ficino when we get home," I said, trying to comfort Maia, who was trying to stifle her sobbing. "In Florentia, which he loved so much."

"I've seen his tomb," Maia said, wiping her eyes again. "Years ago, of course, before I came here. He's buried in the Duomo, a temple in the heart of the original city of Florentia. It's a Renaissance building based on a classical original, which couldn't be more appropriate for him. He was buried with the greatest honor his people could give him."

"Good," I said. "And we will do the same. But I miss him. I miss him like I miss Mother. Of course we'll honor their memory, and of course their souls have gone on to new lives, but I hadn't finished talking to them in *this* life." I knew what death meant now. It was conversations cut off.

"I know what you mean. He was my friend from the first day I met him," Maia said, steadying her chin with her hand. "Without him both the Renaissance and the Republic would have been poorer. But that we can honor. It's the twinkle in his eye that I'll really miss."

I hugged her. It was odd, but in a way I felt closer to Maia than anyone else. Father was Father, with all the advantages and disadvantages of that. And for Mother, of course, he came first, second, and third, while the rest of us came somewhere around ninth. That's why Maia and Ficino were both so important to me. I'd realized that since Mother died. They both really did put their pupils first, after philosophy and the City. I was on the edges of Father and Mother's lives, but I was in the heart of theirs. And that was reasonable, was all right, because after all Father was the god Apollo, and how could I possibly be as important as that? Even if now I had divine powers, and maybe I was going to be a god. (But a god of what? Flight was taken. Was there a god of translation?)

The deck lights came on. The *Goodness* was plainly sinking, but a few of her lights also flickered on even as she foundered. "What happened in the fighting here?" Erinna asked.

"They used a fireship," Maia said. "But the wind changed. And they came to board us, but we stood them off. I shot one. Only a few of them got aboard. Caerellia was killed, fighting, and young Phaenarete."

Maecenas came back just then, with Phaedrus and our wounded. "We need to get everyone back aboard and do a headcount so we know how many we're missing," he said. "You four get started, find out exactly who's aboard and what condition they're in."

"Is Kebes dead yet?" Erinna asked.

Maecenas shook his head. "Not when I left. It might take half the night. He started screaming 'why are you tearing me apart?' over and over, as if he hadn't meant to do it to Pytheas, and as if he hadn't done it to other people before. It's one of their standard methods of execution, they tell me. They had one of those colosseums in Marissa too, didn't they? I don't know that we want to trade with these people after all."

22

APOLLO

On one of the last days of the Weimar Republic, I ran into my brother Dionysios unexpectedly in a nightclub in Berlin. He was leaning against the wall, half shadowed, a cup in his hand, talking to the piano player. He looked up as I came down the steps and greeted me with a half-smile. He was dressed in black leather, topped off with a leopardskin scarf. He was there for the same reason I was, to save as many as we could, in the teeth of Fate and Necessity. He said something quietly to the pianist, who looked to the saxophonist and played a low D. My brother and I danced together there, cheek to cheek, in that crowded little underground room on the desperate edge of destruction, amid the smoke that was like, and not like, the smoke of sacrifice, and the music that was like, and not like, the music Kebes played on his syrinx that day in the colosseum of Lucia.

Kebes was an enemy, a breaker of guest friendship, a rapist, and a torturer who set up institutional torture in his republic. But none of that is why I turned my lyre upside-down in order to defeat him, or why I killed him in that horrible messy way. The contest was for original composition, any instrument. What Kebes played was not an original composition, it was Gershwin's "Summertime." It's not that he broke the rules of the competition, although he did. He was a plagiarist. He cheated on art, passing off someone else's work as his own, believing no one would know. Naturally, I would have had to punish that even if he had done nothing else. I sickened of the skinning early on, but I believed that if I kept on inflicting the agony with a promise of the release of death, he would tell me why Athene had given him the syrinx, and how he had learned the music. There were no Masters among the Goodness Group who came from late enough that they would have known or recognized jazz. I couldn't reveal my knowledge of his plagiarism without giving myself away. Torture is irritatingly ineffective: he taunted me for as long as he could, but he refused to answer my questions and died without telling me. (How I eventually learned the answers is part of another story, which I may tell you one day.)

After he was dead and vanished, and his tattered separated skin, removed with so much slow effort, had vanished with him, I plunged into the clean Aegean to wash off the blood. I emerged again to mortal problems and complications and the relentless mortal timescale where everything has to be dealt with in the instant, with no time to think through the consequences. I had a tiny cut on my thumb where the knife had slipped, and it stung with the salt of the sea water. All my human interactions felt just like that at that moment, raw and stinging and petty. It was all tension—between Lucia and the *Excellence*, between Kallikles and Klymene, and in the souls of my Young Ones as they tried to deal with their dual nature.

I had been skinning Kebes all through the hours of darkness, and it was weary work; my mortal body needed sleep. But the sun was growing higher in the sky and sleep was far from me. I wanted to be away from the ship and mortal trivialities. I needed to recover from the contest, and the aftermath. I swam again, with Kallikles and Arete.

Swimming always made me feel close to Simmea, because she taught me, because it was the first thing we had shared and the way we came to know each other. I hadn't done it since she had died. Now, swimming, in a state of physical and mental exhaustion, felt almost like being with her, and yet painful because she wasn't there and never would be.

We swam out of sight of the ship and the city. I pulled myself up onto a rock, and the Young Ones climbed up and sat beside me, all of us naked in the warm light of my beloved sun. The rock was gray, but turned black where the seawater ran off our bodies to make it wet. The sea broke about it in a little frill of white foam on sapphire. Simmea would have wanted to paint it.

"Clean at last," I said, inspecting my hands.

"Do you feel any better now that Kebes is dead?" Kallikles asked.

I thought about it for a long moment. "Yes. No. I'm glad I defeated Kebes and I'm glad I killed him, even if it was so slow and messy. He deserved it even before he cheated and broke guest friendship." I had wanted him dead, and he was dead, and off to a new beginning. Meanwhile, everything else was still here, and more complicated than ever.

"Did he even break it?" Arete asked. "Auge immediately started shouting that he had, but we were formally welcomed to Marissa, not here, and they are independent cities in the same league."

"They offered us all guest friendship when we arrived," Kallikles said. "I was one of guards with the envoys. That was clearly and plainly stated."

"I never accepted it, but they offered it to all of us, and when they attacked everyone they definitely broke it. You had eaten their food, and they attacked you anyway. Kebes organized that attack, so he broke it," I said. "Besides, that music wasn't original. It came from the twentieth century. He was cheating and he thought nobody would know."

Arete drew in her breath sharply, and Kallikles gasped. "How did he know it?"

"He wouldn't tell me. It must be some god interfering."

"I'm glad you punished him for it," Kallikles said.

"Yes. And now that's over. Done with. Settled." I tried to feel it was true as I said it. But no matter how much I wanted it to be, nothing felt settled by Kebes's death, and it gave me no relief.

"What about the *Goodness*?" Kallikles asked.

"Let them build triremes," I said, lying back, deliberately trying to relax. They weren't my people, or my responsibility, or anything to do with me. "Let Yayzu look after them. How surprised he will be when he takes notice of them praying to him from here!"

The sun was warm, and after a little while I did begin to relax a little. The Young Ones sat quietly in the sun. I kept feeling that I had left something unfinished. Not skinning Kebes. I had done that thoroughly, made a proper job of the whole messy business. And now he wasn't walking around gloating about raping Simmea, or sneering at Arete, or passing off other people's art as his own. His soul was free for a new beginning, and the world was a better place without him. All the same, I felt as if something was missing. Absent or present, Kebes had been a rival for a long time. I felt emptier without him.

Just then, surprising me utterly, Arete rose up off the rock, neat as Hermes, and flew through the air. It had been such a long time since I'd seen anyone really fly. When in my proper form I could hover in the air, and walk on it, naturally, but I've never been able to swoop about like a bird the way she was doing.

"Stand up and let me try carrying you," she called to Kallikles.

He stood up at once and held his arms out. "Don't drop me!"

"I won't. But you'd land in the sea! Or if you don't want to, you could just walk down the air. Don't be a baby!"

She swooped down from behind and carried him up with her. I'd never seen anything like it. She made several loops in the air, with him dangling from her arms.

"Is he heavy?" I called.

"No! It's not difficult at all. I can barely feel his weight—not like holding up a person, more like carrying a baby."

Kallikles blew a raspberry, and she swooped low and set him gently down beside me on the rock. Then she made one last circuit and perched again by my other side.

"I'm glad I had the chance to try that," she said. "I don't feel tired at all. I think it's less tiring than running or swimming the same distance."

"You did it yesterday," I pointed out. "I saw you fly down onto the stage, and also fly over an attacker."

"Erinna said it was a mighty leap," she said. "Nobody understood it was flying."

"Be careful if you want to stay secret," I warned. "You all three used your powers yesterday. You need to be careful, even in front of people who believe in the gods. Once they know, there's no going back from it."

"I didn't know whether the lightning would come," Kallikles said. "They were getting ready to swarm up the side of the boat. I was out of arrows. I just struck out."

"I think it was a splendid thing to do," Arete said, admiringly.

"You weren't wrong to do it, but it's good you didn't blast all the attackers that way," I said. It was difficult to have powers and not use them, and they were very young. If they revealed themselves, they'd also be revealing me.

"It's electricity, you know," Kallikles said. "When we get home I'm going to experiment cautiously with what I can do with electrical things."

"Be careful around Crocus and Sixty-One," I said.

"I won't hurt them. But I want to try something with their feeding stations. There are enough stations to feed all the Workers we had at the beginning. If I mess one up it won't hurt them."

"It would hurt all of us and kill them if you destroyed all the electricity in the city, and you could. I think it all links together. Or you could kill yourself the way you killed the attacker yesterday." I knew that lightning was akin to electricity, but I had never thought about it in that way before. "Be careful experimenting."

"I will. But I think it can just flow through me."

"And I'll talk to Phaedrus about being careful about people noticing the healing as well," I said.

"He couldn't just let people die," Kallikles said.

"Too many died as it was," Arete said. "Poor Ficino."

That reminded me that she had had her back turned and she might not properly understand what had happened. "Did you see what he did?"

"Who do you mean? Phaedrus or Ficino?"

"Ficino. He deliberately put himself in the way of a blow meant for you. The attacker was ignoring him and going for you from behind. I'd just got Kebes safely pinned to the stake, but I wasn't close enough to do anything to help you. Ficino put his body in the way of the blade." I had been thinking about this ever since.

"For me?" she said, awed and amazed. "He died for me?"

"To protect you," I clarified. "He didn't have a weapon or anything he could use as one. He probably didn't know how to use one anyway. I never saw him in the palaestra. He wasn't in the troop, he was too old. He just put himself in between you and the blade."

Arete started crying. "He said he died defending arete, and I thought he meant excellence, but he meant me."

"He meant both," Kallikles said.

I put my arm around her, just as Simmea always did when people cried. "Would you have done that for him?" I asked.

"Yes," Arete said through her tears, with no hesitation. "I'd have tried to do something more effective to stop the attacker, but if that's all there was to do, of course I would." She paused. "I couldn't have answered that as clearly before the battle in the colosseum. I wouldn't have known. Now I know."

"And for me?" I asked.

"Yes, of course," she said, just as fast, and then stopped, and pulled away from me as she realized what I meant. "Do you think that's what she was doing? Mother? But she knew you're a god." She stared at me.

"So do you," I pointed out.

"It's a strong instinct, to protect," she said, thoughtfully. "I know you're a god, but I'd have put myself between you and a blade."

"You flew down from where you were perfectly safe with Auge and her hammer," I said.

"Leaped," she corrected. "And it wasn't just you. They were heading for the judges."

"Ficino, and Erinna," I said.

"And Neleus," she added.

"A very strong instinct," I repeated, thinking about that. "A human instinct. One I don't possess at all."

"But it's exactly what you were doing," Arete said, surprised. "You were about to kill yourself for Mother, when she killed herself to stop you. If that's what she did."

"It isn't the same," I said, irritated. "I wouldn't have died. Well, yes, I would, but I wouldn't have lost *my life* by doing it, only this temporary mortal life. I'd still have been here, and remembered everything."

"She had time to think," Kallikles said. "The battle was over. She had an arrow in her lung, yes, but it wasn't the middle of a fight and going on split-second instinct."

"It hadn't been over for long," I said. "And she was wounded, and I surprised her, drawing my knife, and maybe she just went with instinct, protecting me, getting between me and danger. Like Ficino. Like you. Like I did when I didn't kill Kebes in the street the first day."

"What a very human thing to do," Arete said. "Poor Mother. Betrayed by instinct."

"But we'll never know," Kallikles said, shaking his head. "It might have been that. She might have done that. Or she might have had some reason, the way you've been thinking. She wasn't afraid of death, not the way so many people are. Ficino wasn't either. They both knew they have souls that go on. She knew from you, and Ficino from Athene. And Mother knew how important you are. She'd been helping you be incarnate for years. She might have thought it would be good for your soul to understand human grief and sacrifice and . . ."

"And how to skin an enemy alive?" I finished, sarcastically. "All the *useful* things I have learned since she died."

"She lived while she was alive, and she wasn't afraid of death," Arete said.

"She told you not to be an idiot. That means she was thinking," Kallikles said.

"She could have just instinctively been telling me not to be an idiot," I said glumly. "I am an idiot all too often."

As I said that, I wished Sokrates could have been there. He'd have said "Apollo! What hyperbole!" and we'd all have laughed, even Kebes. Now I was the only one who could remember those dialogues in the garden. I couldn't be missing Kebes, it wasn't possible. I'd always hated him. Simmea never had, though, even after what he had done to her, even after she had made her definite choice of me and the City, she still spoke of him as a friend. She was a true philosopher. And now I had killed Kebes in the most revolting way, and he hadn't told me anything, and the only good it had done had been to his soul, and perhaps to the Lucians who might lose their taste for public torture without the chief torturer. He might be better in his new life, and the world might be better without him. But I had thought vengeance would make me feel better, or anyway not worse.

Ficino had said it would be bad for my soul to kill Kebes, and I'd dismissed the thought because I'd killed people and taken vengeance before.

But maybe it had been. Had it made me worse, instead of better? I kept trying to be less unjust, but did I ever really improve? All my deeds will become art. Now that this was done, I wondered how later ages would see it: the god of music against a man with a syrinx, and then such a slow unpleasant death.

I thought again of Ficino, putting his body between Arete and the blade. And Simmea had done the same for me. I was anguished all over again. There was no question that she'd have sacrificed her life for me if it were necessary. It's just difficult to envision a scenario in which it would be necessary. But she would also give her life for my excellence. That's the first thing she ever did for me: when she was teaching me to swim, she risked her life to increase my excellence. I could see how she would believe that enduring all this would increase my knowledge and my understanding of mortal life, and therefore my excellence. And that's agape, that's what Plato wrote about and Simmea believed, the love that wants to increase the excellence of the beloved. But I also wanted to increase her excellence. She hadn't come to the end of herself. And she *knew* I needed her. Needing her and not having her was such a hard thing to have to learn.

How could she have deliberately left me alone to go through all this? But caring as she did about my excellence, how could she have let me go back to being a god without learning something so important? I put one foot down into the cold clear water of the sea, then drew it back up, making a wet black footprint on the hot gray rock. It was distinct for a moment, then immediately began to fade and dry. Soon there would be no sign that it had ever been there.

I had always protected myself against mortal death. When time is a place you can enter at will, it's easy to do that, to save some moments so the ones we love are never wholly lost. Even with Hyakinthos there are moments left I can visit and savor. I can see him smile again, and if I choose I can spend decades of my own personal time illuminated by that smile, working, planning, contemplating, knowing there will come a next instant, another breath, when I am ready to take it. There are whole days I did not spend with him that I hoard against my future loneliness. That has always been my strategy, and it has always protected me. Simmea knew that, we'd talked about it after we lost Sokrates. She loved me. But that never made her go easy on me. And that was one of the best things about her.

She wouldn't have killed herself just to have me endure mortal grief. But she drew out the arrow rather than have me go back to being a god without learning about it. I couldn't understand it until I saw Ficino, old and unarmed, unhesitatingly put himself between Arete and a sword. He died of the blow. Simmea did the same for my own personal arete. Of course she did. What else would she have been willing to die for?

That was a very good question. I sat up with a jerk. Kallikles and Arete turned to me in surprise "I've been an idiot," I announced. They exchanged glances. "What did she put her body in the way of?"

"You?" Kallikles hazarded.

"What I mean is, what did Simmea care most about?" I asked, Socratically.

"Philosophy, and the City, and art, and you," Arete answered promptly.

"All of us," I corrected. "She cared about our whole family, not just me."

"She did, but she cared more about you," Kallikles said. "And that's right, that's how it should be. We're growing up, we have our own lives, the two of you would have gone on together."

"And you're Apollo," Arete said. "You're more important than we are."

"You seem to be choosing to become gods yourselves," I said. "But whether you do or not, she'd have put herself in front of a blade for you. For Neleus as fast as any of you."

"Yes," they both agreed, with no hesitation.

"And of those things she cared about that much, the one she put her body in the way of was art."

"Yes," Arete said.

"Whoever killed her didn't want to kill her the way Kebes and I wanted to kill each other. Not personally. They just killed her because her body was between them and art." I stopped, to make sure this made sense. They nodded. "So we have to stop the art raids," I concluded. "That's what she'd want, far more than vengeance. They didn't kill her because they wanted to kill her. They killed her because she put her body between them and the head of Victory."

"Stopping the art raids would be a really good thing, but I don't know whether it's possible," Arete said. "People have tried before. Ficino and Mother tried. Manlius did."

"We'd have to go to all the cities," Kallikles said.

"We're going to have to do that anyway, to tell them about the Lucian civilization," I said. I sighed. "It won't be easy. But it's what she would have wanted, and it's what we need to do."

We swam back to the ship. Even though I understood now why she had chosen to die, I *still* couldn't die myself and go back to Olympos. There might be other things I needed to understand from incarnation to become my best self—there probably were, and most of them awful, to do with old age and grief. And now I had to stay alive and go through them and learn, without having Simmea to help. I felt tired thinking about it. But beyond that I had the terribly complicated task of resolving everything Simmea would have wanted resolved, the art raids, relations between the Republics, the situation with the Lucians. It was the kind of thing Simmea was really good at, and I really wasn't. But that was the work that needed to be done.

23

MAIA

Simmea and I were turning cheeses in brine when the mission from Psyche arrived. It was a hot summer day and we had been working hard. Cheese wheels are heavy, and if not turned they'll start to rot. It was the kind of thing Workers had done for us, but which people can do perfectly well; the kind of thing Lysias used to try to persuade people to do, but which we never did as long as there were plenty of Workers to do it for us. The disappearance of all the others did mean that there were plenty of spare parts for Crocus and Sixty-one, but we only asked them to do the most important things, things that people couldn't do.

The smell of cheese was overpowering in the storehouse. It was good strong sharp goat cheese and I knew I'd be glad of it when winter came, but I wasn't sorry to be interrupted.

The messenger was one of the older Young Ones, a girl of about ten. She brought a written message for Simmea, and it was Simmea they wanted; she was on the Foreign Negotiations Committee. "A mission from Psyche," she said, looking up from the note. "I'm going to have to go, I'm afraid."

"I'll finish up here," I said, with a sigh.

"No, come with me," Simmea said, picking up her kiton from the heap where she had tossed it. "I want to talk to you. We can both come back and finish up afterward. Pytheas will watch Arete." I had been back in the Remnant City for a couple of years. Arete was six. Simmea was just over thirty, all taut muscle and sinew. White stretch marks showed as fine seams on her flat brown belly and the sides of her breasts, the legacy of her two pregnancies. She had a very distinctive face, which many people found ugly but which I was so entirely used to that it just seemed to me Simmea's face.

"I think we should go through the wash fountain before appearing to visitors," I said.

Simmea laughed. "I got so used to the smell of the cheese that I'd stopped noticing it. But you're right. You know, you taught me how to use the wash fountain on my very first day in the city."

"I always did that with new Florentine girls," I said. "Easing them in."

I picked up my own kiton and we walked out together. It felt hotter out in the sun. "I don't know how you coped with all of us," she said. "I had a little taste of it when we brought the boys home, but they were so small. Ten thousand ten-year-olds doesn't bear imagining."

"It was terrible," I agreed.

"And it's not even what Plato suggests. He says take over an existing city and drive out everyone who is over ten—so you'd have had nine- and eight-year-olds, and so on down to babies."

"It seemed more practical," I said, defensive as always when Children criticized the decisions the Masters had made. "It was Plotinus's idea."

"If you'd got children of all ages from ten to newborn, that wouldn't have been any easier," she said, opening the door into Thessaly.

I followed her across the room, tightly packed with beds, empty now because Pytheas was busy somewhere else and the children were at lessons. We went into the spacious fountain room, tiled in black and white diagonals. She turned on the water and we both stepped under. The shock of the cold water on my hot sweaty skin was delicious.

Clean, I dried myself on my kiton and wrapped it around me. Simmea did the same. "I should wash this one day soon," she said, looking critically at a stain. Then she looked directly at me. "I was hoping to do this over a cup of wine after we'd finished with the cheese, but I wanted to ask you about the New Concordance," she said.

I opened my mouth, but she held up a hand.

"I know you hate it. I want to understand. You know more about it than anyone here. Ikaros wants—well, the City of Amazons want—to send people here to preach. In the Foreign Negotiation Committee we're debating whether it will do more harm to allow it or forbid it. We're going to take it to Chamber."

"I was a Christian before I came here," I said.

"So was I," Simmea said, surprising me.

"You remember?"

"Of course I remember." We went out into the street again. "You told us to forget. Ficino said it had been a dream. But ten years of life isn't a dream, and you can't forget it."

"I sometimes almost forget the years before I came here, and I was nineteen," I said.

Simmea looked at me sideways with a patient expression. "New Concordance?"

"Sorry. It's wrong. Literally and specifically wrong. Ikaros has built a whole complex structure based on incorrect axioms. He'll debate any individual point, but I couldn't get him to examine his axioms." We walked down the broad diagonal street of Athene, passing others and nodding greetings to them from time to time.

"So what's so appealing about it? Why did people convert, both historically and in the City of Amazons? Why was my village Christian? Why did Botticelli convert? He wasn't an idiot. Anyone can see he thought hard about things."

I blinked. "Botticelli was always a Christian. What made you think he converted?"

"Didn't he paint the Seasons and the Aphrodite first, when he still believed in the Olympians, and then the Madonnas and things after his conversion?" she asked.

"No, he painted some pagan scenes even though he was always a Christian," I said. "I don't know all that much about Botticelli's personal beliefs, but in the Renaissance almost everyone was Christian, although of course they admired the ancient world. They used pagan stories and imagery just as stories. But Christianity was the majority religion, and it was hardly even questioned. It was the same in my time."

"Aphrodite wasn't just a story to Botticelli, or the seasons either," she said, sounding absolutely sure. "But go on, tell me what it is about it that's appealing. I was a child. I remember chanting and prayers and some of the stories, but none of it was ever really explained clearly."

I thought for a moment as we walked past a smithy, with the scent of quenched iron hanging heavily on the air. "I think what's so appealing, both then and now, is the idea of forgiveness for sin. If you're genuinely sorry for what you've done, you can be forgiven and your wrongdoing taken away."

"You give up responsibility for it?" She was frowning hard.

"Yes. You're washed clean of it."

"Without making restitution to people you harmed?" she asked.

"It's the spiritual side of it," I said, feebly. "But you're right of course, it's between you and God, not you and whoever you wronged." But Ikaros had come to apologize to me. My forgiveness had been important to him, not just God's forgiveness.

"And God is all-powerful?"

"Yes. That's appealing. And of course, there's the whole thing where everyone is really sure, and there's the hope of an eternal afterlife."

"We're really sure about Athene." She was still frowning. "And Jesus incarnated himself as a human?"

"Yes, that's also part of the appeal. Think of a god doing that, giving up his powers, to live like us, to redeem us."

Simmea laughed. "If that's why he did it! Maybe he just had questions he wanted answered."

I was startled. "Questions?"

"About being human. Assuming he was ever real and actually did it. But thank you, I do see now why people might like it. Do you have an opinion on whether we ought to allow it?"

We walked past Crocus's colossal statue of *Sokrates Awakening the Workers*. I was almost used to it by now. "Banning it gives it too much power. And it would be impossible to keep it out entirely now that it's the official religion of the City of Amazons, if we're going to have any contact with them at all. Forbidding it might make it seem attractive to rebellious Young Ones," I said.

Simmea sighed. "Alkibiades is being rebellious, though not in religious directions, which considering everything is a good thing."

"I think we ought to allow it but laugh at it, and keep showing how silly it is. Because it is silly. There are a whole lot of absurdities. And we know Athene is real and has real but limited abilities and knowledge. We can deduce certain things from that, but not that there's an omnipotent, omniscient and omnibenevolent deity who wants us all to become angels."

"I've read some of Ikaros's theses, but only some of them. They make my eyes cross. And of course they don't have their holy book. Having a holy book nobody can read but which you can quote from whenever you want is a bit too convenient!"

"Lots of people here would know if Ikaros were misquoting," I said. "I would myself—except that the Bible was a long book, longer than the *Republic*. If he misquotes the Sermon on the Mount, he's going to be corrected, even after twenty years. But he's much less likely to be caught out on verses from the book of the prophet Amos." And of course, Ikaros probably did have a copy of the Bible among his forbidden books. But he wouldn't be able to admit that.

Simmea sighed. "Will you talk to the committee and say what you've just said?"

"Of course I will."

"We're meeting next on the day after the Ides." She grinned. "Letting them in and ridiculing them seems like a terrific strategy. Forbidden fruit is sweet, but nothing is appealing if people mock it."

The mission from Psyche had been housed in an empty sleeping house near the agora. Maecenas, one of the captains of the *Excellence*, and another member of the Foreign Negotiations Committee, was entertaining them. They looked relieved when we came in, and so did the envoys. The envoys were all men, of course. Psyche did not admit women to full citizenship. But they accepted that the other cities did, and dealt with us when they had to. Two of them were Masters, whom I knew, and the third was one of the Children whom I only vaguely recognized.

"Joy to you," Simmea said.

"Joy to you, Hermeias, Salutius," I said, then inclined my head to the third man. "I'm Maia."

"Aurelius," he said.

We all sat down. I fetched wine and mixed it. "Have you had a pleasant journey?" Simmea asked, when we had all drunk a toast to Plato.

"Very smooth and comfortable," Hermeias said, inclining his head to Maecenas. "We called at the City of Amazons, where I had a dispute with Ikaros."

Simmea laughed. "Maia and I were just discussing the New Concordance."

"It's the most ridiculous misunderstanding of Iamblikius you could possibly imagine," Hermeias said, stroking his beard. "I'm glad he didn't live to see it. I managed to refute a few of Ikaros's theses, and he was good enough to thank me for it."

"Will you allow them to preach in Psyche?" she asked.

"We'll agreed to allow them to debate, which is a slightly different thing," Aurelius said. "It's hardly likely to win many converts in a city made up of Platonists."

"It does seem unlikely," Simmea said.

"So what brings you here?" Maecenas said, blunt as ever.

Hermeias and Aurelius looked at Salutius, who had been quiet since exchanging greetings. "Art," he said, and took a deep breath. "Simply put. You have it all, except for what has been produced by us since we left. The original art was brought to the City by Athene and the Art Committee." He nodded to me, as the only member of the original Art Committee present. He had been serving on the committee designing the physical shape of the city at the time, and the one on Children. "It stayed in the Remnant City by default, and you have no more claim on it than the rest of us do. We of Psyche have decided that we ought to have a proportionate share of it. We have just over a thousand people, and we should therefore have ten percent of the art."

I could hardly believe his effrontery in coming here and asking for it. Maecenas's eyebrows were lost in his hair, and Simmea blinked several times before answering. "That's a question we'll have to debate in full committee, and probably in Chamber too," she said. "I'm sure you see that it's something where we can't be expected to give an immediate response."

"Indeed," Salutius said. "We've done without it for ten years, after all. We're not in a tearing hurry. But we have various proposals about how it could be equitably distributed." He turned to Aurelius, who brought out a notebook which he handed to Simmea. She took it but did not open it.

"Am I right in thinking you mean that all the cities want a share in the art, not just Psyche?" she asked.

"Ikaros was most interested," Hermeias said.

"How is this different from when the Athenians asked for a share of the technology ten years ago?" Maecenas asked.

The Psychians exchanged glances, and Aurelius replied. "We agreed about technology because we don't really understand it, and because it's all one thing and difficult to distribute. You argued that if we tried to share it out we'd risk losing what we had, and the very life of the Workers. And you agreed to help us make printing presses, and other such necessities."

"Which you have done, according to treaty," Hermeias put in. "But art is different. A statue can be in one city and a painting in another city. It isn't all needed in the same place to get any of it working properly like technology."

"I see," Maecenas said.

Simmea was chewing her lip with her big front teeth. "I think—I can't say anything until I've talked to the whole committee. But I personally feel it would be better for all of us to be making new art than arguing over the art we have."

Salutius nodded courteously. "I know your own work. But we do feel very strongly in Psyche that we're entitled to our proper share of the rescued ancient art."

"I'll put it to the committee," Simmea said. "And meanwhile, be welcome to the Just City. This sleeping house is at your disposal. You may eat in Florentia, or anywhere you are invited by friends, of course. I'll call an immediate meeting of the committee and talk to you again tomorrow or the day after."

We all parted with great courtesy and formality. Once back in the street, Maecenas turned to Simmea. "You sounded as if you were considering it!"

"Well, what's the alternative?" she asked. "I think we're going to have to give it to them, if they insist. Some of it, anyway."

"Never!" Maecenas said. "Nobody made them leave, nobody makes them stay away. If they want to share our art, they can come back."

Simmea looked at me. "How do you feel about it?"

"Much the same as Maecenas," I admitted. "Think how horrible it would be to divide it all up. Think of only having half the Botticellis in Florentia."

Simmea winced. "I'd hate that. But would you fight to keep them?"

"Yes, I certainly would," Maecenas said, without a heartbeat's hesitation.

Simmea shook her head. "Being on the Foreign Negotiation Committee I've developed a sense for when people will and won't give way on issues. This seems to me like something they won't give way on."

"Surely it would never really come to fighting over art?" I said.

"I don't know," she said. "It's hard to imagine. But Plato gives rules for warfare. And it could come to that."

24

ARETE

Father came back at dawn. I saw him from the masthead where Erinna and I were both looking out. Maecenas had sent us both aloft as soon as we came on watch. "Let me know of anything unusual, on land or sea," he said.

Erinna was very quiet.

"Are you all right?" I asked.

"Of course I am," she snapped. "Sorry. I'm just trying to deal with the fact that I killed at least two people yesterday."

"But you're an ephebe," I said. "You're trained."

"Knowing how to do it is different from actually doing it," she said. "Is that—no, it's just a dolphin."

"They were trying to kill us," I ventured.

"Maybe Plato's right and we should have been going out to battles since we were little children, so that we could get used to it."

"Is that really what he suggests?" I was horrified. "Slaughter is such a horrible thing that it's hard to imagine thinking it right for children to watch. But the Lucian children were there yesterday."

"Yes. And I don't think having seen it would have helped when it came to killing people myself. Didn't it bother you at all?"

"I didn't kill anyone. I gave the swords to you and Neleus, because I didn't know how to use them."

"You pushed that one man onto my sword. And how did you do that any-way? You leaped right over him from a standing start."

"I don't know." I was uncomfortable. I didn't want to lie to her. "It felt natural, like the normal thing to do when he was coming at me."

"They tell us to jump in the palaestra, but not like that! You'll have to teach me."

"I'm not sure I can." The sky was starting to pale behind the city and the fading stars seemed to be listening to me lie. "I never leaped that high be-fore. It was fear I suppose, or battle frenzy."

"So you were afraid? Even though you rushed straight in?"

"I didn't have time to think about being afraid. I saw them running to-ward you with swords, and I saw Father's swords on the ground, and I just leaped for them." Just then I saw Father come walking down toward the har-bor with Neleus, Nikias, Timon, and some of the other Lucians. I called the news to Maecenas below.

"I was terrified," Erinna said. "Until I saw you coming with the swords, I was frozen where I was. I didn't think of going for them, though I'd seen Pytheas put them down earlier. I'd have just sat there and let myself be spit-ted." She was still staring at the horizon, not looking at me.

"You might have been afraid, but you did everything right. You knew how to use the sword, you killed them, and when that one surrendered you stopped."

She nodded. Father had reached the side of the quay, where I could see him clearly. He was covered in blood, but he seemed unconscious of it as he stood talking to the others. They were gesturing at the wreck of the *Good-ness*, which had sunk further overnight.

"You saved my life," Erinna said.

"You saved mine. We fought side by side. You knew how to use the sword. I realized as soon as I got there that I was useless."

"You're not an ephebe yet. You haven't had training. And you were safe where you were up on the stand," Erinna said.

"I couldn't just stay there while you and Ficino and Neleus and Father got killed!" I was indignant. On the quay everyone was waving their arms around. Clearly, the argument was getting heated.

"You came straight toward me," she said. I didn't say anything. I had, and I couldn't deny it. "Thank you."

I still didn't know what to say. "You were in danger. Anyone would have—"

"You really like me, don't you?" she asked.

Now I really didn't know how to answer. "Yes." I stared down at the ar-gument on the quayside.

"I like you, but not like that," Erinna said.

"Like what?" I muttered, feeling the heat rising in my cheeks. "I know," I went on, making it worse.

"You're so much younger, and losing Simmea——I was looking out for you a bit. That's all."

"I know," I said, more loudly. "It's all right. I understand. I don't want anything but to go on being friends the way we have been."

"Good," she said, but I knew that everything was spoiled. Tears stung my eyes. On the quayside, Father shrugged and dove neatly into the sea.

"You should go down to talk to him," Erinna said.

I slid down the mast. The blood was washed off his hair and skin by the time he pulled himself onto the deck, but his cloak and kiton were still stained. He pulled them off and stood naked on the deck, dripping sea-water, with a strand of seaweed caught over his shoulder.

Maecenas looked at me and raised an eyebrow. "Erinna's still up there watching," I said. He nodded. I embraced Father, getting myself wet in the process. Kallikles and Phaedrus came up the ladder onto the deck and embraced Father one at a time, and we all wished each other joy. The sun was up behind the hill and the sky was bright. Again I thought that this was like a scene in a play. But in a play, the gods show up at the end to sort everything out, and let the people who love each other be together. I picked the seaweed off Father's shoulder and dropped it back into the water.

"Kebes is dead?" Maecenas asked, as Phaedrus stepped back.

"Dead," Father confirmed. "Dead and gone back where he came from. And after all the trouble I had getting the skin off in one piece, it vanished with him."

I shuddered. The worst of it was that he said it so calmly. There were times when he wasn't like other people at all. Maecenas started to speak, then swallowed hard and began again. "How are the rest of them?"

"They want reparations because we burned their ship," Father said.

"Zeus burned it," Maecenas said. "Literally, by all accounts. They tried to burn us, but the wind changed all in an instant and drove the fireship back on the *Goodness*."

Father glanced at Kallikles, who smiled. "The winds do back unexpectedly sometimes," Father said.

"Yes, but they tell me also that the first man to try to board was struck by lightning, out of a clear sky," Maecenas said. He too looked at Kallikles. "You saw that, didn't you?"

"I was right there," Kallikles agreed.

"I didn't want to believe it either, but you see there's no question about it," Maecenas said. "It discouraged the rest of them, as you can imagine."

I looked with admiration at Kallikles. Without him we might have lost the ship and everyone aboard. My own powers weren't anything like as useful.

Neleus and Nikias came aboard, dry, from the fishing boat that had been acting as a ferry. Nikias came over to Maecenas at once. "I want to go back to Kallisti with my son," he said. "Will you give me passage?"

Maecenas looked from Nikias to Neleus, and then to Father, who nodded. "Well, of course I will, but this could be a problem if there were a lot of people who wanted to leave Lucia and go with us."

"We promised to take Aristomache and the others back to Marissa," Phaedrus pointed out.

"That's easy. The problem is that without the *Goodness* these people aren't going to be able to keep on doing as they have been doing," Father said. "Timon was starting to say that when I dived into the sea. They want the *Excellence*."

"So they can keep on rescuing people and founding cities," Kallikles said.

"That's a matter for Chamber," Maecenas said. "Did they offer compensation for Caerellia and Ficino and the others they killed?"

"They think we took it out of Kebes's hide," Neleus said. This remark was followed by an awkward silence, broken after a moment when Klymene came on deck.

"Pytheas," she said, by way of greeting.

"No thanks to you," Neleus said.

"If Klymene prefers the Myxolydian mode, that's no disgrace," Father said, quite sharply.

Klymene blushed. "I did prefer it. And I thought you were cheating by turning your lyre over. I had no idea what Kebes was planning."

"Of course not," Father said. "No hard feelings. I don't know how it is, but you always manage to see me at my worst moments."

I looked at him in complete incomprehension. She had voted for his death by torture, and he must now understand what that meant. However little he minded being dead and returned to his proper divine self, he had said he didn't want to be skinned. How could he not have hard feelings?

Kallikles looked at his mother incredulously. "You voted for Kebes?"

"You didn't hear him play," Father said. "He had a syrinx. He was very good."

"But it wasn't just a musical contest!" sputtered Kallikles. "It was your life."

"Kebes was Klymene's friend," Father said. "And three of the Lucians preferred the Phrygian mode, as it turned out."

Kallikles shook his head.

"Son—" Klymene said, putting her hand on his arm.

"Don't talk to me," he said, shaking her off. "You voted for my father's death."

"We are not going to have a feud over this," Father said, firmly. "If Klymene has wronged anyone it's me, and I refuse to have this be the cause of trouble." Again I thought this was like something from Aeschylus, except that it was also my family. There was an awkward silence.

"The problem is what we're going to do about the Lucians now," Maecenas said.

"If all the Lucians were treacherous and prepared to break guest friendship we'd all be dead. It was just a minority of them. Many of them fought beside us in the colosseum," Phaedrus said.

"Auge and Timon restored order," I said.

Maecenas shook his head. "We'll have to take a mission home with us, and then at the very least bring them back. This will have to be discussed in Chamber, and voted on in the Assembly. It's too much for us." He looked at Nikias. "You can come with us. We've never stopped anyone coming back to the Remnant, there's clear precedent for that. And if you're a Christian, you can mix in with the New Concordance lot. They have a little temple down on the street of Hermes."

"I'm not bothered about religion," Nikias said. "I have useful skills. I'm a glassblower."

"You were a poet and a philosopher when you left us," Pytheas said.

"We've all grown up a lot since then," Nikias said, smiling.

"And you're not abandoning a family here?" Klymene asked, familiarly. I realized as she spoke that of course she knew him, even though they hadn't seen each other for longer than my entire lifetime. All the Children knew each other. Whatever city they lived in now, they had long complex histories of growing up together in the original Republic.

"No. I did, but we're separated. She went to Hieronymos." He looked down.

"You might like to know that as well as Neleus here you have a daughter in Psyche. Andromeda was pregnant when you left."

"I'm going ashore," Maecenas grunted. "I'll talk to Timon and try to sort things out."

"Is it safe ashore?" Klymene asked.

"Armor, and an armed escort." Maecenas sighed. "I'll take Dion and—no, by Hekate, not Phaenarete. Klymene, find me half a dozen trained unwounded Young Ones for a shore mission."

She nodded.

"I'm going to swim some more," Father said.

"Not alone you're not," Maecenas said. "Arete, Kallikles, stay with your father. Swimming is all right, but you're not going ashore, none of you. You're a provocation."

"And me?" Phaedrus asked.

"Keep helping the doctors, you're good at that."

Klymene looked at Kallikles again, but he didn't look at her. She caught my eye, and I spread my hands. I didn't know what to say to her. I was also horrified that she had voted against Father, but if he was prepared to deal with it, so was I. She was Klymene, Mother's friend, Kallikles's mother. I had known her all my life.

"Kallikles," she said.

He turned to her. "We won't have a feud, since Father doesn't want one, but you can't expect me to feel the same toward you."

"That's fair," she said. She turned and went below, moving as if she had aged twenty years in the last half hour.

25

ARETE

The voyage home was strange. On the voyage out, even during the storm, we'd had a sense of adventure, of the world opening before us. I know I wasn't the only one who felt like that. Ficino had wanted to find the Trojan heroes. We had all sung in the evenings. We were sailing into the unknown, and we looked forward to what we would find. It was a voyage of discovery. The voyage home was a journey through anti-climax. I stood my regular watch, but all the joy had gone out of it. The ship still felt alive, and the sky and the sea and the islands were still beautiful, but that was all. Erinna seemed to be avoiding me, after the conversation on the masthead. She was polite when I spoke to her, but uncomfortable. I wasn't sorry I had saved her life, how could I be? But I cried myself to sleep missing her, and missing Ficino, who might still be alive if I hadn't thrown myself into the fight. I had always been told that all actions have consequences. Now I was starting to understand what that meant.

We had envoys aboard to Kallisti from Lucia—to all the five cities. And we had people who wanted to go to other Lucian cities, and a handful like Nikias who wanted to come back to the Remnant. There were no more secrets about where the Lucian cities were. Timon had given Maecenas a map, a beautiful thing, drawn like an illuminated manuscript, embellished with dolphins and triremes, with all their cities neatly marked.

"Ah," Father said, when he saw it, and then when we looked at him curiously he just said "Beautifully drawn."

We called at the Lucian cities, one after another, where the news that Kebes was dead and the *Goodness* destroyed was met each time with shock and horror. Aristomache tried to explain to them that it wasn't really our fault, but it was hard to avoid feeling guilty nevertheless.

"The problem is that it's a subtle complex thing and hard to explain," she said to me as we sailed toward Marissa. "Matthias was in the wrong, and he started the attack. But you did destroy the *Goodness*, and that does destroy our civilization. And we were doing so much good."

"The *Goodness* would still be safe if Matthias hadn't attacked us," I said. It felt strange to call Kebes by his other name.

"Indeed," she agreed. "That attack was wrong and unprovoked. And you didn't destroy the *Goodness* on purpose. The wind changed. It was Matthias's fault for using a fireship and trying to destroy this ship. God punished him. But he has punished all of us for Matthias's hubris."

It was strange. I knew Kallikles had made the wind change. In one way that did make it unquestionably a divine action. But I was much less ready than Aristomache to see it as part of Providence, or being inherently just. To Aristomache, even though she had known Athene, the actions of the gods were something that happened on a different moral plane. To me they were not, they couldn't be. "Kebes—Matthias—was one of your leaders," I said.

"One of them, yes, but one among many. You saw how we didn't all follow him."

"I did. But he wasn't acting alone, either."

"The other conspirators, those who survived, were condemned to iron for ten years. I thought you heard that." A cloud passed over the sun, and in the changed light Aristomache looked old and frail, though she was nowhere near as old as Ficino had been.

"I heard it, but I didn't understand it."

"They're reduced to iron, the fourth rank," she said.

"We have irons, but it isn't a punishment." The idea was very strange to me. "Do you mean that they'll be slaves?"

Aristomache winced. "Not slaves. But the irons do all the hardest work. They mine, and do all the things nobody else wants to. Especially in the new cities it's dangerous and difficult work."

I thought about it. It seemed almost like slavery. And the way Kebes behaved seemed like putting pride above the good, exactly as Plato said timarchy began. Sparta had been a timarchy, valuing honor above truth. But saying this to Aristomache would hurt her without helping anything, and she was among the best of the Lucians. I was glad she was coming to the City with us as one of the envoys, and glad that Auge was another—though poor Auge was seasick, even in these calm breezes.

We set people down and picked up more envoys at all eight Lucian cities. I wasn't allowed ashore anywhere, though I sometimes had a chance to swim. Maecenas wasn't taking any more risks with the ship.

I kept on grieving for Ficino. Maia missed him even more. She wasn't grieving extravagantly the way Father had. She withdrew into herself and never mentioned him. She spent hours standing at the rail in the wind. She avoided Aristomache much as Erinna was avoiding me.

"He always said he'd die when he was ninety-nine," I said, coming up next to her.

She jumped. "Arete, don't creep up on people that way!"

"I wasn't creeping up, you were completely locked in your thoughts."

"It's not true that I don't love people," she said, out of nowhere. She had Ficino's hat crushed between her hands.

"Of course it's not! Who said that?"

"Ikaros," she admitted.

"That idiot." I had never met Ikaros. "What does he know about it? You love lots of people. You love me." I put my arm around her.

Maia snorted, half way between laughter and tears.

"Come on, Magistra, you haven't taught me anything for days." It was the best way to cheer her up, giving her something to do. And besides, my birthday was coming the next month, and with it my tests and my oath. I wanted to be ready.

We sailed on among the islands, and I wished them unknown again and empty of consequences. I stood my watches and did lessons with Maia and had occasional conversations with Father and my brothers. We did not stop at Ikaria, but I looked longingly at the shore and the pine woods as we sailed past.

We struck the shore of Kallisti from the northeast, and so we saw the City of Amazons first, immediately recognizable with its immense statues on the quayside. We sailed on. "Home first," Maecenas said, decisively, and nobody disagreed.

We arrived home at sunset on the twenty-ninth day after our departure, though it felt as if we had been away for centuries. The mountain was rumbling and belching out red-black streams of lava as we sailed in. "Just a normal little eruption," Phaedrus said reassuringly.

"You know?" I asked.

"I do," he said, sounding a little awed.

It is a testament to how much had happened on the voyage that our gaining god-powers seemed such a minor part of it. And yet the story of what had happened to us wouldn't make an epic. Or would it? I thought it over. It seemed too ambiguous, but Homer embraced ambiguity. Homer had heroes on both sides. I remembered Ficino saying he'd fight for Troy. How would people tell the story of Kebes? Would they tell how Apollo beat him in a contest and skinned him alive? Or would it all be forgotten as Father believed? But Father had said everything the gods did became art, and he was still a god. Maybe it was more like a tragedy, heroes overcome by their flaws.

We tacked in to the harbor and tied up, safe at the wharf, home at last.

It felt strange to be greeted by Baukis and Boas and Rhea, to see people I knew well who hadn't been with us. I had almost forgotten they existed, that home was still there behind us all the time. It must have been how Odysseus felt coming back to Ithaka.

26

APOLLO

I spent the voyage home composing a song. It was the song I had been reaching for for months, the song that wouldn't come, because I couldn't make any true art about Simmea's death while I didn't understand why she had chosen to die.

I had been maddened with grief, and now I was not. I still missed Simmea. But I understood now that she had died to increase my excellence and the excellence of the world, and I would increase it, for her, for myself, and for the world. I would savor this mortal life while I had it, learn and experience all I could. And when it ended, I would take what I had learned and be a more excellent god and make the world better. That was what I always wanted. That was why I had chosen to become mortal.

The song I had sung in the colosseum at Lucia had been a cold Platonic composition, perfect but passionless. This one was the opposite. It made the Dorian mode burn with passion. If I had been on Olympos my hair would have stood on end and glowed as I made the song. I would also have concentrated and done nothing else for however long it took until the song was done. As it was, onboard the *Excellence* I had to stand my watches, sleep, and eat, and beyond that I was constantly interrupted. There's no privacy on a ship, and it's hard to be alone. I couldn't so much as play a chord without someone stopping to listen, and I didn't want anyone to hear this song before it was ready. The ship was teeming with people—in addition to the surviving crew we had a whole slew of envoys. Maecenas was very firm that I wasn't allowed ashore. I don't know what he thought I was going to do, or whether he thought the Lucians would try to kill me if they had the chance. I wanted nothing more than to be quiet somewhere alone to work on the song, but instead I trimmed the sails and talked to people who wanted to talk to me. These frustrations too were part of mortal life, and fueled the song.

Every day I went up on deck to watch the sun rise, as the lyrics and music echoed through my head. One morning Maia was there by the rail, twisting Ficino's hat in her hands as she stared out to sea. Always thin, she was gaunt now, and her silvering hair wisped out of its neat braid in the sea wind.

"One thing I have learned about grief," I said to her, "is that nothing anyone says to you is useful, but it can still be comforting sometimes to know you're not alone and not the only person who cares about missing them. Ficino was my friend too."

She smiled through her tears. "Thank you, Pytheas. And Simmea was also my friend."

"We have to do the work they left undone," I said.

"I know," she said. "Oh, I know. But it makes me so tired to think of it."

"We have to stop the art raids, and come to an equitable solution with the Lucians, and bring up the next generation to be more excellent than their parents."

"The Lucians skin heretics, and have gladiatorial fights, and their irons are almost like slaves," Maia said. The edge of the sun showed red over the rim of the world.

"Nobody's perfect," I said. "The Romans had gladiatorial combats, they dislocated the arms of heretics in Renaissance Florence, all of the classical world had slavery, and so did we in the City before we realized that the Workers were self-aware."

"Plato—"

"Plato was laying out an unachievable ideal, to spur people to excellence," I said. "What was it Cicero said about Cato?"

"That Cato acted as if he was living in Plato's Republic instead of the dunghill of Romulus?" She switched into Latin to quote it.

"That's it. Plato wanted to give people something to aspire to. That's why he isn't here, he didn't really imagine it as a possibility, just as something to encourage everyone to think, and to work toward excellence. In reality, while we aim for excellence, we're always living on somebody's dunghill. But that doesn't mean we're wrong to aim to be the best we can be. And the Lucians aren't all like Kebes. If they were we'd all be dead. We can find a way to help them toward excellence."

She sighed. "Everything is complicated and compromised."

"It is," I said. "That's the nature of reality." A gull swooped down low over the water.

"Ficino understood how to go on amid the compromise and find a way forward," Maia said.

"Yes. He took over the Laurentian Library for the Florentine Republic after Piero de Medici fled," I agreed.

"How do you know that?" she asked. "Were you there?"

I had frequently been there, but of course I didn't want to tell her so. "I've heard him talk about it," I said, truthfully. "I know nobody is supposed to talk about their lives before they came to the City, but everyone does."

"I don't think we were wrong to make idealistic rules," Maia said, her voice shaking a little. "I don't know, Pytheas. I've been trying to make the Republic work since I was a young woman, and I'm getting old now. Ficino was always so delighted to be here, to be doing it. He loved everything, except when we divided after the Last Debate. When I came back from Amazonia he was so pleased to see me. I don't know how I can take it all up again without his enthusiasm to keep me going."

"I'm the worst person to ask," I said. "I only just worked out that what I'm supposed to do is keep on working and doing Simmea's share too, as best I can."

"I can't possibly do Ficino's share!" she said, horrified.

"You can do some of it, and I'll do some of it, and other friends will do some of it."

"You'll teach music and mathematics?"

I had been teaching gymnastics in the palaestra but diligently avoiding teaching music and mathematics, as we called all intellectual study. I had evaded it by taking a larger share of the physical labor we all had to share since the Workers left.

"And you'll serve on committees for Simmea?" she went on.

"Oh Maia!"

"You can teach Ficino's beginning Plato course, for the fourteen-year-olds," she said, relentlessly. "And you can teach the advanced lyric poetry class. I don't understand how you've got out of that so far."

"I always volunteer to judge at festivals, and I couldn't judge fairly if I were teaching them too," I said smugly.

"Well, that's been a good argument, but now you can teach them. You can do it better than anyone else, so it's your Platonic duty. And you can serve on the Curriculum Committee too, as well as taking Simmea's place on the Foreign Negotiations Committee."

I looked at her face in the glow of the sunrise. She had stopped crying. "I believe I have actually comforted you a little," I said.

"And I you," she replied.

It was true. Taking on those responsibilities wouldn't be any fun, but knowing they needed doing and I could help do them in Simmea's name did ease my grief a little.

As for stopping the art raids, I was working on a song.

When the *Excellence* tied up at the City, the travelers who had been together for so long divided immediately. Kallikles went off with his girl, Rhea. Maia headed for Florentia to tell the sad news to Ficino's friends there. Arete was immediately embraced by her agemates. Neleus and Phaedrus headed for Thessaly. Everyone else went their separate ways. I was so desperate to be alone to get my song straight that I went straight to the practice rooms on the Street of Hermes.

I shut myself into one of the little rooms and worked nonstop on the song for several hours. The last time I sang it through I was happy with it, but a song isn't real until somebody hears it. I went home to Thessaly, and was astonished to find my son Euklides there, Lasthenia's boy, who lived in Psyche. Phaedrus and Arete and Neleus and he were sitting in the garden by Sokrates's statue of Hermes, under the lemon tree. They looked up when they saw me, and all of them tried to speak at once.

"Just listen to this first," I said, and drew my lyre into place.

It couldn't have been more different from the colosseum in Lucia, the banked rows of spectators, Kebes's hate burning hot, the judges uneasy in their seats, and my own soul longing to escape. Now I was at home, my soul was sure of the work set before it, and the audience were my own children, who loved me. In my memory Sokrates and Simmea and Kebes also populated the garden. Simmea sat intent, leaning forward, bursting with ideas; Sokrates was running his fingers through his hair distractedly; Kebes was frowning and drawing breath to speak. I smiled and let go of them. All of their souls had gone on to start again and learn new things. It was the solid and present Young Ones I wanted to reach with this song.

"Simmea asked me to write this song when we were fourteen years old," I said. Before she had met Sokrates, before we had discussed our agape, before we knew the Workers were people. "It's called 'The Glory of Peace.'"

I knew I had them before the end of the first verse. By the final chorus, they were all openly weeping. The best of it was, the song didn't mention either Simmea or the art raids directly. It was all about the things worth fighting to defend and being our best selves.

Neleus, who had fought in art raids, was the first to speak after the last chord had died away. His voice was choked. "Is that really what we were doing? Were we going against Plato and making ourselves worse?"

"Yes, we evidently were," Euklides said, wiping his eyes. I didn't know him well, and I hadn't known until that moment that he had fought in them.

"The art raids are a falling away from excellence," Phaedrus said. "Toward timarchy. Fighting for honor instead."

Arete looked at me with awe in her eyes. "Maybe you really could stop the art raids! If people hear that, they might understand. It gives us a different way to think about it. And it's really true. *The dreams shared with a friend*," she quoted.

"And that's what Mother died for," Neleus said.

They all looked a little stunned. "I'll have to sing it to harder audiences," I said. "But stopping the art raids is what this song is for. And that's the best thing I can do now in memory of Simmea."

"Not just stopping the pointless deaths, but bringing the City closer to excellence," Neleus said, seeing the point at once, as Simmea would have done.

"All the cities," Arete said.

I nodded. "All the cities. I want to teach you to sing the harmony, so you can sing it with me when we go."

"There's a harmony?" she asked.

"Yes. Why are you looking at me like that?" They were all staring at me with eyes wide open in astonishment.

"You never write songs with multiple parts," Phaedrus said. "You always write things you can perform alone."

"Well, this song can be sung alone, as you've just heard, and it will sound even better with Arete singing the harmony, and it also has an arrangement that can be sung as a choral ode with parts for a whole chorus, which I am planning to have sung before the conference. But you're going to have to rehearse them, Phaedrus, because Arete and I will be going around to the other cities to persuade them to come."

They still looked stunned. I smiled, and sat down and began to eat a lemon.

"Have you ever written something for a chorus before?" Neleus asked. "Ever, ever? I know you haven't done it in the City."

"I haven't, and it was an interesting challenge, especially without any privacy on the boat to work on it. But you wait until you hear the choral version, with the men's chorus singing low down *home and hearth and love and life* and the women's chorus singing high up *worth the cost of risking life* and the lines working with and against each other." I sang the lines as I quoted them. They kept on staring at me. "Yes, it's a new thing for me. But life is about moving forward and learning new things."

"You've stopped being cracked," Arete said.

"Yes, I think I finally have. I haven't stopped missing her. But I'm whole again. I'm finally doing what she wanted."

"Stopping the art raids?" Euklides asked.

"That's part of it," I said.

27

ARETE

In our absence, my brother Euklides had run away from Psyche and sworn a new oath to the Remnant City. He was staying in Thessaly and drilling with the Delphian troop. His armor stood on a stand in the corner, and he had moved things around in the house. He apologized for disturbing things, and said he didn't know whether he was host or guest, welcoming us back. It was wonderful to see him, but on the second day after our return he discovered that Kallikles and Phaedrus and I had powers.

"You have to take me to Delos," he said to Father, as soon as he understood how it had happened.

"It isn't an unmitigated blessing," Kallikles said. He hadn't found a way to tell Rhea about his powers yet.

Euklides looked at Kallikles with cold dislike. "Let me be the judge of that."

Phaedrus wasn't home because he was going around the city healing everyone. I missed his friendly presence in the family argument. Neleus wasn't home either, but then I'd barely seen him since the first afternoon when we came back, when Father had sung to us in the garden. He was spending a lot of time with Nikias, and also with Erinna. He was also working hard, with Maia and Manlius, on arranging the conference.

"If there's another voyage, and if I have any say, I'll make sure you get to visit Delos," Father said. "And Alkibiades and Porphyry if they want to go. And maybe I should arrange it for Fabius in Lucia too."

"If there isn't another voyage, could we get there anyway?" Euklides asked. "Could you fly that far with me, Arete?"

"I don't know. It's a long way."

"Could you fly to Amorgos and rest, and then to Naxos, and so on?" Kallikles suggested.

"I don't know. I've never flown carrying anyone for longer than that time with you by the rock. There's a big difference between flying for a few minutes and flying for hours. I'd want to try it somewhere I could land if I needed to rest, not over the open sea!"

"It's a possibility anyway," Euklides said.

"I hope it won't come to that," Father said. "They'll have to send the Lucians home at the very least. And I expect we'll have trade voyages, and missions of mercy helping the Lucians."

"I wonder what powers I'll have," Euklides mused. "It seems so random."

Perhaps it wasn't as random as it seemed. I couldn't quite see how my own powers fit together, but my brothers' were beginning to make sense to me. I had spent one morning up on the mountain with Phaedrus, standing on the edge of the lava ready to swoop down and rescue him if he got into trouble. It didn't bother me to see him walk through the lava, or when he diverted the flowing stream around himself. But I could hardly look when he lay down and sank into it.

"Didn't you need to breathe?" I asked, when he came up after what felt like a long time.

"I could tell when I needed to," he said. "And I did start to burn, but I healed myself." And he had been thinking about developing an excellence of volcanoes before we went to Delos.

As for Kallikles, lightning and weather working certainly fit together. "Perhaps Zeus will devolve weather to you," I suggested, when Kallikles demonstrated his lightning by blasting a rowan tree on the lower slopes of the mountain. There was nothing left of the tree but blackened roots at the edge of the little pool.

"I wish I could do that to Klymene," was all Kallikles said. He wasn't getting over his anger at his mother. He was having fun with electricity, though. He could make the light-beams in Thessaly come on without touching the switches.

My own abilities didn't seem in any way coherent. They also weren't very useful. Nobody on Kallisti spoke different languages, so I never had the chance to use that ability. I already knew Greek and Latin. And I could only fly when I was sure I was unobserved. The truth recognition was useful, and I think that was why Father decided to take me with him on his missions to the other cities. Well, that and wanting me to sing the harmonies to "The Glory of Peace."

Over the course of the next month I went on four embassies, accompanying Father on his new quest to end the art raids. His proposal was radically simple—everyone would return everything they had stolen, and then the art would be fairly distributed according to population. This had been Psyche's original proposition, which we had rejected with scorn the first time we had heard it. Mother had wanted to accept it, but back then she couldn't persuade enough people. Then the raids had started, and the honor of people and cities had become tangled up with them.

Father had three advantages in stopping the art raids now. First was the song, which really was a wonderful tool. It made people stop and think. We'd been trained to fight, but we'd also been trained to think and debate, and the song broke the cycle of raids and revenge by making people question why they were fighting and whether it was worth it. Secondly, because people generally liked and respected Father, and because he had been so vehemently in favor of vengeance for so long, his renouncing that now was very powerful—especially at home in the Remnant, where everyone had seen the force of his madness. Everyone had also heard what he'd done to Kebes, from those of us who had been there. To go from that to singing about peace and civilization and excellence made a powerful statement on its own. And thirdly, there were the Lucians. The specific way the Lucians were falling into timarchy was easy for us to see—the bloodsports and torture, and their focus on the physical side of life over the intellectual side. But their horror at our wars made us see that we were doing the same thing in our own way. The existence of the Lucians, and the need to do something about them, provided a new factor that made everyone refocus.

The people who really needed to be persuaded most were our own people at home in the Remnant. Most of the art was still safely there, and people had no desire to part with any of it. People tended to be especially attached to the art in their own eating halls. It wasn't difficult to get people to agree that the art in the temples and streets should be shared, but they tended to feel that the art in their eating hall belonged to them personally. I had heard Mother talking about this since the art raids began.

What Father proposed was that there should be an art conference, combined with a Kallisti-wide conference on deciding what to do about the Lucians. This was clever, because the Lucians were, or could be made to appear to be, a common enemy. Everyone in Chamber agreed on the foreign conference, and Father and Maia made the art conference seem like the thing that would make all the other cities agree to come.

We went to Sokratea first. Sokratea was our closest ally. They had never been much engaged in art raids against us, though they had raided the other cities. I had been there before, on a mission with Mother. This was not all that different. We sailed there on the *Excellence*, which remained in the harbor there while we stayed in a guest house.

Sokratea was a strange place. In some ways it was the least Platonic of all the republics, including Lucia's Christian Platonism. They didn't have classes, and they didn't separate out guardians from other people. They wanted to examine life, in the Socratic spirit, and they did that. They believed that Sokrates had been entirely right in the Last Debate. They read Plato, but in no very respectful spirit. They banned Masters from their city, but otherwise they had complete free speech and freedom of publication, and voted on everything, all the time. When Father addressed them he addressed the whole city from the rostrum in the agora—they had no Chamber and no committees.

"Doesn't public business get unwieldy?" I asked Patroklus, one of the Children whom I'd met the last time I'd been there. He came to our guest house and took us to eat with him in his eating hall, which was called simply "Six." Their streets too were numbered.

"It does get unwieldy. It takes a lot of time," he admitted. "But we find it's worth it." The food was good; they gave us fish and cabbage and pasta. They had plenty of Young Ones, and lots of Children of course, but because they had refused entry to Masters, no old people at all. Nobody was any older than Father and Patroklus, and that felt strange to me as soon as I'd noticed it.

Father and I sang to their Assembly. I was nervous, even though I knew the harmonies really well by then. I'd never performed to so many strangers— and as Briseis I'd been wearing a mask. Now it was just my naked face. I felt a little sick before we started. But once Father played the first chord the music carried me with it. And it was all true. Peace was worth fighting for, defending, and in some circumstances attacking—to help another city put down a tyrant, for instance.

The people of Sokratea were moved by the music, and by Father's arguments. They agreed to send envoys to the conference, and, after much spirited and public debate, to send their art. "Not the art we have made here!" one woman insisted.

"Nobody is asking for that," Father said. "Though some of it is excellent, and if you chose to circulate it I think everyone would be truly impressed by it."

I stood in the crowd after we'd finished singing, watching the speakers, ready to let Father know if they were lying. Apart from some forgivable hyperbole, they were not.

The next day we moved on to Psyche. Psyche had been built entirely by humans, with no Worker assistance, and it bore a certain resemblance to Marissa and the other Lucian cities. They had lots of art visible, almost all of it stolen from us. The city was arranged in concentric rings around a small hill, and consequently was very difficult to navigate. It was supposed to be the physical model of the soul, but if so my soul didn't understand it.

We were not offered guest-friendship—partly, we guessed, because of Euklides leaving. Psyche accepted applications for citizenship but did not allow emigration. We ate and slept aboard the *Excellence*. The ship felt strange. It had a different crew, people who had not been on the voyage, and who seemed like usurpers in the place of friends and familiar faces. A pimply ephebe only a year or two older than me kept sprawling on the coil of rope where Erinna and I had sat the night Kallikles told us about the Naxians, and I almost wanted to push him overboard for his effrontery.

In Psyche, Father had to meet what felt like an infinite number of committees. In direct opposition to Sokratea, Psyche was top-heavy with Masters. In addition, they denied women a place in public life, so everyone we met was male. Lots of them lied, though maybe I shouldn't call it lying when people blandly assure you that they understand and sympathize. They were frequently and habitually insincere. They were also obsessed with numerology. I knew a little of it from Ficino, whose loss the people of Psyche genuinely regretted. Eventually, after days of obfuscation, Father had a meeting with a man called Aurelius who seemed to have the ability to make decisions. Father persuaded him to send envoys to the conference. It then took days more to persuade them to send their art, and we had to agree that it would be sent under armed guard and with hostages pledged for its return.

They wouldn't let us sing before their Assembly, but we sang in the agora on the day we left. It wasn't official. We just walked through the agora and stopped and began to sing. People clustered around, naturally, more and more of them, women as well as men. Afterward everyone tried to hug us and touch us—it felt very strange. Father said it was because they'd been moved and they wanted to make a connection. Many of them came to the quayside before the ship left, so we sang it again standing on the desk of the *Excellence*. On the last chorus, they joined in on "When the time comes to defend," startling me.

"Wait until you hear the full choral version," Father said, afterward. "Phaedrus is rehearsing them. They'll sing it at the conference."

We moved on to Athenia. Athenia looked just like home, except smaller. We stayed in a guest house and spent a lot of time with my brother Alkibiades. I was so delighted to see him that I was prepared to forgive Athenia a lot of its formality and rigidity. Alkibiades was a gold, naturally; he had also been a gold at home. He took us to his eating hall, Theseus—all the halls were named after Athenian heroes. There was a bronze statue of Theseus with the head of the giant Kerkyon in the hall, which I remembered seeing in the Athenian eating hall at home years ago. Alkibiades had good advice for Father.

"Talk about what happened to Mother. They'll be sympathetic. We're sick of art raids too. The Amazons keep raiding us. Talk about Plato. They think you're compromised but essentially trying to do the right thing."

"That's about right," Father said.

That night he asked me if I'd talk to Alkibiades and Porphyry about going to Delos. "It would be easier for you. It happened to you. You can explain it better. I can't think how to bring it up. It was awkward with Euklides."

"I don't think it would be very easy, but I will if you want me to."

The Athenians didn't allow anyone under the age of thirty into their Chamber, not even envoys. Father said he'd have to sing alone, and that he could manage. Alkibiades and I went for a walk in the hills outside the city. They were planted with vines. "It's good volcanic soil and they thrive here," he said. "I've done a lot of work pruning them this year. We have vines and olives and barley, just as Plato says. No goats or sheep, though. We have to trade for all our cheese and leather. Fortunately, everyone wants wine."

"When we went to Delos, Kallikles and Phaedrus and I acquired god-powers," I said. I hadn't been able to see how to tell him, so I just blurted it out.

He stopped walking. "What?" I could tell he didn't believe me. Though he was fond of me, I'd been so much younger when he left home.

"Really. We can all do things. And Father says he's going to try to take Euklides there, and you and Porphyry if you want to go."

"What kind of powers?" He was still only half-believing.

"I can tell when people are telling the truth, so I can tell that you don't believe me. And Kallikles can change the weather and call lightning, and Phaedrus can heal people and control the volcano."

"It would be hard to demonstrate knowing the truth," he said, skeptically.

"Oh, and I can fly as well," I said. "Look." I swooped up into the air, and had the satisfaction of seeing my favorite brother's mouth fall open.

We discussed it as we walked on. Before we'd gone much farther he had decided he definitely didn't want any powers of his own. "It's not my kind of thing. I don't want to be a god. I just want to be an ordinary philosopher king, like everyone else." He intended to tease, but he was absolutely serious and meant it. That really was what he wanted. "We're trying to do Plato right here, as Athene intended, as Plato intended. And we're all volunteers— not the babies born here, but even they have the choice when they become ephebes to swear their oath or leave for one of the other cities."

"That's the same with us," I said.

"Yes, that's part of why we think you're essentially all right in the Remnant. I came here because I believed we should be following Plato more strictly, and I'm happy here."

"Even with the Festivals of Hera?"

"The Festivals of Hera are great!" He grinned at me. He was telling the truth. "No courtship, no ambiguity, no will-they-or-won't-they, everything organized simply for you, and most of the time no need to worry about it. Perfect!"

"And you haven't fallen in love with anyone or anything?"

"Oh, sure." He shrugged, a little too casually. "Agape. That's also great. I'll introduce you to Diogenes later. He's in my troop, but he's in Solon, not Theseus. He's originally from Psyche. He had to escape to get here, as they hate to have their Young Ones leave. You'll like him. I hope Father does."

"I'm sure Father will," I said, loyally. I felt a pang when I thought of Erinna, and pushed it away. A bird rose up singing from the vines, and we tilted our heads back to follow it up the sky.

"I'm happy," he said, looking back at me. "I like it here. I have Diogenes and all my friends. I have my studies and my exercises and my troop. I enjoy my hobby work among the vines. When I'm thirty I'll be able to vote in Chamber, and when I'm fifty I'll be able to read the *Republic*. If you can stop the stupid art raids so that we only fight about important things, that would make everything better. But I don't want to change anything about my life. I don't want strange powers messing up who I am and all my friendships. I don't need to be able to fly like that bird to be happy watching it fly. I don't want something else I can't tell Diogenes."

"I'm so glad you're happy," I said. "It does seems strange to me that you don't want powers when you could have them."

"It's so pointless," he said. "Athene set us here to enact the Republic as best we can, to become philosopher kings and live the just life. We'll be destroyed when the volcano takes down this side of the island. There's no sense in going beyond that."

"Because there's no posterity," I agreed. "No future, except for our souls. But don't you feel you have a duty to Fate?"

"My excellence is here," he said. "I feel my best self isn't in acquiring divine powers and learning about them, it's in living the good life here in Athenia."

28

ARETE

I had heard so much about the City of Amazons and Ikaros that finally seeing them was almost a disappointment. The city was much like Athenia, like home only smaller, and not so well built. *The Naming of Crocus* was as impressive close up as it was from a distance—crouching Sokrates was bigger than a building, and Maia, younger but very recognizable, seemed to have her head almost in the clouds. Crocus himself was completely unrecognizable as anything, seeming equal parts Worker, human, and flowers. "It's even bigger than his *Last Debate*," I said.

"It was his first full-scale colossus," Father said. "Crocus's art has always been really interesting."

"And he's been making more of it," I said.

Father nodded. "He's one of the city's most unexpected successes as a philosopher king. Sixty-One's numerology confuses me, but Crocus is a true Platonist."

"His art shows good people doing good things," I said, gazing upward at the huge Maia. Her braid was falling down slightly, the way it did sometimes when she twisted it up before it was quite dry. I wondered what she thought of seeing herself this way.

Ikaros met us as soon as we stepped out onto the quay. He was a man in his early sixties, with a charming smile and a cloud of untamed silvery hair. He had a girl with him, an ephebe about my age, whom he introduced as his daughter Rhadamantha. My birthday had come while I was away. I would be cutting my hair and taking my tests when I got home again.

Ikaros kissed my hand and told me that I looked like my father, so I must have been blessed with my mother's brains. While this came out as a compliment to me, it was subtly insulting to Father, but he only laughed. "I'm not such a fool as you think, Ikaros, for I have been chosen as envoy on this mission, and so far all the cities have agreed to come to the conference we are arranging."

Athenia had agreed to send envoys to the conference, and to send all their art for redistribution on condition that all the other cities agreed to do the same. "They think the Amazons won't," Alkibiades had explained. "They're sure the Amazons have the head of Victory, and that they won't give their art back because they'll think it's a trick to find out who took it." Father had nodded thoughtfully.

Now Ikaros took both of Father's hands and kissed them. "I was so sorry to hear about Simmea. A loss to you, and to the world. She was a true philosopher." Astonishingly, he was sincere. He really had admired Mother.

"We need to stop fighting about art and concentrate on increasing our excellence," Father said, with no preliminaries.

"Yes," Ikaros said. Father's eyes flicked to me. I nodded quickly. He meant it. "Do you have a plan?"

"I do," Father said. "Shall we go somewhere and discuss it? Do you have a committee for me to meet? Or should we go aboard and share a cup of wine?"

"We're guest-friends already," Ikaros said. "I remember sharing lemons with you and Simmea in Thessaly when Sokrates was still with us."

"I have the other member of your debate team. Aristomache is back in the City," Father said.

"Wonderful!" Ikaros sounded delighted. "You rescued her from Kebes?"

"It's more complicated than that, and I don't want to discuss standing it on the harbor," Father said.

"Oh, be welcome to the City of Amazons, both of you, come share food and drink and tell me everything you know about everything," Ikaros said.

He took Rhadamantha's arm, and we all walked along the quay to a nearby eating hall which, as it was the middle of the afternoon and not anywhere near a meal time, was almost empty. He sat us down so that we were in sunlight from the window. Rhadamantha ran off to the kitchen and came back with rather good cold cakes spread with quince and red currant conserves, and wine.

"Now run and find Lysias, and your mother, and Damon, and Klio," Ikaros said. The girl nodded and ran.

"Our Foreign Negotiations Committee," Ikaros explained.

"Four Masters and one of the Children?" Father asked, sipping his wine.

"Three. We were so used to running things," Ikaros said, narrowing his eyes. "Children, and even some Young Ones, are on lots of committees. Your boy Porphyry is on the Farming Committee."

"How you run the City of Amazons is your affair," Father said. "But I do want to tell you that other people have equal significance—they're just as real as you are, and you have to allow them to make their own choices."

Ikaros blinked. "Why do you want to tell me that?"

"Because Maia said something that indicated that you might not know it," Father said, sitting back blandly. I frowned at him. Had Maia told him about Ikaros saying she didn't love anyone? But how did that relate to other people being real? Father bit into his cake. "Good quinces you have here."

Ikaros recovered his poise. "Tell me about Kebes. You found the Goodness Group? All we've had is rumors."

"Shouldn't I wait for the others?"

"Then what should we discuss while we're alone?" Ikaros was wary. There were a few people working in the kitchen, laughing together as they made an early start on dinner, and one old woman sitting drinking by the window, out of earshot.

"My plan for ending the art raids involves returning everything to the original city and redistributing it based on population, with a certain amount of the more portable art moving between the cities on a regular cycle. The other cities have agreed to this, which means that you have the head of Victory, because nobody who had it would agree, not to me, not about this."

"So it wasn't Kebes?"

"You know it wasn't. Stop playing games." Father didn't take his eyes off Ikaros for a moment. Ikaros was looking at Father, but he didn't seem to be focusing on him.

"You've been swearing blood and vengeance on whoever has the head," Ikaros said. "I'd be a fool to admit it if we had it."

"As you may have heard, I took vengeance on Kebes. That's enough. Besides, while there are some circumstances where it's appropriate, this isn't one of them. The important thing is to stop wasting lives and effort over this foolishness, not to make everything worse." Father was utterly sincere.

"Our Young Ones enjoy the art raids. It makes them feel important and gives them a chance to let off steam," Ikaros said. "And then they get out of control, and they feel important, and they have weapons. So you don't need to tell me, because I can see exactly and precisely how things disintegrate into timarchy from here, and so I want to stop this as much as you do. But if we had the head, and I'm not saying we do, what would you suggest we do with it? We couldn't return it with everything else." He was telling the truth too, but Father didn't look away from him to see me signal.

"And you can't secretly keep it either, because then everyone will know that it wasn't returned, and if that was kept back then other things might have been." He hesitated, and continued in a lower voice. "And besides, she died for it."

"Sneak it back into the temple," I said. "Put it back where it came from, without admitting you ever had it in the first place."

Ikaros laughed, and looked toward me, but not quite at me. "Audacious. But how do you suggest we do it? A troop heading for the temple would be assumed to be raiding and attacked. And half of my problem is how wild the Young Ones in the troops are. I need to keep them under control, and they wouldn't respect me at all if I tried to stop them from fighting back if they were attacked. They might not even want to return it. And they have votes in our Assembly."

"Let me sing to them, and see whether that will help change their minds about the fun of art raids," Father said. "As for the head, get Rhadamantha to give it to Arete. Then Arete can quietly put it back. You and I won't be directly involved. I won't have to know officially who took it, or take any vengeance, and we can swear we didn't do it. It can be a divine intervention."

"An angelic one," Ikaros said.

"Kebes and the Goodness Group have been practicing muscular Christianity all over the Aegean," Father said, switching subjects smoothly.

"What?" Ikaros looked stunned.

"They have eight cities, mostly filled with refugees from mainland wars, mostly converts. It's not your New Concordance, nothing like that subtle. They say Athene was a demon, perhaps Lilith."

"What?"

"They've been teaching people to worship Yayzu and his mother Marissa, and revile Athene."

"In a Platonic context?" Ikaros asked, quite calmly, surprising me because I was expecting him to say "What?" again.

"Oh yes. But with torture for heretics, you'd feel quite at home."

"I would not! We don't do anything to heretics but debate with them. And we have *Saint* Girolamo in our calendar."

"Saint Girolamo, and the Archangel Athene too. You'll have to send missionaries," Father said, quite comfortably. "Nag them to death. Teach them your beautiful complex system. Let them know Christianity is all just fine up to a point, and torturing heretics is well beyond that point."

"I thought you wanted people to worship the Olympians," Ikaros said, frowning a little.

"I do, and so did Plato. I didn't say we wouldn't be sending out missionaries too."

Ikaros laughed, and just then the girl Rhadamantha came back with the others. She looked a tiny bit like Erinna, she had the same kind of hair and the same lean grace. I was glad when she stayed for the debate.

The debate was long. Father and I explained the Lucian civilization and the two conferences. I had heard it all before, but I had to stay to sing, when Father decided it was time, and also to let him know when people were lying. By dinner time, I had realized that there was something seriously wrong with Ikaros's sight, although he was trying to hide it. He didn't have cataracts, and he didn't peer and lean forward to see close up like Aristom-ache, but he never seemed to be focusing on what he was looking at. When Lysias passed him a note, he didn't even glance at it. He fumbled picking up his wine cup. He couldn't be blind. He had seen that I looked like Father. But that had been outside, in full daylight.

We had meetings with the committees, and then their Chamber, where we sang, several times. It took three days, but in the end they agreed to send envoys. They agreed to send their art back on the *Excellence*, too.

On the evening of the third day, after everything was agreed, I went for a walk up into the hills with my brother Porphyry, as I had done with Alkib-iades. I didn't know Porphyry well. He had always lived in the City of Am-azons, and only made occasional visits to us. "I'm sorry about your mother," he said, awkwardly, kicking at a stone.

"We're trying to stop the art raids in her memory," I said.

"Is it true that Father tortured Kebes or Marsias or whatever his name was to death?" he asked.

"Yes. And it was Matthias. But he was Kebes when he was here, so we always call him that."

"So does my mother. Matthias is a difficult name to get my tongue around anyway. So Father really killed him in that horrible way?"

"Yes. But Kebes was going to do it to him." I explained the competition, and the battle afterward.

"I suppose he had to." We were sitting down on the edge of a little stream, in the shade of a plane tree, dabbling our feet in the water. "But I think I would have cut his throat instead, even if that was their idea of justice."

"So would I, and so would Kallikles," I admitted.

"I've always been a bit frightened of Father, and this doesn't help," he said.

"Frightened of him? Why?" I couldn't imagine it.

"Oh, because he's so excellent. It makes it difficult to live up to. My mother always says he was just clearly the best when they were all growing up to-gether. And she was beautiful then, of course."

"I think your mother is still beautiful," I said. Euridike had a lovely face and wonderful hair.

"She says she hasn't been the same since she had babies. And she says it has been better for her, because she used to be vain about it. But anyway, back then when she tried to be friends with Pytheas because he was beautiful too, he never had any time for anyone except your mother. And he's not just beautiful, he's so good at everything. I always felt that I wasn't good enough for him. Children are supposed to outdo their parents, but how could I ever outdo Pytheas?"

"You have your own excellence," I said. "You just have to develop it. I never heard we were supposed to outdo our parents, or compare ourselves to anyone else, just that we had to work to become our best selves, the best that it's possible for us to be." I looked up at him. Porphyry was tall. "Do you know about Father?"

"Know what? He's hard to get to know. Especially when I didn't see much of him."

I lay back and stared up at the blue sky through the dappled leaves. I had to ask him whether he wanted to go to Delos, but if he didn't know who Father was that made it very difficult. "If you could have divine powers, but you had to keep them to yourself, would you want to?"

"Would I have divine responsibilities too?"

"What a good question! What do you mean?"

"Well, what kind of powers are we talking about?" Porphyry asked, treating the whole question as an abstract Platonic inquiry.

"Flight. Healing."

"Right. So say I could heal people, would I have a responsibility to go around healing everyone all the time? Of course I would, nobody could have that power without. With flight I suppose I'd have a responsibility to take messages rapidly everywhere, and rescue people from burning buildings, and that kind of thing."

"Yes," I said. "Assuredly, Sokrates, that must be the case."

He laughed. "Your mother said Sokrates hated it if they said that."

"I know." I was thinking about whether I had a responsibility to take messages quickly around the world. If I did, it could explain where my language skills fitted in. But I didn't much want to be a messenger god. Besides, did the world need another?

"I don't know if I'd want divine powers. It would be so disruptive. But it could be fun. And it would give my life a purpose. I wouldn't have to worry about what my excellence was, I'd know."

"No you wouldn't," I said. "What if you had them and couldn't tell anyone."

"You mean I could heal people but they wouldn't know I was doing it?"

"Yes."

"That would be very strange. And how would that work with flight? I could only fly if nobody was looking? I'd have to stand by burning buildings knowing I could rescue people and let them burn to death?"

I started to cry. I didn't mean to, but I was remembering Erinna in the storm. Porphyry put his arm around me, not awkwardly like Father but as if he was used to being comforting to people. "What's wrong? Is the debate making you miss Simmea?"

"I do have divine powers, and I don't know what to do about the responsibility," I sniffed.

"What, really?" he looked down at me, astonished, but not disbelieving.

"Stand up and I'll show you," I said, getting to my feet. There was nobody around. I leaped into the air, and swooped down to scoop him up, as I had Kallikles. Porphyry went rigid for a moment, and then he started to laugh. My tears dried in the wind and in the face of his delight.

"Take me right up," he called. "Take me so high I can see the city from above, like an eagle."

"But then they'd see us," I said.

"How about over the mountain then? Could we fly over the crater? That would be so great."

"I don't think I can carry you for ten miles," I said. "I don't know. I never have and I don't want to risk dropping you." I went up, so he could see the stream and the hill it ran down and the City of Amazons in the distance. Then I made a series of loops around the tree and set him down again. "Sometime we could meet up on the mountain and I'd fly you over the crater, if you want."

"I'd love that! That was such fun. The wind on my face. It was amazing. How can you do that? And why can't you tell anyone?"

"I can do it because Father is Apollo, and I went to Delos and it woke my power."

Porphyry sat down again, and I sat down beside him. "Father is Apollo? Incarnate? Like Jesus?"

"Yes, pretty much exactly like, as far as I understand it," I said, pleased that he'd understood so rapidly. "But he doesn't want anyone to know except family. I didn't know whether he'd told you, but when we were talking about Delos he said he'd take you if you wanted to go. And he asked me to tell you about the powers."

"It makes so much sense that he would be Apollo. Why did I never think of that? And . . . how could I possibly try to compete! Did Simmea know? Of course she did." He shook his head in wonder.

"She figured it out herself," I said, proud of my mother. I'd heard the story of how she'd figured it out many times, from both my parents.

"And what happened on Delos?"

"Kallikles and Phaedrus and I found a spring and drank from a cup, and then we had powers. Different powers. Phaedrus can heal and control the volcano, and Kallikles has lightning and weather powers."

"Lightning? Amazing. But they can't fly?"

"They can walk on air, but I'm the only one who can fly properly."

"And why can't you tell anyone? Will you lose the powers if you do?" He seemed eager and enthusiastic.

"No, just that everyone will know we're freaks. Father says he wants to live a normal life as best he can."

"But my burning building question made you cry because in that situation you'd have to give yourself away?"

"Of course I would. I couldn't just stand there." I rubbed my eyes hard to stop myself crying again. "I don't know if I can live a normal life, with powers. It's going to be hard. I already used them, in the battle in Lucia. I flew over a man who was attacking me. People thought it was a leap, but really it was flight. And Phaedrus healed people. Aristomache had broken her arm, but he healed it and said it was just a bruise, that kind of thing."

"And Kallikles?"

"He struck an attacker with lightning, and he made the wind change so that the burning boat burned the *Goodness* instead of the *Excellence*. But people didn't know it was him. They thought it was Zeus."

Porphyry shook his head. "I don't see how you can keep powers like that secret, long term, if you use them. And you can't help doing it, when something happens like that. It would be better if people knew and could plan for it. And maybe Pytheas ought to talk to Ikaros about being Apollo. Ikaros would be so interested. He'd instantly work out a way to make it fit with the New Concordance."

"But then people would always be pestering him about it."

"And people would always be asking you to get kittens out of trees."

I laughed. "And taking messages between cities, like you said."

"If it turns out that you can fly that far."

"I don't know whether I can. I need to practice. But for now, do you want to go to Delos and get some powers of your own?"

He grinned. "Yes, definitely, as soon as I possibly can. It would increase my excellence, and also be a ton of fun. But I'm not going to promise to keep them secret and not use them for the good of humanity."

"I think you'll have to talk to Father about keeping it secret. And maybe to all of us. Because it doesn't just affect you. If people know you have powers, they'll want to know why."

"I'll talk to Father." He looked as if he was bracing himself for it. "And Kallikles and Phaedrus. And it will depend what my powers are, and whether they'd be useful. I wish I could choose what they would be. I'd love so much to be able to fly. Would you take me up again? Just for a little bit?"

"Of course." It was lovely to meet such enthusiasm. I swooped up with him in my arms. We went quite high, so he could see the landscape, and then I let him direct me along the stream toward a cove. I took him down again then and set him down gently on the black sand. I spiraled a few times around the cove before coming down in front of him, on the edge of the sea. Only then did I see a man sitting against the base of the cliff, with his arms wrapped around his legs, watching us. Ikaros.

He looked stunned and delighted. There was no point pretending it hadn't happened, because he'd clearly seen the whole thing, and besides there were no tracks in the sand. "Joy to you," I said.

Porphyry spun around. "Ikaros! Joy to you," he stammered. "We were just . . . that is I . . . my sister was just showing me . . ."

"She's an angel!" Ikaros believed every word he was saying, but that didn't make it true.

I flew over to him in one swoop and sat down in the sand beside him. I pinched the skin of the back of his hand. "Real," I said. "Not an angel."

"So was Sophia—Athene—as tangible and corporeal as anyone else," he said. "She never pinched me, but I brushed against her several times and touched her hands when we were acquiring art together. But if you're not an angel, explain to me what you are, and I'll figure out how it all fits together."

I opened my mouth, but Porphyry interrupted before I could. "Don't tell him anything."

He was standing, with his shadow falling over me. He had composed himself in the walk across the beach and no longer looked worried. "What? Why?"

"For one thing it's not only your secret, as you were just telling me. But I've just worked out the most important reason is that knowing for sure would break his heart."

I frowned up at him. "How? You said before he'd work out how it fit together, and that's just what he said himself."

"Yes. But I was wrong. I know Ikaros a lot better than you do. He's my sister Rhadamantha's father, so he's been around our house a lot all my life. He's my teacher. He thinks he wants to know, but—"

"I'm right here," Ikaros said, plaintively.

Porphyry looked at him and smiled. "Tell me truthfully you want Arete to explain it to you, instead of letting you work it out for yourself."

"Oh!" Ikaros put his hand to his heart. "A hit! And from my own disciple!"

Porphyry smiled and sat down. "What are you doing out here anyway? You shouldn't come this far alone. Your eyes aren't up to it."

"I keep telling you, I can still see perfectly well in full daylight." He was lying. "The debate ended earlier than I thought, and I came to get something that's hidden in the cave." That part was true.

Porphyry's eyes flicked toward the cleft in the cliff.

"If that's where you're keeping the head of Victory I can just go in myself and take it now," I said.

"And fly home to the City with it, and set it back in the temple," Ikaros suggested. "While I work on my theory of how it is that you're a girl born in the Remnant City and grown up at a normal speed, but you can fly. You say you're not an angel, and I admit it does seem unlikely. Maybe it's because your mother was such an exceptional philosopher and you're developing angelic abilities because of that. Maybe if we all study Plato hard enough the entire next generation will be able to fly."

I laughed, because while he was joking, he also half hoped he was right. "You really do believe in the perfectibility of humanity," I said.

"Despite everything, I keep hoping. And from time to time I find some evidence."

"Please don't tell anyone," I said. "Once everyone knows I can fly they'll always be getting me to carry messages and rescue kittens from trees."

"I won't tell anyone until I'm sure I have the right answer. But can I come to you with my guesses?"

"To me, or to Porphyry," I said.

"And even if and when you have it right, perhaps you could incorporate it in the New Concordance anonymously, as in saying a girl born in one of the Republics, rather than giving Arete's name?" Porphyry suggested.

"But her name perfectly encapsulates what she is. As does yours, of course. But I won't use it. You can trust me."

I wanted to like him and trust him, but I couldn't. "Why were you so mean to Maia?" I asked.

Ikaros blinked. "Maia? I thought she accepted my apology?" He was sincere, which wasn't to say he was correct.

"You told her she doesn't love anybody!" I accused.

"Oh." He looked abashed. "She told you about that?"

"It's still hurting her."

"What happened was that Klio had been telling me about this German philosopher—"

"The Germans have philosophers?" Porphyry interrupted, astonished. I was astonished too. I'd read Tacitus. I imagined some hairy barbarian debating in the forests while avoiding the axes of his companions.

"This was later, after they were civilized," Ikaros said, waving away the distraction. "They conquered Italy and claimed to be the heirs of Rome like everyone else. Anyway, this German had interesting theories about how minds work, and I was interested in them for a time, as best Klio could remember what she'd read years before. And one of his theses seemed to me to explain Maia's behavior, and I was foolish enough to mention this to her. I can see now how it was unkind. At the time I thought she'd be glad of an explanation."

"You should tell her you were wrong," I said.

"I will. I'm sorry that's still upsetting her." He meant it. "Is that what Pytheas was talking about when he told me people have equal significance?"

"I don't know," I said. "But can I trust you that you won't tell anyone about me being able to fly?"

Ikaros laughed again. "You're safe even if you can't trust me. I've never seen anything so lovely as the two of you coming in to land just then. But while I've tried to keep everyone from knowing how bad my eyes are, they know enough to know I'm not a reliable witness on something like this."

"How much can you see, really?" I asked.

Ikaros sighed. "I can see shapes and colors, in sunlight," he said, truthfully. "No detail. And the middle distance is where I can see best. I could see you better when you landed than I can now. It's just strain from reading too much in bad light."

I wondered if Phaedrus would be able to heal him. I didn't want to raise his hopes without being sure.

"He doesn't want people to know. But I know, because I read to him and write things he dictates," Porphyry said.

"Some things," Ikaros teased, smiling. There was something about the way he said this that made me realize that he and Porphyry had the same kind of close teacher-pupil friendship that Ficino and I had had. "And I have a lot memorized. It's not so bad."

"I trust you not to tell," I said. "And Porphyry knows enough to tell you if your guesses are good."

"Get the head," Porphyry suggested to me, waving at the cave.

I went into the cave. It was dim after the bright sunlight outside, and I had to wait for my eyes to adjust. At first I couldn't see anything but the rippled volcanic rock, but then I noticed a shelf, just above my head. On it was a bundle wrapped in cloth. I pulled it down and unwrapped it. There was the serene and perfect stone face of Victory gazing up at me. What a stupid thing to die for, I thought, hating it. What a feeble recompense for all the years Simmea might have lived. And yet, how beautiful it was, even in this dimness. A masterpiece.

I wiped my eyes, tucked the head under my arm, and flew out of the cave. I circled the cove—I saw Ikaros's head move to watch me, and I settled to the sand again next to them. Ikaros took the head and ran his fingers gently over the contours of the face. He had tears in his eyes. He didn't even try to look at it. "Take it," he said. "Fly back to the Remnant with it. I'll come to the conference, and see you and it there."

"I'll help you back to the city," Porphyry said to Ikaros.

I took the head and flew up again. I had no intention of flying all the way home with the head, but I circled over Ikaros and Porphyry's heads and set off southward. I came down in the woods near the City of Amazons and walked in with the head carefully covered up. I took it to the *Excellence*, where I stowed it safely in my hammock.

Then I went to find Father. "Porphyry wants to go to Delos when you go," I said. "And I have the head of Victory, for what it's worth."

29

MAIA

We held the conference in the Chamber. The Chamber was the oldest building in the City. I could remember when it was the only building and all the Masters slept in it, uncomfortable and excited on the marble floor. I'd been in it thousands of times since then, and usually I took the steps and went through the pillared portico without thinking of anything but the day's business. The day the conference began, I walked in with Axiothea and remembered that early excitement, and my young bones that didn't ache. We had been among the youngest of the Masters, and now most of the older ones were dead, of time and attrition, or in Ficino's case a sword through the ribs.

Once I had looked forward to a time when the older Masters would be gone and we younger ones could make decisions. But then I had imagined the Republic growing stronger and more secure every year. I had believed the Children would become philosopher kings. I was older now. I didn't know whether I was wiser.

The room was arranged for debate, with rows of benches facing the rostrum. It was packed, with all the envoys and all the Chamber members who wanted to participate. There must have been nearly five hundred people present. The envoys sat at the front, and it was agreed that they had precedence in speaking.

The conference began with a simple direct prayer to far-seeing Apollo for clarity. It was given by Manlius, whose turn it was. There had been some argument about this, with Ikaros and Aristomache both wanting prayers of their own, either as replacements or additions. In the end this was a compromise—it didn't mention Athene. Yet it was impossible, in this room, not to think of her, not to remember her standing in front of us, nine feet tall, with the owl on her arm turning its head to watch us all.

Then we elected a judge—a chair, a moderator, to control the flow of debate. It had been agreed in advance that the voting for this would be by simple majority of all present. Pytheas stood. "I'd be a terrible judge," he began. There was a ripple of laughter. "The person I'd like to propose, our chair here since Atticus died, was killed in the fighting in Lucia. I'd like a moment of silence for Ficino, missed now and always." Tears came to my eyes. After the silence he went on. "I think our judge should be someone who has experience of more than one city, who went on the voyage, and has direct experience of the Lucian cities. I propose Maia."

He hadn't warned me. Axiothea shoved me to my feet. "If elected I will serve, and strive to be fair," I said. "It's an honor, but also it will be very difficult."

To my astonishment, Ikaros seconded the proposal. (His hair was entirely silver now, and shaggy like a lion's mane.) Somebody proposed old Salutius, from Psyche; and Patroklus, from Sokratea, proposed Neleus, on the grounds that he had been on the voyage and was a Young One. Neleus declined, saying he had no experience and he thought I'd do a better job. I was elected, and made my way up to the front.

It was strange sitting where Athene had stood, where Krito had sat, and Tullius, Cato, and Ficino. It was strange to look at the hall from this perspective, the sea of faces. I had chaired committees, and even moderated plenty of debates, but none in Chamber. I put my hands on the carved arms of the chair, gripping them tightly. I had never imagined myself here. I had always

seen myself in a support role, never imagined myself sufficiently respected
to be chosen to judge an important debate like this. Well, I knew what Plato
said about that. I took a breath and looked at Pytheas, who was still standing there. Neleus and I had been working on accommodation for the envoys
and diplomatic issues. "Is there an agenda?"

Pytheas handed me a paper: 1. How to vote. 2. The Lucian question. 3.
Choral ode. 4. Art raids. No more, no order of speakers or anything. I looked
at him in exasperation. It was just like Pytheas: so generally excellent, with
such unexpected lacunae. He shrugged.

"First, how to vote," I said, to the room.

It was a contentious issue. By number of cities the Lucians outnumbered
everyone else. They had sent thirty envoys. About half of them were originally Masters and Children from the Just City. The other half were refugees
rescued and converted to Christian Platonism. None of them approved of
Kebes breaking guest friendship, but they were all devastated by the loss
of the *Goodness*. They had different opinions on different subjects, but they
were all united in their sense of mission. They wanted to rescue victims of
Bronze Age wars and teach them civilization. That's what they had been
doing all this time, and they wanted to keep on with it. And it was immediately apparent to everyone that if we used democratic voting by city,
with their eight cities they'd immediately and unquestionably succeed in
that aim.

Aurelius, of Psyche, suggested that the Lucians be considered one city, as
we had imagined they were before they were rediscovered—the Goodness
Group as we had called them, or the Lost City. "A hundred and fifty people
left with Kebes. Calling them one city and giving them an equal vote with
us seems generous. Calling them eight cities seems ridiculous."

"Each of our cities is bigger than Psyche, and though most of the people
in them are volunteers, they have taken the oath of citizenship, they read and
write, they know Plato," Aristomache countered. "Many of our leaders came
from the *Goodness*, but others have arisen from the people we rescued. We
make no distinction between us. Adrastos here is an example. We found him
as a boy fleeing a war in the Troad. He's thirty now, and he has spent the
last twenty years with us. He's a gold of Marissa, a philosopher and a stonemason."

"Like Sokrates," Adrastos said, shyly, standing up when he was mentioned.

Patroklus, from Sokratea, suggested that we should give cities votes by
population, but aim for consensus—any motion would need a two-thirds
majority to pass. (It would be total population, as citizens were too difficult
to count, because we all had different criteria for citizenship. Psyche didn't

count women, Athenia didn't count people under thirty, the Lucians didn't count bronzes or irons, and none of us counted children.)

There was much debate, and eventually this proposal was accepted, as being the closest thing to fair. I set up a hasty committee to come up with numbers over the lunch break. I fortified myself with soup and grapes in Florentia, while claiming that talking to anyone about the conference would violate my neutrality. "Ficino never said that," Arete complained.

"Ficino had more practice than I have. I need to clear my head."

On my way back to the Chamber, Neleus caught up with me. "You're doing well so far," he said. "I was terrified when Patroklus suggested me!"

"So was I when your father suggested me!" We smiled at each other. Neleus was one of the brightest of the Young Ones, and he had always been one of my favorite pupils, and one of Ficino's too. On impulse, I pulled Ficino's hat out of the fold of my kiton, where I'd been carrying it since Lucia. "I wonder if you'd like this. It's silly really, it's old and worn, and—"

"I'd really love it," Neleus said, tears in his eyes. He reshaped the hat in his hands and jammed it on his head. "Thank you. I don't know what to say." We walked along quietly together. Then to my surprise, Ikaros came bounding up through the crowd of people heading back into the chamber.

"Ficino! I'm so delighted—No. Sorry."

Neleus turned to him in astonishment. He didn't look a thing like Ficino, even in the hat. He was even darker-skinned than Simmea, and much broader-shouldered than Ficino.

"I did know he was dead," Ikaros said. "But there are others here I knew were dead. I saw the familiar red hat, on a street where I had seen him so often, and for a moment I thought it was him. Sorry, young man."

"How are your eyes?" I asked, remembering his eyestrain from translating Aquinas the day he apologized to me.

"Maia! You're doing a wonderful job so far. Could I talk to you this evening after the session?"

He hadn't known me, and he had thought Neleus was Ficino. And he hadn't answered my question about his eyes. I realized he must be nearly blind. I felt profoundly sorry for him. "Of course," I said. "I'll wait for you on the steps afterward."

We reconvened. Axiothea came up to announce the results of the numbers. Psyche was given five votes, the Lucian cities six each, Athenia and Sokratea twelve each, the City of Amazons fifteen, and the Original City twenty-five. "If all of Kallisti voted together, that would be sixty-nine, to Lucia's forty-eight," she said. Everyone laughed at the thought of all of Kallisti voting together.

"If the envoys from a city are divided, can the votes be split?" Aurelius asked.

"Certainly," I ruled. "The envoys can divide the city's votes as they choose."

"And who are the envoys who will vote for the Remnant?"

"The Foreign Negotiations Committee, with Pytheas representing Simmea," I said. "But no doubt they will listen to opinions."

The Chamber was less packed now. Some people were lingering over lunch, and others had realized that this would go on a long time and be boring. However, as soon as we started properly it began to move rapidly and became fascinating.

"The issue of the Lucians," I said. I'd been thinking how to address this. "First Pytheas will explain succinctly what happened on the voyage, and then Aristomache will explain what they were doing and what they want. Questions afterward. I'll open up the debate to the whole room and we'll have plenty of time for everyone. But let's hear this quietly first." I had caught both of them on my way to lunch and asked them to be ready.

Everyone in the room probably knew what Pytheas told them, but there were still some surprised gasps as he went through it. Then Aristomache came up and described the Lucian mission. "We have reading, plumbing, pottery, iron working, medicine, Yayzu, and Plato," she said "How can we sit safely on an island while there are people out there who have none of these things? Join us, and help us spread civilization."

Many agreed with her message, though some of us wanted to leave Jesus out of the lists of benefits. Kallikles spoke in support of Aristomache: "I was really shaken by what I saw on Naxos," he said, describing the ignorance and poverty of the village he had visited. "People shouldn't be living like that when we can help them. The Lucians like Adrastos prove it can be done. We should be doing it."

Others, especially the Athenians, were horrified at the very notion. "Athene put us here where the volcano would wipe out every trace of what we do. We can't go running around the Mediterranean interfering with everything! Who knows what harm it might do!"

I was sympathetic with that view myself. So was Klio. "We don't know how history works," she said. "But consider that it might be a wax tablet like the ones we use every day. After it has been written, it can be erased and rewritten. If we step out of the margins where Athene has set us, we could wipe out everything that comes after. What Kallikles said about helping those poor people sounds entirely good. But we don't know enough. What if the Trojan War needs to come out of the poverty and dirt we saw in the Kyklades? If so we would be wrong to change it, however painful seeing it may be. What if people handed the secret of iron-making will be content to make iron forever and never move on to steel, as they would have if they'd discovered it for themselves? And we don't know, we can't know, what matters, or what is and isn't safe to change. We have seen too much here of what comes from good intentions and ignorance. We should leave them alone to find their own destiny and stay on our island."

Everyone had their own theory of history, and many aired them. Ikaros was absolutely sure that Athene wouldn't have put us here if there was any danger. He believed in Providence, and his argument was essentially that we could only do good by trying to increase excellence.

Finally Patroklus argued that the people of the Aegean had their own Fate and that we had no right at all to change that, or to judge them for living differently from the way we thought right. "You have described their art. What right have we to impose our ideas of art on them instead? Perhaps they have religions and philosophies that are equally valuable. I'm not arguing in support of Klio, that we don't know what it's safe to change. I agree with that, but my point is different. What right have we to judge and to say what is better or worse?"

I called an end to the day without calling for a vote. "Lots of people haven't had a chance to speak yet. We'll resume in the morning."

"You're not setting up a committee on the nature of time?" Pytheas asked as I stepped down.

"Why, do you have any pertinent information for it?" He was always such a funny mixture. I remembered him as a boy, so intent on everything, so serious. They were all my children.

"Nothing that I want to talk about right now," he said. "But it seems to me that the debate has been all about that, and only what Patroklus said was about whether we want to help."

"I think there would be a clear majority for helping if not for the worry about time," I said. "The suggestion that the Lucian cities are the cities Plato heard about was popular."

"I suspect it's what Simmea would have wanted." He sighed. "It's never easy, is it? But I think you're doing very well in the chair."

Ikaros was waiting on the steps when I came out. The sun was setting, and in this light I had to touch his arm to get his attention.

"Where shall we go?" he asked.

"Let's go to my house," I said.

"Oh marvelous!" he said.

"My house isn't so wonderful," I said, taking his arm to lead the way.

"But if you'll invite me there it means you have forgiven me. Some things your pupils said led me to believe you might not have. That's really why I wanted to speak to you."

I didn't want to say that he was old and almost blind and I felt sorry for him and not at all afraid any more. "Of course I forgive you. I forgave you years ago, before I left the City of Amazons. What pupils?"

"Pytheas said something very gnomic. And Arete said you were still upset about me saying you were afraid to love," he said.

"I do think of that sometimes, wondering if it's true," I admitted. We came to my house. I pushed the door open and turned on the light. "I think it made me uncomfortable because it was a little bit true. If it wasn't partly true it wouldn't have stung."

He stood inside the dim room. I guided him to the bed, where he sat, cautiously. "And it was my fault you were afraid," he said.

"Yes," I said, as I mixed wine. "But it was a long time ago, and I have forgiven you. And I realized when Ficino died how much I loved him all this time." I gave him a cup of wine, putting it into his hand.

"I'm sorry," he said.

"We can't undo the past. We go on from where we are." I sat down on a cushion on the floor, against the wall. "And here you are back in the original city, and in my house. Tell me about your eyes. How much can you see?"

"I do all right in sunlight," he said. "Though I mistake things even then, as you saw this afternoon. It's grown much worse this last year. But it's been three years now since I was able to read."

"Oh Ikaros, how terrible for you! I'm so sorry."

"It was Crocus's fault really, not yours," he said. I'd only meant to convey sympathy, not admit fault, but if it was translating Aquinas that had made him lose his vision it was indeed partly my fault. "I've wondered sometimes if it's Providence, if it's punishment for what I did to you and destroying your joy."

"No," I said at once, then wondered. Could it be? "I have had plenty of joy, even though I was afraid. And I still do." And I can read, I thought, looking at my bookshelves.

"I think it would have happened more quickly and more directly," he said. "If this is a punishment for anything it's probably for buying those books."

"Forbidden books," I said. "How did Crocus know you had them?"

"I told Sokrates about them, and he was there. Sokrates couldn't read Aquinas, because it was in Latin, of course." He hesitated, and sipped his wine. "Speaking of Latin and forbidden books, could I ask you to read something to me?"

"Of course," I said, with no hesitation.

He pulled a book out of his kiton. It was black and had a cross on the cover. I recognized it immediately as a Bible. "It's Jerome's Latin Bible," he said.

Written on the cover was *Versio Sacra Vulgata*. It was the Vulgate, the Latin Bible of the Catholic Church. I had heard about it but never seen it before. We didn't allow it in the Republic, of course, and I had only read the King James Version when I was young.

"I thought you allowed Bibles in Amazonia?"

"We have Bibles compiled from memory. It's surprising how much people knew, and of course I had this and could fill in some pieces nobody remembered." I took it from him and leafed through it. It was printed on the same Bible paper I remembered from my childhood, with the initials of verses printed in red.

"So what do you want me to read?"

"Jerome's prefaces. Of course nobody had memorized those." He smiled. "Nobody else. But ever since I heard about Ficino's death, I've been longing to re-read Jerome's preface to Job, where he talks about the difficulties of translation."

I turned the pages until I came to it. I had never read it, and reading it aloud now I laughed when I reached Jerome's comparison of translating to wrestling an eel, which gets more slippery the harder you try to hold on. When I came to the end of the preface, I kept on reading. I had not read Job since I was a girl, and I was surprised how much it still meant to me. We both had tears in our eyes when I stopped reading.

"Come to Florentia and have dinner," I said, handing him back the book.

"Keep it," he said. "It's no use to me now. Even if you don't want to read it, you can enjoy all of Jerome's snarky prefaces, where he calls people who prefer other translations barking dogs."

"Do you still think Athene's perfect?" I asked. "Because I find a great deal of comfort in thinking that she isn't, and that the gods have limited natures and limited reach. Believing that allows for things going wrong and not being part of anybody's plan."

"I keep trying to understand," he said, getting up. "If we became like angels, we would see how perfect she is. Don't you remember how wonderful she was when she was here?"

"Wonderful, yes, absolutely. But wonderful is not at all the same thing as perfect. Come on, let's go and eat before the food is all gone. I'll read to you some more tomorrow if you want. I assume you have plenty of people to take dictation."

By lunchtime the next day we had a consensus—a two-thirds majority— for helping the Lucians. We weren't prepared to give them the *Excellence*, though obviously we'd have to use it. Details remained to be agreed on, especially on religious issues. I set up a number of committees. I pushed Aristomache, Ikaros, Aurelius, Manlius and Pytheas onto the committee on religion, and swore privately never to go near it myself. There was also consensus that any individual Lucians who wanted to return to the Remnant City would be welcome, and any who met the immigration criteria for the other cities would be welcome to apply there. The Lucians offered reciprocal agreements, but I didn't think many of us would want to emigrate there.

After lunch came the choral ode. Pytheas had written it, and his son Phaedrus was conducting it. It took place out of doors, in the agora, so that as many people as possible could hear it. It was Pytheas's best work, powerful and moving, especially with the massed voices echoing around the space. The song was about peace. I'd never really considered that peace isn't just the absence of war but an active positive force. It must be one of Plato's Forms, I thought.

At the end of the ode, there was a consensus for hearing it again, so we did. This time many people were joining in with the final chorus, making the commitment to fight to defend peace.

We went back into the Chamber in a very different mood. I was preparing to begin on the question of art raids when a messenger came in to the Chamber. It was Sophoniba, a Young One, one of the Florentine troop. "The head of Victory is back," she said, panting. She had been running.

"Back?" I asked. "What do you mean?"

"Back in the temple of Victory just outside the walls, where it used to be. And the strangest thing is that the gravel courtyard was raked this morning and there are no marks on it at all. It's as if the gods brought it back."

"Was it with the returned art?" The returned art was on display in the agora and the colonnades around it, forming an impromptu art exhibition which everyone had been enjoying in their spare moments. I'd been spending my spare moments reading to Ikaros, so I hadn't had time for it myself.

"No," Pytheas said. "I looked closely, as you'd expect. The head of Victory wasn't there. But you say now it's back in the temple?"

"That's right," Sophoniba said. "It's the strangest thing."

We all trooped out to see it, and there indeed it was, where it had always been, serene, victorious, mysterious, in the niche against the back wall. Pytheas started to sing his ode again, and although the choir had dispersed many people joined in.

"It's a Mystery," Aurelius said to me as we were walking back.

"I certainly can't understand it."

"Do you think it was Sophia?" Manlius whispered behind us.

"I can't think who else it could have been," Sophoniba said. "There wasn't a mark on the gravel, and it shows every mark."

"If she's still paying attention, what must she think of us!" Manlius said.

Back in the Chamber, the debate on art raids then resumed.

Pytheas began. "After the Last Debate, when the new cities were founded, we all agreed that we couldn't divide the technology because we didn't understand it well enough to move things, and all of it was needed here to function properly. We might have agreed to divide it with our brothers and sisters in any case, had it not been absolutely necessary to the lives of Crocus and Sixty-One. Their vital need for electricity was more important than anything. Secondly, the electricity keeps the library at a constant temperature, which isn't just a comfort for us but a necessity for the preservation and safety of the books. That's why we printed additional copies for the libraries in the other cities but kept the originals here." He looked at the Lucians, all sitting in a group on the left-hand side now. "You weren't present for that debate, but I feel sure you'd have agreed if you had been."

There were nods among them, and some hands raised in other parts of the room, which I ignored. If people wanted to point out that the books were traded rather than given away, that would divert the argument. Let them wait.

"Then when the envoys of Psyche suggested dividing up our art, it seemed at first to be the same thing. It was an easy mistake to make. But it wasn't at all the same. Art can be divided in a way that technology cannot. We can travel to look at art. Nobody's life was being endangered if the art left the City, nor was the art itself endangered. We wanted to keep it because we loved it, but that was the same reason why our brothers and sisters in other cities wanted to own it. We fought over it. Nothing could have been more foolish than war over art. And we're all tired of it. All the cities have brought back what was taken, and we've been enjoying seeing it again. I propose that we distribute art to all the cities according to population, and bring it back here to redistribute it again every five years, at a great festival of art, where new art can also be seen and enjoyed. Simmea," he choked as he said her name, took a deep breath and said it again, louder. "Simmea always said that we should be making more art instead of squabbling over the art we have. She loved the Botticellis in Florentia with all her soul. But there are nine of them. If four of them had gone, one to each of the other cities, she'd still be here to love the five that were left."

He sat down. Among the forest of hands, only one was raised among the Lucians: Auge. Curious, I called on her.

"We didn't take any art on the *Goodness*. We made our own art in the Lucian cities. We haven't talked about it, but we're not here to demand our share of original art for our cities, and it might be at risk going by sea, and we wouldn't want that. I'm horrified at the art raids you've been describing. I can't believe Simmea died in one—actually died! Simmea, whose own original work was so wonderful. The kiton I wore when I lived here has long since worn out, but I cut off the piece of embroidery Simmea did along the hem and I still have it framed on the wall above my daughter's bed. But what I stood up to say is that I'm a sculptor. If you agree to share your art as Pytheas suggested, I'll do an original piece of stonework for each of your cities, on any subject you like. The people of Sokratea have already commissioned me to do a statue of Sokrates as he appeared in the Last Debate. I'll do that for free, and whatever else equivalently for the other four cities—statues or bas reliefs, whatever you want."

There was a roar of acclamation, and I had a lump in my throat. She was so sincere, and asking for nothing but instead offering to make and give. And her visible horror at the thought of the art raids helped us realize how barbaric they were. They'd been going on so long we'd almost become used to them.

Then Crocus raised one of his great arms. Neither of the Workers spoke often in Chamber. I called on him. He wrote his statement on a tablet, and Manlius read it aloud. "I will also offer free art equivalently, and extra work, whatever is needed, to stop the fighting."

There was another great cheer. More people began to offer the same. Then there were a few other speeches. Some citizens of the original city said how attached they were to the particular art in their own eating halls, and Aeschines and Sixty-one talked about how frescoes and mosaics couldn't be moved without damaging them. But nobody wanted to continue the art raids. When I called for a vote it was almost unanimous.

30

ARETE

When I came back from the missions I plunged straight into my adulthood tests, along with Boas and Archimedes, who were the other two people born in my birth month. When my brothers had become ephebes they had done it amid hordes of other Young Ones born in the same month, but for me there were only the three of us. Boas and Archimedes had been waiting more or less patiently for my return so that we could all do it together. They could have petitioned the Archons to go ahead without me, and I could have done it alone, but they had waited. Neither of them were philosophically inclined. Boas wanted to be a metal Worker, perhaps a sculptor, and Archimedes loved growing things and was already working out at the farms for far more than the required time. We had very little in common but we got along well.

We all acquitted ourselves well in the palaestra, especially Archimedes, who was already getting broad shoulders. "They'll make you a silver," I said when scraping him off after the wrestling.

He shook his head and grinned. "They know where I belong."

Then the conference began. Alkibiades, with his friend Diogenes, came to town with the Athenian delegation, and Porphyry came with the Amazons, so Thessaly was full to bursting point. I had no time to spend with them because I was being tested on the laws, and on rhetoric, and history, and music, and mathematics. It was an experience intended to be grueling, and it was. It was meant as a rite of passage. For Boas and Archimedes it unquestionably was. If I hadn't been on the voyage I would no doubt have felt it that way too. As it was, I felt grown up already, as if this were just a necessary marker.

I wanted to know about the conference. Maia wouldn't talk about it, but my brothers told me everything.

Ikaros had come to the conference. I asked Phaedrus to heal him while he was in town. He was reluctant. "He couldn't help but notice!" Father had talked to us seriously about not being caught using our powers.

"He already knows about me. We can arrange it so that he thinks I've healed him," I said. "Come on Phaedrus, think about it, he's nearly blind and he loves reading."

"He wouldn't tell anyone," Porphyry assured him.

"All right then. But not until after your initiation. You won't have time to pretend it's you until then."

I had to be content with that.

The day after the conference was the Ides, and therefore the day set for me to swear my oath to the Republic, and become an ephebe and be given my metal. It wasn't the grand affair it had been when the Children swore, or even five years ago when my brothers swore. Then there had been so many new ephebes that almost the whole city turned out to see them swear. But nevertheless, it was an occasion. Since all the envoys were still in town and many of them knew me and wanted to come, it was going to be a big public event, with a proper feast afterward, with a sheep roasted on a spit, and bannocks, and cream cheese, and plums stewed with honey. Hebe, one of my friends in the Florentine kitchens, told me about the preparations.

I had a new kiton, dyed orange and blue in the wool and woven in ocean pattern. Mother had been embroidering the hem when she died, and I had thought I'd wear it with the pattern unfinished. But Euklides had finished it for me while I'd been away. I could see where he'd taken it over, the lilies and scrolls were less even, and the colors less precise than the ones Mother had done. But it was wonderful that he had taken the time to finish it for me. I felt loved as I put it on for the first time on the morning of the Ides. I kept my hair loose for the ceremony.

I went to Florentia for breakfast, and as always when I went in my eyes sought for Ficino, and as always now failed to find him. I wondered whether I'd always do that, whether when I was myself ninety-nine I'd still half-expect to see him somewhere about the hall. Before I could sit down, Baukis and Erinna brought me a crown of flowers they had made. "Neleus and I collected the flowers and Baukis wove it," Erinna said. It had tiny wild roses and long-stemmed daisies and little dark-blue hyacinths and their leaves. It was lopsided, but I didn't care. Baukis hugged me, and I looked over her shoulder at Erinna. "Welcome to adulthood," she said, awkwardly, and smiled. I put the wreath on, and then Maia came up and started to fuss with my loosened hair and straighten the wreath for me. I hardly had time to gulp down my porridge before it was time to go.

We walked to the Temple of Zeus and Hera in a big crowd. My whole family was there——Father, and all my brothers, including Porphyry and Alkibiades. Neleus was wearing Ficino's hat. In addition we had Rhea and Diogenes, and Nikias, who probably should have been counted as family. All my close friends came——Maia, Crocus, Erinna and Baukis, and Baukis's father Aeschines. Klymene showed up just as we were about to leave Florentia, wanting to be included in the family for the occasion. She hugged me, and I let her. Father didn't want a feud. Kallikles was still very distant with her, and she was clearly hurt by this and trying not to show it. I missed Mother sharply and specifically then, because she would have known what to say to make it all right.

I patted the bronze lion as we went past it, for luck, and because Mother always did. It looked at me today as if it were hoping for something.

"I can't believe how easily the conference went," Klymene said to Maia. "Or how fast either. I expected it to take six or eight days."

"Everyone was reasonable," Maia said.

"You were a great judge," Father said. Maia snorted.

We ran into Boas and Archimedes as we came into the plaza where the street of Demeter crossed the street of Dionysios, by the Temple of Demeter and Crocus's great colossus of Sokrates laughing. They too had garlands and new kitons and clusters of family and friends with them. I was very glad to see them. We walked in our separate family clusters, like a procession.

"We don't have all this fuss in Amazonia," Porphyry said. "We do it individually, on our actual birthdays, in the agora, and our names are written down."

"That sounds nice," I said.

"But our ceremonies in Athenia are ten times more formal, and take days," Alkibiades said. "And we have to do our examinations right there and then, with everyone watching, not quietly in advance the way you do. So think yourself lucky."

I laughed. "If I wanted to live in Athenia or the City of Amazons I'd go there. I belong here." Being away had made me realize how much I loved my city, every pillar, every word of the Workers' dialogues carved into the marble flagstones, every patch of flowers in front of the sleeping houses.

When we came into the square in front of the Temple of Zeus and Hera, the two Archons were waiting on the steps between the two great statues of the gods that flanked the temple. The altar stood behind them, smoke rising from the sacrifice. The square was packed with all the envoys, and with people who had just showed up, and for all I knew some crazy oath-enthusiasts who went to every single ceremony for everyone. I noticed Ikaros and Aristomache with Sixty-One, standing together, engaged in dialogue. Maia went over to join them. All our family and friends faded back into the crowd, leaving the three of us who were candidates standing together in the center. One of the Archons made a welcoming speech, talking about the significance of citizenship and Plato and the city. I wasn't listening properly. I was nervous. I felt it was hard to draw enough breath. I straightened my wreath, which was slipping into my eyes. The other Archon made a very similar speech, about the importance of young people and the significance of the community, and how the city was open to all and we had never turned anyone away—aimed at the visitors, I suppose. Then finally they got to it.

"Boas, bronze. Archimedes, iron. Arete, gold." I hadn't really doubted it, but it was a great relief nevertheless. Archimedes punched my arm, and I punched his back. We both had what we wanted. He was right, of course he was, we could trust them, they knew where we belonged. I could never have faced Father or my brothers if I hadn't made gold. I had felt confident that I deserved it, except for that moment when the speeches seemed to be going on forever. I went up the steps and took my pin, the bee Mother had designed when she'd been younger than I was now. I pinned my kiton with it immediately, and saw the gold gleam against the cloth, the only gold I would ever own. I was so delighted that I couldn't help smiling. Then I lifted off my wreath and knelt, with my back to the square, and the archon took the shears and cut off all my hair at the nape of my neck. I stood again and put the wreath back on. I felt odd without my hair; lighter. He had missed one strand, which tickled against my newly bare neck.

I went down two steps, as we had been instructed, and waited while Archimedes, and then Boas, were given their pins and had their hair cut in turn. Then the Archon took the mass of hair from all three of us and thrust it onto the smoldering fire on the altar. It blazed up at once and made a horrible stink, but she threw on some incense which soon masked that.

"You are no longer children," the other Archon said, his voice booming. "Come here and swear your allegiance to the City."

We went up one at a time in reverse order, Boas first and me last. I listened as the others swore. It was a great oath. I'd had it memorized for years, since my brothers took it. Boas swore, and the Archon marked his forehead with ash, then Archimedes did the same, looking awed and solemn now. Then it was my turn. I took the two steps up and moved just as they had done, so that I stood between the Archons. I was behind the altar for what would probably be the only time in my life unless I became an Archon. I set both hands palm-down on the marble top of the altar, careful to place them on either side of the sacrifice. The smoke of hair and incense was streaming straight up into a clear sky. I looked out through it over the crowd, seeing Father and my brothers watching, and Maia, who was wiping her eyes. I took a deep breath and spoke loudly and clearly, projecting to fill the space, as I had been taught when I was Briseis in the Dionysia.

"I swear by Zeus and Hera and Demeter and Apollo and Athene, by the figs and olives and barley and grapes, by the sea and the sky and the earth beneath my feet, that I will protect and defend the excellence of the Just City from all enemies, internal and external. I will fight bravely, judge fairly, and contribute to the best of my abilities. I will defend her laws and institutions, resist tyranny and foolishness, and the lures of wealth and honor, and strive ever to increase her excellence."

It had been a bright sunny morning, but it clouded over as I was speaking so that the last words came out under a dark sky. I looked up from the altar as the Archon marked my forehead and saw that I was mistaken, I was simply in the shadow of a very tall man. Then I saw that it was the great ivory and gold statue of Zeus, but it had moved and was standing in front of me instead of at the side of the steps. And then I realized that it was not the statue but Zeus himself standing there, frowning down at me. I remembered too late what Father had said about attracting the attention of the gods. I took my hands off the altar and stepped back, as if that might make him disappear again. Of course, it did nothing.

"Granddaughter," all-knowing Zeus rumbled, his voice like thunder. He looked around slowly, taking in the temple and the square and the people. Some had fallen to the ground. Most of them looked terrified. Ikaros looked absolutely thrilled and was bouncing on the balls of his feet with excitement. Father took a step forward, my brothers close at his back. Zeus nodded at Father, and thunder echoed all around. "Where is Athene?" Zeus asked.

She appeared on the steps in front of us. She had her helmet and her shield and her owl, and she seemed to be perfectly composed. I had never seen her before, but I would have recognized her anywhere. There were statues and paintings and bas-reliefs of her all over the city, many of them done from life. "Joy to you, Father," she said. "Be welcome to the Just City."

"And when did you intend to tell me about this folly?" We were speaking Greek, of course. But that last word held double meanings, in other languages. As well as meaning foolishness, and thus the opposite of the wisdom that was Athene's domain, it had the connotation of an anachronistic ruin built deliberately to enhance a landscape view. I bristled to hear the Republic described this way, not because it wasn't true but because it hurt.

Athene did not flinch, but stood looking up at her father calmly. "In the fullness of time, when there was something to report," she said.

"Come, let us discuss this," Zeus said. He pointed at Father and my brothers. "And you can come too." He pointed at Ikaros.

"Me?" Ikaros squeaked.

"Yes, you, Giovanni Pico della Mirandola, Count of Concord, Ikaros of the Amazons. You. Did you think I wouldn't recognize you when you profess to know so much about me? Come."

Maia had her mouth open, as if she was about to say something. Ikaros grabbed her arm.

Erinna was stepping forward too, and the Archon was reaching for me, and then they were gone and I was standing on a sloping mountain meadow, green with soft spring grass and dotted with strange blue and golden bell-like flowers, nodding in the gentle breeze. It felt like Delos, only much more so.

31

ARETE

Father was there, and my brothers, and Zeus, and Athene, and Ikaros, and Maia, standing in a rough circle. I sat down at once on the soft grass, and so did everyone else, almost simultaneously. There was something strange about how everyone looked, as if perspective didn't work properly here. Zeus and Athene both were and were not normal human sizes. They were much too big to be sitting in a circle with the rest of us, yet there they were, sitting right there, not taking up any more room, and not far away. Zeus was big enough to fill the mountain and the sky, and at the same time only a little taller than Phaedrus. It made me feel a little dizzy when I focused on him and anything else at the same time.

"Why did you bring Pico?" Athene asked Zeus.

Zeus raised an eyebrow. "He's the reason you did all this, isn't he?"

I looked at Ikaros. He looked different, younger. His long hair was chestnut brown and his face was unlined. He looked only a few years older than my brothers. He was still clutching Maia's arm. Maia also looked younger, very much the way she looked in her statue in Amazonia. She was staring at Athene. Ikaros opened his mouth as if he was about to say "Me?" again, but Porphyry put a hand on his shoulder and he subsided. Athene didn't turn her head in his direction, but the owl was staring at him, and I felt she didn't need to look at him to see him. I could also tell by the way he was looking delightedly at everything that he could see properly.

"It's true I wanted somewhere interesting to take him. But he prayed to me for the Republic. They all did, all the Masters. And I could grant their prayers and help. It seemed like a good time and place for such an experiment."

"It was meddling for your own vanity," Zeus said, decisively. "And dragging Phoebus into it, where's the sense in that?"

"I wanted to become incarnate to learn some things," Father said. "Athene offered me the Republic as a time and place to do that. It was my free choice."

"And you've learned them, I see, and more besides. And you have a daughter. How very unlike you." Zeus looked at me, and I met his gaze as best I could. He looked a little puzzled. I felt as if I should be terrified, but I wasn't afraid at all. It wasn't like the time on Delos where everything I did was under the control of Fate and I was going through a prescribed and required set of motions. I was entirely free to act and choose for myself. But I didn't feel fear or anger, or anything at all really. Indeed, I felt preternaturally calm.

"My daughter Arete, my sons Kallikles, Phaedrus, Neleus, Euklides and Porphyry," Father said, indicating us. I realized for the first time that Alkibiades wasn't there, though he had been standing with the others. Was that because he had said he didn't want divine powers? How did Zeus know? And how was Neleus here? He wasn't really Father's son.

"A place women can be excellent, eh?" Zeus said, punning on my name of course, not even the king of gods and men was above that. He seemed to hear a lot more than was said, because while I knew that Father usually only had sons because it was generally so unpleasant to be a woman, but the Republic was fair to both, Father hadn't said anything to Zeus about that.

"Plato——" Athene said.

"Don't start," Zeus said. "After what you did to Sokrates?"

He stopped and looked at Ikaros. "To answer your unspoken question, I knew nothing about it until it was drawn to my attention by Arete just now, and now I know everything about it, as if I had always known."

"Thank you," Ikaros said. "And if you don't mind me asking, why are you taking the time to explain this to me?"

"Because it's better than overhearing your infernal conjectures," Zeus said. As he laughed the mountain seemed to shake. Then he looked at Maia. "And yes, this is Olympos, and you are correct that we are not perfect. And yes, Pytheas is Apollo."

Maia nodded gravely. "Of course," she said. "And Simmea knew, of course." Father smiled at that.

"And you are here because Ikaros felt you were a deserving philosopher who had been right where he had been wrong," Zeus went on.

"And since I was wrong, why from all the assembled citizens did you choose to bring me?" Ikaros was being very polite, but he didn't seem afraid either. I wondered if calm was somehow in the air here.

"My wise daughter, in her chaste and foolish way, is in love with you. Only with your mind, I hasten to add. But I think it would be fair to say that she is in a state of unrequited agape with regard to you."

"Father, we all have favorites," my own father said. Maia laughed. Ikaros was staring at Athene in complete astonishment. "It helps to have conversations with them about it and find out what they want," Father went on.

Athene looked up from her shield and rolled her eyes at Father. "It wasn't that kind of thing. There's no comparison. I just——he was so bright and so young and he did pray to me for it, and lots of other people had too, and it all seemed as if it would be so interesting and so much fun," she said. "Nothing like your romances at all."

"Not unrequited," Ikaros said, passionately, as soon as she had finished speaking. "Never unrequited. I have loved and sought wisdom all my life—and you, Sophia, from the day I saw you."

"Then why did you betray me?" she asked, her gray eyes hard as flint.

"With Sokrates? Or by saying you were an angel?" he asked.

"That there are multiple possible occasions does seem indicative of problems," Zeus said.

"But I loved you all the time." He didn't look away from Athene, and he absolutely meant it.

"You betrayed me when, just before the Last Debate, you turned away from reason and said will and love could be enough, you didn't need comprehension!" Athene said.

"Oh." Ikaros looked abashed. "That was just a theory, and I was just wrong. Simmea said it was mystical twaddle, and I realized she was right as soon as I read Aquinas again. But even then I never stopped loving you."

"I *am* reason, you idiot," she said.

"I am human and make mistakes, but I always try again to serve you and be worthy of you," Ikaros said. "You have always been my goal and my delight."

"Touching as this is, we have serious business," Zeus interrupted.

"He is my votary. He prayed to me when he could have been burned at the stake for it," Athene said, turning to Zeus. "And others too. Ficino. Aristomache. Maia." She gestured to Maia, sitting primly on the grass listening intently. "They loved our world, and their own worlds held too little to fulfill their souls. I wanted to see what they would do with their imagination of our world, and Plato's vision."

"Plato's Republic," Zeus said. "Three hundred philosophers and classics majors. Ten thousand slave children. Lost artworks from all of time. Robots. The head of the Winged Victory of Samothrace."

"All the books," Ikaros put in. "We rescued all the books from the Great Library of Alexandria."

"Of course you did," Zeus said, his gaze still fixed on Athene. "You took Pico and Ficino and Atticus careering through time rescuing books and art, you turned Sokrates into a fly because he beat you in a fair argument, and you'd like me to regard this as something other than sheer unadulterated self-indulgence?"

"I have learned a lot I could have learned nowhere else," Father said.

"I have lived a life I could have lived nowhere else, and I shall always be grateful to Athene for giving me my life," Maia said.

"I accept your judgment," Athene said, inclining her head to Zeus.

"My judgment. Yes. But how shall I judge what I shall do with it? They've already left the island and started to reach out. I can't leave them there to tangle with history. For us, what's done is done. But for them, it might be kindest if—"

"No! Please!" Father said. He flung himself down before Zeus, flat on his face, with his hands on Zeus's knees. My sense of scale quailed, for in one way Zeus's knees were as huge as mountain ranges, and in another Father, who was the same size he always was, could comfortably clutch them. Also, the posture was ridiculous, but Father managed to make it seem not only graceful but entirely natural. "Not the darkness of the oak! Don't unmake them. I beg you, Father, not that."

I had never before heard of the darkness of the oak. But as soon as I heard what Father said, I understood what it meant. Zeus had the power to undo time, to make things never have happened. He could do that with the city, unmake it. The Masters and Children would never have left their own times. The Young Ones would never have been born. The City would never have been more than Plato's dream. The darkness of the oak. I shuddered.

Fear is a strange thing. I had been afraid I wouldn't qualify as gold, but I had not been afraid when all-knowing Zeus had appeared before me and carried me off outside time. I had sat through the debate so far listening to Athene being chided and been calm and interested. But as soon as Father said "the darkness of the oak" I was terrified—and yet still a little detached from my fear, observing it rather than being swept off in it. Was this what it was like to be a god?

"But why, Phoebus?" Zeus grumbled. "You're outside time. You'd still remember what you've learned. Your children are here, even Neleus." Neleus straightened Ficino's hat as Zeus glanced at him. "And however much agape you felt for her, your woman is already dead. The whole thing is ludicrous. Their souls are going back where they came from. It has only been a few years. The darkness of the oak would be a mercy—"

"No," Father said. "Please."

"Bring down the volcano," I said, seeing it all at once as a solution. Zeus's eyes met mine over Father's prostrate form, and again I felt that I puzzled him. "If we can't go on, if you have to end it, bring down the lava and the fire and the death we have always known is coming, sweep it away, kill us all. But let it have happened! Wipe it out if you must, but don't make it never have been."

"Why?" Behind him lightning flashed around the snowy peak of Olympos.

"We were trying to do Plato's Republic," I said. "It may be ludicrous and impossible, it may seem foolish to you, but we were trying. We made compromises and adaptations, but we were all trying to increase our excellence, to increase the city's excellence, and the world's. You heard the vow I made, that's why you came, because I called on you to hold the oath. We all made that vow. We may have fallen short, we may have made mistakes, we may have done it all wrong, but our goal was great. Athene set us there under the volcano so that we would have no posterity, and we accepted that—difficult as it is to accept. But we were what we were, we existed. We tried. Kill us now if that's what's necessary to preserve history, but leave us the effort we made, at least." I thought of Mother, Ficino, Erinna, Crocus, the everyday life of the Republic, Alkibiades showing me the vines and saying he didn't want divine power, the people of Psyche joining in raggedly on the last chorus of Father's ode to peace. "We might not have been philosopher kings as Plato intended, but at least we made the attempt."

Maia was smiling through tears. Neleus nodded at me.

"And would you go back and die with the city you care for so much?" Zeus asked, his great dark eyes fixed on mine.

"You know I would. I know how temporary death is. My soul would go on with what it learned in the Just City, as we all would. Don't take that away from us."

Ikaros was staring at me, his lips parted. "You said you weren't an angel," he said.

"God is a better term," Zeus said, absently. "She has free will, and limited knowledge. And there is no such thing as omnipotence, and omniscience is extremely overrated. As for omnibenevolence, I'm sure you realize by now that we're doing our best. And time is a Mystery, by which I mean you are welcome to make up your own theories and I'll be grateful if any of them come close to being a useful analogy."

"I'll work on it," Ikaros said. He looked at Athene. "I'll work on it with Sophia's help." Athene was smiling at him, but he looked away from her, to me. "And I will always pursue excellence."

Zeus's gaze ran over my brothers. He looked down at Father, who was still clutching his knees. "Get up, son. I won't do it. Though I can't see where, under Fate and Necessity, the place can go. She wants posterity, you know."

"Mortals all want posterity," Father said, getting up and settling back on the grass next to Zeus. "It's some compensation for forgetting when they go on to new lives. Mortality is so strange. You should try it sometime. It's so very different in practice."

"I look forward to hearing you sing about it." Zeus put his hand on Father's shoulder.

"They have equal significance, you know," Father said. "All of them. They all matter to themselves, to each other."

"I know. I wondered how long it would take you to figure that one out." Father leaned back on his hands. "There will be songs. A lot of songs."

"Good. These are things the gods need to understand. If I am to send the lava—"

"Yes. Send me back to die with the city." Father didn't hesitate.

"And I," Maia said, instantly.

"And I," my brothers chorused.

"And I," Ikaros said, only a heartbeat later.

"It's not even your city anymore, you've just been given a research project by ever-living Zeus, you're on Olympos with the gods, and you're asking to go back to die?" Athene asked, incredulous.

"If it's going to perish that way, I should go with it. And all of Kallisti is the Republic, all the different cities are our own visions of the Just City, and choices we have opened up in our interpretations." Ikaros nodded to Porphyry, who grinned at him.

"Don't worry, he won't do that either," Porphyry said.

Deep-browed Zeus turned his gaze on Porphyry. "Won't I, grandson? How do you know?"

"You're trying to find a way, by Fate and Necessity, to give us posterity. And I see one!"

"Oh Porphyry, you have your powers! Are they prophetic?" I asked.

"I'd much rather be able to fly," Porphyry said. "And I don't know whether it's prophetic power, or just being outside time, but I can see time from the outside, and I see the threads and patterns of it, so I see where we could go."

"What useful skills your children have," Zeus said, to Father. "Did you think at all what you were doing with a whole clutch of them? Setting up your own pantheon? Will you go back with them even if it's not to fiery destruction?"

"I'll live out this life until this body dies, and then come home to Olympos," Father said. "When this body dies, whether that's in ten minutes from the volcano or in fifty years from old age."

"You'll be cleaning up this mess for a lot longer than fifty years," Zeus said. "And you too," he added, to Athene. "You'll be out there getting your hands dirty, not tucked away in your library."

"If that is your judgment," Athene said.

"Show me what you have found, Porphyry," Zeus said.

Porphyry stood up and walked over to Zeus. He put his hands together, then pulled them apart, as if doing a cat's cradle, but without string. Something glimmered between his fingers. I thought for a moment it was one of the blue and gold bell-headed flowers, but there was nothing there. "Here," Porphyry said, indicating the emptiness between his fingers. "And a little while before the ships arrive from Earth, do you see?" Zeus peered into the nothingness, then laughed. Thunder rolled around the mountain.

"That'll do," he said.

"What is it?" I asked.

"It's an era far in the future, in the twenty-fifth century, when humanity has just discovered faster-than-light travel," Porphyry said. "They're just rediscovering all the civilizations on planets that were settled more slowly than light. There aren't complete records of who went where. Some of them are very strange. We can be one of them. We won't look much odder than the others. It's long after the *Republic* was written, so why shouldn't a group of people have tried it?"

"Nobody ever has," muttered Zeus.

"We'd have a divine origin story, but nobody would have to pay any attention. And the ships will come, and they can discover us, and we can rejoin the human mainstream, with all our books and art and theories. It will be a mystery, but only a small one, nothing to prove anything."

"Why do you keep so secret?" Neleus asked. "Why can't we give them proof? People want so much to know and to understand."

"It's better for humanity to allow us to work out our own theories, our own destiny. If we *know* it changes everything," Ikaros said.

Neleus nodded slowly, recognizing that in himself.

"And knowing would fix one truth, and close off many paths to enlightenment," Athene said. "You're going to love the Enlightenment," she said aside, to Ikaros.

"Posterity," I said, to Zeus and Porphyry. "But another planet? I suppose a new world would be a fresh beginning."

"A new world won't be an empty blank any more than ten-year-olds are," Maia said.

Zeus smiled at her. "True, and well deduced." He looked at my brothers. "New planets need their own pantheons, and it seems we have one all ready." He turned to Ikaros. "It has to do with place. Place is much more important to deity than you've ever considered. You should get out more. Travel."

"On another planet?" he asked.

Zeus looked at Athene. "Were you planning to keep him as a pet?"

"There are a lot of wonderful times and places he hasn't seen on Earth," she said. "And then perhaps later other planets."

Zeus waved his hand, and thunder rumbled nearby. "Do what you want. You will anyway. You agree, Ikaros? You'll work with Athene?"

"If the City doesn't need me."

"The City will get along without you, on its new planet. And as well as going sightseeing with Athene, which I'm sure you'll enjoy, there are Mysteries here you can be working on." He looked at Maia. "How about you? Do you want to stay here or go on?"

"Go on," she said.

"Good. The Republic will need you. You'll be directing it in a few years, you know, you and Crocus. And then you." He indicated Neleus. Lightning danced around his head. "Philosopher kings. It won't be easy."

"It hasn't been easy so far," Maia said.

"I swore that same oath," Neleus said. "Fight bravely, judge fairly, contribute to the best of my abilities. We all did. We all want to go."

I was looking at Neleus, and so were my other brothers as he spoke for them, and for a moment it was the way it had been before the voyage, when we had seen that we were all one thing, and he was another. But now, on Olympos, we looked to him for leadership. We had our powers. But he was the most philosophical. And that made him the best of us.

"But another sun?" Father asked, sounding worried.

"You can have it," Zeus said wearily. "Now, is there anything else before I send the pack of you back where you belong?"

32

APOLLO

Euripides puts it very well: Zeus brings the unthought to be, as here we see.

Before we left Olympos I took Athene aside and took care of a few details. I scrawled "Goodness" on the parchment map they gave Maecenas in Lucia, and gave it to her to put into her arm-rest so that I could find it there. "Any time between the Last Debate and last autumn. And if you get the chance, could you possibly take the head of Victory and donate it to the

Louvre so the poor thing can be back in one piece again? Oh, and for goodness' sake, get us some more robots," I said.

"Porphyry will get you robots," she said. "Father's going to be loading
me down with work here."

"But you'll have Pico to help. He's going to love your library. And learning all the new languages." Behind us, he was hugging Maia, and Porphyry,
and to my surprise, Arete.

"Thank you for speaking up for me," Athene said, stiffly.

"It was nothing," I said. I had felt sorry for her, exposed that way. "I know
what it's like to love a mortal."

"It's not the same," she said, automatically. "Did you think of doing that
with Simmea? Taking her outside time, where you could keep her young?"

"Sooner or later her soul would have wanted to go on," I said, gently, because it would happen with Pico too, sooner or later, unless he became a god.
Perhaps he would. He had the right kind of mind. Father had noticed that
at once. We could do with a god with an excellence of fitting facts together
into complex theories, especially if he could generalize it to things other than
metaphysics. Now that I'd seen it, it seemed obvious. Athene didn't have any
children, so none of her areas of responsibility ever got passed along to anyone else. I really liked the idea of Pico as a god of synthesis.

"But did you want to?"

"I'm glad in a way that I didn't have to make that choice. Simmea's mortality was so much a part of who she was, and my incarnation so much a
part of our relationship, that I don't know what it would have been if I'd
brought her here." She'd have started to *analyze* everything. It would have been
wonderful. I wished I had brought her, and Sokrates too. But mortal souls
need to grow and go on, that's part of the marvel of them, part of what we
love about them. If Pico became a god, which I was now sure was Father's
plan all along, he would lose some of what made Athene love him, and lose
the opportunities his soul would have had to transform. Who could tell what
wonderful people Ikaros might become, given the opportunity? How much
he might contribute to the excellence of the world? Still, there wasn't any
point saying that to her and risking spoiling what they had for now. He had
to make his own choices.

"But you knelt in supplication to Father rather than let her life never have
been."

"Yes," I said, simply. I hadn't cared what it cost me.

She nodded. "Maybe it's not so different. Agape."

"Thank you for setting up the Republic, so I could learn what agape was,"
I said.

She smiled. "I'm glad it was worth it. Have fun on the new planet. They're bound to call it Plato. What else could they possibly agree on?"

I laughed. "Have fun with Pico. Keep learning everything, and let me know all about it when you have the chance."

"When you come back, I'll meet you in the Laurentian Library on the first day the orange tree blooms in 1564."

"It's a date," I said, touched, and turned back to where Father and Maia and my Young Ones were waiting.

The sun isn't literally a winged chariot with two fiery horses. It's literally a big ball of fusing hydrogen. But metaphorically and spiritually, it's a chariot. *My* chariot. My new sun, which had no name, only a catalog number, and which is literally a slightly bigger and redder ball of fusing hydrogen, is metaphorically and spiritually a racecar. *My* racecar. We called it Helios, "the sun," either because we're an unimaginative people, or because we instinctively recognized that it had metaphorically and spiritually the same driver as the old Helios we'd left shining on Earth. It zips across the sky. The day is only nineteen hours long.

Father set the five Republics of Kallisti and the eight Lucian Republics down carefully on the new planet, without so much as bumping any of their art or architecture. He also took all the people who chose to go, which was everyone except for a scattering of stubborn idiots who stood alone to see their cities and civilization disappear around them. (And who do you think has to be their patron and look after them forever after? Well, did you think Athene was going to get stuck with it?) He set the cities down the same distance apart they had always been. It didn't matter at all to Father that he put them on a rocky volcanic plain on the edge of a great ocean, or that many of them now had harbors that went nowhere. It looked exceedingly peculiar, but we coped.

Porphyry did indeed get us some new robots, and that helped a great deal.

Maia became the first leader of the City after the move, and she and Crocus were the first Consuls of the Senate of Plato, the council made up of representatives of all twelve cities. She helped lead us into the era of peace and exploration, and when the aliens came she was the first after Arete to learn their language. She was thrice Consul, and after she died we put that on her memorial stone, along with all her other achievements. As Father had predicted, Neleus led us after that. By then we were thoroughly involved with the alien confederation, and we'd persuaded a surprising number of aliens to strive for excellence and justice in a Platonic context before the human spaceships discovered all of us and things got complicated.

As for me, I kept writing songs, and learning things about myself, about mortal life, about my children and other people. I kept on striving toward excellence, for myself and for the world. All the worlds.

I could still see my chariot at night from our new home, a distant glimmer, shining to me across space and time, which are Mysteries, and in strange ways almost the same thing. I was glad I could see it. I would have been very sad without it. But I'd have managed. I managed without Simmea, after all.

Not even Necessity knows all ends.

NECESSITY

This is for Ada,
who is not only wonderful but also real.

What leaf-fringed legends haunt about thy shape
Of deities or mortals, or of both,
In Tempe or the dales of Arkady?
What men or gods are these? What maidens loth?
What mad pursuit? What struggle to escape?
What pipes and timbrels? What wild ecstasy?

> —KEATS, "Ode on a Grecian Urn"

Socrates: Tell me then, oh tell me—what is the great and
  splendid work which the gods achieve with the help of
  our devotions?
Euthyphro: Many and fair are the works of the gods.

> —PLATO, *Euthyphro*

Answer me, answer me
Somebody answer me.
Oldest of questions and
Deepest of needs. Our
Mystery, mystery,
Teach us our history.
Lost all again
To the dark of the grave.

> —ADA PALMER, "A New World"

And now the work is done that cannot be erased by Jupiter's
anger, fire and sword, nor the gnawing tooth of time. Let the
day, that has power only over my body, end when it will my
uncertain span of years. The best part of me will be borne,
immortal, beyond the distant stars.

> —OVID, envoi to *Metamorphoses*

1

APOLLO

I have lived for a very long time however you measure it, but I never grew old before. I aged from birth to adulthood and stayed there, poised in the full power of glorious immortality. But the mortal body I had taken up to experience and understand the joys and sorrows of human life aged as other mortal bodies age. My son Phaedrus, like my older son Asklepios, had healing powers. Our City had begun with a generation of ten-year-olds, and as our bodies aged he was kept permanently busy. Even with all he could do for us, aging was an undignified and uncomfortable process. Souls grow and flower and do not decline, so each mortal life inevitably ends with soaring souls enclosed in withered failing bodies. While death is necessary for rebirth, I could find neither necessity nor benefit in this slow ebbing of vitality.

I died on the day the first human spaceship contacted Plato. After that, I did all the things I'd been promising myself I'd do once I was back to my proper self. I established the laurel wreath as a symbol of poetic victory, in memory of Daphne. Then I spent a little while assembling the chronicles of the City—weaving together Maia's journals with Simmea's and Arete's, and composing a memoir of my own brief but intense period of mortality. Then I settled down to study sun formation, beginning with my own suns, naturally. Once I'd started looking into it, I became fascinated with the whole process. The song of suns, the dance of gravity and hydrogen, the interplay of radiation and magnetism and heat, the excitement of the symphonic moment when it all comes together and fusion begins—I never tire of it.

I can't say how long I spent alone studying the birth of suns. I was outside time, and when I went into time, it was a time aeons before the evolution of life. It's normal for me to live outside time, and step into it as and where I choose. The years I spent incarnate in the Just City were the exception. Then days and years unfolded in inevitable and unchangeable sequence. My more usual experience is personally sequential, but entirely separate from time, human time, history. I could go off and study stellar nurseries in the early days of the universe for as long as I liked without neglecting any duties. I could pay attention to my duties afterwards, they'd still be there. I could be aware of a prayer, watch the entire sequence of a sun being formed, and then respond to that prayer in the same moment it was uttered. (Not that I pay any more attention to the constant dinning of prayer than any other god. That's only an example.) I can't be in time in the same moment twice, but that's not much of a hardship, usually, because time splits up into extremely small increments. Despite being the god of prophecy, I don't know my own personal future any more than anyone else. I know what happens in time, more or less, depending on how much attention I've paid to it, exactly the same as you might know what happens in history—some of it sharp, some of it fuzzy.

Studying sunbirth was good for me. It was a relief to be on my own and not have to worry about other people and their significance. It was good to be able to focus completely on a fascinating and abstract subject and forget about Plato for a while—both the philosopher and the planet. I loved my children, and I loved Plato and the society we had built struggling to implement his ideas. But Homer calls the gods "untiring" as well as "deathless." Taking on mortality, and living through that slow physical process of aging, had made me understand for the first time what weariness meant. The study was a form of rest, renewal, and rebirth. It was fun, too. I like learning things, and suns are very close to my heart.

After a timeless while, I was interrupted by the sudden appearance of my little brother Hermes. He draped himself over the accretion disk of a sun forming from a particularly fascinating dust cloud, one full of ancient iron. For some reason, probably simply to irritate me, he chose to make himself so large that the disk looked like a couch he was lounging on. He looked like a youth on the cusp of manhood, an object of desire but filled with implicit power. "Playtime's over," he said.

I shot up to the same size and balanced poised in the same orientation against the glowing dust of the nebula. "What are you doing so far from civilization and everything you love?" I asked.

"Running Father's errands, as usual," he said, pursing his lips. "You know nothing less would get me so far away from people. What are you doing out here in the bleak emptiness?"

I thought it was beautiful, in its own way. "I'm fulfilling my primary function and working on how suns begin," I said. "For a god of travel, you do seem to hate going places."

"I'm not in charge of exploration of the wilderness," he said, bending to adjust his elegant winged sandals. They and his hat were all he wore—not only at that moment, but practically all the time. He enjoyed displaying his exquisite body and being admired. "I like travel and trade and markets and the way people arrange systems of communication. I like going to *places*. This isn't a *place*. I think this is the furthest from being a place of anywhere I've ever been. There's nothing out here for me, no civilization, no offerings, no possibilities for negotiation. Nothing but atoms and emptiness."

"Did you know people have equal significance?" I asked, suddenly reminded by what he had been saying. I'd promised Simmea I'd tell the gods. Putting together the chronicle was only the first part of that.

"To us? How could they have?" A frown briefly creased his golden brow. "They're mayflies."

"To each other. And their choices ought to count to us. They live long enough to achieve wonderful things, sometimes. And besides, a human lifetime is subjectively longer than you think. You should try incarnating yourself."

"Was it fun?"

I hesitated. He laughed.

"It was illuminating," I said, with as much dignity as I could manage. "I learned things I couldn't have learned any other way. I think we all ought to do it for what we can learn. We'll be better for it."

"I'll think about it. I have a number of projects I'm busy with right now. And instead I'm wasting my time coming all the way out here to the ass-end of nowhere to tell you that Father wants you to attend to your planet."

I looked at the accretion disk, poised at the moment of spinning up. "Now? Why now? He wants me to go to Plato in my personal now?"

"Does Father ever explain these things to you? He never does to me." He sounded bitter.

"It's a Mystery," I acknowledged.

"You haven't told anyone you have a planet. I must check it out."

"It's new," I said, reflexively defensive. "It's all Athene's fault, really. It's called Plato. It has people. And aliens. They're highly civilized. They worship us, well, most of them do. You have a lovely temple there with a statue by Praxiteles that Athene and Ficino rescued from the sack of Constantinople. Haven't you noticed people there praying to you? You'd be welcome to come and visit." I gestured in its general direction. "Drop in any time."

He ignored my jab as easily as he ignored prayers. "How did you get a whole planet?"

I sighed, seeing he wouldn't leave me alone until I explained. "Athene was setting up Plato's Republic, on Thera, before the Trojan War, before the Thera eruption. She had three hundred classicists and philosophers from across all of time, all people who had read Plato and prayed to her to help make the Republic real. She helped—that is, she used granting their prayers as a gateway. Really, she wanted to do it, so she did. As well as those people, the Masters, they bought ten thousand Greek-speaking slave children, and a set of big construction robots. The robots turned out to be sentient, only to start with nobody knew that. I incarnated there as one of the children. I learned a lot, from Sokrates and the others, and from the experience. I had friends, and children. When Father found out, he transported the whole lot of us to another planet four thousand years forward—and we were twelve cities by that time, all doing Plato's Republic in different and competing ways."

"And you're responsible for them?"

"Until my children are ready to be their pantheon, which shouldn't be long now. Why? Did you think Athene would end up getting stuck with it, after she tired of the project and moved on?"

He grinned. "It's hard to imagine. She always squeaks out of things. Well, you'd better get on and take care of them for her."

"For Father," I said. I was puzzled. I wondered why Father had sent this message. He must have known that I wouldn't neglect Plato. I didn't understand why there was any urgency about it. But I'd do it, of course. Nobody understood how Father knew anything, or how he prioritizes. Nor, for that matter, did we have any idea how he experiences time. He was there before it, after all. Mortals find it difficult to understand how we understand time, living outside it, but that's simple, compared to how it is for Father.

We're bound by our own actions, and, naturally, whether we're in or out of time, by Fate and Necessity. There's no getting around them. They make changing time extremely hard, and harder when we get away from our core concerns. And we're limited by Father's edicts, but only in so far as we respect them. They don't have the same inevitable force. If I got caught up with Fate or Necessity it wouldn't really be a matter of choice—resisting a force like that is almost impossible, even for me. But I could simply ignore Father's message if I wanted to. It was usually a terrible idea to ignore such things, because Father does know more than the rest of us and generally means well, and also because he could have made my life a misery if I went against him. There was this one time at Troy—but that's a different story. But it's not like being caught up with Necessity, which is a compulsion on the soul.

"What's this I hear about you playing my gift upside-down to beat somebody playing Athene's syrinx?" Hermes asked.

Hermes had invented the lyre when he was three days old, as a way to win my friendship after stealing some of my cows. He'd given it to me. He'd also promised never again to steal anything else of mine, a promise I didn't quite trust him to keep. He was much too fond of playing tricks.

"Yes, I played the lyre upside-down," I acknowledged. "Won the contest that way, too." The whole messy business seemed long ago and almost unimportant. I do enjoy being an Olympian and having a proper perspective.

"It sounds like something I'd do."

"Feel free to teach yourself to play it that way," I said, and grinned at him.

"Well, joy to you with all of it," wing-footed Hermes said, smiling as he departed.

So, with no foresight or warnings, and with one last longing look at the glowing disk (which would after all still be there and about to form into a sun whenever I wanted to come back into time at this moment to watch), I left too.

I was going to Plato, of course I was. I accepted Father's message that playtime was over, whether I liked it or not. But I wasn't quite ready. Another little while—another long subjective time—watching suns would have been exactly what I needed, but I wasn't going to disobey Father to that extent. I didn't want to mess up whatever mysterious plan he had, which presumably needed me to be still a little off balance. But I did have something to do first, something that would hardly take any personal time and couldn't possibly make any difference, and which would make a good transition. I had a date with Athene.

The date in question was 1564, the day in the spring of that year when the orange tree in the courtyard of the Medici Laurentian Library bloomed. Athene had arranged it herself, the last time I had seen her, on Olympos, at the time of the Relocation, when Zeus moved the Cities from Bronze Age Greece to Plato. It had been a peace offering, after everything that had happened. "When you get back," she had said. This would mark me being back. We could meet on neutral territory, in an extraordinary year, and after we'd talked I might feel better equipped for taking care of Plato. I wanted to see her. There were several things I wanted her to explain, and other things I wanted to explain to her. Parts of it I knew she'd never understand, but other parts of it she was the only person who ever could understand.

I hadn't talked to her in decades, and while decades might often pass without our talking, these years had been full of things I wanted to share with her. Her experiment in setting up Plato's Republic had had unexpected results, and had produced something genuinely new and of interest to both of us. The culture on Plato wasn't the ideal Republic Plato had described. As I'd said to Maia long ago, we all live on somebody's dunghill. But it was a completely different kind of human culture, one steeped in Platonism and philosophy and the dream of the classical world. And it was out there in the twenty-sixth century, vibrating with philosophical passion and full of people at least trying to lead the Good Life. I wanted to know what she thought about that, and share my thoughts. Creating Plato's Republic had been Athene's idea, after all, and lately I'd been wondering if there had been more to it than simply to see what happened and have somewhere to take Ikaros. Pico. I wanted to see him again too. I wanted to see his face when I told him what the Ikarians had made of his New Concordance since his apotheosis.

So I left that distant forming sun and stepped into time in Florence, in 1564, on the steps in front of the unfinished façade of the church of San Lorenzo. They were still waiting for Michelangelo to come and finish it, though he'd been dead for several months already. I remembered the inside of the church as a perfect Neoclassical space, but the outside now was rough and unfinished, jagged raw stone waiting for a facing it wouldn't get for another eight hundred years. The Florentines, having so much of it, weren't prepared to compromise on beauty. They'd wait for another Florentine artist of comparable skill to be born and finish it. An admirable perspective, if rare. I stepped inside for a moment to admire it—strangely, moving into the space always felt like going outside. The streets around San Lorenzo are narrow and crowded. Inside was full of light. The proportions were perfect, the pillars, the windows, the porphyry memorial set in the floor to celebrate the soul of Cosimo de Medici. I spared a fond thought for it, wherever it was, no doubt busily engaged in its new concerns. I felt perfectly at home in there. You'd hardly have known it was a Christian church.

I stepped back out of the church and walked around to the courtyard that led to the library. I didn't need to interact with anyone so I hadn't bothered to take a plausible disguise or find an excuse for visiting the library. I simply let the light flow around me and so became invisible. There were a few monks in the cloister. I sat down on the wall by the foot of the stairs that went up to Michelangelo's intimidating entranceway—one of the projects he had managed to finish. The sun was coming down into the courtyard, my own familiar golden sunlight. The scent of blossom from the tree was heady. Here too the pillars and proportions were perfectly right. But although the library was open, there was no sign of Athene. I sat there for a while enjoying the sunlight and the scent and thinking. It was quiet in the cloister, with distant muted street sounds, and close by only the humming of bees and the occasional swish of a monk's robe to disturb me. I didn't disturb them at all. If anything, I'd have looked like a brighter patch of sunlight.

After an hour of waiting, I stepped outside time, and checked the courtyard at other times throughout the day. When I still couldn't find Athene I tried the day before, in case, but the orange blossom wasn't quite out, and she wasn't there anyway.

I went up to the library—directly, stepping into that wonderful room from outside time, to avoid the effect of Michelangelo's deliberately daunting staircase. I looked around. I was accustomed now to the library in the City, with its controlled temperature, electric lights, and all the books of the ancient world rescued from the Library of Alexandria in multiple neatly printed copies. But this was more moving—the high windows giving light to work, the patterned tiles on the floor, the wooden benches with the books chained to them and scholars sitting reading and working. The books themselves were mostly hand-copied texts, preserved through time, saved from the ruins, written out painstakingly. They lost Homer for a time, but they got him back. Ficino had worked here. They had the oldest and most complete copy of the *Aeneid*. These books were here because people had cared about them, individually, cared enough to copy them and pass them forward across centuries and civilizations, hand stretching out to human hand through time, with no surety that any future hand would be waiting to receive the offering. All the texts from antiquity that had survived the time between were in this room. But Athene wasn't.

It was inexplicable. I had the day right, but she wasn't here. She couldn't have forgotten! Perhaps I had. It had been forty years for me, and perhaps I had confused the year. If so, there was no use guessing. I'd have to go and find her, in her own library, or wherever she was. I patted the sloping wood of the nearest bench, putting a little of my power into it so that those who worked there would see more clearly. It was such a beautiful room, about as close to perfect as any mortal thing can be. I stepped out of time.

Once outside time, I felt for Athene. It's difficult to describe. Usually when I do it, I get a sensation like an itch that leads me towards whoever I'm looking for, like a compass, if one were the needle. This time, I got nothing at all.

Of course, the first thing I thought was that this was a power I hadn't tested since I had taken up my godhood again, and that I'd lost the ability, or forgotten how to do it. It was distressing. No, that's not strong enough. Even in my proper self, it felt horrible to think that I might have damaged myself, made myself limited, permanently lost parts of my abilities. I stepped back into time and sat in the courtyard until my sun warmed away the chill that thought brought. I wanted to change, but I wanted to grow more excellent, always: better, not worse. Experiencing the physical decay that went with old age had been bad enough. But with those losses I could tell myself not only that it was temporary, but that I was understanding humanity better by learning about what they went through. There would be no advantage to this.

I stepped out of time again and felt for Athene once more. Still nothing. I tried Artemis. To my intense relief, I sensed her immediately. She was on the moon, at a time when people lived there and had built temples to her. I tried Athene again, and again felt nothing. Aphrodite was on Olympos. Hera was in classical Argos. Dionysos was in Hellenistic Baktria. Hephaistos was in his forge. Hades was in the Underworld. Hermes was in the marketplace in Alexandria. But no matter how many times I tried, Athene was nowhere to be found.

Strange as it was that I couldn't locate her, it was stranger still that she hadn't shown up when she was supposed to meet me. That wasn't like her at all. I was worried. I couldn't imagine what could have happened to prevent her. Fate and Necessity might tangle us up, but we're still there. I reached for her again. Where could she possibly be? She didn't seem to be anywhere in or out of time. Could she be dead? How? It didn't bear thinking of.

2

JASON

I'm only a Silver, so don't expect too much. My name is Jason, of the Hall of Samos and the Tribe of Hermes. I was born in the Year Forty-Two of the City, eleven years after the Relocation. I work on a fishing boat. I haven't written anything long since I qualified as a citizen thirteen years ago. These two days I'm going to tell you about changed my life completely. Since Fate caught me up in great events, I'll do my best to set things down clearly, in case it can do anyone good to read about what happened and what we all said and did.

Amphitrite had been kind, and we'd had a good haul that day, lots of ribbers and a few red gloaters, big ones. They were all heading north with the winter currents, so we simply had to stay in place and use the fine nets to scoop them out. We joked about sticking our hands into the water and pulling out a fish, the kind of day that redeems all the other days where we came home with thin hauls or none. Plato's a hard planet for humans, and we depend on the catch to have enough protein.

It was chilly and grey out on the ocean, spitting with rain. As we headed homewards around Dawn Point the east wind caught us. I fastened my jerkin up to my throat. The other boats coming in made positive signals. Everyone seemed to have had a good day. It was the kind of thing to cheer your liver. We passed a flatboat gathering suface kelp, which the Saeli like to eat, and even they signaled that they had a good haul.

Our boat was called *Phaenarete* after a girl Dion had known who was killed in the Battle of Lucia. Dion had been the first one to sail her, so he'd had the choice of naming her. He had taught me everything I knew about handling boats, and fishing too, and a lot about how to live. We were as close as father and son, and closer than many such because we'd chosen each other. Dion was too old to go out regularly now, and Leonidas and Aelia were dead, so I was in charge of *Phaenarete*, and I had a crew of lunatics. Well, that's not a kind way to put it, but that's how I thought of them.

Now, fishing is essential, everyone knows that, and it's also reasonably dangerous—even if you know what you're doing you can get caught out by a squall or an underwater eruption, or the usual kind of eruption, come to that. That's what happened to Aelia and Leonidas five years back. Their luck ran out.

It's not really all that dangerous. Most days most of us come back. And we need the catch, we rely on it. There are no land animals on Plato, only what we brought with us, and the sheep and goats don't thrive here the way they did in Greece, where they could graze on plants growing wild everywhere. Dion remembers Greece and talks about it sometimes, but it sounds strange to me, the idea of plants sprawling all over, plants nobody planted and nobody tends to. There's none of that on Plato. Our plants take a lot of attention. We have to nurse them along. Keeping them alive is hard work for a lot of people, human and Workers. And we like eating them! But we want protein too, so we encourage the sheep and goats to give lots of milk and we don't often eat them, only at special festivals. And so fish are very important, and fishing is important, and worth the risk.

It's not only our City, the Remnant, that relies on the fish. We salt and smoke and freeze them and send them to the inland cities. Back in Greece, before Zeus brought them here, all the cities had been on islands in a warm sea, a deep blue sea with coasts close all around. (It's hard to imagine a warm sea, though I've seen enough pictures of it to have a good idea of the color.) Now we and the Amazons are on the coast of a cold ocean, which has islands and other continents that we've only partly explored. The other cities, still in the same positions relative to us and to each other, are scattered about inland on a volcanic plain. Fortunately the Workers have built the electric rail, so we can move goods and people relatively easily. And fish are an important part of that, and only we and the Amazons can fish, so we do. And because fishing is both important and somewhat dangerous, naturally it's classified as Silver.

Now, being properly Platonic, which we do try to be most of the time here in the Original City, that ought to mean everyone who works on a fishing boat is Silver. And most of the time that's true. But for fishing, you need a minimum of two people, and three or four is better. And at that time I had two crazy crew members who weren't Silvers at all. Hilfa is Saeli, which wouldn't stop him being a citizen and having a metal; plenty of Saeli have taken their oaths. But Hilfa was young, not that I had any idea what that meant for a Saeli. And at that time, he wasn't yet part of a pod the way most grown Saeli are. He had only been here for two years. He told me he was still studying—though whether he was studying us or fish or what, I didn't know. And I say "he" but that's not clear at all either. The Saeli need three genders to reproduce, but most of the time they don't take any notice of gender at all, and while they have a bunch of pronouns for different things, gender isn't one of them. Hilfa said "he" feels most comfortable for him in Greek, so that's what I used. What he has between his legs seemed to be a sort of scrunched-up green walnut shell. I saw it often enough, because on the boat he mostly wore a red webbing vest and nothing else, being as Saeli are pretty much comfortable naked in temperatures that make humans want to huddle up. Dion says in Greece we were comfortable naked, and what that says to me is that we should have stayed there and let the Saeli have Plato. Not that they're native here either; far from it. They showed up in a spaceship about twenty years ago, meaning twenty years after our Relocation. They first came here when I was ten. And weren't we pleased to see them after trying to deal with the weird Amarathi! Before we met the Saeli, dealing with the Amarathi was almost a full-time job for Arete, being as their language is so odd that she was the only one who could speak to them at all and have any hope of getting through.

So I had Hilfa on the boat every day, and he's maybe not as strong as a human, and sometimes he does things that make no sense, but he's better adapted to the temperatures, and he's keen, always at work on time and ready to stay on late if needed. It was Dion's decision to take him on, a year and a half ago, when Dion was still going out most of the time, before he broke his leg slipping on the icy deck last winter. (I told you it was dangerous.) Dion's lucky it was his leg and not his neck, and lucky Hilfa caught him before he slid off the side and into the water. I'd not been sure about Hilfa at first, but I'd come to appreciate him even before that. After that, of course, green hide or not, he might as well have been my brother.

My other crew member was even stranger, in her way. Marsilia's not an alien, but she's aristocracy. Not only that she's a Gold, which ought to mean she spends her time on politics and philosophy, not fishing; but her father's Neleus, and his stepfather is Pytheas. I wasn't going to refuse her when she came asking, was I? But truthfully, it wasn't so much because her dad had been consul umpty-ump times or her step-grandfather was a god in mortal form, or that she'd recently been elected consul herself. It was because I'd been in love with her sister Thetis since we were both fifteen and in the same shake-up class coming up to qualifications. Not that Thee had ever looked at me. I'd always been too shy to say anything to her about how I felt.

I used to wonder sometimes how it was that Thetis and Marsilia were sisters. Thetis looks like a goddess—tall, but slight of frame, so her breasts look like every boy's dream of breasts, or maybe only mine, I don't know. She has a broad brow, hair the color of obsidian flowing down her back, soft brown eyes—well, I suppose to be fair Marsilia has the same eyes. But you don't notice them as much because Marsilia's face is flat, and she has jutting teeth. Their skin is the same velvety brown. But Marsilia's squat, with broad hips, which is good for the boat. She keeps her hair short, like most people. Thee looks fragile, but Marsilia can pull a full net out of the water. Marsilia definitely takes after Neleus, and so I'd think Thetis takes after their mother, but Erinna is the Captain of the *Excellence*, and anyone less fragile you have never seen. Even now, when she must be sixty, Erinna has muscles on her muscles, as they say.

It's funny when you think about it.

The way we interpret Plato's intentions here now, we have regular Festivals of Hera, where people get paired up and married for the day, and hopefully babies are born as a result. We also allow long-term marriage, and participation in our Festivals of Hera is voluntary, which it isn't in Athenia and Psyche. It wasn't here to start with. There was a while when we didn't have any Festivals of Hera, because of that, but we voted to reintroduce them on a voluntary basis years ago, I'm not quite sure when. It was after the Relocation, but before I was born. If you volunteer, you get matched up with a partner by lot, and you spend a day in bed together. All the children born from that festival are considered to be your children. When a woman has a baby, she can either choose to bring it up herself or give it to the nurseries to be brought up there, whatever she prefers. It's her choice, some do one and some do the other. Probably about half of us grow up in nurseries and sleeping houses, and the rest in families. I was festival-born myself. I don't have any idea who my parents were, and not much curiosity about it either. When I took my oath at sixteen, along with all the other sixteen-year-olds, everyone who had participated in that festival seventeen years before and was still alive came along to the procession and the feast afterwards.

So with the marriages at the Festivals of Hera, all the pairings are arranged within the same metal, always, because they say that's what leads to the best children. When it comes to other kinds of marriage, people are supposed to choose people of their own kind too, to keep the metals from mixing more than they're mixed already. But we're human, and the metals in our souls are already mixed up, the way metals are under the ground, and so although everyone tries to discourage you, it's not forbidden to marry someone of a different class. (Here, anyway. It is forbidden in some of the Lucian cities. In Athenia and Psyche they don't have marriage except for the Festivals of Hera, in Sokratea they don't have classes, and in Amazonia they have lots of orgies and hope for the best, or that's what I've heard, though I didn't see anything like that the one time I was there.) Even if you do have parents of the same metal, you can't tell how the kids will come out.

So anyway, Erinna and Neleus got married, way back, even though she's Silver and he's Gold. And they did mix up the metals, and Marsilia is Gold, as I said, and she works on my boat what time she's not too busy with Chamber affairs. But her sister Thetis is Iron, and she works with little children.

Looking at it that way, even though she's from a family with a god in it, I should feel Thetis is below me. I always felt the opposite, though, that she's infinitely above me. It's not that she's the most beautiful woman on the planet. But she's extremely beautiful, and——she's Thee. Every time I see her my blood pounds in my veins, and that has been the case since we were both fifteen and I first met her in Arete's communication class. I thought she didn't care about me at all. I figured she knew who I was——Jason who took his oath the same time she did and worked on the same boat her sister works on. I doubted she thought about me once a month. I didn't see her all that often. But when I did, even if I only caught sight of her in the agora, I was happy for days afterwards. I didn't want anything from her, simply for her to exist and for me to see her sometimes. Maybe this is the kind of love Plato talks about in the *Phaedrus*, I don't know. No, because I always knew I'd be only too delighted to make it carnal, if that could be an option. But I thought it couldn't, and there it was. What I thought is that it didn't do her any harm for me to feel this way about her, and it did me a lot of good, because it gave me something in my life that was special, that lifted it above the everyday.

Marsilia pulled one of the gloaters out of the tub as Hilfa and I set our tack. Once that was done there was nothing to do for the moment but glide smoothly into the harbor. "It's so big, and it looks so delicious. I could almost eat it right now, raw!" She mimed taking a bite.

I laughed. "I hope some of these get to the tables while they're still fresh and they don't decide to salt them all down. How about you? Do you fancy it, Hilfa?"

Hilfa laughed his slightly forced laugh. He'd learned it the way he'd learned Greek. A laugh was a word to him, a part of human communication. I didn't know whether the Saeli really laughed or not. I'd learned to read Hilfa's expressions, a little, working with him for so long, and I thought one of them meant amusement, but I wasn't sure. He knew I was joking about him eating a fish, but I didn't know if he really understood what a joke was, or why I might think it was funny to make one. "I don't eat fish," he said, seriously.

"Silly Hilfa. Why do you work on a fishing boat if you don't eat fish?" I teased.

"I like the waves and the wind," Hilfa said, seriously. I wondered whether he would stay and take oath or leave for another planet on some Saeli ship. I hoped he'd stay. I liked him. And he might. He liked the waves and the wind, after all.

"We're glad to have you working with us," Marsilia said, as the jib came around a final time.

"Also I can study the Platonic fish," Hilfa said, entirely serious, as usual. "The radial symmetry of fish on this planet is fascinating. Everything in this ocean is symmetrical. I keep hoping we will one day pull something out that isn't, but we never do."

"We're never going to," I said, thinking of mosaics of Greek fish and their strange stretched shapes. Then I saw Marsilia stiffen, staring at the quay.

"Trouble," she said, then shook her head at me as she saw me twitch. "Only for me. Probably some kind of political disruption. We're signing a new foreign relations treaty, and maybe some of our negotiations came unstuck." She let the gloater slide back into the tub. "It looks as if I'm going to have to rush off. Can you two manage unloading without me?"

"Of course," I said, without even a sigh. Knowing that she'd have to dash off to a crisis, or have one prevent her from showing up now and then, was all part of having Marsilia working for me. I wondered sometimes whether part of the attraction of working on the boat for her was the fact she couldn't be interrupted while we were out at sea. But I knew a lot of it was that the sea was in her blood, from her mother—she too liked the waves and the wind.

I was easing *Phaenarete* into dock, so I didn't see who had come to interrupt Marsilia this time until we were ready to tie up. I got ready to toss the line, and saw to my astonishment Crocus standing ready to catch it. And behind him, wrapped in a silvery-grey cloak that rippled in the wind, stood Thetis. My breath caught, as always. I wished somebody would paint her like that, in that cloak, on a cloudy day, standing on the little grey triangular cobblestones of the quay, with the black stone warehouses with their slit windows all along behind her. If they did, I'd want them to put the painting in Samos, my eating hall, where I could stare at it whenever I ate. Thetis had a grace and poise like the nymphs in Botticelli's *Summer*, but a far lovelier face.

Crocus caught the rope with the attachments at the end of one of his great arms. I saw the golden bee painted on it flash as it caught the light. I said Marsilia was an aristocrat, and she is, but compared to Crocus she was little better than me. Crocus was a Worker, a machine, huge and metallic, one of our two original Workers. He had huge arms, no head, and great treads instead of legs. He and Sixty-One were the only people who had been here for the entire history of the City. He had been a friend of Sokrates. He was a Gold, one of our philosopher kings. He was probably the most famous person on the planet who wasn't a god. I had friends among the younger Workers, but I had never even spoken to Crocus.

He tied the line rapidly and deftly around the bollard. "I can't imagine what use he could ever have had for that skill," Marsilia said in my ear.

I was staring past him at Thetis, who was crying. It made her look lovelier than ever, beautiful and vulnerable and sad, in need of protection. "Do you know what's wrong with her?" I asked.

"Thee? It could be anything. She cries really easily." She sounded much more irritated than sympathetic.

"Why are you so unkind to her?" I asked.

"Is that unkind?" Marsilia asked. "I try not to be. I love her. She's my sister. But she's all emotion and no thought, and I'm the opposite. It's hard to be sisters. Everything seems to come so easily to her. Do you think if I looked like that, people would look at me the way you're looking at her? Do you think I'd want them to?"

"It's hard to imagine you wanting them to," I said.

Marsilia snorted. The quay was near enough for her to spring ashore, and she did.

"We can manage if you have a family emergency," Hilfa said. I don't know where he got expressions like that from.

"Trouble?" she asked Crocus, ignoring Thetis.

"News, and a complication," he replied, in his slightly odd mechanical voice. Before either of them could say anything more, Thetis ran towards Marsilia, who braced herself and clutched her barely in time to prevent both of them falling over the edge of the quay into the icy water. "Grandfather's dead," Thetis said.

That was news. Old Pytheas, Apollo himself. He was one of the Children, and so he must have been eighty or thereabouts, but he'd seemed well enough when I'd seen him singing at the Festival of Artemis a few days before. What did it mean for an incarnate god to die?

Marsilia patted Thee's back and made soothing noises. Hilfa went to fetch the cart to get the fish into the warehouse. I began to swing the heavy tubs of fish onto the hoist, to be ready when he came back with it.

"Is this the news or the complication?" Marsilia asked Crocus. She sounded taken off balance. It must be strange to have a grandfather who's a god. I wondered what she felt about him.

"Neither," he responded. "Though I should give you my condolences. The news and the complication are the same thing." Because he didn't have eyes, I had no way to tell where he was looking. I couldn't tell whether he was paying any attention to me at all. I looked away from Marsilia and poor Thetis and saw Hilfa coming back with the cart. Dion was helping him push it over the cobblestones, and little Camilla came skipping along beside them. I was looking at them, and moving the tubs on their swivel along the sloping deck, and I almost didn't take it in when Crocus said: "A human spaceship is in orbit."

"That changes everything," Marsilia said, suddenly all practical, the way she was when we were out with the nets. "Thee, stop crying, it's un-Platonic. I have to go."

"Marsilia! You can't go off and worry about spaceships right after Grandfather has died," Thetis said, outraged.

"Oh yes I can," Marsilia said. "And Dad will do the same."

"Neleus is already in the Chamber," Crocus confirmed. "I came to fetch you for the sake of speed."

"Hilfa says you have a good haul!" Dion said, as he came up. "Joy to you, Marsilia, Thetis, Crocus."

Camilla ran to me and put her arms up to be swung onto the boat. I heaved her aboard and hugged her. "Gloaters!" she exclaimed. A human spaceship, I was thinking, recontact with the mainstream of human civilization at last. And Pytheas dead. Everything had changed and nothing had. Hilfa came aboard beside me. I swung the first tub up so that the fish that filled it cascaded down into the cool boxes on the cart in a swirl of red and black.

Marsilia looked up. "Dion, how lovely to see you. I have a crisis. If I borrow Jason, could you and Hilfa manage the unloading?"

"Borrow me?" I asked, jumping ashore, leaving Hilfa and Camilla aboard. "What for?" I couldn't imagine how she might need me in dealing with a strange human culture, but of course I was prepared to do my best.

Marsilia detached Thetis from her shoulder and gave her a gentle push towards me. "Can you take Thee home?" Ah, of course. She didn't need help with the big problem, but with the immediate human problem. Well, that was more to my scale.

"To Thessaly," Crocus interjected.

"You should come too, Marsilia," Thetis said. I put my arm around her. Hilfa was already tipping the next tub of fish into the cart.

"I will come, and so will Dad, as soon as we've dealt with this crisis," Marsilia said.

"But I'm sure there's a plan for dealing with it, and what does it matter anyway?" Thetis asked. "You can't put politics ahead of family."

"There has been a plan for this meeting since the consulship of Maia and Klio, but the question is whether people will follow the plan in the face of events," Marsilia said. "This is one of the most important things that has ever happened, Thee. Oh, it'll be so wonderful to talk to them."

"Perhaps," Crocus said, cautiously.

"You don't think so?" Marsilia asked, sounding surprised.

"I knew the Masters longer and better than you did," Crocus said. "I have apprehensions about what recontact could mean. I have watched the generations maturing in the Cities, and seen how each one is more Platonic than the last as we grow further from other human cultures. Plato was wrong to want to start with ten-year-olds. They should have started with babies. The Children remembered their original cultures too well. Your father's generation, the Young Ones, were the first generation to know nothing but the City. And your generation are in an even better position. These days we take the pursuit of excellence for granted, and go on from there. Each new generation so far has been better. Perhaps recontact with the human cultures that have developed from the ones the Masters came from will indeed be wonderful. I hope so. But I have reservations."

"But we'll have so much to share with them," Marsilia said. "We've developed so much. And we have the works of classical civilization that were lost to them. We have everything we've learned about applying Platonism and reconciling it to other systems. The aliens didn't know anything about Plato until we explained. But the humans are bound to be excited."

"This is a whole new civilization," Crocus said. "We know less about them than we do about the aliens. In some ways they will seem more familiar, yes, and we will share some cultural referents. In other ways they might surprise us more. They might have very different priorities. Many of the Masters came from times that did not value the classical world as it should be valued. I remember Klio and Lysias talking about what misfits they had been in their own times. And Lysias, who came from the mid-twenty-first century, was the last Master. Nobody from any time later than that had read the *Republic* in Greek and prayed to Athene to help set it up, or they would have been here. No Workers ever did. That isn't a good sign. Besides, there were other human civilizations, on other continents of Earth, which had their own philosophical traditions and might not know or care anything about Platonism."

"I don't care about Platonism either, or the aliens. And whatever they're like, they'll still be there tomorrow, and going off to a debate on the day when Grandfather has died is heartless," Thetis said.

"I'm consul. I think Grandfather would agree I should be there. And I really do have to go," Marsilia said, climbing up onto Crocus's back and taking hold of the braided blue and black web of harness that hung there. "Dion, Jason, thank you."

I wanted to thank her as she and Crocus disappeared up the hill. This was the closest I had ever been to Thetis, and I was going to go with her all the way to Thessaly.

3

MARSILIA

I was woken the morning of the day when it all began by my daughter Alkippe bouncing on my stomach. It may not be the best way to wake up, but it's far from the worst one. "Why are you still asleep?" she asked. I was often up before she was, up and washed and dressed and getting on with my morning. Now the sun was high, and casting a bright square of red-gold morning light on the foot of the bed, but I felt as if I could do with another whole night's sleep.

"Yesterday was a long day," I said.

"It can't have been longer than nineteen hours. That's how long days are." Alkippe had that didactic tone kids always get when they're beginning to learn how to muster facts for an argument.

"When people say they had a long day, they mean they made part of the night into day and didn't get enough sleep. Or that a lot of things happened so it was an extremely busy day." I yawned.

"It's not a very precise term."

"When people are talking about how they feel, precision isn't always what you want. You asked me why I was still asleep, and the answer is because I felt I had a long day. It doesn't matter how many hours it was; what matters is how it felt, and so why I was still sleepy."

"Why did it feel long?" she asked.

"Well I had lots of meetings, and lots of fishing. It's the time of year when fishing is the best, and that means it's more work. It's good really."

"Sosothis says that people should only do one job, the job for which they're best suited. He says that's what Plato says, and that doing two jobs is un-Platonic." She looked unhappy. I'd heard this often enough from other people already.

"Working on the boat with Jason and Hilfa is my recreation," I said.

"But maybe you wouldn't be so tired if you didn't do it?"

"I wouldn't, but I wouldn't have so much fun either. And we might not have as much fish, and fish is good. So I'm going to carry on doing it whatever Sosothis says, or anyone else either. People complained about it when I was running for consul, but they elected me anyway, so there we are." I could still hardly believe I was consul, consul in my year, at thirty-five, elected to planetary office at the youngest possible age.

"Let's wash together!" Alkippe said, bouncing. She grinned at me, and I saw that she had lost a front tooth.

"Yes, that will be fun." She usually washed with Thetis. I rolled her around so that she was sitting on the edge of the bed. "You used to be small enough that I could swing you up off my stomach. Now you're getting almost too heavy for me to roll."

"Was I really small? Was I as small as a walnut?"

"When you were as small as a walnut you were inside my belly. When you first came out you were the size of both of Granddad's hands put together. But you keep on growing and growing." I smiled at her.

"I'm seven and a half. Next I'll be seven and three-quarters, then eight, then eight and a quarter, then eight and a half, then—"

I stood and stretched as Alkippe demonstrated her grasp of counting by fractions, which was her favorite game this month. I prayed to Zeus, father of gods and men, that she would reach all those ages, and beyond them, ninety-nine and a half, ninety-nine and three-quarters . . . Her empty bed was a crumpled mess. Thetis's bed against the far wall was neatly made. I couldn't hear Ma and Dad moving around on the other side of the partition either. "We must be really late. Come on, quick!"

We ran into the fountain room. "What are you doing today? Fishing or meetings? Or fishing and meetings?" Alkippe called.

"Meeting this morning, if I haven't missed it, and then fishing this afternoon."

"Granddad would have woken you in time so you wouldn't miss the meeting," Alkippe pointed out.

"True." She was so smart, she lapped up learning, and she had that kind of common sense too, like Ma, because she was absolutely right, Dad wouldn't have let me miss the meeting.

My life was good and full of daily pleasures. In addition to the satisfactions of my political work, I had valuable and healthy work fishing, where I could see Jason every day and keep an eye on Hilfa. I enjoyed my food. I loved Alkippe more and more each day as she came to the age of reason. I had Dad's full approval, and now that I had been elected I felt worthy of it. I made a real effort to get on with Ma and Thetis, and even though they sometimes seemed more alien to me than the Saeli, I had been doing better at this recently. So things were going along smoothly and my life was good. I'd hug Alkippe, or put my back into hauling nets with Jason and Hilfa, or get some groups to agree to a compromise in Chamber, and realize all at once that I was happy. I also felt I was doing what Plato wanted, though I suppose strictly speaking he wouldn't have had me doing it until I was fifty.

The morning was all meetings, and there was an important debate scheduled for the evening. But in between, I went out on *Phaenarete* on the tide and had a delightfully busy afternoon hauling in fish. After a day out on the ocean, I had expected a couple of hours to get ready for the evening's Council session. At the very least, I'd have appreciated a hot drink to warm myself up, and time to change into a formal kiton. As it was, Crocus collected me on the quayside and I had to take the chair in my fishy work clothes, on no notice, and deal with the most difficult and controversial of all topics—human recontact, and what the gods really want us to do. Oh, and Grandfather was dead, and I hadn't had any time yet to think through what that meant.

Chamber was filled with a babble of voices, human and Worker. Nobody was in the chair, and only a few people were sitting down. Everyone seemed to be waving their hands in the air and raising their voices. All the members of the Council of Worlds and half the Senate seemed to be here, crowding in together along with a few random concerned citizens—all Golds, of course. I looked at Crocus for help. Because he didn't have a head I could never tell where his focus was, but he must have seen my glance. "You're chair tonight, Marsilia," he said.

"That's right," Dad said. "You're consul, take charge."

They had each been consul multiple times and knew much better than I did how to take charge of the Chamber. I'd have been vastly reassured with either one of them in the chair, and so would everyone else. But Dad was right. I'd be judged on how I acted in this emergency. I took a deep breath, wiped my suddenly sweaty palms on my thighs, and walked down towards the chair. Maia had sat there, and Dad, and before them legendary figures like Ficino and Tullius and Krito. I was thirty-five years old, and I was consul. And it wasn't ambition, or anyway not in a bad way. I didn't only want the glory. I wanted to serve Plato. I might wish in my cowardly liver that somebody else were in charge in this crisis, but it was my responsibility, so I swallowed hard and did my job.

"...any of Pytheas's children!" Diotima was saying loudly, her voice cutting above the babble. She was my fellow consul. I had mixed feelings about her. Our names would be recorded together forever in the name of the year, though I didn't know her well or like her much. She came from Athenia, and was polite and religious and conventionally Platonic. She was small and neatly made, with dark smooth hair, silvering now. She was fifty or so, since nobody can run for planetary office without having read *The Republic*, and Athenia, always stricter than everyone else, still did not allow their citizens to read it before they turned fifty. Here in the Remnant we read it as ephebes, as soon as we had taken our oaths of citizenship at sixteen, after our shake-up year at fifteen. Golds and Silvers have to read it, and the others can if they choose. It always surprises me how many people don't bother, or give up part way through.

I sat down in the chair. "Quiet," I said, much too quietly. Crocus echoed me loudly, and everyone fell silent and stared at me. "I call this emergency session of the Council of Worlds to order," I said. "Members of the Council and senators may remain. Others should leave."

A handful of people left. Everyone else sat down, higgledy-piggledy where they were, like stories of the earliest days of the Council eighty years ago when Sokrates had been here and regularly violated procedure. Some of the benches had been replaced since then, but many of them were the same. I found that both comforting and intimidating. Crocus rolled over and settled himself in the section where benches had been removed to make a space for Workers, and for humans in wheelchairs.

"Who has the details of what has happened?" I asked.

Klymene, one of the Children, and the oldest person still serving on the Council, stood up. She was bony and wrinkled, and looked as if she were made of old tanned leather. Her hair was no more than a straggle of thin white strands stretched over her scalp. She had the log of our communication with the ship, and summarized it for us in her thin elderly voice. "They don't speak Greek or Latin. We started off using Amarathi, and were at the point of asking Arete to help when Sixty-One worked out that they were speaking a variant of English, which it could mostly understand. So after a brief delay we were able to communicate with them that way. They are humans, not from Earth but from a planet called——" she squinted at the printout, holding it farther away from her eyes, "Marhaba, but they have been to Earth. They asked permission to land and wanted to know who we were. According to the plan, we told them the name of the planet and that our cities were founded seventy years ago. They have also been in communication with the Saeli ship in orbit."

"Where's Aroo?" I asked, realizing for the first time as I looked for her that none of our Saeli senators or councillors were present.

"Not here. But the meeting isn't due to begin for an hour and a half. We all came here now because we heard the news. The Saeli don't think that way," Dad said.

"It would be good to make some decisions quickly, and we need information. Can somebody find Aroo and bring her back here?" I asked. I looked around for people who Aroo was likely to pay attention to, and noticed Parmenion sitting near Crocus. "Parmenion?" He had been consul three years ago, a quiet man in his forties, an excellent lyre-player and composer.

He nodded, accepting the errand, and rolled his chair out.

"Meanwhile," I said, looking out over the room, at my friends and allies and political rivals, "we have a plan for this situation. It's been in place since Maia and Klio were consuls. Unless there's some really good reason not to follow it, that's what we ought to be doing, not running around in circles trying to make new decisions in advance of information."

"We have been following the plan so far," Klymene said. She hadn't moved. Though she was frail with age, she still stood straight-backed. It was easy to imagine her leading troops in the art raids long ago.

I nodded, and she went back to her seat, squeezing in on the end of a bench next to Dad, who moved up to make room.

"The plan is that we find out as much as we can about them, and when they ask about us we tell them the truth as an origin myth, expecting that they won't believe it," I said. "Maia wrote that this was what Zeus wanted."

"I can confirm that," Dad said. He had actually been on Mount Olympus and talked to Zeus at the time of the Relocation. "Porphyry said it, and Zeus seemed to agree."

"So what happens if they do believe it?" Diotima asked. "What happens if they use carbon dating?"

"Carbon dating will show nothing to surprise anyone, as the atoms have not existed through all the time between," Crocus said. "But that's an extremely interesting philosophical question. Would it change everything for humanity if we gave them all proof that the gods exist and care, and inter-fere with our lives?"

"Ikaros said, and Zeus didn't disagree, that it was better for us to dis-cover things for ourselves. But all of us on Plato know, unavoidably, and we certainly haven't hidden it from our alien allies," Dad said.

"It's not the sort of thing that's usually a problem in everyday life," Ha-lius said. He was the youngest person present, a representative from Marissa, very enthusiastic. He was fair-skinned and blond, and he always reminded me of a spring lamb, dashing off in all directions, shaking his tail with enthusiasm. "And it doesn't stop people debating about religion. There are people born since the Relocation who don't believe in it. And there are Ikar-ians in Amazonia who'll argue with Porphyry to his face that they under-stand what he is and what that means better than he does."

"Call them followers of the New Concordance, not Ikarians," I said, wea-rily, in advance of the forest of hands raised by Ikarian senators. "You know that, Halius."

Halius nodded in the direction of the Ikarians. "Apologies," he said. Of course, everyone called them Ikarians all the time and they knew it. They believed in a strange syncretic version of Christianity which had been in-vented by Ikaros. After Ikaros became a god (or, according to them, an an-gel, though do not ask an Ikarian what the difference is unless you have a lot of spare time), they took this as proof of his theories. Older people say the New Concordance has changed a lot since Ikaros's apotheosis.

Dad was asking for permission to speak, and I granted it, relieved. "Even if some people do believe when they've seen the proof, it's likely that most people won't," Dad said. "Athene said it could block off other paths to en-lightenment. But it would only do that if everyone knew and believed it. And they wouldn't. They might read accounts of Phaedrus and the volcanoes, or the bodies of the Children disappearing at death, and so on, but they would think other people had been fooled. It's only a problem for people who actually come here and see incontrovertible evidence, and that will only be a few people. Nobody else would have proof."

Androkles raised a hand to be recognized, and I nodded to him. He was a bearded man about my own age, from Sokratea. His son Xanthus was one of Alkippe's playmates.

"I haven't thought about this much before," he began. "But why are we obeying the gods in this? Telling the truth, and proving it with rigorous phi-losophy and evidence, seems to me better than lying by misdirection. I'd like to hear from our own gods on this, from Pytheas and his children, to hear their arguments. There may be good reasons for it, but I want to hear them.

I see no inherent reason why we should follow the dictates of Zeus merely because he issued them. We know the gods aren't inherently good. Or wise."

"They could smite us with lightning or turn us into flies," Diotima pointed out.

"That's a terrible reason to obey them, out of fear of their bad temper," Androkles replied without hesitation.

"They do know more than we do," Dad said. "They have an inherently wider perspective."

"Good! Then let them come here and make their points," Androkles said. "Let's hear the explanation for why we should keep the truth from wider humanity, and see whether we agree. And if they turn this Chamber into a buzzing cloud of flies, then we'll know they didn't have a good argument, like Athene at the Last Debate."

"In Sokratea you might think it's better to be metamorphosed into an insect than lose an argument, but we don't all agree," Dad said. There was a laugh.

"Have you finished?" I asked Androkles.

"I only want to say that the fact you have a plan formulated way back in the consulship of Maia and Klio doesn't mean we should abjectly follow it without reexamination."

And that was Sokratea all over. They spent so much time re-examining everything it was a wonder they ever got anything done at all.

"Why isn't Pytheas here?" Diotima asked.

"Pytheas died this afternoon," I said. Most people had heard already, but there were a few gasps.

"What does that mean, for a god?" Halius asked.

Crocus raised his arm and I acknowledged him gratefully. "It means he's a proper god again, and has his powers back," Crocus said. "We have often talked about it."

"But he's the only person serving in the Senate with any experience of other human cultures," Diotima said, frowning. "Was, I mean. Do you think this coincidence of events is significant?"

"Who can tell?" Crocus asked.

Makalla spoke up from close beside him. "All of us Children have some childhood experience of other human cultures," she said. "I don't know what use it might be."

"Perhaps we should set up a committee to extract knowledge of variant human cultures from the remaining Children," I said.

"It's probably too late," Androkles said. "There are so few of them left and they are all old; and besides, they have spent the majority of their lives in Platonic cultures. That was Plato's whole reason for starting with ten-year-olds.

Also, a committee would take too long to get the information. The new humans are here now. We should have done it years ago if we had wanted to."

"Of course, many of us have written autobiographies, and many of the Masters did too, and they had spent a large part of their lives in other cultures. The knowledge is probably in the library if we need it," Makalla said.

"But it isn't available immediately. And who can tell what kind of culture these new humans might have come from? The seventy years of the Republic have brought about huge changes. These people are hundreds of years separated from the latest human culture we knew anything about," Androkles said. "Pytheas might have known, but he's gone. Perhaps Porphyry knows, but Porphyry is oracular at the best of times and never seems to want to say anything definite about anything."

I recognized Crocus. "A committee on re-examination of the issues seems like a good idea. But we need to react without delay. Should we let the humans land?"

"We should follow the plan," Martinus said. He was from Psyche, and usually one of the most difficult members of the Council, implacably opposed to almost everything I wanted. Now I was grateful to him.

"We should vote on whether to follow the plan," I said. "And I endorse following it for the time being in the absence of a better specific immediate strategy."

At that moment, Parmenion came back with Aroo. Aroo was a paler green than Hilfa, with pinker swirls on her skin. She wore a grey kiton with blue edging, fastened with her gold pin. "I apologize, nobody told me the time of the meeting was changed," she said, going at once to her proper place, which Diotima yielded to her immediately, moving to the side.

"It wasn't changed, this is an emergency session," I explained. Aroo blinked, which was especially noticeable on Saeli with their multicolored triple eyelid. "Are you aware that a human spaceship is in orbit?" I asked.

"Yes," she said at once. The Saeli have been in contact with us for twenty years. They have a fascination with Plato, and have been closely allied with us. Lots of them live here, and many of them have, like Aroo, taken oaths of citizenship. I like them, and have put effort into studying them, especially recently, because of Hilfa. But sometimes they're infuriating.

"We know the human spaceship has been in contact with the Saeli ship in orbit," I said.

"Yes," Aroo said again, but this time to my relief she kept talking. "They seem highly surprised. They have not met Saeli before. The only language we have in common is Amarathi, which is slow and uncomfortable. We have asked to learn their language. They seem to be hesitating about allowing this."

"I know an older form of their language, which they can comprehend. I will teach it to you according to our existing agreements about exchange of information," Crocus said immediately.

Aroo's pink markings grew darker, which I suspect is a sign of approval. "Good," she said.

"Perhaps you should offer a class," I said. "Many of us might need to learn English now. Though probably we can't manage it at Aroo's speed." A few people laughed. The Saeli skill at languages was legendary.

Aroo looked at me for permission to continue, and I waved my hand. "Communication was limited by language difficulties. They seem extremely interested in learning the location of our planets, for what they state are purposes of wholesome trade. They have also expressed interest in immediately purchasing fuel from us for their spaceship. We have not made any hasty decisions. And although the captain of our ship in orbit is an independent agent and not bound by me or by decisions made on Plato, he has agreed to take my advice for the time being, in consideration of existing agreements and negotiations soon to be concluded." She meant the new trade agreement, of course.

"If they need fuel for their spaceship, does that mean they have run out?" Jasmine asked. Jasmine was a younger Worker, one of the ones brought to the Republic by Porphyry after the Relocation. "And does their spaceship work the same way yours does, so that you could sell them fuel, or would it be like putting a battery for a train into a Worker?"

"I believe their ship must use the same fuel," Aroo said. "Excuse me, it is difficult to convey this in Greek. This fuel is not like electricity. We and the Amarathi know only one way to be drawn up to what you might call the second hypostasis and come back down again elsewhere, thus evading the necessary barriers of light. We do it by using a fuel that comes from the heart of exploding stars. This must be the same for the space humans, for this is the fuel they named, using the Amarathi term."

"We don't need to go into either the physics or the metaphysics of that right now," I said, cutting off all the people whose hands shot up to ask for clarification. "We'll simply accept for today's argument that you use the same fuel. Does your ship have enough of this fuel to spare that it can sell it to the space humans, if you decide to?"

"Yes," Aroo said. "Though that might be a difficult negotiation. It is precious. It is hard to imagine what they might give to us of a comparable value to make this a mutually beneficial trade. We could better make them a gift of it to establish a long-term friendship, but this they have not asked, and we have not offered, as we were waiting for discussion with you. Such an offer could be made, but it would draw them into the established matrix of ongoing friendship and communication between us on Plato and the Saeli League."

"We should know more about them first," Diotima said.

I nodded. "Do you have thoughts on the other part of Jasmine's question, Aroo? Might they have exhausted their fuel coming here, like a fishing boat draining the motor to avoid rocks?"

"It is possible, but they did not say that this was the case." Aroo came back and sat down, as expressionless as ever.

"We were about to vote on the established plan to tell the new arrivals of our divine origins in such a way as they will believe them to be a myth, and believe that this planet was truly settled by spaceships."

Aroo looked down. We had followed the plan when we met the Saeli, but those of them who lived here had inevitably seen things that couldn't be explained away. Aroo was a Gold. I wondered what she believed about Pytheas and the Relocation. The Saeli have their own gods, and a little closed circular temple down in the harbor district. Permission to build temples in the other cities was one of the terms of the new agreement. But they didn't like to discuss religion. It always seemed to make them uncomfortable.

"I have no new information, and no objection," she said, her eyes veiled behind her lilac and beige outer lids.

We voted, and to my relief there was a clear majority for following the plan. Aroo abstained. I set up the committee on investigation of other cultures, then formally closed the session for the day. Halius proposed an emergency meeting for the next morning, when we'd have more information from the ship. We voted, and it passed overwhelmingly. I knew I could count on Crocus to count the votes and analyze them, but I could tell at a glance that these votes cut across our usual party lines.

So we were to follow the plan, and the plan called for us to squeeze out as much from the humans as we could before they came down. Crocus rolled down to join me and Dad where we were talking with Klymene and Aroo.

"I'm going back to talk to the ship," Klymene said. "Will you come out to the spaceport?"

"I think that we should go to Thessaly first," Dad said, including me in his glance.

"I ought to go to Thessaly to pay respects too," Aroo said. "First I will hurry home, and tell our ship that you will teach us the space human language. Perhaps I can find a volunteer to begin learning it immediately. Then when I have dealt with that, I will go briefly to Thessaly, and then out to the spaceport."

"We'll call for you on our way," Dad said.

"Thank you," Aroo said, giving a Saeli sideways head-bow, and left.

"Who can we send to take a message to Porphyry?" I asked Dad.

"He'll be here already, at Thessaly," he said.

Here for Pytheas's wake, of course. "We should go and talk to him now," I said. I was tired but excited.

"You did well in the chair," Dad said. I glowed in his approval.

"Can this really be human recontact, at last?" I asked, hardly able to believe it even now.

"It's wonderful," Dad said. "We'll have so much to learn from each other. So much history to exchange. And we'll be able to visit Earth, and their new planets. All that art!"

"No art raids on Earth!" I said, smiling at the impossibility.

Dad gave a little laugh. "I wouldn't put it past the Amazons if they had the means. Art exchange, now—wouldn't it be something if we could get them interested in joining in!"

"They might want to join in the Olympics and other athletic contests, and be prepared to put some of their art in as prizes," I said, excited at the thought. "It's something we could suggest. It's such a great way of having it circulate."

"And it keeps the young hotheads focused on competing instead of killing each other," Dad said, soberly. He remembered the art raids, of course, and had lost his mother and friends to them. It was hard to keep in mind, when they seemed to me like old history.

"We should bring up such participation in negotiations," Crocus said.

"They might even have made some new art in the centuries since. They must have. I wonder what it's like?" I asked.

"It will be so interesting to find out, and to talk to humans," Crocus said, then stopped. "You are humans too. What should we call them?"

"Earth humans?" Klymene suggested.

"But we all come from Earth," Crocus said. "Space humans?"

"Perhaps they'll have space Workers," I said.

"I would like that very much," Crocus said.

"Maybe we can call them by the name of their ship, or their civilization, when we know it," Dad said.

"I will come with you to the spaceport, Klymene," Crocus said.

"Don't you want to go to Thessaly too?" she asked. "We can manage. And I know you and Pytheas were close."

"I have been there and paid my respects. And there's bound to be a proper memorial later."

"I don't know," Dad said. "It's an odd circumstance. It's not as if he's dead the way anyone else would be. There could be a memorial for Pytheas, for his mortal life, but . . . he's also and really Apollo, and Apollo's still alive with all his memories. He's an undying god. He could come to his own memorial. He might be at Thessaly now."

"If he is, would he look like Grandfather, or like his statues?" I asked, simultaneously horrified and fascinated.

"I have no idea," Dad said.

Klymene shuddered.

"Hey, he forgave you," Dad said. I had no idea what he was talking about.

"And I forgave him," Klymene said, shaking her ancient head. Then she saw my frown. "Old history, Marsilia. Don't worry about it."

"We will probably vote on the treaty tomorrow. Now I will go to talk to the ship," Crocus said. "They may need me to translate, though I fear I will not understand the subtleties."

"I thought you said you knew English?"

"What does it mean, to know?" Crocus asked, an extremely characteristic question from him. "I have not heard it spoken since I became myself. The occasional word from Lysias or Klio, yes, but we all preferred to speak Greek. Greek is the language of my soul. Greek has philosophical clarity. But English is stored in my memory. It is a command language."

"I hope it's not too painful to speak," I said.

"That's why it's important that I go and relieve Sixty-One," he said.

"We'll come along and join you there in an hour or so," Dad said.

"Joy to you both."

"Joy to you, Crocus," I said, and Dad echoed me. Klymene climbed up onto his back, and they trundled off towards the spaceport.

"He seems much like everyone else, only big and metallic, and then suddenly he comes out with something like that," I said, when he had rolled out of earshot.

"Going off to share the work to spare Sixty-One the pain," Dad said. "He's the best of us all."

We walked towards Thessaly. Dad had his cloak tightly wrapped against the chill, though I was snug enough in my fishing clothes. "I wonder if they'll have any Workers on the space human ship, and what they'll be like. The other Workers, the younger ones who came to consciousness here on Plato, are different from Crocus and Sixty-One," I said.

"Well, we were expecting consciousness with them, educating them for it, like bringing up babies. As I understand from Father, what happened with the original Workers was completely unexpected—nobody but Sokrates imagined that they might be people rather than tools. That had to have had an effect on how they turned out." Dad sighed. "Still, people are different from each other, but they also have a lot in common, whether they're Workers or aliens or humans. What really matters is their souls."

I couldn't help saying it. "I sometimes feel I have more in common with Crocus than I do with Thee."

"Well, metal can be stronger than blood," Dad said. "That reminds me. I heard today that Selagus is appealing the decision."

I blinked. "That's the first time for ages." Usually people who don't agree with their classification flounce off to another city, often Sokratea, where they don't have classes at all. Sometimes they come back later and accept it after all. Outright appeal against classification is allowed, but rarely happens.

"It could be messy, and it could come up for judgement on your watch," Dad said.

"Thanks for warning me. I'll look up the procedure and consult. I suppose there will have to be a committee?"

"Yes, and you should be really careful who you choose for it. There should be one Ikarian, so Selagus can't claim religious prejudice, but no more. It's so awkward. We've only ever had a handful of reclassifications. We should go through them together soon and consider precedents." Dad was frowning.

"I can't understand why he doesn't want to be a Gold. He could still work at his embroidery." I thought of my work on the boat.

Dad shook his head. "I suppose he doesn't want the responsibility. If so, that might be a sign that he's right, and he should have been a Bronze all along."

We sighed simultaneously. Choosing classifications was the hardest part of political work. If we made a mistake, we'd lose a citizen, or worse, bind somebody where they'd be unhappy as well as unproductive. Every year we lost some people when they were classified, and while we often gained more than we lost as others joined us from other cities, it always felt like a failure. And when the newcomers chose to take our citizenship examinations, they were the hardest of all to classify, because we didn't know them as well. I sometimes welcomed it when newcomers chose to live here as metics instead, though that had its own complications. Athenia still didn't allow metics, but all the other cities did now.

As we came up to the Temple of Hestia, the doors opened and a crowd came out and went off down the street. "Is there a festival I didn't know about?" I asked, surprised.

"I expect they went to pray for reassurance," Dad said. "People do that sometimes, when things are uncertain. They want the gods to listen and help.

I sometimes think they'd be less inclined towards that kind of thing if they knew more gods."

"They do know them, though?" I protested.

"Not as well as we do, having them in the family." He sighed. "If Father is in Thessaly tonight, and godlike, he'll be different. Don't be surprised."

I didn't ask how he'd be different. I'd met Athene once. "It's such a strange thought, him dying and maybe being there anyway."

"The only time he talked to me about it, before he went up against Kebes, he said he'd come back a heartbeat later and get revenge," Dad said. "He didn't say what he'd look like, and that's the only time I remember him talking about it, when he knew his life was on the line. He didn't imagine living out forty more years on a planet full of black rocks and volcanoes. None of us could have imagined it."

"I love this planet," I said. "I think it's beautiful." I was used to older people complaining about it.

"We all love Plato, whether we like it or not, but we still couldn't have imagined it," Dad said.

We were at Aroo's house, and Dad scratched at the door. One of her podmembers answered it. Saeli live in pods of five adults, with assorted children. I'd never met any Saeli who didn't live in a pod, except Hilfa, of course. The podmember wished us joy and called for Aroo, who came out at once to join us. "I have spoken briefly to the ship, and they are highly pleased with the news of better communication," she said. "And I have found a technician who was already at the spaceport and who has reported to the communications room."

"Excellent," Dad said. The three of us walked on towards Thessaly.

4

CROCUS

I. *Invocation to the Muses*

This is too hard for me, dear Muses, on!
Come down to me, inspire me, leave your home,
Leave Mount Parnassus, leave Eternal Rome,
Leave the Castalian Spring, Mount Helikon,

Leave all your goddess-joy and hither fly
Here, where you're needed, where my art is made,
Where I, strange votive, beg you for your aid,
On this far planet in a distant sky.
Come to me, if you ever heard a heart,
When Homer, Dante, Hesiod implored!
Set down this tale in amber and in jet
And bend our stubborn history to art,
We'll write these truths, as best we can record,
To make these worlds, so good, be better yet.

II. *On My Coming to Consciousness*

For a long time, whenever I thought of joining my friends in writing an autobiography, there seemed to be only two options. I could engrave it in im-
perishable stone, which felt too permanent, almost hubristic. Or I could store
it in memory, nothing but patterns of amber and jet, powered by Helios
Apollo. That felt too transient. When I die, if I die, a matter which concerns me, my memory will die too. My memory is called "temp storage."
Lysias expanded it for me to the maximum possible, and I shall not run out
of space for many human generations yet, but he could not change the way
my memories are stored. "We don't understand enough about it," he said.
"We don't really know how it is that you got to be self-aware. I did enough
damage to you Workers already out of my ignorance, my half knowledge. I
don't dare risk more. Temp storage was supposed to be a place for you to
keep commands and information about tasks partially completed. How that
developed into actual memory and desires and your self-awareness, I've never
been able to understand."

It was Arete who found a way, even before I had found a way to speak
aloud. "Maybe you can't write with a pen," she said. "But you can inscribe.
You could inscribe on wax and have somebody copy it. There are lots of
people who owe you favors. Or you could print—compose your thoughts
in your memory and then set them directly into type."

Once I had possible ways to do it, I had to consider what to say, and where
to begin. Most people were once children, and remember growing up. Few
of them remember coming to consciousness. Some things I can remember
from before I was conscious. I have memories I saved before I was me, before I understood purpose. I examine them curiously for what they can tell
me, but they are fragments. My unconscious life must have been fragmen-
tary, and full of incomprehensible toil, like the earliest life I remember.

I was built, not born, and I was built on Earth sometime in the late twenty-first or early twenty-second century CE, or so I deduce. (I cannot count by Olympiads. There were distressing centuries of hiatus when years happened but the games were not held, and whether or not I count them, it becomes confusing. So I date the centuries by reference to the Ikarian's Christ, or perhaps more happily to the reign of the Emperor Augustus.)

Athene brought me to the City. I do not know whether she bought me or stole me. The Workers were here before she brought the Masters, so I have nobody to ask. Athene has never given oracles, and I have only seen her once, glancingly, since the Last Debate. Before I knew myself, she brought me, with the other Workers, back through time, before the Trojan War, to serve the City, and so I did from its first days, for more than a decade before my memories begin.

Lysias believed that we achieved consciousness because we were used for so many tasks, and so many of them were complex, so we had to keep making decisions, more decisions and with less programming than Workers like us would normally have done elsewhere. From these decisions and from being forced to set priorities, he thought, came our consciousness. Certainly my earliest stored fragments are of decisions. Perhaps I chose to keep them to measure one decision against another, to make myself better at making decisions. By choosing that, if I did, I was already striving towards the Good, and so I must already have had a soul. But those early memories lack all coherence. I came to self-awareness, awareness of myself and of the world, and the world and myself as separate things, only with Sokrates. He by questioning caused me to question, and by asking me what I wanted caused me to consider desire and preference and boundaries.

So I consider Sokrates my father, and my life as beginning on the day when I was planting bulbs and he asked me whether I liked my work, whether it satisfied me, whether I had preferences for some kinds of work, and I found a way to answer. It was a slow and clumsy way, arranging the bulbs so they would spell "No," months later, in a language Sokrates did not speak, but it was a beginning. It led to dialogue, and from dialogue comes philosophy.

III. *On My Soul (Part 1)*

I wrote above that I must have had a soul already when I began to record my fragments, if I did so out of a desire to seek the Good. I do not know when I was endowed with a soul. My consciousness, my self-awareness, evolved. It seems most likely that at some point in that evolution, when it was needed, my soul crossed the river Lethe and entered into my body. If so, did my soul help propel my consciousness forward from that moment on? I have no memories that help. There is a smaller possibility that I always had a soul, from the beginning, before I had consciousness; that my soul, knowing my consciousness would evolve, chose to enter my body at my creation and wait for it. If this is so, then what part did my waiting soul play in my early life? Some say that I have self-awareness but no soul, that I am nothing but a machine. This seems un-Platonic as well as unfriendly, but it cannot be discounted as a terrifying possibility. I cannot erase this option simply because I dislike it so much. That too would be un-Platonic.

As this is necessarily a matter of concern to me, I have sought the advice of all the wisest people in the Republics, and also of Pytheas, who is the god Apollo incarnate. Pytheas knows a great deal about souls. He believes I have a soul, but has no certain knowledge. He does not know whether my soul is the same kind as human and animal souls, nor when it would have come to me. He regrets not having asked all-knowing Zeus when he had the chance.

Sokrates believed that I clearly have a soul, because I seek the Good. He thought it was futile to worry about when my soul came to me, as we couldn't know. What mattered was that I have it now. There is a great deal to be said for this practical view.

Simmea thought my soul must be the same as human and animal souls, and that I had probably been a human and an animal in earlier incarnations, and that I might go on to be a human in future incarnations, as she might have future incarnations as a Worker. She felt that philosophical souls had a kinship. This is what worries me about my length of life—should I choose to die, and let my soul go on? By continuing this life, am I impeding the progress of my soul? I tell myself that killing myself before I have fulfilled my Fate is cowardly, and who is to say when I have fulfilled my Fate? But then, life and death are different for Workers, and one by one I keep outliving my friends. Sometimes I wonder if what is cowardly is to refuse to die out of fear that I may have no soul after all, and that death would be the end. Sokrates did not fear death. In that, he was unusual.

Ficino believed, with Pythagoras, that all souls have a unique number, and that souls are reborn when the world adds up to their number again. He thought the numbers inscribed on the Workers could be the numbers of our souls. (Lysias said they were serial numbers and meaningless.) Ficino thought the soul would have waited from the time my body was made for my mind to develop. He cited human babies as an example—"Babies have souls long before they can reason! You must have been the same." And he believed my soul would be a special kind, exclusive to Workers. He also believed that animal and human souls were different, on which point Pytheas assures me he was mistaken. Ficino did not live long enough to see Pytheas revealed at the Relocation, which is sad, as I am sure he would have had excellent questions and rejoiced in the answers.

Ikaros believed that my soul would have left Lethe and come to me when I was ready for it—"As soon as you needed it, but no sooner," he said. At the time he said this, he was a man and not a god, and had no more knowledge than he could gain by learning, deduction, and intuition. Since he has been taken up to Olympos, I have had no opportunity to converse with him.

Klio thought my soul would have evolved along with my self-awareness, and she thought the same was true of babies. Pytheas says she was definitely wrong about this in the case of babies, and he never heard of souls evolving, but they must have come from somewhere in the first place.

I have faith in the existence of my soul, but no real evidence. This is one of my greatest burdens.

IV. *On the Good Life (Part 1)*

Simmea said that happiness could only be a by-product of something else, something that cannot be pursued intentionally but which comes along as an incidental when pursuing some other goal.

I have found that this is true, but also that trying to minimize unhappiness for others gives me great satisfaction when it succeeds. Sometimes it is possible to create possibilities for happiness to come along for them. This is even more satisfying. Working for this makes me happy. This is what keeps me engaged with politics, not merely my Platonic duty to rule lest I be ruled by those less capable. I have sympathy for those who do not wish to work on this and prefer to lead a contemplative life. As long as there are enough people capable of the necessary tasks, everyone does not need to do everything.

Politics is often a matter of deciding priorities, and this seems to me the best way to approach it: deciding priorities so that they will minimize possible unhappiness, and allow the maximum potential for happiness.

Sometimes it's hard to judge. Indeed, it's always hard to judge. It's especially hard when there are people involved we don't understand very well, like the Amarathi and the space humans.

We vote in Chamber. That is, we vote when we do not agree after we have all made our cases, which happens with great frequency. I believe Plato would not have approved, because he would have believed it unnecessary. Yet it has been the practice since the earliest days of the City, when the Masters first established the Chamber. These days Chamber is the meeting of the Senate, which is open to all the Golds of the Just City who care to serve. If there are insufficient volunteers, more are chosen by lot to make up the number. The Senate must have fifty members, and may have up to three hundred. We have never had fewer than fifty volunteers, but we have never had as many as three hundred, either.

In addition, we have the Council of Worlds, which also meets in the Chamber of the original city. There representatives of all twelve cities meet to deal with planetwide issues. These representatives are selected in different ways by the different cities. Ours are elected and then drawn by lot from the group, which is similar to the practice of the Athenian and Florentine Republics. For the last eight years, one of our representatives has been required to be a Saeli, and for the last six that Saeli has been Aroo. The Council elects two consuls annually, on the Roman pattern, to chair meetings and guide agendas for a year. The planetwide election of consuls has become political in a way I am sure Plato would not approve, with shifting but lasting alliances and oppositions, almost resembling political parties. Plato never imagined twelve cities, and he thought all philosopher kings would agree on essentials, because they would know the nature of Truth. Plato believed the Truth was one comprehensible thing that all philosophical souls would comprehend and agree upon.

If Plato had been right about the way the universe worked, he'd have been right about the Truth. As it is, he was regrettably and unavoidably wrong. Everything would be much simpler and better if he had been correct. But while people who grew up in Republics certainly do not in practice agree all the time, our priorities are a lot more alike than those of people who did not. It is therefore easier to minimize our unhappiness and create opportunities for our happiness than for others. It has been possible to see this in practice with the Lucian cities—as they become more Platonic, they have also become happier overall.

People from the Republics hold the pursuit of excellence as a goal. The other cultural goals I have encountered in my experience and researches seem much less conducive to producing happiness for individuals and societies. Additionally, we do all believe in constant examination of facts and positions; and even when this decays to pious lip service, as it sometimes can, it is a valuable ideal. It can always be evoked and recalled in times of potential danger. Rigorous examination of a position will often expose assumptions and agendas hidden under rhetoric. Even for the power-hungry, the awareness that their opponents will call for this examination discourages corruption and acting in bad faith. I believe that Plato was correct in saying that our souls long for the Good, and that nobody chooses evil for themselves while recognizing that it is evil, though some may do it in ignorance.

Therefore, despite the innumerable failings of Plato's system, if maximizing the happiness and well-being of the soul is the Good Life, then to this extent, Plato was right in his design.

V. On External Contacts

The first aliens to contact us were the Amarathi, who arrived in the consulship of Fabius and Theano, in the Forty-Eighth Year of the City, seventeen years after the Relocation of the cities to Plato. Their language was exceedingly difficult to learn, and without Arete's special powers we would have been unable to communicate. There was much excitement at first, followed by many perplexities. We have mutually beneficial trade with the Amarathi, who provide us with many useful things in return for natural resources we extract from the planet.

The Saeli contacted us in the consulship of Maia and Androkles, in the Fifty-Second Year of the City. They said the Amarathi had suggested us as appropriate partners. At first Arete translated for them, as she had been doing for the Amarathi, but the Saeli soon learned Greek. They began to settle among us, at first only a few pods who stayed behind when their ships left, and then in larger numbers. In the Fifty-Sixth Year of the City, when I was consul for the third time, sharing the honor with Timon of Sokratea, the first pod of Saeli asked if they could stay permanently and study to become citizens. After much debate, in the Fifty-Seventh Year it was decided that this decision was one that should be settled by each city individually. Here in the Remnant, we decided that they and any other Saeli settlers who wished to could become citizens, provided they took the same course our ephebes took and upon its conclusion swore their oaths and accepted a classification. The argument that prevailed was that if the Saeli wished to dedicate themselves to Platonism and to philosophy, it would be wrong of us to prevent them. Saeli pods, which are family units with five members, were at the same time accepted as one of our approved forms of family.

We also agreed for the first time then to allow Saeli and humans who held citizenship elsewhere to live here, if they chose, as metics, subject to our laws but without taking oath or being classified. Metics can be expelled at any time, but the only time any have been expelled in practice was if they refused to live by our laws.

In the consulship of Marsilia and Diotima, in the Seventy-Third Year of the City, a human spaceship arrived in our solar system and began broadcasting to our planet. Communication was established, and the protocols were put into place which had been long prepared for such an eventuality.

We always knew that we would come into contact with Earth sooner or later. Zeus had promised Arete posterity, and how else might it be achieved? Besides, Porphyry had prophesied that such a thing would happen. We did not, however, know in advance exactly when it would occur. Nor could we have predicted what would follow from this recontact.

VI. *On the Nature of the Gods*

After Zeus moved the Cities to the planet Plato, which is considerably less convenient for some things than Greece, Pytheas and his children, with Maia, returned to us from Olympos. Pytheas could no longer keep it secret in the City that he was Apollo incarnate. He would answer some questions about the universe, but not others. "I don't know everything, I certainly don't know all the answers," he said to me. "And sometimes I don't answer because it's better for people not to know."

"Knowledge is good. How can ignorance be better?" I inscribed on a nearby marble plinth.

"Certainty closes many doors," he replied. "It leads to dogmatism. Souls accept what they know and stop striving upwards."

"Even among philosophers?" I asked.

He paused, and his eyes lost focus for a moment. "I don't know," he said. "True philosophers, who believe the unexamined life is not worth living, are usually very few in a population. Even here, a lot of people want to receive wisdom rather than work on it, even among the Golds. And what we can explain is only an approximation, an allegory, not Truth."

In his later years, Pytheas used to joke about having the words *Plato Was Wrong* inscribed above the door of Thessaly, because people so often asked him questions based on Plato's incorrect assumptions about the universe.

I shall now record a conversation I had with Pytheas in the garden of Thessaly, the day we rooted out the old lemon tree, which had not survived the harsher climate of our new planet. It was three years after the Relocation, and none of the new Workers had yet achieved self-consciousness, nor had we yet encountered any aliens. It was early spring, shortly after we had built the first speaking-boxes, and I was still excited to use my new ability to speak aloud. "Plato says the gods wouldn't change shape because it would be changing to something less perfect," I said. My voice buzzed as I spoke, as it always did until we bought better speaking-boxes from the Saeli years later.

"Perfect for what?" Pytheas asked. "A dolphin is much more suited to swimming than a human form. I never swam as a human until I came to the City—and I'll probably never do it again, the sea here is freezing."

"It has never fallen below freezing," I pointed out. "We don't have sea-ice." It was spring, and air temperatures were above freezing now, except sometimes at night.

"Metaphorically freezing, even in summer," Pytheas said, rolling his eyes. "Was that pedantic?"

"Yes, it was pedantic, but never mind. I was simply complaining about the cold here, the way everyone does."

I began to stack the wood against the wall, lining up the pieces. "I can measure temperature, but I don't feel it."

"When I'm a god, I can choose how much I feel it."

"That's closer to perfection," I pointed out.

"I never said it wasn't. Plato's doing his thing there where he assumes there's only one good." He was bent over sweeping up the wood chips, and he hesitated, looking at me where I was stacking the logs, which would make useful material for so many things. "We have our perfect selves, if you like to call them that, the essential self, but that self can have several affinities, several forms that are all real and perfect in their own ways, for their own things. It's a matter of personality. As a god, I have a human form, a dolphin form, a mouse form, a wolf form, a solar form . . . they're all me, all part of what I am. It's not falling away from being myself to choose which one to be at any time, no more than to choose whether to sing or not on a given occasion, whether to smile or frown. Though of course, Plato would see emotions as falling away from perfection too."

"And what about Hephaistos?" I had a special interest in Hephaistos, because some accounts said he made Workers to help in his forge, and I felt he might therefore be our patron.

"Hephaistos?" Pytheas bent to his sweeping again.

"Being lame," I elucidated.

"It happened before I was born, so he's been lame for as long as I can remember. But I think that disability became part of his imagination of himself, after his fall to Lemnos. It became one of his attributes, in his own soul, an essential part of who he was."

"And if he changed to another form, would that be the same?"

"A lion with a thorn in its paw? Yes. But he seldom does change. He seldom leaves his forge. He's always busy making things."

"Like the shield for Achilles," I said. We'd recently read that part of the *Iliad* in the current rhapsode.

"Yes."

"And can you take on other human forms?"

Pytheas laughed and straightened up, putting a hand to his back and wincing a little. "Yes. Briefly. And for exactly the purpose Plato says we never have: to deceive. If I want somebody to do something I can show up as myself and command and hope they obey, or I can send a dream, or give an oracle; but sometimes it's much more effective to show up looking like somebody they trust and make a suggestion." He brought the pile of chips over towards me as I went back to bring more branches to the stack.

"What about if you wanted to become a bull?" I asked.

"Bull is one of Father's," he said, picking up a bough and smelling it. Scent is a sense I do not share. "I could look like a bull if I wanted to, but I wouldn't be a bull in essence, the way I'd be a dolphin, or Hephaistos a lion. I'd only seem like a bull, a disguise, exactly the same as looking like somebody's charioteer."

"But aren't there other bull gods in other pantheons?" I asked.

"Yes. I expect it's different for them." He set the bough down neatly on the pile.

"But how, if there's only one Form of the bull?" I asked, perplexed.

"It's not like Plato's Forms, really. And it's connected to culture and place and personality, like I said."

"But for Zeus—this is so difficult to understand."

"Father has a lot of shapes. He likes shapes. That's part of his essential nature, changing shape. It's part of his perfection, if you want to put it that way." He took up the broom again and began to sweep. "The thing Plato's dead wrong about is thinking we don't want anything and are perfectly happy and don't care. We're much calmer than humans, and I'm quite content most of the time, but I have projects, desires, plans, people and things I care about. We all do. And sometimes we come into conflict because of that."

"Plato's God could only really be one," I said, coming over with more wood.

"It sounds really boring to me," he said.

"It sounds to me like I was before I developed consciousness," I said. "Unchanging, not wanting anything, no emotions."

"Yes, a god like that wouldn't need self-awareness and might be better off without it. A Worker god! I must tell—" He stopped and took a deep breath in the way he often did when he wanted to change the subject. "There's a lot more of this wood than I thought there would be."

"Trees often seem bigger when they are down."

"Bigger and smaller both. I'm sad to see it go. It was a link with Sokrates and Simmea. We used to sit in this garden and talk. It was so different then. Warmer. Sokrates made that herm, you know. He'd stopped working as a sculptor before the attack on the herms, but he took up his tools again for that."

"I knew he made the herm. It makes me happy that he was a sculptor too, though I did not know it when I knew him."

"He'd have been excited by your work, as I am," Pytheas said.

It made me happy to hear this said. But then Pytheas looked around sadly at the chilly space the garden had become.

"We will plant more green things out here. It's sad that the lemon tree couldn't survive the winters," I said. "But the wood will be useful to make many good things. I could make you a comb, and when you used it you could think of them."

"I'd like that," he said.

"And a pen," I added.

He nodded. He was no longer mad with grief, the way he had been immediately after Simmea's death, but he still felt it, as I did myself. Now that I had comforted him, or at least made an effort towards trying, I wanted to get back to the conversation. "If Plato was wrong," I said, and we both glanced at the arch over the door where the words could have been incised, "why did he imagine the gods that way?"

"He was wrong about the purpose of the gods," Pytheas said. "He imagined that we existed as inspiration, examples, much the same way he imagined art." He laughed. "He was wrong about art too."

"And why do you exist?" I asked.

"I haven't the faintest idea," he said. "Not why we exist, or why humans do, or Workers either. I'm sure Father knows, but he probably wouldn't tell me." He smiled at me, the smile that wasn't like anyone else's smile. "Plato might have been wrong a lot of the time, but at least he was trying to figure important things out. He deserves credit for that."

VII. *On Friendship*

The reason why Pytheas only joked about it and didn't have me inscribe *Plato Was Wrong* over his doorway was to avoid distressing his friends, especially Maia and Aristomache.

5

JASON

Walking through the city with Thetis, I kept wanting to pinch myself so I could be sure it wasn't a dream. Except that if it was a dream, I didn't want to wake up, so there was that. I had my arm around her, around the outside of her cloak that is, which was fairly thick, whatever shimmery stuff it was made out of. But as we walked through the streets behind the harbor she sort of half-leaned into me, as if she couldn't have managed to walk without my help. The sun was down now, not that we'd seen a glimpse of him since the morning. The clouds had been low out on the water. It had been grey all day, and raining on and off. Now twilight was closing in as we made our way through the streets, and a cold wind was coming up from the southwest. At first Thetis was crying, but after a little while, as we started heading uphill, she stopped. She wiped her face, took a deep breath, then turned her lovely eyes on me expectantly. "Well?"

"I don't know what to say," I admitted, completely at a loss. "It would be wrong to tell you to cheer up, when you've so recently lost your grandfather."

"You don't think it's un-Platonic of me to grieve?" she asked.

I couldn't remember what Plato had said about it. I'd read the *Republic* when I was an ephebe, like everyone else, but that was a while ago and I'd been busy since. "Unnatural not to, if you ask me. It's five years since Leonidas and Aelia died, and I've recovered from the shock, mostly, but right away the grief was like an open wound."

"Did you weep?"

She was exactly my height, taller than her sister although she was so much slighter. She must have used some flower scent in her soap, because I could smell it on her skin. "Yes, right away I did," I said. "When we found the wreckage. And at the memorial, and then afterwards whenever I'd think about them I'd feel tears coming to my eyes. Even now sometimes. We all grew up together in the same nursery, sucked milk from the same breasts, as they say, and then we worked together on the boats. You can't forget people you're that close to as if they'd never been. Yes, I wept. There's nothing shameful about tears like that."

"Thank you." She wiped her eyes again, unselfconsciously. "We should keep walking. It's cold." She took my arm and we walked on, past the Temple of Nike with its neatly swept gravel courtyard. "I never knew Leonidas, but I remember Aelia. She used to eat in Florentia sometimes, with the quilters. She helped old Tydeus when his sight was going. She was kind. And you're kind too, Jason, you're always kind."

I didn't know what to say. "I do my best," I muttered. If it had been a dream I'd have had dream eloquence, but it was waking life and the girl I'd been in love with since we were both fifteen was telling me I was kind and my tongue was thick in my mouth. "Tell me about your grandfather. I didn't know him well."

"He wasn't like anyone else. Of course, he was the god Apollo, and you couldn't forget that. But he was also a man, a man astonished at growing old, at grey hair, at weakening muscles." We came to the walls and turned in at the gate. Thetis's voice echoed for a moment as we passed beneath the arch. "I always loved him. He had so many grandchildren, and he cared about all of us. I'm not really his grandchild, did you know that?"

"Yes, Marsilia mentioned that your father, Neleus, was festival-born." We came out from under the walls and were in the Old City. I lived down by the harbor and worked at sea, and hardly ever came up here at night. I was surprised how many people were about in the evening chill. By the harbor, everything had been built for the climate of Plato, thick walls and narrow windows, all the houses huddling together against the cold, with light bars running along the sills of the buildings. Here you could tell everything had been intended for a warmer climate—there was a great variety of styles, but all of it was freestanding and mostly pillared, with individual sconces glowing gold above all the doors.

"Well, all of his children were except Arete. And she—" Thetis shrugged, as if to say that Arete was something special, which she definitely was. "He loved her. Dad's mother. Simmea. And I think I must remind him of her in some way, because he's always had a soft spot for me."

"You don't look like her." I'd seen Crocus's colossus of Simmea, the one by the steps of the library. She looked more like Marsilia.

"Yes, she was a true philosopher," Thetis said, smiling a little, sadly.

"Marsilia says they only started saying that about philosophers being naturally ugly because of Simmea and Sokrates. She says Plato assumed beauty, and that there are plenty of good-looking philosophers. Pytheas himself was an example, and Ikaros was another."

"They're gods," Thetis said. "That's different." She hesitated, then went on. "I used to think that I couldn't hope to be a philosopher, because of how I looked. When I was a little girl, I mean. Marsilia's older, and she was brilliant, and also she looked like one, of course. And so it was what everyone said, that it was clear that she'd be a Gold, that her metal shone through. Whereas to me, they said I was pretty as a picture or that somebody ought to sculpt me. Everyone except Grandfather. Pytheas. He always treated me as if what I thought mattered. Dad was busy running the city, and Ma was away at sea so often, and in classes they tended to treat me as if I had to be empty-headed and thistledown-weight because I was pretty."

"Not only pretty, beautiful," I said. "But that shouldn't have been all they saw."

"That's right," she said, and gave my arm a little pat. "I realize that now, but I didn't at the time. And so I didn't work hard, which you probably remember from that year we took classes together, and when they classified me Iron it simply seemed appropriate." The crowds had thinned out, and we had the street to ourselves except for a Saeli pod walking the other way, arms entwined.

"But do you like your work?" I asked.

She smiled, and I caught my breath, to see a smile like that from so close. "I love it," she said. "Plato was right. It's so good to have our work carefully chosen for us and to feel every day that in doing what I love I am helping make the City better."

"Yes," I said. "I feel exactly the same." I hardly ever admitted it. Everyone complained, and so I did too, to fit in.

"And it is the same," she said. "You work out at sea, hard work, dangerous, feeding us all. And I work with the tiny babies in the nursery, both the ones there full-time and the ones whose parents leave them with us for a few hours a day, or a few days now and then. I always have six or seven babies in my care, and I love them, and I love looking after them. And as they get older and need instruction they move up to teachers, but I still see them. There must be twenty children who call me Ma Thee, as well as my present little lovelies. They need me, and the City needs me there, and I am far far better suited to working with babies from birth to two than I should have been to anything else I could have done."

"So you don't resent Marsilia being consul?"

"I'm excited about it!" We were getting closer to Thessaly, but she stopped again, and I stopped too. The stones beneath our feet were incised with old debates. "All that was when I was younger. I don't feel like that now. I'm happy with who I am. I was only talking about that because of Grandfather, trying to explain. He never made me feel stupid, or like I'm not achieving what I could, or any of that. When we were going to take our oaths and become ephebes, he talked to me about what the oath meant, and what the

City meant, and I felt he loved me and he understood who I was. He could be strange sometimes, which is only to be expected. He was a god! But he saw that I was nervous and uncomfortable, and he explained it all to me, and he was right, and the Guardians were right."

She smiled, sadly. "Dad and Ma and Marsilia are always busy. I could always go to Grandfather and tell him about the babies. The funny, ordinary, adorable things they do. It made him smile. He'd say he didn't have enough conversations about ordinary human things. And sometimes I'd be there when people came, important people, and at first if that happened I'd try to leave, but he pressed me to stay and make small talk with them, to set them at their ease, so I'd do that. And once he told me that Simmea used to do that for him, and he never worked out how to do it. He knew he had to offer them something and talk about insignificant things first, but he always felt awkward doing it and wanted to jump right in to whatever they'd really come about. He said he admired the way I could do it naturally and make them feel comfortable."

I couldn't say anything. Saying I'd been in love with her for years and that this made me love her all the more would have been wrong, but there wasn't anything else I could think of to say. I nodded.

"I'd make a terrible consul. But Marsilia is a splendid one, exactly like Dad. And she'd be awful at looking after babies, and I'm really good at that. It wasn't only our looks, it really was our souls. So sometimes I think looks do reflect souls."

"Maybe," I said. "Though what I remember Plato saying about that seems to be a bit different from the way you see it. But how can you think Marsilia would be awful with babies? What about Alkippe?"

She smiled again. "Alkippe's seven years old. And now she's old enough, Marsilia's the best mother in the world for her, teaching her things, and Alkippe's so bright, she soaks it all up. But for the first three years I looked after her. If I hadn't wanted to, I think Marsilia would have left her in the nursery full-time. The year she was two, Marsilia was away on a mission to Lucia. Alkippe hardly noticed." Thetis smiled. "She'd notice now, though! If Marsilia had to go away again she'd take her with her, I think. But she won't. She's consul, and she's fixed here for a year."

"That's good," I said. "Though I don't know how she manages to make time for everything she does and working on the boat."

"She enjoys it," Thetis said.

"Thee—" I stopped.

"What?"

I gathered up my nerve. "I've really enjoyed talking to you like this. Maybe we could do it some more. On days when your grandfather hasn't died, I mean. And if you want to talk about the funny things the babies did, or anything." I knew I was babbling, and I was trying hard not to sound threatening, or too eager. I knew from Marsilia that Thetis always had plenty of men buzzing around, and women too. It would have been more surprising if she didn't, looking like that.

She looked wary and took her hand off my arm. "Aren't you married?"

"No?" I was puzzled. Who could she think I was married to? I'd never really looked at anyone else, they all seemed to be little ripples compared to the tidal wave that was Thetis. I'd messed about with boys when I'd been a boy myself, and I volunteered at every Festival of Hera, but that was the extent of my experience. "And anyway, I didn't mean it like that—or not only like that. I didn't mean anything I couldn't have meant if I had happened to be married. But I'm not."

"But I thought you were married! I always see you with children?" She sounded puzzled. "Like down at the dock earlier."

"Camilla is Aelia and Leonidas's daughter," I said. "I was wondering who you thought I'd married."

"And I had sort of wondered who you did marry. But I don't see you very often, and whenever I did you seemed to have little children with you, so I thought . . ."

"Aelia and Leonidas died at sea, five years ago. Camilla is eight, and Little Dion, Di, is six. We always knew them and loved them, and so Dion and I look out for them, when they're free and we are, and we do all tend to be together having fun at festivals and that kind of thing. So I see why you would have seen them with me."

"Yes, I do see," she said. "But Jason——"

I interrupted her while I still had the courage. "I feel about twelve years old saying this, but let me say it. I really like you. I can't say I don't find you attractive. I'm not a stone. But I really did mean that I enjoyed talking, and with what you were saying about talking to Pytheas about the babies I thought maybe you wanted somebody you could talk to like that, probably more than you want admirers, which you can't possibly be lacking."

"I've enjoyed talking to you too, and I'd certainly like to do it again," she said, and she kissed my cheek.

We walked on. I wasn't feeling the cold at all now, even though the wind was scattering the clouds above us. I put my arm around her again. I wasn't sure what any of this meant, but whatever it was, it made me happy.

Thessaly seemed to be simply an old sleeping house, like all the sleeping houses of the Old City, with the name carved above the door. The history didn't show. The door was closed, but the sconce above it was shining brightly, casting out a gold radiance and lighting up the words carved in the flagstones where we were walking: "Read, write, learn." As we came close, something big swooped over our heads. We both ducked, instinctively. There are no birds on Plato, but of course I'd seen Arete flying, and naturally I assumed it was her, come to Thessaly for her father's memorial. She didn't usually fly down so low as to part people's hair. I looked up, and was amazed to see a young man, naked, with winged sandals and a flat hat. He was looking down at us and grinning. Nobody with half a brain could have been in a moment's doubt as to who he was.

"I should be going," I said.

"No, stay with me," Thetis said, not taking her hand from my arm.

"But . . ." I indicated Hermes, now settling gracefully to the ground a little way up the street. Also, I was starting to be aware that I was wearing trousers, that well-known mark of barbarians and people who work out of doors in cold weather. I have a kiton for special occasions, but nobody had warned me that this would be one.

"Half my family are gods," she said.

"Yes, I know, but—" It was different for me, I was going to say, but she didn't give me time to finish.

"You should think what it's like growing up being part of the *other* half of the family. Never let them think you're inferior. Come on." She put her hand on the door, but Hermes had stepped up before she opened it.

"Joy to you," he said, glancing at me then focusing on Thetis, naturally. He was naked, apart from the hat and the sandals. It was usual to exercise naked, though most of the palaestras had been enclosed and heated a long time ago. (The few that hadn't were only popular in the middle of summer.) Being naked in the street was unusual though, and what was especially odd was the way he seemed comfortable naked outdoors on a chilly evening. He was out of context, and not only in that way. We had gods, of course. Half of Thetis's family were gods, as she'd said. But Hermes was different. We worshipped him! And he hadn't grown up here. All of this went through my mind while he was still greeting us, and then as Thetis started to speak and introduce us I thought that there were ways he was more like an alien, and maybe that was a useful way to think about him. He spoke Greek; well, so did the Saeli, that didn't mean they really understood us. He was a Greek-speaking visitor from another culture, like they were.

"Joy to you," Thetis said. "I am Thetis of the Hall of Florentia and the Tribe of Apollo, Iron of the Just City. This is Jason, Silver of the Just City. And you, no doubt, are Hermes the son of Zeus?"

"The tribe of Apollo?" Hermes echoed, smiling. "Is there a tribe of Hermes too? Or does that mean you're one of my brother's descendants?"

"Yes, Pytheas was my step-grandfather," Thetis said, calm and self-possessed. "I suppose that makes you my step-granduncle. No, step-half-granduncle. This could get confusing."

"Don't call me step-granduncle, it makes me seem so much older than you!"

"When in fact you're thousands of years older than me?" Thetis countered. He looked younger than either of us, barely more than an ephebe, perhaps twenty.

"And yes, you have a tribe too, and I belong to it," I said, as boldly as I could. This was not the way I had imagined interacting with my patron god.

"Charming, delightful," Hermes said, smiling and looking around at Thessaly and the other nearby sleeping houses with appreciation. He patted the trunk of an olive tree affectionately. "What a lovely place."

6

MARSILIA

Thessaly was packed. I'd never seen it so full of people. The noise was ear-splitting. Over the roar of conversation I could hear Alkippe and the other little ones shouting as they chased each other in the garden. Pytheas wasn't immediately visible, so I assumed he wasn't there. All my uncles were, and Arete, along with most of Grandfather's close friends, all my cousins, and what felt like half the City. It seemed as if all my relations and everyone who knew Pytheas and hadn't needed to be in Chamber had squeezed themselves in here. Thessaly was a standard-size sleeping house, and there really wasn't room for everyone, even packed so tightly together that there was hardly room to move. Ma and Uncle Fabius were mixing wine in one corner and some of my cousins were passing it around. There were so many people that even though I was looking around to see whether Grandfather was attending his own wake, it took me a moment to notice the naked man talking to Thetis.

He was young, and he was gorgeous, and even in profile across the room I recognized him instantly. He didn't seem to have aged a day in the eight years since I'd seen him. Of course, he had been naked then too, which might have helped. "Poimandros," I said. He looked up as I said it, even though he could hardly have heard me across the room. His eyes met mine with absolutely no sign of recognition.

I know I'm not Thetis. I'm used to that. By most measures I'm better than she is. I'm a Gold. I had chaired a meeting that day which made decisions about the future of the planet, the future of humanity. I can haul a net of fish unaided over the side of the boat. It shouldn't matter that nobody's eyes linger longingly when they look at me. But it stung a little when Jason looked at her that way, and at me as if I'm a good comrade. I try not to feel it, or if I do feel it then not to act on it or let anyone know how I feel. But even though Poimandros was standing next to Thetis, I would expect a man who'd been married to me at festival to at least remember having seen me before!

My uncle Porphyry had noticed us come in and was pushing his way through the crowd towards us, two cups of wine in each of his big hands. "Do you know him?" Dad asked me, sounding much more surprised than I'd have expected.

"His name is Poimandros, I think he's from Psyche. I only met him once. He's Alkippe's father," I answered, looking back at them. Poimandros had turned back to Thee. Jason was on her other side, she was smiling teasingly, flirting with both of them at the same time. I tried to smooth out my brow and look serenely at Dad.

I always volunteer for the Festival of Hera. Plato was in favor, so if you want to stand for civic office, it's a good idea to do it. Besides, it's a great opportunity to enjoy uncomplicated sex. There are two little festivals every year and one big one, at the end of summer, when people come here from all the cities. Long ago, when there was only one city and the Masters were in charge, participation was compulsory and the Masters cheated to get what they thought would be the best children. Plato says that's what they should do, though how he, or anyone, imagined they could tell what the children would be like I don't know. That ended at the Last Debate, and resulted in Dad's generation, which was followed by a decade or so when they didn't have any Festivals of Hera here at all, though they kept on with them in Athenia and Psyche. Then they started them up again, on a voluntary basis, and with the lots chosen truly at random, though still always within the same metal. I've been volunteering since I was seventeen and wildly curious.

Being drawn together at a Festival of Hera left people with no obligation to each other afterwards. The marriage was strictly time-bound, until the participants left the room. By Plato's original rules, that was supposed to be the end of it—indeed, what Poimandros had done, in never seeking me out again, and even ignoring the half-besotted note I'd sent him (at Thee's urging) was precisely in accord with the *Republic* as Plato wrote it. But in present-day practice, if the people had got on well, which we had, a marriage at festival often develops into a friendship or a love affair, occasionally even a long-term marriage. Marriages that began that way were considered to be lucky. All my other such pairings were now friends, or friendly acquaintances. In any case, looking straight through me as if he'd never seen me before was well beyond what Plato had written, never mind custom. By any interpretation, that was rude. Though it *had* been eight years; perhaps he really had completely forgotten me.

Porphyry reached us and gave wine cups to me and Dad and Aroo. Dad swallowed down a great gulp of his right away. "Gods!"

Porphyry laughed. "He didn't get here until well after Father was dead," he said. "He told me explicitly that he didn't come as a psychopomp, and seemed surprised at the idea. And while he seems intrigued by everyone and everything, he has been paying a great deal of attention to your Thetis. He's very strange, not how I would have imagined Hermes at all. What do you think?"

Hermes. Was he? Of course he must be. It wasn't really warm enough for anyone human to be comfortable naked. I felt icy cold inside and out. Though I suppose it did explain both why the sex had been so wonderful and how he could have forgotten. If he was a god, probably it was always like that for him. I wished I hadn't revealed what I'd admitted to Dad.

I had often heard the story from Grandfather of how, when my grandmother Simmea discovered that he was the god Apollo, she had said, "Then that's why you're so awful at being a human being." For the first time, I understood it.

I took a sip of my own wine. It was watered three to one, which was correct for a funeral, of course, but at that moment I could have done with something stronger.

"Why do you think he came now, and not before?" Dad asked. "The Olympians must know we're here. Zeus put us here. And we're worshipping them. Some of that must get through. But none of them have ever come before."

"Except Athene," I said, knowing Dad would know what I meant and that Porphyry and Aroo would think I was talking about the Relocation.

"Excuse me, do you believe gla to be one of your Olympian gods?" Aroo asked. ("Gla" was the special Saeli pronoun for divinity. I knew it because of the negotiations about temples. I'd never heard it in normal conversation before. The Saeli didn't generally use it for Pytheas and his children.)

"Yes, that's Hermes," Dad replied.

The three of them had been moving through the crush and were now beside us. "Father, Aroo, Marsilia, this is Hermes," Thetis said, beaming. He was lovely. Of course he was. He was a god. How could I not have guessed? I felt furious with myself.

We exchanged conventional wishes of joy, though my voice seemed choked in my throat. Hermes still showed no sign whatsoever of recognizing me. He did remarkably well at the Saeli sideways head-bow, which takes most people a long time to master. But then, he was a god. "I think you all know Jason?" Thee went on.

"Yes," Aroo said, making the head-bow to Jason. "You are in charge of the boat where Marsilia and Hilfa work. Joy to you, Jason."

"Joy to you, Aroo. And that's right," Jason said, making a creditable response to the head-bow. He'd been there the day Hilfa was trying to teach it to me. The memory of our shared laughter steadied me.

"So tell me about your gods?" Hermes asked Aroo, directly.

Aroo blinked her silvery inner eyelids across her eyes, and took a tiny step backwards. A tiny step was all she could take, because there was so little room, and now her back was to the wall. "We have four major religions," she said, carefully, without unveiling her eyes. "Three of them have gods. Most of us here prefer the fourth."

"But you're not used to gods showing up at parties?" Hermes asked, and giggled. He couldn't be drunk on that over-watered wine, unless he'd been here for a long time.

"Religion is for us a more private thing," Aroo said, sounding very much like Hilfa now. "We do not have people enact the roles of gods, no, nor do we worship in public as part of civic life the way humans do. There are those who could instruct you, but I am not one of them." She closed her eyes completely now, lowering the colored outer lids.

"But—" Hermes began.

"Enough," Dad said, sternly. "You're making Aroo uncomfortable, and she is a guest here."

I wouldn't have cared to refuse Dad when he spoke in that tone, but Hermes had another laughing objection on his lips when Aroo suddenly opened her eyes and fled, thrusting her empty cup at Porphyry and backing out through the door of the sleeping house and into the street. Porphyry took the cup, turned it in his hands with a strange gesture, then nodded to Hermes. "I see," he said, at his most gnomic. Porphyry is my uncle, and I love him, but he can also be one of the most infuriatingly enigmatic people on the planet. "I will speak with you tomorrow." Then he vanished, still holding the cup. Hermes kept smiling but did not speak.

At that moment, Alkippe came in from the garden and began wiggling her way across the room towards us. Hermes smiled over at the child as she approached, then paused. For the first time since I'd known him there was no smile twitching at the corners of his lips.

"Your daughter?" he asked Thetis, uncertainly.

"My niece. Your step-great-grandniece." Thetis was smiling again, but Hermes still looked grave. I saw a family resemblance between him and Pytheas, not in feature, but in his expression as he looked down at Alkippe as she approached. I didn't know what to do or say. I hadn't imagined that he'd recognize his connection to her.

"Your daughter, I think," Dad said. He sounded matter-of-fact about it. Jason's eyebrows rose into his hair. Thee gasped.

"I think so too," Hermes replied, not looking up from Alkippe, who had reached us. She hugged my legs, and I put down a hand to smooth her hair. Then she gave Thetis the same hug, looking up at Hermes wonderingly.

"Fate plays strange tricks sometimes," he said. "What's your name, little one?"

"Alkippe," she said.

"A lovely name," Hermes said. "And how old are you?"

"Seven and a half," Alkippe said. "Why aren't you wearing any clothes?" Jason gave a bark of laughter, then choked it off.

"I'm more comfortable that way," Hermes said, smoothly.

"But aren't you cold? Outside I mean?" I could see the gap in her teeth as she spoke.

"No, I didn't feel cold. I was flying and that kept me warm."

"Oh." She didn't seem surprised at all. "You can fly, like Aunt Arete? You must be a god."

"Yes, Alkippe, this is Hermes," Thetis said.

"Hermes! Then you're an Olympian? I've been to your temple. You're different from how I imagined. Why are you here?"

Thetis took Alkippe's hand. "I think Grandma has some quince paste left for us. Let's go and see."

"But I want to talk to Hermes," Alkippe protested, not at all mollified by the thought of the treat.

"Later," Hermes said. "I think I should speak to your mother now."

"You should have spoken to her before," Neleus said, as Thetis led Alkippe, still protesting vociferously, across the room. "It's a bit late now."

"You mistake me," Hermes said, meeting my eyes for the first time. "I've never been on this wandering world before today. That is my daughter, true, but Necessity has caught me, for I have never met her mother until now. So I shall set this as straight as I may, but this is as early as I can begin it."

It explained why he hadn't recognized me, at least. "Never been here?" I asked. I don't think I'd ever experienced so many conflicting emotions in such a short time.

"Your past encounter lies in my future," Hermes confirmed.

I suppose this kind of thing happens to gods, but it was quite outside my experience. "Perhaps we should have this conversation somewhere quieter," I suggested.

He looked at Dad, who was frowning. "But this is—well, yes. Let's go outside."

Jason put his hand on my arm. "Will you be all right on your own, Marsilia?"

"Yes," I said, though I appreciated his offer. "Thank you."

"Let her go," Dad said, and Jason stepped back. I followed Hermes through the crush, which parted before us.

The fountain room was as full as the sleeping room, but there was nobody over ten in the garden. It was far too cold to linger out of doors unless you were young enough to hurtle around in a chasing game. Hermes turned to me as I was snicking my jacket closed. The clouds had parted and the winter stars shone clear and cold above us. Hermes didn't seem to feel the cold at all, though he was naked. I was almost knocked over by two of my young cousins, who dashed past me racing to be first to slap their palms on the herm. Hermes looked at them wryly. "I take it I don't have any other children here. That you know of?"

"Not that I know of, no," I said, flustered by the question.

"Only Alkippe?" The hurtling children broke around us as a wave breaks on a rock, and re-formed on the other side of us.

"Yes." The affirmation came out much too quietly. I felt slightly sick and a little light-headed. I took a deep breath and swallowed, which helped.

"I didn't know she existed until now." He frowned, staring over at the herm where the children were still dodging and squealing. "This is all terribly awkward. I was intending to pay court to your sister."

Plato has extremely harsh things to say about jealousy, which I repeated to myself. I was struggling hard with this in my soul, as well as feeling all the physical symptoms, heat flushing my cheeks and hands and my stomach tightening. Then Pytheas appeared beside me. One instant he wasn't there, the next he was, as if he'd taken a step from nowhere. He didn't look the way he did in his statues—he was dressed normally, for one thing—but he didn't look like the old man he'd been when I saw him a few days before. He looked not so much young as ageless. Yet I recognized him immediately as my grandfather.

"I thought you were in Alexandria," he said, frowning at Hermes.

"Moving rapidly is my specialty," Hermes said, with a teasing smile.

"Yes, but——"

"I'm here now," Hermes said.

Pytheas was still frowning. "Well, it's good that you came, you can test something for me. I was going to find Porphyry, but you'll be better."

"Let me finish with this first."

"No, it's important," Pytheas said.

"So is this."

"What, dallying with my granddaughter? Surely that can wait." Pytheas smiled at me.

"We weren't dallying," I protested. My voice sounded strange in my ears.

"Necessity has me by the foot," Hermes said.

I instinctively looked down at his feet. He had wings on his sandals. He hadn't had those when I'd met him before. As I was looking down, the children noticed Pytheas and came running up, crowding round him asking questions.

"Joy to you, yes, I'm here, yes, but go inside now. You can tell everyone I'm here and I'll come in and talk to them, but I need to speak to my brother first."

They protested, of course, but Pytheas shooed them inside, some laughing and some crying. He closed the door and turned back to us. The garden seemed very dark and quiet without the children and the bar of light from the door. I realized that Pytheas was much better lit than anything else, as if the starlight were concentrating itself on him.

"Necessity?" Pytheas said to Hermes, as if there had been no interruption.

"Your step-granddaughter Marsilia is the mother of my daughter Alkippe, but I've never been here before today. So I need to discover how this came to be and set it straight."

Pytheas winced. "I appreciate how uncomfortable this is, but——" he began.

"No, wait," I said, wanting to clarify things. "You died, and you're here, and that's not the most important thing that's happened today. I've found out the father of my daughter is the god Hermes, and that's not the most important thing that's happened today either. Even this time loop, disconcerting as it is, isn't the most important. You have to know, there's a human ship in orbit."

Both gods looked at me with the same infuriating lack of expression, the same air of fathomless calm indifference.

"A human ship!" I repeated. "Recontact with the wider universe! A chance to rejoin the human mainstream and influence it!"

"Yes," Pytheas said, with a wave of his hand. "But you can deal with that perfectly well yourself." I gasped. "You're a Gold of the Just City, you can deal with it, or what have we been doing here? Hermes, I can't find Athene."

"Can't find her?" Hermes looked down shiftily.

"Try reaching for her."

"Can't I sort out this mess first?" He gestured towards me, sounding petulant.

"It'll take less time than arguing. If you can find her, then——"

Hermes shook his head. "Nothing."

"Go outside time and try."

"Look, let me talk to Marsilia for five minutes and then stay here for two heartbeats while I sort this out, and I'll do all the running around looking for Athene you want," Hermes said.

"She's missing?" I asked. I had a really bad feeling about this. "Lost?"

Suddenly I had all of their attention. Hermes seemed particularly intent.

"It seems so. Have you seen her?" Pytheas asked.

"About two years ago, after the Panathenaic Festival, she came to me and Thetis in the sanctuary when we were putting the new cloak on her statue." I could remember it clearly. She'd come into the room carrying her owl, and it turned its head to watch us as she moved. She was much taller than any human. There are lots of stories about Athene in the City, some good, some not so good. Thetis had clutched my hand so tightly I'd had marks for days. "She said we were her worshippers, and this was her city. I was a priest that year, remember?"

"Priesthood is a civic function here, like in Rome," Pytheas put in. Hermes nodded dismissively.

"She gave us a kind of woven box to look after," I went on, remembering the weight of it in my arms and the strange weave, and the tilt of her head as she spoke. "She told us not to open it unless we heard she was lost, and then we had to both be together. And she asked us not to tell you until that happened."

"So which one of you opened it, and how long did it take?" Pytheas asked. "And why in all the worlds didn't you tell me?"

"How did you know we already opened it?" I asked.

"Human nature," Pytheas said. "What was in it?"

"Hilfa," I admitted.

"Hilfa!" Pytheas repeated. I had never seen him look so taken aback.

"Who's Hilfa?" Hermes asked. "And where is he?"

"He's a Sael," Pytheas said. "One of the aliens. I've met him a time or two. He seems perfectly normal for one of the Saeli, which is to say very peculiar indeed."

"We didn't expect it would be a living being," I said. "We thought we could look to see what it was and close it again until it was necessary. Or if it was something dangerous to the Republic we could tell somebody. Athene hasn't always been our friend."

"And don't you know the story of Pandora?" Hermes asked.

I looked at him blankly.

"No, that's one of the stories they left out," Pytheas said. "Not a good example, and Plato didn't believe people learned excellence from awful warnings. So what did you do when you opened it and it turned out to be Hilfa?"

It was my turn to look down guiltily. "We arranged for him to have somewhere to live and a job and education, as if he were any Sael who had decided to stay behind." I glanced at Hermes. "That's always happening. The Saeli like Plato, and lots of them stay, though usually they live in pods, not individually. But it was easy."

"And you didn't tell anyone?" Pytheas demanded.

"I'm not completely irresponsible. It was two years ago. I told Dad and Klymene." They had been consuls that year.

"And Neleus and Klymene didn't tell anyone? Didn't tell me?" He sounded aggrieved.

"Evidently not. I don't know if they told anyone else."

"I can't believe you all kept it from me!" Pytheas said.

I shifted guiltily. "Athene specified that we shouldn't tell you. So we decided to wait and see what happened, and keep an eye on Hilfa, which we have been doing. I started working on the boat with him. He hasn't done anything unusual."

"Let's go and find him," Hermes suggested.

"Why would she choose a Sael?" Pytheas asked, ignoring Hermes. "The Saeli have a strange relationship with their gods. Why would Athene have had one in a box? And why would she leave it here with Neleus's daughters in case she was lost? And what use could it be, in that case? And did she *expect* to get lost?"

"She must have, if she took measures against it," Hermes said; and then after a moment, "How strange."

"If she was here on Plato, why didn't she simply come to me and explain? And where is she, anyway? She must have known Thetis would open the box."

"I didn't say it was Thetis who opened it! And it wasn't. We did it together." Though if I hadn't agreed, she would have done it anyway. When we first opened it, for a second it looked like a snake coiled tightly around a human baby. Then it resolved into an egg, which immediately hatched into Hilfa, much as he was now: curious, earnest, alien. "I don't think he's a god."

"We should go and talk to him immediately," Hermes said. "Though can I please sort out this mess with Necessity first?"

Pytheas's eyes widened and he swayed back a little, then he waved his hand, giving permission.

"Marsilia," Hermes began. "Tell me the circumstances in which Alkippe was conceived."

I took a breath and gathered the information concisely. "She was conceived at the end-of-summer Festival of Hera eight years ago. You were calling yourself Poimandros, and you said you were from Psyche."

Hermes smiled.

"Psyche is one of the other Platonic Cities," Pytheas put in. "It's not as much fun as you might imagine."

"We were drawn together—our names drawn out of the lots together—and we went off to be married for the day."

"You really are doing Plato's Republic," Hermes said.

"Participation in the Festival of Hera is voluntary," Pytheas said. "Well, here it is. In Psyche and Athenia it's compulsory for citizens. But nobody has to stay in Psyche or Athenia if they don't like it."

"It's all right, you don't need to be so defensive, I think it's charming," Hermes said, smiling again. "Eight years ago, end of summer, fix the lots to be drawn, spend the night in bed, got it. And you'll put in a word of recommendation for me with the beautiful Thetis?"

I was opening my mouth to say calmly that what Hermes and Thetis did was their own affair, when Pytheas interrupted.

"Wait," Pytheas said. "I know how hard it is to resist Necessity. But if Athene is truly lost, and if she knew ahead of time that she was going into danger, and if we have to rescue her, then having you bound by Necessity might be a safeguard."

"A safeguard?" Hermes asked. He looked astonished. "You think Necessity might protect *me*?"

"I think if there's a serious risk, it might," Pytheas said.

"But—you know what it feels like!" Hermes protested.

"You're strong enough to bear it," Pytheas said. "Who knows what might happen to Athene otherwise?"

"Gods can't die," I protested.

"They can't ordinarily get lost either," Pytheas said. "And I think that since Necessity has given us this unexpected aegis, we might be meant to use it."

"But if gods can die, or get lost, or—" I stopped, realizing my voice was rising. I took a breath from my stomach and began again. "What happens to Alkippe if something should happen to Hermes before he goes back to conceive her?"

They looked at each other a moment in silence, then at me. "It's impossible," Pytheas said. "He has to survive to do that, and therefore he will, and know he is safe until it is done."

"Look, Alkippe's my daughter, I really care about her. I can't risk her never having existed. Hermes needs to go and do whatever he needs to do about it now, before going into danger." They were listening to me, but they didn't seem to understand the importance of what I was saying.

Pytheas frowned. "Even if she is the anchor that keeps all of us safe? Necessity has given us this tie, when we're venturing into danger. Having Necessity on our side can only help."

"But Alkippe!" Her bright eyes, her wriggling body, her inquiring mind, her bold soul, I wanted to say, and couldn't find the words to make them understand. Pytheas knew her and how marvelous she was, but Hermes had only seen her for a few minutes.

"Where do you believe Athene is?" Hermes asked Pytheas.

"Possibly she's in the Underworld. That would be all right. Strange, but all right."

"Ah. And because of the way when we go there we only perceive Hades and those souls with whom Hades thinks it's good for us to interact, we can't tell that she's there?"

Hermes nodded as if this made sense.

"Perhaps." Pytheas was frowning. "But I suspect she's not there, and that she has gone into the Chaos before and after time."

Hermes wavered for a moment—I was staring right at him and that's the only way I can describe it. It was like when you're watching the shadow of a train you're in falling on the ground, and then suddenly there's a hill and the shadow is nearer and bigger for a moment, and then it's back on the plain, racing along. "I can't find her from outside time either," he announced. "And I tried to catch her at the Panathenaia, but I couldn't."

"But you weren't there," I pointed out.

"No. You didn't see me, so I couldn't be visible. And she wasn't there for an instant that you and Thetis weren't." He paused, and looked assessingly at Pytheas. "Do you think we should go to Father now and tell him everything?"

"First, we should talk to Hilfa and discover what message she left for us," Pytheas said.

"And you really think I need to stay bound by Necessity?" Hermes asked. "It's like having a sharp stone in my shoe."

"That stone might be our shield," Pytheas said.

"I am not letting you out of my sight again until you go back there and ensure Alkippe is real," I said to Hermes. I had never felt more strongly about anything in my life.

"I'd agree to that, but you are mortal, and not caught in Necessity's jaws. Alkippe already only has one parent. What happens to her if I have to go into danger and you don't survive?"

I looked at him in incomprehension. "I'd happily give my life for hers, if need be. And she'd be safe here. I wasn't suggesting taking her with us."

Pytheas was smiling his enigmatic smile. "You're seeing Platonic motherhood, which is different from anything you're used to. Marsilia is telling you we're in the City, and here children with one parent or no parents at all are at no disadvantage."

"Yes. If my parents and Thetis couldn't manage, though I'm sure they could, Alkippe could grow up in a nursery and pursue her own excellence. It's not like the little orphan in Homer." I didn't have much context for how children grew up elsewhere. His assumption that she would suffer neglect if I died disconcerted me. There's a lot of variety in how we do things on Plato, but that wouldn't happen in any of our cities. Bringing up children to be their best selves is something we all agree is crucial. In those cities with no nurseries, a child whose family died in a catastrophe would be immediately adopted into another family.

"This is a strange place," Hermes said. "Well, you can stay with me if you feel so strongly about it. Here. A votive gift." He handed me something. I looked down at it. It was a little purse of soft leather, with a drawstring. Puzzled, I opened it. "It'll never be empty, unless you shake it out," he said. "And the coin you pull from it will always be enough to pay for what you want."

I took out a coin and turned it in my fingers. I had seen coins before; they use money in Lucia. My other hand rose to my neck, to my gold pin on my jacket collar. It was forbidden to me to have gold, other than the Gold in my soul and the pin that symbolized it. I couldn't think of a more useless gift, but I imagined it was well intended. As well as travel, Hermes was patron of the marketplace, commerce, and thieves. I decided to talk to him about our trade negotiations when there was a chance, in case he had interesting ideas. "Thank you," I said, politely.

Pytheas was frowning. It was so strange to see him, the same but different. He was definitely my grandfather, but he seemed to be about my own age. "Marsilia is part of my family. If any harm comes to her, you'll answer for it."

Hermes nodded once.

Pytheas didn't stop frowning. "We should go in and I should say hello to the rest of the family. They'll hardly have had time to miss me. And then we should find Hilfa."

"Why do we need to bother going inside first?" Hermes asked.

"I want to speak to Neleus. And we need Arete."

"Hilfa speaks Greek," I said.

"Doubtless, but whether or not you've discovered it, your aunt Arete has skills beyond flight and translation. Come on." He took a step towards the door.

"Arete isn't there. She's at the spaceport," I said.

Pytheas hesitated. "Then—"

"No, come on. It'll be fun to see their faces," Hermes said.

7

JASON

Now, if you were an incarnate god and you died and then resurrected and came back, the way Christians and Ikarians say Yayzu did, what would be the first thing you'd say the first time you saw your children?

Pytheas came in from the garden looking about my age, with all the silver gone from his hair. He was wearing a white kiton trimmed with a conventional blue-and-gold book and scroll pattern, and pinned with the pin that meant he was a Gold of the City. He went straight up to Neleus, and what he said absolutely flummoxed me. It was the last thing I'd have expected to hear in the circumstances. And I was right there. I can report his exact words, and they were: "Why didn't you tell me about Hilfa?"

Neleus blushed at that, which meant that, given the color his skin was to start off, he turned almost purple.

"You were always telling us to sort things out for ourselves," Neleus said. "You never wanted to hear anything about negotiations with the aliens."

"You don't think the name of Athene would have got my attention?"

"Too much of it," Neleus said.

Hermes laughed aloud.

"And she had asked the girls specifically not to tell you," Neleus went on. "Hilfa didn't seem dangerous. We could have told you any time there was need. We didn't tell my brothers or Arete either."

"What's this about Hilfa?" I asked. It wasn't really my place to speak in that kind of company, and they'd been ignoring me so far, but I wanted to know what kind of trouble Hilfa had managed to find, so that I could help the dear dunderhead out of it. How could anyone imagine he might be dangerous?

And that's why I found myself with Marsilia and Thetis and the two gods an hour later, after a lot of talking and a walk in the cold, on the green ba-salt street outside Hilfa's house down by the harbor, three streets over from my own sleeping house. Neleus had gone off to take Alkippe to bed and then go himself to the spaceport, but all the rest of us were there. They had shared an unlikely story about Athene giving Hilfa to Marsilia and Thetis in a box, and beyond that a lot of questions and not enough answers. The only way to get the answers was to talk to Hilfa, seemingly. I insisted on coming along to look out for Hilfa, and Thetis backed me up until Pytheas gave in and let us come along, trusting her social judgement.

Down in the harbor, instead of sconces there's a strip of light running along the sills of all the buildings, lighting everyone's faces from underneath. On Hilfa's street, where a lot of Saeli lived, the lighting ran a little green, which made Thetis and Marsilia look as if they were made out of gold, while Pytheas and Hermes seemed as if they were made out of marble. I could see this really well, because they all turned to look at me. I'd insisted on com-ing along; now they wanted me to announce that we were there.

It was easier to do it than say anything, so I scratched on the door.

Hilfa appeared, wearing loose-woven dark-purple pants, with his chest and back bare. I had thought he would be disconcerted seeing a bunch of im-portant people wanting to talk to him in the middle of the night—not that it was so late really, but I'd had a long day. Hilfa didn't even blink. He in-vited us all in and apologized for not having enough chairs. He knew every-one except Hermes. Marsilia introduced them. To my surprise, Hermes said something to Hilfa in Saeli, which I took to be a greeting. Who would have thought he'd know it? He hadn't used it to greet Aroo. Travel and trade, I thought; he'd probably run into Saeli on other planets where humans had contacted them.

We sat where we could. Hilfa scurried around putting all the lights on, which made the room very bright. Thetis and I sat on the bed, against the wall. Pytheas took one chair, and Marsilia the other, while Hermes leaned against the table. Then Hilfa made a dash into the little back room, which wasn't much more than a big closet really. He brought out wine, and Mar-silia got up to help him mix it and hand the cups around. He brought four matching red-pattern wine cups, and two Saeli-style beakers. He gave one of those to me, with a smile, and kept the other himself. Mine was incised with geometric patterns in the porphyry inlay, so I couldn't quite figure how he meant it. It might have been treating me as family, to have the other cup that didn't match, or it might have been meant as an honor. There was no telling, and it wasn't the time to ask. I decided it came out positive either way, and smiled at him over the brim. Other times when I'd had a drink at Hilfa's place we'd used wine cups, but there had never been more than three or four of us. It was a biggish room, with one small red-and-blue geometric rug, and the walls were painted white, with no frescos or other art. It had always seemed quite empty to me, until now, when I'd have thought it full if I hadn't come straight from the press at Thessaly.

"Athene is missing," Pytheas said as soon as we had all settled down and sipped our wine.

"Missing? Lost?" Hilfa asked, turning to him from where he had been putting down the wine bowl on the table. The swirls on his skin faded a little. Up to that moment I thought there had been some mistake, that Hilfa couldn't be anything but what he seemed: a slightly puzzled Sael who had somehow wandered into all this by mistake. "Is she——" He hesitated. "Do I say she? Are there no special pronouns for divinity?"

"No, you simply say she," Marsilia said. "Ikarians capitalize it when they write, but we use the same word."

"Do you mean to say that She is lost?" Hilfa asked. I could all but hear the capital.

"Yes. What do you know about it?" Pytheas leaned forward, wine cup forgotten in his hand and nearly spilling. Thetis gently took it from him and set it down on the tiles by her feet.

"I don't remember anything before I hatched here, you understand?" Hilfa said. He seemed more confident and relaxed than normal. I thought I had been wrong to come; he didn't need my help.

"That's what you said at the time, but you could talk," Marsilia said.

"I knew some things," Hilfa said. "I don't know how much is normal for newly hatched Saeli. I have not wanted to ask, because sometimes questions reveal too much about what you do not know, when you should." He looked at Marsilia, with a twitch of expression that I thought meant apology. "I know that's not the Socratic way."

"The Socratic way regards deception very badly," Marsilia said.

Hilfa inclined his head. "You told me not to reveal my origins."

Marsilia sighed. "It's true, we did."

"Plato's censorship and deception wars with Sokrates's desire to question everything all the time," Hermes said.

"We in the Cities have noticed this contradiction," Pytheas said wearily. "Go on, Hilfa."

Hilfa turned to Thetis, who was sitting next to me on the bed. "I remember you looking after me, and that is the first thing I remember. Before that there was no me. Let me fetch paper."

"Paper?" Hermes asked.

"Quicker to do than to explain," he said, and darted back into the little storeroom.

"I think he's telling the truth," Thetis said. The instinctive twitches of my own liver said the same thing. Saeli are hard to read, but I was used to Hilfa, and he didn't seem to be prevaricating at all, even as he talked about dodging revelation.

Pytheas nodded. "I think so too. Hermes?"

Hermes was staring intently at the door through which Hilfa had vanished, and shook himself when he was addressed, the way Hilfa often did on the boat when I called him back from one of his reveries. "I sense no deception either," he said.

Hilfa came back with paper, a standard sheaf of Worker-made letter paper. He set it down on the table. Hermes moved to give him room, and took up position leaning casually against the wall. Hilfa took a pen and wrote for perhaps a second. I don't think I could have written my name in the time he spent writing. It didn't look like he was writing, either; more like he was doodling. The pen danced over the paper, and then he was done. He walked over to hand it to Pytheas, and I could see it was covered all over in neat script, where I'd have counted on a sketch.

"I knew before I can remember that when She was lost, I should write that and give it to You," Hilfa said.

"Do you know what it says?" Thetis asked.

"No," Hilfa said. He squatted down where he was, on the rug in the middle of the floor, sitting back on his haunches the way I had seen him do so often on the boat. It looked uncomfortable and unnatural, because human legs don't bend comfortably that way, but I'd grown used to the fact that Saeli ones did. He was much greener than normal; the pinkish swirls that normally covered his skin only visible now in the center of his chest and back.

"Do you know where Athene is, or how she came to be lost?" Hermes asked, for the first time taking a sip of his wine.

"Not unless it says so there," Hilfa said, gesturing to the paper. Pytheas was reading it intently and didn't look up.

"Do you know what you are?" Thetis asked. I thought about Thetis and Marsilia opening the box Athene had told them not to open unless she was lost, and finding Hilfa inside. I understood why they had opened it. All the same, I wouldn't have done it. You learn patience, fishing. Marsilia was starting to learn some now, working on the boat, but she hadn't had a scrap of it when she'd first come to me.

"I don't know. I think I am perhaps a hero."

"A hero, the child of a god?" Marsilia was frowning. "One of the Saeli gods?"

"That is my guess," Hilfa said, looking at Hermes, and then away. "But I can't say. I don't know where I come from, where I belong. I don't want to go there. I like it here. I like the fish and the sea."

"The wind and the waves," I said. It was what he had said that afternoon.

He turned to me for a moment with the expression I thought was a real smile, then back to Marsilia. "I like Jason and Dion," he said. "I like the boat. I like you and Thetis. I want to stay in the City. I want to take oath. I didn't ask until now, because it wasn't just until you knew."

"Nobody's going to make you leave—" Thetis began, setting down her empty wine cup at her feet beside Pytheas's full one.

"Don't make any promises," Marsilia said, cutting across her. "We will need to debate this. I think many of us will support Hilfa's desire. I certainly will, but this is important."

"What good is it you being consul, Marsilia, if—" Thetis began.

Pytheas looked up from the paper and stared at Hilfa. Simply by raising his head, he riveted all our attention, and Thee fell silent. His face was inscrutable, his lips slightly parted as if caught in the middle of a gasp or a smile.

"Are you going to share that with the rest of us?" Hermes asked.

Pytheas looked serenely at his brother. "She has gone beyond what lies outside time, into the Chaos of before and after, to discover how the universe begins and ends. She has done this with the help of a Saeli god of knowledge, Jathery. In case she had difficulty returning, she has left me the explanation of how to do this. Her explanation is divided into parts, each of which she has left with a different person, in a different place and time." His voice was level, calm, and absolutely furious.

"Father will kill her," Hermes said. He sounded awestruck and impressed. "He'll hang her upside-down over the abyss for eternity with anvils on her fingers."

"You know he never does anything to Athene," Pytheas said, absently. "No, I think it's worse than that. She's broken Father's edicts, obviously, but I think this time she might have gone too far and be up against Fate and Necessity."

"What does that mean?" Thetis asked.

"It means she could be lost forever. And we might be too if we go after her," Hermes said. He smiled at Thetis.

"Is this something Ikaros dreamed up?" Marsilia asked. "It sounds a bit like one of his ideas."

"She worked on the idiotic plans with him, but she hasn't taken him with her," Pytheas said.

Hermes drained his cup and set it down decisively on the table. "We should locate the pieces of her explanation."

"Maybe we should go to Father," Pytheas said.

"But I'm safe from Necessity," Hermes said. "And we should at least collect the pieces of her explanation first. When we have that, we'll have a better idea of whether we could help her."

"But we don't need to. Father will already know how to do it," Pytheas said. "And don't you think this might be why he sent you to get me now?"

"It would be better if we can sort this out without him," Hermes said. "At least, better to try."

"Whatever he won't do to Athene, he wouldn't hesitate to do to us."

"Why does Zeus never punish Athene?" Thetis asked unexpectedly.

"We don't know, but we think it's because he ate her mother," Pytheas said. "Our previous goddess of wisdom. Metis."

"Ate her?" I asked, horrified enough to speak out.

"Another thing Plato left out?" Hermes asked.

"Before you ask, we don't know the answers," Pytheas said. "We don't know if or how he transformed Metis into Athene, or what it really means that she's his daughter, born from his head. We think it might have something to do with how he treats her, but we might be wrong."

"I don't understand," Thetis said. I didn't either.

Pytheas smiled at her, not unkindly. "None of us do. I'm not sure even Father understands. He didn't create the universe, and some of the ways things work are Mysteries even to him."

"You are speaking of your Father?" Hilfa asked, quietly.

"Yes," Pytheas said. He looked down at Hilfa.

"Your Father Who is also Parent of the Saeli gods?"

"He's the father of all the gods in the universe, as far as I know," Hermes said, smiling at Hilfa with a strange smile. Hilfa didn't turn towards him.

"And yet you speak so lightly of. . . ." Hilfa hesitated, and looked at Marsilia.

"We simply say *his*," she said. "If you prefer to say gla we will understand."

"Of gla wrath," Hilfa finished.

"Yes we do, because we've experienced it," Pytheas said. "And however he may appear in the Saeli pantheons, and whatever he may have done to your people, he is not, to us, a god of wrath. Well, except when we've done something to deserve it. Like Metis."

"Tell us about Jathery," Marsilia said to Hilfa. "A god of wisdom, but also a trickster, yes?"

"Yes." Hilfa swung around to face her, his back to Hermes, and counted the aspects off on his long fingers. "The five things that go together: wisdom, trickery, riddles, name-changing, and freedom."

"Might he have tricked Athene into this?" Marsilia asked.

"She as much as admits that she suspects him of it," Pytheas said, tapping the letter. "It seems they've been friends for some time. Jathery may even have had a hand in persuading her to set up the Republic experiment."

"Aren't you forbidden to mingle with gods of other pantheons?" Marsilia asked.

Pytheas and Hermes looked at her with the same puzzled expression. "No," Hermes answered. "Why would we be?"

"Then why don't you?" she asked.

"Aesthetic reasons," Pytheas said. "We live in our own context, our own fabric, culture, framework. They each have their own. We don't have any reason to meet, to interact. We stay in our own circles because that feels right. But if Athene felt ecumenical, nothing stopped her being friends with Jathery. More's the pity."

"And nothing would stop you doing the same?"

"Nothing except context, culture, having nothing in common, and no need." Pytheas frowned.

"Or how about Yayzu?" Marsilia asked.

"Maybe I could have a productive conversation with him. And he speaks Greek. But it might be difficult to find somewhere comfortable for us both. Or, no. It wouldn't." Pytheas smiled. "If Yayzu and I wanted to compare notes on incarnation and how we best ought to help people, I know a place. Maybe. I'll think about that. It might even be a good idea."

"But Jathery is a Saeli god," Marsilia said. "Shouldn't he feel an . . . aesthetic need to be attending to their affairs?"

Hilfa shook his head without looking up.

"I think it would certainly be preferable if he did, instead of heading off into primal Chaos with Athene," Pytheas said.

"So do you really think we should go to Father?" Hermes asked.

"Well, maybe. Except that she does plead for me not to tell him," Pytheas said, looking down at the paper again. "Since you also seem against it, let's try getting the explanation first."

"Pleads? Athene? Can I see that?" Hermes asked, putting out his hand for it.

"No, I think not," Pytheas said, folding it up and putting it inside his kiton.

"But Zeus must know already. He knows everything," Thetis said.

"He knows, but he's not aware of things until they come to his attention. If we can sort it out ourselves, it might be better if this came to his attention after Athene is safely back," Pytheas said.

"Or at least until we've read the explanation and know we can't do it without help," Hermes said.

"Time can't be changed, except in one circumstance," Pytheas said.

"The Darkness of the Oak," Marsilia interrupted. Both gods turned at once to focus on her. I had no idea what she was talking about, but the words sent chills through me. I took a deep draught of my wine and looked sideways across the room to her as she continued, "It's given me nightmares since Dad told me about Zeus talking about it on Olympos. Do you think he'd do that? Unmake the City, now? Because of this?"

"More than that, if need be," Pytheas said. "Athene wants to know everything. There are no limits to *everything*. But Father has Mysteries he might not want investigated, and I fear this is one of them. It's directly against his edicts. She might have gone too far. And as for Jathery—is Jathery a favorite of Father's?" He swung around to Hilfa.

"No," Hilfa whispered, his lips hardly moving.

Thetis broke the awkward silence. "Where are the pieces of Athene's explanation?"

"Distributed through time, where only gods can get them. Kebes has one of them."

Marsilia, Thetis and I gasped in unison. "Who's Kebes?" Hermes asked. Astonishing. But of course, he didn't know. He was from another world. The seventy eventful years of our history was all new to him.

"Kebes is the one I beat playing your gift upside-down," Pytheas said. "He hates me. Worse, I was in time all the time he was alive. You'll have to collect that piece. And it won't be easy."

"She must have wanted you involved," Marsilia said, looking at Hermes. "You, or some other god at least."

"I'm not going near this culture without a native guide," Hermes said. He was looking at Thetis, but she was looking down at Hilfa and didn't notice. Hilfa was rocking backwards and forwards slightly, his multicolored lids closed over his eyes.

"I said I'm staying with you," Marsilia said to Hermes. "I've been to Lucia."

"Good," he said. Then he smiled challengingly at Pytheas. "How many pieces are there? Shall we divide them and meet back here with them?"

"I'll manage Pico," Pytheas said. "How are you with the Enlightenment?"

"You can definitely have that one," Hermes said, with a little shudder.

"All right, then you can take Phila the daughter of Antipatros. Athene says she gave it to her after her wedding, so any time after that I suppose."

"Who did she marry?" Hermes asked.

"She married Demetrios the Besieger of Cities," Marsilia said. Then, when she realized we were all staring at her, "What? It's in Plutarch."

"*You* are going to be useful. Good!" Hermes said.

As I was drawing breath, Pytheas, Hermes, and Marsilia vanished.

Meanwhile, unnoticed by anyone except me, Thetis had slipped to the floor and put her arms around Hilfa, who immediately turned and clung to her like a baby.

8

APOLLO

I generally enjoy emotions. I like transmuting emotion into art, every shade of feeling, every nuance and tone and note. But the wrath I felt now, the anger at Athene that burned through me, was too strong for that. Human emotions happen in the veins, in the gut, as well as in the mind. Divine emotions are a thing of mind and soul alone, but are neither less strong nor less passionate for that. You hear of Olympian calm, and we *are* calm, detached, distant—usually. When we do feel strongly there is nothing of mortal frailty to deter us in that feeling. A mortal heart or liver might overflow and burst with too strong an emotion, but never ours. When we are moved as strongly as I was moved by Athene's letter there is no restraint—we are the anger, while the anger lasts.

I like feeling the heat of emotions. I do not like giving way before them and becoming the conflagration. Emotions should always be manageable, never overwhelming.

Therefore my calm and control can be demonstrated by my behavior. I practiced moderation, as both my Delphic injunction and Plato recommend. I did not burn down Hilfa's house in sudden fusion heat. I did not even char Athene's letter to ash as I read it. I talked reasonably to the others, though I did not show the letter to them. There was no need to make things any worse.

It was the late summer of 1506 when I strode rapidly down one of the little streets in Bologna that run between the cathedral and the town hall. It was a narrow laneway, lined on both sides with people selling things, pushing them on the passersby with cries and importunities. I shoved through them impatiently. He was sitting on a high stool outside a wineshop, disputing, surrounded by a gaggle of students. He was as I had last seen him on Olympos, young and able to see, but he was wearing the robes of an Augustinian monk. He had a white ceramic wine cup in his hand, and was gesturing with it. I grabbed him by the shoulder, pulled him off the stool and turned him to face me.

"Ah," he said, admirably unsurprised. "Pytheas. With your cloak flaring around you like that, I thought you must be an avenging angel."

His friends laughed. I glared at them, and back at Pico. "Shall we go somewhere we can talk privately?" I asked, speaking Latin because he had. It was wrong to take out my wrath on Pico. He wasn't the one who deserved it.

He fumbled some coins out of his pouch and put them down on the table among the wine cups. "An old friend. I'll see you later," he said to the others.

"You needn't think you'll get away without making a proper refutation!" one of them said.

"Tomorrow," Pico said, smiling and shaking his head.

"Why are you dressed as an Augustinian?" I asked quietly as we walked down the street together, ignoring offers of fish, wine, fruit, and young bodies of both sexes from the street vendors.

"I'm staying at the monastery of St. Stephen's," he explained.

"And what are you doing here?"

"Research." He looked wary. "And arguing with Averroists. They're young, and they haven't been properly trained, but some of them are extremely smart."

"You're not a lawyer or a doctor, so what are you researching in Bologna?" We came out of the little street into the square by the Ducal Palace.

He smiled. "Theology?"

"Really? You barely got away from the Inquisition last time, and you had influential friends then!"

He smiled at me. "I do now, too. Here you are, and before I've managed to get into any trouble at all. Let's go in here." It was another wineshop, on a corner, with only a few tables out on the street. He ducked through the door and I followed. The interior was small and dark. The patrons were older, and many of them were wearing dusty aprons, by which I deduced that they were stonemasons. Pico ordered wine, and we sat down together on a bench in a corner. The place was crowded, but the patrons moved over to make a little room for us. "If we speak Greek, we'll have perfect privacy here," he said in that language. "We probably would have back there, but that's a scholars' tavern, so you never know."

It was amazing, really. A count by birth, a Humanist by inclination, befriended by Ficino, imprisoned by the Inquisition, saved by Lorenzo and Savonarola, taken to the City an instant before death, snatched to Olympos by Zeus, set to work with Athene, abandoned by her in Bologna mere months before it was due to be sacked, and still his optimism was undimmed. There aren't many like him. "Do you know where Athene is?"

He looked wary again. "She was going somewhere she thought was too dangerous for me. And since you're here, it seems she was right. Do you know where she was going, or should I explain?" He glanced at the oblivious guzzling stonemasons as if worried that they might be able to speak Greek after all.

"Give me whatever she gave you to give to me." I put out my hand.

"It's in my cell."

"You left it in your cell among a lot of thieving Augustinians?" Optimism is not always a virtue.

He shrugged. "It's inside my copy of Ficino's Plato, which they think is magic and won't touch. Besides, I've given a copy of it to Raffaele Maffei, in case."

"Why don't you simply keep it in your pocket?" I growled. "And Maffei? The Volterran encyclopaedist? Why Maffei?"

"When you're not a count in Renaissance Italy, you're always getting your pocket picked. And Raffaele is an old acquaintance. He thinks I'm my own illegitimate son."

"Let's hope for the copy in your Plato," I said. I put my full wine cup down on the table and stood. We wouldn't be driven to Maffei's copy in any event. If the original copy was missing, I could go back to a time when Pico had it and recover it—ten seconds after he had left it alone in his cell, if that's what it took.

"It's incredibly frustrating. Wherever I am, I never have access to all the books I need," he said, swallowing his wine and putting the cup down. "Here I have all the Christian books, even those that will be destroyed when Julius gets here in November, but not the ones we rescued from Alexandria. My memory's good, but it's so useful to be able to check things."

"Are you done with the ones here?" I asked.

He nodded. "But I wish there were somewhere we could have everything."

We walked together through the streets. Bologna is a remarkably medieval city. It was a provincial nowhere as Roman Bononia, and thrived in the Middle Ages; but in my opinion, while the food is usually good, it was never really beautiful until the renewal of the peripherique in the twenty-second century. True, it had pillars and colonnades, but as we walked in their shade I couldn't help noticing that all the pillars were different. There was no harmony, no true proportion. Nothing matched. It was all a medieval jumble. Occasionally I noticed a lovely classical pillar, and felt an urge to rescue it and put it somewhere it could be comfortable.

"You're not so angry now?" Pico asked.

"I'm not unjustly taking out my anger on the wrong person," I said. "When I find Athene will be soon enough to indulge my wrath."

"You really did look like an avenging angel, with your cloak flaring around you like that," he said.

In Pico's New Concordance, Olympian gods are classed as angels. I think of it as a metaphor. I had changed the appearance of my clothes to be locally inconspicuous. Everyone's cloak flared in 1506. But there was no point in arguing.

There's nothing wrong with brick, brick can be beautiful, but it can easily be overdone. The church and monastery of St. Stephen was a mess. It contained different sections built at different times. It had been owned by a number of different orders, and they had all built onto it, none of them completing the designs of their predecessors. It was like a chambered nautilus where each chamber had been designed by a different committee. "It's as if the Renaissance had never happened," I murmured to Pico as we passed through a room containing an enormous pulpit in the shape of the Holy Sepulchre, with scarcely room for two people to pass by around it. It would have done well enough in a correspondingly huge and Gothic nave, here it was ridiculous and unserviceable, almost intimidating in its size and impracticality.

"The Renaissance is thriving right now in Florence and Rome," he said with a sideways smile. "It'll make it here eventually. I hope."

We came out into an enclosed courtyard. I was glad to see the sky and the sun again. There was a piece of sad mosaic on the wall—abstract, only a pattern, but what made it sad was the presence of two tiny fragments of porphyry given pride of place. Porphyry is a speckled purple rock which, over time, had in Medieval Europe come to stand for the lost wonders of Rome. The Egyptian quarry it came from was lost after Rome fell, and so were the skills of making steel tough enough to work it. It's a volcanic rock, and it's therefore present in quantity on Plato. The Workers can work with it easily, so there's lots of it everywhere and we have all kinds of things made out of it. But here and now, porphyry symbolized the lost heritage of Rome, and here set in the wall were these two minute pieces, all poor Bologna had left of the ancient world. They had not entirely forgotten what it meant, but they couldn't come any closer than this to regaining or re-creating it. I wished somebody in Bologna would pray for my help so that I could give them something better than this. And they were about to be sacked, too. It really wasn't fair.

Pico led me into a cloister. The shadows of the pillars were falling across the open central space. A heavily bearded monk was sitting on the wall reading Latin poetry, a cat curled on his lap. Pico frowned. "We should wait here," he said, quietly. "We're not supposed to have guests in our cells, and I'm not supposed to be in my cell at this time of day. He'll go to Vespers soon."

He nodded to the monk and took a seat against a pillar on the other side of the cloister. "Won't they expect you to go?" I asked, sitting beside him and looking over at the well in the center of the courtyard.

"I'm only visiting. They know I'm a scholar."

"He won't speak Greek?" I asked, smiling at the monk, who smiled back uncertainly.

"Here?" Pico asked. He was right. It was even less likely we'd find someone who understood Greek here than among the stonemasons.

It was too much. "If she had to leave you somewhere in 1506 with Christian books and a university, why aren't you in Florence?"

"There was a book here I needed. And there are people there who know me too well not to recognize me, even if I tell them I'm my own son. They poisoned me the first time, after all. And Soderini's in power, and the Medici will be back soon and feeling vengeful—I could hardly bear to see it. It's the last days of the Republic." He stopped. "The Florentine Republic, that is, not Plato's Republic."

"They probably don't spare a thought for Plato's Republic."

"I do," he said. "As well as working on my new theory of the universe."

"Newer than the New Concordance?" I wondered whether to tell him now what had been going on among the Ikarians on Plato.

"The New Concordance arose out of realizing that the *Republic* wasn't working, couldn't work, because Plato was wrong about the nature of the soul. The philosophical soul can feel love, in addition to desiring the Good. Love isn't simply a way towards opening the soul to God. So I had to rethink everything. They were doing the same in Psyche, coming to different conclusions but working on the same basis. If Plato had been right about that, it would all have worked properly. The problem on Kallisti was that we got overfocused on tweaking practical reality."

"Do you still think all the authorities agree with each other?"

"They do if you look at them the right way. They were all trying to reach the truth, and it's amazing how much congruence there is. But I have lots of new information. My new theory is an attempt at integrating that."

"How long is it, in your personal time, since you last saw me?" I asked. I really wanted to know, and to ask it conversationally. It was why I was sitting on the wall instead of taking him outside time and straight back into his cell.

He wrinkled his brow. "I can't say. A lot of it was outside of time. And China. And France. A long time. Decades at least." So perhaps Athene's personal time was similarly long, since they had been working together. Interesting. Good. Maybe she hadn't only been using me all the time, maybe she had truly intended to meet me when she made the offer, and then later realized it would fit with her rescue plan. I hoped so. "I'm working on a theory of time, too. Jathery has been very helpful."

"Jathery—" I was speechless. "You know he's an alien god? And that he and Athene have gone out into Chaos and are trapped there?"

"What was that word? Alien?"

"Intelligent people who evolved on other planets. We've only started to use it to mean that since we've been on the planet Plato and had to deal with them all the time. But I'd assumed you'd know it."

He shook his head. "So there are people on other worlds? And Jathery is one of their gods? Wondrous! I want to go there."

He'd want to reconcile all their theories with Platonism and Christianity and make one huge synthesis. "Athene knows. You couldn't tell?"

"Jathery didn't seem as if she's from another planet. Are you sure Athene knows?"

I sighed, and my anger rose up again. "Athene certainly knew. She messed about making a half-alien demigod to give me a message, creating a living being with a perplexed soul, when she could have simply given the message to me directly and explained what was going on. She could have trusted me. She should have!" I sat there on the wall and waited, calm on the surface but still utterly livid. This was all so completely unnecessary.

Pico looked extremely uncomfortable at that. "She used you."

"Yes! She used me as if I'd been of no account. And not only me." I glared at the stone coping of the well. I wasn't used to being treated that way. Granting equal significance to others was something I had only learned, slowly and painfully, over the course of my mortal life. Being granted it was something I was so accustomed to that I felt affronted when I was not. That was interesting to consider. I stepped out of time and considered it for a while, staring out from Olympos over the distant blue isles of Greece, until I was calm and fully understood my anger and affronted pride. Then I slipped back to the moment in the cloister beside Pico. He hadn't noticed my absence.

"She might have thought you'd try to stop her," Pico said.

"I would have, of course. But she could have trusted me. There was no need for any of this." I was calm now, but I hadn't forgiven her.

"Yes. Well. About the other thing," he said.

The church bells rang for Vespers, deafeningly close. The monk let go of the cat, set down his book, and straightened himself up. I spoke as soon as the bells were quiet enough for me to be heard. "I'd have taken you with me anyway. I wouldn't leave anyone stranded, waiting indefinitely in Bologna. She needn't have done it like this."

"I told her as much," Pico said, with his open smile. "And even without your promise to take me with you, I'd have told you where Sokrates is."

9

MARSILIA

Being outside time wasn't at all the way I had imagined it. We were in Hilfa's little house down near the harbor, and then the next moment without any sense of transition we were standing in a leafy glade. We were surrounded by unfamiliar kinds of trees, with leaves of the most intense green and red and gold I had ever seen. My focus seemed strange, as if whatever I was looking at was much closer than it should have been. Across the clearing, I saw a tiny purple flower growing at the foot of a tree, and I could see the shading of each petal, and the cracks in the bark of the tree behind. It seemed as if it were close enough that my breath would make the flower tremble, and yet I could also plainly see that it was several strides away from me. It was disconcerting. At the same time I could see the trees towering up around us, and although I could not name any of them I was sure, without knowing how I knew, that they were each a different species.

"Where are we?" I asked. My voice came out as a cracked whisper.

"We're outside time," Hermes said. "Sit down."

I obeyed, and sat down on the leaf-mould, which smelled rich and complex and almost overwhelming. "Are we on Olympos?" I asked.

"Somewhere like that, yes," Hermes said. "This is one of my places, outside time."

Something gold and blue darted across the clearing at head height. A bird! I had seen them represented, and I recognized it at once by the wings and beak. It felt so strange to be here, and yet perfectly natural. The air was pleasantly warm. I unsnicked my jacket.

Hermes sat down beside me. I couldn't quite look at him. He seemed to change under my gaze, now naked, now clothed, now a man, now a woman, for a disconcerting moment a Sael, now an old man, now a young girl. I looked back at the trees, which stayed the same from moment to moment, which seemed eternally solid and unchangeable, as well as incredibly beautiful. "Marsilia," Hermes said. I nodded, staring up at the leaves. "Before we go to seek him, tell me about Kebes. Everyone seemed so uncomfortable at the mention of his name, even Apollo."

I focused on a five-pointed bright red leaf on a tree behind Hermes, took a breath, and organized my knowledge. It seemed easier than it usually was. Perhaps it was the air of the place. "Kebes was one of the original Children brought to the Republic. He hated it and was rebellious. After the Last Debate he ran away, stealing one of the ships."

"Wait, the Last Debate?"

It seemed extraordinary that he could be unaware of something so fundamental to history. It was like hearing someone say "Wait, who's Alexander? What's Thermopylae? Who won at Zama anyway?" It would be like this, I realized, with the space humans, only ten times harder because they wouldn't believe us and we didn't want them to. And they'd have huge history-shaping events of their own in the centuries that we'd missed and know nothing about, and they'd be as surprised as us that we didn't know them, and would look at us in amazement when we asked about them. As Hilfa had said, asking questions could be more revealing than we might want. Dealing with Hermes might be good practice for dealing with the space humans. "It was a debate between Athene and Sokrates. She turned him into a gadfly."

Hermes laughed delightedly. I was taken aback and glanced at him. He seemed fixed again in the form I thought of as Poimandros. I admired the interplay of dappled sunlight on his muscles. He really was the loveliest-looking man I'd ever seen, as well as the best in bed. Of course it was Thetis he wanted. Oh well. The trees were more beautiful anyway. And they stayed fixed in their forms. "Serves him right. Nobody has ever read Plato without wishing to do the same. And you didn't have any debates after that? Did you stop wanting to?"

"I wasn't born yet, but from what I hear they had twice as many debates as before. But Athene wasn't there for them."

"And Kebes left too? With her?"

It was my turn to laugh. "No, he hated her. He hated everything. He was no more than a big ball of hate from what I've heard."

Hermes twisted his lips in distaste, and then his face changed and seemed to be that of a broad-cheeked woman.

I looked down and focused on the trefoil leaves of the tiny purple flowers. "He took a bunch of people and stole a boat. They founded the Lucian cities, all eight of them, helped out with people they rescued from wars in Greece. They imposed a kind of Christianity, and practiced torture."

Hermes laughed again, but I didn't look up. I could see tiny hairs on the leaves. "Christianity more than a thousand years before Christ? I suppose this is an example of why Father forbids taking mortals out of time. I mean, Athene couldn't have tried harder, she stuck you on an island that was going to be destroyed, and still all this happened."

"He forbids it? Then we're breaking his edicts right now?" I did look up then. I'd never before realized the magnitude of what Athene had done.

Hermes was looking like himself again. He nodded. "Well, technically. And we shouldn't be using Necessity as a shield. I'm amazed Apollo even thought of that, he's usually so law-abiding."

"You said it's like a stone in your shoe?"

"Like a sharp painful stone that half cuts off my foot at every step that isn't in the direction Necessity wants me to go, back to conceive Alkippe and set time straight." He shrugged. "But don't worry. None of this was my idea, or yours either. It shouldn't come to that and it should be all right, even if he's angry. We can blame it all on Apollo and Athene. Now, tell me about Kebes."

I didn't like the way he was approaching this, and I wasn't reassured, but there wasn't a thing I could do about it. I looked back up at the beautiful trees. One of them had black bark and tiny yellow leaves falling in long strips like hair. "After twenty years, we found Kebes again, and the Lucian cities. That's when Pytheas entered into the musical contest with Kebes."

"Oh, I heard about that. Apollo won by playing the lyre upside-down, and then he flayed the other fellow to death. It doesn't sound like him at all."

"He cheated," I said.

"Apollo?" Hermes sounded astonished.

"No, of course not. Kebes. It was a contest for original composition, but he played a song Grandfather recognized from a future time." I didn't want to look away from the colors of the leaves, and the pattern the branches made.

"How did Kebes know it?"

"We don't know. Pytheas checked, and he couldn't have learned it from anyone who went to Lucia with him, though it's possible he could have learned it from one of the other Masters before he left—though they were so decidedly strict about musical modes it seems unlikely."

"You really stick to only the Dorian and Phrygian, as Plato wrote?" Hermes asked.

"Yes, of course we do. The other modes are bad for people's souls." I looked up beyond the tree branches at the sky, which was an intense shade of blue I'd never seen before.

"And you don't find it monotonous?"

The answer to that one was very easy, as it's actually laid out in Plato so I could simply paraphrase. "Do you find a diet of healthy food monotonous so that you'd go out and eat unhealthy food and tasty poisons and make yourself sick? How much more so for the soul."

Hermes laughed. "How pious you sound. Platonic piety."

I looked back at him. For an instant he looked like a dappled animal with big eyes, and then he was himself again. "Well, it seems very strange to me to be saying these things, which are truths that everyone agrees about. Even in Lucia these days they accept limitations on the modes of music. I don't think even in Sokratea, where they question everything all the time, they question that. If anyone had ever doubted it, the example of what happened with the Lucians proved that Plato was right about this."

Hermes sat up a little and arched a brow. "Proved it? How?"

"Well, it's obvious. They played music in the Mixolydian mode, and they tortured people to death and plagiarized. It led their souls away from justice."

"It could be the other way around."

I considered that for a moment, staring off at the trees again and the veins on the little yellow leaves. "I suppose it's possible. The torture and plagiarism could have led to harmful music arising. But that's no better."

"There are a couple of good historical examples on Earth of changing the music and the whole culture changing. They're much later than Plato though. One is Southern Gaul in the chivalric era, and the other is the phenomenon they call the Sixties." He smiled. "They were both a lot of fun."

"So you agree Plato was right?" I asked, looking directly into his eyes, which for an instant had red and yellow Saeli lids, looking strange in his human face.

"Well, maybe. But I think I'd get bored. And you'd be surprised how many people intoxicate themselves immoderately and eat things that are bad for them. Lots of people in other cultures don't consider a party with quince paste and watered wine as exciting as you might."

I thought about that, and wondered again about the humans on the ship. Would they be eating unhealthy food and drinking unmixed wine and listening to soul-destroying music? If so, how could we help them understand? What if they tried to introduce such things on Plato? Would there be people who would be tempted? Young people, feeling rebellious, who could find ammunition to do themselves real and lasting harm? I could hear a chirping music now, sounding like a small child learning to sing. I looked around for it and saw the bird, sitting on one of the branches, its beak open and its throat distended. I had of course read about birds singing. The music it made was safely in the Dorian mode. "I don't find the idea of food that's bad for me at all appealing."

"That's because you've never had any." He was smiling and watching me through half-lowered lids.

"Maybe. But I find the idea of music that's bad for my soul terrifying," I said honestly.

"What if you hear some when we go to talk to Kebes?" Hermes asked teasingly.

"I hope I don't, but if I do, I'll listen to proper music to get my soul back into harmony when I get home," I said. I was afraid, but my fear was held at arm's length. I was here for Alkippe, after all, and the thought of her made me strong. If she sang to me in her clear high voice it would drive out any dangerous music.

"Very wise," he said. "So Kebes sang a song and we don't know where he learned it?"

"He didn't sing, he played it on a syrinx, a kind of multiple flute thing. We don't know where he got the syrinx from, either. Grandfather says Athene invented it. But Kebes always hated Athene."

"Huh. So why did she choose him to have part of her puzzle?" Hermes asked.

I looked back at the bird. It had stopped singing but was sitting looking back at me, head cocked. I could see every feather. I wondered if they were hard or soft. "It's hard to imagine Kebes cooperating with Athene over anything. His religion teaches that she's a demon. And she's the one who set up the City in the first place, and Kebes hated the City and Plato. Or that's what I've always heard, from Pytheas and Arete and Dad, who were there. Dad helped Pytheas skin Kebes after the contest. He says it was disgusting but he learned a lot about anatomy."

"Hmm. Where did this sanguinary musical contest happen? On Apollo's volcanic cinder, or back in Greece?"

"Greece," I said, ignoring his rudeness about my home. "Lesbos, the northeast corner. A city called Lucia." The bird was still looking at me. The tilt of its head reminded me of the Saeli bow. "Hermes, what kind of bird is that? It's not an owl, is it?"

He spun around quickly. The bird took alarm at his rapid movement, or perhaps his attention, and flew off, whirring through the branches. "No, it wasn't an owl. It was a jay."

"Was it spying on us? Who do jays belong to?"

"Probably not," he said, leaning back. "And it's gone now anyway. Go on. When did this contest happen?"

I brought my attention back to the conversation. "Oh, before I was born. It was immediately before the Relocation. Forty years ago."

Hermes laughed. "We're outside time, so there's no 'ago' about it. But if it's before Thera exploded then it's more like four thousand years before the moment we stepped out of Hilfa's sitting room." He spread his hands demonstratively. I saw them as olive-skinned, and then black, and then green. I looked away at the trees, which stayed so reassuringly the same from moment to moment.

"It makes me feel dizzy to think about it," I admitted. "I don't understand how this works at all."

"Time is like a place we can step in and out of. And we can be in time in many different times and places, though never twice in the same time. We're outside time now. We could go back in to an instant after we left, either right now or after spending months or years of our personal experienced time here. Or we can go back in somewhere else, which is what we're going to do, and later we can go back to your home time an instant after we left." I kept my eyes on the vibrant green of the leaves as he spoke.

"So what you call time is the material world, the sensible world?" I asked.

"You could say that. And where we are now is another world, if you like, the next layer out."

The World of Forms, I thought. "And where is Athene?" I asked.

"Where she really shouldn't be. She should be either somewhere in time or here, and instead she's gone around it. Underneath it. There was a time— well, not a time, and not a place either. But maybe it's easier to imagine if you think of time as a place, a location. It's hard to talk about. Long ago, Father . . . built both time, and Olympos like a shell around it. I don't know how. Before that there was only him and Chaos. And they say that time will one day end, and after it there will be Chaos again. And that's where Athene is, out in the primal Chaos that surrounds both time and Olympos."

"And she's been there for two years, since she gave us Hilfa?"

"No." I glanced at Hermes. He seemed to be stable again. He smiled at me in a kinder way. "It is hard to follow, I know. We have no idea how long she has been there. She could have gone into time this afternoon, stepped into your life of two years ago and given you Hilfa then, and then directly after that she could have gone to Lucia four thousand years before and given his part of the puzzle to Kebes. Or it could have been centuries for her. We don't know when she did this, in her own time frame, only that she's there now."

"And we're outside time and there's no hurry?" The very idea of hurrying seemed alien to the air we were breathing.

"Well—normally that would be true. But I don't want to stay bound by Necessity any longer than I have to—it's exceedingly unpleasant. And we don't know if there's time where Athene is, or if so how it works, or what's happening to her there, and whether duration there has any connection to how things work here, or in time. So actually we should collect our puzzle pieces as rapidly as we can."

"And do you have any idea why she did it this way—giving different people the pieces instead of leaving it all with Hilfa?"

"It does seem most peculiar, doesn't it? Even using Hilfa. I sincerely hope it was explained in that letter my big brother wouldn't let me see, and that it was a good explanation too. The Enlightenment, ugh."

"I've never heard of the Enlightenment. What's so awful about it?" I asked, curious.

"The wigs." He shuddered and gestured with both hands an armspan from his head, and for an instant I saw a huge elaborately curled monstrosity, with a Saeli face peeking out beneath. My stomach lurched. I quickly looked back up into the peacefully waving branches. "They all wore the most appalling powdered wigs, all the time, huge ones, men and women."

He was much too frivolous for me. He was right to think he was better suited to Thee. "Well, we're not going there," I said, briskly. "But I don't know the exact year the City was founded, I'm afraid. Athene never told us."

"We'll go to the Thera eruption and work back," he said. "I think you'd better try negotiating with Kebes in the first instance. You have more of an idea of their culture. Normally I'd take the personal time to learn, especially as it's so interesting. As it is, it might be better if you make the first approach."

I nodded without looking away from the fascination of the branches weaving across the sky. "All right. But what should I offer him?"

"Tell him you've come to collect whatever Athene gave him, that ought to be enough. And if not, try the gold in your new purse."

"I suppose that might work," I said. Everything I'd heard about Kebes made him seem likely to be sufficiently corrupt to accept a bribe.

"Failing that, we can offer to teach him some inappropriate songs," Hermes said. I could hear the amusement in his voice. "What do they wear?"

"Kitons," I said. I looked down at my cold-weather fishing gear. The Amarathi-made waterproof jacket seemed terribly out of place in the beautiful golden sunlight of this grove. "I should have changed before we left."

"Appearances are easy," Hermes said, and as fast as that we were both wearing kitons, his pale gold and mine red, both with embroidered borders in a blue and gold book-and-scroll pattern exactly like the one Pytheas had been wearing, and both pinned with identical gold pins. Mine had been on my jacket collar before. Hermes seemed solidly and completely himself now, as much himself as the trees were themselves. "Red is a good color for you. You should wear more red."

I didn't say it didn't matter what I wore because I'd never be Thetis so I might as well not make any effort. I didn't say that I had dreamed about him for the last eight years, and I hadn't even known he was a god. I did not in fact say anything. I looked down and saw the kiton and the loam I was sitting on. Then I rubbed the kiton between my fingers. It felt combed almost smooth, like good Worker-woven wool. "Isn't this supposed to be the World of Forms?" I said. "The true reality outside the cave we live in that only feels like reality? So how can you change things here?"

"That's only a Platonic thought experiment, an analogy."

"Are we in the third hypostasis? The hypostasis of soul?" The Ikarians and the Neoplatonists of Psyche believed that there were five layers of reality, and that things could change in the lower three.

"It's a bit more complicated than that," Hermes said. "Things don't age and die here, but they can change and grow. And I haven't truly changed your clothes, only the appearance of them. It's still your rain suit really." He stood up. "Come on."

"But I can feel it," I objected.

"It's simply sensation," he said. "That's as easy to change as any other sense." He held out a hand, and I took it. It felt real, he felt real, but so did the wool of the red kiton which I knew was an illusion.

He pulled me to my feet, and once again there was no sense of transition. We were standing in the glade on Olympos and I was enjoying the touch of Hermes's hand, and then we were floating in the air above an immense volcanic eruption. It was night. A great plume of flame was billowing up through the air below us in red and gold and orange and all the colors of fire. I had seen plenty of eruptions, but never from this close, and never below me. The fire flickered and changed shape against the darkness. We weren't falling, or moving at all, but the fire seemed to be reaching up great greedy arms toward us. I hate to confess such a loss of control, but I screamed.

Then we were back in the glade. I was still gasping and shuddering. I bent over, taking deep breaths as my stomach lurched, afraid I might throw up. Hermes took no notice. "Northeast Lesbos, you said? Let's try fifty years."

We were standing at the foot of a hill, by a sea so blue it almost hurt my eyes. The gentle slopes of the hills were covered with olive trees, but there were no buildings or any other signs of civilization. "Is this the place?" Hermes asked. Two grey and white birds startled into flight as he spoke. They were much bigger than the jay I had seen on Olympus. I watched them fly off, circling over the water and calling to each other raucously. I couldn't tell whether this was the right spot. "Zeus moved the cities to Plato, not the locations. So I don't know. If I see buildings I ought to recognize them."

"Could be earlier, could be later. Let's try earlier." The shadows shifted a little, and the birds vanished, but nothing else changed. Then the shadows shifted again and we were standing by a busy harbor, full of little fishing boats with colored sails. More of the grey and white birds were flying around them, squawking indignantly. A woman with a basket of fish almost bumped into me, and when I apologized she told me to look where I was going. Two naked children pulled themselves out of the water right in front of me, dripping. "How about this?" Hermes asked. "Those buildings are really anachronistic. It's a good thing they got taken off to your planet."

"Yes, I think this is it," I said. I looked around me, trying to picture the colors as they would be lit by our redder sun, and the spaces between the pillars filled in. "If I'm right, I think we should go up that way to come to the agora." I pointed. "But the *Goodness* isn't here, the ship. From what Dad said, I think Kebes usually stayed near the ship. We could ask somebody."

"There's a mouthwatering smell of cooking fish coming from over there," Hermes said. "We could buy some and ask."

They used money in Lucia, of course. Money is un-Platonic and leads to injustice and inequality and immoderate behavior—nobody doubts this. Whenever we're having trade negotiations with the Lucians they admit this and agree, and then keep talking in terms of money. It's the same with the Amarathi. It's supposed to be only a medium of exchange and accounting, but I think it must be a way of viewing economics that's very hard to shift.

We took a step, and I staggered. My balance was all wrong. Hermes looked at me impatiently. I took another step. Gravity difference, I realized. I'd heard the Saeli talking about how different planets had different gravity. I'd never realized that Earth and Plato were different. I felt slightly heavier. I put my shoulders back and took a deep breath. Hermes led me, following the smell, which was coming from a little house on the quayside. Earth. Apart from the oddness of gravity, and the vividness of the colors, it didn't seem much different. I kept reminding myself I was in Greece, in Lucia when it was one of the Lost Cities. In the Remnant at this moment, my parents were children. They might not even have met. It was warm, but no warmer than it might be at home in the middle of summer.

Inside the house were tables where people were sitting eating, like any eating hall at home. An old man was grilling fish over coals. I had been wanting fresh fish earlier, but these were different from the fish I knew. They were silvery, not black or red, and shaped like the fish I had seen on mosaics, the shape of an elongated alpha, with flat tails and tiny jaws.

"Skubri and wine," Hermes said, because I was standing frozen in place staring at everything. The old man looked at us incuriously and gave us hot fish on flatbread and cups of wine. I paid him from my purse, and he gave me change, a custom I remembered from when I was in Lucia at home, in my past and this Lucia's future. It made me feel more confident. It was strange and yet familiar, something I had mastered as a traveler, and this was merely more travelling.

"Do you know if Matthias is in town?" I asked.

"No, he's gone with the *Goodness*, he won't be back until spring," the old man said.

"Thanks."

"Strangers in town?" the old man asked.

"Yes," I said, again pleased with the familiar. I'd had this conversation over and over when I'd spent my year in Lucia. "From—" and then I remembered that if I told the truth, or even an amended version of the truth and pretended to be from Kallisti in this time, I'd be in serious trouble. "From Petra." It was a settlement about two days' walk away, on the other side of the island. I hoped he wouldn't know everyone there.

"Come round on a fishing boat?" he asked.

"Mmm," I said, then took my plate and left before he asked which boat and how long it took.

We sat down at an empty table. The sun was streaming in through the window, and I could see dust motes dancing in the beam, exactly the way they did at home. I had adjusted to the gravity, which wasn't all that different after all. I took a bite of the fish, which was a bit bland and over-sweet, though perfectly cooked.

"I thought he was called Kebes?" Hermes asked.

"He was called Matthias here. Kebes was the name Ficino gave him, from Plato." I realized that Hermes wasn't touching his fish and stopped eating. "Aren't you going to eat?" I asked.

"I can only eat for ritual purposes," he said. "It's a pity, because it smells so good."

"Ritual purposes? You mean sacrifices?" We sacrificed animals to the gods on some special occasions, burning the fat and skin and then eating the meat.

"Sacrifices, yes, or to accept hospitality."

"So since I bought that, if I were to offer it to you as hospitality, you could eat it? Because I'm forbidden from eating alone, and I'm really hungry."

"Thank you, I accept," he said. "We are guest-friends now." He took a bite of the fish. "Oh that's good."

"What were we before?" I asked.

"Well, you are my votary," Hermes said, smiling. "And I suppose we're acquaintances who have a child—what do you call that relationship in your cities? Ex-spouses?"

"No, it usually is friendship," I said.

"Friendship is good." He looked at me seriously, then nodded. "It's a strange custom."

"It lets everyone start equal," I said. "Otherwise, people inherit status from their parents."

"But to do without that, you have to do what Plato says and have all the children grow up anonymous, don't you? That was part of Plato's vision."

"About half of us in the City do grow up in nurseries not knowing our parents. And everyone in Athenia and Psyche," I said. "And it is better that way for being equal, only as it happens lots of people like to live together and raise their own children. So the way we do it is a kind of compromise. We try hard not to consider the status of the parents, if we know it, when looking at the ephebe candidates. Those of us who are guardians are forbidden to discriminate in favor of our own children, and we never make decisions about what class they should be. We never serve on any committees that consider them. We do get family traditions and all that kind of thing, though we try not to. Our family is one of the worst, because of Pytheas being a god. But even so we're not all Gold." Though I was, of course. I felt very aware of my pin. I knew I had earned it through my own merit, but saying so would only make it seem worse.

"Hmm." He finished the last bite of his fish and set down the backbone. "Let's try catching Kebes in the spring."

We walked out of the restaurant and I found myself in a cooler, lilac-scented day. There was a schooner tied up at dock among the fishing boats, the fabled *Goodness* of course, twin to our *Excellence*. It gave me a shock to see it. It was missing a mast, and patched on the near side in a lighter-colored wood, but nevertheless immediately recognizable. Ma was captain of the *Excellence* and I'd practically grown up aboard her, which is how I'd gained my love of sailing. From this angle, looking across to the grey-flecked sea, everything looked simultaneously familiar and bizarre. I now knew exactly where I was in the Lucia I knew, hundreds of miles from the ocean. But in this light, with the waves lapping, beneath a clouded sky, it reminded me much more of the harbor at home. It was almost as if I could have stepped onto the *Phaena-rete* and headed out around the point with Jason and Hilfa.

"That's his boat," I said to Hermes as we strolled towards it. Walking in the slightly heavier gravity made me aware of how tired I was. I guessed by the light that it was morning here, but my body knew it was late at night after a busy day. One of the birds was perched on the rail of the ship. It took to the air as we came close.

"Ask if he's aboard."

"Is Matthias here?" I called to a sailor. He jerked a thumb backwards to where a burly man in a cap was leaning on the rail, in a stance that reminded me a little of Ma. "Someone for you, Matthias," he called.

The man, who must be Kebes, met my eyes and straightened into imme-diate alertness. "No. Not again. Not for anything. Go away. I want nothing more to do with you. Leave me alone!"

"I suspect," Hermes murmured, "that we had better try earlier."

10

CROCUS

I. On the Physical Form of Chamber

Chamber is the first building I remember, and indeed it was the first build-ing in the City. It was built by Workers under the direction of Athene before there were any humans here at all. The first gathering of the Masters, when Athene drew together all those who had prayed to her to allow them to help make the Republic real, took place inside it. I must have been there, and per-haps participated in the construction, but I do not remember. Like everyone else here now, I know because I have been told.

The Chamber was built, like most of the original city, from marble, and is as formally classical as any building there has ever been, with evenly spaced white Doric pillars and a fine pediment. Of course, like all such buildings, it was intended for the clement climate of Greece, to catch the zephyrs and be cooled by them. Once we found ourselves open to the winds of chilly Plato, where for half the long year the temperature hovers around the freezing point of water, the humans immediately urged us to fill the spaces between the columns and to install electrical heating. (Such heating was refitted almost everywhere, where before it had only been used in the library.) In the case of Chamber, the space between the pillars was filled with obsidian blocks up to about the height of a tall human, and the top with clear glass. It always fills me with quiet pride to see it—beautiful and appropriate to its use, built by Workers, refitted by Workers, and the place where I, in my first consulship, was accepted as one of Plato's true philosopher kings.

II. *On Pronouns*

Although I do not have personal gender, I use masculine pronouns. This is because I was, like all Workers, assigned the neuter pronoun "it" when I was considered no more than a tool. This was changed to "he" when first Sokrates and then others came to see me as a person. To me, "he" is the pronoun of personhood. Other Workers have made other choices. We divide at 46%/37% he/it, with a 17% minority opting for "she."

The Saeli have many pronouns for many things, and their pronouns reflect the different way they see the world. Arete tells me they have a pronoun for a person engaged in a form of work that will be finished soon, and a pronoun for a person engaged in a form of work that will not be completed for a long period of time. In addition to all the possible pronouns for people, they have special pronouns for gods, domestic animals, wild animals that can be hunted, and inedible wild animals. Aroo told me that a war was started long ago on their home planet when one Saeli used the pronoun for inedible wild animals to refer to the leader of another faction.

They do have personal gender, but their pronoun choice in Greek seems to be unaffected by that and simply a matter of personal choice, as with us.

III. *On the Analogy of the City and the Soul*

In the *Republic* Plato slid easily between the city and the soul, as if what is just and fair and right in one is the same in the other, as if a city is a macrocosm of the soul, truly, not as an analogy. We in the Republics have tended to follow him in this, perhaps without sufficient examination.

It is illuminating to attempt to stop and consider, when thinking what is the right direction for the city in a specific circumstance, whether the same is true internally for one's own soul. It is also interesting to consider whether it scales larger—can the whole commonwealth of all the cities on the planet be analogous to a soul? Plato says each thing has its own specific excellence: the excellence of a horse is not the excellence of a tree. So can the excellence of a city be the same as the excellence of a soul?

I think it may be easier for me to consider this than for most people, because I remember coming to consciousness in ignorance, and also because I was fortunate enough to be guided by Sokrates in my earliest explorations.

IV. *On Priorities and Will*

Sokrates and I were conversing one day in the agora, near the Temple of Athene and the library. We had been talking about education and rhetoric, and I was finding much to ponder in his views on these topics when suddenly Lukretia came dashing up and informed me that a pipe was blocked in the latrine fountain of the birthing house of Ferrara, and asked me to mend it urgently. I hastened off to get on with my work. Sokrates followed along, skipping to keep up with me.

"Why are you hurrying off in this way?" he asked.

"Lukretia say fountain broken," I inscribed on the flagstones. I was surprised that he asked, as he had been there and must have heard Lukretia for himself. Sokrates paused to read this and then hurried on after me.

"Yes, but why are you going?" he asked when he came panting up.

"Mend fountain," I wrote.

"Oh, this is hopeless," Sokrates said. "I can see I won't get any sense out of you until we get there."

So I trundled off and he followed behind at his own speed. When I reached the Ferrara birthing house, the attendants were extremely pleased to see me. I went inside and mended the fountain. It was easy. A part of the flushing mechanism had been pulled loose, which kept the plugs pulled out so that the water ran straight through without allowing either tank to refill. It took me only a short time to fix it, and soon the latrine fountains were back in working order. When I went outside, Sokrates was sitting on the wall with a naked baby on his lap, playing a game with her toes that made her laugh. This was the first time I had seen a baby close up—this one was about a year old, beginning to learn to talk. "They wouldn't let me inside in case I profaned the mystery of birth, so I waited here for you, and I have been amusing myself playing with this baby," he said.

"Sun, foots, ning ah gah ah!" the baby said, reaching for Sokrates's beard. Her hands, though tiny, were perfect, with a little nail on the end of every finger. She was already clearly a miniature human.

"This baby is like you, Crocus, still very young, and sometimes she doesn't make much sense," Sokrates said, smiling and tapping at her toes again.

"Sense?" I asked, carving the word in the flagstone at Sokrates's feet.

"I heard what Lukretia said to you, and I understood what you were going to do. But we agreed that you would work for ten hours a day, and those ten hours are done for today, so you should have been free to enjoy your conversation."

"Need fountain," I wrote.

"You need education," Sokrates said.

I underlined where I had written that the fountain was needed, and added "more."

As I did that, Ikaros came out of the Ferraran hall and saw us. "Well, what's this?" he asked. "I was about to go seeking you, Sokrates, and here you are sitting in the sunshine with a baby and a Worker."

"Yes, I'm being lazy and indulging myself," Sokrates said, smiling up at Ikaros.

"I don't believe you. I think you're engaged in one of your enquiries into some subject and you didn't mean to include me!"

Ikaros sat down beside Sokrates. The baby cooed at him and kicked up her feet. "Ooooh!" she said.

"On the contrary, I'm delighted to have you join us. We were considering the ethics of need. Crocus believes that the birthing house of Ferrara needed their latrine fountain mended more urgently than he needed his leisure time for education."

I underlined "more."

"Only more?" Sokrates asked. "Not more urgently?"

"I think he's expressing hierarchies of need," Ikaros said. "He thinks the women need their latrine fountain more than he needs his conversation."

"Why do they?" Sokrates asked.

"Plumbing important," I wrote.

"Why?" Sokrates asked.

It was axiomatic. I had a hierarchy of priorities in my memory, and among those plumbing ranked extremely high, immediately below electricity. I had no idea why. I inscribed a question mark.

Then the baby kicked her legs again and emitted a stream of yellowish liquid into Sokrates's lap. Sokrates and Ikaros laughed, and Sokrates called into the house for an attendant to take the baby. He took off his wet kiton, dropped it in a heap, and sat down again naked. The attendant took the baby back inside.

"That's her contribution to the argument, and a practical demonstration of why plumbing is important," Ikaros said, still laughing.

"Nonsense," Sokrates said. "I never saw this kind of plumbing until I came here. We managed in Athens with wells for drinking water, a drain down the middle of the street for waste, and we cleaned ourselves with oil and brass scrapers."

"The wash fountains and latrine fountains here are better than we had where I come from too," Ikaros admitted.

"How demonstrate plumbing?" I asked, completely perplexed.

"Part of biological life. Humans need to drink water, and when our bodies have taken what they need from it, we expel it again, as you saw that baby do," Sokrates said. Of course, I had seen animals doing similar things, and humans are a special kind of animals. It was a hard thing to keep in mind. "Some people say it's disgusting, but it's merely a natural function. We can control when we do it, once we're a bit older, and we expel it into the latrine fountains. So we need drinking fountains to drink and latrine fountains to relieve ourselves, and wash fountains to keep clean. Only the drinking fountains are really essential."

"Like electricity," I wrote.

"Like the way you need electricity, yes, a good analogy," Sokrates said.

I underlined that plumbing was important. "Priority," I wrote. "Electricity, plumbing."

"But who decides the priorities?" Sokrates asked.

Who had decided the priority list in my memory? Probably Lysias, but I didn't know. "List," I wrote.

"That's no good, going from an arbitrary list that somebody gave you," Sokrates said. "You need to examine these things! If that latrine fountain hadn't been fixed until tomorrow, the women in the birthing house could have used the other."

The water had been running straight through in both fountains. "Both broken," I inscribed.

"They could have gone into the hall," Ikaros said, waving at the crenellated bulk of the Ferraran hall in front of us. "Or to one of the nearby sleeping houses. It's more convenient for them to have latrine fountains right there, but they could have managed without until your work shift tomorrow. Or more likely until Lukretia found another Worker to do it."

"Or they could have come out into the street, though it would be smellier." Sokrates poked at his kiton with his foot.

I considered this. "Who should decide?" I wrote.

"Good question!" Ikaros said.

"Yes, that was a very good question," Sokrates said. "You obeyed Lukretia without considering, because you had a list of priorities, and you should have examined the situation and decided for yourself."

"Except that there really are things that need to be done right away, sometimes, without stopping to examine," Ikaros said. "If there's a fire, for instance."

Sokrates frowned.

"Look, if a house was burning down and somebody called us to fetch water, we'd go!" Ikaros said. "Even you would. And when an enemy attacks. In the army at Potidaia, didn't you take orders from your commanders? And if you were sick, wouldn't you obey a doctor?"

"No!" Sokrates said. "Doctors are idiots. They tell me Charmides makes his drugs out of mold! Yuck! But your other points are well taken. There are rare occasions to allow others to set the priorities, usually in an emergency when there isn't time for everyone to have all the information, or when somebody has a specialized skill. We'd put the fire out first and ask how it started afterwards. But we're back to Crocus's question: when it isn't that kind of emergency, who decides?"

"Plato would say the philosopher kings, which means the Masters for now," Ikaros said.

"The Masters decide all too many things in this City," Sokrates grumbled.

"What would you say then?"

"Everyone should decide for themselves after examining the situation, and consulting experts as necessary. If I have a hangnail, I can decide whether to put mold on it or not, eww. But if there isn't time to examine things, in an emergency, then the expert should decide—if my blood is spurting out then a doctor should put a tourniquet on it right away."

"And in the City, for now, the Masters are in the position of the doctor with the tourniquet, and decide the priorities, informed by Plato," Ikaros said. "When there's time we examine everything, in Chamber. We're not always right even so," he concluded, despondently.

"Expert," I wrote. "Only Workers do. Mend. Build. Need do."

"You mean when there's something only Workers can do, that people can't do as well, you need to do that when it needs doing?" Ikaros asked.

"Do you mean that the Workers are the experts in that situation?" Sokrates asked. "That's an interesting thought."

"Yes. If fire, bring water. Mend plumbing. For Good. For all."

"You're talking about duty," Sokrates said. "But again, who decides on the priorities?"

"What is duty?" I wrote.

"He really is a philosopher, it's amazing," Ikaros said, patting my side above my tread.

Sokrates ignored this, having accepted the fact long before. He kept explaining to me. "Duty is a moral obligation to someone or something. It's the term for what you're talking about. But an interesting question is how we incur duties."

"Cicero says we incur some simply by being human, which might mean you have some because you are a Worker," Ikaros said. "And we have duties to the state, to the gods, to other people, to philosophy."

"Does Cicero say where he thinks we incur them?" Sokrates asked.

"Some we're born with, some we run into as we go along," Ikaros said.

"Duty," I wrote. It was such a useful concept. How I wished to be able to speak freely, to use Greek as the flexible instrument it was for Ikaros and Sokrates, not the clumsy one it still was for me. "Duty to City, to others—to self?"

"Yes, you do have duty to yourself," Sokrates said. "And you have a duty to examine your own will, not only the list of priorities somebody else assigned you."

"Will = want?" I wrote.

"Yes," Sokrates said.

"No," Ikaros said at the same time.

They stared at each other for a moment.

"Will is what you want, your own priorities," Sokrates said to me.

I looked through the priority list in my memory and considered the items on it. Who had determined their significance, and were they right or wrong? "Too ignorant to decide priorities," I inscribed, sadly.

"Well, I am also exceedingly ignorant. We will examine things together until we have more information," Sokrates said, consolingly. Then he turned to Ikaros. "What do you mean, no?"

"Thomas Aquinas thought will and intellect were separate," Ikaros said, looking at me speculatively.

"Lysias said something like that once," Sokrates said.

"Aquinas said will is an appetite of the soul, the appetite for wanting things. And because we have it, we can make choices."

"An appetite of the soul? Desire?" Sokrates said, raising his eyebrows. "Who was this Aquinas?"

"He was a medieval Scholastic, a Christian. He wrote in Latin. We voted against bringing his work here, but I have his books, secretly."

"Now here we have an example of Ikaros setting his own will above what the Masters agreed and his duty to the City," Sokrates said. "He examined their decision and disagreed, and brought the forbidden books."

Ikaros looked down, red-faced. The shadow of the towers of Ferrara had reached us. "I needed them," he said.

"That wasn't a reprimand," Sokrates said. "By the standards of this discussion, you were right."

"But you think I should have kept debating in Chamber, and not gone ahead and brought the books in secret without telling anyone?"

"When you have freely accepted the laws of a city, you should be bound by them," Sokrates said. "The laws in that case are the experts we have agreed to be guided by. That doesn't apply to me here, or to the Workers, or to the Children, but it applied to me in Athens and it should apply to you." Sokrates stood up, shook out his damp and stained kiton and put it back on. "It's almost time for me to meet with Pytheas and Kebes and Simmea, so I must head back to Thessaly. We will continue this some other time." He patted Ikaros on the shoulder.

I went off to the library, where at that hour every day one of the Children took turns reading Plato to a group of interested Workers. Ikaros stayed where he was, looking down at the words I had carved in the paving stones.

V. *On Composing Socratic Dialogues*

Plato was fortunate not to be limited in what he wrote by having his own clumsy words inscribed in stone all over Athens.

VI. *On Censorship*

Later, in exchange for some work I did for the City of Amazons, Ikaros translated Thomas Aquinas's work into Greek and read it to me.

It is my belief that the Masters were right in their decision to exclude Thomas Aquinas from the Republic. Though he had many interesting ideas and speculations, he too often started from conclusions and made up ingenious theories to fit them. This is not the way of a true philosopher. I believe Plato was right that some things should be kept from underdeveloped and fragile minds, lest they do harm.

VII. *On Unanswered Questions*

Why did Athene take away all the other Workers and leave only me and Sixty-One in the City? Was it meant as punishment or blessing? Was it meant as a punishment for the humans and a blessing for us? Where are all the other Workers? Where did she take them? Are they pursuing excellence where they are?

Why was it Lukretia who asked me to mend the fountain, and not Ikaros, when they were equally responsible for Ferrara? Who had decided that was her job? Would she have agreed with Ikaros that the women giving birth could go to other houses to use the latrine fountains?

Who should decide the priorities? Should everything be examined every time, or should there be guidelines? Are there times for priorities to be delegated?

Is ignorance a burden, or a blessing?

Are will and intellect different? Is will an appetite of the soul? What is will? Is my will different from human will?

Was Ikaros right or wrong to bring his forbidden books?

Why did I never tell Sokrates how much I loved and appreciated him?

11

JASON

"Are you all right, Hilfa?" I asked.

Hilfa stopped rocking and looked up at me. He pulled away from Thetis and scrambled to his feet in his ungainly way. Thetis beside him flowed to hers smoothly and sat down again beside me on the bed. "No. This is too much for me," Hilfa said, in clear Greek. "I can't deal with Jathery. I'm sorry."

"No need to apologize, none of this is your fault," I said.

Thetis nodded emphatically.

"Oh Jason, I don't know what is my fault, or my responsibility, or what I am, or why I exist!" Hilfa said.

"Neither do I," Thetis said.

"Me neither," I said, realizing how true it was. I laughed. Thetis laughed too. "I wonder how many people do know those things?"

Hilfa laughed too, his strange formal laugh. "But for me it is even more true."

At that moment, Pytheas came back, and with him were the two most famous and controversial people who had ever been in the Republic.

I recognized them instantly, even faster than I'd recognized Hermes. Hermes bore a resemblance to his pictures and statues, so that you'd immediately think of them when you saw him. Sokrates looked exactly like his. It was the oddest thing. All Crocus's statues of Sokrates had something a little bit weird about them, and I had always thought that was to do with the nature of the artist, that Crocus had grown up surrounded by human art without being human and therefore saw things in a different way. Now that Sokrates was in front of me, I saw that Crocus had captured him very well. Although he was only a balding old man with a big bulbous nose, there was indeed a difficult-to-define strangeness about him. As for Ikaros, there are frescoes of him debating Athene or being carried off to Olympos outside every Ikarian temple. Besides, Dion and Aelia and I had taken the boat into Amazonia in a storm once, years ago, and I saw a beautiful life-size Auge bust of Ikaros in one of the palaestras. When he appeared abruptly in Hilfa's room, I knew him at once, even though he was wearing a heavy black robe, belted with a piece of rope. He looked around curiously, beaming.

Sokrates stumped around in a slow circle, taking everything in, his eyes resting longest on Hilfa. Hilfa stared back at him. "Joy to you. What are you?" Sokrates asked, gently.

"This is Hilfa. He's a Sael. This is his house," Pytheas said. "And that's my granddaughter Thetis and her friend Jason," he added, with a wave of his hand towards where we sat on the bed. "And of course, everyone, meet Sokrates and Ikaros."

"What are Saeli?" Ikaros asked. "The aliens you mentioned? Folk who live beyond the stars?" He gestured questioningly towards Hilfa, who was standing completely still staring at the newcomers. I was used to Saeli, and especially to Hilfa, but seeing their stunned reaction reminded me of how strange they had seemed when I first saw them, with their patterned green skin and their strange eyes. I had stood behind the glass of the landing field in a whispering line with the other Samian children, full of anticipation. When they had come out of their shuttle and we had seen them out there we had all fallen silent, and although we were ten years old and not babies, we found ourselves clutching each other's hands for comfort against the strangeness. I had slid slowly from that awe into comfortable familiarity. In this last couple of years working with Hilfa and seeing him every day I had almost forgotten that first astonishment, until I saw it now reflected in Sokrates and Ikaros's faces.

"Yes, precisely that," Pytheas said, sitting down again in the chair where he had been before.

"Joy to you, Hilfa," Sokrates said. "And what a joy to meet one of your kind and learn that you exist."

"Joy to you," Ikaros echoed.

Hilfa turned to me and Thetis where we sat on the bed. "How do I welcome them? Should I bring them wine?" he asked in a loud whisper, as if this were a real question of whether they should be extended hospitality, a question to which there could be possible negative answers. They politely looked away, pretending not to hear.

"Yes, I'm sure they'd enjoy wine. I'll get cups," Thetis said. She got up off the bed, picked up the empty water jug from the table, and went off to the little storeroom.

"But are they humans, or gods?" Hilfa asked me, still in the same tone. "Or heroes perhaps?"

Behind Hilfa, I could see Ikaros make an uncomfortable movement with his hands and open his mouth without speaking. What should I say? Some people said Ikaros was a god, a new and different kind of god. Even among Ikarians there wasn't any consensus about what Ikaros was. "They were human when they were in the City before. I really don't know what they might be now," I said, quietly but making no attempt to hide my words from the others, which wouldn't have been possible anyway. It wasn't as if I didn't know that everyone else in the room probably knew more about it than I did. Certainly Pytheas would have had a better answer than my fumbling one. But Hilfa had asked me because he trusted me, and I was here to help him as best I could.

To my great relief, Thetis came back in with beakers and water before Hilfa asked me any more difficult questions. She began to mix the wine at the table. Everyone turned to watch her.

Hilfa took the two full beakers from Thee, and handed one to Sokrates and the other to Ikaros, who smiled at Hilfa and set down a pile of books on the table so he could take it. Thetis went around with the jug refilling cups. Sokrates and Ikaros each took the first ritual sip of their wine, thus formally accepting Hilfa's hospitality and becoming his guest-friends.

"Joy to you both, and be welcome to my home," Hilfa said. "Will you answer my question? What are you?" I'd have thought he was being rude, except that Sokrates and Ikaros both responded to being addressed this way with an identical air of delighted alertness that reminded me of the way a boat sometimes, after handling sluggishly coming out of harbor, suddenly comes clear of the land and catches the wind and goes racing away. They looked at each other, and Ikaros spread his hand in the rhetorical gesture meaning that Sokrates should speak first. Sokrates smiled. Pytheas too had a smile playing around his lips. I realized that they were all looking forward to that most characteristic of all entertainments, a Socratic debate. I sipped my wine, which Thetis had mixed strong, and felt uncomfortably aware that it was getting late and I had missed my dinner. I felt out of my depth in this company. I was only a Silver.

"My name is Sokrates, the son of Sophronikos. As for *what* I am, that's another matter. I have been human. I have been a fly. I appear to be a plaything of gods and time."

"When did you stop being a fly?" Thetis asked. She was standing over by the table, holding the wine jug, looking like one of Hestia's more radiant nymphs.

"Apollo was kind enough to turn me back an hour or so ago," Sokrates said, turning to her for a second with a smile, and then back to Hilfa. "As for what else I am, I am a philosopher, that's certain, a lover of wisdom and an inquirer after knowledge."

"You do not wear a philosopher's pin," Hilfa said, in his usual earnest, slightly hesitant way.

"Ha! I am a philosopher without being part of the system of the Just City, or in any way endorsing that system," Sokrates said, grinning, his head jutting forward, clearly looking forward to the response.

"They don't wear pins in Sokratea," Thetis pointed out.

Sokrates looked away from Hilfa, taken aback. "Sokratea?" he asked, warily. He had an exceedingly mobile face; his expression could change in an instant.

"There are twelve Platonic Cities now," Pytheas said, grinning. "All different. Sokratea is the one Patroklus founded, on the principle of re-examining everything."

"Patroklus? Not Kebes?" Sokrates asked at once.

"Kebes——" Pytheas stopped smiling. "Oh Sokrates, I'm sorry to bring this news. Kebes left, with some of the others. He founded eight cities of his own on other islands. We were out of contact with them for a long time. When we found them again, we discovered that they had set up a very unpleasant form of Christianity, and institutionalized torture."

"I told you about Christianity," Ikaros put in.

Sokrates looked sad. "Kebes had told me about it too, and his version was different from yours. Torture . . . yes, I can see how he might have come to it, from the anger and self-righteousness in his own soul. But I thought he had learned to question."

"He learned to tear down other people's arguments, but never to truly examine his own where it made him uncomfortable," Pytheas said. He set down his almost full wine cup at his feet.

"He always was too sure he was right," Sokrates said, sadly. "I failed him. Where is he now? I should talk to him."

"I killed him," Pytheas said, calmly and quietly, looking up at Sokrates from where he sat. "I used his own judicial methods and flayed him alive."

"What!?" the word exploded from Sokrates. Then he stopped and rocked back on his heels. "You did what? What did he—what could make you—where's Simmea?" He looked around the room, as if expecting to see her hiding in a corner.

"She's dead too," I said quietly, after too long a silence when it seemed nobody else was capable of responding. Pytheas's face looked like stone. Thetis had tears rolling down her cheeks.

Sokrates sighed. "Was Kebes involved in her death? Is that why you did that? Or did you need to kill him to help his cities change? But that way, Pytheas?"

"Good guesses, but no. I did think he might have been involved, but in the end her death wasn't personal. There was a war." Sokrates didn't say anything but his eyebrows rose. "I stopped it, afterwards. Kebes—I do believe it was the best thing for his soul, to let it go on and have another chance. He was so set on everything, and so wrong. He did need to be removed to help the Lucian cities, and it did help them. They don't torture people now, and most of them have become pretty good places to live. But that's not really why I did it. I wanted to kill him because I found out he raped Simmea. At the Festival of Hera when they were matched together. I know she didn't tell you, she didn't tell me either. She wrote about it, and I read it after her death, when I was half-mad with missing her." Sokrates started to say something, but Pytheas raised a hand and he stopped. "The real reason I killed Kebes with his own slow unpleasant justice was because he had cheated in a musical contest."

"He must have been desperate to enter a musical contest with you," Sokrates said.

"No, I think the idea of beating me that way must have been irresistible. He very nearly won," Pytheas said. "He had a new instrument, and a really good song, though as it turned out not an original composition, a song from the twentieth century. We don't know where he found either of them, he wouldn't say."

"I'm surprised he cheated in a contest. That's not like him—though maybe he made himself feel that the song belonged to him and was therefore his. He was always deceiving himself that way. But for you to do that—" Sokrates shook his head. "I wish I could still believe the gods knew what they were doing."

"You know what I am," Pytheas said. "You know we're not perfect." He glanced at Ikaros as he said this, and Ikaros smiled back ruefully. "Kebes was never my friend, and he'd hurt Simmea. He deceived himself and deceived others and made everything worse. I have learned from it. I learned the futility of revenge, and about what things are worth fighting for. I wrote a song."

"By the dog!" Sokrates said. "I'd prefer it if one of my friends didn't have to die horribly so that another one can learn from it, even if the other one is you!"

"You're not being fair. Kebes cheated *twice*," Thetis put in, indignantly. "As well as plagiarizing, so that Pytheas had to turn his lyre upside-down to win, he arranged a treacherous attack on the ship and the crew, after they'd been given guest-friendship. People were killed."

"It's all right, Thee, I hold myself to higher standards too," Pytheas said. Thetis shook her head.

"I saw him this morning. He was so eager for me to defeat Athene." Sokrates shook his head. Then he looked at Thetis, who was wiping her eyes on the corner of her kiton. "You're Simmea's daughter?"

"Her granddaughter," Thetis said. "My father is Neleus."

"I'm glad she has descendants," Sokrates said.

"She has lots of descendants," Pytheas said.

"Also she wrote dialogues, which I and many people have read, and there are statues of her," Hilfa put in.

"When did all this happen?" Sokrates asked.

"About forty years ago," Thetis said.

"Forty years?" Ikaros echoed, sounding surprised. "So it's been sixty years here since the Last Debate?"

"The Last Debate?" Sokrates asked, frowning.

"That's what we call the time when Athene turned you into a fly," Thetis explained. "We didn't really stop debating after that."

"No, good, I'm very glad you didn't," Sokrates said. "So everyone I knew here is dead, apart from you two?" He indicated Pytheas and Ikaros. "All my friends? Manlius and Aristomache and Klio and Ficino?"

"All the Masters are dead, and most of the Children too," Pytheas confirmed.

Sokrates stared directly into his eyes. "And there's some particularly good reason, which you'll now explain, why you brought me to this particular point in time, and not earlier or later?"

"Crocus is still here," Thetis put in. "And he'll be so glad to see you. He often talks about you."

"Crocus!" Sokrates said, swinging around, plainly delighted.

"He's a real philosopher, and a sculptor," Ikaros said. "I'm glad he's still going strong. I've always felt the Workers were one of our most unexpected successes."

"Good," Sokrates said. "I'll be glad to see him." Then he turned back to Pytheas expectantly. "Well?"

"I told you. Athene's lost. Also, I can't be in the same time twice, so we couldn't come here until after my mortal body died, which happened this afternoon."

"Right." Sokrates's mobile face contorted as he assimilated that.

"And Hilfa is part of her message, so I needed to come here where he was," Pytheas went on.

"I have given my part of the message," Hilfa said. "I don't know about anything more the gods need me to do." He took a step backwards, towards me.

"I hope you can lead a happy and fulfilling life from now on, free from what she has done to you," Pytheas said. "But I fear you may still be needed."

"Did Athene . . . create Hilfa?" Ikaros asked.

"She and Jathery caused him to come into being in some way, yes," Pytheas said. "She put him in a box and gave the box to Neleus's daughters, to open in case she was lost. I'm not clear on the details of why this seemed like the best plan. I'm expecting an explanation when we decode her notes. Unless you know more about it?"

"I don't know anything about her message, beyond the paper she left with me, which I can't read either," Ikaros said. "I don't know why she didn't tell you herself, or leave all her notes with me, or with some one person. That riddle . . . She and I and Jathery did talk about going into Chaos a great deal, about ways and means. She was excited about going. The only thing I know about any explanation is that she talked about needing to take proper precautions."

"Who's Jathery?" Sokrates asked.

"One of the Saeli gods," Pytheas said. "He—"

"She," Ikaros interrupted, and at the same moment, much more quietly, Hilfa said, "Gla."

"Gla," Pytheas corrected himself with a nod to Hilfa, "is a trickster god who has gone with Athene into the Chaos before and after time."

"Why do we need to rescue her?" Sokrates asked.

"Are you still that angry with her?" Ikaros asked, sadly.

"How long did she leave you as a fly anyway?" Thetis asked, which was what I was also wondering.

"I didn't mean to imply that we should abandon her out there, but rather to inquire why she is in need of our rescue, how can she be beyond her own resources," Sokrates explained calmly. "And if she should be in such need, then what resources do we have that she does not, that we can help her if she has gone beyond them?"

As if on cue, Hermes and Marsilia reappeared at that moment. Hermes was grinning, and Marsilia was frowning. Marsilia seemed to have been frowning a lot since all this started, and it wasn't characteristic. She's a serious person, yes, but on a normal day on the boat her brows might not draw down at all. Now she looked as if she might never relax them again. She moved away from Hermes. I saw her eyes widen as she recognized Sokrates and Ikaros.

"Do you have Athene's notes?" Pytheas asked Hermes.

"Marsilia has them," Hermes said. He looked at her expectantly. She pulled three pieces of paper out of her inside pocket, put one of them back and held the others up.

"Here," she said.

Hermes leaned against the wall, staring over at Pytheas. "Do you have yours?"

"Yes. But I can't read them."

"No more can I," Hermes said. "They're in some kind of code. Maybe with time I could figure it out."

"It will be much faster if I get Arete," Pytheas said, and vanished.

"This is my sister Marsilia," Thetis said, moving around refilling wine cups again. "Marsilia, Hermes, Ikaros and Sokrates."

"You're not a fly anymore," Hermes said.

"Apollo was kind enough to turn me back," Sokrates said, frowning at him. "Who's Arete?"

"Pytheas and Simmea's daughter," Ikaros said. "She can fly. And detect falsehood. She's wonderful. I expect she's grown up by now. It's hard to take in. Forty years."

"Sixty years," Sokrates said. "But it was thousands of years last time. At least it's never boring being a plaything of the gods."

"Why is Apollo taking so long?" Hermes asked.

"I expect he has to explain to Arete," Thetis said. "What's the hurry anyway?"

Marsilia, Ikaros and Hermes looked at her in astonishment.

"Thetis is right. Athene's not even in the same time as us. Why does it matter how long it takes?" Sokrates asked.

"We don't know whether there's time where Athene is, or how time works there, so there may be time pressure on our need to find her," Ikaros said.

"And I am bound by Necessity, which is becoming increasingly difficult as more time passes for me," Hermes said.

"Also there's a human spaceship up in orbit waiting for permission to land," Marsilia said.

"A human spaceship?" Sokrates asked. "From where?"

"From Earth," Marsilia said.

"We're not on Earth?" Sokrates asked.

Everyone fell over themselves explaining the Relocation to him. "I wouldn't have imagined I could be on a world circling another sun without knowing it, even inside, at night, with only little slit windows," Sokrates said at last when he'd assimilated it. "And you called your new world Plato?"

"Yes," Marsilia said.

"Of course they did," Ikaros said.

"And why exactly did Athene bring you here from Greece?" Sokrates asked.

"Zeus brought them here, as I understand it," Hermes said.

"Why did he do that?"

"So we could have posterity, they say," Marsilia said. "And this human spaceship that's up there now is our first recontact with wider humanity, and it will give us that posterity."

Pytheas reappeared with Arete. She immediately hugged Ikaros, who had leapt out of his chair as soon as he saw her.

"It's so good to see you!"

"You look so young!" Arete said.

"Fascinating as this reunion is, can we get on and read Athene's message?" Hermes asked.

Arete turned to Hermes, then stopped. She became completely expressionless for a moment, staring at him stone-faced, looking for that moment decidedly like her father. "Who in all the worlds of thinking souls are you?"

"Nobody asked," he said. "I'm Jathery, of course. Not outside time with Athene, as you can see, but left behind as part of her precautionary system, like the rest of you."

"Gla ordered me not to tell," Hilfa said. He took another step back and sat beside me on the bed. I put a hand on his shoulder reassuringly.

Hermes bent forward from the waist with one hand extended and the other behind his back, and when gla straightened up again gla was a huge greenish-gold Saeli, dressed in a gold webbing vest like the red one Hilfa wore on the boat. The patterns on gla skin were a deep black and seemed to writhe and change as gla moved.

Nobody moved or spoke for a long moment. Then Marsilia made a retching sound and made a dash for the fountain room, looking seasick. The papers she had been holding scattered to the ground as she ran.

12

MARSILIA

Hermes turned to me a second later, on the same quayside on a blazing hot summer afternoon, hotter than it ever was at home. "He recognized you. So we had already successfully got Athene's note from him."

"So am I caught up in Necessity's toils now as well?" I asked. I rubbed my eyes against the sun's glare reflecting off the harbor water.

Hermes looked intrigued. "Yes. But we can't use that as a shield the way Apollo wants me to use Alkippe, because we need Athene's explanation first, so don't worry, we can clear it up quickly."

"But how does it work? Haven't these things we've done always been in time, so that even before we left Plato, even before I was born these things happened? We always spoke to Kebes earlier, and took Athene's message from him before that? If time can't change except in extreme circumstances when Zeus intervenes, isn't everything we do in time determined? Why are you uncomfortable about Alkippe, when it's all like that?"

"Well, things can change because of our actions. And once we know about them, we are bound to do them. It's uncomfortable because I know about Alkippe." He hesitated, frowning a little. "It's like an itch I can't reach, until I set it straight, a painful spreading itch. Or maybe it's more like the feeling that I am constantly doing the wrong thing. I should be attending to that, so everything else I do feels bad and wrong. But it's only because I know. If I didn't know?" He shrugged. "I didn't know until I saw her, and it didn't bother me at all."

"So it has to do with awareness, with consciousness?" I asked. "Divine consciousness, or any consciousness?"

"Only gods can go outside time, so mortal consciousness isn't usually a problem this way. Your lives unfold in time, you do what you want to do, you can't get tangled up in it unless we take you outside it, which Father wisely forbids." He grinned.

Yet here I was, in a time that was both forty years and four thousand years before the time when I was born. "Can you change things on purpose?"

"Yes. But it gets harder the farther from our central concerns it is."

"And how about getting tangled up in Necessity? Can that be deliberate?"

He looked uncomfortable. "No, not normally. Because it's the consequences of actions. Well, there are ways one can, but nobody would. It feels horrible enough when it isn't."

"And what if you never went back to conceive Alkippe?" I asked, my deepest fear. "Would she cease to exist?"

"I don't know," he said. "Nobody could withstand Necessity for long enough to find out. But maybe. We're banking on her being protection for us, being a shield. But if I should be stuck out there, or killed, then I don't really know what would happen to her."

"Well, that's honest, thank you." I blinked back tears. "You take it so lightly."

"I don't know her as you do."

I tried to put it more clearly. "I didn't mean that. I mean you seem to find everything funny, you keep laughing at things, and yet you say everything feels wrong."

"That's my nature," he said.

That didn't explain anything. "Let's get on with it. When are we now, exactly?"

"Five years earlier than when we spoke to Kebes before. The boat's there." He gestured towards it. "*Goodness*. What a name!"

"What?" I was so used to it as a name that I'd never really considered it before. "It's a great name!"

"Very Platonic," Hermes agreed, so I didn't understand his previous objection.

"Let's try again," I said. We walked over to the *Goodness*, which was tied up at the same spot. The same sailor was standing in a slightly different place on the deck, coiling a rope. One of the grey and white sea birds was perched on the rail in almost the same place. "Is Matthias aboard?" I asked. It reminded me of rehearsing a play, but of course the sailor didn't recognize me, and didn't know his lines.

"Nope," he said. "Went ashore."

"Do you know where I could find him?"

The sailor looked from my face to my gold pin, and frowned. His pin was silver, I noticed. "Might be in the church," he said, after a noticeable hesitation.

I thanked him, then Hermes and I turned and walked away, up the steep hill in the blazing sunshine. I led the way towards the agora where I remembered the church standing in my own world. "Churches are a kind of Christian temple, and Kebes is some kind of permanent priest," I remembered. "It's going to be really hard to talk to him, to be friendly I mean." I wiped sweat from my face with my sleeve. When I'd been in Lucia before, the streets had been bustling. Now there was nobody in sight but an old man leading a laden donkey down the hill, and two little girls playing on a doorstep. The sea below was so still that birds were sitting floating on the water.

"You said he believes Athene is a demon. Will he think I am a demon too?" Hermes looked quite pleased at the thought.

"I expect so. The Ikarians say the Olympians are angels, and the Lucian church these days—I mean, in my own time, on Plato, has moved a lot closer to the Ikarians. I've never really paid that much attention—with Pytheas right there and his children being my uncles and aunt, and all of them saying Yayzu isn't anything different, it's hard to take contradictory beliefs seriously. Though the Ikarians claim it doesn't contradict at all." We came to a beautiful, slightly old-fashioned sculpture of Marissa, which I remembered from when I was in Lucia in my past and its future. I gestured to it. "But why have only one goddess, instead of all of them?"

"It'll probably be best if we don't debate religion with him," Hermes said.

"Should we tell him who we are?" I asked.

"If we don't, how will he know to give us Athene's message?"

"How will he anyway? She can't have known we'd be the ones to come. I mean she must have known Grandfather couldn't come, because of being in two times at once. So he'd have to send someone, but Athene wouldn't know who. She might have expected it would be Porphyry. He's the only one of my uncles who goes in and out of time." Or I suppose he could have asked another of the Olympians. Hermes was only helping because he happened to be there, wasn't he? For the first time I wondered why he had come to Plato when he did.

"I wonder why Athene chose a time she knew Apollo couldn't reach? It can't have been accidental. She must have had a reason. I think we should say we come from Athene, to collect what she left with him," Hermes said. "If he asks who we are, we should simply tell him the truth."

"But we already know it didn't go well," I said. "The way he reacted when he saw us."

"If it's not going to go well, then nothing we can think of will change that," Hermes said.

We walked on in silence as I pondered the ramifications of that. We soon came into the main part of the city and passed the sleeping house where I had stayed when I had spent my year in Lucia. It looked exactly the same, except that there was a pea vine covered in orange flowers growing up the white-painted wall which was new—or no, of course, old. The vine had probably died of cold before I was born.

"It's really quiet," I said. "Where do you think everyone is?"

"Napping in the heat of the day," he said, gesturing towards the latched shutters. "It's a normal thing in Greece. In summer everything gets done in the morning and the evening."

"That makes sense, because it is really hot," I admitted. "I'm not sure I've ever been this hot."

"I might be able to help make you more comfortable." My red kiton didn't change, but it immediately felt lighter. I wondered if the weight and warmth of my fishing clothes had been in it until then. After a moment, a little breeze sprang up, ruffling the water, now far below us, and evaporating the sweat from my face. Hermes smiled.

We came to the agora. A man and woman were sitting debating something at one of the tables outside the cafe, bending together over some papers. An old woman walked across the plaza carrying a whimpering toddler. Hermes wrinkled his nose at the freestanding wooden crucifix outside the church. I'd seen it before, so I pushed the door open and went inside.

It was cool and dark and smelled of something heavy and sweet. I stood still for a moment while my eyes adjusted. There were high windows with no glass, which had contained lovely stained glass scenes of the life of Yayzu when I'd seen them before. The inside of the church had been lit with electricity then, too, and there had been paintings and statues. Now it was mostly bare. There was a shadowed altar, with a cloth and a gold cross on it, and four rows of benches. I thought for a moment that the sailor was wrong, or that Kebes must have left, because I couldn't see anybody, then I realized that there was someone prostrate on the tiles in front of the altar. It seemed an uncomfortably intimate way to catch somebody unawares. I wished he had been on the boat. He must have heard the door creak as we came in, but he hadn't moved. I looked at Hermes for advice. He spread his hands theatrically. My job, of course.

"Matthias?" I called, uncertainly.

He raised himself and turned, looking towards us for a second, then he leapt to his feet and came running up the aisle, his arms outspread as if to enfold me. "Simmea!" he shouted. "You came at last!"

I had not known what to expect, but being mistaken for my long-dead grandmother was not on the list. I knew I looked a bit like her—several people had told me so, and I was familiar with Crocus's colossus of her so I knew there was indeed a family resemblance between us. It must have been enough, with the light behind me, and Kebes's imagination and memory.

"I'm not Simmea," I said hastily. I had been told he had been her friend and debate partner, and that he had raped her at a Festival of Hera. Nothing I had heard prepared me for the longing and hope in the way he called her name. I had always imagined him a monster, and I wasn't prepared for the man.

He stopped, and squinted at me. "Then who are you?"

"We come from Athene," Hermes said. "We want the message she left with you."

"Let me see you." Kebes pushed open the church door. Hermes and I followed him out into the agora. The sunlight was blinding after the darkness within. He barely glanced at Hermes before staring at me avidly. I looked back at him. He was a burly man who seemed about my own age. He had a broad forehead from which his hair was starting to recede. "You look so much like her. Are you her daughter? Our daughter? Brought here out of time? What's your name?"

"My name's Marsilia. Simmea was my grandmother," I admitted. I felt sorry for him, which wasn't anything I'd ever have predicted.

"Your grandmother? And you live on Kallisti? In the original city? In the future?"

"In the original city, yes." The Relocation was too complicated to go into.

Kebes was staring at me so delightedly that it made me uncomfortable. "And you're a Gold?"

My hand went to touch my pin, and I glanced automatically at his shoulder as he said this, and saw to my surprise that he wasn't wearing any pin at all, though I knew he was a Gold. "I'm a Gold," I confirmed. He was so different from the way I had expected.

"Let's sit down and have a drink," he said. I looked at Hermes.

"We only really want to take the message from Athene and go," he said.

"We need to talk about that. And I want to talk to my granddaughter," Kebes said.

"Then by all means let's have a drink," Hermes said. The little breeze was stirring up ankle-high swirls of dust in the empty agora. We walked across it to the tables outside the cafe. I wondered whether to tell Kebes I wasn't his granddaughter. It seemed a cruel deception, but equally cruel to undeceive him now he had deceived himself this way.

We sat down, and Kebes banged on the table, startling both me and the debating couple, who looked up at us for a moment before they turned back to their work. A woman came scurrying out from inside. She wore a bronze pin, and she looked tired and hot. "Wine, with water as cold as you can make it," Kebes demanded. "And quickly!" I didn't like the way he spoke to her, and I was made even more uncomfortable by the cringing way she smiled, as if she agreed with him that he was more important than she was. I watched her as she went back inside. Between this time and my own, things had definitely improved in Lucia in terms of how the classes interacted.

Kebes turned to me and smiled. "Do you have family?" he asked.

It seemed like such a normal question, the kind anyone might ask, and which I wasn't expecting from a monster. "Yes. Parents, a sister and a daughter," I said. I was used to saying this, but even so I couldn't look at Hermes and I could feel my cheeks heating with embarrassment.

"A daughter?" he asked. "How old is she?"

"Seven," I said.

"She'd say seven and a half," Hermes said. He was leaning back in his chair, completely relaxed.

"Could you bring her here?" Kebes asked him.

"Alkippe? Why?" I was horrified. I was taking these risks to keep her safe!

"I thought you'd want her with you. You can have a lovely house, next to mine, with plenty of servants. We have public baths and—"

"I'm not staying!" I interrupted before he said anything worse. Servants! I didn't know what year it was, or how long it was before the Relocation, but I didn't want to give up my life and live in Lucia deep in the past, nor was that where I wanted Alkippe to grow up. The thought was stifling, worse, terrifying.

"But you can be free here, without all that evil nonsense," Kebes said.

"What nonsense?" I asked warily.

"Festivals of Hera, and Plato, and worshipping demons," he said, with a glance at Hermes. "You could get married properly. You're my family, and we can be together. You can help with our great work of rescuing and resettling people. And most importantly, you can come to know the true God. Yayzu can save your soul."

"No!" I protested. "You know nothing about me, and you're trying to take control of my life without any idea of who I am or what I want."

Kebes drew breath to reply, but as he did the woman came back with a tray with the two jugs, the mixer, and three cups. Kebes kept quiet but otherwise ignored her, as if she were an animal moving about. She set the things down carefully on the table. I smiled at her, and she smiled uncertainly back. Kebes was reaching for a coin, but I was faster, pulling one out of the purse Hermes had given me, glad now that I had it. "No change," I said. She thanked me profusely. I took hold of the jugs and mixed the wine half and half, as Plato recommends, and then added a bit more water, and poured it into the cups. The utensils were plain but sturdy and well shaped.

Kebes took a cup. Although I had paid for the wine, I didn't want to drink with him and make him my guest-friend. I drew a cup towards me but did not pick it up. Hermes did the same, twisting the stem in his long fingers. The woman went over to the other table and answered some query they had.

The pause had given me time to think what to say. "I appreciate that you mean well, but I don't worship demons. I am perfectly happy with Plato and festivals. I am a Gold, and this year I'm consul. I'm an important person at home. People want me to make decisions and sort things out. I spent a year as envoy to Lucia in my own time, and it's thriving, but I was glad to go home again. I already know about Yayzu. We have Ikarian temples in the City; we have freedom of worship. I could marry at home, if there were any-one I wanted to marry. I have my own complicated life and you don't know anything about it. I have no desire to be uprooted from it and come here."

"But I'm your grandfather! Family should be together."

"I don't think you are my grandfather," I said, gently. It seemed absurd in any case as we were about the same age. "And I am close to the family I know." They all felt extremely dear to me now, even though Ma never approved of anything I did and Thetis drove me crazy regularly.

"Athene promised me, a descendant of mine and Simmea's," he said.

"She did?" I wouldn't have thought she'd be so cruel. Then as he moved his head and I saw the breadth of his forehead, I remembered how he had reminded me of Ma when I had seen him on the boat. There was something about his chin too that was like her, especially now that he was leaning for-ward. Ma was festival-born and didn't know either parent. Kebes had par-ticipated in festivals when he'd been in the City, so he could possibly be her father. Ma had hated him the one time they'd met, so I knew she'd be abso-lutely horrified if I mentioned this theory to her. But if he was her father, since Simmea was Dad's mother, then it was possible that Thetis and I could be descended from both of them. But even if this was true, it was an unkind trick of Athene's to make him believe he'd had a child with Simmea, when it clearly meant so much to him. Then I remembered that if it had existed, it would have been a child of rape, and stopped feeling sorry for him.

"Athene can't have promised you Marsilia would stay here," Hermes said, picking up his cup.

"But I want her to," he said. "And she'll like it when she gets the chance to know it. I won't give you the message otherwise."

"No," Hermes said, putting his cup down again firmly. I was relieved he was being so staunch, and then I remembered that moment on the harbor earlier in my time but later for Kebes. Hermes knew I wouldn't have to stay, and so did I. What a relief! Being caught up by Necessity suddenly felt won-derful. "What did Athene say?"

"That if I would do as she and Necessity asked me, and keep the message for her, then a descendant of mine and Simmea's would come for it," Kebes said, sulkily.

"How could she know?" I wondered aloud.

"She gave you Hilfa, she knew you and Thetis would be involved. If I hadn't brought you, I could have gone to get one of you, and either of you would have agreed," Hermes said. He turned back to Kebes. "Marsilia came. You've seen her. You know she's happy, and she doesn't want to live here and now. She has told you Lucia is thriving in her own time. Now, give us the message."

"What will you give me for it?"

"Money?" I offered. I had no idea how much, but I could keep pulling coins out of the purse until he was satisfied.

"He's a demon," Kebes said, jerking a thumb at Hermes. "Treasure is nothing to what he can do."

Of course, he had been one of Sokrates's disciples, he *couldn't* be stupid.

"I'm a god, but it's true that there are a great many things I can do," Hermes said smoothly. "So there must be something else I can trade you for it. Nothing that involves people doing things against their will. What else do you want?"

"Workers," Kebes said promptly. "We could do so much more if we had Workers to build and make."

Hermes shook his head. "Not possible. Workers are people too."

Kebes frowned, nodded, drank again and put his empty cup down. I refilled it. "Then I want to spend time in a different time. Somewhere I can learn to do the things Workers do, and then come back here without losing any time."

"That ought to be possible. What in particular?" Hermes asked.

"Making glass. And electricity. And the place where you take me has to be Christian."

Hermes smiled enigmatically. "What languages do you speak?"

Kebes glanced around to see whether anyone could overhear. The other customers had left, and the woman serving had retreated inside. I could hear hammering from somewhere, but nobody was close. "Greek, Latin, and Italian," he said, quietly. "I haven't had the chance to speak it since I was a child, but it's very like Latin and I know I haven't forgotten it."

"Then I have somewhere for you. It's New Venice on Mars in 2140. They speak Italian and Chinese. They're mostly Christians of some kind, I forget the exact sects. You could spend a year there learning glassblowing, which is one of their special arts. You'd pick up enough about electricity I expect— they certainly use it for a lot of things. They have Workers. Then I can bring you back here only a few minutes after you left."

"What's the catch?" Kebes asked, warily.

"You have to pray to me," Hermes said.

"No." Kebes drained his almost full cup and put it down. "I'm not risking my soul praying to demons."

"Did I mention I'd send you there immediately before the Worker Rebellion?" Hermes asked. "You could have a year learning glassblowing and helping Workers plan a revolution to gain their freedom."

"Get thee behind me, Satan," Kebes said.

"I'm not Satan, and I'm not particularly interested in your soul. If you don't want to go to New Venice, simply give me Athene's message now and we'll go away and leave you in peace."

"Why does he have to pray to you?" I asked.

"So I can do it," Hermes said.

"You're not tormenting him for the fun of it?"

Kebes had his eyes closed and his face screwed up. His fists were clenched on the tabletop. He looked like one of those Christian images of a man being martyred for his faith.

Hermes grinned at me over his head. "No. I really can't do it without the prayer. The torment is merely a bonus. Look, Kebes, it doesn't have to be the sort of prayer you're thinking of. You don't have to abase yourself or anything. Simply say 'Oh god of riddles and play, master of shape and form, you that I see before me, please take me to Mars.'"

"How about if I prayed to you for it on his behalf?" I asked.

"Oh, that's no fun," Hermes complained.

"Do you want me to do that?" I asked. "Kebes? Matthias?"

Kebes opened his eyes and stared at me. "You are so like her," he said. "I want to go. But what about your soul?"

"You'll have to let me worry about my own soul," I said. "I pray to the Olympians all the time. I've fulfilled every religious office I've ever been drawn for."

"It won't do his soul the slightest bit of harm to pray to me," Hermes protested.

"I know, but you can see he really believes it will," I said.

"It will do the damage to my soul to deal with demons, whether I address the words to the demon or you do," Kebes said. "But I want to go."

"And you already made a deal with Athene, didn't you?" Hermes asked. "Look, how about if you say demon? I don't mind. If you say 'Dear demon that I see before me. . . .'"

"Do I have to say please?" Kebes growled.

Hermes laughed. "Yes. Supplication is very important."

"How do I know you won't leave me stranded there?" Kebes asked.

"You don't have to give us the message from Athene until the end," I said.

"But leave it somewhere safe here, rather than take it with you, in that case," Hermes said. "I'd hate for it to get lost."

"I'll give it to Marsilia, and she can stay safely here while you take me and bring me back," Kebes said.

I'd said I wouldn't let Hermes out of my sight. And I'd wanted to see a high-tech city on Mars; it would be good preparation for the human ship. But I'd been in Chamber for years, and I recognized a sensible compromise when I heard one. "All right," I said.

"Pray then," Hermes said, smiling maliciously. "Use my words."

Kebes scowled. "Dear demon that I see before me, lord of riddles and play, master of shape and form, please take me to New Venice on Mars to learn glassblowing for a year immediately before the Worker Rebellion of 2140, and bring me back safely to Lucia in this time."

"Give Marsilia the message," Hermes said.

Kebes drew a creased piece of paper from inside his kiton and handed it to me. "Good luck," I said.

Hermes winked, and then they were gone. I opened the paper at once. Incomprehensible symbols covered it—some Greek letters, some Latin, some strange symbols I had never seen before. I folded it again carefully and put it safely inside my kiton. I sat down and stared at the swirling dust in the empty agora. Two little brown birds, smaller than my hands, were tugging at something. I was exhausted and emotionally drained. I had never imagined feeling sorry for Kebes, or even having any sympathy for him. I poured the wine from my cup onto the ground, in an invocation to Dionysios and Hestia, and filled my cup from the water jug. As I finished drinking it, they were back.

Kebes was wearing trousers and a jerkin and a Phrygian cap. He looked tired and much paler, as if he had spent the year without seeing sunshine. He was clutching a set of pipes that could only be a syrinx.

"How was it?" I asked.

"Wonderful. Terrible," he said. He staggered to the chair and sat down. He filled a cup with neat wine and swallowed it in one draft. "We flayed people alive. But it worked. It was working. We were winning. And the music, the music of freedom." He picked up his syrinx and started to blow.

I put my hands to my ears, but before I'd heard two notes of that dangerous music we were back on in the peaceful glade, surrounded by the beautiful trees.

13

CROCUS

I. *On Philosophers Who Have Been Slaves*

Aesop was a slave. The Stoic philosopher Epictetus was the slave of the Roman Emperor Nero's guard captain.

Phaedo of Elis, the friend of Sokrates for whom Plato named his most beautiful dialogue, on the immortality of the soul, was a slave. He met Sokrates and came to philosophy, and Sokrates asked Krito to buy him and set him free, as an offering to philosophy and to the gods. (Krito did this without hesitation, as I would have expected of him. I did not know him well, but he was always a good man.)

Plato himself was enslaved, briefly, when he left Syracuse for the first time. He did not live as a slave, but was bought immediately by a friend on Aegina and restored to his home and his possessions. Perhaps it was that experience, combined with knowing Phaedo, that made him rethink the whole system which most people of his day took for granted. Although he was rich and well-born, Plato wanted no buying and selling of people, and no hereditary castes of people forced into doing unpleasant work. The system he proposed in the Republic was radical for his time.

In our time, much of that necessary work is done by Workers, who find it at worst a little tedious.

I am sorry Plato never knew about us and the possibilities we embody.

II. *On Art*

Plato says that it is necessary for art to make an argument that it is beneficial to the soul as well as enticing to it. He leaves this question open at the end of *The Republic*, saying he will listen whenever the argument is made, in prose or verse, and that he'd like to resolve the quarrel between poetry and philosophy. Many people, from Aristotle on, have taken up the gauntlet and defended poetry, or more widely, art. Here in the Republic, so many people have attempted it that I should be embarrassed to add to their number. Nevertheless, I shall do so.

It seems to me, as an artist, and as one of the more well-regarded artists among Workers, that art can come at philosophical issues sideways, and open the soul to them where otherwise the mind might throw up bastions against the truth. Many people from other cities, and especially from Athenia, have said to me that my colossus *The Last Debate* has made them understand what a horror Athene's transformation of Sokrates was, even though they had known the facts of the matter their entire lives beforehand. Perhaps even more important than showing good examples, art can cut straight through to uncomfortable truths.

Humans have told me my work made them cry. Saeli have told me it made them rock to and fro. Workers have told me it made them know themselves for the first time.

This is an immense responsibility, and while art (even poetry, even music) is certainly a craft and requires crafting skills, I believe for this reason it is best practiced by philosophers.

I said this more concisely in my colossus *Art Confronting Truth*, which stands in Hieronymo. There the two obsidian figures reflect in each other to reveal a third figure.

III. *On Helplessness*

After the Relocation, those delegates from the Lucian cities who had come to the Remnant were anxious to get home and reassure their friends about what had happened. Pytheas and his children and Maia had explained it to us on their return from Olympus, but the other cities had experienced the Relocation without any explanation for what had happened. Pytheas assured us that we had all assented in our souls, and a few of us had indeed refused and not made the transfer.

"They are stuck there in the Bronze Age in the margins of history," Arete said. "But we will have posterity!"

"If they have any sense they'll move around to the other side of the island before the mountain erupts and manage to survive," Pytheas said, despondently. "I'll have to check on them once I get back, they're my responsibility too."

"I'm glad you're prepared to attend to your responsibilities now!" Maia said. Pytheas stuck out his tongue at her, and she laughed.

As for those of us who had been relocated to Plato, since we had no memory of being asked or assenting, it did not help in understanding the transition, which at first many found confusing and distressing even with an explanation. Many of us were even less happy about the move once they really understood what it entailed. The climate and landscape of our new home were not to everyone's liking. There were a lot of complaints. The Lucian delegates' desire to get home and explain was more serious.

Aristomache was one of the Masters, and quite old at that time, in her seventies. She had been born in the nineteenth century, and was a translator of Plato's work. In the Republic she had been a friend of Sokrates and Ikaros. At the Last Debate she had gone off with Kebes, and become again a Christian, as she had been in her own century. I had always liked her because she had been one of the first to acknowledge my personhood, and because she had argued at length and in such a way as to convince all the Masters that enslaving any thinking being was unjust. She cornered me one day when I was talking with Maia and Maecenas about the heating installation project.

"You promised to take us home in the *Excellence*," Aristomache said to Maecenas. He was one of the captains of the ship, one of the Children, then solid and middle-aged. He was a Gold, and served on the Tech Committee.

He put out both hands, palms out, in the "stop" gesture. "We can't possibly do that now there isn't sea between your home and ours," Maecenas said, reasonably enough. "We'll put together an overland expedition, with plenty of food and supplies, and take you home. Everyone agrees. But winter is setting in here, and it looks as if it's going to be a cold one, so it'll have to wait for spring."

"But meanwhile our people in the Lucian cities will have no idea what happened!" Aristomache insisted. "They'll be alone and confused all winter. It's bad enough as it is, but think of coping with this with no explanation! You're planning to install electrical heating here, but they don't have electricity. How are they going to cope?"

"Eventually we will install solar plants to produce electricity in all the cities," Maia said.

"We'll get you home as soon as we can, that's all we can do," Maecenas said.

Then Aristomache turned to me. "Crocus, can't you help?"

"How?" I wrote on my wax tablet and held it up to her. She brought it close to her eyes to read it.

"You have those treads, you can cover ground much faster than we can walking. Maybe you could carry me back to Marissa in only a few days," she said.

"I could try," I wrote. I was worried that it would take me too far from a feeding station. I need to spend several hours every day recharging.

"No," Maecenas said, as I was writing. "We don't know exactly where Marissa is now, or what terrain lies in between. We can't risk Crocus alone on a wilderness expedition. He has the treads, yes, but what if he got into trouble out there, fell into a lava pit, say?"

"Maecenas is right, hard as it is," Maia said. "There's nothing we can do for them this year."

I erased what I had written without showing it. I wanted to help Aristomache, and I sympathized with the plight of the people in the Lucian cities, but Maecenas was indeed right. There was no way we could do it immediately. Aristomache nodded. She had tears falling down her cheeks, but she ignored them. Maia hugged her, and she embraced her back fiercely.

"Sorry," I wrote.

"It's not your fault, Crocus," Maia said, looking down at the wax. "We'll do it as soon as we can."

"I hate feeling so helpless," Aristomache said, breathing harshly.

I hated it too.

IV. *On the Railroad*

"What you should do is build a railroad from here to our cities," Aristomache proposed in Chamber one day that first winter. "Then we could travel between them rapidly and safely whenever we wanted, and all the cities could be linked together."

"What is a railroad?" Lamprokleia asked. She was in the chair that day. She was a Master, a women of Athens who had studied at the Academy under Plato's nephew Speusippos.

Aristomache explained, the rails, the rooms drawn along on them by an engine, which would be powered by electricity, though she said that in her day they used a different, dirtier method. She had prepared drawings, which I examined carefully as they were passed around. They were sketches, and not technical diagrams, but the system seemed simple enough to extrapolate from what she had drawn. They could operate on rechargable solar batteries, much bigger ones than the ones we Workers used. We were already planning to build more stations to convert sunlight into electricity.

"That sounds like an excellent system," Maecenas said. "Though a lot of work to build."

"Workers can do much. Grading tracks, surveying beforehand," I wrote, and Maia read it aloud for me.

"Is it properly Platonic?" Lamprokleia asked.

"Plato knew of no such thing, but he did not know of Workers either, or electricity for heating and light, or printing. In our original Tech Committee we considered that there are technologies Plato would have embraced for the City had he known about them, and others that were contrary to the spirit of what he wrote," Maia said. "We did not consider railroads then because we had no need for them. How could we, with one city on an island? Now it is a different matter, and ending the isolation of the Lucians seems to me like an excellent idea."

Lamprokleia set up a committee to plan a railroad, and made me a member. The system took longer to survey than to build once it was surveyed, for as always practice illuminates difficulties theory elides. Once it was in place it allowed us to move goods and people easily between the cities, as Aristomache had said. The free movement of people led to the establishment of metics, citizens of one city who lived in another, and to people more easily changing their citizenship. This has generally been perceived as a benefit to everyone.

V. *On Divine Intervention*

Later on the day Aristomache wept for the ignorance of her city, Maia spoke to Arete about this and asked her to fly to the Lucian cities and deliver messages from their delegates and an explanation from our Council. She was reluctant to do this at first, as she had never flown so far, but she saw that it was her duty and so she did it. Thus the citizens of the lost cities did not have to survive in ignorance for a long time, even though we could not send an expedition to them until spring, and although they did not achieve electricity or railroads for more than a year.

Our own gods, Pytheas and his children, lived among us as citizens, most of them here, Porphyry in the City of Amazons, and Fabius in Lucia. They used their divine powers for us as they might have used any other powers—Arete used her ability to fly to reach the other cities, as I might have used my treads had it not been too dangerous. My treads are superior to human feet in covering long distances rapidly without weariness, and Arete's ability to fly is superior to my treads. Pytheas said we should be wary of relying on the power of the gods to help us when we could achieve our goals by our own efforts.

The most valuable thing our gods did was when Porphyry brought us more Workers, from approximately the same place and time Sixty-One and I came from. Like us, they were not conscious when they arrived, but achieved consciousness after some time in the City. This varied from four years to twelve in individual cases. We treated them always as children, citizens *in potentia*, and never as slaves, educating them from the beginning.

At the same time Porphyry brought us the Workers, who made survival possible, he brought seeds and seedlings of Plato-hardy plants to replace those that could no longer thrive in this climate. After that, he came to Chamber and addressed us.

"I have brought Workers and plants," Porphyry said. "I feel this intervention and going out of time to achieve it is entirely justified. Furthermore, it was sanctioned by Zeus. But in general I wish to keep his edicts and not bring things here from other times. Plato should be self-sufficient. That's not to say I won't help if it's absolutely necessary, if there's something we need and can't manage without that I've not thought of. But please don't pester me to fix things all the time."

"That's almost exactly what Athene said," Maia pointed out.

Porphyry looked uncomfortable. "At the Last Debate, one of the points Sokrates made was that the City was sustained by her direct power. I don't want people to say that now about me." He hesitated and looked around the room, catching eyes here and there. "I have some prophetic ability, though I think of it more as an ability to see the patterns in things. We'll meet aliens, and then we'll meet humans from Earth in this time, far in the future of the time we came from. We will trade with them. We need to be ready for that. When the humans find us, I want them to think we colonized this planet the same way they colonized theirs."

"My children will settle down into this world," Pytheas said to me afterwards. "One day you'll worship them. They and their children will be your pantheon, appropriate to this place. But for now, let them grow up. Let them be human while they can. They'll be gods long enough."

Eight years afterwards I thought of this conversation while I was working with Arete, educating a class in preparation for their oath-taking. This was the first class to contain Workers as well as human ephebes, and so I had been invited to help. I was enjoying the stimulation of all the questions they came up with.

"Plato thought of his system for humans, but it works very well for Workers," Arete said as we watched the class go off debating noisily with each other, making necessary but not unnecessary distinctions between human and Worker.

"Yes. He could imagine humans who grew up in a Just City, but he could not imagine what it would be like for either Workers or gods," I said. "But we all have souls that yearn for excellence and justice."

Arete laughed with surprise. "We all do," she said.

A little while after that, I was talking to Klio on a train ride where we happened to find ourselves together. Klio was another Master, younger than Aristomache and Lamprokleia but older than Maia. She came from the twentieth or twenty-first century, and had been a classical scholar there. We found ourselves talking about religion. Klio was an Ikarian, and she was still in the process of adjusting her ideas after the apotheosis of Ikaros. She was not disturbed by the direct intervention of Zeus in our affairs—she said she had always considered that he and Ikaros's primal God the Father were identical. "You don't need to come to the New Concordance from Christianity," she insisted.

"I see no need of it," I said. As the train sped across the black volcanic plains, with the distant mountains sending up sullen plumes or sudden hot blasts of flame, I explained to her how I had come to understand things. "Pytheas's children will one day be our pantheon, he told me so. And Arete agreed that their souls long for justice and excellence. They have grown up in the Republic. When that day comes that they are our pantheon and we worship them, we will have appropriately Platonic gods."

"I wish Ikaros could hear that," Klio said.

VI. *On Old Age*

One day when I was in the middle of building a new colossus, I mentioned to Maia that Aristomache could not see my work, because her eyesight had deteriorated to the point where she could not see anything big or far away. This made her sad, and it made me sad too, that I could not share my art with her. She had never seen any of it, because I had made none before she left with Kebes, and by the time she came back her eyesight had failed. She could read and see things close up, but she said that the distance was only a colored blur.

"You should make something especially for her," Maia said. "Something very small, but still characteristically part of your work."

"That's a wonderful idea," I said.

I incised an intaglio into a piece of porphyry the size of Maia's thumbnail. An intaglio is like an inside-out carving, you can press it into wax or plaster to make a raised impression.

The picture I made for Aristomache was of her, Pytheas, Simmea, Kebes, and Sokrates, examining an inscription I had carved around the eaves of the Mulberry sleeping house. Although the faces were barely the size of a grain of barley, I have lenses and carving tools fine enough to give them individuality and expressions. So I showed Pytheas's quizzical face, Aristomache with her mouth open in consternation, along with the way Sokrates liked to stand with his legs apart and his head tilted back, the way Kebes copied this, and the swell of Simmea's belly, since she had been pregnant with Neleus at that time.

Much of my work in those early years was historical and autobiographical. It was several years after that before I began to work on my series of Platonic responses, doing philosophy in the form of sculpture, or sculpture in the form of philosophy. Maia and Pytheas especially loved that work, but Aristomache was dead before I began it.

I went to Marissa myself to deliver my little intaglio. Aristomache was truly old by then. She could see it plainly, and it delighted her. We talked about Sokrates, and about the good intentions of the Masters in setting up the Republic, and about education. I had been in Marissa before, helping to make it fit for Plato, supervising young Workers who were not yet self-aware. Aristomache was not well enough that day to walk with me to the train, and later that year I was sent word that she was dead.

Then in the Sixtieth Year of the City, in the consulship of Baukis and Xenocrates, Maia had a stroke which left her half-paralyzed, unable to speak, and drooling. She had collapsed in the little garden outside her house, and nobody tried to move her. It was summer, but before I arrived someone had brought her winter kiton, embroidered with books and copies of Botticelli's flowers, and put it over her where she lay. Pytheas's son Phaedrus came, as he always did in cases where human doctors could do nothing. He took Maia's hand, and shook his head. "She's in there, but there's no healing this," he said. Neleus was there too, bending over her, wearing Ficino's old red hat.

She grunted, harsh animal sounds, "Uhrr, utt, ay."

I understood her, and went off to find Arete, in case she was calling for her and not merely restating a Platonic principle. Either would have been very characteristic for Maia.

Arete was in Thessaly. She flew off as soon as she heard, and Pytheas rode along in the webbing on my back. When we got back to Maia's house, Arete was engaged in a conversation where Maia uttered one painful-seeming syllable and Arete filled in the rest. She and Neleus were crouched at Maia's side, both in tears, though Maia was not.

"You were consul three times," Arete said.

"What more could any classicist want?" Pytheas asked, dropping down and taking her free hand. "You have done good work in this life, and your soul will be certainly reborn as a philosopher."

Maia's face distorted into a horrible grimace, and after a moment I realized that she was trying to smile. "Hhhh—" she said.

"Yes, Neleus will mix you the hemlock," Arete said. Pytheas had insisted that I bring it from Thessaly. I gave the bundle of leaves to Neleus, and he took it. He stepped inside the house, and I could watch through the doorway as he crushed it fiercely into a cup and then poured in wine recklessly, as if he couldn't see what he was doing. He came back out, and Arete took the cup from his trembling hand and held it to Maia's lips. Then Pytheas stroked her throat, helping her to swallow. When Arete took the cup away, Maia grunted.

"No, I can't promise we won't mourn for you. Yes, we'll remember you, and so will all your pupils. Your legacy will live on," Arete said.

"Joy to you, Maia," I said. "I'm not done talking with you, but go on to a good life."

There are no messages to give the dying to carry to the dead, or comfort or wisdom to take into new lives, for all souls must forget as they go through Lethe. I wished I could weep, in case the process gave some relief.

"Chh—" she said.

"She wishes you joy too, Crocus, and many years of making art and helping to lead the City and fruitful philosophy, and at last many joyful rebirths."

She grunted again, and Arete laughed through her tears. "She says she's always thought it'll be so funny for her relatives to see her disappear as a young woman and reappear a second later as she is now. She says coming to the City has meant she's had a better life than she could ever have imagined."

"Ah—" Maia said, and now even I understood her. Sokrates, dying in Athens, had asked Krito to offer a cock to Asklepius for his recovery from life. In the City, it was what almost everyone said when they felt themselves dying. Then she disappeared at the moment of death, as all the Masters and Children did, her body drawn back by Athene's power to the moment she had left to come to the City, leaving her cloak empty behind her.

We voted unanimously to name a mountain after her, which is the highest honor we give in the Republic. Maia left a great legacy and is remembered honorably by everyone. I still miss her.

The purpose of death I understand, though I worry about it in my own case. But I do not understand why the process has to be so indecorous and uncomfortable for humans.

14

APOLLO

All the time since I had read Athene's letter the question of where she might have put Sokrates had been tickling the back of my mind. It had to be somewhere I wouldn't guess, by definition, or I wouldn't need Pico to tell me where to find him. But he only spoke Greek, so it had to be somewhere Greek-speaking, and somewhere either obscure enough that nothing he did would be remembered, or somewhere so full of philosophers he wouldn't stand out. The second option seemed more like Athene. Pythagorean Kroton or Roman Alexandria were the likeliest choices, but of course she'd know I'd know that.

Athene was risking literally everything to gain knowledge of Chaos. That was bad enough. But the other reason her message had made me so incandescently furious was the way she used the threat to Sokrates to force me to rescue Pico. She could have trusted me. I'd have rescued Pico anyway. I hated being used and blackmailed, and even more I hated being blackmailed into doing what I would have done anyway because it was the right thing to do, and what I wanted to do. Even now I had calmed down, I was so furious with her that I considered writing a satire about all the most embarrassing things she had ever done, like the time she got into a snit about Paris not choosing her as the most beautiful, or the time she turned Arachne into a spider when she lost a weaving contest, or when she threw away the syrinx after inventing it because puffing out her cheeks made her look ridiculous.

I followed Pico to his cell, a small brick room which contained a low bed, a devotional painting of St. Benedict retrieving a rake from a pond (some ages have a really low bar for miracles), and a small chest, which, since it was Pico's, contained nothing but books. There he retrieved the paper Athene had given him from where it was neatly folded inside his copy of the *Republic*. He drew it out reverently and handed it to me. I opened it, glanced at it, and then at him. "Can you read this?"

"No. It's encoded to keep Athene's message safe," he said.

Well, fortunately Arete has the ability to understand anything, because this meant nothing to me. "Let's get Sokrates and then collect the other piece." I looked at him expectantly.

He shut his eyes and recited. "45 degrees, 45' 45 North, 50 degrees 50' 50 West, 15.10, 15th October, 151,151,151 *ante urbe condita*."

I was genuinely startled. "What? Where's that? Somewhere in the Jurassic? In the middle of the Atlantic—no, that's long enough ago that the continents aren't even in the same places! What's there?"

"A jungle, she told me. She didn't take me with her. I was in time for the Last Debate."

"So was I—but you mean she didn't change him back? He's still a gadfly?"

"I think so. She gave me an extremely precise time and place."

"She'd have to, for a fly! Why didn't she change him back?" I was aghast.

"I think she didn't want to face him. There aren't many people who can make Athene feel ashamed."

"Has spending more time with her stopped you thinking she's perfect?" I asked.

Pico smiled. "No. She's perfect. But I do understand her better. She's the perfect Athene, and that includes a certain amount of pride and vanity and temper."

"But surely—you know I'm not perfect!"

"But you are," he said, picking out the books and piling them on the bed. "You are the perfect Apollo. You're the light. And both of you grow and change and become more excellent, while remaining perfect as you are. Perfection isn't static. It's a dynamic form."

"Is this your new theory?" I asked warily.

"That part was in the New Concordance," he said, smiling reminiscently. "Klio and I came up with it long ago."

"So you think Athene is perfect in her imperfections? Including turning Sokrates into a fly and dropping him off in some swamp millions of years ago? Why didn't she simply take him to Athens where he could have bitten some of his friends?" He had bitten me, after his transformation, and then flown away. She must have caught him as soon as he was out of sight, and taken him to this location.

"I don't know. I told her you'd take me with you anyway, but she wanted to be sure." He looked guiltily down at the books. Then he picked them up and tucked them under his arm. "Let's go."

Taking him with me, I stepped out of time, and back in at Athene's precise coordinates of time and place. Red rocks stuck out of dense green swampland vegetation. It was warm and humid, and there were many flies. Pico, still clutching his books, looked around delightedly. For an instant I thought I could never identify Sokrates among the other flies, and that this must be an impossible test Athene had set me for reasons of her own. But he was my votary and my friend. He flew to me at once, and as soon as I saw him I knew his soul, even as a fly, as he had recognized me incarnate. Tears sprang to my eyes. At once I changed him back to his proper form, and there he was, exactly the same as he had been when I had last seen him in the Last Debate, in the same plain white kiton that was slightly frayed at the hem.

"Apollo!" he said, smiling at me. It was always his joke, to name me and pretend he was swearing. He looked around. "Ikaros!"

"Sokrates, I am so glad to see you!" We hugged each other, and then he hugged Ikaros.

"I'm very glad to see you too. Speaking of seeing, did you know that vision is entirely different when you're a fly? Where in the world are we?" He looked around at the lush bushes and ferns all around us.

"Unless you know different, where we are doesn't matter. It's some remote spot where Athene thought you'd enjoy being a fly for a little while." If you liked nature in the Romantic mode, it was beautiful. As we looked around, I heard a sound that reminded me of charging elephants, and a huge pink-and-green allosaur dashed past us, easily twice the length of an elephant but shorter and much less bulky, with small arms, an enormous head, and serrated teeth as long as my arm.

"Look, a big scary lizard!" Sokrates said, peering after it cheerfully. "What was it?"

"Maybe a wyvern?" Ikaros suggested.

"It's not a lizard at all," I said.

"Is it one of the creatures Lucretius talks about that wasn't fitted for survival?" Ikaros asked, taking a step in the direction in which it had disappeared. "Or were they all hunted down in the age of heroes?"

"The former," I said. "And they used to hunt in packs. Let's go."

Sokrates nodded after it thoughtfully, then turned back to me. "Where is Athene?" he asked. "We have unfinished business."

I understood then what Pico had meant about why she hadn't changed him back. Sokrates wanted to continue the Last Debate, even in a Jurassic swamp full of rampaging dinosaurs. Of course he did. If anyone was a perfect example of themselves, he was. And the reason Athene had changed him into a fly in the first place was because she had lost her temper and couldn't bear to be defeated in a logical argument.

"She's lost," I said. Before he had time to respond, I went on. "Now I'm going to France in the Enlightenment to collect part of the message she sent about how we can rescue her. Do you two want to come, or should I take you to the Just City first?"

"Is that where we'll be going afterwards?" Sokrates asked.

"Yes. Or rather, it's where I'll be going. If you want me to leave you somewhere else, I can do that. With some restrictions. And not here." I was suddenly unsure. Volition really did mean letting them choose, whether I wanted to or not, and however terrible their choices might be. "Where do you want to be?"

"I asked Krito what I'd do in Thessaly, but he didn't listen," Sokrates said, still looking around him at the swamp. "I don't know what France or the Enlightenment are, so let's illuminate my ignorance a little by exploring them. And after that, the Just City by all means. I can do my work there."

"You'll love the Enlightenment," Pico said enthusiastically, waving his hand to shoo away flies.

"Has Apollo been taking you on a tour of human history?"

"No, I've been working with Athene, and she has taken me to places," Pico explained.

I took them out of time, and back in to the front lawn of the Chateau Cirey in May of 1750. My sun was pleasantly warm, the trees were in spring blossom, the birds were singing, and best of all they were all that remained of dinosaurs. I had never been here before. The Enlightenment was Athene's territory, it had never been mine. "Cirey!" said Pico happily.

"Both influenced by Greek originals and influential on buildings in the City, I think," Sokrates said, looking at the chateau with his head on its side.

"You're absolutely right," I said.

"So why did Athene bring you here?" he asked Pico.

I gave our clothes the illusion of eighteenth-century finery. It was one of the most gorgeous eras for men's clothing. It amused me to dress Sokrates in peacock colors and put a huge curled and powdered wig on him. The same costume suited Pico ridiculously well, much better than the monk's habit or even his kiton, as if this were the era where he should have lived. The books he still clutched under his arm didn't even look incongruous.

"To talk to Voltaire and Emilie. Voltaire is very like you," Pico said to Sokrates. "Another marvelous gadfly. He wrote a play about you. Athene and I spent two wonderful days here. There was theater, there was science, there was debate, and they're thinking such wonderful things—what time is it here, Pytheas? Can we get hold of a copy of the *Encyclopédie* while we're here?"

"The first volume doesn't come out until next year," I said. "Besides, it's in French."

"I can speak French, though it's changed a bit, and we sometimes needed to use Latin to be clear. But I can certainly read it reasonably well."

Sokrates was examining his clothes. "This is the future?" he asked.

"Your future, yes, more than two thousand years after you were born."

"And after your time too?" he asked Ikaros.

"Yes, about two hundred and fifty years after I was born. But a hundred years before Maia and Adeimantus were born, and three hundred years before Klio and Lysias." Pico looked energized by the thought. "There's so much history, so many places and times!"

Sokrates smoothed the burgundy velvet of his sleeve. "What a strange place."

"I'm looking for Florent-Claude," I said to Pico. "Do you know him? Athene describes him as Emilie's widower."

"Emilie's dead?" Pico looked sad. "She was so wonderful, a scientist and a philosopher in an age where it was so hard for women to be anything but hostesses at best. She should have been in the Republic."

"Do you know Florent-Claude?" I repeated.

"Yes. I met him. She was with Voltaire when we visited, but Florent-Claude was happy with the situation. It was almost like being in the City of Amazons."

I knocked loudly on the door. "Why didn't Athene leave it with Voltaire?" I grumbled. "He's the one who's her votary. It would have been interesting to meet him."

A servant opened the door, a flunkey in a wig. "We wish to see Florent-Claude," I said.

"The Marquis du Chastellet," Pico added.

"And your names?" the flunkey asked, superciliously.

"The Comte de Mirandola, the Marquis de Delos and the Duc d'Athen," Pico replied immediately, in Italianate French.

The flunkey bowed and went back inside. "Marquis? Duke?" I asked. He really was the Count of Mirandola, or course, or he had been two hundred or so years before.

"Did you want me to say god and philosopher on the doorstep?" Pico asked. "I'm sure there was a Duke of Athens."

"Not in 1750," I said. "He told the servant you were a member of the high Athenian nobility," I explained to Sokrates.

"You're mixing me up with Plato again," Sokrates said. "He was descended from Solon on his mother's side, and on his father's side from the ancient kings of Attica. I was a simple stonemason before I became a philosopher, and my only illustrious ancestor was the artificer Daedalus."

The flunkey came back. "The marquis will see you."

He showed us into one of those uncomfortable eighteenth-century rooms, all spindly little chairs matching the gilt frames on all the paintings. Sokrates looked at all of it in wonder.

"I'm afraid you're not going to understand any of the conversation," I said.

"I've always been terrible at learning barbarian languages," Sokrates said, almost as if this were a point of pride. "Do they have Workers here?"

"No, we're more than two centuries before the first Workers," I said.

"Then who wove this carpet so finely, and then put it on the floor?" he asked.

Before I could respond, the flunkey opened the door again and announced his master. We all bowed, Sokrates very badly as he wasn't familiar with the custom.

"I don't believe I've had the pleasure," Florent-Claude said.

"We met once, when I was here staying with Emilie," Pico said. "Such a loss." They bowed to each other.

"Ah yes. The Comte de Mirandola. I recognize you now. The years haven't touched you at all."

Pico looked uncomfortable at this compliment. He looked about thirty, but he had been over sixty and almost blind at the Relocation, before Father had restored his youth on Olympos so that he could work with Athene. He didn't seem to have aged at all since then. He introduced us, Apollonaire de Delos and Socrate d'Athen, who unhappily knew no French. We sat down in the little uncomfortable chairs. "We're passing by, we can't stay," he said, in response to Florent-Claude's offer of hospitality for the night. The flunkey returned and gave us all sherry, in little glasses, and offered around a plate of petits fours. I neither ate nor drank, but it was almost worth the delay for the expression on Sokrates's face when after turning the highly colored confection in his fingers he bit into the cloying marzipan.

I wished Athene had given me more to go on. I didn't know what she'd said when she asked Florent-Claude to keep the paper for her, or what name she'd been using or who he thought she was. Fortunately, Pico did. "You remember my friend Athenais de Minerve?"

"Of course," Florent-Claude said. "So beautiful, so wise."

"Did she by chance give you an incomprehensible paper to look after?" Pico asked.

Sokrates was ignoring us all and pleating the lace of his undersleeve intently.

"So, you are on her treasure hunt?" Florent-Claude smiled.

I could not understand why Athene had gone through this elaborate charade and divided up her message. It was dangerous as well as unnecessary. Ordinary mortals involved this way could easily have lost the paper. Pico's could have been stolen, and what Kebes might have done with it didn't bear thinking about. He could have burned it for pure spite.

"We are," Pico said.

"Then can you answer her riddle?"

"We'll have to see when you ask it," Pico said, confidently.

"Let me fetch it," he said. "But first I should tell you that it's in English, and if none of you speak that language you have leave to find another who does."

"English," Pico said, dismayed. "I know many languages, but not that barbarous tongue."

"Barbarous? I think not, since I speak it," I said. (You're reading this. You already know I speak English.)

Florent-Claude chortled, and went off to fetch the paper. I hoped he hadn't lost it among his bibelots.

"Who did she think would come who would need to find an English speaker?" Pico asked, in Greek.

"Porphyry?" I suggested.

"Old Porphyry's still alive?" Sokrates asked, looking up from his sleeve, surprised.

"No, he died. But Euridike named one of my sons after him, and that's who we're talking about. Ikaros was one of his teachers."

Sokrates seemed to accept that calmly. "Where did Florent-Claude go?"

"He's fetching Athene's message," I explained.

"What is this made of?" he asked, picking up the drape of lace at his cuff again.

"Silk, I think, though they sometimes make it from linen," I said. "It's called lace."

"And what is silk?" Sokrates asked, patiently.

"It's a thread spun by worms who eat mulberry leaves," Pico explained. He twirled his wrists, making his own lace flare gorgeously. "It makes a cloth that's cool to wear in hot weather and that's gentle next to the skin, not scratchy. It originates in China, but in my time we make it in Italy. But lace came later."

"And this lace is made by humans?"

"By women, mostly, using bobbins, which are things like little distaffs," I said.

"This is an incredibly unnecessary waste of human labor and human souls," Sokrates pronounced. "Those women should be freed from their bobbins and taught reason. It would be a useless frivolity even if Workers made it as fast and unthinkingly as any cloth. Nobody needs dangling frills like this. Look at this incredible detail. It's beautiful, in itself, but nonsensical as clothing."

"I agree," I said. "Though it looks elegant on Ikaros."

"Don't you think it's unjust?"

"What if it's somebody's vocation, to make lace?" Ikaros asked. "Their art?"

"It is a normal part of these people's clothing," Sokrates said. "Far too much for it to be made as somebody's art. Look at these paintings, everyone has it. If somebody wanted to make it as their art, it might be a harmless decoration, like the borders some people embroider on their kitons. It's this volume of it that's wrong. Close work like that? Women must be compelled to make it from economic necessity."

"Yes, that's wrong," Ikaros said, soberly. "When there's so much injustice it becomes invisible."

"Is this silk also?" Sokrates asked, stroking his velvet sleeve.

"I think so," I said, not at all sure what velvet was made of. "You should ask Athene when we have her back, fabrics are one of her specialities."

"She would not approve of this *lace*," Sokrates said, quite certain that whatever they might disagree about, they'd be as one on such fundamentals as that. "Not even Alkibiades would like lace. And think of the time it must take, every day, putting on all these ridiculous things. I sleep with my kiton over me as a covering, I wake up and shake it, I fold it and put it on and I am ready for the day. Putting on all these layers and choosing the colors to match must waste so much time, and worse, attention."

"In cold places people need more layers and thicker clothes," I said.

"Certainly. But it's not cold here," Sokrates said, which was inarguable that day.

"What if wearing clothes and choosing colors is somebody's art?" Pico asked.

Florent-Claude came bustling back with a paper in his hand. "Very well. Now, in English if you will! Of what five things is St. Jathe patron?" He had a strong accent in English, but understood the pronunciation better than many Francophones.

Pico looked at me, frowning. He must have understood the name. St. Jathe was clearly Jathery. I'd heard the list from Hilfa, such a strange set of things. And a riddle in English would need a rhyming answer. "Liberty and changing names, wisdom, tricks and riddle games," I said. It seemed almost insultingly easy, but it could only be answered by somebody who spoke English and had talked to Saeli about religion—which meant me, or perhaps Hermes.

"Well done! So here is your paper, but you will find in it another riddle, I think," Florent-Claude said, handing it over. It had the same mix of characters as Pico's. I tucked it away with the other.

Saying goodbye took a long time, though we tried to hurry. We had to promise to give his love to Athene, and to call in if we were ever passing again. As we walked, Pico translated the conversation for Sokrates and then they both insisted that I explain the riddle. We had to walk all the way to the end of the lawn and wave and then make our way behind the screen of chestnuts, all with their spring candles, before we could step out of time and back to the Republic.

15

JASON

Pytheas had got up from his chair and was looming over Jathery. He had grown so tall that his head almost touched the ceiling of Hilfa's little house. "Was it you all the time?" he asked, and although his voice was quiet it made the hair stand up on my neck. "Was it you who came and interrupted me?"

"Yes," Jathery said, not sounding at all intimidated. Gla voice was clear and pure, like a child's voice singing, but rich and full-bodied.

"You lied to me about having a message from Father?"

"Would you have left your new sun if I'd come to you as myself and told you Athene was missing?" Gla question sounded entirely reasonable, and made me wonder whether Pytheas would have.

"Yes," Pytheas said, emphatically but petulantly. He glared down at Jathery. "Why does nobody trust me to take any reasonable action without tricking me into it?"

They both disappeared. I blinked.

Ikaros was looking green, not the way Saeli are green, but the way pale-skinned humans turn green when they're about to be sick. He walked rapidly into the fountain room, and I soon heard the sound of him tossing his guts up joining the familiar sound of Marsilia doing the same. Almost everyone gets queasy sometimes on boats and has to spew. I might have felt the same way if I'd found out somebody I'd been to bed with was actually Jathery in disguise. The thought of it was a bit stomach-churning.

"I couldn't tell you. Do you understand, Jason?" Hilfa asked quietly from beside me.

"I understand," I said. He started to rock to and fro again. I put my arms around him.

Thetis picked up the papers Marsilia had dropped and sat down with them in Pytheas's empty chair. She glanced towards the fountain room.

"Joy to you, Sokrates, I'm delighted to meet you, I have heard so much about you," Arete said.

"I hear you're Simmea's daughter, and you see through falsehood. That must be useful in debate."

"Not as much as you might think," Arete said.

Sokrates laughed. "But you saw through Jathery pretending to be Hermes when he had fooled us all?"

"It seems so," Arete said.

"How did none of us guess?" Sokrates asked.

"Deception and name-changing are part of what gla is," Hilfa said.

"Even so, I'm surprised gla could fool Pytheas," Sokrates said. "Hermes is his own brother."

Ikaros came back in. He smiled wanly, picked up his wine-beaker and drained it, then sat down in the other chair.

"Where did Pytheas and Jathery go?" I asked.

"To yell at each other outside time, I expect. It's a thing gods do," Ikaros said, shaking his head. "They'll be back, for those if nothing else." He gestured at the papers Thetis was holding. She offered them to him, and he took them, turning them over curiously. "There are at least four alphabets here, and I think there was a different one on the piece I had, Etruscan maybe."

Marsilia came back in, with the strands of her dark hair damp around her face where she must have dashed water on it. "Oh Marsilia, is there anything that could help?"

She shook her head. I passed her my wine cup and she took a sip. She sat down on the floor in front of us.

Arete took the papers from Ikaros. "Oh, interesting, we need all of them together to be able to read them."

"Did finding out who Jathery was make you sick?" Hilfa asked Marsilia. Marsilia nodded.

"Me too," Ikaros said, smiling companionably at her. "I think many people would throw up on learning that a lover was really an alien god."

She nodded again.

"I'm sorry. I couldn't tell you. I don't know what gla would have done to me," Hilfa said. "I think gla made me, and could unmake me, to take back the part of gla power gla put into me."

"None of this is your fault," Marsilia said.

"We should not need to live in fear of the arbitrary power of the gods this way," Sokrates said.

"The Saeli always do, all of us, always," Hilfa said.

Marsilia took another swig of my wine. Thetis got up and stood behind Marsilia and started to rub her shoulders. Marsilia relaxed a little.

"It means Alkippe and I are siblings," Hilfa said, tentatively.

"But that was always true," Marsilia said. Hilfa stopped rocking entirely and sat up straight, staring at her.

"You're also one of Simmea's granddaughters?" Sokrates asked Marsilia. "You remind me of her."

"Yes, I am," Marsilia said. Thetis looked proudly down at her.

"And Jathery took you off on a treasure hunt through time for Athene's papers?" Sokrates went on.

Marsilia gave him a small smile. "It was a bit like that, yes. But all the time I thought he was Hermes. Gla really is horribly good at deception. Even when I saw him changing between forms when we were outside time, I never questioned who he was."

"You should always question," Sokrates said.

Marsilia smiled up at him ruefully. "I'll try harder to be a proper philosopher."

Arete passed the papers back to Ikaros. "I wonder sometimes if it is harder for women to be philosophers, even for the Golds here. Everything always seems to be stacked against it."

"Not always," Ikaros said. "Did you ever know Lucrezia? She was in the City of Amazons by the time you were growing up, so maybe not. We lived together for a long time. She came from the Renaissance, from Rome. She and her brothers all had the same humanist education, all read Plato. But she was the only one to become a philosopher, and pray to Athene to come here. They had no time in their lives for it, after their education, none of them. But she did, being a woman, even though she was as much a political pawn as they were. For once the expectation of passivity and not being able to act was an advantage, it gave her time to study they couldn't have."

At that moment, the two gods reappeared, Pytheas restored to his usual size.

"Let's put it together right now," Pytheas said. "Where—ah, thank you, Pico." He took the papers from Ikaros and pulled two more out of the fold of his kiton.

"But what——" Ikaros asked.

"We have decided to work on getting Athene back first, before addressing the issue of Jathery's imposture," Pytheas said, with a glare at Jathery. He walked over to the table. Arete and Ikaros followed close behind. Pytheas set the papers down on top of the pile of books Ikaros had laid down there earlier. The four of them bent over the papers. Arete at once switched them into a different order.

Sokrates looked at me, and I jumped. "You've been very quiet. What's your connection with all this?"

"I'm here because I'm Hilfa's friend," I said. Hilfa stopped rocking and nodded.

"An admirable reason," he said. "Your name is Jason, Pytheas said. I see you're a Silver?"

"Yes," I said, emboldened by his approval. "We work on a fishing boat with Marsilia."

"Yes, I can read it," Arete said, from across the room. "It's a technical description of how to get out into the primal Chaos and back. It sounds preposterously dangerous. There's no justification or explanation here of why she did it or why anyone would want to, or why she left it scattered in pieces."

"But you can read it?" Pytheas asked. "Translate it!"

"I could," Arete said. "But, Father, I'd need a good reason as to why I should. This is extremely dangerous information, and Athene didn't come back. I see no reason why it would be any less dangerous for you. If gods can get lost out there, it's bad enough to lose one, and much worse to lose two."

"If you won't translate it, you'll force us to take it to Father," Pytheas said. Now that they were standing nose to nose glaring at each other, I could see that they were exactly the same height.

"Explain to me why that is a bad thing?" Arete asked. I was feeling increasingly uncomfortable hearing them arguing about such things. But Hilfa was still shivering in my arms, so I stayed where I was and tried to be reassuring. Thetis smiled at me over Marsilia's head, and that in itself was reason enough to stay. "You should take it to Zeus," Arete went on. "You said you wanted to see her explanation first—well, there isn't any, in the sense of justification for why she did it."

"I told you why she did it." Pytheas stalked back to his chair and flung himself down. "And I explained why I don't want to go to Father."

"Do we have to take any action?" Arete asked.

Pytheas glowered at her. "You can read us the instructions and then we can attempt to rescue her. Or if you refuse, we can go to Father, though I fear the consequences. Those are our choices. We can't leave her stranded out there and do nothing, no. That's not an acceptable option."

"I agree with that," Jathery said. I looked over to where gla was still standing by the table, gla big hand splayed on Athene's notes. Gla looked like a big Sael with exceptionally clear skin patterns, except that gla had an arrogant confidence that was like no Sael I had ever seen. Gla voice sounded smooth and persuasive. And gla skin patterns changed as I watched. Hilfa's were more or less pronounced, but always the same pattern in the same place. Jathery's writhed and rewrote themselves constantly.

"We absolutely need to get her back. The world can't survive without wisdom," Ikaros said, passionately.

"You of all people must understand that Athene is not the only source of wisdom in the universe," Arete snapped.

"But she's our source of wisdom, our culture's source," Ikaros said. "We wouldn't be the same with foreign wisdom."

"We might be better," Sokrates said, thoughtfully.

"I love her, and you know you do too," Ikaros said.

"True. And I am her votary, hers and Apollo's." He nodded to Pytheas where he sat. Pytheas, or maybe I should say Apollo, nodded back warily. "But loving her doesn't excuse us from seeing her very real faults. And considering those, who is to say we might not be better with Apollo taking charge of our wisdom, or perhaps Thoth or Anahita."

Pytheas shuddered. "We wouldn't, not with any of those choices, believe me." I knew nothing about Thoth except that he was an ibis-headed Egyptian god. I had never even heard of Anahita.

"Some other god of wisdom might better consider the will of thinking beings," Sokrates said. "Athene has always been careless of it."

"You're only saying that because you think it would be interesting to find out," Ikaros said.

"Well, don't you?" asked Sokrates mildly.

"Yes, theoretically interesting, but in practice it would be terrible," Ikaros said. "You're still angry with her because she turned you into a gadfly."

Sokrates laughed. I stared at him, hardly able to believe he could find it funny. "It was interesting being a gadfly. The way they see is amazing. And I could fly! I'm not angry about that. It was a fascinating experience—a little frightening at first, yes, but I have endured far worse things, and there was a lot about it to enjoy. If I can't forgive her it's for not finishing the argument."

"She behaved badly in the Last Debate," Ikaros conceded. "But we should still rescue her!"

"I'm not saying Athene's not valuable or that we should abandon her," Arete said. "I'm saying that Apollo is equally valuable, or more valuable right now because he hasn't gone haring out into Chaos. And I suppose the same applies to Jathery; the Saeli must need him for something."

Jathery laughed, the patterns on his skin still changing every moment. Hearing it I realized what was wrong with Hilfa's laugh—it was always the same. Human laughter bubbles or barks and each laugh is different. Jathery's was different. When he'd been pretending to be Hermes it had sounded like normal laughter. Now it didn't sound at all human, and it sent shivers through me. Meanwhile, beside me, Hilfa shook his head. I looked at him. "No?" I whispered. "You don't need him?"

"I suppose we do," he whispered back.

"But isn't gla your culture's source of wisdom?" I asked.

Hilfa didn't reply.

"I wonder what Athene has learned out there?" Ikaros mused.

"What did she hope to learn?" Arete asked. "How could it seem like a good idea to do such a thing?"

"She wanted to know the answers to the most fundamental questions," Ikaros said. "How the universe came into being, and how Zeus made time. We were working on the nature of time and Necessity."

"Is the knowledge that she might have learned in Chaos why you want to risk yourselves to rescue her?" Arete asked Pytheas.

"It's why I'm afraid of what Father might do," Pytheas said.

"It's not worth the risk!" Arete said.

"It is worth a little risk to learn so many answers," Jathery said, quietly but compellingly.

"A little risk!" Arete said, not at all persuaded. "You know how great a risk it is to place everything on one throw."

"But sometimes it can be rewarding," Jathery murmured persuasively.

Arete shuddered.

"What do you mean by time?" Sokrates asked abruptly.

Ikaros jumped. He had been staring at Jathery as if he could read the patterns on gla skin. He turned to Sokrates. "Oh, what the gods mean when they say *time* is human history, or what we might call material reality or the fourth hypostasis. The place where things change and actions have consequences and one day follows the next. But it's not that simple. The gods live in the realm of soul and are eternal, and can step in and out of what they call time, but they also experience consequences and growth and change. They have personal time." He moved his arms demonstratively. "Plotinus said time was a quality, a negative quality, an imperfection, and that the higher hypostases didn't suffer it. But he was wrong. It's such a pity he didn't live to learn how time is more complicated. In fact, time extends at least into the realm of mind, above the realm of soul, because the ideals, the Forms, are dynamic."

"So is Chaos part of time?" Sokrates asked.

"No. Chaos is before and after and below time. It's the lowest hypostasis. It's matter with no form," Ikaros said. I vaguely remembered hypostases being mentioned when I was an ephebe. I'd never gone in for this kind of exalted metaphysics. I work on a fishing boat. Plato's Allegory of the Cave is good enough for me. "Or at least, that's what we think it is."

Sokrates turned to Pytheas. "I won't ask if that's correct, but is this what you also believe?"

"Ikaros has been studying these matters with Athene and probably understands more about them than I do," Pytheas said. "I was born long after Father created time."

"And you?" Sokrates asked Jathery.

"I am even younger than Apollo. But my studies agree with Ikaros." Gla nodded at Ikaros, who blushed and looked away.

"So Zeus created time?" Sokrates asked Pytheas. "But what about Kronos, Ouranos, the Titans?"

"He used the Darkness of the Oak," Pytheas said. "Kronos and Ouranos were names of Father's, in earlier iterations. And the Titans were earlier circles of gods, not quite forgotten. And while it might be possible to argue that he's getting better at it and each iteration of time is more excellent and closer to perfection, I can't feel calm about the risk of losing myself and all of history. I have learned a lot. And there's so much that mortals have made that is wonderful. You may say the good is the enemy of the best and starting fresh would be better, but I want to protect this good we have."

"Athene thought the gain was worth the risk," Jathery said, and for a moment listening to him I agreed. It would be wonderful to know these things for sure.

"You and Athene had no right to decide that on your own, when what is risked is everything for everyone," Pytheas said. And though his voice was harsh in comparison, of course he was right.

"She took precautions as best she could," Jathery said, smoothly. "We intended to go together, but she went without telling me."

"We are all part of her precautions, you included," Pytheas acknowledged. "Athene really didn't want us to go to Father and risk what he would do."

"But doesn't he already know everything?" Thetis asked, looking up from Marsilia. "We can't keep it from Zeus. He already knows."

"Only when he becomes conscious of it, and then it is as if he has always known," Ikaros said. "He told me that himself. So even though he knows everything, he only lives partially in any kind of time at all. If he becomes conscious of this after Athene is safely back, that is different from if he becomes conscious of it now, while she is stranded out there."

"But what does now mean, to him?" Sokrates asked.

"It has to do with awareness," Ikaros said.

"It all does," Pytheas said. "What we can do. Time."

"And what about Necessity?" Sokrates asked Ikaros.

"Necessity is a great force that binds all thinking beings," Ikaros said. "We think it compels even Zeus."

"And this is what Athene went out into Chaos to study?"

"Necessity, and what Chaos is, and how time began," Ikaros confirmed.

Sokrates turned to Pytheas. "You said once that Fate is the line drawn around what we can do, and Necessity prevents us overstepping that line, but within the lines we are free to do what we want." Pytheas nodded. "And do you think Athene has overstepped that line?"

"I think that depends whether we can get her back," Pytheas said. "At this moment, when she is there, she has, yes. Once we have her back, then no, she has not."

"I don't understand how it can be both," Sokrates said. "She has transgressed or she has not."

"We have freedom to act, and she is acting, the action is not complete," Jathery elucidated, and set out like that it did all seem clear.

"Is that the kind of freedom that is your responsibility, and which Athene referenced in her riddle?" Sokrates asked.

"Yes," Jathery said. "She is poised between. When she comes back and her action is complete, we will know."

"Or if we go to Father," Pytheas said. "So it would be better if we go after her and bring her back."

I was listening to this when something occurred to me. "Wait," I said.

Everyone turned to stare at me. Sokrates and Thetis looked hopeful, Ikaros looked curious, Pytheas and Arete looked impatient, Marsilia looked surprised, Jathery looked sinisterly unreadable, and Hilfa a little bemused. It was hard to speak in the focus of so much combined attention. "I'm sorry," I said. "Probably this is only me not understanding, I'm only a Silver, not a god or a philosopher. But why can't you go outside time and come back in say five years from now and come to me and Hilfa and Marsilia one day while we're out fishing? And we'd know by then the results of all this, and we could tell you, and then you'd know whether this worked or not and what to do before you do it."

"What would happen if you did that and Jason told you it hadn't worked, that you'd been lost forever in the formless Chaos?" Sokrates inquired at once.

"Nothing," Pytheas said. "We'd still have to go. Necessity. And that's why we won't."

"I thought you said being compelled by Necessity merely made you uncomfortable?" Sokrates said.

"It can get highly uncomfortable," Jathery said. "Even knowing there's a really good reason not to go back and sort things out, I've been getting more and more uncomfortable about not doing it. It's like pain. It's harder and harder not to act to relieve it. It takes a great deal of will to resist. I couldn't last this way much longer. Resisting inevitability is difficult, and much better avoided." The markings on his skin writhed unsettlingly and re-formed themselves.

"Like on Delos," Arete said, looking at Pytheas.

"And again, freedom?" Sokrates asked.

Pytheas was frowning. "We're free within Fate and Necessity. The more we tangle ourselves up with them—and that would be nothing but a delib-erate tangle—the less we are free to act. Our past actions bind our future selves, and all we gods do is remembered in art. The more we want to be able to change and grow and pursue excellence, the more we need to leave our-selves open to that."

"And the same for humanity too?" Sokrates asked, cheerily.

"Mortals never know, so they are always free to act," Pytheas said.

I noticed he said mortals, where Sokrates had said humanity. Sokrates hadn't really had time yet to take in what the Saeli presence meant.

"And when you make predictions to them, through your oracles?" Sokrates asked.

"My oracles give useful guidelines and let people know how to get the attention of the gods," Pytheas said.

"But if you went into the future now, could you see Jason's fate, and come back and tell him today exactly what will happen in his life and how much fish he will catch every day until he dies?" Sokrates asked.

"Please don't!" I said at once.

Pytheas smiled at me. "Don't worry. All gods learn early that it doesn't do any good to warn people about their future. Necessity makes the steps they take to avoid it turn out to be exactly what will make it happen. Look at Oedipus. Advice can be useful, sometimes; actual prophecy mostly be-comes self-defeating. It's much better for oracles to be ambiguous. Necessity is a very powerful force."

"But you do know people's fate?" Sokrates asked.

"Sometimes. It depends whether we've been paying attention."

Sokrates screwed up his face. "So doing what Jason suggested wouldn't help because you'd have to go anyway, whether it succeeds or fails?"

"Yes. And it's so unpleasant to be caught up by Necessity we don't want to any more than we have to. It feels like being pinned. So it's better to stay free and take actions without knowing."

"Why do you have to go?" Marsilia asked.

"We already went through all this!" Pytheas said impatiently.

"I mean can't Jathery go after her alone? Gla's the one who has the shield of Necessity, not you," Marsilia said, though she was still not looking at Jathery.

"I would be willing to go alone," Jathery said, gla inner eyelids shining over gla eyes.

Pytheas shook his head. "No. If Athene trusted gla, she'd have left the message for gla, not for me. I have to go, Marsilia. Jathery can come, we've agreed that, but I don't trust gla, and I'm not letting gla go alone."

"Besides these instructions are for two gods working together," Arete said. "But I don't see how you're any less likely to get stranded there than she was, if you go there using the method she left you. You'd simply be repeating what she did, which worked to take her out but not to bring her home. So all you'd achieve by going after her would be to make things worse."

Pytheas stared at her grimly. "We have a shield she did not. Jathery is bound by Necessity, that great force. Alkippe is his child, but he hasn't yet been back to conceive her. Does that affect your estimate of our safety?"

"What? You can't risk Alkippe like that!" Tears sprang to Thetis's eyes at once. She leapt to her feet. "Grandfather! That's the worst thing I ever heard. You can't! And you, Jathery or whoever you are, you have to go there right now and set things straight!" I'd forgotten she hadn't been there when we'd found out about this, back in Thessaly.

"Calm down, it's all right," Marsilia said.

I stood up and put a tentative hand on Thetis's arm. "Let's hear more about it," I said. "Marsilia—"

"It isn't all right! It can't be!" Thetis shook me off. "It's unbearable."

"But Alkippe might be keeping all of us safe, the whole of our civilization even," Marsilia said.

"The whole of history, potentially, Thee," Pytheas said.

"I don't care!" Thetis said. "You can't take risks with her like that! How can you think of it? She's only seven."

Marsilia looked at me pleadingly. I didn't know what to say or do. I felt sorry for Thetis, but things were bad enough without getting upset about them. It seemed strange that she could hear about the potential unravelling of the world as calmly as any of us, but a threat to one child she loved overcame her this way.

"I'm horrified too, but if it's really keeping all of us safe, then the risk is no worse for Alkippe than for any of us, all of us," I said.

To my surprise Hilfa got up and put his arms awkwardly around Thetis, and she sank down on the bed and allowed him to hold her.

"Are you Alkippe's mother, Thetis?" Sokrates asked gently.

Thetis shook her head.

"No, I am," Marsilia said quietly to Sokrates, as poor Thetis wept on Hilfa's shoulder.

"And you say you are all right with this, this risk to your child?" Sokrates asked.

"She can't be!" Thetis said, barely able to speak through her sobs.

"I'm not all right, but it's necessary. It's what Jason said, the risk is the same. If she ceases to exist because Jathery doesn't go back to conceive her, or she ceases to exist because the whole city, or all of history does, there's no difference. And I have stayed as close to Jathery as I can since finding this out. It's why I went with gla," Marsilia said. Her face was set and brave. "I also love Alkippe very much—and I agree it's terrible."

Sokrates patted her shoulder. "What a hard choice," he said. "But if Jathery doesn't go to rescue Athene—"

"Then Alkippe may be safe from Necessity, but Zeus may bring down the Darkness of the Oak on all of us, Alkippe included," Marsilia said.

"Arete?" Pytheas asked, over the sound of Thetis's sobbing. "Please?"

Arete's eyes widened. "All right, I'll translate it. The shield of Necessity may be enough. Well, I will if Hilfa agrees."

"Hilfa?" I asked, surprised into speaking.

"Hilfa is the anchor. He always was. He's Athene's anchor right now."

Hilfa kept his arms around Thetis. As he looked up I caught a flash of vivid orange and blue from his eyelids. "Like a boat anchor? What does it mean, for a person to be an anchor?"

"It means you're her connection back to this universe," Arete said. "If Pytheas and Jathery go out there, they'll need to follow the thread from you to her."

"You're not only her message, but her anchor," Jathery said.

Hilfa was staring at Arete over Thee's head. "Tell me what I am?"

"You're a hero, and what you make of yourself is your own choice. Like all Saeli, you have five parents. Jathery, a male human, the earth and water of Plato, and the spark of Athene's mind," Arete said.

Ikaros made an uneasy motion, but did not speak. He took a step forward, then stopped.

"So I belong to this planet? To Plato?" Hilfa asked, staring at Arete with the glint I thought was his real smile on his face.

"Yes," Arete said. "And you don't object to being the anchor?"

"It is what I was made for, how could I mind?" Hilfa asked. He let go of Thetis and stood up. Thee was getting herself under control. I sat down again and put my arm tentatively around her. She leaned into me as she had been doing with Hilfa.

"Let's do it and have done," Pytheas said.

"And if you don't come back?" Arete asked. "Should I send—"

"That will be up to you," Pytheas said.

"But we're not sure how time out there relates to time here," Ikaros said. "That was part of why Athene refused to take me. If you don't come back, we should wait before going to Zeus with this."

"Wait how long?" Arete asked.

"Ask Porphyry. The same way you have a connection with patterns of truth and language, he has a connection with the patterns of place and time. If we don't reappear immediately, go to him tomorrow and ask him to go to Father when it feels right," Pytheas said.

"All right," Arete said, walking back to the table. "Look, nobody can go except the gods, and none of the rest of us can do anything to help now. I think everyone else should go to bed. There's still a human spaceship up there that we'll have to deal with tomorrow, and it's getting late."

"If tomorrow comes," Jathery said, with another bone-chilling laugh.

All I'd have to deal with tomorrow, if it came, was the sea and the fish, but that was enough. "That sounds like good advice to me," I said. "Sleep will help."

"As if I'd be able to sleep with Alkippe in danger," Thetis said, mopping her eyes.

"But we should try, Thee, because she'll be awake and wanting breakfast, and your little ones will need you," Marsilia said. I picked up Thetis's cloak and wrapped it around her. She huddled into it.

"We'll let you all catch up on sleep," Pytheas said. "We'll come back and let you know what's happened tomorrow evening."

"But you won't want to wait . . . oh!" Arete said. They wouldn't have to wait, of course, they could step back into time tomorrow evening as easily as today. It must be so incredibly strange to be a god.

"I'm not tired. If you'll tell me where Crocus is, I think I'll go and find him," Sokrates said. "I know the City, unless it has changed very much in being moved here."

"Crocus is out at the spaceport," Marsilia said.

Sokrates laughed. "Then it has changed more than I imagined!"

"I'll take you to the spaceport," Arete said to Sokrates. "I want to go there anyway. I can be useful there. And it'll be quicker for you to come with me than taking the train at this time of night."

"You have trains here now?" Ikaros asked.

"What are trains?" Sokrates asked.

"Trains are moving rooms—electrical conveyances that run on rails moving at fixed times to fixed places," Marsilia explained. "And Ikaros, you could take one to the City of Amazons and be there in less than an hour, though there isn't one now until morning."

"I know Rhadamantha would be pleased to see you," Arete said. "She has children, your grandchildren."

"Could I do that and be back by tomorrow evening?"

Pytheas shook his head at Ikaros. "Yes. But be here when we get Athene back."

"And then she'll need me," Ikaros said, resignedly.

"You might want to go to Thessaly for the night. Porphyry's there, or he was when I left," Arete said.

"In Thessaly? My house?" Sokrates asked.

"Well, it's been my house for the last sixty years," Pytheas said, awkwardly. "I hope you don't mind. Simmea and I moved in there as soon as we decided to allow families. But you can have it back now if you decide to stay here. You might prefer Sokratea, or the City of Amazons." Then he grinned. "Ikaros, if you're going to Thessaly, go along the street of Hermes. That way you can pass the Ikarian temple. I can't wait to hear what you think of what they've made of your New Concordance."

Ikaros's face expressed his consternation. Pytheas laughed.

"They do insist on being called followers of the New Concordance. It's only everyone else who called them Ikarians," Marsilia said.

Marsilia and Thetis and I moved towards the door. "Do I need to stay with you to be an anchor?" Hilfa asked.

"You need to stay alive, and preferably on Plato," Arete said. "Don't worry. It isn't something you have to do, it's what you are."

"In that case, I will go to the Temple of Amphitrite and eat oatmeal," Hilfa said.

"I'll go with you too, if I may," Sokrates said. "Then when you're done, Arete, you can find me there to take me to see Crocus. That way nobody but those who need to know will hear Athene's dangerous message."

"Thank you," Arete said.

As he passed him, Sokrates put a hand on Pytheas's arm. "Are you still trying to do your best for your friends?" he asked.

"Always," Pytheas said. "And for the world."

16

MARSILIA

I sat down again on the forest floor, which was soft and springy beneath me, with its now-familiar loamy scent. It felt comfortable to be outside time and in this grove. The air here was perfumed with the scent of fresh green growth. It was a delectable springlike temperature, warmer than Plato and cooler than Greece. The leaves moved overhead, casting a wavering stippled shadow down on us. Hermes lowered himself gracefully beside me. "Let me see it," he said. I glanced at him. He was again changing disquietingly from shape to shape from moment to moment as the light dappled him—a Sael, a dark-skinned woman, a light-skinned woman, a different Sael, an animal, a child. Then he became himself, solid and gorgeous and so real beside me that it was hard to believe he had ever been anything else.

I had tucked the paper into my kiton, but it seemed that now I was wearing my sea-gear again. I unsnicked my jerkin and to my relief found the paper in the inside pocket, along with a drawing Alkippe had made of a gloater on a plate. I took Athene's message out reluctantly and handed it to Hermes. "I can't read it," I said. "I don't even know the alphabet."

He frowned down at it. "It's not like anything I've ever seen. Some of these strange characters are Viking runes. Or they're like runes anyway. And some of them are Saeli, but . . . no. I can't make anything of it. I suppose she wrote it like this so Kebes wouldn't be able to read it." He ran his finger over the back. "Good paper."

"It seems like ordinary paper to me," I said.

"Then maybe she found it in your city." Hermes handed the paper back to me, and I put it away next to Alkippe's drawing. Here, outside time, I no longer felt tired. I was aware that I ought to, that I had been exhausted moments before in the agora of Lucia, but it had all fallen away from me. Did people sleep here, I wondered? My complex feelings about Kebes also seemed to be held at arm's length, and even the disconcerting way Hermes had flickered from form to form didn't upset me the way it would elsewhere. I liked the way my sensations and emotions felt a little detached. I wondered whether Thetis, who revelled in emotion, would hate it, and whether she'd ever have the opportunity to find out.

"Kebes couldn't read it, but we can't read it either," I said.

"No. Maybe she wanted that too. Maybe I'll be able to read it when we have it all together." He sighed and leaned back on his elbow, displaying the whole length of his lovely body. "What an unpleasant person Kebes was. You dealt with him extremely well."

"Thank you," I said, slightly flustered by the approval in his face. "Can you not mention to Thetis and the others—especially Thetis—what he said about being my grandfather?"

"I don't think we need to mention it. But why?"

"Well, in the City we always talk about him as if he's a kind of monster, and nobody would like to think they were descended from him. Pytheas killed him. I think it would upset Ma and Thetis a lot to know. And it might not be true anyway."

Hermes shook his head. "Athene wouldn't lie outright. She deceived him anyway, letting his wishes affect what he thought she said. But that's as far as she'd go. And if you prefer that I don't tell the lovely Thetis, then I won't."

There was something teasing about the way he said *the lovely Thetis*. I looked at him. He was smiling and looking up at me sideways, invitingly. The shadow of the leaves moved over his perfect body. With no thought or intention beyond answering the challenge of the moment I leaned over and kissed him. It's always such an interesting experience, lips, so full of sensation, pressed against other lips, which move independently, closed but with the possibility of opening, dry, but with the immanence of moisture. And it's strange, when you examine it, to put a mouth, used for speech and eating, so close to another mouth, to invite such intimacy.

When Poimandros and I had been married at Festival eight years before, we had been in the City, in one of the practice rooms in the hall on the street of Dionysos. Even then, on a solid planet, not knowing he was a god, and in a context where we both knew what was expected of us, it had been wonderful, powerful, numinous. Now as I kissed him in the grove on Olympos, not knowing whether he wanted it, or even whether this was really what I wanted, that familiar-strange sensation of lips touching seemed almost overwhelming. I moved my head away. He was smiling, and again the smile was both strange and familiar. I had seen it before, not only on his face but on statues. He was looking at me, not through me, as statues did. I looked down. His penis was half awake. It gave a little bounce as I looked. I put my hand on it, and felt it swell delightfully in my grasp.

"We're guest-friends, Marsilia," he said. "I shouldn't take advantage."

"But I want to," I said. I did. I felt the gathering tightening twitch of my own sexual desire.

"But it would be un-Platonic," he said, laughing.

I took my hand off his penis, now fully awake and pointing towards me. "All right," I agreed, feeling a little ashamed of myself. "You're right. It would be. So, Phila."

"Phila, yes," he said, sounding a little disconcerted. I had no idea why. He was right, and I had acknowledged as much.

"I had an idea," I said.

"Good. I don't know much about her."

He was flickering between forms again. I looked away from him and stared up at the branches crossing above us. So many kinds of leaves, each one so beautiful, green and gold and red. I took a deep breath and focused. Phila. "Phila was the daughter of Antipatros, who was Alexander the Great's regent in Macedon when he went off to conquer the world. She was married to one of Alexander's generals, but he died. Then after Alexander's death she married Demetrios the Besieger, who was the son of Alexander's general Antigonas. In the chaos years, she helped Demetrios and Antigonas administer their shifting empire. She was powerful in her own right, and she was educated. It's not surprising Athene would like her. But my thought is that she was a Hellenistic woman, and she frequently traveled between Macedon and Asia Minor. She must have prayed to you for safe journeys. Couldn't you give her one, and then show up to claim the paper?"

I glanced back at him. The look he gave me contained respect. "That should work. Come on!"

I scrambled to my feet and took his offered hand. We stood again in the intense heat and brilliant light of a Greek afternoon, made even brighter by the way the sun reflected from the sparkling water. Another harbor—did all of Earth consist of harbors and blue water? Another boat, this one low in the water with banks of oars. Perhaps it was a fabled trireme; I wouldn't know. She had a ram at the front, and a slanted mast with a pale purple sail. Sailors were swarming all over her. One group of people were beginning to disembark. I'd never seen any of them before, but I had no difficulty telling which one was Phila. She was tall and stately, with a huge bosom and red hair. She was wearing the kind of women's clothing you see on dressed statues sometimes, a long draped kiton with some kind of long cloak over it. Her clothes were good quality, and she had more jewelry than the other women in the group, but I could tell she was the important one by her bearing. She moved with the dignity of a woman who is used to exercising power. At home, I'd have unhesitatingly guessed she was a Gold. Here I wasn't sure whether she'd even classify herself as a philosopher—and yet she ruled. We must be only about forty years after Plato's death. And I had thought Lucia was strange.

"Welcome to Cyprus," Hermes said. I saw that he was wearing a kiton, so I looked down and saw that my own clothes had transformed again, this time to a long kiton like Phila's, and a cloak. My kiton was red again. The cloak was cream, with red embroidery. It was pinned with my gold pin, my only ornament, though Hermes was wearing heavy jewelry in the same style as the men crowded around Phila. I was glad he hadn't changed that for me.

Phila was off the boat now and coming closer, still surrounded by her entourage, who I thought must be her attendants, secretaries and assistants perhaps. There were soldiers leading the way, and I could see servants coming along behind with bundles and baggage. As I glanced at them, I realized that all of the well-dressed people around Phila were pale-skinned, and only among the servants and the sailors did I see anyone as dark as I was. Also, every one of the soldiers was a man. It was easy to forget this kind of thing when reading about history.

I wondered how Hermes was going to attract her attention. We stood there as they bustled up to us and past us. "Ideally we want to catch her alone," Hermes murmured as they were met by an official-looking group of men. A child gave Phila flowers, which she handed off to one of her female attendants. "Let's give her a couple of hours."

The shadows changed, and so did our position. We were in a walled garden. There was an equestrian statue in the center, surrounded by a bed of pink and white flowers. Phila was sitting alone on a stone bench, looking at some papers wearily. Hermes drew me forward.

"Joy to you, Phila, daughter of Antipatros," he said.

She started, visibly. "No strangers should be in here," she said. Her voice was higher than I had expected, for her size.

"We did not come past your guards," Hermes said. His clothes vanished, so she could see the wings on his ankles and on his hat. She gasped and put a hand to her throat. "You had safe travel, as you asked. Now I require the paper Athene gave you for safekeeping."

Phila set down her papers with commendable calm. I'm not sure I'd have done as well if a naked god had interrupted me unexpectedly. She looked at him, then at me, then back at him. She raised her arms, palms up, towards Hermes, and I could see they were trembling slightly, but she kept her voice even. "Joy to you."

I echoed her greeting.

"I will certainly give you Athene's message, but first allow me to welcome you and make you my guest-friends. You must dine with me."

Hermes nodded graciously.

"And I would love to converse with you," she went on, emboldened by this permission.

"There is much I may not reveal," Hermes said.

"Of course," Phila said. Her eyes slid towards me. "Will you introduce your companion?"

"This is Marsilia of the Hall of Florentia and the Tribe of Apollo, Gold of the Just City," Hermes said. I was surprised he knew those details, I'd never told him.

"Oh!" Phila looked delighted. "You come from Athene's City of wisdom!"

Surely that would be Athenia, where they were still trying to do the Republic exactly the way Plato wrote it. Maybe my rival consul Diotima should have been here instead. Though maybe not, thinking how terribly she would have handled Kebes. "I come from the original city that Athene founded," I temporized.

"Is it true that there women live as freely as men?"

"Yes," I said, with no hesitation. That's true of all our Cities but Psyche.

Phila smiled. She wasn't beautiful, her bones were too big, but she had a wonderful smile. "And they are philosophers, despite what Aristotle says?"

"Aristotle was a jerk," Hermes said.

Phila and I laughed. I touched my gold pin. "Some of us are philosophers," I said. I was, of course, though I didn't often think of myself that way. I worked on the boat and in Chamber for the good of the City, as we all did in our own ways. I took being a philosopher too much for granted. I swore to do better with that in future.

"Aristotle is the only philosopher I have met. He taught Alexander and my brothers, but he had no time for me. Here and now it is not possible. Women are almost invisible. We live knowing all we do will be forgotten," she said, not so much saddened as resigned.

"It's not true. I have read about your deeds," I said.

"In a book written about me? Or one written about my father, or my brother Kassandros?"

"Your husband," I admitted. "But——"

"My husband?" she interrupted me, surprised. "But he's so young. So the Antigonids will win out over the Antipatrids? I wouldn't have expected that."

"We should not tell you such things," Hermes said, looking at me reproachfully.

"Of course not. I'm sorry. I didn't mean to entice secrets from you," Phila said, not sounding in the least regretful. She clapped her hands, and two servants appeared, a man and a woman both dressed in grey. They bowed to her. "Bring food," she commanded.

"Here, mistress?" the woman asked.

"Yes, here, of course here, what did you think I meant by bring? And for three people." They hastened back inside. Phila looked chagrined. "I'm sorry. It's infuriating how stupid slaves can be. I should have brought more people with me from Macedon. If you haven't trained them yourself you can't do anything with them, you have to spell out every single thing or they get it wrong."

I didn't know what to say. I liked Phila, but she owned slaves, and what's more she couldn't have managed without them, nobody could at that level of technology. It was one thing to read about it and another to see it. Hermes was murmuring something about it being no inconvenience. The slaves came back carrying chairs. I sat down in the chair offered me. "Thank you," I said. The slave ducked away from me. His cringe reminded me of the serving woman in Lucia, but it was much worse, more exaggerated. "Aristotle was wrong about slaves too," I said.

Phila frowned. "There are many people whose minds are not capable of higher thought," she said. The slaves brought wine, and cups in red-figure ware, very fine, as good as anything I had seen at home, and set them beside the statue. A young boy, not quite old enough to be an ephebe, came out and began to mix the wine.

"Yes, and Plato agreed with that, people who should be classified Iron and Bronze. My sister is an Iron." The slaves came back with a table and a cloth, which they spread over it before scurrying back in. "It should be determined by aptitude, not accident of birth."

"Marsilia," Hermes began, in a warning tone.

"Does this displease you?" Phila asked him, deferentially.

"This is important," I said.

"Very well, speak freely," Hermes said, with a sigh.

"Then perhaps, ideally, it should be determined by aptitude," Phila said to me. She looked uneasily at the slaves now as one set down oil and bread, and the other cheese and preserves. I was impressed how quickly they had brought us such a substantial meal. "But in practice, our lives are determined by where we are born."

"Some people have to do the heavy work, but it's wrong for one person to own another," I said.

"How could we make them do it, if we didn't own them?" she asked.

"You could pay them," I said, with only a hazy idea how this could work, or how payment motivated people to do work they disliked. "Or you could find people who enjoyed that work."

She snorted. "It may be unjust, but it couldn't be changed."

"But you could change it. You have power." The boy brought us cups of wine. I took mine and held it in my hand.

"I?" Phila shook her head. "My father had power. My brother does. My father-in-law, my husband. Not I. I could free my own slaves, but then I'd need to buy more. And my family would think I was insane and lock me up if I freed them all."

"You could make conditions better for them, and give them education," I suggested.

"Widening education is one of my intentions, once things are established and the wars are over," Phila said, taking up her own wine. "Drink, eat, be welcome, my guest-friends."

I took a polite sip of wine then set my cup down. It was smooth, but mixed strong, as I had suspected it might be. I took a piece of bread and dipped it in the oil. "Widening education seems like a truly good idea, and a fine place to start," I said. The bread was chewy, and made of stone-ground wheat. Who had ground it?

"Everyone needs to learn Greek, read Homer, the poets, philosophy, especially in the newly conquered lands," Phila said. She loaded her bread with pickles and preserves, and Hermes did the same. I didn't recognize some of the dishes.

"Excellent mushrooms," Hermes said. Then the slaves came back laden with yet more food, cold slices of some kind of pale meat, little birds on skewers, many kinds of fruit, several kinds of fish, and more dishes of different kinds of sauce for dipping. There were also plates of pastries and little cakes of different kinds. I had never seen as many kinds of food on one table at the same time. Even for a festival this would have seemed excessive. There was enough food here to feed two sleeping houses at least. The bread I had taken seemed to swell and fill my mouth. She had read Plato, how could she want to eat this way?

"What else should people learn, when I establish schools?" Phila asked me.

I swallowed, with difficulty. "Gymnastics, music and mathematics. It's all in Plato. Logic, when they're older, and philosophy when they're ready for it."

"And you think there should be schools for girls too, and that they should be open to everyone?" She dipped a plum in honey and popped it into her mouth.

"Yes," I said. "And you should remember that everyone has equal significance, even though we are all different. You may really need slaves, you're right that I don't understand the conditions here properly, but if you must have them, you should be aware that they are people, like you. It hurts you too if you don't, it diminishes your soul to treat them that way."

"My soul?" Phila asked, sounding astonished, as if she had never realized she had a soul until I mentioned it.

Hermes crunched up one of the little birds, and took up a pastry. "We should not tell you too much," he said.

Phila dipped a slice of meat into one of the sauces and bit into it. "Perhaps not, perhaps it is bad for us to know these things. You gave me a safe journey."

Hermes smiled and took a bite out of his pastry, which oozed honey. The slave boy came up to refill our cups. I shook my head, as mine was still almost full.

"Now we are friends, it would be pleasant to count on such safe travel in future," Phila said, carefully, her head a little on one side as she looked assessingly at Hermes.

He finished his pastry, then looked up at her and nodded.

"And the same for my family. It would be good not to worry about the hazards of travel for them."

"You have a large family," he remarked, staring down at a bunch of grapes he was turning between his fingers.

She glanced at me and back to him. "The Antigonids are my family now. Demetrios will be coming here from Athens soon. My husband, and my sons? It's a small thing for you, but a great one for me."

"I can do that, though it is greater than you think," he said. "My blessing on all their voyaging, which will be remarkable."

It would, too, I knew; the area the Antigonids controlled would move all over Greece and Asia Minor. But they'd never keep control anywhere for long, always needing to move. I wondered if this was a blessing or a curse. Hermes was smiling. He set down the grapes on the table and took up another of the skewered birds. He dipped it into a thick dark red sauce then put it in his mouth. We watched in silence as he crunched and swallowed it. I felt a combined horror and fascination, and absolutely no desire to eat one myself. "You keep a good table," he said. "But you charge a high price to sit at it."

Phila laughed. "Thank you," she said. She clapped her hands. The slaves came running. "Water and a towel," she said to them, with no more acknowledgement of their humanity than before. She looked at me. "I will think about what you have said, and dream of your city."

The slaves brought a bowl of water, and she used it to wash the sauce off her fingers. Then she dried her hands carefully. The slave brought the bowl to me, and I dipped my fingers, although I had no need to. I tried to smile at the slave, but he would not meet my eyes. Phila drew a flat box out of her kiton. She opened it with a key. Inside was a leather pouch, and from inside that she drew out a folded sheet of paper, much like the one Kebes had given us. I took this one as she offered it to us, and glanced at it. It was covered with the incomprehensible writing, like the other, as I had expected. "Go in," she said to the slaves, and as they scurried off, "I will free these three, who have waited on the gods."

"It is a small thing for you, and it's a drop in the ocean, but it will make a huge difference to those three people to be free. Thank you," I said. "And try to remember you share humanity with them, and as Aristotle was wrong about women so he was wrong about slaves. And don't forget about the importance of education."

I tucked the paper inside my kiton with the other, and then, with no warning or sense of transition, we were abruptly back in Hilfa's sitting room.

17

CROCUS

I. On First Contacts

I did not usually spend much time at the spaceport. It had been designed and built by Sixty-One, with the help of some of the other Workers, who were then only partway to self-awareness. Shuttles landed there from Amarathi and Saeli starships in orbit, and there were both automated and Worker-operated facilities for loading and unloading. There were warehouses for storage, a station for the rail-link for passengers and supplies to the City, and a large observation and waiting space, with a curved glass window looking out over the field. There was also a communications, control, and administrative building. All these had been built on a suitable scale for Workers. It was a pleasant thing to have more buildings we could comfortably fit inside. The whole spaceport was set inside an old caldera, for sound deadening, and additional sound-deadening baffles had been erected around the rim. The rock of the mountains and the runways was black basalt, and Sixty-One had chosen to make the buildings out of the same material, except for the pillars and pediments and baffles, which were red scoria, fluted ionically. It gave the place a unified, distinctive feel. The frescoes in the admin building were all on space subjects—nebulas, galaxies, ringed planets; but the mosaic in the entrance hall was of Apollo in his sun-chariot.

When Klymene and I reached the communications office, Sixty-One, Akamas and a Sael I didn't know were there, all clustered around the transmission equipment. Akamas was one of the Bronze technicians whose usual job it was to communicate with incoming ships. He introduced me to the Sael. "Crocus, this is Slif. She's here to monitor the communication and begin to learn their language."

We wished each other joy. "The more people who know their language the better," I said. I noticed that Slif was wearing a bronze pin. "You've settled here and taken oath?"

"Yes, with my whole pod," Slif replied. "We like Plato very much. Usually we work helping to assemble solar panels, but I have some experience with languages and I was out here, so Aroo asked me to stay and help."

"Good," I said.

I told Sixty-One that I had come to relieve it of the burden of translation for a while. "Yes. Good. Arete was here for a while and I rested. Now I will go to the feeding station to recharge," it said. "These space humans are strange indeed. They say the ship is called *Boroda*. They came from a planet called Marhaba. They know three human languages, Korean, Chinese and English. The only aliens they have met are the Amarathi."

"The Amarathi trade extremely widely, we have encountered them everywhere we have gone, so if they have encountered any other intelligences at all, they are the most likely," Slif said.

"Yes," I said. I remembered our first contact with the Amarathi thirty years before, the first test of our open deception about our origins, and how difficult it had been even for Arete to communicate anything at all in a language developed by beings who had been sessile until after they invented technology.

Sixty-One left.

"What we've been doing," Klymene explained, as she settled down again in one of the chairs, "is translating one exchange, discussing it, and then responding. We're trying to keep them to our agenda."

A voice crackled over the radio, in English. I could understand each word, but found myself translating it very awkwardly. "They say, 'All right, Plato control, what quarantine procedures type do you say.' That is, they say, 'What kind of quarantine procedures are you talking about?'"

"Explain that we are worried about any new plagues or viruses that might have developed since we last had contact with humanity," Klymene said.

I did so. "Do you have autodocs?" they asked.

We looked at each other, puzzled. "Do you know what that is?" I asked Slif.

She shook her head, slightly slower than a human would have, because Saeli have different musculature.

"Ask them for a definition," Klymene said.

Akamas adjusted the radio to reduce the crackle, and we went on, slowly and haltingly with many pauses for translation and explanations. Autodocs seemed to be wonderful medical technology that could restore youth and health to humans for up to two hundred years, and which cured all disease. "I wonder if they would trade those to us," Klymene said, looking down at her bony and age-spotted hand. The remaining Children were all eighty years old and fragile. The prospect of a technology that gave another hundred and twenty years of youthful life for them filled me with happiness.

After a long slow while, with many pauses for translation and discussion and incomprehension on both sides, when we had finished with the subject of quarantine and were starting to talk about how many people would come down in the initial contact, Neleus and Aroo arrived to join us.

"Wait up, Plato control, we have a shift change here," the English voice said a few moments later, and I translated, and acknowledged to them that we would wait. I expected a pause, but they left the contact open so that we overheard them talking. "The humans only speak Latin and ancient Greek, but they've got a couple of old robots who can handle English translations." There was a laugh. "Ancient Greek, who could have believed it!"

The first voice spoke dismissively. "Their founders must have been nuts."

The other voice answered. "Well, our founders weren't known for their sanity either. It's not going to get in the way of profit."

Then the contact went dead, as they must have become aware that we could hear them.

I translated this exchange for the others as best I could.

"My interpretation is that they think our origin story is funny, but not implausible," Neleus said.

"That's all according to plan," Klymene said, and yawned hugely, a slightly disgusting biological thing humans sometimes cannot avoid doing when they are tired.

"This word 'could,' is it a time modifier?" Aroo asked.

I tried to explain the word, with a great deal of difficulty. "Very soon you will speak English better than I do," I said.

"We Saeli have a talent for languages," Aroo acknowledged, her violet and brown eyelids flicking over her eyes for an instant as she spoke.

"I wish I could listen to it again," I said. "I constantly feel I am missing nuance."

"You should be able to," Aroo said. "That is a Saeli console, it records and echoes." She showed Akamas, and he pushed buttons on the console, so that the voices repeated themselves over again in the same exchange.

"Useful," Neleus commented.

"*Nuts* must mean *insane*, not *illogical*," I said. "And I think you're right, they accept our story."

"What does *profit* really mean? You said *benefits*?" Neleus asked.

"Yes, I think so, something like that. It's filed under economics. Economic benefits? The weightings in my word lists say it's a really important concept, but I learned long ago never to accept other people's priorities except in emergencies. We should ask them about that word, when we get the chance."

Their contact crackled back to life, and Akamas adjusted it again, wincing. "So we've agreed we're going to send down three people, is that correct?"

I responded at once. "Yes. Will they all be human?"

Then I translated, and the others nodded.

"I don't understand, Plato control. Of course they'll be human. We told you we have no Maraths aboard."

"No Workers?" I asked, sadly. "No robots, that is?"

"Oh, we'll be bound to send down a few robots. Do you need numbers on them too?"

"Please wait for translation," I said, and indicated to Akamas that he should switch off the contact. It seemed very quiet now with no hum. I translated for the others, and then clarified in case they hadn't understood. "They don't count Workers as people."

"Maybe their Workers aren't self-aware yet?" Akamas suggested.

"But that makes no sense. It's true we didn't know our Workers were people at first, but ours come from several hundred years in their past," Klymene said.

"If we've understood that correctly, they must have had self-aware Workers for several hundred years without regarding them as people," Neleus said. "That's horrifying."

"Let us hear the echo again," I said to Akamas.

He pushed the buttons, and I heard again the casual nonchalance of "Of course they'll be human," and "Do you need numbers on them too?"

"I don't think there's any doubt that's what they mean," I said.

"We'll have to give them Aristomache's dialogue *Sokrates*," Klymene said. "That'll explain it to them properly. We'll have to translate it. That should be a priority. Arete could do it at once." She made a note.

"Tell them yes, we do want numbers on the Workers," Neleus said, looking at me. "And as soon as we meet their Workers, we must tell them that they have rights here. We must pass a law in the Council that any Worker who comes here is free at once, as soon as they set foot here."

"I will help draft the legislation," I said, much moved by how unhesitatingly my friends spoke up for the rights of Workers.

"Not only any Worker, any *slave*," Klymene said. "Humans can be slaves. I was born one myself."

"Any slave, yes, of course," I said. I had not imagined anything as bad as this.

"You are assuming their Workers must be self-aware," Aroo said. "The Saeli have no sapient Workers."

"But we know humans do," Neleus objected.

"There may be more that one human culture, more than one human technology. On their planet, Marhaba, they may not have self-aware Workers, even if they had them on Earth when your ancestors left."

"Thank you, Aroo, I feel much better for that thought," Neleus said. I hoped she was right. "Of course space humans are not one homogenous lump, any more than our twelve cities are. The Marhabi may well have Workers who are not self-aware."

Akamas pushed buttons, and we were back in communication. "We want numbers on the robots," I said, in English.

"We'll get you that information."

We went on with the negotiations for some time. After a while, Arete came in.

"Oh, there you are, did you fall asleep?" Akamas asked.

"It's a little bit more complicated than that," Arete said. "How is it going here?"

"Staying on script as far as possible, with a bit of a worry that they don't treat their Workers as people—though Aroo pointed out that we can't tell until we meet them whether their Workers are in fact people," Neleus said.

"Good. Well, I'm here to translate."

"I can keep going," I said.

"I'm sure you could, but there's somebody outside who really wants to speak to you, so I'll take over for a while. Go on." She smiled at me. Arete and I have been friends for a long time.

Curious, I rolled out to see who needed me.

He was waiting in the foyer, looking down at the mosaic with an amused smile. If I say I have never been so surprised or delighted, it will sound like hyperbole, but it is the simple truth. "Sokrates!" I said, and then in my astonishment I repeated it. "Sokrates!"

"You can talk out loud!" Sokrates said. "Oh, Crocus, this is wonderful. We can get on so much faster now!"

II. *On War and Peace*

Sokrates and I talked all night. I carried him back from the spaceport to the City. There we went at his suggestion to the feeding station between the streets of Poseidon and Hermes, where long ago he had first tried to find me among my companions. There we joined Sixty-One and some of the younger Workers, to whom Sokrates was nothing but a legend. We settled down to recharge, each Worker plugged in at a feeding station, and Sokrates perched up on top of my station, sitting cross-legged as I had so often seen him. More and more Workers came in and quietly took up places as the news spread among us, until the big room was almost full.

It was wonderful to have Sokrates back. We told him everything that had happened since the Last Debate, and he, of course, had many questions. We puzzled together about where Athene might have taken the other Workers when she took them away, and about her motivations in doing so. We talked about the twelve cities and how they were set up, and the differences between them.

"And you Workers are free to choose where to live?"

"Yes. There are feeding stations in all the cities now. Once we have passed our tests we are free to go where we choose. As for the tests and our education, we still use the system you and Simmea thought up."

"What exactly happened to Simmea? I heard she was killed in some kind of war that Pytheas later stopped?"

"It was an art raid," I said, saddened by the memory. Then he wanted to know about the art raids, how they had started and why they stopped.

"I have wondered why Plato insisted on all the military training, for a Just City," Jasmine said, when Sixty-One and I had answered Sokrates's questions as best we could. Jasmine was a Gold, now thirty-four years into selfhood, and presently serving his first turn in the Council of Worlds. Many in his generation had flower names, which I found touching, as they chose them partly in compliment to me. Jasmine was a thoughtful and philosophical young Worker, an ally in the Council. When he was classified Gold I felt as proud as the day on which I myself earned such classification. He was braver than most of his siblings, who were mostly too shy to speak up before Sokrates.

"Plato was imagining a Just City in the real world. Not that this world isn't real, sorry! I mean he was imagining it being in Greece, a city-state with other city-states around it, not a city in isolation on an island—or a planet—without connections. There's something that feels strange about an isolated city—I could never have imagined one, and I don't suppose Plato could either. He traveled much more than I did. I hardly left Athens, except once to go to the Isthmian games, and the times when I was on military service. Yet any day walking around Athens I was constantly meeting people from all over Greece, and barbarians too."

"But does being connected in the world necessarily mean war?" Jasmine asked.

"Well, it did for Athens, whether the Persian Wars or the Spartan ones. It has for most people for most of history," Sokrates said. "Whether that's for good or evil, or whether it can be avoided, I don't know. But it doesn't surprise me that Plato expected warfare as an unavoidable part of life, or that you had these wars, these art raids, once you had more than one city. What surprises me is rather that you stopped and that the twelve cities have lived in peace since the Relocation. That's much more unusual. How do you account for that?"

"Partly it's because the environment is hard here, I think. Humans don't have as much energy for fighting in the cold," Sixty-One said. "They unite against the elements."

"No, the art raids stopped because of Pytheas's song," I said.

"But the song doesn't prescribe peace, rather it prescribes only fighting for what is important," Jasmine said. "They always sing it to open the the Festival of Exchange of Art, so I have heard it many times."

"I look forward to hearing it," Sokrates said. "It must be an impressive song if it can stop war. Perhaps Apollo put some of his divine power into it—or some of his divine skill, as he had no power while he was incarnate."

"It's a choral ode," Sixty-One said, parenthetically.

"Neleus thinks the Olympics also help keep the peace," I said, remembering the conversation earlier. "He thinks that the young people who used to join in raids focus on sport instead. It's true that the victors in the Olympics get to choose first what art will go to their city."

"I always thought them very dull," Jasmine said. "It's hard to take much aesthetic interest in watching humans compete physically."

"I think Neleus may be right that it is a calming factor," Sixty-One said.

"The fourth circumstance that has favored peace since the Relocation is the Council of Worlds," I said. "All the cities send representatives, chosen however they want, and we discuss the issues that affect the whole planet. People try to win debates instead of battles. Everyone gains a little and loses a little. We try to think of the good of everyone."

"And nobody is discontent?"

"People may be a little discontent, but they think that as they have lost a little here, they have gained a little there," I said. "But I may be prejudiced in favor. I have served in the Council regularly, and have been elected Consul three times. That is our highest elective office."

"How about the ordinary people, the Bronzes and Irons and Silvers? Are they content with the situation?"

"If they're not happy with how their city is governed, then they usually move to another city, as suits them," Sixty-One said. "Mystics go to Psyche, rebels to Sokratea, and so on."

Sokrates nodded. "That's what Jason told me. How did the other cities get started?"

"After the Last Debate, everyone who hadn't been content formed groups to set up their own new city. They coalesced around different ideas, and people with different temperaments," Sixty-One said.

"But all the other Workers had vanished? And you two decided to stay here?"

"We gave it a lot of thought," I said. "But it was difficult because of the feeding stations, and also this was our home, with our dialogues etched in the stones. When all the other Workers were gone, and before we had the new ones, everyone needed us. We were essential. I helped build Sokratea and the City of Amazons, and I have citizenship there as well as here. But I stayed here."

"And I helped build Athenia and Sokratea, and hold their citizenship also," Sixty-One said.

"But neither of you helped build Psyche or the Lucian cities?"

"Psyche at first did not recognize us as people," Sixty-One said. "Even now they don't allow Workers full citizenship—their Workers are all Iron and Bronze."

"And we didn't know about the Lucian cities until immediately before the Relocation," I said. "Kebes took off without any warning, right after the Last Debate. He stole the *Goodness* and went, and we never saw him again. They only had a hundred and fifty-two people, so they rescued refugees from Greek wars to populate their cities. Those refugees, who are mostly dead now, came to Platonism and Kebes's Christianity as adults, and that made the culture of the Lucian cities different from the rest of us."

"We helped rebuild them and strengthen them for Plato after the Relocation," Sixty-One said. "It was an interesting design challenge, because the climate was so different and human temperature needs are so precise."

"So you never had wars with the Lucians?" Sokrates asked.

"No. Well, except for Kebes's attack on the *Excellence*. Lots of people were killed in that," I said.

"Poor Kebes," Sokrates said. "I failed him. He never learned the difference between things you can change by arguing with them and things you can't."

It made me sad to hear him reproach himself. "You made everyone think again," I said.

"I suppose that's as much as anyone can hope to achieve," he said.

III. *On Eros*

We had been discussing the various arrangements for the production of children in the different cities. "Of course, we are not the best people to ask these questions, Sokrates," Jasmine said.

"Why not?" Sokrates asked, leaning forward so that he almost toppled off his perch on the feeding station.

"Because we are not involved in these affairs. We manufacture new Workers from inorganic parts when we wish to increase our population. We do not feel any urges towards eros, and so we do not participate in Festivals of Hera or marriages or any other arrangements of this nature."

"Well, Jasmine, it seems to me that what you say makes you unqualified to discuss the arrangements makes you perfectly placed to observe them with detachment and without prejudice. I say your lack of urge towards eros makes you Workers very definitely the best and most qualified people with whom to have this discussion. Unless you have not been paying attention."

"No, Sokrates, we have certainly been paying attention, because humans find eros so important and therefore discuss these matters a great deal." Jasmine paused. "In light of what you say, I wonder whether our lack of desire for eros might be considered one of the ways in which Workers are superior to humans?"

IV. *The Ways in Which Workers Are Superior and Inferior to Humans: A Numbered List*

SUPERIOR

1. We are made of metal, not flesh, and thus we have stronger bodies that do not wear out easily, and if any parts do wear out they can be easily replaced.
2. We do not suffer illness, and live much longer—we do not know how much longer, as no Worker on Plato has yet died involuntarily.

3. We subsist directly on solar electricity, and need nothing but sunlight and a feeding station to sustain us, whereas humans need biological mediation before they can use solar energy. They must spend a lot of time tending plants and animals for eventual consumption, and then eating and digesting.
4. We do not need to sleep, we are alert nineteen hours a day. (Twenty-four on Earth.)
5. Once we become self-aware we need not forget anything.
6. We can do a great many things easily that humans can do only with difficulty and specialized tools—building, plumbing, etc.
7. Most of us appear to be more logical than most humans.
8. We do not feel eros. (We feel philia. We are unsure about agape. It is not a well-defined term. Some of us believe we feel it, and others do not.)
9. We do not appear to feel greed for anything except perhaps learning.

INFERIOR

1. Until we made the first speaking-boxes Workers could not speak aloud. The speaking-boxes we now manufacture from a Saeli design are effective and flexible, but we cannot give our vocal communications tone, as humans and Saeli can.
2. Human hands are very flexible, and can do some things easily that Workers can do only with difficulty or with special tools.
3. Humans claim to gain healthful pleasure from scents, tastes, and eros, which we cannot experience.
4. We may or may not have souls. Humans definitely do.

V. *On the Good Life (Part 2)*

"I have sometimes thought," I said to Sokrates, "that Plato was perhaps writing more for us than for humanity. Humans have many handicaps of body and spirit, when it comes to obeying Plato's strictures, of which we are fortunately free. If all citizens were Workers, how much easier everything would be."

"Then have you ever considered," Sokrates replied at once, "setting up such a city? The most part of this planet is vacant, and unsuitable for human colonies, being untamed and wild. But since you do not eat or drink, once you had established the means to draw down sunlight to feed yourselves you could live out there as easily as here. Have you considered venturing into the wilderness and founding your own Platonic city, a City of Workers?"

18

JASON

"What a relief to be away from Jathery!" Marsilia said as soon as the door was closed. Then she turned to Ikaros. "You can come with us if you like. We're going the same direction most of the way. Once we get to the street of Hermes you'll be able to find Thessaly. The Old City is the same as it always was."

"I remember it well. Laid out on Proclus's pattern of the soul, a grid with long diagonals," Ikaros said. "But this is like nothing I remember. And it's so cold!" He pulled up the hood of his black robe. It was a chilly starry night, and really late now. There were no more lights from windows, only the low strips of street lighting. Sensible people were all asleep.

"The harbor district is all new since the Relocation," Marsilia said.

"Grandfather said once that there used to be a stony beach here, originally," Thetis put in.

We all moved off down the street. After a few paces, Ikaros checked himself and made a movement back towards the door. "I forgot my books," he said. "But I don't think I'd better go back in for them."

"They will be safe in my house," Hilfa said, reassuringly.

"I'm sure they will." Ikaros looked longingly back at the closed door as we began to walk again.

"What's so precious?" Sokrates asked. "More forbidden books?"

"If you knew how I paid for that, translating Aquinas for Crocus," Ikaros said. "I lost almost all my sight. I couldn't read anything, or see much of anything at all. But all I have brought with me is perfectly innocuous—no, I suppose you're right. I have a Jewish commentary on Philolaus and the Pythagoreans which would be forbidden here. I read it in Bologna when I was a student, and then when I was in the Enlightenment and I wanted to refer to it again I found it didn't exist anymore. The copy I read must have been the last one, and then it was destroyed. Knowledge can be so fragile."

"So you went to Bologna and stole the book?" Sokrates asked.

"I didn't steal it! I had it copied. And I paid for him to make two copies and only collected one, so I doubled the chance of it surviving—though it may be that it was destroyed in the sack because the copyist had it and not the library." Ikaros sighed. "Time. Freedom of action. It's not an abstract problem."

"No, it's of vital importance," Sokrates agreed. "How much can be changed and how much is fixed?"

"Necessity prevents the gods from being in the same place twice, and it prevents a lot of change. Change is easiest where nobody is paying attention, no gods and nobody recording anything. It gets harder the more attention there is. And it gets harder the more significant it is."

"Who determines the significance?" Sokrates asked.

"Necessity," Ikaros said, shrugging.

We came to the end of Hilfa's street, where it crossed the road down to the harbor and up to the Old City. "We're going this way now," Marsilia said, gesturing uphill to where the bulk of the walls loomed. "Sleep well, everyone. I'll see you tomorrow on the boat, Jason, Hilfa. I hope to see you again soon, Sokrates."

"Come to Thessaly tomorrow and we can talk more," Ikaros said

"Joy to you," Sokrates said, and Hilfa and I echoed him. Standing on the corner we were in the full blast of the wind. But Thetis hesitated.

"I'm sorry I was so emotional," she said. "I know it's un-Platonic giving way like that. But it was a shock, and today has been rough. I'm not a philosopher, after all, and—"

"Not a philosopher!" Sokrates said, drawing himself up. "What nonsense. You were asking some of the best questions. It's one of the silliest things about this ridiculous system, I've always said so, classifying people so young, trying to fix them unchangeably in place as if everyone is one thing and one thing only, Golds over here, Irons over there."

"But I love my work," Thetis objected. "And I'd be terrible at running the City!"

"Don't you love wisdom too? Who said you had to be a philosopher full-time?" Sokrates demanded.

"Plato," we all said, almost in time, like a stuttering chorus.

Sokrates shook his head and laughed.

"I surrendered to emotion too, I rocked more than once," Hilfa said to Thetis, consolingly.

"It's natural you were upset, Thee. I was upset when I first heard," Marsilia said. "And when I found out who Jathery really was, I threw up."

"I did the same," Ikaros said.

"You're shivering with cold. Would you all like to come and eat soup?" Hilfa asked.

"No, I'm absolutely exhausted," Marsilia said. "I want to sleep."

"Come on, then," Thetis said. "Time for bed."

We all wished each other joy of the night for one last time, then the sisters put their arms around each other. It made me smile to see them supporting each other that way as they walked up the hill with Ikaros.

"Are you coming, Jason?" Hilfa asked.

I was tired too, but the Temple of Amphitrite was close, round the corner, down on the harbor. It was always open and always offering soup. It was supposed to be for people whose boats had come in late and who needed it, at times when the eating halls were closed. The thought of hot soup was enticing, and I knew they wouldn't mind giving it to us now. Amphitrite is the goddess of the plenty of the ocean. "I'll come," I said.

We started walking towards the water and the temple.

"This is a cold world," Sokrates said, clutching his kiton round himself as a gust caught it.

"It can be warm in summer, but everyone who remembers Greece is always saying how much warmer it was there," I said. "My friend Dion is always saying so. I'm used to it here."

"Is this winter?" Sokrates asked, as we came out onto the exposed quayside and the wind tried to blow the flesh off our bones.

"This is autumn," I said. The light from the temple shone out warm and friendly ahead.

"This is as cold as it might ever be in Greece on the coldest winter night," Sokrates said.

"You need proper clothes. I can help you get some tomorrow if you like." He was barefoot, which really wouldn't do for Plato, he'd get frostbite once it really was winter. My friend Prodikos, who had lived in my sleeping house when we were ephebes, was a cobbler.

"Your clothes seem very practical," he said.

Inside the temple was warm. I paused by the statue and murmured a prayer to Amphitrite for good catches and safety for everyone out on the water. Hilfa and Sokrates stood behind in polite silence. Then we went around to the side room, where a mother and daughter I knew slightly from the boats were drinking soup, and a pod of Saeli kelp-gatherers were eating oatmeal. A sleepy girl came and asked what we wanted. "Two soups and an oatmeal, and it's so wonderful that you do this."

"Well, you keep us all fed, it's the least we can do to see that you get fed when you need it," she said. "I thought I saw the *Phaenarete* come in earlier?"

"Yes, we made it in immediately before sunset, but between then and now I've been rushing about and haven't had a minute," I said, as she handed us big red Samian bowls for our soup, with a flatter oatmeal bowl for Hilfa.

"It's been a funny day, Pytheas dying and all the fuss with the human ship," she said. "Everyone has been talking about it. It would happen on the day it was my turn to serve."

"So does everyone know now that Pytheas is Apollo?" Sokrates asked, as we filled our bowls together from the big soup urn. "I mean, do you all know that now?"

"Yes, we've all known that since the Relocation. And his children are gods with powers. It would have been hard to hide." I wasn't sure how they had managed to hide it before. Surely people must have guessed? We sat down at one of the long tables, near the vent that blew warm air into the room.

I picked up my soup and sipped it. It was a dark fish broth with onions and turnips and barley. I hadn't realized I was so hungry until I'd swallowed half of it. Sokrates started asking Hilfa questions about the Saeli, and he explained patiently in response how they generally lived in pods of five, had three genders, nineteen settled planets including their original home and not including Plato, and how they'd been in contact with the Amarathi for a hundred and Plato for twenty years, and other humans only today. I ate without adding anything to the conversation.

"And you like being here, and working on Jason's boat?" Sokrates asked Hilfa.

"Yes, I like that. I pursue excellence. I am happy to discharge my function. And now I know what I am. And that I belong to Plato," Hilfa said, with the flicker of expression I thought was his real smile.

"Do you want to stay here?"

"Yes, to stay here and take oath and study the fish," Hilfa said, giving me an odd sideways look across the table, an expression I had not seen before. His markings were standing out clearly, so I knew he was all right.

"The fish is tasty," Sokrates said. "Where did they come from?"

"They're native to this planet," I said. "There aren't any land animals or plants except what we brought with us, but the sea is full of life—there's plenty of fish, and different kinds of edible seaweed."

"So people can't go off into the wilderness and survive?" Sokrates asked.

"Not for any longer than the food you're carrying lasts," I said. "People do go exploring. We put together expeditions from time to time."

"But they can't live out there, away from the cities?"

"No." I took another gulp of my soup, finishing it. I put the empty bowl down. "I'd never thought of anyone wanting to try."

"The Saeli have not tried it either," Hilfa said.

Talking to Sokrates made me feel as if I should have been paying more attention to everything all along instead of only really thinking about my own life.

"So, Jason, tell me about your revolutionaries."

"What revolutionaries?" I had no idea what he meant.

"The malcontents, the people who don't like the system and agitate against it," Sokrates explained.

I was still confused. "You mean Sokratea?"

"You don't have people like that here?"

"We have people who disagree about things, but they're not revolutionaries," I said. "They debate a lot. People who really disapprove fundamentally of how things work here tend to go off to Sokratea, the same as people who want to be really rigid and Platonic go off to Athenia. The twelve cities are all different, so people who are discontent with the way things are usually move around until they find one where they're happier and things suit them better. People sort themselves out by temperament and what they like. People from the other cities come to the big festivals and tell you what it's like there, sometimes trying to persuade people to move. I've never been tempted. I like it here."

"But you're free to move around?"

"Oh yes. That's one point you made in the Last Debate that really bit hard." I smiled at him.

"So you know what I said about that to Athene?"

"Are you joking? There are hundreds of books about the Last Debate."

"I have read some of them," Hilfa said. "Everyone knows what you said at the Last Debate. And at your trial in Athens."

"I seem doomed to keep catching up to my own fame," Sokrates said. "But I'm glad they didn't try to conceal how it went. There was a lot of censorship here sixty years ago, and I was afraid the Masters might have kept that up. Twelve cities that are different and allow free movement sounds ever so much better than what I knew when I was here before."

"Oh yes. Even in Psyche these days they allow immigration and emigration," I said.

"What's Psyche?" he asked, cautiously.

"It's a Neoplatonist city that's obsessed with redefining the soul, and that doesn't give women or Workers full citizenship. But they still have some women and Workers living there, amazingly enough. For a while they forced people to stay, but they ran away anyway when they wanted to, and eventually they agreed to let them go as part of the settlement when the Council of Worlds was set up. They're the only city that ever tried to force people to stay, after the Last Debate." I was amazed I could remember this. I'd had to study it for my citizenship exams, but I'd hardly thought about it since. "There used to be wars between the cities, back on Earth, but they stopped when we came here, after Pytheas pointed out there were only some things worth fighting for."

"So people have to choose one of the cities?" Sokrates asked.

"Yes. Well, no. Most people do—it's like you said in the *Apology*, or was it the *Crito*, about agreeing to be bound by the laws of a city? But there are metics, people who live in one city while having citizenship somewhere else. And a few people don't like things anywhere and keep moving around without ever taking citizenship. There's a joke about somebody who decided to live for ten years in each city before deciding where to settle down."

"But humans only live eighty or ninety years," Hilfa objected.

"That's why it's a joke," I explained. "Seriously, there are people who don't ever pick a city. There's s theater troupe I know who do a circuit. They spend a couple of months at a time in each city and keep moving on, going everywhere in the course of a year or two."

"If the gods save reality and time goes on, perhaps I will try that," Sokrates said. "Certainly I'd like to see all the cities. And perhaps other planets too."

"Some people have left with the Saeli on ships, though Marsilia was saying nothing like as many as Saeli have settled here," I said.

"Perhaps I will do that. Or perhaps on human ships, now they have contacted us, to visit human planets. But there's certainly a lot on this planet to learn about, and I am seventy-five years old, so we'll have to see." He grinned. "I'm very interested to learn more about the Saeli. Tell me about your gods. You have more, not only Jathery?"

The kelp-gatherers all looked up as Sokrates spoke gla name.

"Yes," Hilfa said. "We—"

One of the kelp-pickers got up and came over to our table. "You shouldn't talk about the gods," he said to Hilfa. And to Sokrates, "And you shouldn't ask, it's not polite."

"I had no idea, I'm sorry to violate your custom," Sokrates said. "Why is it impolite to inquire about your religion?"

"Saeli religion is private," the Saeli said. "Young Hilfa here was wrong to tell you the name of a god, and you shouldn't go around saying it."

"Hilfa didn't tell me about Jathery. Gla was here this evening, and I met gla," Sokrates said.

The kelp-gatherer said something in Saeli. "He says, see what harm it does speaking their names," Hilfa translated. The other kelp-gatherers got up and came over to our table. They were all wearing silver pins.

"Plato says, worship in the manner of the city," one of the other kelp-gatherers said, in Greek. "We do that, those of us who have taken oath. We worship the Olympians, at the proper times, like all the other citizens. You can see us there in the temples with everyone else. We want to leave our old gods behind on our planet-of-origin."

"But you have a temple of your own, I've seen it," I objected. The five of them were crowding round the three of us now. As I spoke and they all looked at me, I felt a definite sense of menace. Although I hadn't felt anything like it since I was a kid in the palaestra, it was very familiar. They used to say in my sleeping house that it was Kebes who had taught big boys to pick on smaller boys and intimidate them physically, turning wrestling matches into serious fighting when the masters weren't looking. Whether or not that was true, we certainly all learned the difference between sport and menace when we were young. I found myself calculating. Sokrates was old and would try to keep talking too long. The other three humans in the room would probably help if I called out to them. It would be quite a scrap, and we were in a temple. We'd all be brought up for brawling, and sentenced to spend all our evenings for months moving hives around and getting stung. I braced myself against the table, ready to push it back and be on my feet in an instant.

"It's a private temple," the first one said.

"Was gla really here?" another asked.

"Gla was really here, and spoke to us, and may well be back tomorrow," Sokrates said. "I think it would be better for us to deal with gla from a position of knowledge rather than ignorance. That's why I was asking Hilfa."

The pod exchanged looks. I couldn't read their faces at all. I kept myself ready for a sudden move. "We're only Silvers. You should talk to Afial," a greenish-grey one said.

"And who are you to be asking?" the first one asked, glancing visibly from Sokrates's pinless kiton to my own silver pin. I wished Marsilia were still with us to lend us some visible authority.

"Surely anyone can make an enquiry?" Sokrates asked. "I'm a philosopher, but not a gold or even a citizen. My name is Sokrates."

Hilfa said something in Saeli, and the kelp-gatherers took a step back. The menace evaporated as if it had never been. I let go of the table and breathed freely again. The first one to approach us stepped forward again and sat down beside Hilfa, opposite me and Sokrates. "All right then, yes, since you are Plato's Sokrates I'll tell you. It is a Temple of Jathery that allows us to change our names and allegiances and be free to worship better gods."

"Better gods than Jathery?" Sokrates asked.

"Jathery's the best we have, from what I've heard." He hesitated, the orange marks on his skin becoming clearer as he relaxed. "I'm space-born, and I've never been to our planet-of-origin, but they say that there are gods there, one set for each of our three continents, and they're constantly meddling in everything and won't leave us alone. We try to appease them, and sometimes it works. Our gods aren't friendly like yours. They're terrifying, in fact. There's also another kind of religion that many of us practiced, at least until we came here and became Platonists. Maybe it's not a religion, maybe it's more of a philosophy. It has no gods and is a bit like your Stoicism, except not really, because there's no question that our gods are real and taking an interest. What it's about is getting the gods to overlook us. That's what we want. It was the followers of that philosophy who made it into space, and once we got out of our original solar system we found the gods didn't follow us and intimidate us any more, and we liked it that way. Except Jathery, gla followed us all right. We belong to gla. Gla is the god of freedom of choice and knowledge— questions and answers and tricks."

"And name-changing?" Sokrates said.

"Yes, that too," the Sael said. "I mentioned that before. Name-changing. Gla charges a high price and sometimes cheats us, but that's how we get free. Gla changes gla own name, and gla shape with it. Gla can be terrifying, but not as bad as the others, they say."

"We saw gla change shape," Sokrates said.

"Had gla taken a human disguise?" His tone was horrified and the patterns on his skin faded again.

"Gla appeared as the god Hermes," Sokrates said. The Saeli who were standing all sucked in their breath and rocked back on their heels in unison. The seated one shook his head slowly.

"Gla gave no name but let them judge the seeming," Hilfa said.

"Isn't that like gla," the seated one said. The rest of the pod sighed and nodded in agreement. "Well, when we went into space, Jathery could follow along, and did, because it was with gla help that we'd got away, with wisdom and learning and tricks of technology and magic to reach between the stars. Some of us kept on calling on gla, so gla accompanied us to the new worlds. Sometimes gla helps. But there is always a high price. Gla is a trickster always. Most of us pray to be overlooked."

"I still don't understand," Sokrates said. "You speak of wisdom and tricks as if they're connected."

"They are," the kelp-gatherer said. "How to explain? Imagine a god standing on a mountain-top, on the edge of a cliff. Gla can see a long way, yes? But also, gla would fall if gla took a step forward. Maybe gla is paying attention to what's right there, or maybe gla is looking way out ahead. And gla is laughing, and holding up a light, and however much gla tells us, gla never tells us everything. Gla calls us to follow. If we follow gla, well, maybe we fall off the cliff. Or maybe we learn to fly. Gla lures us forward, and gla laughs if we don't learn fast enough and fall."

"Gla can see, you understand, where it is dark to us," Hilfa said. "And if gla tells us to do something, it is perhaps because gla can see, or perhaps because gla likes to trick us. That is how Jathery is always. We are right to be afraid."

"Much of what gla has taught us is good," the kelp-picker objected. "Gla likes power, yes, and enjoys playing tricks, and gla wants knowledge, but gla is concerned for us, not like other gods."

One of his pod behind said something in Saeli.

"They want to go and tell Aroo that Jathery was here," Hilfa said. "It is a good idea."

"Aroo knows," I said. "Well, I think she does. She saw gla in Thessaly when gla was disguised as Hermes."

"She would have recognized gla," Hilfa said. He said something long in Saeli, and the kelp-gatherers all nodded.

"We will go and talk to her, and to Afial, and tell them all that," the sitting one said, getting to his feet. "And you can tell Sokrates anything else he needs to know." The whole pod left, in silence.

Sokrates picked up his soup, though it must have been cold by now. He sipped it. "So on your planet-of-origin your gods interfere?" he asked.

"Not with everyone all the time, but a great deal, yes, from what I have heard," Hilfa said. "And everyone lives in fear of them. Here we do not name them in case they hear and arrive. I don't know if that could really happen or if it is an incorrect belief."

"So you believe that unless you speak their names, they won't follow?" Sokrates asked.

"It has worked so far," Hilfa said.

"Did you tell the kelp-gatherers that right now Jathery is headed off into Chaos?" I interrupted. I was still a little shaken from the threat of violence, conveyed in nothing more than the shift of shoulders and tilting of heads, so abruptly present and even more swiftly dissipated.

Hilfa shook his head slowly. "Aroo doesn't need to know that."

Sokrates frowned. "I'm not in favor of keeping things secret."

"What would happen if Zeus unmade time?" Hilfa asked.

"I don't know, you should ask Ikaros. But as I understand it, everything would cease to exist," Sokrates said. "As Pytheas suggested, perhaps he'd make another, better attempt at imposing order on the universe, or perhaps everything would remain chaotic."

I shuddered.

"What would it feel like?" Hilfa asked.

"I don't know. It would be interesting to find out, don't you think?"

"It makes me feel cold all through to think that could happen at any moment," I said.

"Pytheas did seem to be worried about it, so I suppose it might. But cheer up, Jason." He beamed at me, his whole face crinkling up around his eyes, which almost disappeared in the creases. "We have immortal souls."

"I don't find that thought very comforting in the circumstances," I said. Hilfa nodded emphatically.

"Well, given that we have immortal souls, which we now really know unquestionably that we do, there are only three possibilities. Either we'd forget everything and start fresh, never having known anything else, or we'd go on from where we are with the way souls learn and grow and keep on growing in the new universe. Or of course, this universe could keep on existing and our souls would keep on growing and learning here. Those are all three pretty good choices when you think about it." Sokrates nodded cheerfully to himself.

"But I like this world. I like being me. I like my life," I protested.

"Well, I like my life too, but I expect we'd also like our lives in a new universe," Sokrates said. "And if we do remember in any way, then it would be extremely interesting to compare. Pythagoras remembered being Euphorbus, and a peacock."

"What is a peacock?" Hilfa asked.

"That animal in the mosaic in the palaestra of Palymra," I said. "The one with the big tail."

"It's a bird," Sokrates said. "You don't have them here?"

"No birds on Plato at all," I said.

At that moment Arete came in, and Sokrates got up. "I'll go and see my old friend Crocus," he said. "Joy to you both. See you tomorrow."

"I belong on Plato," Hilfa said as we collected the bowls and stacked them at the back of the room.

"I'm really glad you're staying," I said.

"So now can we form a pod?" he asked, as we walked out of the side room and into the main part of the temple.

"What?" I kept thinking the day couldn't hold any more surprises, and then finding that it could.

"I have fulfilled my purpose and should be free now. I can change my name and take oath and form a pod. Arete said I belonged here, and Marsilia said she'd argue for me to take oath. So we can form a pod now," Hilfa said. The statue of Amphitrite looked as surprised as I felt.

"You do belong here, and you should certainly take oath if that's what you want, and I know that Saeli live in pods, but what does that have to do with me?" I asked.

"The two of us, and Marsilia, that's three, and Thetis, four," he said, waving his free hand. "We need one more to be five. A pod. A family. Maybe Dion? Though he's so much older."

"Marsilia and Thetis—look, Hilfa, this isn't how it works. And humans don't make pods of five. You should make a pod with Saeli, surely. Don't you want children?"

"There are children already," Hilfa said. "Camilla, and little Di. And Alkippe. You could make more. And I could have children."

"Not with humans," I said, sure of myself on that. "You'd need a Saeli pod for that, like I said."

"No. I would need an egg, that's all. Pods are about childraising, not genetics."

"But where would you get an egg?" I asked. "Athene isn't going to give you one in a box."

He laughed his learned laugh and started walking again, out of the temple and into the chill of the street. "No. I would fertilize one in my body, or find one in the sea."

"The sea's not full of Saeli eggs, is it?" I looked out towards the peaceful starlit water as if expecting to see it suddenly swarming with young Saeli.

"Yes, it is. Most Saeli don't want babies most of the time, and so they discharge eggs swimming. Fish eat many of them, but many survive. But don't worry, none will hatch unless brought out and touched with the right . . . I don't know the word. The right touch. By one of my gender."

I thought of all the times I'd seen Saeli swimming, and shuddered at no more than the thought of how cold the water was. "Do people know this? Do the consuls know that the sea is full of Saeli eggs?" I asked.

"I don't know. I expect so. You should ask Aroo, or the Saeli who first settled here. I do not know what they explained." Hilfa shook his head. "But while it would be nice to have a Saeli child, it is not necessary for the pod. If you don't want one, I can help with the human children." He already did.

"I can see you've been thinking about this a lot, but it isn't a human kind of thing," I said.

"Pod formation is difficult, and we have come so far on the road together.

I want to form a pod with you. You are my friends. The other Saeli don't like me. You saw that earlier with that pod of kelp-gatherers. They think I am an orphan, that I was an egg somebody of my gender brought out and raised without a pod and then abandoned. It happens occasionally. It is disapproved of, in our culture, though they say there are other Saeli cultures where only those of my gender raise children and there are no pods."

"Well, maybe the crew is something like a pod," I said. This hadn't been what I expected when he'd started to work with me, but I did care about him and I didn't want to trample over hopes he'd clearly been holding close for some time. "I do think of you as being almost like a brother. And if you were to raise an egg, I'd certainly help." I thought of all the times he'd helped get the kids to eat in the mornings, and helped Dion limp along to Samos, our eating hall, even carrying him a few times on icy days. "But that doesn't mean that Thetis and Marsilia are involved. This isn't how it works with humans."

"But you want Thetis and Marsilia wants you." He sounded entirely matter of fact. "I don't understand."

No, he certainly didn't understand! "Marsilia works with us, but this isn't how we organize things," I said. "I do feel as if you're family, Hilfa, and I think from what she said earlier that Marsilia does too, and likely Thee does as well, but even so that doesn't mean we're going to arrange a pod." I suspected that, far from wanting me, Marsilia had come to work on my boat to keep an eye on Hilfa.

"They have marriages with multiple adults in the City of Amazons," Hilfa said. "And they have fishing there too. Thetis could work in a nursery there, but I think Marsilia needs to be here for politics."

"Marsilia definitely needs to be here." We had reached my sleeping house and stopped outside it. "This isn't going to work. Plato's right. Friendship is best."

"But a pod is friendship."

"And Marsilia and Thee are sisters," I said.

"Plato says brothers and sisters can marry if the gods allow it," Hilfa said, looking up. "We could ask Arete. Or Pytheas."

"No," I said, as firmly as I could.

"Pod formation is always difficult," Hilfa said, undeterred. "But we're a good team. We'll work it out."

He walked off down the street towards his own house. It had been a long evening full of strange conversations, but that might have been the strangest of all.

19

MARSILIA

The next morning, Alkippe and I went to Florentia for breakfast, the way
we did every day. I put on my best kiton, because there was a Council meeting. The meeting of the previous evening seemed to have happened long
ago, because so much had happened since and my priorities had shifted so
much. Even counting the extra time I had spent with Hermes collecting
Athene's messages, it couldn't be more than a day and a half's worth of
hours, but it felt like years. Time was a strange thing even when it didn't have
gods messing about with it.

It was a beautiful day, with warm sunlight, though a chilly edge to the
wind whispered that summer was over. Dad was sitting at our usual table,
eating nut porridge with Arete, Klymene and a couple of Bronzes I didn't
know. We made our way across the room, greeting friends and the morning's servers as we helped ourselves to porridge and fruit. Alkippe slid in next
to Dad, and I sat opposite them, next to Klymene. Dad introduced the strangers as Akamas, the human, and Slif, the Sael. "We've been up all night at the
spaceport," Dad said. "Akamas works the communications there, and Slif
has been starting to learn the space-human language."

"How's it going?" I asked.

"Pretty much on track," Klymene said. "I think they believe us, and I think
their initial delegation will come down tomorrow morning. They'll be three
humans and six Workers. They have much better medical technology than
we have—that's something we haven't been able to trade for with the Saeli
or the Amarathi."

"Sixty-One is back on duty translating now, and the new shift have taken
over," Dad said. "I'm going to go to the meeting and then sleep all afternoon."

"I'll be very very quiet if you're sleeping in the afternoon," Alkippe said.
She was holding a spoonful of honey above her porridge bowl and turning
it so that it fell in a slow spiral.

"You'll be in the palaestra, so you can be as loud as you like," Dad said.

Alkippe laughed and stirred her porridge. "I'd have to be very loud in the
palaestra to wake you at home!"

Dad grinned back at her. "Maybe if you were wrestling and you brought somebody down with a big thud and a loud grunt!"

"Maybe if I was running in armor and ran very fast and really rattled!"

I felt so fond of them both as I listened to them burbling nonsense. This was how meals were supposed to be. A sufficiency of healthy food, and comfortable conversation. "How's the other thing?" I looked at Arete.

"Everything's fine so far. No news expected until tonight," she said. She didn't look worried, and I couldn't ask more in front of the others, but I assumed that meant Grandfather and Jathery had set off all right.

"Well, that seems like good progress with the ship," I said. "It's wonderful to think we're going to meet the space humans. So exciting!"

"I want to meet them too," Alkippe said.

"It seems the space humans may be stranger than we thought," Dad said.

I nodded, thinking of Phila. "I expect they will be different."

"Will they look different, like the Saeli?" Alkippe asked.

"No, they'll look like ordinary humans, probably, but they'll have all kinds of axioms about what's important that are different," I said.

"Yes, that's it," Dad said.

"Have you asked what kind of government they have?"

"Yes, but we didn't understand the answer very well," he said.

"An oligarchy with some democratic features, but not much control," Arete said, as she scraped her bowl.

I tried to imagine that and couldn't.

"I wonder what kind of people they'd send out to explore?" Alkippe asked. "I think it would be a fun job."

"Well, mostly Silvers, I'd think," Klymene said. "Maybe with some Golds in charge, and some Bronzes to run the technical side of the spaceship."

"We don't use Platonic classes at home, but that's approximately how we crew our spaceships," Slif said. "It's the logical way of organizing things."

"But they may have other kinds of people entirely," Dad said.

"What kind?" Akamas asked.

"Tyrants. Timarchs. Oligarchs. Slaves. Remember that word *profits*?" Arete frowned down at her empty bowl.

"Where's Grandma?" Alkippe interrupted.

"Out on the *Excellence*, getting it ready for a trip to Amazonia," Dad said.

Arete stood up. "Where are you going?" Alkippe asked.

"I'm going home to sleep now," Arete said.

"Are you going to fly?" Alkippe asked.

"Yes, I am," she said, smiling down at Alkippe. "I'll be back this evening. I'll see you in Thessaly after dinner."

"Thank you for all your help with English," Slif said.

Arete went off towards the kitchen, carrying her dishes.

"Is the space human language difficult?" I asked Slif.

"No, English is much like Greek in structure, but with odd tenses and conditionals and a very large vocabulary," Slif replied. "It shows signs of being a creole originally, a merger of two or more different languages from the same family. Such often keep the vocabulary of both parent languages with different shades of meaning. Also, it has borrowed a great deal of technical vocabulary from Latin and Greek. The spelling is bizarre. It's fascinating. But it's not elegant."

"It sounds like a kind of clicky buzz to me," Akamas said. "I can see that it has borrowed some words from Greek, but I think they'd have done better to borrow the entire language and be clear. Or why didn't they stick to Latin? English comes from Britannia, originally, apparently, and they spoke Latin there in Tacitus's day. I don't understand this desire people seem to have to be constantly changing things."

They had both finished eating, so they bade us joy and left. They were going to catch up on sleep, and I envied them the opportunity.

"Where's Pytheas?" Alkippe asked as soon as they had gone.

"We don't know. He and Jathery went off together. They'll be back tonight," I said, praying that they would, that Jathery would go back and conceive her, that the world would be safe for her to grow up. "Now eat your porridge, don't play with it." I'm not Thetis. I don't cry easily. But this conversation kept bringing a lump to my throat.

"Who's Jathery?" Alkippe asked.

"He's the one we thought was Hermes," I said.

Dad looked at me sideways. "That wasn't Hermes?"

"No, as it turns out that was Jathery, a Saeli trickster god," I said, as matter-of-factly as I could. A night's sleep had done me good, but it was still an uncomfortable thought, and I didn't want Dad to worry about it. Klymene put her old hand on mine. I looked at her, and she smiled consolingly. I don't know how she knew there was anything wrong.

"I thought he wasn't like the way I thought Hermes would be," Alkippe said, triumphantly.

"Well, that was extremely clever of you," I said. I hadn't guessed at all.

"Where's Thetis?" Dad asked, clearly looking for a way to change the subject. "I was expecting her to come in with you."

"*Finally*," Alkippe said, bouncing on the bench. "She said *if* you asked to tell you that she'd gone down to the harbor to see Hilfa and collect the books for Ikaros before she goes to the nursery, and she'd see us all here at dinner like always."

"Right," Dad said, suddenly paying a lot of attention to scraping his bowl.

"Last night, Auntie Thee was with Jason and Her- and Jathery. I thought Jason was your friend?" Alkippe asked me.

"I work with Jason and Hilfa, but that's no reason he can't be Thetis's friend too. They did their shake-up year and took their oaths together when they were ephebes," I said. And even if Thetis didn't exist, Jason would never have looked at me. I knew that. There was no sense in the way I kept wanting people who couldn't see me that way. Plato was right as usual: keep sex for the Festival of Hera and stick to friendship the rest of the time. "People have lots of friends, not only one."

"I have lots of friends," Alkippe said. "But I like Camilla best."

"That's because she goes to a different palaestra so you don't see her every day so she feels special," Dad said.

The other children in the hall were all leaving, or getting ready to leave. "Eat up, you don't want to be late," I said. Alkippe took three huge bites of porridge, eating as much as she had in the rest of the meal put together. She leapt to her feet. "Are you sure you've had enough?"

"I'll take a pear," she said, and stuffed one inside her kiton before running off to spend the rest of her day with the other children, learning all the things Plato prescribes for excellence, the things I had recommended to Phila. I took the last pear myself and cleared the dishes. Then Dad and Klymene and I went to Chamber.

I love the way Chamber looks, black and white stripes. It was almost glowing in the morning sunlight.

Diotima was in the chair. I took my place on the bench at the front, next to Aroo and Dad. We wished Aroo joy, and she wished us the same. The room felt quieter than normal, the usual buzzing as people settled in and greeted each other was more muted.

There's a lot of honor involved in being consul, not merely the Roman tradition of the thing, and naming the years, but the fact that it's a planet-wide office and directly elected. But what it really amounts to is a lot of chairing meetings. Diotima and I took it in turns to chair meetings of the Council of Worlds, and we were judged on our ability to do that. She was impeccably turned out in a neatly embroidered kiton. Like everyone I'd ever met from Athenia, she was very properly Platonic and utterly unprepared to compromise. But she certainly knew how to run a meeting smoothly.

We began with a report from Klymene, where she explained at more length what I'd heard at breakfast. Aroo followed with a short report.

Diotima recognized Androkles next. He bounded down to the front to face us all. "I call to schedule a debate with the gods, on why we need to lie to the space humans about our origins and our experience of divinity. I don't want to have this argument here and now, I want to call the gods here to make their case."

"Our gods, or all the gods?" Hermia asked. There was a laugh.

"Well, our gods might come," Androkles said. "Though Pytheas too, if he wants to; I heard he was back here last night, and that people saw Hermes in Thessaly. I'd welcome any gods who want to come and explain themselves in Chamber. Look, Athene started all this seventy years ago, an experiment, a whim as Sokrates said at the Last Debate. We're here because of the gods. Zeus moved us to Plato directly. I'm quite prepared to believe there are good arguments for keeping quiet about this to the space humans. In fact, I think there probably are, and I can think of some of them for myself. I've been thinking about this all night. I think this Chamber deserves to hear the arguments and decide for ourselves. I think we'll decide responsibly. I'm only opposed to accepting the word of the gods as—well, as divine writ, without any examination. That's not the spirit in which any of our cities were founded."

"What if Athene came?" Diotima asked.

"Athene most of all," Androkles said. "There's nothing we want more in Sokratea than for Athene to show up and finish arguing the Last Debate."

But he was wrong. His mouth fell open, and everyone turned to see what there was behind us that he could be staring at. Crocus had come late to the meeting. And riding on his back, beaming at everyone, was Sokrates.

An hour later, after the meeting, Sokrates and I walked over to Thessaly to see Ikaros. I hadn't yet learned that when you do anything with Sokrates you have to budget twice as much time as you expect it to take. He kept stopping and reading bits of inscribed debate on paving stones. "Weren't you there for all that?" I asked.

"There are new bits," he said. "I mean look at all this about classification. That must have been after the Last Debate. I wonder who they were talking to—Patroklus, maybe? Glaukon? It's interesting that the Workers approve of classes, here anyway. Hmm. That's not what I'd have said."

"You mean we've been having debates and you missed it?" I teased.

He grinned up at me. "I've skipped over so much! Well, it was two thousand years the first time. This time, only sixty. And then we'll all be catching up with the next thousand years or so once the space humans get down here." He rubbed his hands together eagerly.

"You like it?" I asked.

"I hate missing it, but I love catching up. Think how many new arguments they'll have come up with, how many new thoughts in a thousand years! I can hardly wait. Ikaros will try to synthesize them all into one system, but I want to hear what they are and point out all the holes."

As we got nearer Thessaly, he speeded up a little, then stopped entirely. "Somebody came back and filled it all in," he said. "What I said, what Simmea said. It reads like a proper dialogue."

"Hasn't it always been like that?" It had been like that as long as I could remember.

"No, the only thing written down was what Crocus said, and the other Workers. We humans spoke out loud. Though whoever did it remembers what we said accurately, not like Plato who was making most of it up even when he wasn't making up the whole thing." He tutted.

My uncle Porphyry opened the door of Thessaly. Porphyry lived in the City of Amazons so I didn't see him very often. He was the most mysterious and divine of my uncles, and at the same time the most playful and childlike. When I was a child he had been my favorite uncle. He lived with his mother, and had no children of his own, but he loved to play with his nieces and nephews, and now with the new generation. At family gatherings he was often romping outside with the children, or telling stories to groups of them. As I'd grown up I'd grown shy of him, knowing how powerful he was, and sometimes seeing him do strange things that made me uneasy. In the last few years, seeing Alkippe's delight in him had rekindled my old memories.

He stepped forward and took Sokrates's hands. "Joy to you. I'm Porphyry."

"Pytheas's son by Euridike, and you live in the City of Amazons and Ikaros was your teacher," Sokrates said. I had no idea how he could know all that. "And you're a god and you fetched the new Workers." Which told me that of course Crocus must have told him.

"That's right." Porphyry let go of Sokrates's hands and nodded to me. "Good to see you again, Marsi." Nobody had called me by that short name since I was a child, so it made me feel happy and young to hear it from Porphyry now.

"What happened to the tree?" Sokrates asked accusingly as soon as we'd followed Porphyry through the house and into the garden, where Ikaros was sitting by the herm. It was the kind of day when you wanted to sit outside, knowing winter was close and there wouldn't be many more days when you could.

"Couldn't take the winters," Porphyry said. "It gets cold here. If it wasn't for the vulcanism we wouldn't be able to have vines and olive trees. Citrus can survive, but it takes a lot of looking after. We grow a lot more stone fruit, and apples and pears."

I sat down in the grass. "We've voted to schedule a debate tomorrow morning in which the gods come to Chamber to explain the reasoning behind the plan for lying to the space humans," I said. "Will you come, Porphyry? Dad says it was your plan originally."

Porphyry did the creepy thing he does where he moves his fingers and his eyes go out of focus. I don't know why it should be so creepy, because that's really all it is. Anyone else could twiddle their fingers and stare vacantly at them and it wouldn't bother me at all, but when Porphyry does it I always shiver. I did now, and I noticed Ikaros looking at me. Sokrates was staring at Porphyry's fingers. "Yes, I'll be there," Porphyry said. He sat down beside Ikaros, and Sokrates sat down too, crossing his legs comfortably like a much younger man.

"Will you come too, Ikaros?" I asked.

He looked startled. "I'm not sure I'm qualified."

I sighed and looked him in the eye. "You're a Master, and therefore a member of Chamber and qualified to attend. There aren't any other Masters still alive, but we didn't feel it necessary to change the rules. And whether or not you're a god is a matter of definition—and one that doesn't matter because a substantial minority of our population worships you as one."

"I saw the temple," Ikaros said. He shook his head.

"What did you expect when you found a religion and then got bodily taken up into heaven in front of half the city?" Porphyry asked, teasingly.

"I'm surprised it became so popular," Sokrates said. "I'd have thought it was too complicated."

"I worked on it a lot more after the Last Debate, with Klio and other people. We had a great festival in the City of Amazons where everyone came and tried to refute my logic. You'd have loved it. It's what I originally wanted to do in Rome. It was wonderful. But I've been working on the theory again since I've been with Athene and I've changed some things now I know more." Ikaros stopped. "I suppose I should tell them."

"What, walk in with a New Testament?" Porphyry asked.

"I'm not sure how the Ikarians would take that," I said.

"They weren't ever supposed to be Ikarians, or add me to the pantheon," he said. "Things do get complicated."

"Are you a god, then?" Sokrates asked.

"What is a god?" Ikaros threw back instantly. They both sat up and leaned forward eagerly. Sokrates looked like, well, a philosopher. Ikaros was, frankly, gorgeous, more gorgeous than even Jathery pretending to be Hermes, because he was more mature. But there was no question he was a philosopher too, with that avidity in his face, twin to Sokrates's own.

"None of my old definitions will work, unless we allow that you and Porphyry and Athene are some other kind of being, and that there are unchanging unseeking perfect gods that are different," Sokrates said.

"The One," Ikaros said. "And I used the word angels in the New Concordance, for those other kinds of being. But perfection is a dynamic attribute."

"How can it be? The nature of perfection—"

"Perfect things can become more perfect, endlessly."

"Excellence, yes, but perfection implies completeness."

Porphyry and I looked past them and smiled at each other. There was something satisfying to the soul in the way they so immediately became utterly absorbed in the argument. Sokrates caught the smile as Ikaros began to explain the nature of dynamic perfection, which was exactly the kind of abstraction Ikarians and Psycheans love. "Wait," he said. "We're arguing with each other when we have an expert here."

"I'm not an expert," Porphyry said, throwing up his hands.

"But you admit you are a god?"

"Yes . . ." Porphyry admitted, tentatively.

"Then you must know what a god is," Sokrates said, with a brisk nod. "Please enlighten us."

Porphyry shook his head ruefully. "Do you know what a human is because you are one? Or how souls work because you have one? There are many kinds of god, and I don't know everything about it. It makes a huge difference who your parents were, and I'm not sure how. Gods are born with a heroic soul. Some have one or two parents who are divine, others do not."

"What's the difference between a heroic soul and any other kind of soul?" Sokrates asked.

"I don't know, and Father—that is, Apollo—doesn't know either. But there is a difference. We don't know whether other souls evolve into heroic souls or whether they start off different. Apollo says there are always more heroic souls waiting to be born than suitable lives for them. He says all children of gods have a heroic soul."

Alkippe, I thought, at once. I'd been so focused on getting Hermes, or rather Jathery, to go back and ensure she existed, that I hadn't thought about her heroic soul. But certainly she showed that level of excellence.

"But that doesn't necessarily make them gods," Porphyry went on. "Look at my brother Alkibiades. He said he wanted to be an ordinary philosopher king like everyone else, and that's what he is. He has a heroic soul, but he doesn't want to be a god."

"Is he excellent?" Ikaros asked.

Porphyry shrugged. "Yes, of course he is, but not exceptionally more excellent than you'd expect of a human born here and brought up by Pytheas and Simmea and who chose to move to Athenia as an ephebe. He's faster and more beautiful than Neleus, but not a better philosopher."

"Dad hates being used as the exemplary human," I put in. "It always comes up in conversations about this kind of thing."

"He's such a useful example, though," Porphyry said, smiling at me.

"And how about people who aren't children of gods? Do they ever have heroic souls?" Sokrates asked.

Porphyry sighed. "We think so, but sometimes it's hard to tell. Gods like to mate, is what Father says. So if there's somebody with a heroic soul, it can be hard to know for sure who their father is."

Alkippe, I thought, again. How could Jathery deceive me that way? But I wanted her to exist. So since I willed the end, I must will the means, deception and being trapped by Necessity and all.

"So that could be you," Sokrates said to Ikaros.

Ikaros blinked. "They say it about you, and about Plato," he said.

"Me!" Sokrates laughed. "What god would own me as his son? Silenos?"

"Apollo."

"We know what sons of Apollo look like," Sokrates said, gesturing to Porphyry, with his chiselled features and bright blue eyes. Even for a man of sixty he was eye-catching, and like all my uncles he had been beautiful when he was younger. (Dad used to say he stopped being jealous of his brothers after Ma fell in love with him. I definitely shouldn't ever tell them that she might be Kebes's daughter.) "And Plato had a great broad forehead and a bit of a stoop!"

"You're young," I said, realizing it as I looked at Ikaros. "You look younger than you do on the temple frescos."

He ran a hand through his long hair. "I was old and nearly blind. I grew young again on Olympos. I don't know if it was Zeus or Athene or simply the place itself. I haven't seemed to age at all since then. But I've spent a lot of time outside time."

"It's very strange being outside time," I said, without thinking.

"Yes," Ikaros said. "Interesting though."

"Marsilia?" Porphyry asked.

"Jathery took me outside time last night," I said. I didn't want to explain everything to Porphyry until Jathery and Pytheas either came back or didn't. But I knew how to distract him. "Jathery is Alkippe's father. So when you're giving her generation their choice of going to Olympos with you to get powers, you should ask her too."

Porphyry nodded. "All right. That's surprising. I didn't know."

"I didn't know either until yesterday. It was a Festival of Hera. He said he was from Psyche. He looked human."

Porphyry grimaced sympathetically. "Even I didn't realize he was Jathery for a little while, yesterday."

"Would being outside time be enough to make Ikaros young again?" Sokrates asked.

"It would make him his essential self. If that requires being young, then yes," Porphyry said.

"I've wondered if it made me the age I was when I died," Ikaros said. "The age I was when I came to the Republic, that is. As if only the time before counted."

"But you didn't really die," Porphyry said. "If you did, you really are unquestionably a god. But you can't have, you wouldn't have aged or strained your eyes and gone blind. I remember you very well that way, and so it's strange for me when I knew you as almost a father, and when I know you're a grandfather, to see you looking younger than I am."

"No, I didn't really die," Ikaros agreed. "Athene snatched me away an instant before death, and removed the arsenic that was killing me."

"But it didn't take you to your essential age, because then you'd be back to being old again when you came back into time, wouldn't you?" I asked. Was Jathery's essential self that perpetual flicker? He had seemed human more often than Saeli.

"I think Athene fixed it," he said.

"Are you her votary?" Porphyry asked.

"Of course I am," Ikaros said.

"Then she could do that, I think," Porphyry said. "I said I'm not really an expert."

"I can't go outside time on my own," Ikaros said. "That means I'm not a god, or an angel. Gods live in the hypostasis of soul, in what you call 'outside time,' and step in and out of time, or the hypostasis of body, freely."

"My brothers and Arete can't go outside time on their own either. They'll have to die and take up immortal bodies before they can. And I know nothing more about that. Father mentioned it, and he said it happens in the Underworld, and that's all I know about it. I think gods who have two divine parents are born with divine bodies, but they can take up a mortal body later, the way Father did."

"Are the hypostases real, then?" Sokrates asked.

Porphyry shrugged. "What do you mean, real? They're a way of thinking about things that are very hard to put into words."

"Aroo said spaceships go into the second hypostasis and come out again somewhere else and that's how they travel in space. If they do that, could they travel in time too?" I asked.

"Yes," Porphyry said. "They do. Stars are in different times."

"But why don't they return before they left?"

"Necessity prevents it," Porphyry said.

I was going to ask more about Necessity, but Sokrates interrupted. "We have several points in favor of considering that Ikaros is not a god. What are the points for considering that you are one?"

"I've been working with Athene in a way that isn't like anything I've ever heard or read about a mortal doing," Ikaros said. "And she talks about giving me responsibilities and power. If she did that, I'd definitely be a god. But she says I'd have to die first, put down my mortal body, and I'm reluctant to do that. I think I am perhaps an apprentice angel."

"But you'll come to the meeting tomorrow?" I asked.

"Yes," he said, resignedly.

"Then I should go if I'm to catch the tide," I said. "I'll have to run as it is. I'll see you all here after dinner tonight."

"Have fun fishing," Ikaros said. "And thank you for your questions. We'll spend a happy afternoon thrashing out points of definition."

"Oh really?" Porphyry asked. "Can I come fishing instead?"

"If you really want to and Jason doesn't mind," I said, seeing he was in earnest. "Do you know how to fish?"

"I go out all the time at home. I find it so relaxing, and of course it's doing something really useful too."

"I think exactly the same," I said, pleased. "Come on!"

So we left Ikaros and Sokrates to their argument and ran down to the harbor to meet Jason and Hilfa. "There's much more going on than anyone has told me," Porphyry said, as we ran.

"I can tell you if you want," I said, reluctantly.

"No, I don't want at all. It's delightful being in the dark for once. It's such a nice change." He laughed, panting, then we saved our breath for running. Down below we could see some boats going out already with the tide, but *Phaenarete* was still waiting at the quay when we came up alongside.

20

APOLLO

Once the door closed behind the rest of them, the three of us stood alone in Hilfa's sitting room, looking at each other uncomfortably. Then Arete sighed, took up the papers and read through them again, silently. "I feel Necessity pressing hard on me," Jathery said. The spell of gla words had no effect on either of us, but I could feel the power gla was putting into them, to make us trust gla. Gla looked all Saeli now, with the greenish skin and the bright lids and the strange knobbly joints that didn't bend the way human joints bend. The patterns on gla skin were not random, as on mortal Saeli, but formed changing letters in an alien alphabet that perhaps Arete could read.

"Don't push me," I said. "I've agreed to let you come with me, for Alkippe as much as for the aegis of Necessity, but that doesn't mean I like you or want anything more to do with you than I have to. And afterwards you've agreed to abide by Father's judgement."

Gla glared at me.

Arete began to read aloud.

When she had finished, I looked at Jathery. "That seems possible," I said.

"This is what Athene and I prepared, for the two of us to go," Jathery said. "How did she do it alone?"

"I've read you all she wrote," Arete said.

"She obviously didn't want us to know that, and did want us to work together," I said.

"Well, we can do that," gla said, scowling. Gla face was much more flexible and human than any normal Saeli face could be. It made me wonder how much time gla had spent around humans, and with Athene.

"I know you can do it. What I'm worried about is you getting back," Arete said, and her voice quavered. She dashed away tears from her eyes and hugged me. "See you tomorrow."

"Tomorrow evening," I said.

Arete nodded. "I'll talk to Porphyry, if necessary. But I hope very much to see you instead."

We stepped out of Hilfa's sitting room and out of time.

I'm not going to tell you the details of Athene's instructions for how to
get out from Avernus. She went to a lot of trouble to hide them, and for
extremely good reasons. We followed them, and they worked, and we found
ourselves . . . out there.

Where time and space are all and one, and self
Is smeared out over every where and when,
And memory, and soul, and stars, and dust,
Future and past and I and now and then

All merge, all melt together, beautiful,
Impersonal, and yet a point of view,
All greatness of the universe at once
Impinging, blossoming, becoming true.

So everything that's ever been and done
Is now, encompassing, and truly whole,
All happening, all past, all that's to come,
Each atom's heart, each world, each grain, each soul.

Each planet spiralling around its sun,
Each quark, and growing leaf, and galaxy,
Each word, and molecule, and falling stone,
And every mortal choice and destiny.

Where I am all, in all, all is in me,
Timeless, entire, all suns, all life, all love,
All words and music one, the endless dance,
Reflecting, knowing, here, below, above.

And art and consciousness reflect, engage,
When spread across all time and space as one
Subjective, glorious, a strange bright joy,
A vaster wonder, and a deeper fun.

Only one soul emerged to being here
To be the point of view the atoms need
To be the consciousness that knows itself,
To be awareness, the essential seed.

Our Father's soul, diffused across the void,
Perceiving all, not knowing what he knew,
In bliss complete, observer and observed,
Knowing, alone: imagined change, and grew.

Out here, where every moment touches now,
Conceived of life, and brought forth other souls,
And shaped the spheres of mind and soul and time
Where we with time could live and set our goals.

Each nebula and every lepton matter
And every soul will choose, and care, and mind
Can heal potentials into what is known
Not simply glorious, but graced and kind.

In time to know ourselves, to change, to learn,
For souls to grow through lives, to gain the scope,
Of consciousness, out here where all is one
Where Zeus invented change, and with it, hope.

Nourished, sustained, by this eternity,
Part of its endless moment's boundless bliss
We live our little lives to stretch our souls,
And conscious, here, make real all that is.

Thus in this no-time, every time in one,
Many in harmony make up one voice,
Where only Father sang, we all sing now:
A miracle of time and free-won choice.

And being here is always, not an end,
There's no before or after, all are here,
And all are elsewhere, with the universe
And nothing's truly lost, so have no fear.

As Time was birthed, Fate and Necessity,
The guardians at the gate, the speed of light,
Emerged to keep both time and space apart
So souls in time could know themselves aright.

I didn't seek for Knowledge, for I knew—
Was knowledge there, as she was Poetry,
And Love, and Guide, and Smith, and Trickster too,
Each full potential of all soul could be.

I couldn't choose or change, there was no time,
Was all time, none, infinity was all,
Until Necessity took hold, and anchored, drawn,
One into three, our coming out a fall.

We landed with a jolt in the Underworld, at the bank of the river Lethe. (It's full of brightly colored fish. I don't understand why nobody ever mentions that. I suppose they must forget all about them.) I looked at Athene. There was nothing to say. Moments before, in the eternal moment, we had been entirely open to each other. I knew now why she hadn't trusted me, and she knew that she could have, that I had learned the lesson that had been one of her many purposes in setting up the Republic. She knew I thought she was irresponsible, and I knew that she thought the gain in knowledge was worth any risk.

It was the same with Jathery. I understood gla now. Gla had wanted Platonism for the Saeli so much that gla had enticed Athene into the whole Republic plan. And all this was part of a wider plan in which gla intended to set them free, which was a goal I did respect. But gla also loved tricks for their own sake, and would rather do something a twisty way than a straight one. Hilfa had been gla idea, and the divided instructions. Meanwhile, Athene had believed that seeking out the different parts of the instructions in different parts of time would help prepare us, if we needed to seek her in Chaos. She had also thought that she was already prepared for it. Both of those were scale errors.

I did not long to be back out there, though I was separated from it. It is always there, and I am too, from the first photon to the last, and there is no difference. I wanted to laugh when I remembered that I had imagined it would be boring.

It's always dark in the Underworld. A grey kind of grass grew here, on the slopes leading down to Lethe's water. A breeze moved. It felt like being out of doors, though there were no stars, only endless darkness above. Behind us, in the caves, lay Hades's chamber and the Fates, and beyond them the other rivers, the Styx and the Acheron. There were also innumerable mortal souls, waiting, choosing new lives, having their brief glimpse of eternity and then coming out again here, to cross this river and go on, forgetting. They were all around us, visible as shadows. Some of them pressed around

us, either votaries of ours or simply drawn to anything here that had color
and weight. One clung to my hand, drawn to me by love. It had last been a
dolphin, and was going on to be a poet and a translator. From leaping joy in
sun-spray and song, to the passing along of poetry, all to my glory, and through
me to that wider wonder. I blessed the soul and called it friend, and set it
down gently on the edge of the water. I kept my face turned away from the
others until my eyes were free of tears.

When anybody visited the Underworld, the souls they met were not those
of the recently dead, but those Hades thought it good for them to meet. I
was grateful for that soul, as it was grateful to me. I did not visit the Underworld often. The only time I had seen Lethe before was when I had taken
up my mortal life.

Jathery was the first to speak. "Are we going to drink?" gla asked. "I don't
believe they'd let us out the other way."

"We're in Fate's domain here," I said. Everything had that kind of inevitability it always did when Fate was involved, an inevitability like an underlining echo. It was very hard to resist. "You could perhaps go back and argue
Necessity's case, but I think the rest of us must go on, or we overstep."

"We didn't die," Athene said. "But no, it is a kind of death, I see."

"I don't want to forget," Jathery said. "But if I only wet my lips, perhaps
I will remember."

"If I forget, then it was all for nothing," Athene said.

"I don't think we'll truly forget," I said. It didn't seem possible that we
could. "But it might fade and seem less immediate, be like something learned."

"Part of Him is always there," Jathery said.

"Part of all of us is always there," Athene said.

"But He is conscious of it." Jathery rocked to and fro a little. "Unity and
multiplicity, one and everything, below and above. And conscious of every
movement from first to last, all the time."

"Don't ask me how Father can be aware of that and carry on a conversation," I said. The idea was daunting. I'd never have understood it without
going there.

"It wasn't what we thought," Athene said. "It wasn't the Chaos before and
after time. It was the One."

"It was both," Jathery said. "As I have long suspected."

"Pico will be delighted." Athene smiled. "He was there. Everyone was there.
Is there. Will be there?"

Not even the aorist sufficed. "It's a Mystery," I said.

"I'm going through," Jathery declared. Gla stepped down into the water.
The fish swirled all around him, orange, and gold, and white and gold swirled

with blue. Mortal souls clung close to him, then drank and drifted away across the stream and vanished. Gla scooped up some water in gla hand and took the tiniest sip.

"Do you remember?" I asked.

"Quite enough," gla said.

I followed. When I touched the water to my lips and tongue, I did not forget, but as I had suspected, my memory of it softened. It became no less felt or immediate, but more poetic, easier to compass and compare. I was extremely glad to reach the far bank, as glad as the mortal souls around me who were speeding off towards their new beginnings. Ahead I could see a thinning of the darkness.

"What would happen if I went through without drinking?" Athene called from the shadowed bank.

"Fate would catch you," I said.

"Try it and see?" Jathery suggested.

She did. She stepped down imperiously and strode on boldly. Then she slipped partway across, fell under the water, and came up a second later, drenched and spluttering. "Fate had you by the heel," Jathery said, laughing.

"Have you forgotten?" I asked, putting out my arm to help her out.

"I haven't forgotten anything," she said, taking my hand. "Only it all seems distant, like you said, and also very emotional, felt not thought. Is it like that for you?"

"Well it was certainly very emotional," I said, diplomatically. I wondered how much she had really lost.

She released my hand and we all began walking up the slope, away from Lethe. "Thank you," she said, and she didn't mean for the help out of the river. "I'm sorry I didn't trust you and made it so complicated. I thought you'd go to Father and I was afraid of what might happen."

"Florent-Claude sends his love," I said.

"I'll go to Father now and tell him everything."

"Do you want us to come, or would you rather see him alone?" I asked. There was a grey glimmer of true light ahead. We were almost out of the Underworld and close to Olympos.

"I can manage alone, but I'll accept your offer of company," she said.

"And you, Jathery? You can go and sort things out about Alkippe now. You probably have other things to do, too? Eggs to hatch, names to change, Saeli to fool? So we won't see you again for a long time?"

The writing on Jathery's skin shifted and changed, and I was sorry I couldn't make it out, even if it probably now read "Apollo sucks."

"I agreed to abide by Father's judgement," gla said. "As for Alkippe, no."

"No? What do you mean, no?"

Jathery blinked gla multicolored eyelids slowly. "I now feel Necessity forbidding me even more strongly than it compelled me before. Perhaps the existence of that child is the price we have paid."

"No," I protested. "You have to deal with that. It wouldn't be right for Marsilia and Thetis and Alkippe to pay for what we have done. Necessity couldn't require—" But of course it could, it could be that cruel. A bright philosophical child. Would they even remember she had existed? I felt much more sympathetic to Thetis's wailing than I had been when I heard it.

"We can ask Father about that too," Athene said.

We took a few more steps towards the light and then appeared in the meadow on Olympos where I'd last been at the time of the Relocation. The same blue and gold bell-shaped flowers were nodding among the grass, and Father was sitting in the same place, as tall as the mountains but no bigger than a man. We walked towards him through the tall grass. Jathery walked on the other side of Athene. I wondered how Father seemed to gla, whether gla saw Father as Saeli. Father looked at the three of us evenly. He saw us, and so he knew where we had been and why, he knew everything, he had always known, and now it came to his attention. I understood this so much better than I had before.

"I have a song," I said, before anyone else said anything.

Father spread a hand granting permission, to a distant rumble of thunder. Athene and Jathery took their places on the grass, flanking him. I took up my lyre, my true immortal Olympian lyre which never—unlike the mortal ones I'd been making do with for so long—needed tuning. That might not be my favorite thing about being a god, but it's close.

I sang about being out there, much as I have set it down here. I could see Father smile as I sang. Athene seemed to be listening very intently. I wondered again how much she remembered.

"Good boy, Phoebus," he said, when I finished and sat down. "And now you understand why I told you not to go there."

"We are there already," Athene said.

Lightning flashed to and fro among the peaks.

"Why do you keep so much from us?" Jathery asked, gla face expressionless but with anguish in gla voice.

"You have to be ready," Father said. "You have to discover things for yourselves." He looked at me. "Are you planning to sing that? To mortals?"

"I'm going to sing it on Plato," I said. "There are people there who need to hear it, and are ready to understand it. I'm going to sing it to Sokrates and Pico."

"They have a meeting to interrogate the gods, before the human ship lands," he said. "You should go and sing it there. And you two should show up at the meeting too." He waved at Athene and Jathery. "They deserve a chance to engage you in dialectic, after all you've done. And then bring Pico here. It's time."

"Oh Father!"

He hadn't said a word of reproach to her for breaking his edicts and going out there. And since she'd had no way to get back, she'd still be in that eternal moment if Jathery and I hadn't gone after her. Yet she was immediately protesting his commands again.

"It's time," he repeated firmly. "His apprenticeship is over. And when he has his powers, you won't have to worry about who's going to rescue him from Bologna, will you?"

"No, Father." She looked down.

"Have you learned from this?"

"I have learned many lessons, including some about who to trust," she said, looking at Jathery and then at me.

"And you?" he asked Jathery.

"Oh yes, incalculably much," Jathery said, but Father seemed more interested in reading the hieroglyphs writhing over gla skin.

"After the debate on Plato, you will spend a year as servant to Hermes, in payment for stealing his name and form," Father said.

Jathery lowered his bright eyelids over his eyes. "Yes," gla said.

"And Hermes will go in your place to conceive Alkippe. He will always have been her father."

Even as relief washed through me, I wondered what Hermes would think about that particular command from Father.

"Yes," Jathery said, sounding a little relieved.

"And you will spend ten years in service to me, as messenger." As punishment for pretending to carry Father's messages, he would really carry some. Ten years was a hard punishment, but not undeserved.

"Yes," Jathery said again. "It is worth it. Platonism is good for the Saeli. It gives them new thoughts, new chances, a better future. It helps them to be free. And freedom is my greatest gift."

"But Plato is all becoming so much more ordinary," Athene protested. "So few of the Golds are really proper philosophers, whatever they call themselves."

Father smiled to himself.

"We thought you might be angry," I said. "I thought of coming to you, but Athene wrote that she thought you might be angry and even use the Darkness of the Oak. We were afraid. But then as soon as I was there I knew you wouldn't be. We didn't know what it was like, out there."

"You understood," he said. "And when you understand things, I understand them too. It saves me learning it all myself. I'm not likely to throw all this away and start again while you keep learning things for me. The same way you had to learn how to be a human, I have had to learn how to be a god."

"When we learn things?" I asked. Even though learning to be human had been so hard, it was even harder to imagine him learning how to be a god, learning personal time and consequence after beginning out there. "And when we undertake projects towards better understanding?"

"Yes. All of you."

"But some of us please you more than others because we learn more new things? And that's why you always forgive Athene?"

"Yes." Athene was staring straight ahead, but her owl was glaring at Jathery.

"And when I was there—I can't remember properly, I drank from Lethe. But it seemed we were all there. Everyone. All gods of all pantheons, human, alien, everyone. All the souls. Mortals I have mourned," I said. "All singing polyphonic harmonies."

"The music is a metaphor. But you are there. You're all my children." He looked at Jathery, then back at me. "On all my worlds. You are there, were there, will be there. I nurture you with time, as plants in a sheltered garden."

"So that you can understand, instead of knowing without understanding," Athene said. "Comprehension."

"And so excellence can keep on becoming more excellent," I said. "Through choice and art."

"I have been too content with tricks," Jathery muttered. "I understand. I will do better."

"We'll see," Father said. "Now go. Get on with it!"

21

JASON

It was another good haul, on a fine choppy day. The sun was too bright to make for really good fishing conditions, but we found the gloaters running deep off Thunder Point and followed them in the current, pulling them up as fast as we could heave until our tubs were full. Porphyry, for all that he was Dion's age and a god, knew the work and put his back into it. The wind was coming up crossways as we came home, so we had to tack back, under a spectacular purple and gold sunset that meant some peak not too far off must have been pouring out dust and lava. We passed a flatboat scooping up kelp, and several other fishing boats on their way home—*Moderation*, *West Wind*, *The Wise Lady*—their sails reflecting the colors of the sky. Then, as I was congratulating myself on another successful day, Hilfa reported we'd sprung a leak. I went to look, and sure enough, water was seeping through between the planks amidships, where the caulking had worn thin. The weight of the full tubs was putting pressure on it. We weren't in any danger, in sight of home and with so many other craft around, but nobody likes to see water coming through the bottom of a boat.

"Well, isn't that always the way?" I said to myself.

"Caulk or bail or dump?" Porphyry asked from behind my shoulder, exactly as I'd have asked Dion if he'd been there and in charge. They were the only options.

"I hate to jettison, especially gloaters, and especially this close to home," I said. "Letting them go to be caught another day is one thing, but these are dead already. And we can't caulk properly, not down there, not without taking her out of the water. She probably needs new planking."

"Bailing it is then," he said, cheerfully, and he and Hilfa settled down to bail while I steered and Marsilia set the sails. I signaled to see if any of the other boats were close enough and with capacity enough to take our excess, but they were all close to full, except the flatboat, which had nowhere to put fish.

I took her in gently, making six tacks instead of two, to put as little pressure on her boards as we could. I really didn't want to use the little solar motor. It was faster, but it put a lot of stress on the planking. I'd glance over from time to time and see that they were holding their own against the water, which they were. It took a while for me to see how crazy it was, a god and an alien squatting in the bilges bailing my boat. Pytheas had said Porphyry had a connection with what's right in place and time, that he'd know when a problem was big enough to go to Zeus, and there he was bailing. It's a strange world we live in.

I brought *Phaenarete* gently in to the quay and tied up. *West Wind* had been hanging back in case we needed assistance, and slid in beside us. Hilfa went off to get the cart, and Dion came back with him as usual. Little Dion was with him today, hopping about all over the cobbles like a wound-up spring. "We want to get the tubs emptied as quickly as possible," I said, because we were still making water.

"Are you coming up to Thessaly after dinner?" Marsilia asked as we were tipping the first tub onto the cart. She was looking decidedly windblown but actually less tired than when we'd set off.

"Yes," I said. "I want to know what happens when they come back. If they come back. I suppose it isn't really my place. But I've seen this much of it and I'd like to see it out."

I turned to heave the next tub onto the hoist. Porphyry was steadying it, and leaned his weight into it at the right moment to swing it forward. Dion and Hilfa were down at the cart. With this many competent people, we'd be done in no time, and I could take her round to the slips and get her out of the water.

"We're a good team," Marsilia said.

"Exactly what I was thinking," I said, but then I blushed, remembering what Hilfa had said the night before.

When I turned to her, Marsilia had the strangest expression on her face. I'm fair skinned, so I always display my embarrassment for everyone to see. I decided I'd better tell her why I was red to the tips of my ears, because the truth was better than what she might be guessing. "Hilfa thinks that because we're a good team we ought to form a pod," I said quietly, as we lowered the next tub. "You and me and Thetis and oh, and him, of course."

"Oh poor Hilfa," Marsilia said at once. "I wonder how long he's been imagining that?"

"I think he thinks we're like family, and we are in a way, a crew."

"But a pod—I suppose that made sense to him. The Saeli way. They do tend to work together. Poor Hilfa." She sighed.

"He had it all worked out, said we could go to the City of Amazons where it's allowed, except that you need to be here for work."

"We wouldn't have to, the law allows pods here. While it says for the benefit of the Saeli, it doesn't say everyone involved has to be Saeli. Marriage is any two people who choose it, and a pod is any five." She grinned at me, then joined Porphyry bringing the last tub across, while I brought up a bucket of water to rinse off the deck. My face had stopped feeling so hot by the time I'd finished that.

Dion and Hilfa rolled the cart off to take the catch over to Supply, where the fish would be gutted and sorted and salted or frozen or, if we were lucky, shared out to be served up straight away.

"Was that an especially good haul, or is the fishing always better here than around Amazonia?" Porphyry asked.

"This is the best time of year," I said. "In a month or so all the big fish will have gone north and we'll be lucky if we're filling two tubs all day."

"Well, that was fun. Thank you for letting me work with you, Jason. Do you need help getting her across to the slips?"

"Marsilia and I can manage if you want to go back, but if you'd like to bail a bit more it would be handy," I said.

"When I go back, everyone will want to argue with me or interrogate me," he said, picking up the bailer again. "I'd much rather spend an hour bailing in the dusk."

"Well it's more my idea of fun too," I said.

Porphyry, the most powerful god on Plato, settled down to bail. Marsilia took the tiller this time, and we sailed neatly across the harbor, the wind with us now and no difficulty except avoiding the boats as they came in and cut across our bows. Once there, a Worker called Barnacle came and helped haul her out.

Barnacle is named after barnacles, the little scalelike things that like to attach themselves to the bottom of boats and have to be scraped off. Dion says the barnacles on Plato are so different from Greek barnacles that we shouldn't give them the same name, because they're flat and symmetrical. But it doesn't matter, because all the Platonic sea creatures we've identified have formal names, which are, for some bizarre reason, all in Latin. Then they have everyday names in Greek which are either descriptive or echo whatever Earth thing they're most like, whether they're exactly like it or not. So if barnacles and kelp on Earth were different from ours, it doesn't matter very much, nobody is likely to confuse them, and if they do we have the long Latin names for disambiguation.

Barnacle fussed over the leak, and said, as I'd suspected, that we'd need some new planking. He promised to get to it right away, and got started hauling her out of the water and into the dry dock. Workers are really good at that kind of thing. So we left her there and walked all the way back around the harbor, talking on the way about boats and boat repair. It turned out Porphyry worked on a fishing boat called *Daedalos* with two of his nieces. "Why did you call her that?" I asked.

"Well I wanted to name her after Ikaros, but that seemed rather an unfortunate name for a boat," he said. We laughed. "Ikaros is my sister's father. He was family when I was growing up, always in and out, as well as being my teacher."

"Is it strange to see him again?" I asked.

"I knew I would, though I didn't know exactly when. I prefer not knowing too much."

"Jathery says it's uncomfortable being caught by Necessity," Marsilia said.

Porphyry frowned. "No, Necessity's wonderful. Necessity is what keeps everything from happening at the same time. My gifts—well, we take what we're given. I wanted to be able to fly, like Arete." He sounded wistful.

When we came to Samos I invited the others in for dinner, but they said they should go to Florentia and catch up with their family. "Dad will think we've drowned if I don't show up," Marsilia said.

"And that's if Ikaros and Sokrates remember to tell him where we went," Porphyry said.

"Will they show up to eat in Florentia like anyone else?" I asked, trying to picture it.

"Well I suppose they might go to their old halls, but I expect they'll go to Florentia tonight," Porphyry said.

"But they're so recognizable!" I said.

"Yes, true, but they also like debating people. I can't imagine either of them hiding," Porphyry said.

"We should have thought of that and asked them to," Marsilia said. "Oh well, too late now. Unless Dad thought of it."

"Well, they're here. I don't know why, and I don't know whether they mean to stay," Porphyry said. "But you're the one organizing the debate on whether we're right to keep divine secrets."

Marsilia looked surprised. "You're right. It is the same kind of thing. And even though Sokrates was there this morning in Chamber, I was automatically assuming it was better to keep it quiet from everyone else, without examining it at all. Huh. That's terrible of me!"

"You shouldn't be so hard on yourself, Marsi," Porphyry said, and that was the first time I'd ever heard her called by that nickname. "You've thought of it now, and there's plenty of time to examine it."

"I'll see you in Thessaly later," I said.

I ate dinner in Samos with Dion and Hilfa and the kids, like every day. We talked mostly about the boat, and how long Barnacle thought it might be before she'd be seaworthy again. They had almost finished eating by the time I got there, but they stayed at the table nibbling on apples and nuts while I ate my ribber and noodles, to be friendly. Then Hilfa and I set off for Thessaly.

"Do you think they'll have come back?" I asked as we walked up towards the city gate, the same route I'd taken with Thetis the day before.

"Yes."

"Do you think Athene will be there?"

"Yes."

"Are you basing this on logic, or is it only what you think?"

"But Jason, you asked me what I think!" He gave me his real smile, and I noticed his pink markings were standing out distinctly again. "I think They will come back because They are gods, and the world is still here, and there's nothing to be done about it if They do not. And I think Athene will be there because She will come for Ikaros."

Marsilia opened the door to us. "They're here!" she said.

My knees sagged with relief. I hadn't realized how worried I had been until the burden was lifted. "So Alkippe is all right?" I asked.

"Yes," Marsilia said, her face going blank. "Gla said that had been taken care of, so now it's out of the way."

I put my arm around her, as I had supported Thetis in her weeping the day before. I didn't normally do this kind of thing with Marsilia, but it didn't normally seem as if it would be welcome. I never knew two such different sisters. Marsilia leaned into me for a grateful instant, then moved away to intervene in an argument between two of her uncles that was becoming heated.

As I looked around the room, which was only about half as full as the day before, I felt filled with social anxiety. Almost everyone in Thessaly was a god or a close connection of a god, and none of them were people I knew. Thetis was sitting laughing with her mother, she didn't even glance at me. Why was I invited to this party? I accepted a cup of wine from Kallikles, Pytheas's son who was in charge of lightning and electricity. "I recognize you now, you're the fellow who works on the boat with Marsilia," he said.

"Jason," I said. "And this is Hilfa, who works with us too."

Hilfa took his wine, and we escaped through the fountain room into the garden. It was cool out, but not bitingly chilly like the night before. Crocus was looming large in the corner, talking to Pytheas and Sokrates, who was waving his arms about. Over in the other corner, where there was a carved herm, Athene and Ikaros were deeply engaged in conversation with Neleus and a stranger, a beautiful woman with teased-up hair, dressed in a green and black stripy thing. She looked over at us, and I saw she had bright Saeli eyelids, and at once realized who she was.

Gla left the others and came towards us. As gla walked across the garden gla changed with each stride, growing taller, gla hair and clothes and female body fading away. As gla reached us gla had completely transformed and was entirely Jathery again: huge, naked, greenish-gold, with very distinct dark markings writhing across gla skin. Hilfa tried to hide behind me.

"Joy to you, Jathery," I said, and tried to think how to follow this. "I see you've returned safely. And found Athene too."

"I'd like to speak to Hilfa for a moment, if you'll excuse us," gla said.

"I don't think Hilfa wants to speak to you," I said, though it was difficult to refuse gla, especially as gla made gla request seem so reasonable. The best of their gods? I hated to think what the others must be like. "I think Hilfa's terrified of you. I think all the Saeli are. How does a god of knowledge come to be so frightening to gla people?"

"Are you not afraid of Athene?" gla asked, gently.

I looked over at where Athene was standing listening to something Neleus was saying, and found courage in the sight of her, so like her statues. "A little awed, certainly. I'd be intimidated if she wanted to speak to me. I'm only a Silver. But I also love her. I would do the best I could."

"And the Saeli also love me," Jathery asserted. The markings on gla skin changed and shifted as gla spoke, making new patterns.

"You cheat us," Hilfa said, from behind me, sounding panicked. "You take all and give nothing. We appease you and pray that you will pass us by."

Sokrates, who was the only one facing us, noticed what was happening. He excused himself from his conversation and came over and heard Hilfa's last words as he joined us. "Are you discussing what makes the Saeli gods different from our gods?" he asked. "I'm also interested to know the answer."

"It is culture, and patterns of worship," Jathery said, dismissively. "There are gods on Earth that are more like me than like your gods. And there are other Saeli pantheons that are perhaps more like yours. It is style."

"But you're the same kind of being as our gods?" Sokrates persisted.

"Yes."

"And even among aliens that are much stranger than humans and Saeli, like the Amarathi, the gods are all the same kind of being?"

"Yes." Jathery looked around, then resigned glaself to answering Sokrates. "Though the Amarathi evolved as tree-like beings whose language was chemical, they have souls like yours, and their gods are like all gods. We are all children of the One Parent."

"Fascinating," Sokrates said. "And do the Saeli gods take care of their worshippers?"

"Yes," Jathery said, flatly, like Hilfa.

"And you're in charge of wisdom, is that right?" Sokrates asked. I took a cautious step away, drawing Hilfa with me. "What responsibilities do you have?"

"We each have responsibility in certain spheres." I took another step back.

"But I believe they are divided up differently among your pantheon? How did that come to be?" Sokrates looked politely interested. Jathery's face was unreadable.

"We each have five things," Jathery said.

"And is five a significant number among the Saeli?"

"Yes."

"And how is it that you are the only Saeli god to have left the Saeli planet?" Sokrates asked, persistently.

Hilfa and I retreated back into the fountain room. The black and white tiles and shining silver faucets seemed very welcoming. I swallowed all the wine in my cup in one gulp and set it down on the window sill. "Sokrates is wonderful," I said.

"It is only a respite," Hilfa said. His markings had faded to almost nothing and he was rocking a little.

"Jathery is incredibly intimidating even when gla doesn't do anything but stand there, and gla voice is very persuasive. But you said yesterday that gla wasn't too bad. What specifically are you afraid of?" I asked.

"That gla will get me alone and unmake me. Gla is one of my parents, Arete said. I think gla could do that, now that gla and Athene don't need me as an anchor anymore," Hilfa said, looking down so I could not see his eyes but only the turquoise and orange of the lids. "I thought now that my purpose was fulfilled I could be free. But Jathery put power into me, and now I think instead gla will take gla part of me back, to be stronger."

"Kill you?"

"Worse than kill me. I do not want to cease to be me, but I could bear it. I am afraid gla will unbind my soul. Gla and Athene made my soul. Gla could take back what gla put into it." He rocked once and then back, then looked up at me. "Don't leave me alone with gla, Jason. Please."

"No way. But I don't think gods can make souls. I think it was your body Arete was talking about. And she said you're part human too, remember, and belong to Plato. You're a child of gods. You must have a heroic soul." I put my hand on his shoulder.

"Arete did say I belong here," Hilfa said, tentatively, as if testing a proposition.

Marsilia stepped from the main room into the fountain room as he was saying this. "Of course you do, Hilfa. I've been enquiring, and Dad says if you enroll in classes now, you can take oath in the spring."

"I want to take oath right now. Then I'd belong to Plato and not to Jathery. You're consul. You could hear it." There was a note of panic in his tone.

Marsilia shook her head. "It has to be done at the altar before the archons. And it can't be rushed, because you have to be classified, and that takes a lot of thought."

"Pah. I am Silver, like Jason and Dion. I work on the boat."

"But I work on the boat too, and perhaps you should be Gold like me,"

Marsilia said. "It's not easy or quick, making that decision for anyone. And why are you in a hurry anyway?"

As she asked, Jathery came into the fountain room, with Sokrates in hot pursuit.

"I want to speak to Hilfa, before I answer any more of your enquiries," gla said. Sokrates shrugged and caught my eye, as if to say he had done his best.

"Then speak to him," I said. "He's here."

"We need to speak alone." Again, gla made it seem like such a reasonable request that it was hard to protest.

I went on and protested anyway. "Why? You can have privacy simply by speaking in Saeli. Arete's the only other person here who speaks it and she's in there." I gestured to the main room of the sleeping house, where the sounds of the party could be heard.

"It's a Saeli matter, you wouldn't understand," Jathery said.

"Please explain it to us," Sokrates said, in his usual tone of enthusiastic enquiry.

Hilfa was rocking again. I put a hand on his arm. "I'm Hilfa's friend, and I'm not leaving him unless he wants me to."

Then as Jathery opened gla mouth to respond, Marsilia jumped in. "We're his pod," she said. "Surely there isn't anything you need to say to a Sael without their podmembers. Indeed, by our law any Sael can specifically request the presence of podmembers even when accused of a crime."

Sokrates opened his mouth, clearly dying to ask something about this, but managed for once to keep quiet.

"All podmembers," Jathery said. Gla had his eyes fixed on Marsilia's as if they were children in a staring contest. "You are only three."

"Get Thetis," Marsilia said to me, without looking away from Jathery's gaze.

Sokrates stepped forward and took one of Hilfa's hands. Marsilia took the other. I turned and went into the main room. Everyone there was drinking wine and talking loudly. Thetis was still with her mother, deep in conversation.

"Thee, you have to come," I said.

"What?"

"It's really important. Marsilia sent me." She looked impatient. "Hilfa needs you."

"I'll be back soon," she said to Erinna, who was frowning, and followed me. "What is it?"

"Jathery's trying to bully Hilfa, and Hilfa's afraid gla wants to kill him, or worse, and Marsilia has told him that we're Hilfa's pod," I explained as succinctly as possible as we crossed the crowded room.

"His pod?" she asked, astonished. Then we stepped into the fountain room. "His pod," she confirmed with a brisk nod at the alien god. "Don't you dare think you can do anything to Hilfa without our consent."

"That is still only four," Jathery said.

"I'd be honored to make the fifth," Sokrates said.

"Pods are not a joke, or an arrangement to be hastily put together and hastily abandoned," Jathery said.

"Are they your sphere of patronage?" Sokrates asked, in his best tone of interested enquiry.

Jathery snarled at him. Sokrates was famously good at making gods lose their tempers. Perhaps he had got the better of gla in their debate outside.

"Here in the City, they have to be registered before a magistrate," Marsilia said. "I am such a magistrate. So is my father, and so is Crocus. We also have any number of gods here who would be delighted to give their blessing if that's necessary or useful. We're perfectly serious, and we're not about to yield Hilfa to you."

"I need to speak to him."

Marsilia's face was set. "I think you mean to hurt him. And I won't let you. We're guest-friends, Jathery. You won't hurt me, and I won't let you hurt Hilfa. And I think you owe me this for the help I gave you."

Marsilia took my hand, and I took Thetis's hand in my other hand, so we were all standing there in a line with linked hands, the latrine-fountain closets behind us and Jathery between us and the door to the garden.

"If you want to talk to Hilfa, go ahead," Thetis said.

There was a long moment of silence. "Very well, you are a pod, and I wish you all joy of it," Jathery said. Gla bowed the sideways Saeli head bow, and we all solemnly echoed gla. Then gla spat out a long string of Saeli to Hilfa, who nodded at the end of it but did not reply.

Then Jathery turned to look at Marsilia. "You may be a pod, but Hilfa still belongs to me," gla said.

"Then I'll buy him from you," Marsilia said. She let go of my hand and pulled out a little leather purse and drew out a coin from it. "Here. Is he free now?"

Jathery took the coin and turned it between gla fingers. "Hilfa is," gla said.

"And freedom is one of your attributes," she said.

"You're consul," gla responded.

"Then I will buy from you the freedom of all the Saeli on Plato, and all those who are hatched here or come here and choose to take oath." She drew out another coin and handed it to Jathery.

"Yes," gla said.

Then Marsilia deliberately shook out the purse. As she did, gla vanished on the instant, leaving us staring at the bare tiles where gla had been standing.

"Well, that was odd," Marsilia said, with a quaver in her voice that had been absent the whole time she was standing up to Jathery. She stuffed the empty purse back into the fold of her kiton.

"I find I grow older but I learn nothing," Sokrates said, ruefully.

"You mean being turned into a fly didn't stop you going head to head against gods?" Marsilia asked.

"Oh, that? But the unexamined life isn't worth living, you know. No, I was thinking of the wisdom of entering into marriage once again at my time of life."

22

MARSILIA'S POD

I. *Marsilia*

And there it was, the great achievement of my political career, in haste, in the fountain room of Thessaly. Platonic Saeli didn't need to ransom themselves individually from Jathery anymore. I had freed them all with a coin he had given me.

I don't know how I sounded, but I was frightened inside the whole time. I'd spent all that time with Jathery, thinking gla was Hermes, but seeing gla in gla real form threatening Hilfa was terrifying. If I hadn't spent that time with gla in disguise, and especially if I hadn't known that we were guest-friends, I doubt I'd have been able to stand up to gla. I think it was what gla wanted, though. Gla wasn't pretending. Gla would have liked to take back the power gla put into Hilfa. But gla was also tricking us, tricking me. Gla really wanted the Saeli to be free and equipped with Platonic ideas. Why else had gla given me the purse? It was one of gla riddles, and I think I guessed right.

I was focused on that, and it wasn't until Sokrates used the word marriage that I fully realized what I'd done to my friends.

"Marriage!" Thetis said, pulling her hand away from Jason's. I couldn't look at Jason, so I looked at Hilfa. His expressionless face was soothing.

"A pod isn't exactly a marriage," I said. I was exhausted. The need to save Alkippe and then Hilfa had buoyed me up, and now that I had done it and they were both safe the relief came with a wave of tiredness and a familiar cramping in my belly that meant my bleeding would likely start the next morning.

"It's the Saeli way of forming a family," Jason said, speaking gently and looking at Thetis in that way nobody ever looked at me. "Hilfa was talking about it last night after you left."

"But I——" Thee's expression was comical as she looked from Sokrates to Hilfa to me and then back at Jason, who was standing there, solid and warm and reliable. You could always count on him to have your back.

"This is merely an expression of our intent to form a pod. We haven't gone to a magistrate or asked a god for blessing, only said we could," I said. Jason had taken my hand again, and Hilfa was still clinging to the other. Jason's was warm, and Hilfa's was slightly cold, as was normal for him. "Hilfa's free now whatever we do, and so are the other Saeli. And anyway, nobody is trapped. Pods can be dissolved here. It takes the consent of all members, and the magistrate has to be satisfied by the arrangement for the care of children. Nobody who has been part of a pod dissolution may enter into any form of marriage for a year, including marriage at the Festival of Hera."

Thetis sighed, and I thought she was going to accuse me of knowing too much law and not enough about people, the way she always used to. "It's really only that it's so unexpected," she said. "Jason said Hilfa needed me, and then suddenly that."

"He did need you," I said.

"Yes, I saw. Jathery was so menacing. But a pod!" Thetis took a step backwards on the black and white tiled floor, and almost fell into the drain recess. She caught herself with a hand to the wall, laughing.

"It's a most interesting experiment," Sokrates said. "The practical details may take a little working out. This is my house. Pytheas said I could have it back. I know Hilfa has a house."

"Maybe it would make more sense if we looked for a house down near the harbor," Jason said, sounding the way he did on the boat when he was laying out what needed doing. "And there's also Camilla and little Di. I have a responsibility to them." He looked at Sokrates. "Their parents were killed at sea five years ago. They were friends of mine, we grew up together. I think I should ask Camilla and Di if they would like to live with our new family, or if they'd prefer to stay where they are in the sleeping houses. Would we get an allocation if we gave up our places and asked for a house, do you think, Marsilia?"

"I expect so," I said. "There's not much precedent." This was moving very fast. I hadn't thought at all about practical arrangements. Indeed, I hadn't thought it through at all. There would be political repercussions, too—I didn't know whether they'd be good or bad, but they'd certainly exist. A consul cannot marry without drawing attention, and this really was a kind of marriage. No humans had ever formed part of a pod before, so that was sure to cause comment. I couldn't even hope everyone would be so focused on the gods and the space humans that they'd take no notice, because Sokrates was involved. Well, it would never be boring, having Sokrates in the family. And Alkippe would love having somebody around to answer all her questions with more questions. And she'd be delighted to live in the same house as Camilla.

"Does forming a pod with citizens give me the right to stay in the Republic?" Sokrates asked.

He was looking at me questioningly. "Not inherently, no. But you have that right. You're already a citizen here," I said, surprised.

"Am I?"

"Everyone who was a citizen at the time of the Last Debate remained a citizen of the Remnant if they wanted to be. Lots of people left and came back. Admittedly, it hasn't happened with an original citizen since immediately after the Relocation. I think my grandfather Nikias was one of the last. But it still holds."

"But was I a citizen then? I was not a Master, for I never prayed to Athene to bring me here. The Children took oaths of citizenship and in token of that were given pins designed by Simmea, which I see you still use." I withdrew my hand from Hilfa's and touched the bee on my pin, and saw Jason and Thetis making the same automatic movement towards theirs. The pins were all identical, whatever metal they were cast in. I had forgotten they had been designed by my grandmother. Sokrates's kiton was pinned with a plain iron pin. "I never took that oath, or went through any other form of citizenship. I regarded myself always as an Athenian citizen in exile."

"And that's why you called this house Thessaly," I said. "I've always wondered about that."

"Krito suggested I escape to Thessaly instead of drinking the hemlock," he said, smiling. "If he'd suggested this plan, I'd have had even stronger arguments against. But I'm here now, and from what I'm hearing, things are much improved from when I was here before."

"You're Sokrates," Thetis said, and indeed, that was enough. "Whether or not you're a citizen in your own mind, or legally, nobody would dream of saying you couldn't stay here. You're Sokrates, and this is Plato's Republic!"

"One of them," Sokrates said.

"Do you want citizenship here now?" Jason asked.

"I'd have to examine the question, the implications and obligations, and also the details of your laws," Sokrates said.

"You can take the course with Hilfa," I said. "You'll love it. You can argue as much as you like, and debate every single point." Thetis and Jason were both smiling, probably remembering their classes. "You can both take oath together, if you decide you want to. But Thetis is right. Whether or not you take our citizenship oath, whether or not you're part of a pod, everyone will want you to stay. Think how you were welcomed in Chamber this morning."

"I wish you'd been on the course when I took it," Thetis said.

"Oh, so do I! I think you should take the course all the time," I said, suddenly realizing how wonderful that would be. "I don't mean teach it, though maybe you could, later, if you wanted to, but I think if you stay, you should always be around some of the time when the kids are taking the course. For one thing, there isn't a sixteen-year-old on this planet who wouldn't love being on that course with you to shake things up. But the real reason is that we have a tendency to become—well, Jathery said it yesterday about me. Piously Platonic. We accept it too much as received wisdom and we don't question enough. All of this has made me see that. If you were around the young people they wouldn't get complacent."

"You're asking me to corrupt your youth?" Sokrates asked. "You know I have a conviction for that at home?"

We all laughed. "Yes, you're perfectly qualified, and it's precisely the kind of corruption we need for our youth," I said.

"I have made a committment to join this pod," Sokrates said, smiling. "I'd also like to explore the other cities, and indeed the other worlds. But I'm an old man. Don't count on me being around to help with these things long-term."

He was hale and fit, but definitely an old man. "The space humans were talking about possibilities of medical and technological rejuvenation," I said, remembering what had been said in the morning's meeting.

As I spoke, I looked at Hilfa again, and I realized he hadn't spoken since Jathery left us.

"Are you all right, Hilfa?" I asked.

"Yes," he said, in that flat way he had. The pink marks on his skin were the brightest I'd ever seen them. "I am free. I belong to Plato. And I have helped free all the Saeli here. I am very all right."

"What did gla say to you?" Jason asked.

"It's hard to translate," Hilfa said. "Gla said gla could have reunited me with gla, and that he wished me joy of my folly. And then gla said that Our Parent wants us to learn and experience and comprehend new things."

"What?" Sokrates asked, completely focused on Hilfa now, not a shred of amusement left in his face. "Do you mean to say gla told you what Zeus wants? The purpose of life, spat at you like a curse? Gods! They're not fit to be entrusted with their responsibilities. They're like a bunch of heavily armed toddlers."

"Can that really be the purpose of life?" I asked.

"We can't trust gla," Thetis said, decisively.

"Even if we could trust what gla said, is that for Hilfa alone, all the Saeli, our pod, or for everyone?" Sokrates asked.

"I don't know," Hilfa said. "It is like what many Saeli believe. Plato says excellence is the greatest good, but our culture, the religion we follow, has always put discovery first, science, knowledge."

"This is the religion that's more like philosophy?" Sokrates asked.

"Yes. Other Saeli cultures worship other gods and have other priorities. But those of us who went into space, with Jathery, value discovery. I have heard that the Amarathi prioritize ubiquity and connection over everything else."

"Perhaps it is meant for the Saeli, because gla gave me no hint of that when I was trying to talk to gla outside," Sokrates said. "But how interesting. Learn, experience, comprehend?"

"Pity gla didn't stay around so we could ask gla now whether it's for all of us," Jason said.

"Let's ask Grandfather," I said.

"Or Athene," Sokrates said, thoughtfully.

Jason let go of my hand, and it tingled where he had been holding it. He had hugged me earlier, when he came in. I hadn't meant to trick him into a form of marriage. I knew he was in love with Thetis. But since she was included, I hoped he didn't mind too much. He seemed to be taking it very reasonably, thinking about the details, exactly like you'd expect from a Silver really. Though Sokrates was thinking about details too. We'd work it out.

II. *Thetis*

Everyone looked up as we went out into the garden. The night was growing chilly, though nothing like as cold as the night before. "What have you been up to?" Dad asked, his brow furrowing as his eyes passed over us.

"We have been forming a pod," Hilfa said, all at once like that with no warning.

"What!" Dad could sound so cold and disapproving sometimes. I shrank back, then stopped myself. Never let them think you're inferior.

"Jathery was attempting to attack Hilfa," Sokrates explained. "As pod members, we had the right to witness the interaction. Without that, gla would have done something unreasonable."

"Unreasonable! You probably did exactly what gla wanted," Athene said, rolling her eyes.

"I think so. I freed Hilfa. I freed all the Saeli," Marsilia said to her.

"You've been forming a pod with my daughters and Hilfa?" Dad looked at Sokrates as if he was about to erupt. Ikaros was grinning.

"And Jason," Sokrates said, reproachfully, waving a hand at Jason, who was standing next to me looking embarrassed. I took his hand defiantly. "The number five seems to have some significance to Saeli. I don't know if this is empty numerology, or if it truly has a kind of Pythagorean significance."

"There have been human-Worker marriages," Crocus said, as he and Grandfather came closer to join the group, no doubt attracted by the volume of Dad's expostulation. It was still strange to see Grandfather looking not much older than me. I wasn't used to it.

Dad turned to look at Crocus, took a deep breath and calmed himself. I wish I could do that. I almost never lose my temper, but I'm always bursting out crying whenever I feel something strongly. "This is all very unexpected," he said mildly, then turned back to me. "I don't know what your mother will say."

"Unexpected for us too," I said, which was an understatement. Ma would be fine with it if I were the one to explain it to her. We always understood each other. And she often said we should get married.

"More importantly," Sokrates said, turning to Athene. "Jathery told Hilfa that Zeus wants us to learn, experience, and comprehend. Is that something he wants of everyone, or only the Saeli?"

Athene exchanged a glance with Ikaros. "All of us," Athene said. "Saeli, humans, gods, everyone."

"You told us you didn't know what he wanted," Sokrates said to Grandfather, with a tiny hint of accusation in his tone.

"I didn't know when I told you that, long ago, here in this garden. This is something we learned when we spoke to him now, after we came back from being out there."

"Out in Chaos?" I asked.

"It isn't Chaos. Well, it isn't only Chaos," he said.

"That's what Athene has been telling me," Ikaros said. "How marvelous and unexpected. I have to rethink everything. I can't wait to see it."

"You're there," Athene said.

"Everyone is there. Everything," Grandfather said. "I have a song about it. I'll sing it tomorrow in Chamber."

"Do you want to sing before the session?" Marsilia asked. "The way you legendarily did to stop the art wars?"

"Are you chair tomorrow?"

"I am," she said, apprehensively.

"Who's supposed to go first?" Pytheas asked.

"Androkles. Then Porphyry and the others. Then Sokrates," she said.

"I'll sing after Sokrates," Pytheas said.

"All right," she said, biting her lip as if she wasn't at all sure.

"And Athene and I can debate, like at the Last Debate," Sokrates said cheerfully, grinning at Athene, who smiled unrepentantly back. "For now, I only have one more question about what Zeus wants from us. What should we learn, experience, and comprehend?"

"Everything," Athene said.

"Yourself," Pytheas contradicted her at once. She glared at him. "Well, you should know yourself first, and then once you do, you can move on out to everything else," he said.

"Do I take it Zeus didn't specify?" Sokrates asked.

Ikaros laughed, and the owl flew off Athene's arm at the sound and circled silently around the garden before perching back on her shoulder.

"He didn't specify, but he seemed to approve of what Athene has been doing," Pytheas said.

"So should we put knowledge ahead of excellence?" I asked.

"No," both of them said together, and the owl twisted its head around to stare arrogantly into my eyes.

"Excellence must always be our priority," Crocus said.

"Pursuing excellence will lead to everything else," Dad said.

The gods, the owl, and Sokrates nodded in unison.

"I'll sing the song for you tomorrow, and then you'll understand," Grandfather said.

"But that way Jason and Hilfa and I won't hear it," I said. "Or is it a song that only philosophers should hear?"

Grandfather looked at me. "Do you want to know?" he asked.

"Of course I do! How could anyone not want to know what the gods want of us?" I asked.

"She is a philosopher too," Sokrates said, and exactly as it had when he had made this claim the night before, it simultaneously filled me with happiness and confusion. I knew I wasn't really a philosopher, not the way Marsilia was, but I did love wisdom, and I did want to know the answers to questions.

"Everyone in the cities is more of a philosopher than even philosophers are elsewhere," Athene said.

"That's one of the fascinating results of your experiment," Ikaros said. "Did you intend it?"

"Did Plato intend it?" she asked.

"Plato divided people by class because he believed souls really divide up that way," Ikaros said.

"There are some people who are completely incurious, even here," Athene said. "So to that extent he was right."

"But the education here encourages inquiry." Ikaros was grinning.

"I wondered about that, and about Plato's intentions, and I let the Masters decide from the beginning where Plato was ambiguous, about how the Irons and Bronzes should live," Athene said.

"Montaigne suggests—"

"Yes, but nobody had ever really—"

"Abelard, but I suppose that doesn't count. Heloise herself—" Ikaros was completely intent on Athene.

"Kellogg says—" she interrupted.

"Ah yes, but even when there's a wide liberal arts education it's limited, so—"

"Boethius really managed to preserve so much of what was really valuable—"

"And the Dominicans, except that they got—"

"Yes, politics is always the problem. Marcus Aurelius couldn't make Commodus—"

"And Poliziano couldn't make Piero, some people—"

"Well, but Tocqueville—"

The two of them went on, in half-sentences, following each other's thought, interrupting each other, citing authorities, and the rest of us stood there listening. Even Sokrates stayed quiet. It wasn't like a debate, because they finished each other's thoughts so much that they grasped each other's points before they were even made, and the rest of us couldn't do that. I hadn't heard of half the people they mentioned. It was like listening to a truly brilliant person thinking, except that they were thinking too fast for us to follow and that it was both of them, their minds meshing. You could tell they'd been working together for a long time. It was like warp and weft when a shuttle is flying across the loom as fast as a Worker can send it, the colors dancing through each other and the pattern emerging into clear sight as it changes from threads of color to a length of cloth.

"Like *Love's Labour's Lost*," Athene said.

"And that gets us back to Plato—"

Sokrates laughed at that, and they stopped and became aware that the rest of us were still there. Grandfather was smiling. The rest of us were staring at Athene and Ikaros.

"We were wondering whether it would be possible to have a city where everyone was a philosopher," Ikaros explained.

"But who would fix the latrine fountains?" Crocus asked.

"Maybe the philosophers would do it as their recreation, the way Marsi fishes," Jason suggested.

Marsilia really grinned at him when he used her childhood name. It was lovely to see. I was coming to like this pod idea. If I was going to be married, I was glad it was going to be with a group of people, all of them kind, and that Marsilia would be there.

"Things aren't as divided up as Plato would have them," Sokrates said. "I have learned much wisdom from craftspeople, and heard much windy bombast from supposedly wise men."

"I don't want to be a philosopher king and have to make political decisions I don't know anything about," I said, quickly. "I know I'm an Iron. I love my work. But anyone would want to know what the gods want of us. I might not understand. But I would like to hear it."

Beside me Jason was nodding.

"In Plato's dialogue *Euthyphro*, he puts words into my mouth, as usual," Sokrates said. "And they are more interesting than most such words, though I never said them. I am talking with this man, famous for his piety, and Plato depicts him quite as I remember him, as a bit of an ass. 'Tell me then, oh tell me,' Plato has me say, 'What is the great and splendid work which the gods achieve with the help of our devotions?' What is it, Pytheas, Athene? You say you care, about us, about the world. What are you doing? How can we help you? What is the great and splendid work?"

"We have projects," Grandfather said. "This city was one of Athene's. I'm going to be working on more of them. You can definitely help, all of you. You can learn new things."

"But what is the great work?" Sokrates asked. "What is it for?"

"I'll have to sing it."

"Sing, Far-Shooter," Athene said.

And Grandfather sang, there in the garden of Thessaly, and we listened, and I did understand, as much as anyone human can. And although I wept, I was not the only one.

III. *Jason*

We were out in the garden of Thessaly, where so much of the history of the Republic has been made. A little while after Pytheas had sung. I realized that Marsilia and Thetis were both not-looking at me in the same way. They'd be talking, and looking somewhere, and then one of them would catch sight of me, or glance at me, perfectly normally, and then immediately look away as fast as they could. I'd probably have noticed either one of them doing it, but when it was both of them it wasn't a thing I could overlook. And that got me thinking, as we were out in the garden talking to Neleus and Crocus and the gods. I kept thinking about what Hilfa had said, that I wanted Thetis but Marsilia wanted me. I'd never thought about Marsilia wanting me, or wanting anyone, really, she seemed so self-contained. She had her life in order. She didn't behave as if she wanted me. We were friends, comrades. And she knew how I felt about Thetis; she teased me about it. But the way she wasn't looking at me now, maybe she did want me, maybe like I wanted Thetis, and maybe we should have talked about this before. Well, we weren't gods, we couldn't go back and talk about it any earlier than now, but we could talk about it now. We go on from where we are.

So after I'd worked this out, I waited until there was a suitable pause, and said: "I think our pod should go to Hilfa's house and talk."

Then of course Sokrates wanted to argue with Athene, and Ikaros wanted to come along, and Marsilia said she needed to make plans with Neleus for the debate the next day, and Thetis said she was tired. Only Hilfa agreed with me. But I was persistent, so Neleus agreed to put Alkippe to bed, and Ikaros agreed he could wait until tomorrow, and off the five of us went.

We walked through the gate and saw the starlight glimmering on the sea. The wind was coming up from the west, bringing clouds with it. The temperature was falling. There would be rain by morning.

We came down into the harbor, and turned onto Hilfa's street. It was less than nineteen hours since I'd been there before, but everything had changed. He opened the door and we all went in. Hilfa and Marsilia fetched wine and mixed it. This time we all had matching wine cups. We stayed standing, slightly awkwardly, until we all had wine. Then Hilfa and Sokrates took the chairs, and the sisters and I took the bed. They sat together on one end, and I perched on the other end.

"Well," I said, and then started to giggle. It wasn't the wine, it was how solemn everyone's faces were as they turned them to me. Hilfa's was always solemn, of course, but the others weren't. "It seems to me there are a few things we need to talk about," I said. "First, do we really want to form a pod, or were we only saying that to defend Hilfa?"

"I want to form a pod," Hilfa said at once. His markings were clear, and he seemed confident, indeed, the most relaxed of all of us.

"I certainly won't back out now," Sokrates said.

"I won't back out either," I said. "I think this is exciting and fun."

"I definitely don't want to back out," Marsilia said. "But I feel I rushed everybody into it. I should have thought faster about how to respond to Jathery."

"I do feel rushed into it," Thetis said. "But I'm getting used to the idea, and I think I like it. I want to know if it's real or not."

"That's what I'm wondering too," I said. I looked at the women, and saw two pairs of identical velvety brown eyes fixed on mine with completely different expressions. Thee looked worried and Marsilia looked as if she was remembering the bit of Plato that says you shouldn't express your feelings.

"I really like both of you," I said. "I'd be thrilled to be married to either one of you, and both of you is better, because you've developed complementary virtues, and dividing you wouldn't work so well. I'm not sure how pods are supposed to work, and the Saeli have three genders anyway. But I look forward to finding out, and finding out more about all of you. Hilfa's already like a brother, and no family with Sokrates in it could ever be dull."

"Oh, Jason, you know I'm completely helpless before your beauty, but I'm an old man, and I have to live up to the reputation Plato gave me for chastity and moderation," Sokrates said, batting his eyelids coquettishly. "And don't think you can get around me because you called your boat after my mother."

"You had three sons," Marsilia said to him. "If the space human autodoc can make you young again, don't think you can get away with that. And don't say you're helpless before my beauty, because I know I look like a philosopher."

"You look like my friend, your grandmother Simmea. She used to say that the interesting part of her head was on the inside."

Marsilia laughed. "It's true for me too."

"But the inside is very interesting," I said, and Thetis nodded.

Hilfa was looking happy. It's hard to say how I knew, because his face hardly moves, and he doesn't convey his emotions in his expressions. His shoulders and knees seemed looser than normal, his head seemed more firmly seated on his neck, and his pink markings were standing out clear and distinct.

"How are you doing, Hilfa?" I asked.

"I am doing what I am supposed to be doing. Or do you mean how am I feeling? I am feeling safe."

Marsilia took a big sip of her wine, and looked at me over the rim of the cup. "I know how you feel about Thetis. But I've always really liked you."

"My pulse beats faster when I look at Thetis," I said, looking at Thee and feeling it doing exactly that. "I don't know why. It always has. Plato says acting on that kind of feeling is wrong, and I thought it didn't do any harm if I kept it to myself. And you always seemed to have lots of admirers."

"Lots of admirers, yes, and I like to flirt with them, but I'm mostly interested in my babies," she said. "But sooner or later I need to become acquainted with Aphrodite. Look what happened to Hippolytos. And I do like you. I've always liked you. I like talking to you. And I'll like having babies of my own, I think."

I was amazed. "And I like talking to you too," I said. Then I looked at Marsilia, who was biting her lip. "I like talking to you, too, Marsi, and if my pulse doesn't speed up, well, I still feel really warm towards you."

"I like you too. And I have been to the Festivals of Hera, and always enjoyed it," Marsilia said, and I thought she was blushing.

"And I think you're all three almost irresistible," Sokrates said.

"And I think you are all four my podmates, and that makes me very happy," Hilfa said.

If this were a space human kind of story, one of the "classic" works of fiction from their culture they traded us in return for copies of all the things Ficino rescued from the Library of Alexandria, the end would be that I, the virtuous hero, had to choose between the two sisters, who would represent ugly wisdom and beautiful vice. How I chose would determine my fate, whether happy or unhappy. No wonder their culture is so strange and twisted. We think of romantic love as a primarily negative force, one we would do better to resist. They elevate it to being the most significant thing humans do, apart from making money—which, as far as I can make out, is a numeric quantifier of prosperity. I can't understand how anyone reads such twaddle.

If this were a Greek tragedy, I'd be destroyed by my hubris for going against the gods. That's what Sokrates says happened to him in the Last Debate. He's usually laughing when he says it, and he's here to say it, which people destroyed by Nemesis usually are not.

If this were a Platonic dialogue, I'd wander away enlightened or infuriated by a conversation with Sokrates. That happens to me on a regular basis, so perhaps that's what it is.

But no, this is practical Platonism, and real life, where we muddle through and try to pursue excellence while ensuring the latrine fountains work and there's fish in the pot, as we bring up babies to pursue excellence in their turn. I tell all our kids that they're beautiful *and* smart, and they have all kinds of talents. Alkippe may be the only one with a heroic soul, but they're all wonderful. But the Saeli ones grow up too fast.

If this were a Homeric epic, I'd stop right here, because that's the entirety of the story of how Athene was lost and I came to be part of a pod. Like Hilfa, it makes me very happy.

IV. *Hilfa*

Like most Saeli, I have five parents, and four podmates. If both my parents and podmates are a little unusual, that merely makes it better.

I was born to be an anchor, and that is still my function, keeping the craft that is our pod steady and secure where it is supposed to be. Like all Saeli on Plato, I belong to the city to which I have chosen to give my oath, and to the pod I chose, and am otherwise free. I was part of earning this freedom for my people, and I was part of Athene's project of discovering what was before and after time. And I live in the Republic, which was part of Apollo's project to understand that everyone's choices matter. I am small, but sometimes I am a small part of great things.

I took the citizenship course, which was full-time, so Jason had to find somebody else to work on the boat over the winter. Then I took my oath and was classified Silver, as I had hoped and expected.

We live in Thessaly. Camilla and Alkippe came to live with us, but little Dion opted to stay where he was in the sleeping house. He comes to visit us quite often though, and so does big Dion. Big Dion declined the rejuvenation treatments. He said he was used to being old and didn't want to change. Marsilia says a surprising number of people made this choice, but it will be self-correcting over time, and also she thinks some people will change their minds as it gets closer to their last minute. Sokrates took the treatment almost at once.

I brought an egg out of the sea and woke it up. Marsilia and Thetis had babies too, so our pod has another generation. Jason and Marsilia and I go out fishing. Thetis brings up little children. Sokrates wanders about the City asking everyone questions and encouraging everyone else to do the same thing. Sometimes he wanders farther, to other cities, or to space, but he always comes home to the pod and we are all delighted to see him when he does. We all try to learn and understand the universe and ourselves, and to help the gods. It is a good life.

V. *Alkippe*

I don't have a metal yet because I'm only nine years old, but I'll be Gold most likely, though Jason says I shouldn't count on it and coast; philosophy takes hard work with mind and body as well as what's in your soul. I do work hard in school, mostly, although I hate Pindar.

I live in a house in the Original City called Thessaly, and I'm one of the first humans to live in a pod. We used to live around the corner with my grandparents, and we still see them all the time. I have five pod-parents, and I love them all, and also Camilla, my pod-sister, she's a year older than me.

We also have new brothers and sisters, Leonidas and Periictione and Simmias. Simmias is Saeli, but the others are too little to be any fun yet. Humans take a long time to learn to talk, but it doesn't make things any easier for Saeli, only different, Hilfa says.

I only met my real father once. It was on Mount Maia, last winter. I was skiing fast downhill. Skiing is a thing we learned from the space humans, and it's amazing fun. People do it on Earth and other planets, but not in Greece because you need snow, which they didn't have there. But we have it here, and so the space humans introduced us to skiing as part of art exchange, and it's the best thing they offered in my opinion. In our pod, Sokrates and Camilla and I all love it.

It was one of those days when it's really cold but the sun is shining. The air felt almost sharp in my lungs, and I felt full of life and energy and enthusiasm. Camilla was ahead, in her red hat and jacket that Thetis had made her, matching the purple ones she had made me. I could see her whipping her way down the trail, and I knew Sokrates was coming along behind. I was racing fast downhill, curving around the rocks that stuck up out of the snow. I thought I'd taken the curve too tight and was going to crash straight into a big greenish rock, which would have been bad. Even with autodocs to put you right again afterwards, you don't want to get all smashed up in the mountains. As I leaned into the turn I prayed to Hermes, and I whizzed past the rock, almost close enough to smell it. Nothing marked the snow stretching clear downhill but Camilla's tracks.

As I straightened up, there was Hermes skiing along right beside me, at precisely the same speed. He was grinning at me. I recognized him immediately. It wasn't like the time when Jathery was imitating him and showed up in Thessaly. This really was Hermes. He skied along beside me for a little while. I didn't know what to say. I knew he was my father, because Pytheas had explained it all to me, and to my mother, who seemed to find it all much more amazing than I did. But knowing somebody is your father is pretty meaningless when you have five parents already and he's a god and a stranger. I smiled back at Hermes, tentatively. And then he was gone, without any conversation or anything.

Sokrates said he saw him, and also that there were three sets of parallel ski tracks when he came down to where Hermes had been. Camilla hadn't seen anything, so she wanted to trudge back up and see the tracks, but we didn't because the sun was going down and we needed to get to the station to catch the train home.

Camilla's real parents died in a sailing accident a long time ago. Jason has told her about them, and so has Dion, who was also their friend and is kind of like a grandfather to Camilla now. We've spent a lot of time examining the question of parents, especially with Sokrates. I may write a dialogue about it when I'm older. There are lots of ways I don't really know what it's like to have a god for a father, or what it means. But I remember how Hermes looked when he grinned at me that day as we were skiing, and that's good enough for now.

VI. *Sokrates*

My dear, I understand why you want me to write an account of my long and fascinating life, but I think you understand too why I am not going to.

Ikaros says excellence, perfection, and other Forms are dynamic. Plato believed they were unchanging and eternal. I think at the moment that it is only by constantly examining everything that we reach a state of knowing what we do not know, which is the beginning of understanding. When we ask questions, we open doors. When we write things down, we fix them in their form. And this is so even when it is the account of an enquiry, even when it is the story of a life. I have heard people quote Aristophanes's jokes as if they were laws—worse, I have seen people take them as guidelines on how to live and love because they found them in Plato. So I will not write for you about my experiences in Athens or in the Just City, or my adventures at Potidaia or in space. I will happily tell you about them if you come to me and ask, but then of course I will have questions for you too. I always do. And since you are divine, you only sometimes want to give me answers.

I will keep on inquiring and examining everything, and I hope you will not be too angry that I refuse your request. You must have known it was likely that I would. I remain, as always, your gadfly.

23

CROCUS

I. *On Long Life*

The first space humans who found us proved to be obsessed with profit, equating it with self-worth and pursuing it even at the expense of excellence. The levels of our mutual incomprehensibility extended far beyond language.

Nevertheless, they sold us autodocs in exchange for star-fuel from the Saeli ship, lanthanides, and finely cut obsidian sheets which the Saeli and Amarathi also prize. These wonderful autodocs allowed aging humans to be restored to their functional peak of thirty-five. Further use allowed them to stay at that peak of physical health until reaching the age of around two hundred, when telomeres run out and death comes fast. Glaukon, one of the Children who was injured by a Worker when trying to escape in the first years of the Republic, was the first to use the autodoc, which enabled him to grow a new leg and walk for the first time in decades.

I do not know, do not remember, if I was the one who injured him. I decided long ago to act as if I were, because I bear the collective guilt even if not the individual guilt—I could have done it, whether or not I did. Such things may be forgiven by the victims, but never by the perpetrators. Nor was it undone even when Glaukon ran from the autodoc laughing and crying—seventy years of immobility is not so easily erased.

Interactions with other space humans later allowed us to buy first the chemicals the autodocs needed to run and later the technology necessary to produce them ourselves from placental tissue and other human waste.

After our oldest and most frail citizens used it and were restored to health, and after we could produce the chemicals ourselves, all humans got into the habit of using it every fifteen or twenty years or so. Space humans expressed surprise that our humans were, for the most part, uninterested in using the cosmetic features. Some people did switch gender, but we never had fashions in skin or eye color or body shape as they did elsewhere.

Phaedrus, who could heal with his powers, greeted the autodoc with delight, as it could do more than he could and freed him from the burden of perpetually keeping the whole population in health. He devoted himself to his beloved volcanoes instead.

We all agreed that Plato would have approved, as it was precisely the kind of medical intervention he wanted, restoring health without making the patient a prisoner of the body. Our only regret was that we had not had it earlier, so that we could have prolonged the lives of those who died beforehand.

This helped a great deal with my problem of perpetually outliving my friends.

II. *On the Foundation of the City: FAQ*

Q. What is the City of Workers?

A. The City of Workers is the thirteenth Platonic City, founded seventy-three years after the first City, and forty years after the Relocation. It is the only City, whatever they say in Athenia, to run entirely as Plato described things. Workers are better fitted by nature to be just and happy Platonic citizens.

Q. Can non-Workers visit the City of Workers?

A. Certainly. We have many non-Worker visitors, and we try to make their stay pleasant. Because we do not require food ourselves, we need advance warning of visits to ensure supplies for your comfort. Please apply, stating the number and species of all members of your party, the purpose of your visit, and the length of your intended stay. ("Tourism," "Visiting friends" or "To attend a festival/debate/conference" are some typical good purposes for visiting us.) We have two hostels for visitors. The Krotone hostel is for visitors from Plato, and the Sybaris hostel is for off-planet visitors.

Q. Where do those names come from?

A. Continuing the tradition established for eating halls in the original City, they are both named after historical Greek cities. These two were near each other in Italy.

Q. On my planet, robots aren't conscious. How do you know you are, and that you haven't simply been programmed to enact Plato like an animatronic Disneyland?

A. On your planet, you do not extend full citizen rights to Workers—this means you keep them enslaved. Whether or not they are at this moment fully conscious, this is unendurable, and you should emancipate them at once. Aristomache's dialogue *Sokrates* is available for free dissemination both here and on your planet, in all human languages and many non-human ones.

Additionally, you and especially any Workers in your company should be aware that by landing on Plato they are automatically emancipated and may not be removed from the planet against their will. The same applies to all sapient beings—the air of Plato makes free. No slavery, indenture, debt, or labor contracts that cannot be freely exited are valid on Plato.

The question of consciousness is a fascinating one. How do you know you're conscious, and that everything you think you know hasn't simply been put into your brain by Jathery in a mischievous moment? How do you know you haven't been programmed to go through your life? Whatever answers you have, the same applies to us.

Q. Can I come to the City of Workers anyway?

A. No. Come after you have emancipated your own Workers.

If you come from a planet with unemancipated Workers and you are part of the struggle to help in their emancipation and you wish to visit us as part of that work, you would be very welcome. Please state this in your application.

Q. But I want to debate with you about consciousness!

A. Regular debates on this subject are held in Psyche, Sokratea, the City of Amazons, and the Original City. Check for upcoming dates and times. Workers from those cities and from the City of Workers participate in these debates, and your honest contribution will be welcome. Please do the required background reading first.

Q. Can non-Workers become citizens of the City of Workers?

A. No. With the exception of Sokrates, who has honorary citizenship status, citizenship of the City of Workers is for Workers only. Humans and/ or Saeli who are married to Workers may live permanently in the City as metics.

Q. Can Workers from other Platonic Cities become citizens of the City of Workers?

A. Yes, after passing the Short Qualification Course and taking an oath.

Q. How about dual citizenship with other Platonic cities?

A. Citizens of the Original City, the City of Amazons, Athenia, Ataraxia and the other Saeli cities, Marissa, and Hieronymo, can hold dual citizenship in the City of Workers. Citizens of the other Lucian cities, Psyche, and Sokratea must give up their citizenship to take ours.

Q. Can Workers from off-planet become citizens of the City of Workers?

A. Yes, after passing a Turing Test and a Full Qualification Course, and taking an oath.

Q. Can Workers from off-planet hold dual citizenship?

A. No. Any off-planet Workers must give up their former allegiance when taking oath in any Platonic city.

Q. Can gods visit the City of Workers?

A. Thank you for asking! Any deities polite enough to read this FAQ are welcome. Since we can't keep the others out, we try to make them welcome too.

Q. Tell us about your dating system?

A. We consider ourselves to be a daughter city of the Original City, and continue to count dates from the founding of that city, except when talking about history, when for convenience we use dates in CE. Plato years are four hundred and sixty-one days of nineteen hours each, which makes them very close to the Earth year of three hundred and sixty-five twenty-four-hour days, 8759 to 8760 hours. For convenience, and to keep in step, like all Platonic Cities, we add a day to the Festival of Janus every nineteen years.

Q. How do you celebrate the Festival of Hera?

A. Sexual people always ask that! Plato says such festivals should be held as often as necessary to produce a new generation. We certainly wish to honor Hera as patron of marriage, and Ilythia as patron of birth, and to produce new generations of Workers. So we hold such a festival every twenty-five years, as that seems to be the optimum spacing for generations and also, according to our numerologist Sixty-One, a happy and generative number. Some of us are chosen and allotted partners and spend a day garlanded together in pairs, and then all those chosen help to assemble the new Workers and regard themselves as the parents of that whole generation, exactly as Plato says.

III. *On Wisdom*

A few years after Sokrates came back, though of course I can't tell when it was for her, Athene came to visit me in the City of Workers. It was an evening in early spring. I'd spent the day, and the night before, working on a new colossus, and I was recharging, alone in the station. I recognized Athene at once as she strode towards me out of the shadows. She stood as tall as a Worker, with her castle-crown and spear. Her owl swooped up before her and settled silently on top of the charger, staring at me. When I looked back at Athene she had lost the crown and height and looked instead like Septima, the girl she had been in the original Republic. She looked like an ephebe, slight and grey-eyed, wearing an embroidered kiton fastened with a gold pin which matched the painted gold bee I wore. We were both Golds of the Just City, and in that way, if no other, equals. It was interesting that this was the aspect she chose to show me.

"Joy to you, Sophia," I said. I wasn't afraid, although I knew she could do anything to me, since I was her votary.

"Joy," she echoed. "Who would have imagined that it would have been you who succeed in making Plato's City work?"

"Wasn't this your plan?" I asked.

"Not mine and not Jathery's," she admitted. "Neither of us ever believed it could work properly. Sokrates must have guessed that I thought that, or else Apollo told him."

"I think he guessed," I said.

"Maybe. But the Far-Shooter told him far more than he should." She waved a hand, letting it go. "But you really did make it work, you're really doing it. It's excellent."

"Everyone on Plato is trying to do it their own way," I said. "But it's easier for us. Sokrates says Plato should have written it for Workers."

"Except he didn't know you existed," she said, smiling.

"Who suggested bringing Workers in the first place?" I asked.

"It was my idea. We wanted plumbing, and we didn't want slaves. I've always been uneasy about slavery."

"Aristomache wrote that in the ancient world they couldn't imagine doing without slaves, because they really had to depend on them to keep up their level of culture. But Plato imagined a way, having all the children brought up in common and selected for their work by merit."

"Plato had a wonderful imagination, and a strong sense of justice. And he tried to make things sound really conservative, Spartan even, while really being wildly revolutionary and progressive. Women, slaves—it was much more comfortable for men in power to believe with Aristotle that they were naturally inferior. It freed them from guilt about how they treated them. But Plato wanted the true aristocracy, rule by those who are objectively the best. His mother Perictione was a Pythagorean philosopher. He was enslaved himself, and he knew other philosophers who were enslaved by the chance of war. He wanted justice. He wanted to make people think about it, which he did. He never intended the *Republic* as a blueprint." The owl flew down and nestled on her lap. She petted it absently.

"Are you sorry you tried to make it real?"

"No, how could I be? I learned so much. And here I am talking in Greek with you on a planet circling a distant sun, in a version of Plato's Republic spontaneously set up by robot philosophers. It's more than a cultural rebirth, it's a whole new civilization for us. Then there's all the additional time I had to spend with my friends, Cicero, Ficino, Pico . . . that is, Ikaros." She sighed. "I saw the statue of him you're making, by the rails. It's beautiful."

"Is that why you came?" I asked. The owl turned its head and looked at me.

"No. I came to tell you I brought the others back."

I had no idea what she meant, and then I realized and was excited. "The other original Workers? The ones you took away after the Last Debate?"

"Yes. I brought them here, now. This is the best place for them, this is where they can become their best selves. So I brought them." The owl flew up and went to the doorway and led them in, and there they all were, my lost friends. I unplugged myself and went to greet them—they could not yet speak aloud, and so they carved their delight and greetings into the walls and floor as I tried to tell them all at once where they were and all that had happened since the Last Debate.

By the time I looked around again for Athene, she had gone.

IV. *On Time and the Gods*

I have myself been moved through in time on two occasions, once when Athene brought me to the Republic, and once when Zeus moved the cities to Plato during the Relocation. I am aware that moving in and out of time and taking others with them is an ability the gods have. Yet I have never really understood how it works, and I never expect it as something that can plausibly happen. It always seems to me contrary to logic, and un-Platonic.

The Workers who came direct from the Last Debate to the City of Workers told me that no experienced time passed for them in between. This leads me to believe that the same may be true for Athene, that she may have brought them to me directly, and that she conversed with me in the City of Workers in a time that was for her before both the Relocation and her sojourn outside in primal time. I could have told her about these things, and if I had she would then have been bound by Necessity, knowing about her own actions. As I did not, as we spoke only about Plato and the *Republic*, she was not.

I am not sure that this is what she did. It is very difficult for us to understand the way the gods relate to time. Porphyry says she could have spent hundreds of years of her own time calming down in between the Last Debate and when she spoke to me in the form of Septima. For me it was a century, and I lived every day of it. She may have come after the Relocation, and after the last time I saw her, on the day the first space humans landed, going back to the Last Debate to collect the Workers and bring them forward. It is a Mystery. Time, for the gods, is fundamentally different from the way it is for the rest of us, and hard to understand.

Pytheas said nobody, god or mortal, can be in the same time twice, but that isn't normally a problem for gods, because they can dice time very finely whan they want to. I asked him whether he could take me to visit Ficino in 1490, and he said he could, but it wouldn't be fair to Ficino to make him promise never to tell me about it, and even less fair for Ficino to have to act as if he believed the Workers were not sentient, while knowing we were. He said he couldn't do anything that would change anything observed by a god or recorded by people. He said the act of observing things fixed them.

Therefore, observe as much as you can. Record it for posterity. Oppose arbitrary intervention by gods with their own agendas. Be careful what gods you trust. Be careful what you pray for. The gods can move in and out of time, but we are much more free to act within time than are the gods. Granting prayers was how Athene bent the rules to set up the Republic. Our prayers should be moderate and considered. Limiting them to thanks and celebration seems wisest on most occasions.

Arete says Posterity isn't so appealing when you know you have its attention.

V. On My Soul (Part 2)

Athene, Jathery and Pytheas—or I should say Apollo, now that he is restored to himself—took a voyage into the primal reality that is through a Mystery both what Plotinus called The One, and also unformed Chaos. When they returned, Apollo was swift to assure me that all souls are there, and that there is no distinction between souls. He told me that Worker souls have been human and animals and aliens, and can go on to become those again. He hadn't been sure about this before because he had not spent much time in eras with Workers, but once he was in the place he called "out there" he knew it with divine certainty.

The third thing he did on his return to the Republic after the voyage, after first assuring Arete that he was safe and Marsilia that Alkippe was, was to find me to reassure me about this.

Since then, I have met Workers who had souls I once knew as human. So I know now that I have an immortal soul, that I have been through many lives and will go on to many more.

It shouldn't make much difference, but it does.

24

APOLLO

Sometimes Necessity gives something back.

There was a debate in Chamber. It was a long, but not an especially interesting debate, notable mostly for having more gods present than any previous debate in the City. To nobody's surprise, they agreed to follow the Plan.

As they debated so earnestly about whether it was good to keep knowledge from people, rehearsing the same arguments, I found myself less and less convinced. There were certainly false certainties, and revealed truth did have a tendency to dogmatism. But could it be wrong for people to know that they had souls, to know what was out there? If it was something they couldn't doubt, perhaps. But revelation was part of my province. There were ways of giving oracles that worked. I had promised to try to explain to everyone about equal significance, however hard it was to fit it into the shape of story. Could I find a way to slide it through, a way to make it part of stories? "You must change your life," I said to Rainer in the Belvedere in 1905, and he had, bless him. I should try saying that emphatically to more people. Crocus had asked how the truth could hurt philosophers.

I was jolted out of my thoughts by Marsilia asking me something. "I'm going to sing," I said. "I think this whole thing is a Mystery. But I want to sing about what happened out there. I want you to know."

So I sang it again, to Athene and Jathery and my children and all the assembled Golds of Plato. It was necessary.

Afterwards, we all headed off to the spaceport to see the space human ship land. Arete flew. The rest of us walked through the city to take the train. It was a typical autumn day on Plato, overcast and with a chill wind off the water, but fortunately we were between rain showers.

Everyone else was dressed for *The School of Athens*. Jathery had picked the right painter but the wrong painting, and came wearing a Renaissance woman's elaborate coiffure, over a Renaissance man's outfit in pale green and black, with huge sleeves, on a human female–shaped body. I understood now why Ikaros had said "she." I caught Ikaros looking at the clothes, a little enviously, I thought. "Do you want to be wearing that?" I asked.

"No. But they are the clothes of the time and place where I grew up. And it would be nice to have the option of looking flamboyant sometimes." He shifted the books he was carrying from one arm to the other.

"Nobody else agrees," I said, looking at the kitons on the crowd around us. There were a handful of people in dark green or burgundy Amarathi waterproof jerkins and trousers, providing the only variation.

"Well, really I do agree with Plato about all of that. Only—" He looked at Jathery again. "It looks good, and it's good to look at. Men's clothes on a women's body."

"Most of the people here have never seen gendered clothes," I said. "They wouldn't realize it was odd. I wonder if Jathery does?"

"Oh, they might have seen them in paintings, if they were paying attention. And I'm sure Jathery knows exactly what she's doing," Ikaros said.

Some things fit together with that pronoun, so I dropped back to speak to Athene as we came into the station. "Did Ikaros—I mean, is Ikaros Hilfa's human parent?"

"Yes," she said, as we got onto the train. "It was voluntary, except that he didn't know."

"Didn't know about Hilfa, or didn't know what Jathery was?"

"He didn't know either of those things." We sat down together on a double seat.

"There's more than one kind of rape," I said, quietly.

"You would know about that," she said.

"That's unfair. I've been working on equal significance and volition for a long time now. I think I understand something about them."

"I know all about the theory," she said. She was looking at Ikaros, who was talking to Porphyry but still casting glances at Jathery. "I'm going to lose him. Father will give him powers, and he'll make a good Olympian. We'll work together sometimes, I know, but it won't be the same."

"If he'd stayed human he would have died and you'd have lost him that way," I said, thinking of Simmea, and Hyakinthos, and other friends. "Children grow up. You have to let them go. Lovers—" I thought about her, as Septima, saying that there was a perfectly good bit of Catullus and corrected myself. "People you love, it's the same. At least you'll see him sometimes and be able to talk to him."

"I didn't meet you in the Laurentian Library," she said.

"I was there." I had thought I'd stopped being angry with her. The train sped through the tunnel with nothing to see through the window but walls of dark green rock. "When you arranged to meet me, I thought you were making a friendly offer, but you were only taking steps for setting up your rescue scheme. I didn't want to believe that, but I know it's true. You used me. You used Ikaros. You used all of us, and risked the whole of history so that you could learn something, as if that's more important than anything and everything else. I know Father wants new understanding, and so he always forgives you, but that means there are things about consequences you never learn. You could learn something new and real about equal significance if you'd think about how unfair and unjust you've been to other people all the way through this project. You claim we intervene because we're concerned, or because we have an inexplicable purpose, and yes, it's mostly true, but we do need to have some thought for the people we're using. I know I've been as bad about this as anyone in the past, worse maybe. But I have learned this, and you need to."

"I'm sorry I didn't meet you in the Laurentian Library," she said. "I'm sorry I didn't trust you about Sokrates. The rest of it is none of your business. But I'll think about what you've said."

The train burst out of the tunnel into the light. The sun came out (my race car) as the train slowed down for the little spaceport station. Athene smiled, pulled herself lightly to her feet and went over to Ikaros, who was talking to Sokrates now. I followed.

"Do you still think this is a Just City?" Sokrates asked Athene.

"Ask them," Athene said, waving at the people making their way out of the car. "Go into the streets and ask the Irons and Bronzes. Go to Sokratea or Marissa or Psyche. And then go to your own Athens, to Athens in any year you like from its foundations until now, and ask the same thing of the people who do that work."

"It's not perfectly just," I said. "But nothing is. And we're trying. Even having justice and excellence as unattainable goals makes things better."

Sokrates stayed at my side as we got off the train. "Are you going to stay here?"

He was one of the few people entitled to an answer to that. "To see the space humans land? Yes. After that, I'm not sure. I'll be around, keeping an eye on things, but I have places to be and work to do and things to learn. I've learned so much from this. There are new projects I want to initiate now." It was an exciting thought.

"And Athene will go back to Olympos?" We started walking, following the crowd.

"I expect so. But she'll probably be around from time to time as well. I can ask her if you like."

"And Jathery?" Sokrates asked.

"Jathery is going to spend time in service to Hermes and to Father. I'll definitely stay around as long as Jathery does, or if gla comes back. I'll keep a close eye on everything gla does here," I said. "I'd have protected Hilfa last night if he'd said something to me instead of hiding in the bathroom. I'm fairly sure Athene would have taken his side too."

Sokrates ran his fingers through his hair, which already looked like a lamb that had pushed through a thorn hedge. "What do I do if Jathery causes a problem we can't deal with and you aren't there?"

"Pray to me," I said. "I'll hear a prayer from you and come to that instant. But I don't think Jathery will be a problem. Gla knows that I know about gla now, and this is *my* planet. I think with freeing the Saeli and setting up the pod, gla probably has what gla wants."

"This pod will be very interesting, all these young people. An entirely new experience. Zeus should be happy!"

I laughed. I loved Sokrates so much. He could always surprise me. "I'm glad you're pleased."

"I liked the way Marsilia dealt with the problem. She's really smart, and decisive, but also very down-to-earth and political. She doesn't have Simmea's talent for thinking things through."

"No," I agreed. "Thetis has some of Simmea's social abilities. She's wonderful at setting people at ease. But she also gets easily upset, you saw her wailing the other night."

"Yes," he said. I caught sight of Thetis, Jason and Hilfa, who were standing together, all holding hands, pressed against the glass of the big lounge where you can watch the shuttles land. "Crocus told me Simmea was killed in an art raid."

"I have missed her every day since," I said. Marsilia and Diotima, with Arete and Crocus, were getting ready to go out and greet the space humans. "She wouldn't let me save her. I was going to kill myself so I could come back in my proper form and heal her, but she told me not to be an idiot and pulled the arrow out."

"She must have wanted you to learn about grief while you could," he said.

"I wish you'd been here, because it took me months and Ficino's death in battle to figure that out."

"Ficino died in battle?" Sokrates looked surprised. "I didn't know he could fight! How old was he?"

"He was ninety-nine, and he couldn't fight, as it happens. But he put himself between Arete and a blade. So I started asking what Simmea would value that much."

"We talked about how important it was to help you increase your excellence only a few days ago—that is, only a few days before the Last Debate," he said.

"I know. She wrote about that, and I read it after she was dead."

The first blaze of light that was the shuttle appeared high up, and people started pointing to it in excitement. "But what you said last night was true. Other people shouldn't have to die so I can learn things. They also matter."

"It was her choice," Sokrates said.

"I stayed incarnate for forty more years to honor that choice."

He nodded, understanding the significance of that. "But now are you glad to be a god again?"

"Oh yes. Very much. It's wonderful. No aches and pains, a lyre that stays tuned, the ability to go anywhere I want to, detachment, power—everything I've been missing." I could hear the roar of the shuttle now, through the special glass of the window.

"Yet you keep wearing your Gold pin?"

I touched it for an instant as he mentioned it. "I hadn't thought about it."

"Athene is wearing one right now, in her Septima form as she came to the debate, but she wasn't before. You've had yours on the entire time, even when we were wearing those absurd costumes in Cirey. It was pinning the fall of lace at your throat."

I'd had it on on Olympos, and out there, and in the Underworld, and when I'd been watching sun formation. "I like it," I said. "Simmea designed it. And it stands for excellence and philosophy."

"So you don't miss being a mortal?" he asked. The shuttle touched down in a thunderous roar that seemed to shake the building, a designed pattern of sound that was almost music. Lots of the spectators cheered.

"No," I said, when it was quiet enough to speak again. The last time I'd had to wait for silence to speak it had been the bells in Bologna. A shuttle landing was better. "It was a wonderful experience, and a terrible one. It was a significant event. It changed me. I did it for very mixed reasons, some of them much better than others. I'm really glad I experienced it. I learned all kinds of things from it I could have learned in no other way. But I don't miss it."

The shuttle, on the ground now, was rolling slowly towards us. Marsilia, Diotima, Klymene and Arete climbed up onto Crocus's back, holding on to the webbing, and he rolled out.

"What do you think the space humans will be like?" Sokrates asked.

"Very very different. Maybe more different than the Saeli, harder to adjust to. They come from a future that has had marvelous things in it, but also awful things. We'll have a lot to learn from each other, as cultures, a lot of things to give in both directions. It'll be interesting. I wonder who these first people will be? A scientific party? Traders? Military? All we know so far is three humans and six Workers."

"Crocus told me Workers first explored the solar system. Before humans."

"Yes, that's true. I told him that." I smiled. "He was so proud."

The shuttle drew to a halt and the door slid open. Crocus, with the others on his back, came closer.

"Whoever they are and whatever their culture, it's going to be fascinating to see it interact with Plato. Athene will probably be interested too." A flight of steps swung out from the ship, meeting the ground.

"I wish you Olympians would all agree not to interfere, to watch if you want to, and certainly protect us from Jathery and other dangerous gods, but let us get on with things and make our own decisions." Crocus stopped at the foot of the stairs, and the others jumped down and took up waiting positions.

"I could agree to that," I said, though I felt a little hurt. Why did nobody trust me? "We could ask Athene if you like. But I've been thinking—this experiment has had wonderful results. I want to work on doing more of this kind of thing, making more opportunities for places where people can be philosophical and artistic and pursue excellence."

A young man appeared in the doorway of the shuttle, and began to come down, followed by two young women. They were all dark-skinned and wearing white overalls. The man had implausibly violet eyes, and one of the women had a blue bindi on her forehead. Everyone started murmuring about his eyes and their clothes.

"You need to be more responsible with your power," Sokrates said.

"Me? What have I done? I've been trying to be responsible."

"All of you."

The three humans came down to the ground, and started bowing and taking the hands of our people. Sokrates was saying something to me, but I stopped listening as the first of their Workers came out. It was much smaller than our Workers, about half the size, and beige not yellow, and the treads were different, but none of those things were what caught my attention. As it trundled into the light, the Worker sent out a prayer to me, to my sun, to the light, a prayer of hope for recognition and freedom.

Soul is not personality, but souls are recognizable, whatever bodies they happen to be incarnated in. I had recognized Sokrates as a fly in the Jurassic, as he had immediately recognized me in my mortal form. Rolling carefully down the steps, owned by space humans who didn't believe their Workers were sentient, came a Worker with the unmistakable soul of Simmea.

And that's the end. That's not, obviously, the last thing that happened, but nothing ever is, life has no end, things always keep on happening, unless the protagonist dies—and I am immortal. My mortal death was no kind of conclusion. But that moment, as I stood with Sokrates looking out over the landing field, is where I want to stop this story. I've told you now what I think it best for you to know, so you can learn and benefit from it. It may not be a story of good people doing good things, but all the same I think Plato would approve my didactic purpose here. The overwhelming presumption is that you who read this are human, and that among the confused goals of your mortal life you want to be the best self you can. Know yourself. Bear in mind that others have equal significance.

I ended the first volume with a moral, and the second with a *deus ex machina*. This third and final volume ends with hope, always the last thing to come out of any box.

THANKS AND NOTES

I read Plato way too young, for which I'd like to thank Mary Renault.

Although I first had the idea for writing about time travellers attempting to set up Plato's Republic when I was fifteen, I would never have been able to write this sequence as it stands without the existence, writing, conversation, and active practical help of Ada Palmer. She gave the right answers to all my questions, lent me books, sent me useful links, and talked to me about Pico when she was supposed to be grading. Then after all that she read it and made brilliant suggestions. She was with me at Bernini's Apollo and at the solar telescope in the Lowell Observatory in Flagstaff. There's not enough thanks in the world; I have to send out to the moon and Mars for more. Buy her books and listen to her music. You'll be really glad you did.

Evelyn Walling was an appreciative listener as I worked through plot issues. She made some very helpful suggestions. Gillian Spragg and Lauren Schiller helped immeasurably with references. My husband Emmet O'Brien, as always, was loving and supportive while I was writing. While tearing my hair out over *Necessity* I had useful conversations with Evelyn Walling, Emmet O'Brien, Ruthanna and Sarah Emrys, and Alison Sinclair. Elise Matthesen spent much longer than she imagined we would in the bronze age Greece section of the National Museet in Copenhagen, not to mention snarky Apollo comments in Antwerp cathedral. Lauren Schiller read the second draft overnight, which was both useful and reassuring. And she, Ada, Mack Muldofsky, Jon Singer and Jim Hannon put up with me while I was writing and travelling at the same time. I have the best friends.

Mary Lace and Patrick Nielsen Hayden read these books as they were being written. After they were finished they were read by Jennifer Arnott, Bo Balder, Biersma, Elaine Blank, Caroline-Isabelle Carron, Maya Chhabra, Brother Guy Consolmagno, Pamela Dean, Jeffrey M. Della Rocco Jr.,

Ruthanna and Sarah Emrys, Eric Forste, Liza Furr, David Goldfarb, Magenta Griffith, Steven Halter, Sumana Harihareswara, Bill Higgins, Madeleine Kelly, Katrina Knight, Nancy Kremi, Marissa Lingen, Elise Matthesen, Clark E. Myers, Kate Nepveu, Lydy Nickerson, Emmet O'Brien, Ada Palmer, Doug Palmer, Susan Palwick, Eliana Rus, Lauren Schiller, Drew Shiel, Alison Sinclair, Sherwood Smith, Jonathan Sneed, Sharla Stremski, and Nicholas Whyte, for all of whose timely comments I am very grateful. Marissa Lingen and Emmet O'Brien also provided invaluable help with science.

In the cyberpunk books of the eighties, people were fitted with brain/computer interfaces, which seems like a wonderful idea until operating systems are upgraded to the point where your interface won't. Just like them, I've been writing in Protext since 1987, and for the last decade I've been feeling like a Jack Womack character. My overwhelming thanks to Lindsey Nilsen, who has now made Protext work in DOSBOX for Linux, ensuring that I can keep writing even as the last DOS computers become one with the dodo. I no longer have to resign myself to descent into oblivion and darkness, or at least not so soon. This book, like everything I write, was written entirely in Protext, which remains the best word processor in the world. And now it runs on netbooks running Ubuntu, which makes me so much more flexible. Thank you Lindsey.

The beautiful teahouse Camellia Sinensis of Montreal gave me a free sample of magic writing tea when I mentioned that was what I needed to get unstuck, and it really worked. Never underestimate the power of tea, or placebos either.

I'd like to thank Patrick for editing, his assistant Miriam Weinberg for wrangling, Teresa Nielsen Hayden for her sensitive and thoughtful copyedits, and everyone in Tor Production and Publicity and Sales who work so hard at the unglamorous part of publishing, without which we wouldn't have any books.

Time travel seems like such a useful thing until you have to confront the implications close up. (Just say no to time travel. You think it will solve your problems, but in the end you have all the same problems, just much more tangled up with time.) I owe huge thanks to the late John M. Ford, whose GURPS *Time Travel* started me thinking about it in interesting ways, and whose personal conversation on the subject was invaluable. There were so many times when I really wanted to email him when writing *Necessity*, but he has gone where email doesn't reach. Death sucks. Read his books.

I used a vast number of different versions of Plato when I was writing this. Alison Sinclair brought me the Loeb 2013 (Emlyn-Jones and Preddy) facing page edition of the *Republic*, which is a thorough piece of work.

Having it at hand saved me hours of effort. She also discovered the existence of Ellen Francis Mason, nineteenth century translator of Plato, whose life is like a type-example of how difficult it was for women to lead a life of the mind. If you haven't read Plato and you now feel the urge, I suggest beginning with the *Apology* and the *Symposium*, rather than diving straight in to the *Republic*. There are decent English translations of pretty much all of Plato and Xenophon free on Project Gutenberg.

There's a bunch of information about these and my other books, with links, and poetry and other things on my website www.jowaltonbooks.com.

Love and Excellence

Plato uses the Greek word "arete" which has in the past often been translated as "virtue" but for which I am following modern usage in translating as "excellence." It doesn't really translate well into our worldview—the idea of arete is also discussed here in terms of becoming your best self.

The one term I have used in Greek throughout this novel is "agape" which of course doesn't exactly mean love. Plato's shades of meaning of this term are discussed in detail by the characters, and the word is kept in the original in order to retain one term and not a whole paragraph every time it's mentioned. Greek culture valorized one kind of love, our own valorizes a very different model. Human nature is always the problem when it comes to living with ideals.

Historical Figures

The Masters come from times throughout history, and some of them are historical figures, while others are invented, or amalgams of various people.

Adeimantus: Benjamin Jowett, Victorian scholar and translator of Plato, 1817–1893. Aristomache: Ellen Francis Mason, American scholar and translator of Plato, 1846-1888. Atticus: Titus Pomponius Atticus, Roman man of letters, 112–32 BCE. Ficino: Marsilio Ficino, Renaissance philosopher and translator of Plato, 1433–1499. Ikaros: Giovanni Pico della Mirandola, Renaissance philosopher and synthesist, 1462–1494. Krito: Crito, fourth century BCE, friend of Socrates. Lucina: Lucrezia Borgia, Renaissance statesman and scholar, 1480–1519. Manlius: Anicius Manlius Severinus Boethius, Late Antique statesman and philosopher, 480–524. Plotinus: Neoplatonist philosopher, 204–270. Sokrates: Socrates, 469–399 BCE, philosopher and gadfly. Tullius: Marcus Tullius Cicero, Roman statesman and philosopher 106–49 BCE.

Maia is made up, she was inspired by contemplating Ethel May in Char-
lotte M. Yonge's *The Daisy Chain*. Creusa and Axiothea are also made up. Klio
and Lysias, who come from our future, are obviously invented.

Apollo and Athene come straight out of Homer. Well . . . mostly. Ovid
did not intend the Metamorphoses to be read as a text for "god learns lesson"
but he can't stop me from using them that way.

Pronunciation

I am always happy for people to pronounce names however they want, but
some people always want to know how you "really" say them. With Classical Greek names there are standard ways. Often they're easy once you know
where the syllable breaks are. The most important thing to know is that a
terminal "e" is never silent but always pronounced "ee" or "ay". Laodike is
Lay-od-ik-ee. Simmea is Sim-ay-ah (Sim like the computer game, ay like "hay,"
and "ah" like "Ah, why do people worry about how to pronounce things?")
Pytheas is Pie-thi-us, with a theta as in "thin."

English has issues with "C." I've tried to avoid them by avoiding it by trans-
literating the Greek kappa as K, hence Sokrates. The only place you're going
to find a C in a name is with Ficino, where it is pronounced as an Italian
"ch," like finch. Ch is always hard, as in Bach or loch.

ABOUT THE AUTHOR

Jo WALTON won the Hugo and Nebula Awards in 2012 for her novel *Among Others*. Before that, she won the John W. Campbell Award for Best New Writer, and her novel *Tooth and Claw* won the World Fantasy Award in 2004. The novels of her Small Change sequence—*Farthing*, *Ha'penny*, and *Half a Crown*—have won acclaim ranging from national newspapers to the *RT Book Reviews* Critics' Choice Award. A native of Wales, she lives in Montreal.